HOLD THE DREAM

Barbara Taylor Bradford was born in Leeds, and by the age of twenty was an editor and columnist on Fleet Street. Her first novel, *A Woman of Substance*, became an enduring best-seller and was followed by nineteen others, most recently *Unexpected Blessings*. Her books have sold more than seventy million copies world-wide in more than ninety countries and forty languages. Ten of her novels have been made into successful movies and mini-series. She lives in New York City with her husband, producer Robert Bradford.

BARBARA TAYLOR BRADFORD

Hold the Dream

HarperCollins*Publishers*

This novel is entirely a work of fiction. The names,
characters and incidents portrayed in it are the work of the
author's imagination. Any resemblance to actual persons,
living or dead, events or localities is entirely coincidental.

HarperCollins*Publishers*
77–85 Fulham Palace Road,
Hammersmith, London W6 8JB

www.harpercollins.co.uk

This paperback edition 2004

First published in paperback by Grafton 1986

First published in Great Britain by Granada Publishing 1985

Copyright © Barbara Taylor Bradford 1985

Barbara Taylor Bradford asserts the moral right to
be identified as the author of this work

ISBN 0 007 77357 9

Set in Plantin

Printed and bound in Great Britain by
Bookmarque Ltd, Croydon, Surrey

Contents

For Bob – who makes everything possible for me, with my love.

'She possessed, in the highest degree,
all the qualities which were required in a
great Prince.'

GIOVANNI SCARAMELLI,
Venetian Ambassador
to the Court of Elizabeth Tudor,
Queen of England

'I would have you know that this kingdom
of mine is not so scant of men but there be
a rogue or two among them.'

ELIZABETH TUDOR, Queen of England

Family Tree (Emma Harte)

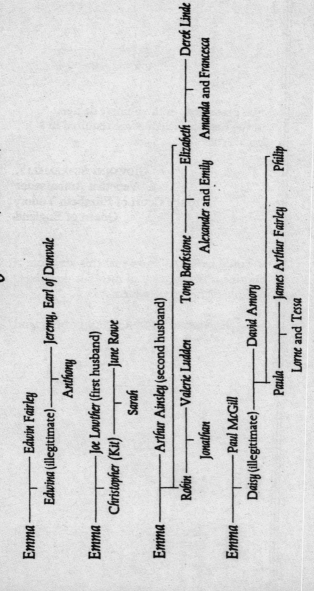

Emma —— Edwin Fairley
Edwina (illegitimate) —— Jeremy, Earl of Dunvale
Anthony

Emma —— Joe Lowther (first husband)
Christopher (Kit) —— June Rowe
Sarah

Emma —— Arthur Ainsley (second husband)
Robin —— Valerie Ludden   Tony Barkstone —— Elizabeth —— Derek Linde
Jonathan   Alexander and Emily   Amanda and Francesca

Emma —— Paul McGill
Daisy (illegitimate) —— David Amory
Paula —— James Arthur Fairley
Lorne and Tessa   Philip

Matriarch

'I speak the truth, not so much as I
would, but as much as I dare; and
I dare a little more, as I grow older.'

MONTAIGNE

CHAPTER 1

Emma Harte was almost eighty years old.

She did not look it, for she had always carried her years lightly. Certainly Emma felt like a much younger woman as she sat at her desk in the upstairs parlour of Pennistone Royal on this bright April morning of 1969.

Her posture was erect in the chair, and her alert green eyes, wise and shrewd under the wrinkled lids, missed nothing. The burnished red-gold hair had turned to shining silver long ago, but it was impeccably coiffed in the latest style, and the widow's peak was as dramatic as ever above her oval face. If this was now lined and scored by the years, her excellent bone structure had retained its clarity and her skin held the translucency of her youth. And so, though her great beauty had been blurred by the passage of time, she was still arresting, and her appearance, as always, was stylish.

For the busy working day stretching ahead of her she had chosen to wear a woollen dress of tailored simplicity in the powder-blue shade she so often favoured, and which was so flattering to her. A frothy white lace collar added just the right touch of softness and femininity at her throat, and there were discreet diamond studs on her ears. Otherwise she wore no jewellery, except for a gold watch and her rings.

After her bout with bronchial pneumonia the previous year she was in blooming health, had no infirmities to speak of, and she was filled with the restless vigour and drive that had marked her younger days.

13

That's my problem, not knowing where to direct all this damned energy, she mused, putting down her pen, leaning back in the chair. She smiled and thought: The devil usually finds work for idle hands, so I'd *better* come up with a new project soon before I get into mischief. Her smile widened. Most people thought she had more than enough to keep her fully occupied, since she continued to control her vast business enterprises which stretched halfway round the world. Indeed, they did need her constant supervision; yet, for the most part, they offered her little challenge these days. Emma had always thrived on challenge, and it was this she sorely missed. Playing watchdog was not particularly exciting to her way of thinking. It did not fire her imagination, bring a tingle to her blood, or get her adrenaline flowing in the same way that wheeling and dealing did. Pitting her wits against business adversaries, and striving for power and supremacy in the international marketplace, had become such second nature to her over the years they were now essential to her well-being.

Restlessly she rose, crossed the floor in swift light steps, and opened one of the soaring leaded windows. She took a deep breath, peered out. The sky was a faultless blue, without a single cloud, and radiant with spring sunshine. New buds, tenderly green, sprouted on the skeletal branches, and under the great oak at the edge of the lawn a mass of daffodils, randomly planted, tossed yellow-bright heads under the fluttering breeze.

'I wandered lonely as a cloud that floats on high o'er vale and hill, when all at once I saw a crowd, a host of golden daffodils,' she recited aloud, then thought: Good heavens, I learned that Wordsworth poem at the village school in Fairley. So long ago, and to think that I've remembered it all these years.

Raising her hand, she closed the window, and the great McGill emerald on the third finger of her left hand flashed as the clear Northern light struck the stone. Its brilliance

14

caught her attention. She had worn this ring for forty-four years, ever since that day, in May of 1925, when Paul McGill had placed it on her finger. He had thrown away her wedding ring, symbol of her disastrous marriage to Arthur Ainsley, then slipped on the massive square-cut emerald. 'We might not have had the benefit of clergy,' Paul had said that memorable day. 'But as far as I'm concerned, you are my wife. From this day forward until death do us part.'

The previous morning their child had been born. Their adored Daisy, conceived in love and raised with love. Her favourite of all her children, just as Paula, Daisy's daughter, was her favourite grandchild, heiress to her enormous retailing empire and half of the colossal McGill fortune which Emma had inherited after Paul's death in 1939. And Paula had given birth to twins four weeks ago, had presented her with her first great-grandchildren, who tomorrow would be christened at the ancient church in Fairley village.

Emma pursed her lips, suddenly wondering if she had made a mistake in acquiescing to this wish of Paula's husband, Jim Fairley. Jim was a traditionalist, and thus wanted his children to be christened at the font where all of the Fairleys had been baptized, and all of the Hartes for that matter, herself included.

Oh well, she thought, I can't very well renege at this late date, and perhaps it *is* only fitting. She had wreaked her revenge on the Fairleys, the vendetta she had waged against them for most of her life was finally at an end, and the two families had been united through Paula's marriage with James Arthur Fairley, the last of the old line. It was a new beginning.

But when Blackie O'Neill had heard of the choice of church he had raised a snowy brow and chuckled and made a remark about the cynic turning into a sentimentalist in her old age, an accusation he was frequently levelling at her of late. Maybe Blackie was right in this assumption. On the other hand, the past no longer troubled her as it once had. The past had been buried with the dead. Only the future concerned her now. And Paula and Jim and their children were that future.

Emma's thoughts centred on Fairley village as she returned to her desk, put on her glasses and stared at the memorandum in front of her. It was from her grandson Alexander, who, with her son Kit, ran her mills, and it was bluntly to the point, in Alexander's inimitable fashion. The Fairley mill was in serious trouble. It had been failing to break even for the longest time and was now deeply in the red. A crucial decision hovered over her head . . . to close the mill or keep it running at a considerable loss. Emma, ever the pragmatist, knew deep in her bones that the wisest move would be to close down the Fairley operation, yet she balked at this drastic measure, not wanting to bring hardship to the village of her birth. She had asked Alexander to find an alternative, a workable solution, hoped that he had done so. She would soon know. He was due to arrive for a meeting with her imminently.

One possibility which might enable them to resolve the situation at the Fairley mill had occurred to Emma, but she wanted to give Alexander his head, an opportunity to handle this problem himself. Testing him, she admitted, as I'm constantly testing all of my grandchildren. And why not? That was her prerogative, wasn't it? Everything she owned had been hard won, built on a life rooted in single-mindedness of purpose and the most gruelling work and dogged determination and relentlessness and terrible sacrifice. Nothing had ever been handed to her on a plate. Her mighty empire was entirely of her own making, and, since it was hers and hers alone, she could dispose of it as she wished.

And so with calm deliberation and judiciousness and selectivity she had chosen her heirs one year ago, bypassing four of her five children in favour of her grandchildren in the new will she had drawn; yet she continued to scrutinize the third generation, forever evaluating their worth, seeking weaknesses in them whilst inwardly praying to find none.

They have lived up to my expectations, she reassured herself, then thought with a swift stab of dismay: No, that's not strictly true. There is *one* of whom I am not really sure, *one* whom I don't think I can trust.

Emma unlocked the top drawer of her desk, took out a sheet of paper, and studied the names of her grandchildren, which she had listed only last night when she had experienced her first feelings of uneasiness. Is there a joker in this pack, as I suspect? she asked herself worriedly, squinting at the names. And if there is, how on earth will I handle it?

Her eyes remained riveted to one name. She shook her head, with sadness, pondering.

Treachery had long ceased to surprise Emma, for her natural astuteness and psychological insight had been sharply honed during a long, frequently hard, and always extraordinary life. In fact, relatively few things surprised her any more, and, with her special brand of cynicism, she had come to expect the worst from people, including family. Yet she *had* been taken aback last year when she had discovered through Gaye Sloane, her secretary, that her four eldest children were wilfully plotting against her. Spurred on by their avariciousness and vaunting ambition, they had endeavoured to wrest her empire away from her in the most underhanded way, seriously underestimating her in the process. Her initial shock, and the pain of betrayal, had been swiftly replaced by an anger of icy ferocity, and she had made her moves with speed and consummate skill and resourcefulness, which was her way when facing any opponent. And she had pushed sentiment and emotions aside, had not allowed feelings to obscure intelligence, for it was her superior intelligence which had inevitably saved her in disastrous situations in the past.

17

If she had outwitted the inept plotters, had left them floundering stupidly in disarray, she had also finally come to the bitter, and chilling, realization that blood was not thicker than water. It had struck her, and most forcibly, that ties of the blood and of the flesh did not come into play when vast amounts of money and, more importantly, great power, were at stake. People thought nothing of killing to attain even the smallest portions of both. Despite her overriding disgust and disillusionment with her children, she had been very sure of *their* children, *their* devotion to her. Now one of them was causing her to re-evaluate her judgement and question her trust.

She turned the name over in her mind . . . Perhaps she was wrong; she hoped she was wrong. She had nothing to go on really – except gut instinct and her prescience. But, like her intelligence, both had served her well throughout her life.

Always when she faced this kind of dilemma, Emma's instinctive attitude was to wait – and watch. Once again she decided to play for time. By doing thus she could conceal her real feelings, whilst gambling that things would sort themselves out to her advantage, thereby dispensing with the need for harsh action. But I will dole out the rope, she added inwardly. Experience had taught her that when lots of freely proffered rope fell into unwitting hands it invariably formed a noose.

Emma considered the manifold possibilities if this should happen, and a hard grimness settled over her face and her eyes darkened. She did not relish picking up the sword again, to defend herself and her interests, not to mention her other heirs.

History does have a way of repeating itself, she thought wearily, especially in my life. But I refuse to anticipate. That's surely borrowing trouble. Purposefully, she put the list back in the drawer, locked it, and pocketed the key.

Emma Harte had the enviable knack of shelving unsolvable problems in order to concentrate on priorities, and so she was enabled to subdue the nagging – and disturbing – suspicion that a grandchild of hers was untrustworthy, and therefore a potential adversary. Current business was the immediate imperative, and she gave her attention to her appointments for the rest of the day, each of which was with three of the six grandchildren who worked for her.

Alexander would come first.

Emma glanced at her watch. He was due to arrive in fifteen minutes, at ten-thirty. He would be on time, if not indeed early. Her lips twitched in amusement. Alexander had become something of a demon about punctuality, he had even chided *her* last week when she had kept him waiting, and he was forever at odds with his mother, who suffered from a chronic disregard for the clock. Her amused smile fled, was replaced by a cold and disapproving tightness around her mouth as she contemplated her second daughter.

Elizabeth was beginning to push her patience to the limits – gallivanting around the world in the most scandalous manner, marrying and divorcing haphazardly, and with such increasing frequency it was appalling. Her daughter's inconsistency and instability had ceased to baffle her, for she had long understood that Elizabeth had inherited most of her father's worst traits. Arthur Ainsley had been a weak, selfish and self-indulgent man; these flaws were paramount in his daughter, and following his pattern, the beautiful, wild and wilful Elizabeth flouted all the rules, and had remained untamed. And dreadfully unhappy, Emma acknowledged to herself. The woman has become a tragic spectacle, to be pitied, perhaps, rather than condemned.

She wondered where her daughter was at the moment, then instantly dropped the thought. It was of no consequence, she supposed, since they were barely on speaking

19

terms after the matter of the will. Surprisingly, even Alexander had been treated to a degree of cold-shouldering by his adoring mother because he had been favoured in her place. But Elizabeth had not been able to cope with Alexander's cool indifference to her feelings, and her hysterical tantrums and the rivers of tears had abruptly ceased when she realized she was wasting her time. She had capitulated in the face of his aloofness, disapproval, and thinly-veiled contempt. Her son's good opinion of her, and his love, were vital, apparently, and she had made her peace with him, mended her ways. But not for long, Emma thought acidly. *She* soon fell back into her bad habits. And it's certainly no thanks to that foolish and skittish woman that Alexander has turned out so well.

Emma experienced a little rush of warmth mingled with gratification as she contemplated her grandson. Alexander had become the man he was because of his strength of character and his integrity. He was solid, hardworking, dependable. If he did not have his cousin Paula's brilliance, and lacked her vision in business, he was, nonetheless, sound of judgement. His conservative streak was balanced by a degree of flexibility, and he displayed a genuine willingness to weigh the pros and cons of any given situation, and, when necessary, make compromises. Alexander had the ability to keep everything in its proper perspective, and this was reassuring to Emma, who was a born realist herself.

This past year Alexander had proved himself deserving of her faith in him, and she had no regrets about making him the chief heir to Harte Enterprises by leaving him fifty-two per cent of her shares in this privately-held company. Whilst he continued to supervise the mills, she deemed it essential for him to have a true understanding of every aspect of the holding corporation, and she had been training him assiduously, preparing him for the day when he took over the reins from her.

Harte Enterprises controlled her woollen mills, clothing factories, real estate, the General Retail Trading Company, and the Yorkshire Consolidated Newspaper Company, and it was worth many millions of pounds. She had long recognized that Alexander might never increase its worth by much, because of his tendency to be cautious; but, for the same reason, neither would he ruin it through rash decisions and reckless speculation. He would keep it on the steady course she had so carefully charted, following the guidelines and principles she had set down years ago. This was the way she wanted it, had planned it, in point of fact.

Emma drew her appointment book towards her, and checked the time of her lunch with Emily, Alexander's sister.

Emily was due to arrive at one o'clock.

When she had phoned earlier in the week Emily had sounded somewhat enigmatic when she had said she had a serious problem to discuss. There was no mystery, as far as Emma was concerned. She knew what Emily's problem was, had known about it for a long time. She was only surprised her granddaughter had not asked to discuss it before now. She lifted her head and stared into space reflectively, turning the matter over in her mind, and then she frowned. Two weeks ago she had come to a decision about Emily, and she was convinced it was the right one. But would Emily agree? Yes, she answered herself. The girl will see the sense in it, I'm positive of that. Emma brought her eyes back to the open page of the diary.

Paula would stop by at the end of the afternoon.

She and Paula were to discuss the Cross project. Now, if that is skilfully handled by Paula, and she brings the negotiations to a favourable conclusion, then I'll have the challenge I'm looking for, Emma thought. Her mouth settled into its familiar resolute lines as she turned her attention to the balance sheets of the Aire Communications

21

Company, owned by the Crosses. The figures were disastrous – and damning. But its financial problems aside, the company was weighted down with serious afflictions of such enormity they boggled the mind. According to Paula, these could be surmounted and solved, and she had evolved a plan so simple yet so masterful in its premise, Emma had been both intrigued and impressed.

'Let's buy the company, Grandy,' Paula had said to her a few weeks ago. 'I realize Aire looks like a catastrophe, and actually it is, but only because of its bad management, and its present structure. It's a hodgepodge. Too diversified. And they have too many divisions. Those that make a good profit can never get properly ahead and really flourish because they're burdened by the divisions which are in the red, and which they have to support.' Paula had then walked her through the plan, step by step, and Emma had instantly understood how Aire Communications could be turned round and in no time at all. She had instructed her granddaughter to start negotiating immediately.

How she would love to get her hands on that little enterprise. And perhaps she would, and very soon too, if her reading of the situation was as accurate as she thought. Emma was convinced that no one was better equipped to deal with John Cross and his son, Sebastian, than Paula, who had developed into a tough and shrewd negotiator. She no longer equivocated when Emma hurled her into touchy business situations that required nimble thinking and business acumen, which she possessed in good measure. And of late her self-confidence had grown.

Emma glanced at her watch again, then curbed the impulse to telephone Paula at the store in Leeds, to give her a few last-minute tips about John Cross and how to deal with him effectively. Paula had proved she had come into her own, and Emma did not want her to think she was forever breathing down her neck.

The telephone rang. Emma reached for it. 'Hello?'

'It's me, Aunt Emma. Shane. How are you?'

'Why Shane, how lovely to hear your voice. And I'm fine, thanks. You sound pretty good yourself. I'm looking forward to seeing you tomorrow, at the christening.' As she spoke, she took off her glasses and laid them on the desk, relaxed in the chair.

'I was hoping to see you before then, Aunt Emma. How would you like to go out on the town tonight, with two fun-loving bachelors?'

Emma laughed gaily. 'And who's the *other* fun-loving bachelor?'

'Grandfather, of course, who else?'

'Fun-loving! He's getting to be an old stick-in-the-mud, if you ask me.'

'I wouldn't be saying that, mavourneen,' Blackie boomed into the phone, having taken it away from his grandson. 'I bet I could still give *you* a run for your money, if I got half the chance.'

'I'm sure you could, darling.' Emma smiled into the phone, her heart warming to him. 'However, I'm afraid you won't get that chance tonight. I can't accept your invitation, Blackie dear. Some of the family are arriving later, and I ought to be here.'

'No,' Blackie interjected peremptorily. 'You can see *them* tomorrow. Ah now, don't be refusin' me, darlin',' he cajoled. 'Apart from wanting the pleasure of your lovely company, I need your advice on an important business matter.'

'*Oh!*' Emma was mildly taken aback by this statement. Blackie had retired and left the running of his companies to his son, Bryan, and to Shane. Not unnaturally, her curiosity was piqued, and she said, 'What kind of business?'

'I don't want to be discussing it on the telephone, Emma,' Blackie said in a softly chiding tone. 'It's not something that's so cut and dried it can be settled in the matter of a few minutes. We have to be going back and

23

forth, you know, dissecting it a bit, and I think we should be doing it over a nice drop of Irish and a fine meal.'

Emma laughed under her breath, wondering how important this so-called business matter really was, but found herself conceding, 'I suppose I can let them fend for themselves. To tell you the truth, I wasn't much looking forward to tonight. Even though Daisy and David will be here, the prospect of a family gathering isn't particularly exciting. So I accept. And where are you and your dashing grandson planning to take me? Out on the town in Leeds isn't too exciting.'

Laughingly, Blackie concurred and said, 'But don't worry, we'll cook up something, and I promise you won't be bored.'

'What time then?'

'Shane will pick you up around six. Is that all right, me darlin' girl?'

'It's perfect.'

'Good. Good. Until later then. Oh, and Emma?'

'Yes, Blackie?'

'Have you given any more thought to me little proposition?'

'Yes, and I have serious doubts about it working.'

'Oh, so you're still me Doubting Emma after all these years, I can see. Well, we'll discuss that tonight, too, and maybe I can be convincing you yet.'

'Perhaps,' she murmured softly as he hung up.

Emma sat back, contemplating Blackie O'Neill. *Doubting Emma.* A faint smile flickered in her eyes. When had he first called her that? Was it 1904 or 1905? She was no longer sure, but it had been thereabouts, and Blackie had been her dearest, closest friend for all of those sixty-five years. For a whole lifetime. Always there when she needed him, loyal, devoted, supportive and loving. They had been through most of life's exigencies together, had shared each other's terrible losses and defeats, pain and anguish; had

24

celebrated each other's triumphs and joys. Of their contemporaries, there were only the two of them left, and they were closer than ever, inseparable really. She did not know what she would do if anything happened to him. She resolutely squashed this unacceptable thought before it took hold. Blackie was an old war horse, just as she herself was an old war horse, and even though he was eighty-three there was a great deal of surging life and vitality left in him. But no one lasts indefinitely, she thought, experiencing a twinge of anxiousness, whilst acknowledging the inevitable. At their grand ages mortality was a given, one which could not be argued with, and impending death was an old, if unwelcome, familiar.

There was a knock on the door.

Emma glanced at it, adopted her normal expression of cool inscrutability, and called, 'Come in.'

The door swung open and Alexander entered. He was tall, lean and trim in build, with his mother's dark good looks, her large, light-blue eyes; but his somewhat serious, saturnine face made him appear older than his twenty-five years, gave him a dignified air. He wore a well-cut dark grey worsted suit, a white shirt and a burgundy silk tie, all of which reflected, and reinforced, his rather sober personality.

'Good morning, Grandmother,' he said, striding towards her. Reaching the desk, he added, 'I must say, you're looking pretty nifty today.'

'Morning, Alexander, and thank you for the compliment. Mind you, flattery's not going to get you anywhere with me,' she responded crisply. Nonetheless, her eyes danced and she regarded her grandson fondly.

Alexander kissed her on the cheek, seated himself opposite, and protested, 'I'm not trying to flatter you, Grandy, honestly I'm not. You do look absolutely spiffing. That colour really suits you and the dress is very chic.'

Emma nodded impatiently, waved her hand in airy

25

dismissal, and fixed her grandson with a keen and penetrating stare. 'What have you come up with?'

'The *only* solution to the Fairley problem,' Alexander began, understanding she wanted to curtail the small talk and plunge into business. His grandmother loathed procrastination, unless it suited her own ends; then she could elevate procrastination to an art. But she scarcely tolerated it in others, so he rushed on. 'We have to change our product. By that I mean we have to stop manufacturing the expensive woollens and worsted cloths that hardly anybody is buying, and start weaving blends. Man-made fibres, such as nylon and polyester, blended with wool. Those are our best bets.'

'And you think this move will get us out of the red and into the black?' Emma asked, her stare intensifying.

'Yes, I do, Grandy,' he replied, sounding sure of himself. 'One of our chief problems at Fairley has been trying to compete with the man-made fibre goods on the market today. Nobody wants pure wool any more, except the Savile Row boys, and they're not a big enough market for the Fairley output. Look, either we produce the blends or shut up shop – which you don't want to do. It's as simple as that.'

'Can we make the changeover easily?'

Alexander nodded emphatically. 'We can. By manufacturing cheaper goods we can capture the more popular-priced markets here and abroad, and do volume sales. Of course, it *is* a question of sales and getting a real foothold in those new markets. But I'm sure we can pull it off.' He reached into his inside breast pocket, pulled out a sheet of paper. 'I've analysed every aspect of the plan, and I'm certain I've not overlooked one thing. Here it is.'

Emma took it from him, reached for her glasses, studied the closely-typed sheet. She recognized immediately that he had done his homework with his usual diligence. He had refined the idea she herself had toyed with, although

26

she had no intention of revealing this, not wishing to undermine him, or diminish his efforts. She looked up, removed her spectacles and gave him the benefit of a warm, congratulatory smile.

'Well done, Sandy!' she exclaimed, reverting to the affectionate diminutive of his childhood. 'You've put a lot of sound thinking into this, and I'm delighted, really delighted.'

'That's a relief,' he said, a smile breaking through. Reserved of nature though he was, Alexander was always completely relaxed and outgoing with Emma, who was the one person he truly loved, and now he confessed, 'I've really bashed my brains out on this one, Grandy, played around with all manner of convoluted ideas, I don't mind telling you. Still, I kept coming back to my original plan for creating the new blends.' He leaned closer to the desk, and gave her one of her own penetrating stares. 'But, knowing you, I have a feeling you'd already thought of the solution before you threw the problem at me.'

Emma was tickled at his perceptiveness, but she stifled the laugh that bubbled in her throat. She looked into his candid blue eyes and slowly shook her head. 'No, I didn't,' she lied. Then observing his disbelief, she added, 'But I suppose I would have. Eventually.'

'You're damned right you would,' he acknowledged. He shifted slightly in the chair and crossed his legs, wondering how to break the bit of bad news to her. He decided to jump in with both feet. 'There is one other thing, though, Grandmother.' He hesitated, worry suddenly clouding his face. 'I'm afraid we'll have to cut down on our running costs at the mill. Really tighten our belts out there at Fairley, if we want to operate more efficiently — and profitably. I hate to tell you this, but a number of men will have to be laid off.' There was a slight pause before he finished gloomily, 'Permanently laid off.'

Emma's face tightened in aggravation. '*Oh dear.*' She

27

nodded slowly, as if confirming something to herself. 'Well, I sort of expected that, Alexander. If you have to do it, you have to do it. I presume you'll be letting the older men go, those who are near retirement age?' she asked, one brow lifting questioningly.

'Yes. I think that's the fairest thing.'

'See to it that they get a special bonus, severance pay, whatever you want to call it. And naturally their pensions will become effective immediately. No penny pinching, and waiting it out until they actually reach retirement age. I won't have any of that nonsense, Sandy.'

'Yes, of course. I second-guessed you on that one. I'm preparing a list of names, and details of our financial obligations to the men. I'll get it to you next week, if that's all right with you.' He sat back, waiting.

Emma made no response. She pushed herself up and walked slowly to the oriel window, where she stood looking down into the magnificent gardens of Pennistone Royal. Concern edged on to her wrinkled face as she ruminated on the mill at Fairley. Her life had been bound up with it in so many different ways. Her father had worked there, and her brother, Frank, when he was only a small boy and should have been at school. Frank had been a bobbin ligger, slaving from early morning until nightfall, hardly able to drag his weary little legs home at the end of the long day, sickly pale from exhaustion and lack of fresh air and sunshine.

Adam Fairley, Jim's great-grandfather and the Squire of Fairley, had been the owner of the mill then. How she had hated him as a girl; for the best part of her life really. With the wisdom of great age, she knew Adam had not been the tyrant she had believed him to be. But he had been negligent, and that in itself was a crime in her eyes. His monumental negligence and his selfish preoccupation with his personal problems and his all-consuming love for Olivia Wainright had caused grievous trouble for others less

28

fortunate. Yes, Adam Fairley had been guilty of abdicating his duties in the most careless and callous fashion, and without so much as a glance at those poor souls who toiled in his mills: The workers who made his cushioned life of ease and privilege possible, who were dependent on him, and were, in a very real sense, his responsibility. Half a century ago, she commented silently. I may understand something of the man now, but I'll never forget what he did. Never.

She glanced down at her small but strong hands, soft and well cared for, the nails manicured to expensive perfection. But once those hands had been red and chapped and sore from scrubbing and polishing and washing and cooking for the Fairleys, when she had been bound in service to them as a child. Lifting one hand, she touched her face, and remembered with stunning clarity Murgatroyd's sharp blows on her cheek. The detestable Murgatroyd, Adam Fairley's butler, who had been permitted by the squire to rule that pernicious and secretive doomed house with a cruelty that bordered on savagery. Despite his harshness and his unremitting persecution of her, Murgatroyd had never frightened her. It was that monstrous house which had filled her with a nameless terror and from which she had wanted always to flee.

Then, one day, *she* had owned that great mausoleum of a place – Fairley's Folly, the villagers had called it – and she had known at once that she would never live in it, would never play the role of the grand lady of the manor. And with a flash of sudden and intense vision she had understood exactly what she must do. She must obliterate it from the face of the earth as if it had never existed. And so she had torn it down, brick by brick by brick, until not a trace of it was left, and she could still recall to this very day the grim satisfaction she had experienced when she had finally razed it to the ground.

Now, across the span of four decades, she heard an echo

of her own voice saying to Blackie: 'And destroy this garden. Demolish it completely. I don't want a rosebud, one single leaf left growing.' Blackie had done exactly as she had instructed, uprooting that walled rose garden where Edwin Fairley had so inhumanly and shamefully repudiated her and their child, which she had been carrying. Miraculously, in the space of a few days, the garden, too, had disappeared as if it had never been there at all, and only then had she felt free of the Fairleys at last.

At this time in her life, Emma had acquired the mill. She had done her utmost to give the men proper living wages and overtime and all manner of fringe benefits, and she had kept the village going for years, often at great financial cost to herself. The workers were part of her in a way, for it was from their class that she herself came, and they held a favoured and unique place in her affections. The thought of letting a single one of them go distressed her, yet she had no choice, it seemed. Better, surely, to operate at half her work capacity and keep the mill rolling, than to close it down completely.

Half turning she said, 'By the way, Alexander, have you discussed any of this with Kit?'

'Uncle Kit,' Alexander exclaimed, his startled tone reflecting the expression flicking on to his face. 'No, I haven't,' he admitted. 'For one thing, he hasn't been around. And for another, he doesn't seem interested in any of the mills, Fairley least of all. He hasn't appeared to give a damn since you dumped him out of your will.'

'That's a crude way of putting it, I must say!' Emma snapped, and returned to her desk with a show of briskness. 'I didn't *dump* him, as you call it. I passed him over. For his daughter, remember. As I did your mother for you and Emily, and your Uncle Robin for Jonathan. And you know the reasons why, so I won't bother elucidating on them again. Also, let's not forget that my will doesn't come into effect until I die. Which won't be for a long time, if I have anything to do with it.'

'Or me either,' Alexander cried swiftly, as always dismayed by her talk of dying.

Emma smiled at him, fully aware of his devotion to her, his genuine concern for her well being. She continued, in that business-like tone, 'Well, so much for Kit. *Mmmm.* Of course, I realized he was being a bit derelict in his duties; on the other hand, I did think he made an *occasional* visit, if only for appearances' sake.'

'Oh yes, he does do that. But he's so morose and uncommunicative he might as well not be there,' Alexander explained, adding, as an afterthought, 'I can't begin to guess what he does with his time these days.'

'Not much, if I know my eldest son. He never was blessed with much imagination,' Emma shot back sardonically, the suggestion of a disdainful smirk playing on her mouth. She made a mental note to talk to Kit's daughter, Sarah, about her father's present mood. Morose indeed, Emma thought, with disgust. He brought his troubles on entirely by himself. No, not true. Robin gave him a helping hand, and Elizabeth and Edwina, his cohorts in the plot against me. Aware that Alexander was waiting expectantly, Emma finished, 'Anyway, since Kit's not around, he's not going to hamper you – as he has so often in the past. Your way is clear. Put this plan into operation immediately. You have my blessing.'

'Thanks, Grandy.' He leaned forward, said with earnestness, 'We *are* doing the right thing.'

'Yes, I know that.'

'And don't worry about the men who are to be retired. They will be all right, really they will.'

She glanced at him quickly, her eyes narrowed under the hooded lids. She thought: I am so glad it's not Alexander whom I suspect of treachery and duplicity. That I could not bear. It would kill me. She said, 'It pleases me that you've always been so involved with the Fairley mill, and on such a personal basis, Sandy. You *care*, and that's important to me. And I appreciate your understanding . . . I mean of my involvement with that particular mill.' She smiled wryly and shook her head. 'The past, you know, is always with us, always reaching out to claim part of us, and I learned a very long time ago that we cannot escape it.'

'Yes,' he said laconically, but the look in his eyes expressed so much more.

Emma said, 'I've decided to go to the Fairley mill next week. I'll be the one to explain the changes we're going to make. Tell them about the retirements myself, in my own words. It's only proper.'

'Yes, it is, Grandy. And they'll be thrilled to see you. They all worship you, but then you know that.'

'Humph!' she snorted. 'Don't be so foolish, Alexander. And don't exaggerate. You know I can't abide exaggeration.'

Alexander swallowed a smile, remained silent, watching her closely as she sorted through some of the papers on the desk, her head bent. She had spoken swiftly, crossly even, but there had been a curious gruffness in her voice, and he knew that she had been touched by his words. He was amused by her mild chastisement. It was a hoot. Her whole life had been an extraordinary exaggeration, for God's sake. Why, she was *larger* than life.

'Are you still here?' Emma said, glancing up, frowning and feigning annoyance. 'I thought you'd be halfway to the office by now, with all you've got to do today. Get along with you!'

Alexander laughed, jumped up and went around the desk. He hugged her to him, and kissed the crown of her silvery head. 'There's nobody like you in this entire world, Emma Harte,' he said gently. 'Nobody like you at all.'

CHAPTER 2

'Nobody in this world but Emma Harte would have come up with such a preposterous proposition,' Sebastian Cross cried indignantly, glaring, his face turning choleric.

'She didn't come up with it, I did,' Paula replied in her coldest voice, returning his angry look with a steady unblinking gaze.

'Tommy rot! It's your grandmother talking, not you!'

Paula felt herself stiffening in the chair, and she suppressed the swift denial that sprang to her lips. Self-control was essential in all business dealings, and particularly with this odious man. She would not permit him to put her down, nor bait her with his inference that her grandmother was manipulating this negotiation from afar.

'Think what you will,' she said, after a slight pause. 'But regardless of whoever formulated the deal, that's it, as I've outlined it. It's a take it or leave it situation.'

'Then we'll leave it, thank you very much,' Sebastian shot back, filled with rancorous hatred for her and her strange yet compelling beauty, her money and her power. His dark eyes blazed, as he added, 'Who the hell needs you or your grandmother.'

'Now, now, Sebastian, let's not be too hasty,' John Cross soothed. 'And please, do calm down.' He threw his son a cautionary look, then turned to Paula, his whole manner unexpectedly conciliatory. 'You must make allowances for my son. Naturally he's rather upset. After all, your proposal came as something of a shock to him. He is very committed to Aire Communications, as I have always been, and he has no desire to leave the company. Neither do I. In short, we both expect, indeed fully intend, to continue in our present positions. I as chairman of the board, and Sebastian as managing director. Harte Enterprises would have to agree to that.'

'I don't believe that is possible, Mr Cross,' Paula said.

'Forget it, Dad,' Sebastian almost shouted. 'We'll go elsewhere for the money.'

'You've nowhere else to go,' Paula could not help retorting icily, reaching for her briefcase on the conference room table. She stood up, announced with finality, 'Since we seem to have reached an impasse, there's obviously nothing more to say. I think I'd better leave.'

John Cross sprang to his feet, took her arm. 'Please,' he said quietly. 'Please sit down. Let's talk a little more about this.'

Paula hesitated, staring at him. Throughout their relatively short meeting, whilst his son had blustered and snarled, John Cross had adopted a stance of inflexibility, displayed a quiet but firm resoluteness to make the deal on *his* terms, despite their original understanding. Now, for the first time, she detected a sign of wavering on his part. And whether he was aware of it or not, the preceding months of tension and anxiety had taken their toll. The troubles of his floundering company were much in evidence, clearly imprinted on his gaunt and weary face, and there was a quiet desperation behind the bloodshot eyes which held a hint of new panic. He knows I'm right about everything, she thought, carefully assessing him yet again, but he just won't admit it. The fool. She instantly corrected herself. The man standing before her had built up Aire Communications from nothing, so she could hardly characterize him as a fool. Misguided, yes; and, regrettably, he suffered from the serious malady of paternal blindness. He had long invested his son with qualities Sebastian did not possess, nor was ever likely to possess, and therein lay his downfall.

'All right,' she said at last, seating herself tentatively on the edge of the chair. 'I'll stay for a few minutes to hear what you have to say. But very frankly, I meant it when I said we'd reached an impasse.'

'That's not strictly true, in my opinion,' he responded, smiling faintly, and his relief at her continuing presence in his board room was barely concealed as he took a cigarette and lit it. 'Your proposition *is* a bit preposterous, you know. We want new financing. We don't want to be taken over and thrown out of our own company. No, no, that's not what we had in mind when we came to you,' he finished, shaking his head several times for added emphasis.

Paula gazed at him in amazement. She gave him a curious smile. 'You've just pin-pointed the crux of the matter. *You* came to *us*, remember. We didn't seek you out. And you certainly knew enough about Harte Enterprises, and how we operate, to understand that we never invest in companies that are in trouble. We take those over, reorganize them, and put them under new management. Our management. In other words, we get them running smoothly, efficiently, and on a profitable basis. We're not interested in financing other people's continuing disasters. It doesn't pay.'

John Cross winced at this unmistakable thrust, but resisted the parry. Instead he said, 'Quite so, quite so. I've been thinking . . . Maybe we can arrive at a workable compromise – '

'*Dad!* Don't!' Sebastian exploded irately, moving violently in his chair.

His father held up one hand, and frowned at him. 'Hear me out, Sebastian. Now, Paula, here's what I think we might do, how we might make a deal after all. Harte Enterprises could buy fifty-two per cent of Aire Communications' shares. That gives you the control you insist you must have. You put in your management, reorganize as you wish, but you must let us stay with – '

'Dad! What are you saying? Are you crazy?' Sebastian bellowed, his flushed face darkening considerably. 'Where would that leave *us*? I'll tell you where. Out in the bloody cold, for Christ's sake.'

'Sebastian! *Please*,' John Cross shouted back, finally losing his composure, his exasperation running high. 'Let me finish for once in my life.'

'Just a minute, Mr Cross,' Paula cut in rapidly, her irritation echoing in her voice. 'Before you go any further, I must point out, *yet again*, that we wouldn't be interested. It must be a *full* buy out. One hundred per cent or nothing. And I told you this right from the –'

'That's the old monster talking again, Dad,' Sebastian interrupted derisively, his mouth contorted into an ugly line. 'Emma Harte! Jesus Christ, the only heart she's got is in her name. Don't deal with them, Dad. They're vultures, both of them, and this one learned well at the knee of the master, that's patently bloody obvious. She wants to swallow us up, in the same way her grandmother has swallowed up companies over the years. I told you, we don't need *them*.'

Paula chose to ignore this unruly and vindictive outburst, deeming it unworthy of a response. She focused all of her attention on John Cross. She was appalled at his deviousness and enraged, but controlling herself, she said as evenly as possible, 'I started to say, that I quite clearly recall mentioning the full buy out to you, Mr Cross, long before today's meeting. I find it hard to believe you've forgotten the protracted conversations we've had about that very matter.' She gave him a hard stare, wondering if he thought she was stupid.

John Cross coloured under her sharp scrutiny. He remembered her initial statements only too well. But he had hoped to get Harte Enterprises interested in the company, whet Emma Harte's appetite, then structure the deal to suit himself. He had been elated when he had realized it was Paula who would do the negotiating. He had believed he could manipulate her, and the situation, to

36

his advantage. His plan had somehow misfired. Maybe Sebastian was right. Yes, Emma Harte was undoubtedly working behind the scenes; all of this had her unmistakable stamp to it. An unreasonable anger surged through him, and he exclaimed heatedly, 'Look here, you're not being fair.'

'*Fair*,' Paula repeated. She smiled thinly, added in a clipped tone, 'The issues of fair or unfair just won't play in this instance.' She held him with her startlingly blue eyes. 'I'm surprised to hear *you* use that word. I told you, at the outset of today's meeting, that Harte Enterprises is prepared to pay you two million pounds for Aire Communications. That's more than *fair*. It's downright generous. Your company is in an unholy mess. It could go belly up at any moment.' She shrugged. 'Well, I suppose that's your affair, Mr Cross, not mine.' She leaned forward, grasped the handle of her briefcase. 'We seem to have nothing further to say to each other.'

The senior Cross said, 'If, and I am saying *if*, we do decide to accept your offer, can my son and I remain with the company?'

She shook her head.

John Cross thought rapidly, came to an unpalatable but necessary decision. 'I would be willing to step aside. After all, I am near retirement age.' He stubbed out his cigarette, fixed his pale eyes on her. 'However,' he went on firmly, 'you must reconsider your decision regarding Sebastian. No one knows this company like my son. Why, he would be invaluable to you. I must insist that he be appointed to the new board of directors and that he be given a contract for five years as special consultant. I would have to have your guarantee on that, and in writing, before we can proceed any further.'

'No,' she said. 'There is no place in Aire Communications for your son if we take the company over.'

The older man was silent.

Sebastian looked pointedly at his father, his expression at once both baleful and condemning. John Cross dropped his eyes, unable to meet that accusatory gaze, toyed with his gold pen, said nothing at all. Sebastian leaped up angrily, seething, and strode across the board room. He stood looking out of the window, his body rigid, and he cursed Paula Fairley under his breath.

Paula's glance followed Sebastian. She felt the malignancy and alertness in him, but intuitively so, for she could not see his face. It was turned into the shadows cast by the window and the buildings outside. Involuntarily she shivered and brought her eyes back to his father. They regarded each other alertly, each wondering which one of them would make the next move. Neither did.

Paula saw a thin, grey-haired man in his early sixties, a self-made man who had pulled himself up by his bootstraps, and who, in the process, had acquired a distinguished air and a degree of superficial polish. He was also a frightened man. His company was sinking like a torpedoed battleship with a gaping hole in its bow, yet seemingly he was prepared to spurn the life belt she had thrown him because of his love for his son. The son who had so badly mismanaged Aire Communications that he had brought it to its present weakened and crippled state. She noticed a muscle twitching in the elder Cross's face and glanced away.

John Cross, for his part, sat facing a young woman of great elegance in her grooming and her dress. She wore a magenta wool suit, magnificently cut and tailored, obviously a pricey piece of *haute couture*, with a man-tailored shirt of white silk. There was an absence of jewellery, except for a simple watch and a plain gold wedding band. He knew that Paula McGill Amory Fairley was only in her mid-twenties, yet she gave the impression of being so much older with her inbred caution, her cool authoritative manner. She reminded him of her famous grandmother, even though her colouring was so different. The glossy black hair, cut in a straight bob that grazed her jawline, the blue eyes flicked with violet, and the ivory complexion were unquestionably striking; but whereas Emma's fabled russet-golden tints had always suggested softness and beguiling femininity, Paula's beauty was somewhat austere, at least to suit his taste in women. Neither were her features quite as perfect as Emma's had once been. Still, they did share the same aura of presence, and she had apparently inherited the old lady's steely toughness as well as that uncommon widow's peak, those sharp eyes that penetrated with a keen intelligence. His heart sank as he continued to study that palely beautiful but obdurate face.

He would never win with her. As this unpleasant realization sank in he did another *volte-face*, made yet another decision, and this one was final. He would seek financing from another source and insist that the deal include Sebastian. He must ensure his boy's future with the company — one which had been built up expressly for him. That was the only thing he could do; the right and proper thing to do. Yes, he must protect his son above all else, otherwise what had his life been about?

John Cross was the one who broke the prolonged silence. 'We are deadlocked, Paula. I have to pass.' He lifted his hands in a helpless gesture, then let them fall on to the conference table limply. 'Thank you for your time. And please tell your grandmother that her terms are too harsh for my palate.'

Paula laughed softly as they both rose. 'They're my terms, Mr Cross, but I won't labour the point.' Being a courteous young woman she thrust out her hand. 'I wish you lots of luck,' she said with studied politeness.

'Thank you,' he said, his voice equally as civil as hers but not quite as steady. 'Let me escort you to the lift.'

As they passed the window, Paula said, 'Goodbye, Sebastian.'

He swivelled his dark head, nodded curtly, and she was

so startled by the naked hatred etched on his cold and bitter face she hardly heard his muttered response. She had recognized a most dangerous enemy.

CHAPTER 3

Paula was blazing mad.

Walking rapidly down the Headrow, one of the main thoroughfares in Leeds, she soon put distance between herself and the Aire Communications building. Her mind was racing. Although she had felt the sharp thrust of Sebastian Cross's vindictive and combative personality, had readily acknowledged that he detested her and had become her arch enemy, her thoughts now centred on his father, and with good reason. Having more or less agreed to her terms right from the start, John Cross had ultimately reneged, and, moreover, in the most treacherous and despicable way.

It did not require much analysis on her part to understand why he had done so. It was apparent that he did not want to lose face in front of his domineering son, whose presence had unnerved him, made him defensive and, very possibly, more reckless than he had ever been in his entire life. Yet surely his honour and integrity were important to him too, took precedence over everything else? And what about retaining his son's respect? She laughed hollowly at herself for entertaining such ridiculous thoughts. A young man of Sebastian's perfidious nature had never made the acquaintance of those particular qualities. During the meeting, when she had understood that John Cross was not to be trusted, she had been momentarily astonished. He enjoyed a good reputation in Yorkshire's business community, had always been considered honourable if not necessarily the wisest of men. That he would go back on his word was inconceivable to her.

Her pace accelerated, and so did her anger, as she recalled the energy and thought and time she had expended on Aire Communications. Her grandmother was going to be as infuriated as she was. Emma Harte would not tolerate being played for a fool; neither could she abide anyone who did not deal from a straight deck. Grandy would handle the situation in one of two ways. She would either shrug disdainfully and turn away in disgust, or she would treat Mr Cross to a tongue lashing the likes of which he had never heard before. Her grandmother had an intractable sense of honour, never went back on her handshake or her word, both of which were as good as a written contract, as the whole world knew.

The thought of Emma Harte putting the duplicitous John Cross firmly in his place brought a flicker of a smile to Paula's violet-blue eyes. He deserved that if nothing else. But in reality he was facing much worse than Emma's acid tongue and her virulent condemnation. He was looking disaster right in the eye. Bankruptcy. Total ruin. Obliteration. She knew he was convinced that he could easily find another conglomerate or company to refinance Aire. She also knew he was absolutely wrong in this foolish belief. She had her ear to the ground, and the word was out. Nobody wanted to touch Aire Communications. Not even those ruthless and rapacious asset strippers who bought companies, plundered them, and then tossed to one side the empty shells which were left.

It suddenly occurred to Paula, as she cut down Albion Street, that, unbelievable though it was, John Cross had no real conception of what was about to happen to him or his company. She thought then of those he would take down with him, and of the many employees at Aire who would be thrown out of work. We could have saved him, more importantly saved *them*, she muttered under her breath.

The man is unconscionable. Ever since she could remember, her grandmother had instilled a sense of responsibility in her, and this was one of the mandatory rules in Emma's special code of ethics.

'Great wealth and power bring enormous responsibilities, and don't you ever forget that,' Grandy had told her time and time again. 'We must always look after those who work for us, and with us, because they help to make all this possible. And they rely on us, just as we rely on them in other ways,' she had constantly pointed out. Paula was well aware that there were those magnates and industrialists who were jealous of Emma Harte, and who, as adversaries, misguidedly saw her as a hard, ruthless, driven and power-hungry woman. Yet even they did not have the temerity to deny that she was eminently fair. That was something every Harte employee knew from firsthand experience, hence their extraordinary loyalty and devotion to her grandmother, and their love for her.

Paula stopped abruptly, and took several deep breaths. She must get rid of the anger boiling inside her. It was exhausting, took too much of her precious energy – energy which could be directed elsewhere and to much better purpose. And besides, rage blocked reasonable and intelligent thought. She started to walk again, but now her step was slower and more regulated, and by the time she reached Commercial Street she had managed to calm herself considerably. She dawdled a little bit, stopping to glance in shop windows, until finally she was drawing to a standstill in front of E. Harte, her grandmother's huge department store at the end of the street. She smiled at the uniformed doorman, whom she had known since childhood. 'Hello, Alfred,' she said, smiling.

''Ello, Miss Paula,' he responded with a benevolent grin, touching his cap. 'It's a right beautiful day. Yes, luvely, it is that, Miss Paula. Let's 'ope t'weather 'olds til termorrer, for yer bairns' baptisms.'

'Yes, let's hope so, Alfred.'

He grinned again and pushed open the door for her. She thanked him, hurried through the perfumery department and took the lift to her office on the fourth floor. Her secretary, Agnes, looked up as she walked in, and exclaimed, with a small frown, 'Oh dear, Mrs Fairley, you've just missed Mr O'Neill. Shane O'Neill, that is, and only by a few minutes too. What a shame. He waited for quite a while, then had to rush off to an appointment.'

'*Oh.*' Paula stopped dead in her tracks, taken aback, but she recovered herself, and asked quickly, 'Did he say why he dropped in? Or leave a message?'

'I gathered he was passing the store and decided to say hello on the spur of the moment. No message though, other than to tell you he would be coming to the christening.'

'I see. Anything else, Agnes?'

'Mr Fairley phoned from London. You can't call him back, he was on his way to a luncheon at the Savoy Hotel. He'll be arriving on schedule, at six, with your parents. The other messages are on your desk. Nothing vital.' Agnes hesitated, then asked, 'How did your meeting go at Aire?'

Paula made a sour face. 'Not good, Agnes. In fact I'd venture to say that it went extremely badly.'

'I am sorry, Mrs Fairley. I know the amount of work you put in on those dreadful balance sheets, and then the hours you devoted to the contracts.' Agnes Fuller, prematurely grey at thirty-eight, plain of feature and with a severe expression that actually betrayed the kindest of hearts, had worked her way up through the ranks of the Leeds store. She had been flattered yet apprehensive when Paula had promoted her to private secretary. After all, Paula was the heiress apparent, and Emma Harte's favourite; also, there were those in the store who thought she was cold, remote, unyielding and something of a snob who lacked Emma's extraordinary common touch. But Agnes had soon discovered that Paula had none of the characteristics so

43

unkindly attributed to her by detractors. She was reserved of nature – even a little shy – cautious and prudent, and a veritable work horse, and these traits had, very simply, been misconstrued. Over the past three years, Agnes had come to love the younger woman, was admiring of her, and considered her to be a brilliant executive who was a warm and caring person and a considerate employer.

As she peered at her young boss through her bifocals, Agnes noticed that Paula was paler than usual, and drawn. She gave her a look of sympathy mingled with regret. 'It's all very annoying,' she clucked in commiseration, shaking her head. 'And I hope you're not going to let it bother you, particularly this weekend.'

'No, I won't, I promise you that,' Paula reassured. 'As my grandmother always says, you win a few, lose a few. We lost this one – ' She did not finish, and a reflective expression settled on her face. 'But, come to think of it, perhaps that's just as well.' There was a thoughtful pause, before she finished, 'Excuse me, Agnes, I'll see you shortly.'

Paula went into her office and sat down at the huge antique partners' desk which dominated the room. After taking the Aire Communications papers out of her brief-case, she picked up a red pen and wrote *dead* in capitals across the front of the bulging folder. She rose, went to the filing cabinet and slipped it inside, then returned to her desk. The deal *was* dead as far as she was concerned. The negotiations had ended in a fiasco, and, in consequence, she had lost all interest in Aire Communications.

More than any other of the Harte offspring, Paula had inherited an unusual number of Emma's characteristics, and those she had not been born with she had acquired by osmosis, from years of working at Emma's side. Chief amongst these was the ability to admit any kind of mistake with openness and candour, and then put it behind her philosophically. Like Emma, she would invariably say: It

44

didn't work. Perhaps my judgement was flawed. But let's go on from here. We mustn't look back.

And this was exactly what she said to herself now. In her mind, Aire Communications was already a thing of the past. If she had gravely misjudged John Cross and wasted a great deal of time and effort on him, she had no intention of compounding these errors by dwelling on them unnecessarily. She wondered whether she ought to give her grandmother a ring, to explain what had happened, then decided against it. Grandy was seeing both Alexander and Emily this morning, and was bound to be busy. Later, she would drive out to Pennistone Royal, as arranged, and apprise her of the situation. Grandy is going to be disappointed, of course, she thought, sorting through the sheaf of messages. But that won't last long, and I'll soon find another project for her.

Picking up the telephone, Paula returned all of her business calls, signed the stack of letters Agnes had typed, and then sat back in the chair, glancing at her personal messages.

Her mother had called. *Nothing important. Don't bother to call back. Will see you tonight,* Agnes had scribbled, then added one of her inimitable postscripts. *Mrs Amory sounded marvellous, elated about tomorrow. We had a lovely chat. She's got a new hairstyle, and is wearing a grey Christian Dior suit for the event.*

Paula smiled at Agnes's comments, then scanned the message from her cousin, Sarah Lowther. Apparently she was fighting a cold and might not be well enough to attend the christening. *But she didn't sound at all sick,* Agnes had written cryptically. How strange, Paula thought, frowning and re-reading the slip of paper. Sarah obviously doesn't want to come. I wonder why? Since she could not hazard a guess, she turned to the last message. Miranda O'Neill was at the Leeds office of O'Neill Hotels International. *Please call her back before lunch,* Agnes had instructed.

Paula immediately dialled Miranda's private number. The line was busy, as it usually was when she was in the city. Like her grandfather, Miranda had what the poet Dylan Thomas had called 'the beautiful gift of the gab'. She could easily be talking for the next hour. Automatically, Paula's thoughts turned to Miranda's brother, Shane, and instantly she saw his vivid laughing face in her mind's eye. She was terribly disappointed she had missed him earlier. Such a visit had become a rarity. For years he had made it a habit to drop in on her both in Leeds and London, and when these unexpected visits had ceased abruptly she had been hurt and baffled.

Shane O'Neill, son of Bryan, grandson of Blackie, had been Paula's closest friend since childhood. They had grown up with each other, had spent all of their school holidays together, and they had been inseparable for most of their lives, so much so that Emma had nicknamed Paula the Shadow. As her mind lingered on Shane, she realized she had not set eyes on him for many, many months. He was constantly travelling these days, dashing off to Spain and the Caribbean, where a number of the O'Neill hotels were located, and when he was in England, and if she chanced to run into him, he had a preoccupied air and a distant manner. She exhaled softly, slowly. How odd it was that their closeness should end with such finality, as it had two years ago. It still puzzled her. When she had eventually tackled Shane, had asked him what had happened between them, he had looked at her in the most peculiar way, and denied that anything had. He had blamed business and his time-consuming schedule for his absence from her life. Perhaps he had simply outgrown her. Childhood friendships often did change radically; very frequently they deteriorated to such an extent they could never be reinstated. Regrettably, she thought. And I do miss him. I wish I'd been here this morning.

46

The buzz of the telephone cut into her thoughts. She reached for it. Agnes said, 'It's Miss O'Neill, Mrs Fairley.'

'Thanks, Agnes, put her through, please.'

A split second later Miranda's lilting voice flowed over the wire. 'Hello, Paula. I thought I'd better call you again, since my phone's been busy for ages.'

'That's par for the course,' Paula said with an affectionate laugh. 'When did you get in from London?'

'Last night. I drove up with Shane. And for the last time, I don't mind telling you. He's a maniac in a car. The tyres sizzled the roads. I thought we'd end up in a ditch. I'll never know how I got here safe and sound. I was so shaken up, and white, when we arrived at the house, Mummy knew immediately what had happened. She's forbidden me to drive with him again. She gave him quite a piece of her mind, and – '

'I'll bet,' Paula broke in, with another laugh. 'Your mother thinks the sun shines out of Shane. He can't do anything wrong in her eyes.'

'Well, he's in the doghouse at the moment, my dear. She really told him off, and so did Dad.'

'Shane came to see me today, Miranda.'

'Hey, that's good news. Like you, I can't understand why he's so aloof with you these days, but then he's a strange one, that big brother of mine. Too much of the Celt in him, perhaps. Anyway, what did he have to say?'

'Nothing, Miranda, since I wasn't here. I was out at a meeting.'

'Too bad. Still, he's coming to the christening. I know *you* had your doubts, but he told me he was definitely going to go. He even offered to drive me.' Miranda groaned in mock horror at this idea. 'I declined. I was going to go with Grandpops, but naturally he's escorting Aunt Emma. So I'll toddle over by myself. Listen, Paula, apart from wanting to say hello, I was wondering if you'd like to have lunch? I've got to come over to the store to pick up a

47

package for my mother. I could meet you in the Birdcage in half an hour. What do you think?'

'That's a nice suggestion, Merry. I'll see you there at noon.'

'It's a date,' Miranda said. 'Bye.'

'Bye.' As she began clearing her desk of papers, Paula was suddenly glad Miranda had suggested lunch. Her friend was a delight to be with, and a very special girl, with her naturalness, her sweetness, her gaiety and effervescence. She had a joyous, carefree disposition, and laughter sprang readily to her lips, undoubtedly the reason why her nickname Mirry had soon turned into Merry when she was small.

Paula smiled to herself, wondering what Miranda was wearing today, what surprise was in store for her. The twenty-three-year-old girl had a penchant for creating the most outlandish outfits – costumes really – but they were put together with imagination and style, and she certainly carried them off with élan. They would have looked perfectly ridiculous on anyone else, but somehow they were exactly right on Miranda O'Neill. Apart from suiting her tall, somewhat boyish figure, they were an adjunct to her 'fey and whimsical personality. Or so it seemed to Paula, who considered Merry to be an original, the one genuine free spirit she knew. Her grandmother was equally fond of Miranda, and said that Blackie's granddaughter was the best tonic in the world for all of them, because she chased their blues away. 'There's not a bad bone in that girl's body,' Emma had remarked to Paula recently. 'And now that she's grown up she reminds me a lot of her grandmother. There's a good deal of Laura Spencer in Merry – Laura's true goodness for one thing. Also, there's a wise head on those young shoulders, and I'm pleased you two have become such good friends. Every woman needs a close and trusted friend of the same sex. I should know. I never really had one after Laura died.'

Remembering these words of Emma's, Paula thought: But she always had Blackie, and she still has him; whereas I've lost Shane. Funny, though, that Miranda and I drew closer together once Shane had dropped out . . .

There was a knock and Agnes poked her head around the door. 'These proofs just came up from the advertising department. Can you give them your okay?'

'Yes, come in, Agnes.'

'They're the advertisements for the spring fashion sales,' Agnes explained, handing them to her.

After studying the newspaper advertisements for a few seconds, Paula initialled the proofs, gave them back to her secretary and stood up. 'I'm going out on to the floor for a while. Could you phone the Birdcage, Agnes, and tell them I'll need my usual table, please. At noon.'

'Right away,' Agnes said as they went out together.

When Emma Harte had first opened the café on the second floor of the Leeds store, she had called it the Elizabethan Gazebo, and had decorated it in the style of an English country garden. Such things as handpainted wallpaper depicting pastoral scenes, panels of white trellis, artificial topiary animals, and antique birdcages combined to create a most enchanting little setting.

Over the years, as she refurbished the café, the name changed to match the theme, or vice versa. But always a garden or outdoor motif prevailed, often with an international flavour, as Emma had given rein to her imagination and fantasies with flair and not a little wit. After a trip to the Bosphorus, with Paul McGill, she had been inspired to create the effect of a courtyard in a Seraglio. Mosaic tiles, silver wallpaper painted with peacocks, potted palms and a splashing fountain were combined in the new design. She had called the café Turkish Delight, and had been delighted herself to witness its instantaneous popularity as a smart gathering place, not only for women shoppers but local businessmen who came in for lunch. Several years later, Emma decided a more homespun motif was in order. Highland Fling was the name she chose, and the setting took on the appearance of a Scottish castle yard, featuring rustic furniture and colourful tartans. Eventually this ambience gave way to one which suggested an Oriental teahouse and drew its inspiration from the elegant decorative elements of the Far East. The café was renamed the China Doll. Then came the Balalaika, redolent of nineteenth-century Russia; after that it was transformed into Riviera Terrace, and in 1960 Emma redid the café yet again. This time she used a sophisticated theme based on the skyline of New York City, lining the walls with giant-sized photographic murals of Manhattan. The decor suggested a big-city roof garden and she called it Skyscrapers. But by the late summer of 1968 Emma had grown tired of this decorative mood, and, as the café needed a complete overhaul at this time, she gave the project to Paula, asking her to create something different.

Paula knew everything there was to know about all of the stores in the Harte chain, and she remembered the photographs she had seen of the original Elizabethan Gazebo. She went into the archives, dug out the original plans and sketches, and was instantly struck by the uniqueness and beauty of the antique birdcages. Since she was aware they were stored in packing cases in the basement, she had them brought up and unwrapped. And so the current theme and the latest name were born.

Paula had the wooden and brass birdcages repainted or repolished and, after finding more to add to the collection, she featured them throughout the restaurant. They stood out beautifully against a background of lime-green wallpaper over-patterned with a sharp white trellis design; white wicker chairs and matching tables with glass tops reiterated the outdoor mood. Paula loved all growing things, was, in fact, a gifted gardener, and so her final, masterful touch was a lush assortment of small trees, flowering shrubs and plants. It was the many pots of hydrangeas and azaleas that gave the Birdcage its cachet, and this real garden within the heart of the store bloomed in all seasons under her personal supervision. Emma had recognized at once that it was an evocation of her own first design and as such a little tribute to her, and she was flattered.

A few minutes after twelve, on this Friday morning, Paula hurried into the Birdcage and as always she was struck by the refreshing sight of the flowers and foliage, one which appeared to cheer everyone up. Moving between the tables, where morning shoppers were settling down to lunch, Paula saw that Miranda O'Neill had already arrived. Her burnished copper hair, cascading in a glorious mass of waves and curls around her heart-shaped face, seemed to catch and hold all the light, was like a shining beacon at the far side of the room. Miranda glanced up from the menu she was perusing, saw Paula, and waved.

'Sorry I kept you waiting,' Paula apologized when she reached the table. 'I was delayed in the Designer Salon. We've been having the most awful trouble with the new lighting, and I wanted to check on it again. It's still not right I'm afraid.' She bent down and kissed her friend, slipped into the next chair.

Miranda grinned a little impishly, and said, 'Oh dear, the trials and tribulations of running a store! I'll swap jobs with you any day. Doing public relations for a chain of hotels can be the pits at times.'

'If I remember correctly, you really badgered your father for that job.'

'That's true. But I wouldn't have, if I'd known what I was letting myself in for,' Miranda grumbled, making a long face. But she then had the good grace to laugh, and admitted, 'I suppose I enjoy it really. It's only occasionally that I feel the pressure. But right now I'm in Dad's good books. He's very happy with my latest campaign, and he even went so far as to say I'd been innovative the other day. That's praise indeed from him. He's not given to paying me compliments, as you know. He even said that if I behave myself he's going to send me to Barbados in a few weeks, to look over the hotel we've just bought there. By the time we've remodelled it and redecorated, it'll be super de luxe and as elegant as the Sandy Lane. We all believe it's going to be an important addition to our chain.'

'That's marvellous, Merry. Really exciting for you. Now, shall we order? I don't want to rush you, but I have to leave the store early today.'

'No problem, I'm a bit pushed myself.' Miranda glanced at the menu again, said, 'I'll have the plaice and chips, I think.'

'Good idea. I'll join you.' Paula caught the attention of the waitress, ordered, and then turned to Miranda, looking her over quickly, at once captivated by her outfit. Today she was wearing a rather theatrically-styled jerkin with a wide, flaring collar and three-quarter sleeves, and it was laced up the front over a white silk shirt with longer sleeves. There was a twinkle in Paula's eyes as she said, 'You look like a female Robin Hood, in all that Sherwood Green suede, Merry. The only things that are missing are a quiver of arrows and a perky little felt hat with a sweeping feather.'

Miranda broke into laughter. 'Don't think I don't have the hat! I *do*. But I didn't dare wear it to lunch, in case you'd think I was bonkers. Everyone else does.' She swivelled in the chair to reveal her legs, which were encased in tight green-suede pants and matching boots that came up above her knees. 'When Shane saw me this morning he said I looked like the Principal Boy in a pantomime. I went the whole hog with this outfit, I'm afraid. *Is* it too theatrical?'

'Not really. And you could have worn the hat. I for one happen to like you in your fanciful costumes.'

Miranda looked pleased. 'Coming from the elegant you that's a real compliment.' Leaning closer, she hurried on, 'Are you and Jim busy tonight? I was wondering if I could invite you out to dinner?'

'I'd love you to join us tonight, if you won't be bored. Grandy's having a family dinner at Pennistone Royal.'

'I'm not sure that that's still on, Paula. *Your* grandmamma has a hot date with *my* grandfather.' Miranda's laugh held a hint of mischief, which was reflected in her eyes, as she said, 'Can you imagine, and at their ages!'

Paula was thrown by this statement. 'Oh, you must be mistaken. I'm certain Grandy intends to be there.'

'I'm not wrong, honestly I'm not. I heard Shane talking to my father a little while ago. Grandfather *is* taking Aunt Emma out to dinner. But I was only teasing when I said they had a hot date, since Shane's going with them.'

'Then Grandy must have changed her plans,' Paula said, dreading the thought of the dinner without her grandmother's presence. 'I expect my mother will play hostess in her place, since I can't imagine Grandy actually cancelling it without talking to me first.'

'No, I don't think she would do that.' Leaning forward again, her manner still teasing, Miranda said, 'When my grandfather and your grandmother get together, they're incorrigible. I told him the other day that it was about time he made an honest woman out of Aunt Emma and married her.'

'If anyone's incorrigible, it's you, Merry! And what did Uncle Blackie say to that?'

'He chuckled, and told me he'd only been waiting for my approval, and now that he had it he was going to pop the question. 'Course, I knew he was only kidding me in return. But to tell you the truth, I don't think it's such a bad idea, do you?'

Paula merely smiled. She said, 'Anyway, getting back to the family dinner, you're very welcome. Come around seven-thirty for drinks. Dinner's at eight-thirty.'

'You are a darling, Paula. Thank you. You've just rescued me from a boring evening with Ma and Pa. All they do these days is talk about the baby.'

'I'm not sure your evening with us will be much more stimulating. My mother has become something of a doting grandma. All *she* does is rave about the twins. I can't seem to shut her up.'

'But I adore Aunt Daisy. She's such a lovely woman, and not a bit like the rest of you – ' Miranda stopped, horrified at her words. Her pale, freckled face flamed to scarlet.

'And what's that supposed to mean?' Paula demanded, a dark brow arching as she pretended to be insulted, but the amusement touching her mouth betrayed her.

'I didn't mean it the way it came out,' Miranda exclaimed in embarrassment. 'I wasn't referring to you or Aunt Emma, or your cousins, but to your aunts and uncles actually. I am sorry, though. It was rather rude of me.'

'Don't apologize, I happen to agree with you.' Paula fell silent thinking specifically of her Aunt Edwina, the Dowager Countess of Dunvale, who was due to arrive from Ireland later that day. It was because of Edwina that she and Jim had had their first truly serious quarrel. Some weeks ago, to her utter astonishment and disbelief, Jim had decided that Edwina must be invited to the christening. When Paula had objected, and strenuously so, and had reminded him that Edwina was no favourite of Grandy's, he had brushed aside her protestations and told her she was being silly. And then *he* had reminded *her* that Emma wanted bygones to be bygones, sought peace within the family. 'Well, you'd better not invite Edwina until I've mentioned it to Grandy,' Paula cautioned, and he had acquiesced to this suggestion, at least. When she had told her grandmother about it, Emma had appeared off-hand, indifferent even, and had told her to accept the situation gracefully, to let him invite Edwina, and to put a good face on it if she accepted. But there had been a strange look in Grandy's eyes, and Paula suspected that Emma had been disappointed in Jim. As she had herself, but she had overcome this feeling, loving him as much as she did; and she had excused Jim, too, because he had no family of his own to invite to his children's christening, and Edwina *was* half Fairley. If only Edwina weren't so hostile to Emma and to her.

Miranda, studying her friend, saw that she looked troubled, and ventured, 'You're awfully pensive all of a sudden, Paula. Is something wrong?'

'No, no, of course not.' Paula forced a smile, and changing the subject, she asked, 'How's your mother?'

'Her health's much better, thanks. Also, I think she's finally recovered from the shock of getting pregnant at forty-five and giving birth to a change-of-life baby. And little Laura is simply adorable. I love to watch Grandfather playing with her. He's quite infatuated, and of course he's thrilled they called her Laura, after my grandmother. They almost gave *me* that name, you know.'

'No, I didn't, Merry.'

'Yes. Then they changed their minds, I suppose. But I wouldn't have minded being named for my grandmother, and I certainly wish I'd known her. She must have been a remarkable woman. Everyone loved her so, especially Aunt Emma.'

'Yes, and Grandy told me, only the other day, that she's never stopped missing Laura since the day she died.'

'We're all muddled up, aren't we, Paula?'

'What do you mean?'

'The Hartes and the O'Neills. And the Fairleys, for that matter. Our lives are inextricably linked . . . we can't really escape each other, can we?'

55

'No, I don't suppose we can.'

Miranda reached over and squeezed Paula's hand. 'I'm glad we can't. I think it's rather nice to have you and Aunt Emma and Aunt Daisy for a second family.' Her huge hazel eyes, sparkling with tiny prisms of gold, overflowed with warmth and affection.

Paula returned the pressure of her hand. 'And it's nice for me to have the O'Neills.'

The arrival of the waitress with the tray of food interrupted this exchange, and for the next fifteen minutes or so the two young women talked mostly about Paula's babies, the christening the next day, and the reception Emma was giving after the church ceremony. But then Miranda, quite suddenly, adopted a serious tone, when she said, 'There's something very important I'd like to discuss with you.'

Paula, at once noticing the change in her friend's demeanour, asked swiftly, 'Do you have problems?'

'Not at all. But I do have an idea I'd like to throw at you, to get your reaction.'

'What kind of idea, Merry?' she asked curiously.

'You and I doing business together.'

'Oh.' This was the last thing Paula expected, and after her initial exclamation she was startled into momentary silence.

Miranda grinned, and not giving her a chance to comment further or brush the idea to one side, she rushed on: 'I had a flash of inspiration last week, when I was going over the blueprints for the new hotel we're building in Marbella. The architect has planned a galleria of shops, and it struck me immediately that we must include a boutique. Naturally, I thought of Harte's, then I realized one boutique wouldn't interest you. So I took the idea a step further . . . Harte boutiques in all of our hotels. There's the new one we're doing over in Barbados, we're about to remodel the Torremolinos hotel, and eventually the entire chain will get a revamp. We could have a

boutique in each one, and Harte's could run them.'
Miranda sat back and searched Paula's face for a clue to
her feelings, but it was unreadable. She asked eagerly,
'Well, what do you think?'

'I'm not sure,' Paula said. 'Have you discussed this with
Uncle Bryan?'

'Yes, and Dad liked the idea. He was very gung ho
actually, and told me to talk to you.' Miranda gazed at her
friend expectantly and crossed her fingers. '*Would* you be
willing to go into the venture with us?'

'I think we might be. I'd have to talk to my grandmother,
of course.' This was uttered with Paula's usual caution, but
she could not conceal the interest quickening on her face.
With a small rush of excitement, she thought: It could be
the perfect project for Grandy. The one I've been looking
for, and it would certainly take the sting out of the Cross
fiasco. Straightening up, Paula said in a more positive
voice, 'Give me some additional details, Merry,' and she
listened attentively as the other girl talked. Within minutes
she began to recognize the endless possibilities and advan-
tages inherent in Miranda O'Neill's idea.

CHAPTER 4

Emma sat up with an abrupt jolt.

I don't believe it. I almost dozed off, she thought with
exasperation. Only old ladies do that in the middle of the
day. She began to laugh. Well, she *was* an old lady, even
though she was loath to admit that to anyone, least of all
herself.

Shifting her position on the sofa, she stretched, then
straightened her skirt, and immediately became aware of
the heat from the blazing fire. The room was stifling, even
for her – she who had always suffered from the cold and

rarely ever felt warm enough. No wonder she had become so drowsy.

With a burst of energy she propelled herself up and off the sofa, and hurried to the windows. She opened one of them and took several deep breaths, fanning herself with her hand. The crisp air felt good, and the breeze brushing against her face soon refreshed her, and she stood there for a moment or two until she was cooler, before turning away and retracing her steps.

Her pace was slower, and she looked around as she skirted the two large plump sofas in the centre of the floor. She nodded with pleasure, thinking how lovely the room appeared at this moment, washed as it was in the golden sunlight now streaming in through the many windows. But then it always did look beautiful to her, and she would rather be here than anywhere else on this earth.

Is it age, I wonder, that makes us cleave to the best-known spaces in our lives, and the well-loved and familiar things? Is it the memories of the years gone by, and of those we cared so much about, which bind us to those places and make them so special in our deepest hearts? She believed that this was true – at least for her. She felt safe, and comforted, when she was in surroundings where so many episodes of her long and colourful life had been played out.

Such a place was Pennistone Royal, this ancient, historic and rambling house on the outskirts of Ripon, which she had purchased in 1932. In particular she favoured this room – the upstairs parlour – where she had spent so many endless happy hours over the years. She had often wondered how it had come to be called the upstairs parlour, for there was nothing parlour-like about it at all. This struck her once again as her glance took in the impressive architectural details and the splendid furnishings.

By the very nature of its dimensions the room had a singular grandeur, with its high, Jacobean ceiling decorated with elaborate plasterwork, its tall leaded windows flanking the unique oriel window, and the carved fireplace of bleached oak. Yet for all its imposing detail, and despite its size, Emma had introduced a mellow charm and great comfort, plus a subtle understated elegance that had taken time, much patience, superb taste and a vast amount of money to create.

Being confident of her original choices, Emma had never felt it necessary to change anything, so the room had remained the same for over thirty years. She knew, for instance, that no other paintings could ever surpass the fine portraits of a young nobleman and his wife by Sir Joshua Reynolds, or the priceless Turner landscape. The three oils were in perfect harmony with her graceful Georgian antiques, collected so lovingly and with infinite care. And such things as the Savonnerie carpet, faded now to a delicate beauty, and her Rose Medallion china in the Chippendale cabinet, were matchless touches that added to the room's graciousness and style. Even the walls were always repainted in their original primrose, for to her discerning eye this pale and delicate colour made the most restful backdrop for the art and the rich patinas of the dark woods, and it introduced the cheerful sunny aspect she preferred.

This morning, the springlike mood of the setting, created by the airy colour scheme and the brightly-patterned chintz on the sofas, was reinforced by porcelain bowls brimming with jonquils, tulips and hyacinth, which spilled their lively yellows, reds, pinks and mauves on to some of the darkly-gleaming surfaces, and their fragrant scents were aromatic on the still and gentle air.

Emma moved forward, then paused again in front of the fireplace. She never tired of looking at the Turner which hung above the mantelpiece, dominating the soaring chimney wall with its misty greens and blues. The landscape was bucolic, evocative, and a superb example of Turner's poetic and visionary interpretations of the pastoral scene.

It's definitely the light, she decided for the hundredth time, as always fascinated by the luminous sky in the painting. In Emma's opinion, no one had ever been able to capture light on canvas in quite the same manner as Turner. The clear cool light in this masterpiece was forever associated in her mind with the Northern skies under which she had grown up, and had lived for most of her life, and which she would love always. She believed them to be unique because of their clarity, and a radiance that seemed unearthly at times.

Her eye now caught the carriage clock on the mantelpiece. It was almost one. She had better pull herself together, and very smartly, since Emily was due momentarily, and everyone had to be on their toes when the volatile, whirlwind Emily was around. Most especially old ladies, she added inwardly, chuckling softly again.

Hurrying briskly into the adjoining bedroom, she sat down at her dressing table. After dabbing her nose with powder, she renewed her pink lipstick and ran a comb through her hair. There, that does it. Passable, she added under her breath, peering into the glass. No, more than passable. I really do look pretty nifty today, as Alexander said.

She swung her head and stared at Paul's photograph standing on one corner of the dressing table, and she began to speak to him in her mind. This was an old habit of hers and one which had become something of a ritual.

I wonder what you would think of me, if you could see me now? Would you recognize your glorious Emma, as you used to call me? Would you think that I have grown old gracefully, as I believe I have?

Picking up the photograph, she sat holding it with both hands, gazing down into his face. After all these years she still remembered every facet of him, and with a poignant vividness, as if she had seen him only yesterday. She blew a mote of dust off the glass. How handsome he looked in his white tie and tails. This was the last picture taken of him. In New York. On 3 February 1939. She recalled the date so easily. It had been his fifty-ninth birthday, and she had invited a group of their friends for drinks at their lavish Fifth Avenue apartment, and then they had gone to the Metropolitan Opera to hear Risë Stevens and Ezio Pinza sing *Mignon*. Afterwards, Paul had taken them to Delmonico's for his birthday dinner, and it had been a wonderful evening, marred only at its outset by Daniel Nelson's talk of impending war, and Paul's equally bleak assessment of the world situation. Paul's mood had been gay later, at dinner. But it was the last carefree evening they ever spent together.

She touched the white wings of his hair with a fingertip, and half smiled to herself. The twins who were being baptized tomorrow were *his* first great-grandchildren too, a continuation of his bloodline. Upon his death, the McGill dynasty had passed into her hands for safekeeping, and she had guarded it well and faithfully, just as she had preserved and multiplied his great fortune, which she had solemnly vowed she would.

Sixteen years, she thought. We only had sixteen years together. Not very much time really, in the span of a life . . . particularly a long life like mine.

Without thinking, she spoke aloud: 'If only you had lived longer. If only we could have shared our later years, grown old together. How wonderful that would have been.' Her eyes misted over and she felt a tightening in her throat. Why you foolish, foolish old woman, she admonished herself silently. Weeping now for something gone so far beyond tears. With a swift and darting movement she returned the photograph to its given place.

'Grandma . . . are you alone?' Emily asked in a tentative voice from the doorway.

Startled, Emma jumped, and turned in the chair. Her face lit up. 'Oh hello, Emily dear. I didn't hear you come through the parlour. And of course I'm alone.'

Emily ran to her, gave her a resounding kiss, and then looked down at her curiously. She said, with a funny little smile, 'I could have sworn I heard you talking to someone, Gran.'

'I was. I was talking to him.' She inclined her head at the photograph, and added dryly, 'And if you think I'm getting senile, you can forget it. I've talked to that photograph for thirty years.'

'Gosh, Grandy, you're the last person I'd ever think of as being senile!' Emily was quick to reassure, meaning every word. 'Mummy maybe, but never you.'

Emma fixed her coolly probing eyes on her granddaughter. 'Where is your mother, Emily. Do you know?'

'Haiti. Basking in the sun. At least I *think* that's where she's gone.'

'*Haiti.*' Emma sat up in the chair, surprise registering, and then she let out a small whoop of a laugh. 'Isn't that the place they practise voodoo. I hope she isn't having a wax doll made called Emma Harte, into which she can stick pins and wish me ill as she does.'

Emily also laughed, shaking her head. 'Honestly, Gran, you are a card. Mummy wouldn't think of anything like *that*. I doubt she's ever heard of voodoo. Besides, I'm sure she's far too preoccupied. With the Frenchman.'

'*Oh.* So, she's done another bolt, has she? And with a Frenchman this time. Well, I must say, your mother is getting to be a regular United Nations.'

'Yes, she does seem to have developed a fondness for foreign gentlemen, Grandy.' Emily's green eyes brimmed with laughter as she stood rocking on her heels, regarding her grandmother with delight, enjoying their bit of repartee. There was no one like her Gran when it came to the caustic jab which got right to the heart of the matter.

Emma said, 'Knowing your mother, he undoubtedly has an uncertain character, not to mention a dubious title. What's this one's name?'

'Marc Deboyne. You might have read about him. He's always in the gossip columns. And you're right on target, regarding his character. But he doesn't have a title, dubious or otherwise.'

'That's a relief. I'm sick to death of all these counts and princes and barons with unpronounceable names, grandiose ideas and empty wallets, whom your mother unfailingly collects. *And* invariably marries. Deboyne *is* a playboy though, isn't he?'

'I'd categorize him as IWT, Gran.'

'What on earth does that mean, dear?' Emma asked, her brows lifting, expressing her puzzlement.

'International White Trash.'

Emma guffawed. 'That's a new one on me. And whilst I get the implication, explain further, please, Emily.'

'It's a term for men with murky backgrounds, even questionable backgrounds, who have social aspirations which they can only hope to fulfil in another country. I mean a country not their own. You know, where inconsistencies won't be spotted. It could be an Englishman in Paris, a Russian in New York, or, as in this instance, a frog in London.' Emily made a disagreeable face. 'Marc Deboyne has been flitting around Mayfair's fashionable drawing rooms for years, and I'm surprised Mummy got involved with him. He's so *transparent*. He must have managed to dupe her somehow. Personally, I think he stinks, Gran.'

Emma frowned. 'Have you met him then?'

'Yes, and before Mummy too.' She stopped short, deciding not to mention that Deboyne had made a pass at her first. That would really be inflammatory to her Gran. She finished, 'He's quite ghastly.'

Emma sighed, and wondered how much this one was

63

going to cost her daughter. For cost her he would. That type of man always came expensive – frequently emotionally, but *always* financially. Dismally she thought of the million pounds she had given Elizabeth last year. Cold cash, too. Most of it had probably been frittered away by now. Still, what that foolish woman did with the money was no concern of hers. She had only been interested in buying Elizabeth off, and in so doing, protecting Alexander, Emily, and the fifteen-year-old twin girls. Emma said, with some asperity, 'Your mother is impossible. *Impossible*. Where are her brains, for God's sake? Don't bother to answer that, Emily. In the meantime, out of curiosity, whatever happened to the current husband? That lovely Italian.'

Emily stared at her in disbelief. 'Grandy!' she shrieked. 'What a switch! You always said you thought he was a gigolo. In fact, you were usually quite unkind about him, and I was certain you detested him.'

'I changed my mind,' Emma replied loftily. 'As it turned out he wasn't a fortune hunter, and he was nice to the twins.' She stood up. 'Let's go into the parlour and have a drink before lunch.' She tucked her arm through Emily's companionably, and steered her across the floor. She asked again, 'So, where is Gianni what's-his-name?'

'He's around. He's moved out of Mummy's flat, of course. But he's still in London. He's got himself a job with some Italian importing company, antiques, I believe. He often telephones me to ask about Amanda and Francesca. He's rather attached to them I think.'

'I see.' Emma disentangled her arm and lowered herself on to one of the sofas. 'I'd like a gin and tonic, Emily, instead of the usual sherry. Do the honours, please, dear.'

'Yes, Grandy. I think I'll have one myself.' Always in a tearing hurry, Emily dashed across the room to the Georgian table which held a silver tray of bottles and Baccarat crystal glasses. Emma's eyes followed her. In the red wool suit and frilly lilac blouse Emily reminded her of an iridescent humming-bird, so small, so swift, so brilliantly plumed, and so full of life. She's a good girl, Emma thought. Thank God she hasn't turned out like her mother.

Mixing the drinks deftly, Emily said, over her shoulder, 'Talking of my baby half-sisters, Gran, are you going to let them stay at Harrogate College?'

'For the moment. But I fully intend to pack them off to finishing school in Switzerland this September. In the meantime, they seem to be happy at the college. Of course, I realize that's because of my proximity. I suppose I spoil them, letting them come home so much.' Emma paused, remembering the fuss and bother and upset the previous year, when her two youngest grandchildren had tearfully begged to come and live with her. Emma had finally succumbed under their constant pressuring, although her acquiescence had been conditional. For their part, they had had to agree to attend the nearby boarding school Emma had selected. The girls had been thrilled, their mother delighted to be rid of them, Emma relieved that she had averted a nasty family contretemps from developing further.

Leaning back against the cushions, she let out a tiny sigh. 'Anyway, spoil them or not, I do feel those two need mothering, and a chance to lead a normal family life. They've had little enough of either with your mother.'

'That's true,' Emily agreed, carrying the drinks over to the seating arrangement in front of the fire. 'I feel a bit sorry for them myself. I suppose Alexander and I got the best of Mummy, I mean her better years. The girls have had a rough time of it . . . all those husbands. It seems to me that ever since she left their father, our mother has been on a downward slide. Oh well, what can you do? . . .' Emily's young breathy voice petered out sadly. She shrugged in resignation, and her whole demeanour reflected her disenchantment. 'There's not much you or I *can* do about *your* daughter, *my* mother, Grandy. She's not likely to change.'

Emily now looked across at her grandmother, her blonde brows meeting in a frown. She said in a fretful tone, 'The trouble with poor Mummy is that she suffers from the most terrible insecurity about herself, her looks, her figure, her personality . . . well, just about everything.'

'Oh, do you think so,' Emma exclaimed in astonishment at this remark. Her face changed and there was a glint of malice in her flinty green eyes as she remarked, with immense coldness, 'I can't *imagine* why.' She lifted her glass. 'Cheers.'

'Cheers, Gran darling.'

Emma settled into a corner of the vast sofa, and, squinting in the sunlight, she focused on the attractive twenty-two-year-old Emily. The girl had a special place in her affections, for apart from being open and uncomplicated, she had a very lovable personality, one that was sunny, cheerful, and perennially optimistic, and she was a dynamic girl, filled with enthusiasm for life and her work. If Emily's pink-and-cream blonde prettiness had the porcelain fragility of a Dresden shepherdess, it was, nevertheless, deceptive, belying an extraordinary drive that had the velocity and power of an express train running at full speed. Emma knew there were those in the family, specifically her sons, who thought Emily was scatterbrained and flippant. This secretly amused Emma, since she was fully aware that Emily purposely chose to give this fraudulent impression. In no way did it reflect her basic seriousness and diligence. Emma had long ago decided that her sons really disliked their niece because she was far too blunt and opinionated – and truthful – for their comfort. Emma had been witness to more than one scene when the intrepid Emily had made Kit and Robin squirm.

Emma looked into the clear green eyes, a reflection of her own as they had once been, saw the expectancy flickering in them, then noted the confident smile etched on Emily's mouth. Emily had obviously convinced herself she was going to get her own way. *Oh dear.* Taking a deep breath, Emma said, with a faint laugh, 'For someone with a serious problem, you certainly don't look very troubled, dear. You're positively glowing this morning.'

Emily nodded, and admitted, 'I don't think my problem's all that serious, Grandy. I mean, it doesn't seem to be today.'

'I'm glad to hear that. You sounded as if you had the burdens of the world on your shoulders, when you spoke to me on Tuesday morning.'

'Did I really,' Emily laughed. 'I suppose things seem so much brighter when I'm with you. Perhaps that's because I know you can always solve any problem, and I just know you'll – ' She broke off when Emma held up a silencing hand.

Emma said: 'I've known for some time that you want to go back to Paris, to work in the store there. That *is* what you want to discuss, isn't it? That is your *problem?*'

'Yes, Gran,' Emily said, her eyes shining with eagerness.

Emma put down her drink on the butler's tray table, and leaned forward, her expression suddenly serious. She said carefully, 'I'm afraid I can't let you go to Paris. I'm very sorry to disappoint you, Emily, but you will have to stay here.'

The happy smile vanished, and Emily's face dropped. 'But why, Grandy?' she asked in a crushed voice. 'I thought you were pleased with the way I handled things in Paris all last summer and through the autumn.'

'I was. Very pleased, in 'fact, and proud of you. Your performance has nothing to do with my decision. No, that's not strictly true. One of the reasons I've formulated new plans for you is because of the way you performed over there.' Emma's eyes did not leave her granddaughter's face as she explained carefully, 'Plans for your future. Which, in my considered opinion, is with Harte Enterprises.'

'*Harte Enterprises!*' Emily cried, her voice rising incredulously.

She froze on the sofa, staring at her grandmother dumbfounded. 'Where would I fit in *there*? Alexander, Sarah and Jonathan are working in that company, and I'd just be a spare wheel! A dogsbody, with nothing to do. Anyway, I've always worked for *you*. In the stores. I love retailing, and you know that, Gran. I'd just hate, positively hate and detest, being pushed into that organization,' Emily protested with uncommon fierceness, flushing bright pink. Breathlessly, she rushed on, 'I really mean it. You've always said it's important to enjoy one's work. Well, I certainly wouldn't enjoy working at Harte Enterprises. Oh please let me go to Paris. I really love that store, and I want to continue to help you get it properly on its feet. Please change your mind. Please, oh *please*, Gran darling. I'll just be miserable if you don't,' she wailed, and her face was as woebegone as her voice as she clenched her hands together in her lap.

Emma made an irritated clucking noise, and shook her head reprovingly. 'Now, now, Emily, don't be so dramatic,' she exclaimed with unusual sharpness. 'And do stop trying to cajole me. I know all about your wheedling. Sometimes it works, other times, like right now, I am quite impervious to it. And incidentally, the Paris store *is* on its feet, thanks, in no small measure, to you. So you're not needed there any more. Very frankly, I need you here.'

This remark, although uttered mildly, caused Emily to sit up swiftly, and she frowned, further taken aback. '*You* need me, Grandy. What for? What do you mean?' Emily's eyes widened and filled with worry. She wondered if her grandmother had a serious problem within Harte Enterprises. Hardly. Her health? That seemed unlikely too. But obviously something was amiss.

'What's wrong, Grandma?' she asked, giving words to her spiralling anxiety, all ideas about Paris swept completely out of her head.

'There is nothing *wrong*, dear,' Emma said with a bright smile, detecting the girl's concern. 'Before I explain my reasons for wanting you here, I would like to clarify my remark about your future. Naturally I realize you like working at the stores, but you can't get much further at Harte's. Paula and your Uncle David have the real power there these days, and Paula will inherit all of my shares one day. Paula respects your ability, and she would love to keep you by her side, but Emily, you'd always be a salaried employee, with no financial interest whatsoever. I do – '

'I know that,' Emily interjected. 'But – '

'Don't interrupt me,' Emma snapped, cutting her off. 'As you learned last spring, I have left you sixteen per cent of Harte Enterprises, and that's a huge interest, since the company is so very rich. And solid. As solid as the Bank of England, in my opinion. Your wealth, your future security, will come from your shares in Harte Enterprises, and I have felt for the longest time that you must have a hand in running it. After all, it will belong, in part, to you one day.'

Emma could not fail to miss the worried expression now settling on Emily's face and she reached across the table and squeezed her arm affectionately. 'Don't look so distressed. I'm not implying that I lack confidence in your brother. You must know that I don't. Alexander will guide, and guard, Harte Enterprises with all of his strength and ability, and with great devotion, I've no fear. Nevertheless, I want *you* to be active there, along with Sandy and your cousins. I really believe that you must direct that considerable energy of yours, and your many talents into the company in which you have such a major stake, and from which you will reap so many benefits.'

Emily was quiet, mulling over her grandmother's words,

and after a longish pause, she said slowly, 'Yes, I see what you mean, and I know you have my interests at heart, but there's nothing about the company that appeals to me. Anyway, Sarah has always enjoyed running the clothing end, and she'd resent it if you shoved me in there with her. As for Jonathan, he'd really get on that high horse of his, if you foist me on *him*. He considers the real estate division to be his little kingdom, and his alone. He'd be in revolt if I started poking around there. So what would I do at HE? The only thing I understand is retailing.' Her voice faltered, for she was on the verge of tears, and she looked away swiftly, staring out of the window, her expression exceedingly glum.

The prospect of leaving the Harte chain of stores, and Paula, whom she worshipped, was depressing and distressing to Emily. And she *would* have to leave. That had already been decided, she had the good sense to recognize. Her opinion wasn't being sought. She was being *told* what to do, told what was expected of her, and her grandmother's authority was unassailable. Besides, that cold and stubborn look was now engraved on her grandmother's face, and it was a look they were all familiar with, one which left nothing to the imagination. It said, in no uncertain language, that Emma Harte would have her own way no matter what. Emily felt the prick of tears behind her eyes, as she contemplated her miserable future. Mortified, she blinked them back and swallowed, endeavouring to hold on to her diminishing composure. Tears, emotion, and any other sign of weakness in business were anathema to her grandmother.

Emma, observing the girl closely, saw how troubled and upset she was growing, and realized immediately that she must allay Emily's worries. Adopting her most sympathetic manner, Emma said, 'Don't take this so hard, dear. It's not half as bad as you imagine. And I certainly had no intention of putting you in either of the divisions run by your cousins. That wouldn't be fair to any of you. Nor am

I considering making you Sandy's assistant – if that idea has entered your agile little brain. No, no, nothing like that. When I said I needed you here, I did mean *here*. In Yorkshire. I would like you to work at General Retail Trading, and learn everything there is to know about that division of Harte Enterprises. You see, Emily, I want you to run it for me eventually.'

For a moment Emily thought she had misheard. She was so surprised she was speechless. She gaped at her grandmother, and then finally managed to ask, 'Are you serious?'

'Really, Emily, that's a stupid question. Do you honestly think *I* would joke about my *business*?'

'No, Grandy.' Emily bit her lip, trying to digest her grandmother's words. The General Retail Trading Company, known within the family as Genret, was one of Harte Enterprises' most important assets, and an enormous money-maker. As the implications behind her grandmother's announcement began to sink in, she was assaulted by a mixture of emotions: she was flattered, overwhelmed, worried and scared all at once. But these feelings were almost instantaneously overshadowed by genuine bafflement.

Sitting forward with a jerk, she asked in a puzzled voice, 'But why do you suddenly need *me*? You have Leonard Harvey. He's been running Genret for years, and brilliantly. Or so you've always said.'

'And I meant what I said.' Emma picked up her drink, took a sip, sat nursing it in her hands. 'However, Len reminded me several weeks ago that he will be retiring in three years. I'd hoped he would stay on, but he insists on going when it's time. He wants a chance to enjoy life, do a few of the things he's always wanted to do, like take a trip around the world, for one thing.' Emma laughed softly. 'I can certainly understand his point of view. That man's worked for me for over thirty-five years, and I don't remember him ever taking a day off, except for his annual summer holidays in August. Naturally, I'd no option but to agree, albeit reluctantly.'

Emma put down her drink, rose, and went to stand with her back to the fireplace. She stared down at Emily, and continued matter-of-factly: 'Len brought up his retirement because he thought it was high time I started to think about his successor. It occurred to me at once that here was the perfect opening for you. I've been racking my brains for months, wondering how to get you situated within Harte Enterprises, in a division you would enjoy. I believe I've found it, Emily, and I'm also convinced Genret could well use your special talents.'

Emily said nothing. She, who had an opinion about everything which she usually had no qualms expressing, was now oddly at a loss for words.

Emma stood waiting, giving Emily a chance to catch her breath and marshal her thoughts. She understood perfectly the girl's unprecedented reticence. She had just dropped a bombshell on her. But as the silence grew, Emma, always in a hurry to settle matters and move on, announced peremptorily, 'I need you to start working at Genret immediately. Len wants to begin his training programme at once. Three years may seem like a long time to you, but it isn't really. Genret is a large company, and you will have a great deal to absorb and understand. So, what do you say?'

Still Emily was mute, and Emma threw her a sharper look. Then she scowled at her. 'Come along, dear, you must have some comment to make. I can't believe that the cat's got *your* tongue permanently.'

Pulling herself together, Emily gave her grandmother an uncertain smile. 'Are you sure? Really sure about me going into Genret?'

'I wouldn't have suggested it, if I'd had any doubts,' Emma retorted crossly.

72

'But what about the group at Genret?' Emily asked quickly. 'I mean, will they sit still for it? For me?'

'I *am* Genret, Emily. Or had you forgotten that?'

'No, no, of course I hadn't, Grandmother. What I meant was, will Len and the top management team accept me? I know you can appoint anybody you want, since it's your company, but surely Len must have a protégé, somebody he would like to follow in his footsteps, who knows the inner workings of Genret.'

'He doesn't. Furthermore, he thinks you're the ideal choice. And he's not just pandering to me. Len's too shrewd and outspoken to fall into that trap. And, whilst he realizes I would *like* a member of the family inside Genret once he goes, he would tell me point blank if there was no suitable candidate. He would insist we look outside the family. It just so happens that he thinks you're ideally suited to head up a wholesale supply company. For several reasons, all of them excellent. Your experience with the stores, your considerable knowledge of retailing, not to mention merchandise, plus your natural business abilities. That you also happen to be my granddaughter is simply fortuitous. It didn't influence him one iota, I can assure you of that. Besides, you're a quick study, Emily, and you've learned a lot in the last five years.'

'I'm glad to have Len's vote of confidence, as well as yours, Grandy.' Emily started to relax, and as her depression also began to lift, she discovered she was excited about the sudden turn of events. She asked, 'And Alexander? Have you discussed it with him?'

'Naturally. He thinks you'll be marvellous.'

'What does Paula say?'

'She's delighted too. She's going to miss you at the stores, but she recognizes the good sense behind my plans for you.'

'Then it's settled!' Emily beamed, and allowed her

natural enthusiasm to surface. 'Genret is a big responsibility, but now that I've recovered from my initial surprise, I'm looking forward to it, I really am. I'll try very hard, and I'll do my best not to let you down.'

'I know you will, dear.' Emma returned her smile, delighted to finally witness Emily's eagerness and her excitement. Not that she had had any doubts about her offer being accepted. Emily was far too clever to thwart her, *or* to pass up the opportunity to head a division. Besides, Emily loved a challenge. This last thought prompted Emma to add, 'I'm quite certain you'll enjoy this new venture as much as you did your sojourn in Paris last year. It's going to be equally as challenging, and ultimately very rewarding.'

'Yes, I know it will be.' With a sudden flush of embarrassment, Emily recalled her outburst of earlier. Looking extremely shame-faced, she apologized, 'I'm sorry I behaved in such a childish way, when you said I couldn't go back to Paris, Grandy. It was ridiculous of me to act like that.'

'I understand. You were disappointed. In any case, you'll be going to Paris quite a lot for Genret, and travelling all over the world on your buying trips. That's certainly something to look forward to, Emily.'

'Oh it is, Grandy. And thank you for your faith in me, and for this wonderful opportunity.' Emily jumped up and hugged Emma tightly. With a happy little laugh, she said, 'Oh Grandy, you're such an inspiration! You make everything seem possible – and attainable. And exciting as well. Do you know what? I feel like rushing down to the Genret offices in Leeds right now, and getting stuck into the work with Len immediately.'

'Len and Genret have managed to exist without you until now, Emily, so I think they'll survive for another few days,' Emma replied, her mouth twitching with hidden laughter. 'In the meantime, I have a much better idea. I think you should come downstairs with me, and have lunch instead. I don't know about you, but I'm famished.'

CHAPTER 5

Emma sat at the table in her splendidly-appointed Adam dining room, sipping a cup of coffee after lunch, smiling and nodding occasionally, enjoying Emily's natural *joie de vivre* and bubbling enthusiasm for everything. Earlier, when they had been eating, Emily had bombarded her with questions about Genret. Each one had been probing and not without a certain shrewdness, and this had pleased Emma.

Now, the twenty-two-year-old was entertaining her with titbits of gossip about the family, and, as usual, Emma found her pithy comments hilarious. Robin and Kit were most often the butts of her barbed wit, and she had already managed to get in a few sharp digs about her uncles.

But here her sarcasm stopped, for she never made astringent or unkind remarks about anyone else. Although Emily tended to be something of a chatterbox, she was not malicious, nor was she a talebearer intent on stirring up trouble. In point of fact, she was anything but this, and Emma was well aware that her granddaughter's predilection for chattering was harmless enough, especially since she knew herself to be the girl's only confidante. To Emma's considerable relief, Emily was not only discreet but extremely close-mouthed with everyone else in the family, and even Paula and Alexander, with whom she was on very intimate terms, were no exceptions to this rule.

Unexpectedly, Emily veered away from her discourse on the family, and launched into glowing descriptions of the outfits she had chosen for the fifteen-year-old twins to wear the next day. Recently Emily had elected to play a motherly big-sister role with Amanda and Francesca, and Emma had assigned to her the task of selecting their clothes and looking after similar details.

But it was not very long before Emma found her attention straying, her mind forever preoccupied with business, and specifically Paula's meeting with the Crosses. She could not help speculating on the outcome, wondering how Paula had fared. If the negotiations had gone well she was facing a fair amount of work. Not that this troubled Emma unduly. She had always thrived on honest-to-goodness toil, and still did, and Paula had laid out foolproof plans for the takeover.

Emma and Paula wanted Aire Communications for its three most important assets: its magazine division, its local radio stations, its huge, modern building on the Headrow. Following Paula's advice, she fully intended to make Aire Communications a subsidiary of the Yorkshire Consolidated Newspaper Company. Once she had relocated the entire staff of Aire in the offices of the *Yorkshire Morning Gazette*, her newspaper headquartered in Leeds, she would sell the Aire Communications building. This would enable her to cut down on Aire's staggering overheads, and at the same time she would cleverly recoup part of the purchase price, possibly a good half of her two-million-pound investment. Yes, that building's worth at least a million, Emma reflected, whatever Jonathan says to the contrary. She would have to have a little talk with her grandson tomorrow, a very serious talk. He was dragging his feet with his second evaluation of Aire's prime bit of real estate. She had asked him for it days ago and he had not yet responded. Once again she wondered why, and her mouth tightened.

'Grandy, you're not listening to me!' Emily shook her arm impatiently.

'Oh sorry, dear. You were saying you'd chosen navy-blue dresses and coats for the twins. I'm sure they're very smart, you have such good – '

76

'Goodness, Gran, that was five minutes ago,' Emily interjected. 'I was already on to another subject. Aunt Edwina to be precise.'

'Now why on earth is *she* suddenly so interesting to *you*?'

'She's not really. I think she's an old sourpuss and a crashing bore,' Emily said in her typical blunt fashion. 'However, I'm positive we're going to be in for a rocky ride with her this weekend. I bet she's going to give us all an earful.'

'What about?' Emma asked, sounding slightly baffled.

'The divorce,' Emily said succinctly.

This reply brought Emma upright in her chair, and she stared hard at Emily. 'So, you've heard about *that*, have you?' Surprise immediately gave way to humour, and Emma chuckled and shook her head. 'Is there anything you *don't* know about this family of ours?'

'Not much,' said Emily, grinning at her. 'But I don't pry, Gran. You know that. Everyone just tells me things automatically. It must be my sympathetic nature.' Her grin widened. 'And then I tell you. Never secrets, though. I don't break a confidence. Ever.'

'I should hope not, dear. Remember what I've always said . . . a still tongue and a wise head. Anyway, who mentioned Anthony's divorce?'

'Jim. He came to see me last weekend. He wanted my opinion about something, my advice really. He brought up the divorce in passing. It was Aunt Edwina who told him. Apparently she's terribly upset . . . scandal touching the sacred name of the Dunvales and all that silly nonsense. As if anybody *cares* about divorce these days. But she'll harp on about it for the next few days, you mark my words.'

'I doubt it, since Anthony will be here himself. In fact, he's already here.'

'In this house?' It was Emily's turn to be astonished.

'No. He's staying with your Uncle Randolph up at Middleham. Actually, he's going to be there for the next week.' A wicked gleam entered Emma's eyes, and she could not resist teasing, 'Obviously there are *some* things you don't know, Emily. Our young earl is staying with the Hartes because he's courting Sally. Very seriously courting her.' Emma was unable to hold back a laugh as she observed the expression on Emily's face.

Emily was so dumbfounded by this piece of news her jaw had dropped. But it took less than a second for her to recover, and she retorted, 'And I bet Aunt Edwina doesn't know either! Otherwise she would have scuttled that relationship ages ago. And she'll still try.'

'She can do nothing,' Emma snapped, her face hardening. 'Anthony is not only of age, he's thirty-three. He doesn't have to answer to his mother, or anyone else for that matter, and I told him so last night. He has my blessing. Frankly, I'm glad he's going to marry Sally. She's a fine girl and quite lovely, and it's a perfect match in my opinion.'

'I second that, about Sally being a lovely person. But then I'm prejudiced. So are you – even more so, because she looks so much like your mother. And Edwina's going to be prejudiced too, in the other direction.' Emily stopped, thinking of her aunt's reaction, which would be violent, and she cried excitedly, 'Oh my God! I can't wait to see Aunt Edwina's face when she finds out he's involved with Sally Harte. She's going to be absolutely furious, Grandma. She has such grand ideas about everything. And after all, Sally's only a generation removed from the working class.'

'And what do you think Edwina is?'

'A countess,' Emily giggled gleefully, 'and a Fairley to boot! She's never been the same since she discovered her father was Sir Edwin Fairley, and a KC, no less. She's an even bigger snob now than she was before. It's a pity you ever told her the truth about you and old Edwin, Gran.'

'I'm inclined to agree with you.'

Emma averted her face, looked out of the window,

focused her thoughts on her eldest grandchild, son of her own first-born child. Anthony Standish was the only offspring of Edwina's marriage with the Earl of Dunvale, and as such he was her whole life. Because Emma had been estranged from Edwina for years, she had not really come to know Anthony until he was eighteen. That was in 1951, when her brother Winston had affected a reconciliation between her and her daughter. More like an armed truce, Emma said inwardly, but at least the boy and I took to each other immediately, and thankfully we have continued to be close. She was extremely fond of Anthony, who, despite his reserved nature and gentle manner, had an inner strength and a toughness of mind that Emma had recognized instantly and privately applauded. Upon his father's death, he had inherited the latter's title and lands in Ireland. For the most part, Anthony lived at Clonlough-lin, his estate in County Cork, but whenever he had the occasion to be in England he never failed to visit her. It was on one of these trips to Yorkshire, six months ago, that he had become re-acquainted with Sally, Winston's granddaughter, who was his cousin. According to Anthony they had fallen in love at once. 'It was a *coup de foudre*, Grandmother,' he had confided shyly last night. 'And as soon as my divorce from Min is final I intend to marry Sally.' Emma, delighted at this news, had indicated her pleasure, and assured him of her full support.

Shifting in the chair, Emma glanced at Emily, and said, 'I wouldn't worry your head about Anthony. He can take care of himself. I told him not to hide his relationship with Sally any more, from his mother, that is, and to behave naturally at the christening. We might as well get this out in the open once and for all.'

'Edwina will make trouble, Grandma. Big, big trouble,' Emily warned, rolling her eyes at the ceiling.

'If she knows what's good for her she won't,' Emma

replied, her voice murderously soft. 'Now, on to other things. You said Jim wanted your advice. What about?'

'The gift he's bought for Paula. It's a strand of pearls, and he wasn't sure she'd like them. But they're beautiful, and I told him she'd be thrilled.'

'That's nice.' Emma glanced at her watch, feeling restless. 'I'll have another quick cup of coffee, and then I'd better go up and do a little paperwork until Paula arrives.'

'I'll get the coffee for you,' Emily volunteered, taking Emma's cup to the sideboard. Returning with it, she said, 'I had dinner with T.B. when I was in London on Tuesday. He sends his love.'

Emma's face softened considerably. She had always cared for Tony Barkstone, Elizabeth's first husband and father of Emily and Alexander. They had remained good friends over the years, and she asked, with a warm smile, 'How is he?'

'In good form. He's as sweet as always, and he seems happy. No, content might be a better word. Or perhaps *accepting* is even better. Yes, that's it. He's accepting.' Emily sighed heavily.

And a little too dramatically, in Emma's opinion. But then Emily was a romantic girl and Emma knew that she had long harboured the desire for her parents to be reunited. A most unlikely event, as far as Emma was concerned. Looking at Emily thoughtfully, Emma's brow lifted quizzically, and she murmured, 'Accepting is a peculiar word to use about your father's life, isn't it, dear?'

'Not really. I think T.B. *is* accepting – of his new family. But I don't believe my father has been really happy since he split with Mummy. To tell you the truth, Gran, I think he's still in love with her.' She confided this in an intense tone, giving Emma a long and knowing look.

'Oh phooey!'

'Well, she *was* his grand passion, that I know for a fact –

because he once told me so. I believe he's carrying a torch for her.'

'That's a bit farfetched, Emily, they've been divorced for donkey's years.'

'Even so, he could have remained shackled to her emotionally.' Emily tilted her blonde head to one side and wrinkled her nose. 'Unrequited love, and all that. Why are you looking so sceptical, Grandma? Don't you believe that's possible?'

'Possible. Not very practical. And I'm quite certain your father has more common sense than to yearn after Elizabeth. He had *her* pegged years ago.'

'I hope you're right. I'm sure that being in love with someone who doesn't care in return is most unsatisfactory, not to mention painful. Very impractical in the long run, as you just said.' A faraway expression flickered in Emily's wide green eyes, and she said, almost inaudibly, 'If only Sarah would recognize that.'

As quiet as her voice had been Emma had heard her. She put down her coffee cup with a loud clatter and gaped at Emily, frowning. '*Our Sarah*. Is she in love with someone who doesn't love her?'

'Oh gosh, Gran, I shouldn't have mentioned Sarah. It's really none of my business,' Emily muttered, her face flushing and filling with chagrin. 'Please don't say anything to her, will you? She'd be ever so upset.'

'Of course I won't say anything. I never do, do I? Who's she carrying a torch for? That's what you implied, you know.'

Emily hesitated. She was suddenly tempted to fib. But she had never lied to her grandmother in her whole life. Still, perhaps in this instance she ought to resort to a white lie.

Emma pressed, 'Who is it?'

There was a moment of silence. Emily swallowed, and knowing herself to be trapped, she mumbled, 'Shane.'

'I'll be damned.' Emma leaned back and focused her keen old eyes on her granddaughter, 'Well, well, well,' she said, and a slow smile spread across her face.

Emily shot up in her chair, her eyes flaring open, and she cried, 'Oh Grandy, don't look like that! *Please* don't look like that!'

'And how am I looking?'

'Gratified. And ever so conspiratorial. I know you and Uncle Blackie have long had hopes that one of us, or one of the Harte girls, would marry Shane O'Neill, and unite our families. But he's not interested in any of us, except for – ' Emily bit off the rest of her sentence abruptly, instantly wishing she could also bite off her tongue. This time she really had said far too much. She jumped up and went to the Hepplewhite sideboard, where she hovered over the silver bowl of fruit. 'I think I'll have a banana,' she said, attempting nonchalance. 'Would you like one too, Gran dear?'

'I certainly wouldn't, thank you very much.' Emma swung her head and studied her granddaughter's back. 'Except for *whom*, Emily?'

'No one, Gran.' Emily wondered how to extricate herself, and adroitly, without arousing her grandmother's suspicions further. She sauntered back to her chair, flopped down, and attacked the banana with her dessert knife and fork, her head studiously bent.

Emma watched her, knowing that Emily was avoiding her eyes. And avoiding answering.

'I know you were about to tell me who Shane *is* interested in, Emily. If anyone knows, it's you.' She laughed lightly, endeavouring to be casual. 'You've always been my conduit for information about everyone in the family. And *out* of it for that matter. So come along, finish your sentence.'

Emily, who was still cutting the skin off the banana with painstaking care, finally lifted her head. Her face was a picture of innocence as she said, 'I wasn't about to reveal a thing, really I wasn't. I'm not in Shane's confidence – I don't know anything about his love life. What I was going to say, before, is that he isn't interested in any of us, except for a one-night stand.'

'Really, Emily!'

'Sorry.' Emily dropped her eyes, then coyly looked up at Emma through her long lashes. 'Have I shocked you, Grandma?'

'At my age I'm shock resistant, my girl,' Emma replied tartly. 'But I am rather surprised by your remark about Shane. It wasn't very nice. Extremely unkind, in fact.' A new thought struck Emma, and she gave her granddaughter a fierce stare. 'Has he ever suggested anything of the sort –'

'No, no, of course not,' Emily burst out peremptorily before Emma could finish. And then she was swift to qualify her previous statement about Shane. 'It's just a *feeling* I have about him,' she mumbled, hating herself for maligning Shane, who was the nicest person imaginable. 'I didn't mean any harm, Grandy, honestly I didn't. Besides, who can blame him for being a bit of a lady-killer, when women fall at his feet like ninepins. That's hardly his fault.'

'True,' Emma acknowledged. 'But getting back to Sarah, I hope this crush she has on him is going to pass soon. I can't bear to think that she's miserable. How does she *really* feel, dear?'

'I don't know, Gran,' Emily replied in all truthfulness. 'She's only discussed Shane with me once, ages ago, and I think she's regretted mentioning him ever since. But I know she's smitten with him, just through my own observation. She always blushes furiously whenever his name comes up, and she gets all self-conscious and sort of dopey when he's around.' Emily levelled her gaze at Emma, and it was direct and candid, as she added, 'No, she'll never say anything to anyone about her feelings. Sarah's basically much too secretive to confide.'

This last comment further surprised Emma, but she decided not to pursue it for the moment. Conscious of the girl's stricken expression, she hastened to say, 'You don't have to be apprehensive about me, darling. Have no fear, I won't mention Shane to Sarah . . . I wouldn't dream of embarrassing her. And she'll come to her senses, if she hasn't already.' Emma's eyes rested on the bowl of spring hyacinths in the centre of the table, and she ruminated briefly on all that had been said. When she raised her head she smiled kindly at Emily. 'I don't want you to think I'm questioning your powers of observation, or your judgement, but you do have a tendency to be overly imaginative at times. You could be wrong about Sarah. Perhaps she has forgotten Shane by now, in view of his lack of interest in her. She *does* have her feet on the ground, you know.'

'Yes, Gran,' Emily said, although she did not agree with her grandmother's assessment of her cousin. Sarah might look as if her feet were firmly planted on the ground but her head was most definitely in the clouds. Emily bit her lip, and she wished more fervently than before that she had never mentioned Sarah in the first place. Embarking on this kind of conversation with her canny grandmother had been a horrible mistake. The trouble was, she was constantly doing it. Emma had always been the most dominant and important person in her young life, and confiding everything in her was a childhood habit which was difficult, if not impossible, to break. But Emily was thankful for one thing – she had caught herself in the nick of time, had managed not to reveal the truth about Shane to Grandy, who doted on him as if he were one of her own.

The realization that she had protected him made Emily feel better, for she liked and admired Blackie's grandson. She smiled to herself as she toyed with the banana in front of her, filled with sudden self-congratulation. For once she had been rather clever, side-stepping Grandy's probing so skilfully. And thankfully Shane O'Neill's secret was still safe. It would always be safe with her. Poor Shane, she thought with a twinge of sadness, what a terrible burden he has to carry. Stifling a sigh, Emily finally said, 'I don't think I want any more of this,' and she pushed her dessert plate away, making a face.

Emma, anxious to bring the lunch to an end, nodded quickly, and said, 'I'd better get back to my desk. What are your plans for this afternoon? You've finished at the Harrogate store, haven't you?'

'Yes, Grandy. I completed the stock inventories you wanted, and selected the clothing for the sales,' Emily explained, relieved that Emma had apparently now dismissed Shane and Sarah Lowther from her mind. 'I'm going to potter around in my room. Hilda asked one of the maids to unpack my suitcases when I arrived, but I prefer to arrange my things myself.'

'Suitcases in the plural, Emily? How many did you bring?'

'Ten, Gran.'

'For the *weekend*?'

Emily cleared her throat and gave her grandmother one of her most engaging and persuasive smiles. 'Not exactly. I thought I'd stay with you for a while, if that's all right with you. It is, isn't it?'

'Well, yes, I suppose so,' Emma answered slowly, wondering what this unexpected move on Emily's part was all about. 'But what about your flat in Headingley?' she thought to ask with a small frown.

'I want to get rid of it. I have for some time, actually. I decided to sell it, or rather that you should ask Jonathan to do so. Anyway, last night I packed a lot of my clothes and other things, because I'd convinced myself you'd be sending me to Paris next week. Now that I'm not going, I might as well stay here at Pennistone Royal. I'll be company for you, Gran. You won't be so lonely.'

I'm not lonely, Emma thought, but said, 'I'm probably being dense, but you seemed awfully taken with that flat when I bought it for you last November. Don't you like it any more, Emily?'

'It's a very nice flat, really it is, but – . Well, to be honest, Gran darling, I have felt rather isolated there by myself. I'd much rather be *here*. With you.' Emily flashed her beguiling smile again. 'For one thing, it's a lot more fun. And exciting.'

'Personally, I find it pretty dull here. Pretty dull indeed,' Emma muttered and stood up, headed for the dining room door. Over her shoulder she said, 'But you're quite welcome, Emily,' and she hoped she had not sounded too grudging. First the twins, and now Emily, she sighed under her breath. Suddenly they're all moving in on me. And just when I thought I was going to get some peace and quiet for once in my life.

As she walked briskly across the vast Stone Hall and mounted the staircase, with Emily trailing in her wake, Emma had another thought: maybe she would take Blackie up on his little proposition after all.

Paula talked and Emma listened.

They sat together in the upstairs parlour, facing each other across the Georgian silver tea service which Hilda had brought up a few minutes after Paula had arrived.

Emma had poured tea for them both, but she had hardly touched her own cup. She sat so still on the sofa she might have turned to stone, and the familiar mask of inscrutability had dropped down over her face as she concentrated on Paula's words, absorbing each one.

Paula spoke well, recounting the meeting at Aire Communications with precision and careful attention to the smallest detail, and her narration was so graphically descriptive Emma felt as though she had been present herself. Several times she experienced a spurt of anger or annoyance, but not an eyelash flickered, not a muscle moved in her blank, impenetrable face, and not once did she interrupt the flow of words.

Long before Paula came to the retelling of the final scene in the board room, Emma's mind, so agile and astute, leaped ahead. She knew without having to be told that John Cross had reneged on the deal. For a moment she was as startled as Paula had been earlier in the day, but when this initial reaction passed with some swiftness she realized she was not so surprised after all. And she came to the conclusion that she knew John Cross better than she had believed. Years ago she had spotted him for what he was, an egotist, puffed up with his own self-importance, a foolish man with immeasurable weaknesses. At this time in his life he was between a rock and a hard place, dealing from fear and desperation and propelled by increasing panic, and it was patently clear that he would be capable of just about anything. Even a dishonourable action, for apparently he was a man without scruples. And then there was that disreputable son of his, goading him on. A pretty pair indeed, she thought disdainfully.

Paula came to the end of her story at last, and finished with a tiny regretful sigh, 'And there you have it, Grandy. I'm sorry it ended in a debacle. I did my best. More than my best.'

'You certainly did,' Emma said, looking her fully in the face, proud of her, thinking how she had progressed. A year ago Paula would have blamed herself for the breakdown in the talks. 'You've nothing to reproach yourself for, and just chalk this one up to experience and learn from it.'

'Yes, Grandy, I will.' Paula regarded her closely. 'What are you going to do now?' she asked, continuing to study that impassive face in an effort to gauge her grandmother's feelings about the Cross situation.

'Why, nothing. Nothing at all.'

Although she was not altogether surprised by this statement, Paula nevertheless felt bound to say, and a bit heatedly, 'I thought that might be your attitude, but I can't help wishing you'd give John Cross a piece of your mind, tell him what you think of him. Look at all the effort we put into this deal. He's not only wasted our valuable time, but played us for a couple of fools.'

'Played himself for a fool,' Emma corrected, her voice low and without a trace of emotion. 'Very frankly, I wouldn't waste my breath, or the tuppence, on a phone call to him. There's not much to be gained from flogging a dead horse. Besides, I wouldn't give him the satisfaction of knowing I'm put out. There's another thing . . . indifference is a mightily powerful weapon, and so I prefer to ignore Mr Cross. I don't know what his game is, but I won't be a party to it.' The look Emma gave Paula was full of shrewdness and her eyes narrowed. 'It strikes me that he might be using our offer to jack up the price with another company. He won't succeed, he won't have any takers.' A cynical smile glanced across her face, and she laughed quietly to herself. 'He'll come crawling back to you, of course. On his hands and knees. And very soon. Then what will *you* do, Paula? That's more to the point.' Settling back against the cushions she let her eyes rest with intentness on her granddaughter.

Paula opened her mouth to speak, then closed it swiftly. For a split second she hesitated over her answer. She asked herself how Grandy would act in these particular circumstances and then dismissed the question. She knew exactly what *her* course of action was going to be.

In a resolute tone, Paula said, 'I shall tell him to go to hell. Politely. I know I could hammer him down, get Aire Communications at a much lower figure, because when he

88

does come back to us, and I agree that he will, he'll be choking. He'll accept any terms I offer. However, I don't want to do business with that man. I don't trust him.'

'Good girl!' Emma was pleased with this reply and showed it, then went on, 'My sentiments exactly. I've told you many times that it's not particularly important to like those with whom we do business. But there should always be an element of trust between both parties in any transaction, otherwise it's begging for problems. I concur with what you think about Cross and that son of his. Their behaviour was appalling, unconscionable. I wouldn't touch them with a ten-foot barge pole myself.'

Despite these condemning words and the stern expression lingering on Emma's face, her overall reaction had been so understated, so mild, Paula was still a trifle puzzled. 'I thought you'd be much more annoyed than you are, Grandy, unless you're not showing it. And you don't seem very disappointed either,' she said.

'My initial anger soon changed to disgust. As for being disappointed, well, of course I am in some ways. But even that is being replaced by an enormous sense of relief. As much as I wanted Aire Communications, now, quite suddenly, I'm glad things turned out the way they did.'

'I am too.' There was the slightest hesitation on Paula's part before she remarked quietly, 'Sebastian Cross has become my enemy, Grandmother.'

'So what!' Emma exclaimed in a dismissive tone. 'If he's your first, he's surely not going to be your last.' As she spoke Emma became aware of the concern reflected in the lovely, deep-violet eyes fastened on hers, and she sucked in her breath quickly. Making an enemy troubles Paula, she thought, and she reached out and squeezed the girl's arm, adopted a gentler tone. 'As unpleasant as it may be, you're bound to make enemies, as I myself did. Very frequently it happens through no fault of ours, that's the sad part.' Emma let out a tiny sigh. 'So many people are jealous and envious by nature, and *you* will always be vulnerable to that kind, and a target, because you have so much. Wealth and power through me, not to mention your looks, your brains and your immense capacity for work. All very enviable attributes. You must learn to ignore the backbiting, darling, rise above it. As I have always done. And forget Sebastian Cross. He's the least of your worries.'

'Yes, you're right on all counts, as usual, Grandmother,' Paula said and pushed away the dismaying memory of those hard eyes which had filled with loathing for her that morning. She felt a shiver trickle through her. Sebastian Cross would do her harm if he could. This unexpected thought immediately seemed silly, farfetched and overly imaginative, and Paula laughed silently at herself, and dismissed such an idea.

Rising, she crossed to the fireplace and stood warming her back for a moment or two. Her eyes swept around the lovely old room. It looked so peaceful, so gentle in the late afternoon sunlight filtering in through the many windows, with every beautiful object in its given place, the fire crackling merrily in the huge grate, the old carriage clock ticking away on the mantelpiece as it had for as long as she could remember. She had loved the upstairs parlour all of her life, had found comfort and tranquillity here. It was a room abundant with graciousness and harmony, where nothing ever changed, and it was this timelessness which made it seem so far removed from the outside world and all its ugliness. It's a very civilized room, she said to herself, created by a very civilized and extraordinary woman. She looked across at Emma, relaxed on the sofa and so pretty in the pale blue dress, and her eyes became tender. Paula thought: she is an old woman now, in her eightieth year, yet she never seems old to me. She could easily be my age with her vigour and strength and zest and enthusiasm. And she is my best friend.

For the first time since she had arrived, Paula smiled.

'So much for my wheeling and dealing . . . skirmishing might be a better way to describe it, Grandy.'

'And so much for my new project. Now that that's flown out of the window, I'll have to find another one, or take up knitting.'

Paula could not help grinning. 'That'll be the day,' she retorted, merriment swamping her face. Stepping back to the sofa, she sat down, lifted her cup and took a sip of tea, then remarked casually, 'I had lunch with Miranda O'Neill today, and – '

'Oh dear, that reminds me, I'm afraid I won't be here for dinner this evening. I'm going out with Blackie and Shane.'

'Yes, so Merry told me.'

'My God, can't I take a breath around here without everyone knowing!' Emma paused, scanned Paula's face. 'Well, you don't seem too upset, so I presume you don't mind that I'm trotting off and leaving you to cope with Edwina. Don't worry, she'll behave.'

'I'm not concerned. I was at first, but I decided she's Jim's problem. He invited her, so he can entertain her. In any case, Mummy's always pretty good with Edwina. She knows how to appropriately squelch her, in the nicest possible way too.' Paula put down her cup and saucer, leaned closer. 'Listen, Grandy dear, Merry has had an idea, one that might appeal to you. It could be just the project you're looking for.'

'Oh, has she. Well then, tell me about it.'

Paula did so, but as she came to the end of her little recital she made a small moue with her mouth, and finished lamely, 'I can tell you're not enthusiastic. Don't you think it's a good idea?'

Emma laughed at her crestfallen expression. 'Yes, I do. However I'm not interested in taking it on as a *personal* project. Still, that doesn't mean you shouldn't pursue the idea and develop it further with Merry. It could be good for the stores. Come back to me when you have it refined. Perhaps we *will* open the boutiques.'

'I'll set up a meeting with her for next week – ' Paula stopped, peered at Emma. 'Out of curiosity, *why* don't you think it's a project for you?'

'There's no challenge to it. I like tougher nuts to crack.'

'Oh Lord! And where on earth am I going to find such a thing for you?'

'I might find my own project, you know.' Emma's green eyes twinkled, and she shook her head. 'You're constantly trying to mother me these days. I do wish you'd stop.'

Paula joined in Emma's laughter and admitted, 'Yes, I am doing that lately, aren't I. Sorry, Gran.' She glanced at the clock, swung her eyes back to Emma, said: 'I think I'd be much better off going home and mothering my babies. If I hurry I'll get back in time to help the nurse bathe them.'

'Yes, why don't you do that, darling. These early years are the most precious, the best really. Don't sacrifice them.'

Paula stood up and slipped into the magenta jacket, found her handbag, came to kiss Emma. 'Have a lovely time tonight, and give Uncle Blackie and Shane my love.'

'I will. And if I don't see you later, I'll talk to you in the morning.'

Paula was halfway across the room when Emma called, 'Oh, Paula, what time do you expect Jim and your parents?'

'Around six. Jim said he'd be landing at Leeds-Bradford Airport at five.'

'So he's flying them up in that dreadful little plane of his, is he?' Emma pursed her lips in annoyance and gave Paula the benefit of a reproving stare. 'I thought I'd told the two of you I don't like you flitting around in that pile of junk.'

'You did indeed, but Jim has a mind of his own, as you well know. And flying is one of his main hobbies. But perhaps you'd better mention it to him again.'

'I certainly will,' Emma said, and waved her out of the room.

CHAPTER 6

They all said that he was a true Celt.

And Shane Desmond Ingham O'Neill had himself come to believe that the heritage of his ancestors was buried deep in his bones, that their ancient blood flowed through his veins, and this filled him with an immense satisfaction and the most profound pride.

When he was accused by some members of his family of being extravagant, impetuous, talkative and vain, he would simply nod, as if relishing their criticisms as compliments.

But Shane often wanted to retort that he was also energetic, intelligent and creative; to point out that these, too, had been traits of those early Britons.

It was as a very small boy that Shane O'Neill had been made aware of his exceptional nature. At first he had been self-conscious, then confused, puzzled and hurt. He saw himself as being different, set apart from others, and this had disturbed him. He wanted to be ordinary; they made him feel freakish. He had detested it when he had overheard adults describe him as *fey* and *overly emotional* and *mystical*.

Then, when he was sixteen and had more of an understanding of the things they said about him, he sought further illumination in the only way he knew – through books. If he *was* 'a curious throwback to the Celts', as they said he was, then he must educate himself about these ancient people whom he apparently so resembled. He had turned to the volumes of history which depicted the early Britons in all their splendour and glory, and the time of the great High Kings and the legendary Arthur of Camelot had become as real to him, and as alive, as the present.

In the years that followed his interest in history had never waned, and it was a continuing hobby. Like his Celtic forebears he venerated words and their power, for filled with a recklessness and gaiety though he was, he was also a man of intellectual vigour. And perhaps it was this extraordinary mingling of contrasts — his mass of contradictions — that made him so unusual. If his angers and enmities were deep rooted, so his loves and loyalties were immovable and everlasting. And that theatricality, constantly attributed to the Celt in him, existed easily alongside his introspection and his rare, almost tender, understanding of nature and its beauty.

At twenty-seven there was a dazzle to Shane O'Neill, an intense glamour that sprang not so much from his remarkable looks as from his character and personality. He could devastate any woman in a room; equally, he could captivate his male friends with an incisive discussion on politics, a ribald joke, a humorous story filled with wit and self-mockery. He could entertain with a song in his splendid baritone, whether he was rendering a rollicking sea shanty or a sentimental ballad, and poetry flew with swiftness from his tongue. Yet he could be hard-headed, objective, outspoken and honest almost to the point of cruelty, and he was ambitious and driven, by his own admission. Greatness, and greatness for its own sake in particular, appealed strongly to him. And *he* appealed to everyone who crossed his path. Not that Shane was without enemies, but even they never denied the existence of his potent charm. Some of these traits had been passed on from his paternal Irish grandfather, that other larger-than-life Celt, whose physique and physical presence he had inherited. Yet there was also much of his mother's ancestry in him.

Now on this crisp Friday afternoon, Shane O'Neill stood with his horse, aptly called War Lord, high on the moors overlooking the town of Middleham and the ruined castle below. It was still proud and stately despite its shattered battlements, roofless halls and ghostly chambers, all deserted now except for the numerous small birds nesting in the folds of the ancient stone amongst the daffodils, snowdrops and celandines blooming in the crannies at this time of year.

With his vivid imagination, it was never hard for Shane to visualize how it had once been centuries ago when Warwick and Gareth Ingham, an ancestor on his mother's side, had lived within that stout fortress, spinning their convoluted schemes. Instantly, in his mind's eye, he saw the panoply unfolding as it had in a bygone age . . . glittering occasions of state, princely banquets, other scenes of royal magnificence and of pomp and ceremony, and for a few seconds he was transported into the historical past.

Then he blinked, expunging these images, and lifted his head, tore his eyes away from the ruined battlements, and gazed out at the spectacular vista spread before him. He always felt the same thrill when he stood on this spot. To Shane there was an austerity and an aloofness to the vast and empty moors, and a most singular majesty dwelt within this landscape. The rolling moors swept up and away like a great unfurled banner of green and gold and umber and ochre, flaring out to meet the rim of the endless sky, that incredible blaze of blue shimmering with silvered sunlight at this hour. It was a beauty of such magnitude and stunning clarity Shane found it almost unendurable to look at, and his response, as always, was intensely emotional. Here was the one spot on this earth where he felt he truly belonged, and when he was away from it he was filled with a sense of deprivation, yearned to return. Once again he was about to exile himself, but like all of his other exiles, this, too, was self-imposed.

Shane O'Neill sighed heavily as he felt the old sadness, the melancholy, trickling through him. He leaned his head against the stallion's neck and squeezed his eyes shut, and he willed the pain of longing for her to pass. How could he live here, under the same sky, knowing she was so close yet so far beyond his reach. So he must go . . . go far away and leave this place he loved, leave the woman he loved beyond reason because she could never be his. It was the only way he could survive as a man.

Abruptly he turned, and swung himself into the saddle, determined to pull himself out of the black mood which had so unexpectedly engulfed him. He spurred War Lord forward, taking the wild moorland at a flat out gallop.

Halfway along the road he passed a couple of stable lads out exercising two magnificent thoroughbreds and he returned their cheery greetings with a friendly nod, then branched off at the Swine Cross, making for Allington Hall, Randolph Harte's house. In Middleham, a town famous for a dozen or more of the greatest racing stables in England, Allington Hall was considered to be one of the finest, and Randolph a trainer of some renown. Randolph was Blackie O'Neill's trainer, and permitted Shane to stable War Lord, Feudal Baron, and his filly, Celtic Maiden, at Allington alongside his grandfather's string of race horses.

By the time he reached the huge iron gates of Allington Hall, Shane had managed to partially subdue his nagging heartache and lift himself out of his depression. He took several deep breaths, and brought a neutral expression to his face as he turned at the end of the gravel driveway and headed in the direction of the stables at the back of the house. To Shane's surprise, the yard was deserted, but as he clattered across the cobblestones a stable lad appeared, and a moment later Randolph Harte walked out of the stalls and waved to him.

Tall, heavy-set, and bluff in manner, Randolph had a voice to match his build, and he boomed, 'Hello, Shane. I was hoping to see you. I'd like to talk to you, if you can spare me a minute.'

Dismounting, Shane called back, 'It *will* have to be a minute, Randolph. I have an important dinner date tonight and I'm running late.' He handed the reins of War Lord to the lad, who led the horse off to the Rubbing House to be rubbed down. Shane strode over to Randolph, grasped his outstretched hand, and said, 'Nothing wrong, I hope?'

'No, no,' Randolph said quickly, steering him across the yard to the back entrance of the house. 'But let's go inside for a few minutes.' He looked up at Shane, who at six feet four was several inches taller, and grinned. 'Surely you can make it *five* minutes, old chap? The lady, whoever she is, will no doubt be perfectly happy to wait for *you*.'

Shane also grinned. 'The lady in question is Aunt Emma, and we both know *she* doesn't like to be kept waiting.'

'Only too true,' Randolph said, opening the door and ushering Shane inside. 'Now, have you time for a cup of tea, or would you prefer a drink?'

'Scotch, thanks, Randolph.' Shane walked over to the fireplace and stood with his back to it, glancing around the room, feeling suddenly relaxed and at ease for the first time that afternoon. He had known and loved this study all of his life, and it was his favourite room at the Hall. Its ambience was wholly masculine, this mood reflected in the huge Georgian desk in front of the window, the Chippendale cabinet, the dark wine-coloured leather Chesterfield and armchairs, the circular rent table littered with such magazines as *Country Life* and *Horse and Hounds*, along with racing sheets from the daily papers. A stranger entering this room would have no trouble guessing the chief interest and occupation of the owner. It was redolent of the Turf and the Sport of Kings. The dark green walls were hung with eighteenth-century sporting prints by Stubbs; framed photographs of the winning race horses Randolph had trained graced a dark mahogany chest; and cups and trophies abounded. There was the gleam of brass around the fireplace, in the horse brasses hanging there, and in the Victorian fender. On the mantelpiece, Randolph's pipe rack and tobacco jar nestled between small bronzes of two thoroughbreds and a pair of silver candlesticks. The study had a comfortable lived-in look, was even a bit shabby in spots, but to Shane the scuffed carpet and the cracked leather on the chairs only added to the mellow feeling of warmth and friendliness.

Randolph brought their drinks, the two men clinked glasses and Shane turned to sit in one of the leather armchairs.

'Whoah! Not there. The spring's going,' Randolph exclaimed.

'It's been going for years,' Shane laughed, but seated himself in the other chair.

'Well, it's finally gone. I keep meaning to have the damn thing sent to the upholsterers, but I always forget.'

Shane put his glass on the edge of the brass fender and searched his pockets for his cigarettes. He lit one, said, 'What did you want to talk to me about?'

'Emerald Bow. What do you think Blackie would say if I entered her in the Grand National next year?'

A surprised look flashed across Shane's face and he sat up straighter. 'He'd be thrilled, surely you know that. But would she have a chance? I know she's a fine mare, but the Aintree course . . . Jaysus! as Blackie would say.'

Randolph nodded, stood up, took a pipe and began to pack it with tobacco. 'Yes, it *is* a demanding course, the supreme test for a man and his horse. But I really do think Emerald Bow has a chance of winning the greatest steeplechase in the world. The breeding is there, and the stamina. She's done extremely well lately, won a few point-to-points, and most impressively.' Randolph paused to light his pipe, then remarked, with a twinkle, 'I believe that *that* lady has hidden charms. But, seriously, she is turning out to be one of the best jumpers I've ever trained.'

'Oh my God, this is wonderful news!' Shane cried, excitement running through him. 'It's always been Grandfather's dream to win the National. Which jockey, Randolph?'

'Steve Larner. He's a tough sod, just what we need to take Emerald Bow around Aintree. If anyone can negotiate her over Beecher's Brook *twice* it's Steve. He's a brilliant horseman.'

'Why haven't you mentioned it to Grandfather?'

'I wanted to get your reaction first. You're the closest to him.'

'You know he always takes your advice. You're his trusted trainer, and the best in the business, as far as we're concerned.'

'Thanks, Shane. Appreciate the confidence. But to be honest, old chap, I've never seen Blackie fuss over any of his horses the way he does that mare. He'd like to keep her wrapped in cotton wool, if you ask me. He was out here last week, and he was treating her as if she was his great lady love.'

A grin tugged at Shane's mouth. 'Don't forget, she *was* a gift from his favourite lady. And talking of Emma, did I hear a hint of annoyance when you mentioned her earlier?'

'Not really. I was a bit irritated with her last night, but . . .' Randolph broke off, and smiled genially. 'Well, I never harbour a grudge where she's concerned, and she *is* the matriarch of our clan, and she's so good to us all. It's just that she can be so bloody bossy. She makes me feel this high.' He held his hand six inches off the ground, and grinned. 'Anyway, getting back to Emerald Bow, I'd intended to mention it to Blackie tomorrow. What do you think about my timing? Should I wait until next week perhaps?'

'No, tell him tomorrow, Randolph. It'll make his day, and Aunt Emma will be delighted.' Shane finished his drink and stood up. 'I don't mind telling you, I for one am thrilled about this decision of yours. Now, I'm afraid I really have to leave. I want to stop by the stables for a second, to say goodbye to my horses.' Shane smiled a trifle ruefully. 'I'm going away again, Randolph. I'm leaving Monday morning.'

'But you just got back!' Randolph exclaimed. 'Where are you off to this time?'

'Jamaica, then Barbados, where we've recently bought a new hotel,' Shane explained as they left the study together. 'I've a great deal of work there, and I'll be gone for quite a few months.' He fell silent as they crossed the stable yard, and Randolph made no further comment either.

Shane went into the stalls, where he spent a few moments with each of his horses, fondling them, murmuring to them affectionately.

Randolph hung back, watching him intently, and suddenly he experienced a stab of pity for the younger man, although he was not certain what engendered this feeling in him. Unless it was something to do with Shane's demeanour at this moment, the look of infinite sadness in his black eyes. Randolph had retained a soft spot for Shane O'Neill since he had been a child, and had once even hoped that he might take a fancy to Sally or Vivienne. But the boy had always been patently uninterested in his two daughters, had remained slightly aloof from them. It was his son, Winston, who was Shane's closest friend and boon companion. A few eyebrows had been raised two years ago when Winston and Shane had bought a broken-down old manor, Beck House, in nearby West Tanfield, remodelled it and moved in together. But Randolph had never questioned the sexual predilections of his son or Shane. He had no need to do so. He knew them both to be the most notorious womanizers, forever chasing skirts up and down the countryside. When his wife, Georgina, had been alive she had often had to comfort more than one broken-hearted young woman, who showed up at the Hall in search of Winston or Shane. Thankfully this no longer happened. *He* wouldn't have known how to cope with such situations. He presumed that if there were any disgruntled young ladies they beat a track directly to Beck House. Randolph smiled inwardly. Those two were a couple of scallywags, but he did love them both very dearly.

Shane finally took leave of his horses and walked slowly back to Randolph standing at the entrance to the stalls. As always, and especially when he had not seen him for a while, Randolph was struck by Shane's unique good looks. He's a handsome son-of-a-gun, Randolph commented silently. Blackie must have looked exactly like Shane fifty years ago.

Putting his arm around the older man's shoulder, Shane said, 'Thanks for everything, Randolph.'

'Oh lad, it's a pleasure. And don't worry about the horses. They'll be well cared for, but then you should know that by now. Oh and Shane, please ask Winston to call me later.'

'I will.'

Randolph's eyes followed Shane O'Neill as he strode off to his car, and there was a thoughtful look on his face. There goes one unhappy young man, he muttered under his breath, shaking his head in bafflement. He has everything anybody could ever want. Health, looks, position, great wealth. He tries to conceal it, but I'm convinced he's miserable inside. And I'm damned if I know the reason why.

Beck House, so called because a pretty little stream ran through the grounds, stood at the bottom of a small hill, at the edge of the village of West Tanfield, about halfway between Allington Hall and Pennistone Royal.

Situated in a dell, shaded at the rear by a number of huge old oaks and sycamores, the manor dated back to the late Elizabethan period. It was a charming house, low and rambling, made of local stone supposedly from Fountains Abbey, and it had a half-timbered front façade, tall chimneys and many leaded windows.

Winston and Shane had originally bought the old manor with the intention of selling it once they had rebuilt the ruined parts, remodelled the old-fashioned kitchen and bathrooms, added garages, and cleared away the wilderness which covered the neglected grounds. However, they had devoted so much time and energy and loving care on the house, had become so attached to the manor during the renovations, they had finally decided to keep it for themselves. They were the same age, had been at Oxford together, and had been close since their salad days. They enjoyed sharing the house, which they used mainly at weekends, since they both maintained flats in the Leeds area to be near their respective offices.

Winston Harte was the only grandson of Emma's brother Winston, and her great-nephew, and he had worked for the Yorkshire Consolidated Newspaper Company since he had come down from Oxford. He did not have a specific job, nor a title. Emma called him her 'minister without portfolio', which, translated, meant troubleshooter to most people. He was, in a sense, her ambassador-at-large within the company, and her eyes and ears and very frequently her voice as well. His word on most things was the final word and he answered only to Emma. Behind his back the other executives called him 'God', and Winston knew this and generally smiled to himself knowingly. He was well aware who 'God' was at Consolidated. It was his Aunt Emma. She was the law, and he respected and honoured her; she had his complete devotion.

Young Winston, as he was still sometimes called in the family, had always been close to his namesake, and his grandfather had instilled in him a great sense of loyalty and duty to Emma, to whom the Hartes owed everything they had. His grandfather had worshipped her until the day he had died at the beginning of the sixties, and it was from him that Winston had learned so much about his aunt's early life, the hard times she had had, the struggles she had experienced as she had climbed the ladder to success. He knew only too well that her brilliant career had been hard won, built on tremendous sacrifices. Because he had been reared on so many fantastic, and often moving, stories about the now-legendary Emma, Winston believed that in certain ways he understood her far better than her own children. And there was nothing he would not do for her.

Winston's grandfather had left him all of his shares in the newspaper company, whilst his Uncle Frank, Emma's younger brother, had left his interest to his widow, Natalie. But it was Emma, with her fifty-two per cent, who controlled the company as she always had. These days, however, she ran it with Winston's help. She consulted with him on every facet of management and policy, frequently deferred to his wishes if they were sound, constantly took his advice. They had a tranquil working relationship and a most special and loving friendship which gave them both a great deal of satisfaction and pleasure.

The newspaper company was very actively on Winston's mind as he drove slowly into the grounds of Beck House. Even so, as preoccupied as he was, he noticed that the little beck was swollen from the heavy rains which had fallen earlier that week. He made a mental note to mention this to Shane. The banks would probably need reinforcing again, otherwise the lawns would be flooded in no time at all, as they had been the previous spring. O'Neill Construction will definitely have to come out here next week, Winston decided, as he pulled the Jaguar up to the front door, parked, took his briefcase and alighted. He went around to the boot of the car to get his suitcase.

Winston was slender, light in build, and about five foot nine, and it was easy to see at a glance that he was a Harte. In point of fact, Winston bore a strong look of Emma. He had her fine, chiselled features and her colouring, which was reflected in his russet-gold hair and vivid green eyes. He was the only member of the family, other than Paula, who had Emma's dramatic widow's peak, and which, his grandfather had once told him, they had all inherited from Big Jack Harte's mother, Esther Harte.

Winston glanced up, squinting at the sky as he approached the short flight of steps leading into the house. Dark clouds had rumbled in from the East Coast and they presaged rain. There was a hint of thunder in the air since the wind had dropped, and a sudden bolt of lightning streaked the tops of the leafy spring trees with a flash of searing white. As he inserted the key large drops of rain splashed on to his hand. Damn, he muttered, thinking of the beck. If there's a storm, we're going to be in serious trouble.

Dimly, from behind the huge carved door, he heard the telephone ringing, but by the time he had let himself inside the house it had stopped. Winston stared at it, fully expecting it to ring again, but when it didn't he shrugged, deposited his suitcase at the foot of the staircase and walked rapidly through the hall. He went into his study at the back of the manor, sat down at his desk, and read the note from Shane telling him to call his father. He threw the note into the wastepaper basket and glanced vaguely at his mail, mostly bills from the village shops and a number of invitations for cocktail parties and dinners from his country neighbours. Putting these on one side, he leaned back in his chair, propped his feet on the desk and closed his eyes, bringing all of his concentration to bear on the matter at hand.

Winston had a problem, and it gave him cause for serious reflection at this moment. Yesterday, during a meeting with Jim Fairley at the London office, he had detected a real and genuine discontent in the other man. Oddly enough, Winston discovered he was not terribly surprised. Months ago he had begun to realize that Jim loathed administration, and in the last few hours, driving back from London, he had come to the conclusion that Jim wanted to be relieved of his position as managing director. Intuitively, Winston felt that Jim was floundering and was truly out of his depth. Jim was very much a working newspaperman, who loved the hurly burly of the news room, the excitement of being at the centre of world events, the challenge of putting out two daily papers. After Emma had promoted him a year ago, upon his engagement to Paula, Jim had continued to act as managing editor of the *Yorkshire Morning Gazette* and the *Yorkshire Evening Standard*. Essentially, by holding down the old job along with the new one, Jim was wearing two hats. Only that of the newspaperman fitted him, in Winston's opinion.

Maybe he ought to resign, Winston thought. It's better that Jim does one job brilliantly, rather than screw up on two. He snapped his eyes open, swung his legs to the floor purposefully and pulled the chair up to the desk. He sat staring into space, thinking about Jim. He admired Fairley's extraordinary ability as a journalist, and he liked the man personally, even though he knew Jim was weak in many respects. He wanted to please everybody and that was hardly possible. And one thing was certain: Winston had never been able to comprehend Paula's fascination with Fairley. They were as different as chalk and cheese. She was far too strong for a man like Jim, but then, that relationship was none of his business really, and anyway perhaps he was prejudiced, considering the circumstances. She was a blind fool. He scowled, chastising himself for thinking badly of her, for he did care for Paula and they were good friends.

Winston now reached for the phone to ring Emma and confide his problem in her, then changed his mind at once. There was no point worrying her at the beginning of her very busy weekend of social activities which had been planned for weeks. Far better to wait until Monday morning and consult with her then.

All of a sudden he felt like kicking himself. How stupid

he had been. He should have challenged Jim yesterday, asked him point blank if he wanted to step down. And if he did, who would they appoint in his place? There was no one qualified to take on such heavy responsibilities, at least not inside the company. That was the crux of the problem, his chief concern. At the bottom of him, Winston had the most awful feeling that his aunt might lumber him with the job. He did not want it. He liked things exactly the way they were.

It so happened that Winston Harte, unlike other members of Emma's family, was not particularly ambitious. He did not crave power. He was not crippled by avarice. In fact, he had more money than he knew what to do with. Grandfather Winston, with Emma's guidance, advice and help, had acquired an immense fortune, had thus ensured that neither his widow, Charlotte, nor his offspring would ever want for anything.

Young Winston was dedicated, hard working, and he thrived in the world of newspapers, where he was in his element. But he also enjoyed living. Long ago he had made a decision and it was one he had never veered away from: *He* was not going to sacrifice personal happiness and a tranquil private life for a big business career. Treadmills were decidedly not for him. He would always work diligently at his job, for he was not a parasite, but he also wanted a wife, a family, and a gracious style of living. Like his father, Randolph, Winston was very much at ease in the role of country gentleman. The pastoral scene held a special appeal for him, gave him a sense of renewal. His weekends away from the city were precious, and recharged his batteries. He found horse riding, point-to-point meetings, village cricket, antiquing and pottering around in the grounds of Beck House therapeutic and immensely satisfying. In short, Winston Harte preferred a quiet, leisurely existence, and he was determined to have it. Battles in board rooms made him irritable, and he found

106

them endlessly boring. That was why Paula continued to surprise him. And it was becoming increasingly apparent to Winston that she was indeed cast in the same mould as her grandmother. Both women relished corporate skirmishing. It seemed to him that business, power, and winning hands-down over a business adversary were narcotics to them. When Emma had wanted him to be Paula's back-up in the negotiations with Aire, he had swiftly demurred, suggested she send Paula in alone. His aunt had readily agreed, much to his considerable relief.

Oh what the hell, he thought, becoming impatient with himself. I'm not going to spend the entire weekend worrying about Jim Fairley's intentions. I'll thrash it out with him next week, once the plans for taking over Aire Communications have been put into operation. Pushing business matters to the back of his mind, he rang his father at Allington Hall and chatted with him for a good twenty minutes. He then dialled Allison Ridley, his current girl-friend. He felt a rush of warmth when he heard her voice, and she sounded equally pleased to hear his. He confirmed that he and Shane would be at her dinner party the following evening, made plans with her for Sunday, and finally dashed upstairs to change.

Ten minutes later, wearing comfortable corduroys, a heavy wool sweater, Wellington boots and an old raincoat, Winston meandered through the dining room and out on to the flagged terrace overlooking the fish pond. The sky had brightened after the brief shower. The trees and shrubs and lawns appeared to shimmer with dewy greenness in the lovely late afternoon light which brought a soft incandescent glow to the fading blue of the sky. The scent of rain and damp grass and wet earth and growing things pervaded the air, and it was a smell Winston loved. He stood on the terrace for a moment, inhaling and exhaling, relaxing and shedding the rest of his business worries, then ran lightly down the steps into the gardens. He hurried in the direction

107

of the beck, wanting to satisfy himself that the condition of
the banks had not deteriorated after the recent shower.

CHAPTER 7

Edwina had arrived.

Emma was aware that her eldest daughter was sitting
downstairs in the library, having a drink and recovering
from her journey from Manchester Airport. In the last few
minutes first Hilda, then Emily, had been up to see her, to
pass on this news.

Well, there's no time like the present, Emma murmured,
as she finished dressing in readiness for her dinner date
with Blackie and Shane. Putting off the inevitable is not
only foolish, it frays the nerves. There's a time bomb
ticking inside Edwina, and I'd better defuse it before the
weekend begins.

Nodding to herself, glad she had stopped wavering,
Emma fastened a pearl choker around her throat, glanced
at herself in the mirror, picked up her evening bag and
sable jacket, and hurried out.

She descended the long winding staircase at a slower
pace, thinking about the things she would say, how she
would handle Edwina. Emma had an aversion to confrontation and conflict, preferred to move in roundabout ways,
and often with stealth, to accomplish her ends. Accommo-
dation and compromise had been, and still were, her strong
suits, both in business and personal matters. But now, as
she approached the library, she recognized there was only
one thing she could do: tackle Edwina head on.

Her quick, light step faltered as she walked through the
vast Stone Hall, and dismay flew to the surface as she
thought of doing battle. But Anthony's happiness was at
stake, and therefore Edwina had to be dealt with before

she made serious trouble for him, for everyone, in fact. Emma took a deep breath, then continued across the hall, her step now ringing with new determination, her manner resolute.

The library door was partially open, and Emma paused for a moment before going in, one hand resting on the door jamb as she observed Edwina sitting in the wing chair in front of the fire. Only one lamp had been turned on and the light in the rest of the room was gloomy. Suddenly a log spurted and flared up the chimney, the lambent flames illuminating the shadowed face, bringing it into sharper focus. Emma blinked, momentarily startled. From this distance her daughter was the spitting image of Adele Fairley ... the same silvery blonde hair, the delicate yet clearly defined profile, the shoulders hunched in concentration. How often had she seen Adele sitting like that, beside the fire in her bedroom at Fairley Hall, staring into the distance, lost in her thoughts. But Adele had not lived to see her thirty-eighth year and Edwina was sixty-three and her beauty had never been as ethereal and as heart-stopping as Adele's once was. So Emma knew this image was part illusion; still, the resemblance was there, had been there since Edwina's birth, and she had always been more of a Fairley than a Harte in many respects.

Clearing her throat, Emma said, 'Good evening, Edwina,' and bustled forward with briskness, not wanting her to know she had been watching her from the doorway.

Her daughter started in surprise and swung her head, straightening up in the chair as she did. 'Hello, Mother,' she replied in a formal voice that rang with coldness.

Emma paid no attention to the tone, accustomed to it by now. It had not changed much over the years. She deposited her jacket and bag on a chair, then proceeded to the fireplace, turning on several lamps as she walked past them. 'I see you have a drink,' she began, seating herself in the other wing chair. 'Does it need refreshing?'

'Not at the moment, thank you.'

'How are you?' Emma asked pleasantly.

'I'm all right, I suppose.' Edwina eyed her mother. 'There's no need to ask how you are. You're positively blooming.'

Emma smiled faintly. Sitting back, she crossed her legs, and said, 'I'm afraid I won't be here for dinner after all. I have to go out. A last minute –'

'Business as usual, I've no doubt,' Edwina sniffed scornfully, giving her an unfriendly look.

Emma winced, but suppressed her annoyance. Edwina's rudeness and sneering manner were generally inflammatory to Emma, but tonight she was determined to overlook her daughter's unwarranted attitude towards her. You don't catch flies with vinegar, she thought dryly; and so she would continue to be pleasant and diplomatic, no matter what. Studying Edwina's face, she at once noticed the tiredness of the drooping mouth, the weary lines around her silver-grey eyes which swam with sadness. Edwina had lost weight, and she seemed nervous, anxious even, and certainly the Dowager Countess of Dunvale, usually filled with her own importance, was not quite so smug this evening. It was apparent she was besieged by troubles.

Emma felt a stab of pity for her, and this was such an unprecedented feeling, and so unexpected, she was a little amazed at herself. Poor Edwina. She is truly miserable, and frightened, but she does bring it on herself I'm afraid, Emma thought. If only I could make her see this, get her to change her ways. Then becoming aware that she was being looked over as carefully as she was scrutinizing, Emma said, 'You're staring at me, Edwina. Is there something wrong with my appearance?'

'The frock, Mother,' Edwina replied without a moment's hesitation. 'It's a little young for you, isn't it?'

Emma stiffened, and wondered if her charitable feelings had been misplaced. Edwina was intent ' on being obnoxious. Then she relaxed and laughed a gay, dismissive laugh, resolved not to let Edwina get her goat. When she spoke her voice was even. 'I like red,' she said. 'It's lively. What colour would you like me to wear? *Black?* I'm not dead yet you know, and whilst we're on the subject of clothes, why do you insist on wearing those awful lumpy tweeds?' Not waiting for a reply, she added, 'You have a lovely figure, Edwina. You should show it off more.'

Edwina let this small compliment slide by her. And she asked herself why she had ever accepted Jim Fairley's invitation, or agreed to stay here at Pennistone Royal. She must be insane, to expose herself to her mother in this way.

Emma compressed her lips, her eyes narrowing as they weighed Edwina speculatively. She said, with the utmost care, 'I'd like to talk to you about Anthony.'

This statement jolted Edwina out of her introspection, and swinging to face Emma, she exclaimed, 'Oh no, Mother! When Emily said you'd be coming down to see me, I suspected as much. However, I refuse to discuss my son with *you*. You're manipulative and controlling.'

'And you, Edwina, are beginning to sound like a broken record,' Emma remarked. 'I'm tired of hearing that accusation from you. I'm also fed up with your continual sniping. It's impossible to have a decent conversation with you about anything. You're defensive and hostile.'

Strong as these words were, Emma's tone had been mild, and her face was devoid of emotion as she pushed herself up and out of the chair. She went to the William and Mary chest in the corner, poured herself a small glass of sherry, then resumed her position in front of the fire. She sat holding her drink, a reflective light in her eyes. After a long moment, she said, 'I am an old woman. A very old woman really. Although I realize there will never be total peace in this family of mine, I would like a bit of tranquillity for the rest of my life, if that's possible. And so I'm prepared to forget a lot of the things you've said and done, Edwina, because I've come to the conclusion it's about time you and I buried the hatchet. I think we should try to be friends.'

Edwina gaped at her in astonishment, wondering if she was dreaming. She had hardly expected to hear these words from her mother. She finally managed, 'Why *me*? Why not any of the others? Or are you planning to give the same little speech to *them* this weekend?'

'I don't believe they've been invited. And if they had, I would hope they'd have enough sense not to come. I don't have much time for any of them.'

'And you do for me?' Edwina asked incredulously, mentally thrown off balance by her mother's conciliatory gesture.

'Let's put it this way, I think you were the least guilty in that ridiculous plot against me last year. I know now that you were coerced to a certain extent. You never were very devious, avaricious or venal, Edwina. Also, I *do* regret our estrangement over the years. We should have made up long ago, I see that now.' Emma genuinely meant this, but she was also motivated by another reason. *Anthony*. Emma was convinced that only by winning Edwina over to her side could she hope to influence her, get her to adopt a more reasonable attitude towards her son. So she said again, 'I do think we should give it a try. What do we have to lose? And if we can't be real friends, perhaps we can have an amicable relationship at the very least.'

'I don't think so, Mother.'

Emma exhaled wearily. 'I am saddened for you, Edwina, I really am. You threw away one of the most important things in your life, but – '

'What was that?'

'My love for you.'

'Oh come off it, Mother,' Edwina said with a sneer, looking down her nose at Emma. 'You never loved me.'

112

'Yes, I did.'

'I don't believe this conversation!' Edwina exclaimed, shifting in her chair. She took a gulp of her scotch, then brought the glass down on the Georgian side table with a bang. 'You're incredible, Mother. You sit there making these extraordinary statements and expecting me to swallow them whole. That's the joke of the century. I might be stupid, but I'm not that stupid.' She leaned forward, staring hard at Emma, her eyes like chips of grey ice. 'What about you? My God, it was *you* who threw *me* away when I was a baby.'

Emma brought herself up in the chair with enormous dignity and her face was formidable, her eyes steely as she said, '*I did not.* And don't you ever dare say that to me again. *Ever*, do you hear? You know that I put you in your Aunt Freda's care because I had to work like a drudge to support you. But we've gone through this enough times in the past, and you'll think what you want, I suppose. In the meantime, I have no intention of being side tracked from what I have to say to you, just because you have the need to dredge up all your old grudges against me.'

Edwina opened her mouth, but Emma shook her head. 'No, let me finish,' she insisted, her green eyes holding Edwina's sharply. 'I don't want you to make the same mistake twice in your life. I don't want you to throw Anthony's love away, as you did mine. And you're in grave danger of doing so.' She sat back, hoping her words would sink in, would have some effect.

'I have never heard anything quite so ridiculous,' Edwina snorted, assuming a haughty expression.

'It's the truth, nevertheless.'

'What do you know about my relationship with my son!'

'A great deal. But despite his love for you, which is considerable, you are hell bent on driving a wedge between the two of you. Why, only last night, he told me how

113

concerned he is about your relationship, and he looked pretty damn worried to me.'

Edwina lifted her head swiftly. 'So he *is* here. When I phoned him at his London club last night they said he'd already left. I couldn't imagine where he was. I had no idea he was coming to the christening. Is he here?'

This was asked with anxiousness, and Emma saw the eager light flickering in her daughter's eyes. She said, 'No, he's not.'

'Where is he staying?'

Emma chose to ignore this question for the moment. She said, 'Anthony can't understand why you're so opposed to his divorce. It seems you're making his life miserable, badgering him night and day to reconcile with Min. He is baffled and distressed, Edwina.'

'So is poor Min! She's heartbroken, and she can't comprehend *him*, or his behaviour. Neither can I. He's upsetting our lives in the most disturbing way, creating havoc. I'm almost as distraught as she is.'

'Well, that's understandable. No one likes divorce, nor the pain it involves. However, you must think of Anthony before anyone else. From what he tells me, he's been very unhappy for – '

'Not *that* unhappy, Mother,' Edwina interrupted, her voice snippy and high-pitched with tension. 'He and Min do have a *lot* in common, whatever he might have told *you*. Naturally, he's disappointed she hasn't had a child. On the other hand, they've only been married six years. She could still get pregnant. Min is perfect for him. And don't look at me like that, Mother, so very superior and knowing. It just so happens that I *know* my son better than you do. Anthony might have strength of character, as you're so fond of pointing out to me whenever you get the opportunity. Nonetheless, he does have certain weaknesses.'

Edwina stopped, uncertain about continuing, then decided her mother might as well know the truth. 'Sex, for one thing,' she announced flatly, staring Emma down with a show of defiance. 'He'll go for a pretty face every time. He got himself into the most awful scrapes with women before he married Min.' Edwina shook her head, and bit her lip, muttering in a low voice, 'I don't know how much Min actually knows, but *I'm* aware that in the last couple of years Anthony has had several affairs, and as usual with the wrong sort of women.'

Emma was not unduly surprised by this bit of information, nor was she particularly interested, and she did not rise to the bait. Instead she gave Edwina a curious look, asked, 'What exactly do you *mean* by the wrong sort of women?'

'You know very well what I mean, Mother. Unsuitable females with no background or breeding. A man in Anthony's position, a peer of the realm with enormous responsibilities, should have a wife who comes from the aristocracy, his own class, who understands his way of life.'

Stifling her amusement at Edwina's hidebound snobbery, Emma said, 'Oh for God's sake, stop talking like a Victorian dowager. We're living in the twenty-first century – well almost. Your views are outdated, my dear.'

'I might have known *you'd* say something like that,' Edwina replied in a snooty voice. 'I must admit, you constantly surprise me, Mother. For a woman of your immense wealth and power you are awfully careless about certain things. Background is one of them.'

Emma chuckled and sipped her sherry and her eyes twinkled over the rim of the glass. 'People who live in glass houses shouldn't throw stones,' she said, and chuckled again.

Edwina's face coloured, and then wrinkling her nose in a gesture of distaste, she said, 'I dread to think of who he'll end up with, if this divorce ever goes through.'

'Oh it's going through all right,' Emma said in her softest

tone. 'I think you would be wise to accept that. *Immediately*. It's a fact of life you cannot change.'

'We'll see about that. Min has to agree before he can do anything.'

'But, my dear Edwina, she has agreed.'

Edwina was shocked and she stared at her mother through horrified eyes, trying to grasp these words. For a split second she was disbelieving, and then with a sinking heart she acknowledged that her mother spoke the truth. Whatever else she was, Emma Harte was not a liar. Furthermore, her information was always reliable, deadly accurate. Edwina finally stammered, 'But . . . but . . .' Her voice let her down, and she was unable to continue. She reached for her glass with a shaking hand, and then put it back on the table without drinking from it. Slowly she said, 'But Min didn't say anything to me last night when we had dinner. How very strange. We've always been close. Why, she's been like a daughter to me. I wonder why she didn't confide in me, she always has in the past.' Edwina's face was a picture of dismay as she pondered Min's extraordinary behaviour, and her very perplexing reticence.

For the first time, with a sudden flash of insight, Emma understood why her daughter was so frantic. She was obviously on intimate terms with Min, happy in the relationship. Yes, she was comfortable, secure and safe with her daughter-in-law. Anthony, in upsetting the matrimonial applecart, had put his mother's world in jeopardy, or at least so Edwina believed. She was petrified of change, of a new woman in her son's life, who may not accept her quite as readily as Min had, who might even alienate her son from her.

Leaning towards Edwina, Emma said with more gentleness than usual, 'Perhaps Min was afraid to tell you, afraid of distressing you further. Look here, you mustn't feel threatened by this divorce. It's not going to change your

116

life that much, and I'm sure Anthony won't object if you remain friendly with Min.' She attempted a light laugh. 'And after all, Anthony is getting a divorce from Min, not from you, Edwina. He would never do anything to hurt you,' she placated.

'He already has. His behaviour is unforgivable.' Edwina's voice was harsh and unrelenting and her face flooded with bitterness.

Emma drew back, and the irritation she had been suppressing suddenly rose up in her. Her mouth curved down in a tight line, and her eyes turned cold. 'You're a selfish woman, Edwina,' she admonished. 'You're not thinking of Anthony, you're only concerned with yourself. You claim your son is the centre of your life, well, if he is, you have a damn poor way of showing it. He needs your love and support at a difficult time like this, not your animosity.' Emma threw her a condemning stare. 'I don't understand you. There's far too much resentment and hostility in you, for everyone, not only me. I can't imagine why. You've had a good life, your marriage was happy, at least I presume it was. I know Jeremy adored you, and I always thought you loved him.' Her glance remained fixed on Edwina. 'I hope to God you *did* love him, for your own sake. Yet despite all the wonderful things life has given you, you are filled with an all-consuming anger. Please turn away from it, put this bitterness out of your heart once and for all.'

Edwina remained engulfed in silence, her expression as obdurate as ever, and Emma went on, 'Trust your son, trust his judgement. I certainly do. You're knocking your head against a brick wall, fighting this divorce. You can't possibly win. In fact, you'll end up the loser. You'll drive Anthony away forever.' She searched her daughter's face, seeking a sign of softening on her part, but it was still closed and unyielding.

Sighing to herself, Emma thought: I give up. I'll never get through to her. And then she felt compelled to make

117

one last stab at convincing her to change her views. She cautioned gravely, 'You'll end up a lonely old woman. I can't believe you would want that to happen. And if you think I have an axe to grind, remember I have nothing to gain. Very genuinely, Edwina, I simply want to prevent you from making the most terrible mistake.'

Although Edwina was unresponsive, sat huddled in the chair, avoiding her mother's penetrating eyes, she had been listening attentively for the last few minutes, and digesting Emma's words. They had struck home, Emma's belief to the contrary. Now, in the inner recesses of Edwina's mind, something stirred. It was a dim awareness that she had been wrong. Suddenly, discomfort with herself over-whelmed her, and she felt guilty about Anthony. She *had* been selfish, more selfish than she had realized until this moment. It was true that she loved Min like the daughter she had never had, and she dreaded the thought of losing her. But she dreaded losing her son more. And that had already begun to happen.

Edwina did not have much insight, nor was she a clever woman, but she was not without a certain intelligence, and this now told her that Anthony had turned to his grandmother in desperation, had confided in Emma instead of her. Resentment and jealousy, her worst traits, flared within her at the thought of this betrayal on her son's part. And then, with a wisdom uncommon for her, she put aside these feelings. Anthony had not really been treacherous or disloyal. *It was all her fault.* She was driving him away from her, as her mother had pointed out. Emma was being sincere in trying to bridge the rift rapidly developing between herself and her son. Emma did want them to remain close, that seemed obvious, if she considered her words dispassionately and with fairness. This admission astonished Edwina, and against her volition she experienced a feeling of gratitude to her mother for making this effort on her behalf.

Edwina spoke slowly, in a muted voice. 'It's been a shock, the divorce, I mean. But you're right, Mother. I must think of Anthony first. Yes, it's *his* happiness that counts.'

For the first time in her life, Edwina found herself turning to Emma for help. Her anger and bitterness now somewhat diffused, she asked softly, 'What do you think I should do, Mother? He must be very angry with me.'

Believing that her attempts to drill some common sense into Edwina had had no effect whatsoever, Emma was a bit taken aback by this unanticipated reversal. Rapidly regrouping her thoughts, she said, 'No, he's not angry. Hurt perhaps, worried even. He loves you very much, you know, and the last thing he wants is a permanent split between you.' Emma half smiled. 'You asked me what you should do. Why, Edwina, I think you should tell him exactly what you've just told me . . . that his happiness is the most important thing to you, and that he has your blessing, whatever he plans to do with his life.'

'I will,' Edwina cried. 'I must.' She gazed at Emma, for once without rancour, and added, 'There's something else.' She swallowed, finished in a strangled voice, 'Thank you, Mother. Thank you for trying to help.'

Emma nodded and glanced away. Her face was calm but she was filling with uneasiness. I have to tell her about Sally, she thought. If I avoid revealing his involvement with the girl, holy hell will break loose tomorrow. Everything I've accomplished in the last half-hour will be swept away by Edwina's wrath when she sees them together. This way, she'll have time to sleep on her rage, perhaps put it behind her. When she's calm she'll surely recognize she cannot live her son's life for him.

Gathering her strength, Emma said, 'I have something further to say to you, Edwina, and I want you to hear me out before you make any comment.'

Edwina frowned. 'What is it?' she asked nervously,

clasping her hands together in her lap. Emma was silent, but her face was readable for a change. It telegraphed trouble to Edwina. Steeling herself for what she somehow knew would be a body blow, she nodded for her mother to proceed.

Emma said, 'Anthony is in love with another woman. It's Sally . . . Sally Harte. Now, Edwina, I – '

'Oh no!' Edwina cried, aghast. Her face had paled and she gripped the arms of the chair to steady herself.

'*I asked you to hear me out.* You just said your son's happiness was the only thing that matters. I trust you really meant that. He intends to marry Sally when he is free to do so, and you are – '

Again Edwina interrupted. 'And you said you had no axe to grind!'

'I don't,' Emma declared. 'And if you think I've encouraged them, you're mistaken. I *was* aware he'd taken her out several times, when he's been in Yorkshire, I don't deny that. But I hadn't paid much attention. Anyway, it seems they are seriously involved. Also, Anthony came to *announce* his plans to me, not ask my permission to marry my great-niece. Furthermore, I gather he took the same stance with Randolph, told him he was going to marry his daughter, and without so much as a by your leave. Randolph can be old-fashioned at times, and his nose was considerably out of joint when we spoke late last night. But I soon put *him* straight.'

Moving to the edge of the chair, the fuming Edwina let her furious glance roam over Emma. She examined that old and wrinkled face minutely, looking for signs of duplicity and cunning. But they were absent, and the hooded green eyes were clear, guileless. Then without warning, a vivid picture of Sally Harte flew into Edwina's twisting mind. They had run into each other nine months ago, at the exhibition of Sally's paintings at the Royal Academy. She had sought Edwina out actually, and had been charming, very friendly. At the time Edwina had thought that Sally had grown up to become one of the most beautiful women she had ever laid eyes on. A Harte though, through and through, with her grandfather Winston's arresting looks, his carefree blue eyes, his dark windblown hair.

Edwina snuffed out the disturbing image of Sally Harte and concentrated her attention on the old woman sitting opposite her, who in turn was observing her acutely and with sternness. Always ready and willing to brand her mother a manipulator, a schemer who contrived to control them and run all of their lives, Edwina decided that in this instance Emma Harte had indeed been an innocent bystander. As much as she wanted to blame her for this . . . this disaster, she could not. She had the most dreadful conviction that it was her son's doing, and his alone. Anthony would be unable to resist that lovely, laughing, bewitching face, which she had been so struck by herself. It was his pattern, after all . . . falling for beautiful features and a shapely figure. Yes, once again, Anthony had managed to get himself involved with the wrong sort of woman, and all because of sex.

With a little shiver, Edwina drew herself up, and said in a clipped voice, 'Well, Mother, I must admit you've convinced me that you've not been a party to this unfortunate relationship. I give you the benefit of the doubt.'

'Thanks a lot,' Emma said.

'Nonetheless,' Edwina continued purposefully, her face set, 'I must voice my disapproval of this match, or I should say mismatch, to my son. Sally is not cut out to be his wife. She is most *unsuitable*. For one thing, she is dedicated to her career. Her painting will always come first with her. Consequently, she most certainly won't fit into his life at Clonloughlin, a life that revolves around the estate, the local gentry and their country pursuits. He is making a terrible mistake, one he will live to regret for the rest of his

121

life. So, therefore, I intend to put a stop to this *affair* at once.'

How could I have ever given birth to such a pig-headed fool? Emma asked herself. She stood up and said, with great firmness, her manner conclusive, 'I must leave. Shane will be here any minute. But before I go I have two statements to make, and I want you to listen most carefully. The first concerns Sally. You cannot point a finger at her, since she is beyond reproach and her reputation is impeccable in every sense. As for her career, well, she can just as easily paint at Clonloughlin as she can here. I might also remind you, silly snob that you are, that she is not only accepted by those ridiculous nitwits in so-called high society, whom you have the desire to kowtow to constantly, but is assiduously courted by them. Thank God *she* has more sense than you, and hasn't fallen for all that worthless, high-falutin clap trap.'

'As usual, you're being insulting, Mother,' Edwina snapped.

Emma shook her silvered head disbelievingly, her lips pursing. Trust Edwina to interrupt a serious conversation because her sensibilities were offended. She said with a small, very cold smile, 'Old people believe that age gives them the licence to say exactly what they think, without being concerned that they may be giving offence. I *don't* mince my words these days, Edwina. I speak the truth. And I will continue to do so until the day I die. Anything else is a waste of time. But getting back to Sally, I would like to remind you that she is an artist of some repute, also, in case you'd forgotten, she is an heiress in her own right, since my brother Winston left his grandchildren a great fortune. Mind you, I'll give you your due, I know money isn't particularly interesting to you, or Anthony, for that matter. Still, that doesn't change the facts, and you're making yourself look ridiculous by saying she is unsuitable. Poppycock! Sally is ideal for him. And let's not dismiss their feelings for each other. They are in love, Edwina, and that's the most important consideration of all.'

'Love? Sex, you mean,' Edwina began, and then stopped, seeing the look of disapproval in Emma's eyes. 'Well, you are correct about one thing, Mother, money doesn't matter to the Dunvale family,' Edwina finished, looking as if she had just smelled something rotten.

Emma said with cool authority, 'Anthony is his own man, and for that I will be eternally grateful. *He will do as he wishes.* And if this relationship is a mistake, then it will be his own mistake to make. Not yours, not mine. Anthony is a man of thirty-three, not a snot-nosed boy in short pants. It would behove you to stop treating him as such.'

Abruptly Emma swung away from Edwina and crossed to the desk in front of the window. She stood behind it, regarding her daughter intently. 'And so, my dear Edwina, if you do speak to Anthony, I suggest you restrict your conversation to motherly words of love and concern for his well being. And I want you to restrain yourself when he mentions Sally, as no doubt he will. I don't believe he will tolerate any criticism of her, or his future plans.'

A horn hooted outside the window, startling both women. Emma glanced over her shoulder, saw Shane getting out of his bright red Ferrari. Turning back to Edwina she lifted the address book off the desk and waved it at her. 'You will find Randolph's number in here. Anthony is staying at Allington Hall. Take my advice, call your son and make up with him.' Emma paused, added with finality, 'Before it is too late.'

Edwina sat rigidly in the chair and not one word passed her white and trembling mouth.

Emma gave her only a cursory glance as she passed the chair, picked up the jacket and evening bag, and left the library. Closing the door quietly behind her she reassured herself she had tried her very best to solve this troublesome family problem and make friends with Edwina at the same time. But she and Edwina did not matter. They would live with their armed truce as they had always done. Only Anthony and Sally were important in the scheme of things.

Emma threw back her shoulders and drew herself to her full height, striking out across the Stone Hall to the front door. And she hoped against hope that Edwina would come to her senses about her son and give him her blessing.

CHAPTER 8

Blackie O'Neill had a plan.

Now, this plan vastly entertained him whenever he thought about it, which had been frequently in the last few days. He was mostly amused because he had never come up with a plan in his entire life.

It had always been Emma who had had a plan. When she had been a little snippet of a girl in patched clothes and worn-out button boots there had been her Plan with a capital P. That had been a plan so grand it had left no room for doubt, and when she had set it finally in motion it had carried her away from Fairley and out into the wide world to seek her fame and fortune. Later she had devised innumerable other plans – for her first shop, her second and her third; then she had created plans to acquire the Gregson Warehouse, the Fairley mills, and yet another for the creation of the Lady Hamilton line of fashions with David Kallinski. And of course there had been her Building Plan, which she tended to pronounce as if this, too, were capitalized. He had been very much a part of that most grandiose plan of all, drawing the architectural blueprints and building her enormous store in Knightsbridge. And this great edifice still stood and it was a proud testament to her most extraordinary achievements.

Yes, his Emma had lived with one kind of plan or

another for as long as he had known her, and each one had been put into operation with determination and carried through with consummate skill in her inimitable way. And with every success she would give him a tiny smile of cold triumph and say, 'You see, I told you it would work.' He would throw back his head and roar, and congratulate her, and insist they celebrate, and her face would soften and he knew that she was giddy with excitement inside, even if she did not really want to show it.

But *he* had never made a plan before.

In fact, almost everything that had happened to Blackie O'Neill in his long life had been by sheer happenstance.

When he had first come over from Ireland as a young spalpeen, to work on the Leeds canals with his Uncle Pat, he had never imagined in his wildest fantasies that he would become a millionaire many times over. Oh, he had boasted that he was going to be a rich 'toff' to young Emma, when she had been a servant at Fairley Hall, but at that time it had seemed unlikely ever to come true. It had been something of an idle boast, and he had laughed at himself in secret. His boasting had proved not to be so idle after all.

Over the years, Emma had often teased him and said that he had the luck of the Irish, and this was true in many respects. He had had to work hard; on the other hand, he had also carried Lady Luck in his breast pocket, and great and good fortune had continually blessed him. There had been times of terrible sadness in his personal life, and sorrow too. For one thing, he had lost his lovely Laura far too young, but she had given him his son, and he considered Bryan to be his best bit of luck of all. As a child Bryan had been warm and loving, and they had stayed close, enjoyed a unique relationship to this day. Bryan had a shrewd, sharp brain, was inspired and fearless in business, a genius really, and together they had parlayed O'Neill Construction into one of the biggest and most important building companies in Europe. When Bryan's wife, Geraldine, had inherited two hotels from her father, Leonard Ingham, it was Bryan who had had the foresight and brains to hang on to them. Those little hotels in Scarborough and Bridlington, catering to family holidaymakers, had become the nucleus for the great O'Neill chain, which was now an international concern, and a public company trading on the London Stock Exchange.

But had Blackie planned all this? No, never. It had simply come about by chance, through the most marvellous serendipity. Of course he had been smart enough to recognize *his* train when it had come rolling through *his* station, and he had jumped on it with alacrity, and he had used every opportunity that presented itself to his advantage. In so doing, he had, like Emma, created an empire, and founded a dynasty of his own.

These thoughts ran through Blackie's head as he dressed for dinner, and he chuckled to himself from time to time as he contemplated *his* first Plan, also with a capital P. Not unnaturally, it involved Emma, with whom he spent a great deal of time these days. *He had decided to take her on a trip around the world.* When he had first suggested this a few weeks ago, she had looked at him askance, scoffed at the idea, and told him *she* was far too busy and preoccupied with her affairs to go gallivanting off on a holiday in foreign parts. His smooth Irish tongue and persuasive manner had seemingly had no effect. Nevertheless, he had made up his mind to get his own way. After a great deal of thought, and pacing the floor racking his brains, he had devised a plan – and the key to it was Australia. Blackie knew that Emma secretly itched to go to Sydney, to see her grandson Philip McGill Amory, who was being trained to take over the vast McGill holdings. He was also aware that Emma had balked at the thought of the long and exhausting trip to the other side of the world, and she was still vacillating about going.

So he would take her, and they would travel in style.

Naturally she would be unable to resist his invitation when he explained how comfortable, luxurious, leisurely and effortless their journey would be. First they would fly to New York and spend a week there, before going to San Francisco for another week. Once they were rested and refreshed they would hop over to Hong Kong and the Far East, and slowly head to their final destination in easy stages.

And he fully intended to make sure she had a little fun on their peregrinations. Blackie could no longer count the times he had asked himself if Emma had ever really had any honest-to-goodness fun in her life. Perhaps becoming one of the richest women in the world had been her way of enjoying herself. On the other hand, he was not sure how much pleasure she had derived from this consuming, back-breaking endeavour. In any event, he was planning all sorts of entertaining diversions, and young Philip was the tempting morsel he would dangle in front of her nose, and if he was not mistaken the trip would prove to be irresistible to her.

Blackie knotted his blue silk tie and stood away from the mirror, eyeing it critically.

It's sober enough, I am thinking, he muttered, knowing Emma would make a sarcastic remark if he wore one of his gaudier numbers. Long, long ago Laura had curbed, at least to some extent, his exotic taste for colourful brocade waistcoats, elaborately-tailored suits and flashy jewellery; Emma had cured him completely. Well, almost. Occasionally Blackie could not resist the temptation to indulge himself in a few jazzy silk ties and handkerchiefs and ascots in florid patterns and brilliant colours, but he made certain never to wear them when he was seeing Emma. He reached for his dark blue jacket and put it on, smoothed the edge of his pristine white collar, and nodded at his reflection. I might be an old codger, but sure an' I feel like a young spalpeen tonight, he thought with another chuckle.

Snowy-haired though he was, Blackie's bright black eyes were still as merry and mischievous as they had been when he was a young man in his prime, and his bulk and size were undiminished by age. He was in remarkable health and looked more like a man in his seventies than one who was eighty-three. His mind was alert, agile and unimpaired, and senility was a foreign word to him, in much the same way as it was to Emma.

Pausing in the middle of the bedroom he dwelled momentarily on the evening ahead, the business matter he would discuss with Emma. He was glad Shane and he had decided to broach the subject to her. Once that was out of the way, and when they were alone, he would move gently into the conversation about the trip. It won't be easy, he told himself, you know she's the stubborn one. When he had first met Emma he had recognized at once that she had the most pertinacious will it had ever been his misfortune to encounter, and it had only grown more inflexible over the years.

A scene flashed, transporting him back to the past. 1906. A bitter cold January day. Emma sitting next to him on the tramcar going to Armley, looking impossibly beautiful in a new black wool coat and the green-and-black scarf and tam-o'-shanter he had given her for Christmas. The green tones in the tartan bringing out the green depths in her eyes, the black showing off the flawlessness of her alabaster skin.

What a pallor her face had held that Sunday, nonetheless, it had not marred her loveliness, he ruminated, remembering every detail of that afternoon so clearly. She had been seventeen and carrying Edwina, and oh how rigid she had been in her obstinacy. It had taken all of his powers of persuasion to manoeuvre her on to that tram. She had not wanted to go to Armley, nor to make the acquaintance of

128

his dear friend, Laura Spencer. Still, when the two girls had met they had taken to each other instantly, and were the closest of loving friends until the day poor Laura died. Yes, Emma's terrible burdens had eased, once she had moved into Laura's snug little house, and he had experienced an enormous sense of relief, knowing Laura would mother her, watch over her. And he had won that day, as he fully intended to win with her now, sixty-three years later.

Opening the top drawer of the bureau at the other side of the room, he took out a small black leather jewel box, stared at it thoughtfully, and then slipped it in his pocket. Humming to himself he strode out and went downstairs.

Blackie O'Neill still lived in the grand mansion he had built for himself in Harrogate in 1919. A handsome wide staircase, so beautifully designed it appeared to float, curved down into a charming circular entrance hall of lovely dimensions, where walls painted a rich apricot acted as a counterpoint to the crisp black-and-white marble floor. The square marble slabs had been set down at an angle, so that they became diamond shapes, and they led the eye to the niches on either side of the front door. White marble statues, of the Greek goddesses Artemis and Hecate, graced these niches and were highlighted by hidden spots. An elegant Sheraton console, inlaid with exotic fruitwoods, stood against one wall underneath a gilt Georgian mirror, and was flanked on either side by Sheraton chairs upholstered in apricot velvet. Illuminating the hall was a huge antique crystal-and-bronze-dore chandelier which dropped down from the domed ceiling, and the setting had elegance without the slightest hint of ostentation.

Crossing the hall, Blackie went into the drawing room. Here a log fire burned cheerily in the Adam fireplace, and the silk-shaded lamps cast rafts of warming light on to the cool green walls, on the sofas and chairs covered in darker green silk. Splendid paintings, and Sheraton and Hepplewhite antiques, added to the graciousness of the room, which exemplified Blackie's sense of style and colour and perspective in furniture and design.

He fussed with the bottle of champagne in the silver wine cooler, turning it several times, shifting the ice around, then he took a cigar from the humidor and went over to his favourite chair to wait. He had no sooner trimmed the cigar, and lighted it, than he heard them in the hall. He put the cigar in the ashtray, and rose.

'There you are, mavourneen,' he cried, hurrying to meet Emma as she came into the room. There was a wide smile on his ruddy face as he exclaimed, 'You're a sight for sore eyes.' He hugged her tightly to his broad chest, held her away and looked down at her. He smiled again, admiration shining in his eyes. 'And aren't you my bonny colleen tonight.'

Emma smiled back at him, love and warmth overflowing in her. 'Thank you, Blackie dear. And I must admit, you don't look so bad yourself. That's a beautiful suit.' Her eyes twinkled merrily as she ran a hand down his arm expertly. 'Mmmm. Very nice cloth. It feels like a bit of my best worsted.'

'It is, it is,' Blackie said, and winked at Shane who was standing behind Emma. 'Would I be wearing anything else now. But come, me darlin', and sit here, and let me get you a glass of champagne.'

Emma allowed him to guide her across the room to the sofa. She sat down, and a brow lifted. 'Are we celebrating something?'

'No, no, not really. Unless it's reaching our grand old ages and being in such good health.' He squeezed her shoulder affectionately, added, 'Also, I know you prefer wine to the stronger stuff.' He glanced at Shane. 'Would you do the honours, me boy? And make mine a drop of me good Irish.'

130

'Right you are, Grandfather.'

Blackie seated himself in the chair facing Emma, picked up his cigar and puffed on it reflectively for a moment, then said to her, 'And I expect you've had a busy day as usual. I'm beginning to wonder if you'll ever retire . . . as you're constantly threatening to do.'

'I don't suppose I ever will,' Emma laughed. 'You know very well I plan to go with my boots on.'

Blackie shot her a chastising look. 'Don't talk to *me* about dying. I've no intention of doing that for a long time.' He chuckled softly. 'I've a lot more damage to do yet.'

Emma laughed with him, and so did Shane, who carried their drinks over to them. He fetched his own, and they clinked glasses and toasted each other. Shane took a swallow of his scotch, and said, 'Would you both excuse me for a few minutes. I have to phone Winston.'

Emma said, 'I hope you have better luck than I did. I was trying to get him for ages, earlier. First the line was busy, then there was no answer.'

Shane frowned. 'Perhaps he'd slipped down to the village. Any message, Aunt Emma?'

'Tell him that we didn't – ' Changing her mind, she broke off and shook her head. 'Never mind, Shane. It's not important. I'll be seeing him tomorrow, and I'm sure we'll have a chance to chat at some point then.'

When they were alone, Blackie reached across and took Emma's hand in his, and stared deeply into her face. 'It's grand to see you, me darlin'. I've missed you.'

Emma's eyes danced. 'Get along with you, you silly old thing. You just saw me the day before yesterday,' she exclaimed, amusement surfacing. 'Don't tell me you've forgotten our dinner at Pennistone.'

'Of course I haven't. But it seems like a long time to me, caring about you the way I do.' He patted her hand affectionately and sat back in his chair, giving her the

131

fondest of looks. 'And I meant it when I said you looked bonny, Emma. You're a real bobby dazzler in that dress, it's very flattering on you, me darlin' girl.'

'Some girl! But thank you, I'm glad you like it,' she answered with a smile of real pleasure. 'My friend Ginette Spanier, at Balmain's, picked it out for me and had it shipped over from Paris last week. Mind you, Edwina was rather scathing earlier. She told me it was too young for me, the colour, you know.'

Blackie's expression altered radically. 'She was just being catty, Emma. Edwina's got a chip on her shoulder the size of that old oak tree out yonder in my garden. *She'll* never change.' He noticed the look of pain flit across Emma's face, and he frowned with concern for her, cursing her daughter under his breath. Edwina had always been troublesome. But then so had most of the others, and there were a couple of Emma's children whom he could quite cheerfully strangle with his bare hands. He cried heatedly, 'I hope she's not been giving you a hard time!'

'No, not really.'

She sounded unusually hesitant, and Blackie spotted this immediately, and shook his marvellous white, leonine head, and exhaled in exasperation. 'I'll never understand Jim. I don't know what prompted him to invite her. It was stupid on his part, if you ask me.'

'Yes, and Paula was upset too, but I decided not to intervene. I thought it would look petty. But . . .' Emma shrugged, and, since she confided most things in Blackie these days, she told him about her conversation with Edwina, her attempts to reason with her daughter.

Blackie listened carefully, occasionally nodding, and when she had finished he said, in a low voice, 'Well, I'm happy for Sally, if this is what she wants. She's a lovely lass, and Anthony is a nice chap. Down-to-earth, and not a bit stuck up, which is more than I can say for that mother of his.' He paused. Recollections swamped him. Slowly, he added, 'She was most peculiar when she was growing up, and never very nice to you, Emma. Always slighting you, if I remember correctly, and believe me, I do. I haven't forgotten how she used to show her preference for Joe Lowther, making it so bloody obvious too. She was a little bitch, and she hasn't changed. Please promise me you'll let this matter about Anthony rest. I don't want you getting agitated because of Edwina. She's not worth it.'

'Yes, you're right, and I promise.' She smiled faintly. 'Let's forget about Edwina. Where are you taking me to dinner? Shane was most mysterious when we were driving over here.'

'Was he now, mavourneen.' Blackie grinned from ear to ear. 'To tell you the truth, Emma, I couldn't think of a nice enough place, so I told Mrs Padgett to prepare dinner for us here. I know you like her home cooking, and she's rustled up a lovely bit of spring lamb. I told her to make new potatoes, brussel sprouts and Yorkshire pudding, all your favourites. Now, me darlin', how does that sound to you?'

'Delicious, and I'm glad we're not going out. It's much cosier here, and I do feel a bit tired.'

His black eyes narrowed under his bushy brows as he examined her alertly. 'Ah,' he said softly, 'so you're finally admitting it. I do wish you wouldn't push yourself so hard. There's no need for it any more, you know.'

Dismissing this comment with an easy smile, Emma leaned closer to him, and no longer able to suppress her curiosity, she asked eagerly, 'What do you want my advice about? You sounded cagey on the phone this morning.'

'I didn't mean to, darlin'.' He sipped his whiskey, puffed away for a moment, and continued, 'But I'd prefer to wait until Shane comes back, if you don't mind, since it concerns him.'

'What concerns me?' Shane asked from the doorway. He strolled into the room, his drink in his hand.

133

'The business matter I want to discuss with Emma.'

'I'll say it concerns me!' Shane exclaimed rather forcefully. 'It was my idea in the first place.' Seating himself on the sofa next to Emma, he settled against the cushions, crossed his legs and turned to her. 'Winston's sorry he missed your calls. He was out in the garden earlier, worrying about the beck flooding. It's dangerously near to it apparently.' His eyes swivelled to his grandfather. 'I just rang Derek and asked him to get a couple of our men over to Beck House tomorrow, to check things out.'

'Aye, that's a good idea. But they'll have to shore up those banks a lot better than they did last year,' Blackie remarked pointedly. 'Now, if you'd both listened to me, it would have been done right in the first place. Let me explain a couple of things.' He commenced to do so, not giving Shane a chance to respond. And then for the next couple of minutes they discussed various methods of reinforcement. They sounded for all the world like a couple of builders about to embark on a major construction project, and Blackie was most vociferous in his opinions, which tickled Emma. He was still a bricklayer at heart.

But she soon lost interest in their somewhat technical conversation. She had become extremely conscious of Shane's presence next to her. His bulk did more than fill the sofa, it commandeered it. For the first time in years she began to regard him through newly perceptive and objective eyes, not as an old family friend, but as a younger woman – a stranger – might. How marvellous looking he was tonight, dressed in an impeccably tailored grey suit and a pale-blue voile shirt with a silver-grey silk tie. He had inherited his grandfather's large frame, his broad sweeping back and powerful shoulders, along with Blackie's wavy black hair and those sparkling eyes so like jet. His complexion was dark too, but *his* light mahogany tan came from winter sun, garnered on the ski slopes of Switzerland or a lazy Caribbean beach, and not from toiling long hours

134

as a navvy out in the open as his grandfather had once done.

His appearance was much like Blackie's had been at his age. The face is different, though, she thought, sneaking another surreptitious look at him, but he does have Blackie's distinctive cleft in his chin, the same dimples when he smiles. And that long upper lip betrays his Celtic origins. I bet he's broken many a heart already, she added silently with an inward smile of amusement. Then she experienced a tiny pang of sadness for Sarah. Easy to understand why the girl had a crush on him. He was a splendid young man who exuded virility and manliness, and there was a unique warmth and gentleness in him. That was the most devastating of combinations, and she knew only too well about men like Shane O'Neill. She had loved such a man herself, had had her heart broken by him once when she had been young and vulnerable and very much in love. But *he* had repaired *her* broken heart, had given her immeasurable happiness and fulfilment in the end. Yes, Paul McGill had had the same kind of potency and fatal charm such as Shane O'Neill possessed in some abundance.

Blackie said, 'Daydreaming, Emma darlin'?'

She shifted her position on the sofa and smiled lightly. 'No. I'm patiently waiting for you two to finish discussing that damn beck, so we can get down to brass tacks about the business you want my advice on.'

'Why yes, of course, it's wasting time we are,' he admitted, his manner more genial than ever. In fact, conviviality seemed to spill out of Blackie tonight, and he beamed first at Emma, then at Shane. 'Now, me boy,' he said, 'please top up Emma's glass with a drop more of that bubbly, and give me a refill, and we'll settle in for a nice little chat.'

And this they did, after Shane had attended to their drinks.

It was Shane who began, concentrating his attention entirely on Emma, his tone as sober as his face had become. He spoke rapidly, but clearly, as he generally did in business, plunging in without preamble. Emma appreciated his directness, and she, in turn, gave him all of her attention.

Shane said: 'We've been wanting to build, or acquire, a hotel in New York for several years. Dad and I have both spent a great deal of time scouting out possibilities. Recently we found the ideal place. It's a residential hotel in the East Sixties. Old-fashioned, of course, and the interiors are in need of considerable remodelling – rebuilding actually. That's what we'll do – most likely. You see, we tendered a bid, it has been accepted, and we're buying the hotel. The papers are currently being drawn up.'

'Congratulations, Shane, and you too, Blackie!' Emma looked from one to the other, her face bathed in genuine delight. 'But how can I be of help to you? Why do you need to talk to me? I don't know a blessed thing about hotels, except whether or not they're comfortable and efficient.'

'But you do know New York City, Emma,' Blackie countered, leaning forward with intentness. 'That's *why* we need you.'

'I'm not sure that I follow you – '

'We need you to steer us in the right direction to the best people,' Shane cut in, wanting to get to the crux of the matter. He pinned her with his bright black eyes. 'It seems to me that you've made that city your own in so many different ways, so you must know what makes it tick. Or rather what makes its business and commerce tick.' His generous mouth curved up into the cheekiest of grins. 'We want to pick your brains, and use your connections,' he finished, regarding her carefully, his cheekiness still very much in evidence.

Amusement flickered in Emma's eyes. She had always

136

liked Shane's style, his directness, his boyish impudence. She stifled a laugh, said, 'I see. Do continue.'

'Right,' Shane replied, all seriousness again. 'Look, we're a foreign corporation, and in my opinion that city's as tight as drum. We can't go in cold . . . well, we could, but we'd have a tough time. I'm sure we'd be resented. We need advisers – the proper advisers – and some good connections. Political connections for one thing. And we'll need help with the unions, with any number of things. I'm sure you of all people understand what I'm talking about, Aunt Emma. So, where do we go? Who do we go to?'

Emma's mind had been working with its usual swiftness and acuity, and she saw the sense in Shane's words. He had analysed the situation most shrewdly. She told him this, went on without hesitation, 'It *would* be unwise of you to start operating in New York without the most influential backing and support. You'll need everybody in your corner, and the only way you'll get them in it is through friends. Good friends with clout. I think I can help.'

'I knew if anybody could, it would be you. Thanks, Aunt Emma,' Shane said, and she saw him visibly relaxing.

'Yes, we're very grateful, me darlin',' Blackie added, pushing himself up out of the chair. He took his drink to the console behind the sofa, plopped in extra ice, added more water to his whiskey, and said, 'Well, go on, Shane, as Emma asked.' He touched her shoulder lightly, lovingly. Emma glanced behind her, questions on her face. Blackie chuckled. 'Oh yes, there's more,' he said, and ambled back to his chair by the fireside.

Shane said: 'We have a solid, well-established law firm representing us in the purchase of the hotel – they're specialists in real estate. However, I feel we are going to need additional representation for other business matters. I'd like to find a really prestigious law firm that has political

137

savvy and a few gilt-edged connections. Any suggestions about that?'

There was a moment of thoughtfulness, before Emma said, 'Yes, of course. I could send you to my lawyers, and to any number of people who would be of use to you. But I've been thinking hard whilst I've been listening, and I believe there is one person who would be of more assistance to you than me and my lawyers and my friends put together. His name is Ross Nelson. He's a banker – head of a private bank, in fact. He has the very best connections in New York, throughout the States, for that matter. I'm sure he'll be able to recommend the law firm most qualified for your purposes, and assist you in a variety of other ways.'

'But will he do it?' Shane asked, doubt echoing.

'He will if *I* ask him,' she said, giving Shane the benefit of a reassuring smile. 'I can telephone him on Monday, and explain everything. I hope I'll be able to enlist his help immediately. Would you like me to do that?'

'Yes, I would. *We* would.' He swung his head to Blackie. 'Wouldn't we, Grandfather?'

'Anything you say, my boy. This is your deal.' Blackie tapped ash from his cigar, looked across at Emma. 'That name Nelson rings a bell. Have I met him?'

'Why yes, I think you did once. It was some years ago, Blackie. Ross was over in England with his great-uncle, Daniel P. Nelson. Dan was a close friend and associate of Paul's, if you recall. He's the fellow who wanted me to send Daisy over to the States during the war, to stay with him and his wife, Alicia. But as you know, I never wanted Daisy to be evacuated. Anyway, the Nelsons only had one child, Richard. The boy was killed in the Pacific. Dan was never quite the same after that. He made Ross his heir, after his wife, of course. Ross inherited controlling interest in the bank in Wall Street when Dan died, and God knows what else. Not millions. *Zillions*, I think. Daniel P. Nelson

138

was one of the richest men in America, had tremendous power.'

Shane was impressed and this showed in his face. He asked quickly, 'How old a man is Ross Nelson?'

'Oh he must be in his late thirties, early forties, not much more.'

'Are you sure he won't mind helping us? I'd hate to think he would regard your request as an imposition. That kind of situation can create difficulties,' Shane remarked. He was intrigued with Nelson, wanted to know more about him. He reached for his drink and took a swallow, observing Emma out of the corner of his eye.

Emma laughed quietly. 'He owes me a few favours. And he won't think I'm imposing, I can assure you of that.' She gave Shane a shrewd look through her narrowed green eyes. 'Mind you, I know Ross, and he's going to expect something in return. Business, I'm sure, in one form or another. Actually, you might consider doing some of your investment banking with him, and let his bank handle your affairs on that side of the Atlantic. You could do worse.' There was a cynical edge to her voice, as she finished, 'There are two things you must remember, Shane . . . one hand always washes the other, and there's never anything free in this world. Especially in business.'

Shane met her cool, concentrated gaze steadily. 'I understand,' he said softly. 'And I learned long ago that anything for nothing is usually not worth having. As for Ross Nelson, I'll know how to show my appreciation, you have no worries there.'

Blackie, who had been following this exchange with considerable interest, slapped his knee and laughed uproariously. 'Ah, Emma, it's a spry one I've got me here.' He shook his head and his benevolent smile expressed his love and pride. 'There are no flies on you, my boy, I'm glad to see, and it won't be the same without you.' A hint of sadness crept on to his face, wiping away the laughter. 'I

139

know it's important and necessary, but I hate to see you go away again, and so quickly. It pains me, it truly does.'

Emma put down her glass and stared at Shane. 'When *are* you leaving, Shane?'

'I fly to New York on Monday morning. I'll be staying there for a good six months, maybe longer. I'll be supervising the rebuilding of the hotel in Manhattan, and trotting down to the Caribbean every few weeks to check on our hotels in the islands.'

'*Six months*,' she repeated in surprise. 'That *is* a long time. We shall miss you.' But perhaps it's just as well he won't be around for a while, she added under her breath, thinking of her granddaughter Sarah Lowther. Out of sight, out of mind. Or so she hoped.

Shane cut into her thoughts, when he said, 'I shall miss you too, Aunt Emma, and Grandfather, everyone in fact. But I'll be back almost before you can say Jack Robinson.' He leaned into Emma and squeezed her arm. 'And keep an eye on this lovable old scoundrel here. He's very dear to me.'

'And to me too, Shane. Of course I'll look after him.'

'Ah, and won't we be taking care of each other now,' Blackie announced, sounding extremely pleased with himself all of a sudden, thinking of his Plan with a capital P. 'But then we've been doing that for half a century or more, and it's a difficult habit to break, sure an' it is.'

'I can imagine.' Shane laughed, marvelling at the two of them. What an extraordinary pair they were, and the love and friendship they felt for each other was a most enviable thing. Sighing under his breath, he reached for his scotch, peered into the amber liquid, reflecting. After a swallow he turned to Emma. 'But getting back to Ross Nelson, what kind of a chap is he?'

'Unusual in many ways,' Emma said slowly, staring into space, as if visualizing Ross Nelson in her mind's eye. 'Ross is deceptive. He has a certain charm, and he appears

140

to be very friendly. On the surface. I've always thought there was an innate coldness in him, and a curious kind of calculation, as if he stands apart from himself, watching the effect he has on people. There's a terrific ego there, and especially when it comes to women. He's something of a ladies' man, and has just been divorced for the second time. Not that this is significant: on the other hand, it's frequently struck me that he might be unscrupulous . . . in his private life.'

She paused, brought her eyes to meet Shane's, and added, 'But that has nothing to do with you or me. As far as business is concerned, I deem Ross to be trustworthy. You have no cause to worry in that respect. But be warned, he's clever, razor sharp, and he has the *need* to get his own way – that monumental ego rears up constantly.'

'Quite a picture you've painted, Aunt Emma. Obviously I'll have to have my wits about me.'

'That's always wise, Shane, whoever you're dealing with.' She smiled faintly. 'On the other hand, you're going to Ross for advice, not pitting yourself against him in a business deal. You'll be able to handle Ross Nelson very nicely. In fact, I think you'll get along with him just fine. Don't forget, he owes me a few favours, so he'll bend over backwards to be co-operative and helpful.'

'I know your judgement is never flawed, always spot on,' Shane replied. He rose, walked around the sofa to fix himself another drink, thinking of the characterization she had drawn in her thumbnail sketch. He was anxious to meet the man. It was obvious that Nelson was going to be invaluable. And he was impatient to get the ball rolling with the New York hotel. He needed to submerge himself in business, to take his mind off troubling personal matters. Ross Nelson might possibly be a pain in the neck in his private life, but who cared about his philandering. As long as he was smart, shrewd, trustworthy, and willing to help, that was all that mattered.

Blackie's eyes flicked briefly to his grandson, and then settled on Emma. 'I'm not so sure I like the sound of this Ross Nelson fellow,' he began.

Emma cut him off with a laugh. 'My money's on Shane. He's a grown lad who knows how to take care of himself very well. Very well indeed, Blackie. I'll even go as far as to say that Ross Nelson might have met his match in Shane.' This observation seemed to entertain her, and she continued to laugh.

Shane grinned, but made no comment.

He was looking forward to meeting Mr Ross Nelson more than ever. The banker would add spice to the New York venture.

CHAPTER 9

They sat in front of the blazing fire in the library – just the two of them.

Blackie nursed a snifter of aged Napoleon cognac, and Emma sipped a cup of tea with lemon. He had poured her a small glass of Bonnie Prince Charlie, her favourite Drambuie liqueur, but it remained untouched on the Sheraton side table next to her chair.

They were quiet, lost in their diverse thoughts, relaxing after Mrs Padgett's fine dinner. Shane had left, and, as much as they both loved him in their individual ways, they were content to have this time alone together.

The firelight flickered and danced across the bleached-pine panelled walls which had taken on a mellow amber cast in the warm roseate glow emanating from the hearth. In the garden beyond the French doors, the towering old oak creaked and rustled and swayed under the force of the wind that had turned into a roaring gale in the last hour. The door and the windows rattled, and the rain was flung against the glass in an unrelenting stream, beating a steady staccato rhythm, and it was difficult to see out through this curtain of falling water. But in the fine old room all was warmth, cosiness and comfort. The logs crackled and hissed and spurted from time to time, and the grandfather clock, an ancient sentinel in the corner, ticked away in unison.

His eyes had been focused on her for a while.

In repose, as it was now, Emma's face was gentle, the firm jaw and determined chin and stern mouth softer, less forbidding in the flattering light. Her hair held the lustre of the purest silver, and she seemed, to him, to be a lovely dainty doll, sitting there so sedately, perfectly groomed and dressed as always, elegance and refinement apparent in every line of her slender body.

She had not changed really.

Oh, he was aware that when the flames blazed more brightly, he would notice the wrinkles and the hooded lids and the faint brown speckles of age on her hands. But he knew, deep in his soul, that she was still the same girl inside.

She would always be his wild young colleen of the moors, that little starveling creature he had come across early one morning in 1904, when she had been tramping so bravely to Fairley Hall to scrub and clean in order to earn a few miserable coppers to help her impoverished family. His destination had been the same place, for Squire Adam Fairley had hired him to do bricklaying at the Hall, and then he had stupidly gone and lost himself in the mist on those bleak and empty Godforsaken hills . . . so long ago . . . but not so long to him. He had never forgotten that day.

Blackie's gaze lingered on Emma.

He had loved this woman from the first moment he had met her and all the days of his life thereafter. He had been eighteen, that day on the lonely moors, and she had been a fourteen-year-old waif, all skin and bones and huge emerald

143

eyes, and she had touched his heart like no one else before or after, and bound him to her forever without even trying.

Once he had asked her to marry him.

She, believing it was out of kindness and friendship, and the goodness of his heart, had refused him. She had thanked him sweetly, her face wet with tears, and explained that she and the child she was carrying, by another man, would only be burdens to him. And she would not inflict such a terrible load on her dearest friend Blackie, she had said.

Eventually, he had married Laura Spencer, and he had loved her well and true. And yet he had never stopped loving his bonny mavourneen, even though at times he was hard pressed to explain that unique love to himself, or articulate it to her, or anyone else for that matter.

There was a time when he had half expected Emma to marry David Kallinski, but once again she had turned down a splendid, upright young man. Later, she had confided the reason to him. She had not wanted to create trouble between David and his family, who were Jewish. Although Mrs Kallinski was motherly towards her, Emma said she had long realized that as a Gentile she would not be considered appropriate as a daughter-in-law by Janessa Kallinski, who was Orthodox and expected her son to marry in the Faith.

Then one day, Joe Lowther had come riding by, metaphorically speaking, and to Blackie's astonishment – and not inconsiderable bewilderment – Emma had plunged into holy matrimony with Joe. He had never been able to fully comprehend their union. In his opinion, it was difficult, if not downright impossible, to hitch a race horse and a cart horse to the same wagon. But Joe had been a kindly man, if plodding and dull and not particularly brilliant or engaging. Still, he and Blackie had liked each other well enough and had gone off to fight a war together. And he had seen Joe Lowther killed in the muddy trenches of the

144

bloody, battle-torn Somme, and had wept real tears for him, for Joe had been too young a man to die. And he had never been able to talk about Joe's ghastly death, to tell her that he had seen Joe blown to smithereens. Only years later did he learn from Emma that she had married Joe, who adored her, to protect herself and her baby daughter Edwina from the Fairleys, after Gerald Fairley had attempted to rape her one night at her little shop in Armley. 'It wasn't as calculating as it sounds,' she had gone on. 'I liked Joe, cared for him, and because he was a good man I felt honour-bound to be a good wife.' And she had been devoted, *he* knew that.

The second time he had wanted to marry Emma he had truly believed his timing was perfect, that he had every chance of being accepted, and he was buoyed up with soaring hopes and anticipation. It was a short while after the First World War when they were both widowed. In the end, though, uncertain of her true feelings for him, and filled with sudden nervousness about Emma's astonishing achievements in comparison to his own, he had lost his nerve, and his tongue, and so he had not spoken up. Regrettably. And she had unexpectedly gone off and married Arthur Ainsley, a man not good enough to lick her boots, and had suffered all kinds of pain and humiliation at Ainsley's hands. Finally, in the 1920s, as he was biding his time and waiting for the propitious moment, Paul McGill had come back to England to claim her at last for himself.

And he had lost his chance again.

Now it was too late for them to marry. Yet, in a sense, they had something akin to marriage and just as good, to his way of thinking . . . this friendship, this closeness, this total understanding. Yes, all were of immense and incalculable value. And Emma and he were perfectly attuned to each other in the twilight of their days, and what did the rest mean, or matter, at this stage in the game of life?

But he still had that ring . . .

Much to his own surprise, Blackie had kept the engagement ring he had bought for Emma so long ago. There had never been another woman to give it to – at least, not one he cared enough about; and for a reason he could not fathom, he had never wanted to sell it.

Tonight the ring had burned a hole in his pocket all through drinks and dinner, in much the same way his Plan with a capital P burned a hole in his head. Putting down his drink, he leaned closer to the hearth, lifted the poker and shoved the logs around in the grate, wondering if it was finally the right time to give it to her. Why not?

He heard the rustle of silk and a sigh that was hardly audible.

'Did I startle you, Emma?'

'No, Blackie.'

'I have something for you.'

'You do? What is it?'

He reached into his pocket and brought out the box, sat holding it in his large hands.

Emma asked curiously, 'Is it my birthday present?' and she gave him a warm little smile of obvious pleasure, laughter sparkling in her eyes.

'Oh no, indeed it's not. I intend to give you *that* on your birthday at the . . .' He curbed himself. The elaborate party he and Daisy were planning was very hush-hush and meant to be a big surprise for Emma. 'You'll get your birthday gift at the end of the month, on the very day you're eighty,' he improvised adroitly. 'No, this is something I bought for you . . .' He had to laugh, as he added, 'Fifty years ago, believe it or not.'

She threw him a startled look. 'Fifty years! But why didn't you give it to me before now?'

'Ah, Emma, thereby hangs a long tale,' he said, and fell silent as memories came unbidden.

How beautiful she had looked that night, with her red

146

hair piled high on her head in an elaborate plaited coil, wearing a superb white velvet gown, cut low and off the shoulders. Pinned to one of the small sleeves was the emerald bow he had had made for her thirtieth birthday, an exquisite replica of the cheap little green-glass brooch he had given her when she was fifteen. She had been touched and delighted that he had not forgotten his old promise, made to her in the kitchen of Fairley Hall. But on that particular Christmas night, in all her elegant finery, with McGill's magnificent emeralds blazing on her ears, he had thought his emerald bow, costly though it had been, looked like a trumpery bauble in comparison to those earrings . . .

Growing impatient, Emma frowned and exclaimed, 'Well, are you going to tell me the tale or not?'

He pushed the past to one side, flashed her a smile. 'Do you remember that first party I gave here? It was Christmas . . .'

'Boxing Day night!' Emma cried, her face lighting up. 'You had just completed this house, finished furnishing it with all the lovely Sheraton and Hepplewhite pieces you'd scoured the country to find. And you were so proud of what you'd created all by yourself. Of course I remember the party, and very clearly. It was 1919.'

Blackie nodded, glanced down at the box, continuing to finger it. He raised his head. Unabashed love shone on his craggy, wrinkled face, giving it a more youthful appearance. 'I'd bought this for you earlier that week. I'd travelled down to London to choose it, gone to the finest jeweller, too. It was in the pocket of my tuxedo. I'd intended to give it to you at the party.'

'But you never did . . . why not? Whatever made you change your mind, Blackie?' She looked at him oddly, through eyes awash with perplexity.

'I'd decided to have a talk first – with Winston. Why, it was here, in this very room, as a matter of fact.' He looked

147

about him, as if seeing that ancient scene being re-enacted in the shadows; seeing the ghost of Winston, as he had been as a young man, lurking there. He cleared his throat. 'Your brother and I talked about you, and . . .'

'What *about* me?'

'We discussed you and your business ventures. I was worried to death about you, Emma, distressed because of the way you had plunged into the commodities market, and recklessly, or so I thought. I was concerned about your rapid expansion of the stores in the North, your determination to keep on building, acquiring other hold-ings. I believed you were over-extending yourself, gambling . . .'

'I've always been a gambler,' she murmured softly. 'In a way, that's the secret of my success . . . being willing to take chances . . .' She left the rest unsaid. He surely knew it all by now.

'Aye,' he agreed. 'Maybe it is. Anyway, Winston explained that you'd stopped the commodities lark, after making a fortune speculating, and he told me you were not in over your head. Just the opposite. He told me you were a millionairess. And as he talked, and ever so proudly, I began to realize that you were a far, far bigger success than I'd ever dreamed, that you'd surpassed me, outstripped David Kallinski, left us both behind in business. It sud-denly seemed to me that you were quite beyond my reach. That's why I never gave you this ring . . . You see Emma, I was going to ask you to marry me that night.'

'Oh Blackie, Blackie darling,' was all she could manage to say, so stupefied was she. Tears pricked the back of Emma's eyes as a variety of emotions seized her with some force. Her love and friendship for him rose up in her to mingle with a terrible sadness and a sense of regret for Blackie, as she envisioned the pain he must have suffered then and afterwards, perhaps. He had wanted her, and he had not said a word. That was his tragedy. At the party in

1919 she had believed Paul McGill was lost to her forever. How vulnerable and susceptible she would have been to her one true friend Blackie in her heartbreak, loneliness and despair. And if he had been more courageous how different their lives would have turned out. Her thoughts ran on endlessly. Why had she never suspected that he cared for her in that way . . . that he had marriage on his mind? She must have been blind or dense or too involved with business.

The silence between them drifted.

Blackie sat unmoving in the chair, staring into the fire, saying not a word, remembering so much himself. It's odd, he thought suddenly, how things which happened to me when I was a young man have an extraordinary vividness these days. More so than events of last week, or even yesterday. I suspect that's part of growing old.

Emma was the first to rouse herself.

She said, in a small, pained voice, 'Were you trying to tell me, a few minutes ago, that my *success* put you *off*? Prevented you from proposing?' She studied that dear, familiar face with infinite compassion, thinking of the years he had wasted, the happiness he had let slip through his fingers, and all because of his love for her. A love unuttered.

Blackie nodded. 'Aye, I suppose I am, mavourneen. I decided, there and then, that you could never be weaned away from your business because it was very much a part of you, *was* you, really. In any event, I lost my confidence. After all, I wasn't half as rich and successful as you in those days. I didn't think you'd have me. My nerve failed me. Yes, that's precisely what happened.'

A deep sigh trickled out of Emma, and slowly she shook her head. 'How foolish you were, my dearest, dearest friend.'

Blackie gaped at her, his jaw slack with astonishment. 'Are you saying that you would have married me, Emma

Harte?' he asked, unable to keep the shock and incredulity out of his voice.

'Yes, I believe I would, Blackie O'Neill.'

Now it was Blackie who began to shake his head, and he did so in wonderment, trying to absorb her words. For a few minutes he could not speak as old emotions took hold of him, surprising him with the strength of their impact.

At last he said, 'It does me good to hear that, even so long afterwards.' His voice took on a quavering treble, as he added, 'Perhaps it's just as well we didn't marry, Emma. I'd have been left high and dry, not to mention broken-hearted, when Paul swept you off your feet again.'

'How can you say such a thing! What kind of woman do you think I am!' she cried, her indignation flaring as she jerked herself up in the chair and glared at him with such unprecedented ferocity he flinched. 'I would never have hurt *you*! I've always loved you, cared about your well being, and you know it. Apologize at once,' she spluttered angrily, and added, as an afterthought, 'or I'll never speak to you again!'

He was so startled by her vehemence he was speechless for a few seconds. Slowly a shame-faced look crept on to his face. He said in a most tender and placating voice, 'It's sorry I am, Emma, I take back those words. I believe you. I don't think you would have left me for Paul. And that's not my ego talking. I know you . . . better than anyone does. No, you wouldn't have betrayed me, you wouldn't have given him the time of day if you'd been married to me. It's not in you to be cruel to someone you love, and then there's your morality and your loyalty and goodness and sense of responsibility. Those would have worked in my favour. Besides – ' He gave her a boyish grin that brought his dimples out. '*I* would have made you happy.'

'Yes, Blackie, I believe you would.'

This was said rapidly, and there was a sudden urgency in her manner as she leaned forward anxiously, needing to clarify the past, to make him understand the reasons which had motivated her and Paul, quite aside from their great love. 'Don't forget,' she began, intent on jogging his memory. 'My marriage to Arthur Ainsley was on the rocks long before Paul McGill returned to this country. I was on the verge of divorce when Paul showed up. Besides, and this is most important, Blackie, Paul wouldn't have intruded, wouldn't have sought me out, if I'd been happily married. It was only because Frank had told him I was miserable, and separated from Ainsley, that he arrived on my doorstep.'

She paused, settled back in the chair, and clasped her hands tightly in her lap. 'I *know* I would not have seen hide nor hair of Paul ever again, *if* my life had been on an even keel. He told me that himself. He came searching for me because he was aware I was unhappy – and also available. He most certainly wouldn't have done that if I'd been married to *you*. Have you forgotten how much he liked and respected you?'

'No, I haven't. And you're correct in what you say . . . Yes, Paul was a fine and honourable man. I always had a lot of time for him.'

Blackie now rose.

'Well,' he said, 'that's all water under an old and decrepit bridge, my girl. There's no point rehashing our troubles of half a century ago. And maybe it was meant to be . . .' he lifted his hands and shoulders in a brief shrug '. . . exactly the way it is. But I would like you to have the ring. It's always been yours, you know.'

He bent over her. She looked up at him, and then at the black leather box in his hands. He lifted the lid, turned the box to her.

Emma gasped.

The ring was exquisite, throwing off the most brilliant prisms of light, and sparkling with life and fire against the black velvet. The central diamond was round and multi-faceted, and very large, at least twenty carats, and it was surrounded by smaller stones which were equally as lovely and superbly cut, and these formed a circle at the base of the mounting.

Even Emma, accustomed to magnificent jewellery, was awestruck and she found herself blinking, truly taken aback by its size and beauty. 'It's stunning, Blackie,' she said a bit breathlessly. 'One of the most beautiful rings I've ever seen.'

His joy at her words was evident. 'It's an old setting, of course, the original, and perhaps it's even a bit outdated. But I didn't want to have it reset. Here, slip it on, mavourneen.'

She shook her head. 'No, you do it, my fine black Irishman.' She offered him her left hand. 'Put it on the third finger, next to my wedding ring.'

He did so.

Emma held out her small, strong hand, her head on one side, admiring the ring glittering so brightly in the fire's glow. And then she glanced up at him, her expression unmistakably mischievous. 'Are we finally engaged to be married then?' she teased in a flirtatious voice, and offered him a smile that was decidedly coy.

Blackie laughed, with delight, hugely amused. He'd always enjoyed her sense of humour.

Bending closer to her, he kissed her cheek. 'Let's just say we're engaged to be – to be the dearest and closest friends and companions for the rest of the time we have on this earth.'

'Oh Blackie, that's such a lovely thing to say, and thank you for my beautiful ring.' She caught his hand and held on to it and pressed it tightly and looked up at him again, and then she smiled that incomparable smile that filled her face with radiance. 'My dear old friend, you're so very very special to me,' she said.

'As you are to me, my Emma.'

He stepped away from her chair as if heading to his own, and then he paused and swung his white head. 'I hope you're going to wear the ring,' he remarked off-handedly but his glance remained riveted intently on hers. 'I sincerely hope you're not going to put it away in that safe of yours.'

'Certainly *not*. How could you think such a thing. I'm never going to take it off . . . ever again.'

He touched her shoulder and returned to his seat, smiling to himself. 'I'm glad I gave you your ring, me darlin'. I've thought about doing so many times, and I've often wondered what you'd say. I know I'm always accusing *you* of being a sentimentalist in your old age, but I do believe *I've* become a sentimental old man myself.'

'And tell me, Blackie O'Neill, what's wrong with sentiment? It's a pity there isn't more of it in this world,' she said, her eyes unexpectedly moist. 'It might be a better place to live in, for one thing.'

'Aye,' was all he said.

After a short while, Blackie cleared his throat, and remarked, 'Now, what about that little proposition of mine, Emma? This morning you said you were doubtful that it would work, but I can't agree.'

'Do you know,' she exclaimed brightly in an enthusiastic voice, 'I was thinking about it again this afternoon. Emily's moved in with me, and it suddenly struck me that the only way I'll get a bit of peace and quiet is to accept your generous invitation.'

'Then you'll come with me! Ah, me darlin', this news warms the cockles of me heart, sure an' it does.' He beamed at her, happiness and excitement welling inside him. He lifted his brandy balloon high. 'Come along, take a sip of your Bonnie Prince Charlie, Emma. This calls for a toast, it does indeed.'

She held up her hand instead. 'Wait a minute!. I didn't actually say *yes*. I can't accept – at least not just yet. I *am* seriously thinking about the trip, but you'll have to give me a few more weeks to settle things, to adjust to the idea of being absent for several months.'

Biting down on his disappointment, he said, 'All right, I'll be patient. However, I will have to start making the arrangements soon, so please don't delay your answer for too long.'

'I'll let you know as quickly as possible. I promise.'

He sipped his cognac, savouring it, and slowly a sly gleam entered his eyes. He was wrapped in thought for a minute or two longer, said finally, 'By the way, Emma, I've recently made a plan, as no doubt *you'll* be surprised to hear. I think of it as my Plan with a capital P, since it happens to be the first plan *I've* ever made.' He was unable to contain himself, and let out a throaty chortle and his eyes became merry and teasing. 'Do you remember that first plan of *yours*?'

'Goodness me, I'd forgotten all about *that*.'

'I never did. And I even recall the day you confided it in me. Such a small slip of a thing you were, too, and I was most impressed. Anyway, if you've got a few minutes, I'd like to tell you about mine. It's a most marvellous plan, me darlin', even though I say so myself. And I'll bet my last quid it's going to intrigue you, sure an' I know it will.'

Amusement touched her mouth. 'I'd love to hear about your plan, Blackie dear.'

He sat back expansively, nodding to himself, and began: 'Well, it's like this. There is this woman I know, and she's the most stubborn creature I've met in all my born days. It just so happens that this stubborn, contrary, maddening but quite adorable woman has a grandson living in Australia. I know she wants to go and see him, and I thought it would be a wonderful treat for her, if I took her out there to see him myself. And so I've made a very *special* plan, and this is how it goes . . .'

154

Emily had fallen asleep on one of the huge sofas in the upstairs parlour.

To Emma, standing over her, she looked small and defenceless and innocent, wrapped in a white towelling robe and curled up in a ball against the pile of cushions. A feeling of infinite tenderness swept through Emma, and she bent down and gently moved a strand of pale blonde hair away from Emily's eyes, and brushed her lips against the girl's smooth young cheek. She straightened up, wondering whether to awaken her or not, decided to get ready for bed herself first, and tiptoed into the adjoining bedroom.

Emma hung up her sable jacket, took off her pearl choker and matching earrings and placed them on the dressing table. After removing her watch and the McGill emerald, she started to pull off Blackie's ring, then stopped and looked down at it. This ring had lain in a vault waiting for her for fifty years, and she had promised Blackie she would never take it off. She pushed the ring back on her finger, next to Paul's platinum wedding band, and finished undressing. She had just put on her nightgown when there was a tap on the door and Emily's smiling face appeared around it.

'There you are, Grandy. I waited up for you.'

'So I noticed, darling. But you didn't have to, you know.'

'I wanted to, Gran. But to be honest, I didn't think you'd be as late as this. It's turned *twelve-thirty*!'

'I'm well aware of the time, Emily. And look here, if you're going to live with me, you mustn't start monitoring my comings and goings. And I don't need mothering either. I get enough of that from Paula at the store,' Emma remarked evenly, putting on her silk dressing gown and knotting the belt.

Emily giggled and skipped into the room, obviously wide awake and full of her usual *joie de vivre*. 'It's not role

155

reversal, if that's what you're thinking. I'm *not* trying to mother you. I was merely commenting on the time.'

'Just bear in mind what I said.'

'I will, Grandma.' Emily hovered near the dressing table. She saw the jewellery strewn across it and her eyes darted to Emma's hand. She noticed the diamond at once, which shone with brilliance in the bright light from the lamps. 'Aren't you going to show me Blackie's ring?' she asked.

Emma's brows shot up. 'And how did *you* know about the ring?' The words had no sooner left her mouth than she wondered why she had even bothered to ask Emily, of all people, such a question.

'Merry and I were Blackie's conspirators,' Emily explained. 'About two weeks ago he asked *her* to ask *me* to check your ring size. He thought your fingers might have shrunk.'

'Did he indeed! I'll have to have a few strong words with him tomorrow. Does he think I've turned into a shrivelled up old crone,' Emma exclaimed pithily.

Emily could not keep the laughter out of her voice as she said, 'Nobody would think that about you, Gran, least of all Blackie. You're still beautiful.'

'No, I'm not. I *am* an old woman,' Emma stated flatly. 'But thank you for being nice, Emily. Of course,' she added with a laugh, 'everyone knows *you're* prejudiced.' She held out her left hand. 'Well, how do you like it?'

Emily took hold of Emma's hand, her bright green eyes huge, and as round as saucers, her excitement apparent on her expressive, mobile face. 'Gosh, Gran, I'd no idea it was going to be so big, and such a beauty! It's fabulous!' She scrutinized the ring more closely, and with an expert's eye, lifted her head and nodded knowingly. 'It's a perfect diamond, Gran. I bet it cost a fortune . . .' Her voice trailed off and she hesitated, then asked in an uncertain tone, 'Does this mean you and Blackie are going to get married?'

Emma burst out laughing and extracted her hand. 'Of course not, you silly goose. Whatever will you think of next.' She touched Emily's face lovingly, 'You're such a romantic girl,' she murmured, sighing softly. 'No, it wouldn't be appropriate. Not at our ages. As Blackie said, we're engaged to be the best of friends for the rest of our lives.' Emma now became aware of the undisguised curiosity and interest lingering on Emily's face, and before she could stop herself she said, 'I'll tell you the story about the ring, if you like.'

'Oh yes, I'd love to hear it, Grandy. Let's go to the parlour, though. I have a thermos of hot chocolate waiting for you. Come along.' She took hold of her grandmother's arm possessively, and shepherded her next door, not realizing she was fussing and bustling like a mother hen. Emma merely smiled, allowed herself to be bullied, secretly amused.

After filling two mugs with chocolate and giving one to Emma, Emily curled up on the sofa she had so recently vacated, tucked her feet under her and gleefully snuggled down into the cushions. Lifting her mug she took a sip and cried with delight, 'This is such fun, it's like being back at boarding school and having midnight feasts.'

Emma's mouth twitched. 'Don't get carried away, Emily,' she laughed. 'We won't be doing this every night. I'm usually in bed by this time. And talking of bed, it's getting *very* late. I'd better tell you the story quickly, so that we can go to sleep. We have a hectic day tomorrow.'

'Yes, Gran.' Emily gave her grandmother her rapt attention.

When the old story was finally told, Emily said, 'Oh Grandma, that's so lovely and touching, and a little sad in a way. And imagine him keeping the ring all these years. Gosh, that's real devotion.' A wistful look swept across her delicately pretty face and she shook her head. 'And you're

157

sceptical about unrequited love! This should prove you're absolutely wrong.'

Emma smiled indulgently, made no comment.

Brightening, Emily rushed on in her breathy voice, 'Just think, if you'd married Blackie instead of Awful Arthur all those years ago, your children would have been very different – it's all a matter of genes, you know. I wonder if the oldies would have been any nicer?' Emily tilted her head and pursed her lips, lost in thought, her mind racing. Several things occurred to her all at once, and she burst out, 'What about your grandchildren? Paula, for instance. And *me*. Goodness, Grandy, I might not have been *me* at all. I could have been someone altogether different . . .'

Emma cut in, 'But I would have loved you just as much, Emily, and Paula too.'

'Oh yes, of course you would, I know that. But your family would have been very – '

'Now you're speculating about things we'll never know. And it's all *much* too complicated for me, especially at this hour,' Emma said with a dismissive yet kindly smile. 'But speaking of my family, what happened here this evening? How was the dinner party?'

Instantly Emily's face underwent a change, became serious as she sat up abruptly, swung her feet to the floor, and leaned closer to Emma. Her manner was confiding as she said, 'You're not going to believe this, but Edwina's behaviour was quite extraordinary – '

'In what way?' Emma asked sharply, dreading the worst.

Seeing the apprehensive expression settling on her grandmother's face, Emily shook her head with some vehemence. 'Don't look like that. It was *all right*. Edwina was nice . . . so nice I couldn't get over it, and neither could Paula. The Dowager Countess was charm personified. Well, that's not strictly true.' Emily made a moue. 'You know I have a tendency to exaggerate.' Emily wrinkled her nose, went on, 'She was sort of . . . *cautious* with Paula and me. She doesn't really like us. She was polite, though, and pleasant to everyone else. I can't imagine what you said to her earlier, Grandma, but it certainly had a drastic effect on her.' Emily searched Emma's face and probed, 'You must have given her an awful lecture. You *did*, didn't you?' A blonde brow lifted quizzically.

Emma said nothing.

Emily volunteered, 'I think Aunt Edwina had been crying before she came down for drinks. Her eyes were puffy and red, and so was her nose. She didn't want a drink. She asked me for aspirins and a glass of water. We'd only been alone together for a couple of minutes when Paula and Jim arrived with Aunt Daisy and Uncle David. Edwina attached herself to Daisy immediately – it's funny, she seems to have a thing about Daisy. Anyway, she didn't say much to anyone else, not even Jim, during cocktails.' Emily's shoulders hunched in a small off-handed shrug. 'I thought she seemed ever so subdued, and she was certainly abstemious. You know how incorrigible she and Mummy are, always tippling. They never know when they've had enough. Edwina didn't touch a drop all night, though, not even wine with dinner.' Flopping back against the cushions, regarding Emma more closely, she pressed, 'What actually *did* you say to her, Gran?'

'Now, Emily, don't be so nosy. That's a private matter between Edwina and me. Anyway, it's not important. What matters is that my words penetrated. Perhaps I drilled some sense into her after all.'

'Oh I'm sure that's true,' Emily agreed. 'And there's something else – you'll never guess what she did before we went in to dinner.'

'No, I'm certain I won't. So you might as well tell me, Emily.'

'She asked Aunt Daisy if she could invite Anthony over for coffee later, and then went to telephone him at Uncle Randolph's.'

Emma stiffened, asked with a frown, 'Did he come?'

'Oh yes.' Emily grinned. 'With cousin Sally. Oh Gran, they're so much in love, and super together.'

'Sally came with him! How did Edwina treat her?'

'With cordiality. *My* eyes were popping, I can tell you that, and I wouldn't have missed that little scene for all the tea in China. Of course Edwina was falling all over Anthony. She was a bit *too* obsequious, if you ask me, you know, Uriah Heapish, but then she's always fawned over her son.' She gave Emma a huge smile, and finished, 'In a nutshell, Grandma, the dinner was a roaring success.'

Emma was flabbergasted and temporarily rendered speechless. 'Well,' she said at last, 'this is one for the books. I never expected Edwina to do such a *volte-face*.' Privately she congratulated herself. Her dire warnings had frightened Edwina into behaving like a normal person seemingly. This is a major victory, she thought, and hoped that her daughter would not have a change of heart. Edwina *was* unpredictable. There was no telling what she might do in a moment of pique. Now, don't go begging for trouble, Emma cautioned herself. Relax.

Smiling brightly, filled with an enormous sense of relief, Emma propelled herself to her feet. 'On that rather surprising but pleasant note I think I'll get off to bed, darling girl.' She leaned over and kissed Emily. 'It looks as if everyone is going to behave with decorum tomorrow. Well, let's hope so. Goodnight, Emily.'

Emily rose and hugged her tightly. 'I do love you so much, Gran. And goodnight, sleep tight.' She picked up the tray. 'I suppose I'd better do the same. I've got to collect the twins from Harrogate College tomorrow, and I've *thousands* of other chores.' She sucked in her breath. '*Phew!*' she exhaled, 'I never seem to have a minute to spare.'

Emma swallowed a smile and disappeared into her bedroom before Emily decided to regale her with those chores she had planned for the following morning.

'Oh Grandy,' Emily called after her, 'I'm glad you're not upset about the Aire Communications deal collapsing.'

Emma came back to the doorway. 'I'd venture to say that it's their loss, our gain.'

'Yes, so Paula indicated when she mentioned it earlier.' Emily glided to the door, and muttered with a degree of terseness, 'Sebastian Cross is simply dreadful. I thought Jonathan might make headway with him. Apparently he didn't, and if Jonathan couldn't succeed, then nobody could.'

Emma stood perfectly still, said with the utmost care, 'What are you chattering on about, Emily?'

Emily stopped in her tracks, swung to face Emma. 'The Aire deal. You asked Jonathan to talk to Sebastian, didn't you?'

'No,' Emma replied in the quietest of voices.

'Oh,' Emily said, looking confused.

'What makes you think I propelled Jonathan into those particular negotiations?' As she spoke Emma steadied herself against the door jamb, her astute eyes glinting darkly as they rested with fixity on her grandchild. All of her senses were alerted, and she remarked tersely, 'Obviously *something* did.'

'Well, yes,' Emily began, and scowled. 'On Tuesday, when I had dinner with Daddy in London, I saw the two of them in the bar of Les Ambassadeurs when we were leaving. We'd had an early dinner, you see, and Daddy was in a frightful stew about being late for a business meeting. He was in such a hurry I didn't get a chance to go over and speak to Jonathan.'

'I see.' Emma was thoughtful for a moment, asked, 'Why did you suggest Jonathan would be able to influence young Cross?'

'Because of their old friendship . . . they were at Eton together. But then you know that, Gran. You once took

161

me there with you, when you went to visit Jonathan at half-term. Don't you remember?'

'Yes. Naturally I also remember that Jonathan went to Eton. What I hadn't realized was that Cross was a pupil there as well, or that Jonathan and he had been friends in those days. I had – '

'I think they're still friends actually,' Emily interrupted.

This bit of information chilled Emma to the bone, but she attempted a smile. 'He probably wanted to surprise me. He might have realized the negotiations were going to be touchy and was endeavouring to smooth the way for Paula,' she said, trying to convince herself this was the truth. But her intuition told her it was not. Emma gripped the door jamb more tightly, and, adopting a meticulously casual tone, asked, 'Did Jonathan see you in Les Ambassadeurs, Emily?'

Emily shook her head. 'He was in deep conversation with Cross.' She pondered, asked swiftly, 'Why? Is it important?'

'Not really. Did you mention this to Paula?'

'I didn't get an opportunity. She had just started to tell me about the Aire fiasco, as she called it, and Cross being horrid to her, when Hilda announced dinner.' Emily bit her inner lip, frowning, beginning to wonder precisely what her grandmother was leading up to with her questions.

Emma nodded, as though to herself, remarked in that same lightly casual voice, 'I'd prefer you not to say anything about this to Paula. I wouldn't want her to think he was interfering, queering her pitch. Unintentionally, of course. And don't bother to bring it up with Jonathan either. I'll talk to him, find out what his aim was, if indeed he had an aim. It might have been a strictly social evening you know, in view of their friendship.'

'Yes, Grandy, whatever you say.'

Emily stood rooted to the spot, studying her grandmother closely, filling with alarm. Emma's face had paled as they had been talking and she noticed that the happy light in her eyes had fled. They were uncommonly dull, lifeless for once. Emily put down the tray hurriedly, and flew across the room. She grasped Emma's arm, exclaimed with concern, 'Are you all right, Gran darling?'

Emma made no response. Her mind was working with that razor-sharp precision and vivid intelligence which were so integral to her great genius. Assessing and analysing with her rare brand of shrewdness and perception, she suddenly saw things with a clarity that shocked. For a split second she recoiled from the truth. I'm making assumptions, she thought, but then her ingrained pragmatism reminded her that she was rarely wrong. The truth was staring her in the face.

Becoming conscious of Emily's hand clutching her arm, her worry and anxiousness apparent, Emma dragged herself out of her disturbing thoughts. She patted the girl's hand, brought a smile to her face that was convincing, reassuring in its certitude.

'I'm just tired,' Emma said in a contained voice and smiled again. But she felt as though something cold had touched her heart.

CHAPTER 10

The medieval church at the top of the hill in Fairley village was filled to capacity, almost bursting at the seams.

Family and friends occupied the front pews and the villagers were crowded in closely behind, for they had turned out in full force to honour Emma Harte at the baptism of her great-grandchildren. And after the ceremony they would troop across the road to the parish hall to partake of the special celebration tea, which Emma had instructed Alexander to arrange.

163

All was peace and serenity within the ancient grey stone walls. Sunshine pouring in through the stained-glass windows threw rainbow arcs of dancing, jewelled light across the sombre stone floor and the dark wood pews. Masses of spring flowers were banked around the altar and on the altar steps. The mingled scents of hyacinths, narcissi, freesia, imported mimosa and lilac filled the air, diminishing the peculiar musty smell of mildew and dust and old wood that was so prevalent in the church. It was the odour of antiquity, and one Emma had detested since childhood: she had automatically chosen the most fragrant of flowers for this occasion in an attempt to counteract it.

She sat in the front pew, proud and dignified, wearing a midnight-blue wool-crêpe dress and loose matching coat. A small velvet beret of the same deep blue was perched at a jaunty angle on her immaculate silver hair, and she wore the McGill emeralds and a long rope of matchless pearls. Blackie was seated to her left, handsome in a dark suit, whilst Daisy sat with her husband, David Amory, to Emma's right. Edwina was wedged in between David and Sarah Lowther, her posture rigid, her expression rather prim, as usual.

Emma had been somewhat taken aback to find Sarah standing on the porch steps when they had arrived. No one had expected to see her, since she was supposed to have a bad cold. They had spoken briefly at the back of the church before taking their seats, and Emma had been immediately struck by her granddaughter's healthy appearance. In her opinion, Sarah had either made a miraculous recovery overnight, or had not been sick in the first place. It was more than likely she had toyed with the idea of not coming in order to avoid Shane. Emma could not hold that against her. She understood, had a good idea how Sarah probably felt. But, she thought, I'll say this for Sarah. She's a cool customer. Sarah had not blinked an eyelash nor displayed the slightest sign of self-consciousness when Shane had greeted them earlier.

Now Emma sneaked a look at him.

He was sitting with his parents in a pew across the nave, his face in profile. Suddenly, as if he knew he was being observed, he turned his head slightly to the right and caught Emma's eye, half smiled and then gave her a conspiratorial wink. Emma returned his smile, swung her eyes back to the altar.

Paula and Jim were standing at the carved stone font which dated back to 1574, and were surrounded by the godparents of their children, totalling six in all. The vicar, the Reverend Geoffrey Huntley, having christened the boy Lorne McGill Harte Fairley, was now preparing to baptize the girl, who was to be named Tessa. Like her twin she would bear the same additional middle names.

Emily, one of Tessa's godmothers, was holding the baby in her arms, and standing on Emma's left were Anthony, and Vivienne Harte, who were the other godparents. Vivienne's elder sister, Sally, was godmother to Lorne and cradled him, flanked on either side by his godfathers, Alexander and Winston.

What an attractive group of young people they are, Emma said inwardly, her eyes lighting up with pleasure, and she saw in her mind, for a brief instant, their antecedents . . . her own parents, her brother Winston, Arthur Ainsley, Paul McGill, Adele and Adam Fairley. How miraculous it was that she and Blackie were still alive and were able to be here today to witness this event, to share in the joyfulness of the occasion.

She shifted her eyes to Paula and Jim.

They do look well together, she thought. He so tall and broad and fair, and the living embodiment of his great-grandfather, Adam; Paula so slender and willowy and dark, and so dramatic looking with her vivid McGill colouring. And Paula's inbred elegance was most apparent in the way she held herself, and in her clothes. She had chosen a tailored wool suit of a deep violet tone, and wore it with a lighter coloured violet satin blouse and a satin pillbox of the same tone. The violet echoed her eyes. She's still too thin, Emma thought, but she has such an extraordinary radiance this afternoon.

Her love for her granddaughter and her pride in the girl were emotions most paramount in Emma at this moment, and her face relaxed into softer lines as she continued to regard Paula. The young woman standing up there at the font had given her nothing but happiness and comfort since the day she had been born, in much the same way her mother, Daisy, had done, and continued to do.

Emma closed her eyes. Paul would have been as proud of Paula as she was, for the girl had all the qualities he had most admired: Honour, integrity, honesty, fairness and an intelligence that frequently startled with its brilliance. Although she had gentle manners, and was inclined to shyness, Paula possessed a certain cool poise, and she had inherited her grandfather's great sense of fun, as had Daisy. Yes, she's a McGill all right, Emma remarked under her breath. But she's a Harte as well. Thank God she has my toughness and astuteness, my indomitability and stamina. She's going to need all of those in the years to come, with what I'm leaving her, with what she has inherited from her grandfather. I hope she never thinks of her inheritance as a terrible burden. It *is* an enormous responsibility, of course . . .

Baby Tessa started to shriek, her piercing wails echoing throughout the church. Emma opened her eyes and blinked. She leaned forward, peered at the scene at the font. Everyone wore expressions of concern. The vicar was holding the baby, sprinkling the holy water on her forehead, christening her now in the name of the Father, the Son and the Holy Ghost. When he had finished he handed the child back to Emily, obviously with some relief. Emily began to rock her, trying to calm and soothe the infant to no avail.

Emma chuckled quietly, knowing it was the shock of the cold water on her forehead which had made Tessa cry. The child was protesting – and most vociferously. I can see it already, she thought, little Tessa McGill Harte Fairley is going to be the rebellious one in *that* family.

Daisy, also smiling, took hold of her mother's arm and squeezed it. She whispered, 'It sounds to me as if Tessa is a chip off the old block, Mummy.'

Emma turned her head to look into her favourite daughter's wide clear blue eyes. 'Yes,' Emma whispered back, 'she's always been the livelier of the two. Another maverick in the brood?' She arched a silver brow most eloquently. Daisy simply nodded in answer, her fine eyes dancing with happiness and some amusement.

Within minutes the ceremony was over and they were slowly filing up the aisle. Emma, her arm tucked through Blackie's, smiled and nodded graciously, but she did not pause to speak to anyone.

Before long the entire family, their friends and the villagers were assembled on the porch, congratulating the parents and chatting amongst themselves.

Several of the local residents came up to Emma, stood talking to her for a few minutes, but very shortly she excused herself and drew Blackie away from the crowd. She said, 'I'll slip away now and I'll be back before anyone notices my absence. Then we can get off to Pennistone Royal.'

'All right, Emma. Are you sure I can't go with you?'

'No. But thanks anyway, Blackie. I won't be a minute.'

As Emma edged away from the busy porch, Milson, Blackie's chauffeur, hurried towards her carrying a basket of flowers. She took it from him, smiled, and murmured her thanks.

She went through the lych-gate leading into the graveyard adjoining the church.

Her feet knew the way by heart, and they led her down the flagged path to the far corner, a bit secluded and bosky and shaded by an old elm tree growing by the side of the moss-covered stone wall. Lying in that corner, beneath the headstones she herself had chosen years before, were her parents, John and Elizabeth Harte. Next to them were her two brothers, Winston and Frank. She took bunches of flowers from the basket and placed one on each of the four graves. Straightening up, she rested her hand on her mother's headstone and stared out towards the bleak moors, a smudged dark line against the periwinkle blue sky filled with scudding white clouds and intermittent sunshine. It was a lovely day, surprisingly warm, balmy even, after the thunderstorms of yesterday. A perfect day to go climbing to the Top of the World. She strained her eyes, but that spot was too far away in the distance to see, and obscured by the soaring fells. She sighed, remembering. Her eyes swept from headstone to headstone, name to name. I've carried each one of you in my heart all the days of my life, she said silently. I've never forgotten any of you. Then unexpectedly the queerest thought entered her mind – she would not be coming back here again to visit these graves.

Emma turned away at last.

Her steps carried her along the same flagged path that curved through the cemetery, and she did not stop until she reached a wide plot of ground at the other side, in the gloomy shadows of the church. This large private plot was encircled by iron railings which set it apart, told everyone that it was special and exclusive. She pushed open the small gate and found herself amongst generations of Fairleys. She glanced at the graves, and finally her eyes came to rest on Adam Fairley's headstone made of white marble. On either side of him were his two wives – Adele, the first, and Olivia, the second. Those two beautiful sisters who had

168

loved and married the same man, and who had, in their own ways, been good to her when she had been a young girl. She had never forgotten their kindness to her, but it was on the middle grave that her gaze lingered for a moment longer.

Well, Adam Fairley, she thought, I won. In the end it was I who triumphed. There is nothing left that your family owns in the village, except this plot of land where you are buried. Everything else belongs to me, and even the church operates mostly through my largesse. Your great-great-grandchildren have just been christened and they bear both of our names, but it is from *me* that they will inherit great wealth and power and position. These thoughts were not rancorous, ran through her mind in a matter-of-fact way, for she had lost all hatred for the Fairleys, and it was not in her nature to gloat, especially when standing next to a man's last resting place.

Slowly she walked back to the church, and the smile on her serene face was one of gentleness and peace.

Coming through the lych-gate, Emma saw Blackie standing to one side, away from the large group of people, talking to her two youngest grandchildren, Amanda and Francesca.

Blackie chuckled as she came to a standstill by his side. 'You might know *these* two would see you do your disappearing act! I had to forcibly restrain them from running after you. Well, almost.'

'We wanted to look at the graves, too, Grandy,' Amanda explained. 'We love cemeteries.'

Emma gave her a look of mock horror. 'How morbid.'

'No, it isn't, it's interesting,' Francesca chirped up. 'We like to read the tombstones, and we try to guess what the people were like, what kind of lives they led. It's like reading a book.'

'Is it now.' Emma laughed, and the look she gave the fifteen-year-old was affectionate. 'I think we should go back to the house,' Emma continued. 'Did Emily tell you we're having a champagne tea this afternoon?'

'Yes, but she said we couldn't have any champagne. We can, though, can't we, Gran?' Amanda asked.

'Just one glass each, I don't want you both getting tiddly.'

'Oh thank you, Gran,' Amanda said, and Francesca linked her arm in Emma's, and announced, 'We'll come with you. Uncle Blackie's car is much nicer than Emily's old Jag.'

'That's not a very nice attitude, Francesca. You came with Emily, and you will drive back with her. Besides, Uncle Blackie and I have things to discuss.'

But they did not really have anything very special or important to talk about. Emma simply wanted to be alone with her dear old friend, to relax before the reception, to catch her breath before she was engulfed by her large and unorthodox clan.

At one point, as they were driving along, Blackie looked at her and said, 'It was a grand christening, Emma. Very beautiful. But you had such a strange look on your face when the vicar was baptizing Lorne, I couldn't help wondering what was going through your mind.'

Emma half turned to face him. 'I was thinking about another christening . . . the one you performed when you baptized Edwina with Armley tap water in Laura's kitchen sink.' Her eyes held his for the longest moment. 'I couldn't help dwelling on the past. You know, Edwin Fairley wouldn't have been permitted to marry me when I was pregnant, even if he had wanted to, and so Edwina could never have been christened here at Fairley. That really struck home today.'

'Yes,' he said in agreement, 'it would have been denied her, no matter what.'

Emma nodded. 'And so, as I thought of everything that

has gone before in my long life, it suddenly occurred to me that this occasion today was a most compelling example of ironic reversal. And that Adam Fairley, more than anyone else, would have appreciated the poetic justice of it all.'

She paused, smiled faintly. 'The wheel of fortune truly has come full circle.'

CHAPTER 11

Jim Fairley, orphaned at the age of ten and raised by his widowed grandfather, had always been lonely as a child.

In consequence, he thoroughly enjoyed being a part of Emma Harte's huge family, one which had become his own when he married Paula in 1968. In a way, being flung head first into this extraordinary clan was something of a novelty to him; also, as yet, he remained unscathed by them and thus had kept an open mind about their individual characters, had not attempted to do a tally of their attributes or their faults. And he had held himself apart from the complex animosities and alliances, feuds and friendships that flourished around Emma.

Because Jim rarely thought ill of anyone, he was frequently startled when Paula came down hard on one of her aunts or uncles, and at times he even wondered if she exaggerated when she listed their imperfections, the terrible wrongs they had done her grandmother. But then she was fiercely protective of her beloved Grandy, whom she doted on. Jim was secretly amused by his wife's attitude, since he believed no one was better equipped to take care of herself than Emma Harte.

A short while ago Jim had decided that Paula's warnings about the Countess of Dunvale were written in water. So far this weekend Edwina had behaved impeccably – as he had fully expected she would. If she was somewhat reserved with Paula she was at least civil, and he had even managed to make Edwina laugh on their way back from church. She was still in an amiable mood, as he could now see.

His aunt was chatting with her son, Anthony, and Sally Harte, near the fireplace and her usually stiff, tight-lipped expression had all but vanished. For once she appeared to be relatively at ease. Poor old thing, she's not so bad, he thought, as always charitable about others, and swung his eyes to the painting to Edwina's left. This hung over the white marble fireplace and it was one of his favourites.

Jim stood at the entrance to the Peach Drawing Room. Pennistone Royal, that lovely mixture of Renaissance and Jacobean design, boasted two formal reception rooms. Paula had chosen this one for the christening party.

He was glad that she had.

He thought it was the loveliest spot in the entire house, with its cream and peach colour scheme and exquisite paintings. Although Emma had depleted her renowned collection of Impressionists by selling some of them off last year, she had retained the two Monets and the three Sisleys that graced these walls. In his opinion it was the works of art that gave the tranquil and elegant Regency room its great beauty.

Jim gazed at the Sisley for a second or two longer, admiring it from this vantage point. He had never coveted anything material in his whole life, but he longed to own this painting. Of course he never would. It would always hang in this house, as Emma had decreed in her will. One day it would be Paula's property, and therefore he would never be deprived of it, could gaze at the landscape whenever he wished. That was why his intense desire for personal possession of it constantly startled him. He had never felt so strongly about anything, except perhaps his wife. His eyes sought Paula without success. The room had filled up during the ten minutes he had been absent with the photographer, who was setting up his equipment in the

Grey Drawing Room. It was just possible she was hidden from view.

He went in rapidly.

At six foot one, well built but trim of figure and with long legs, James Arthur Fairley cut quite a swathe, especially since he was something of a clothes horse, was never anything but faultlessly dressed right down to his handmade shoes. Like his great-grandfather before him, he had a weakness for elegant clothes and a penchant for wearing them with a bit of a dash. Fair of colouring, with light brown hair, he had a pleasant rather sensitive face and soulful greyish-blue eyes. Born and bred a gentleman, he had a natural self-confidence and handled himself easily, and with aplomb, in any given situation. He had a certain quiet charm and a ready smile for everyone.

This flashed as he strode into the centre of the room, glanced about, looking for Paula.

Since he could not find her he took a glass of champagne from a passing waiter, and made a move in his father-in-law's direction. Edwina spotted him and hurried over, cutting him off before he reached David Amory. She at once launched into a rave about the church ceremony, and then engaged him in a conversation that centred on Fairley village. As he listened patiently, Jim realized yet again, and with a recurrence of his initial surprise, that being a Fairley was of tremendous importance to her. Ever since their first meeting, she had continued to ply him with questions about his grandfather, his grandmother and her father, the long-dead Earl of Carlesmoor, and was inquisitive about his own parents who had been tragically killed in a plane crash in 1948.

On the various occasions he had been with his half-great-aunt, for that was what she actually was, he had detected a sense of embarrassment in her because of her illegitimacy, and he had always felt slightly sorry for her. This was one of the reasons he tried to be kind, to include her in those

173

family celebrations about which he had something to say. His mother-in-law had a nice way with Edwina, but apart from this, Jim recognized that Edwina was drawn to Daisy because they had both been born on the wrong side of the blanket. Emma's first child strongly identified with her youngest because of this similarity in their births. But their illegitimacy was the only thing they had in common. The two women were the antithesis of each other. His mother-in-law had the sweetest nature, was a compassionate and considerate woman, and a lady in the truest sense of that word. There was no 'side' to Daisy Amory, and he liked her for her relaxed attitude towards life, her gaiety and her sense of humour. Sadly, his Aunt Edwina was inflexible and sour, tense and standoffish, a dyed-in-the-wool snob, whose basic values were quite alien to him. Yet there was something indefinable in her that touched him, filled him with a curious sympathy for her. Perhaps this was because they shared the same blood. Paula constantly said that blood was *not* thicker than water, but he tended to disagree. He was sure of one thing. His relationship with Edwina, slender and tenuous though it was, annoyed Paula to the point of anger. He found this to be most unreasonable on her part, and he fervently wished she could be less emotional about his aunt. In his opinion, Edwina was a harmless old lady.

'I'm so sorry, Aunt Edwina, I missed that,' Jim said with an apologetic smile, giving her his undivided attention again.

'I was saying that it was a pity my mother had Fairley Hall torn down.' Edwina gave him a long and careful look through her narrowed silvery eyes. 'The house was very old, and by rights it really ought to have been preserved as a landmark in Yorkshire. And just think, if it were still standing, you could have lived there with Paula.'

Jim missed the inherent criticism of her mother in these words. He laughed and shook his head. 'I don't think so. I

174

didn't like the look of Fairley Hall from the photographs I've seen. According to Grandfather it was a hodgepodge of architectural styles and a bit of a monstrosity. He never liked it himself, and personally I think Grandy did the right thing.'

Daisy, who had been hovering close by, caught the tail end of their conversation, and exclaimed, 'I second that, Jim. Besides, Mother put the land it stood on to very good use, by turning it into a park for the villagers. It's a charming spot for them during the warm weather. It was very generous of her.' She glanced across at the Vicar of Fairley who was talking to her husband, and explained, 'And the reason Reverend Huntley is beaming right now is because Mother has just given him a large cheque for the church restoration fund. She keeps that village going in more ways than one.' Having rebutted Edwina, squelched her in the pleasantest way, Daisy gave her half-sister a warm smile. 'I haven't complimented you, Edwina dear. You look lovely, and that's a very smart suit you're wearing.'

'Oh,' Edwina said, startled by these kind words. She hardly ever received compliments, and she preened a little, and a sparkle entered her pale eyes as she automatically reached up and patted her hair. Then remembering her manners, she rushed on, 'Thank you very much, Daisy. You look beautiful yourself, but then you always do. As for my suit, it's by Hardy Amies. I wasn't sure it was right for me, but he persuaded me it was.'

The two women discussed clothes for a few seconds, then Daisy exclaimed, 'You'll have to excuse me, I'm afraid. I can see Mother trying to catch my eye.'

Left alone with Jim again, Edwina began to enumerate the delights of her home in Ireland. 'I do wish you could see Clonloughlin at this time of year, Jim. It's perfectly beautiful, everything's so green. Why don't you and Paula make plans to come over for a weekend soon? You've never seen it, and we'd love to have you. It's only a hop, skip and a jump in that plane of yours.'

'Thank you, Edwina, perhaps we will.' As he spoke Jim knew Paula would never agree. He decided to cover himself, added, 'However, I don't think I'll be able to drag her away from the babies for some time yet.'

'Yes, I do understand,' Edwina murmured, wondering if she had been rebuffed, and to cover her confusion, she went on talking nonstop.

Jim, listening politely and trying to be attentive, wished he could make his escape. Because of his height he towered above Edwina, who was quite small, and now he glanced over her silvery blonde head, looking around, wondering what had happened to Paula. Most of their guests had arrived. *She* was noticeably absent.

Sarah Lowther had just walked in on the arm of her cousin, Jonathan Ainsley. Bryan and Geraldine O'Neill were talking to Alexander Barkstone and his girlfriend. Blackie was standing by the window, engaged in an animated conversation with Randolph Harte, and he appeared to be excited about something, was beckoning to his granddaughter. Miranda floated over to join them, a vision in one of her crazy costumes, her freckled face brimming with laughter, her bright auburn hair gleaming like a copper helmet in the sunshine pouring through the tall windows.

Jim shifted slightly on his feet, surveying the room at large. Emma was perched on the arm of a sofa, being attentive to her brothers' widows, Charlotte and Natalie. These two genteel-looking ladies gave the impression of frailty and great age in comparison to Emma, who exuded vitality and happiness this afternoon. He studied her face for a moment. He had revered and respected this remarkable woman all the years he had worked for her; since his marriage to her granddaughter he had come to know a different side of her, had grown to love her. Emma had

176

such an understanding heart, was kind and generous, and the most fair minded person he had ever met. What a fool his grandfather had been to let her escape. But he supposed things were difficult in those days. Stupid class differences, he thought, and sighed under his breath. Then, quite suddenly, he wished that Edwin Fairley had lived long enough to witness this day . . . to see the Fairleys and the Hartes united at last through matrimony. Their blood was mingled now. He and Paula had started a new blood line.

He became aware that Edwina had stopped her ceaseless chattering and was staring up at him. He said quickly, 'Let me give you a refill, Aunt Edwina, then I think I'd better go and look for Paula. I can't imagine what's happened to her.'

'No more champagne at the moment, thank you, Jim,' Edwina said with the faintest of smiles. She was determined to remain cool and collected and keep a clear head this afternoon. Too much wine would have an adverse effect on her, make her lose her self-possession. That she could not afford. She said, 'Before you disappear, there is one thing I'd like to ask of you. I've been wondering if you would be kind enough to invite me to your house in Harrogate. I know it belonged to your grandfather.' She hesitated, nervously cleared her throat, finished, 'I'd love to see where he . . . where my father lived for so many years of his life.'

'Of course, you must come over for drinks,' Jim said, understanding this need in her. He hoped Paula would not fly into one of her tempers when he told her he had acquiesced to his aunt's request. He began to edge away when Emily, with Amanda and Francesca in tow, breezed up to them, cutting off his escape route.

Smiling brightly, Emily grabbed his arm, glanced at Edwina and cried, 'Hello, you two. Isn't this the most amazing bun fight. I think it's going to be a super party.'

Jim smiled at her indulgently. He was extremely fond of young Emily. 'Have you seen my wife anywhere?' he asked.

'She went upstairs with the nursemaid and the babies, muttering something about changing them. I guess they wet themselves rather thoroughly.' Emily giggled and rolled her eyes in an exaggerated fashion. 'Just be glad they didn't get that elegant Kilgour and French suit of yours drenched with their wee w –'

'Really, Emily,' Edwina sniffed reprovingly, 'don't be so vulgar.' She gave her niece a cold and disapproving look.

Emily, blithely unconcerned, giggled again. 'Babies do do that, you know. They're like puppies. They can't control their bladders. And I *wasn't* being vulgar, Aunt Edwina, merely stating a fact of life.'

Jim could not resist laughing, recognizing that Emily was purposely being provocative. He threw her a warning frown, glanced at his aunt, praying she would not pounce on Emily.

Edwina was obviously annoyed. Fortunately, before she could think of a suitably chilly response, Winston hove in view, made a beeline for them, greeted everyone and positioned himself between Emily and Amanda.

He turned to Jim, and said, 'Sorry to bring up business on such a festive occasion, but I'm afraid I have no alternative. I'd like to get together with you first thing on Monday, to discuss a couple of matters. Will you have time to see me?'

'Of course,' Jim said, giving Winston a puzzled look. Concern edged into his eyes and he frowned. 'Anything serious?'

'No, no, and the only reason I mentioned it now was to make sure you'd keep an hour free for me. I have to go to Doncaster and Sheffield that day, and the rest of the week is impossible. I'm really jammed.'

'Then let's make a definite date, Winston. Say about ten-thirty? I'll have the first edition out on the streets by then.'

'That's fine,' said Winston.

With this matter settled, Jim said, 'Your father seems very pleased with himself, and so does Blackie. Look at them both. They're behaving like a couple of kids with a new toy. What's all the excitement about?'

Winston glanced over his shoulder and laughed. 'My father wants to run Emerald Bow in the National next year, and Blackie's tickled to death about it. I think Aunt Emma's just as thrilled.'

'So I can see,' Jim said.

'Gosh, what marvellous news, Winston,' Emily exclaimed.

'I hope Grandma invites us all to go to Aintree next March.' The conversation now centred around the Grand National and the possibility of Emerald Bow winning the steeplechase. All kinds of opinions were voiced, and even the fifteen-year-old twins had something to say.

But not Edwina. She was silent.

She sipped the last drop of champagne in her glass, eyed Winston with an oblique surreptitiousness. She did not particularly like him. But then she had never had much time for the Hartes. All they had was pots and pots of money. And looks. She could not deny that they were a good looking family – each and every one of them. Suddenly, with a small start of surprise, she saw how closely Winston resembled her mother. She had always been aware they shared certain physical characteristics, yet had never realized how pointed and strong these were. Why, Winston Harte is a younger, male replica of *her*, Edwina muttered to herself. More so than any of her children or grandchildren. The same features, so clearly defined they might have been cut by a chisel; that red hair shot through with gold; those quick intelligent eyes of an unnatural green. Even his small hands holding the glass are like *hers*. My God, it's uncanny, Edwina thought, and looked away quickly, wondering why this revelation disturbed her.

Jim, who had been listening with interest to Winston

179

talking about Steve Larner, the jockey, interrupted him when he exclaimed, 'There's Paula at last.' His face filled with pleasure and he waved to her. 'I'll see you all a little later.' He squeezed Edwina's arm reassuringly and dashed across the room.

Paula watched him hurrying to her, a happy expectant smile playing around her mouth. Her heart tightened. She loved Jim very much and she was so lucky to have found him. He was the dearest, sweetest man, and fine and honourable and good. She would have to try harder with Edwina . . . she wanted so much to please her husband.

Jim caught Paula's hands in his as he came to a standstill by her side. He smiled down into her face. 'You were gone such a long time,' he said. 'I missed you.'

'The babies, darling, they needed me.' Her sparkling bright eyes rested on him lovingly. 'I hope you're not going to turn out to be one of those jealous fathers I keep hearing about.'

'Not on your life. I adore those little moppets.' He leaned into her, pulled her closer and lowered his voice to a hoarse whisper. 'But I also adore *you*. Listen, darling, let's sneak away tonight and have a quiet dinner. Just the two of us. Your parents won't mind. They can have dinner with Emma.'

'Well . . .'

'I won't take no for an answer, my pet.' He bent over her and whispered in her ear, gripped her hands all that more tightly as he did so.

Paula blushed at his words, then laughed a light sweet laugh. 'You're positively wicked. A regular devil.' Looking at him archly, she teased flirtatiously, 'I'll have you know I'm a married woman, sir. What you propose is most indecent. Quite improper, I'd say.'

'Do you really think so?' He laughed, and then he winked, '*I* think my ideas are very *exciting*.'

'Mummy's heading this way,' Paula said laughing and

180

adroitly changing the subject. 'And she's looking very determined about something.'

'Say yes,' Jim demanded. 'To everything.'

'Yes. Yes. Yes.'

Daisy looked from one to the other fondly and shook her head. 'Sorry to break up you two lovebirds, but Mother is champing at the bit. She wants to get the photography out of the way as soon as possible now. I'm rounding everyone up. So come along, let's start assembling in the Grey Drawing Room. Oh, and by the way, Jim dear, I've suggested that Edwina be included in one of the family group portraits, and my mother has agreed.'

'How very nice of you, Daisy,' Jim exclaimed with warmth and sincerity, thinking how typical it was of her to be thoughtful, and caring about another person's feelings. That Daisy had shown such consideration for Edwina was doubly commendable.

Emma Harte had never missed a trick in her entire life.

This afternoon was no exception. Her eyes were everywhere, and from her position near the fireplace she had an overall view of the room, and everyone in it. In much the same way that Jim Fairley held himself apart and took in everything, so Emma herself played the observer much of the time these days.

However, unlike Jim, who only saw things on the surface and, moreover, believed exactly what he saw, Emma had an almost frightening perception, one that pierced any façade to comprehend what actually lay behind it. She understood that nothing was ever the way it seemed, and so she was acutely conscious of the undercurrents in the room – the rivalries, the conflicts, the bad blood that existed between some of those present.

A sardonic smile touched her lips. As usual, cliques had formed. It was easy to see who was allied to whom. And she could read them all like an open book.

Edwina was the one who had surprised her the most, in that she had obviously had the intelligence to accept the inevitable. Her eldest daughter was giving off an aura of cordiality, sitting on the sofa near the window, chatting with Sally. On the other hand, Emma had noticed that she was assiduously avoiding any real contact with the other Hartes in the drawing room.

Randolph, Sally's father, and his two other children, Vivienne and Winston, were most decidedly *persona non grata* with Edwina, and her intense dislike of them was barely concealed behind the stiff and chilly smiles she had given them earlier. Edwina was also cold-shouldering Blackie, although there was nothing new about that. Once, last year, Edwina had referred to him as the grand seigneur, meaning it disparagingly, her voice ringing with sarcasm.

Emma smiled inwardly. She had rather liked the description then: she did so now. It was apt.

Blackie was indeed behaving like the grand patrician gentleman, strolling around as if he had territorial rights, his manner distinctly proprietary, being gracious and charming, playing the genial host to the limit. And why not? He was her greatest friend, and her escort after all, and this was her house, and she was the hostess at this gathering. He had stood at her side during the toasts and the cutting of the christening cake, and after Randolph had finished speaking he had made a toast himself. To her. He had called her the youngest and most beautiful great-grandmother in the world. Now he had paused, was hovering over Paula, who in turn hovered over her babies. Daisy joined them, her serenity and sincerity and goodness a beacon in this room.

Emma shifted her eyes to the far corner, where they settled on her grandson, Alexander.

Always reserved, Alexander seemed particularly so with Jonathan and Sarah, whom he had briefly acknowledged when he had arrived. Since then he had consistently and carefully ignored them. He had attached himself to Bryan and Geraldine O'Neill at the commencement of the reception, returned to sit with them after the photographs had been taken. She did not understand why he was being cool and distant with Sarah and Jonathan. Could they have had a disagreement? Even a falling out? Or was he simply bored by the company of his cousins, with whom he worked at Harte Enterprises? She turned these possibilities over and then let them go. She would know soon enough if there were any real problems between these three. She wished Alexander would make up his mind about that nice Marguerite Reynolds. He had kept that poor girl dangling for too long. Now where was *she* hiding herself?

Emma scanned the room. Ah yes, there she was, near the door, laughing with Merry O'Neill and Amanda. Good God, was that child drinking another glass of champagne. Her *third*? Emily is supposed to be looking after those sisters of hers, and she's not even in the room, Emma thought, and took a step forward, making for Amanda, then stopped in her tracks. Emily had just returned with Winston and Shane, had spotted Amanda and was about to chastise her little sister, who wore a guilty expression. Emma nodded to herself, amused at the little scene being enacted. Emily, for all her youth and gay disposition, could be very tough when she wanted to be.

Shane had detached himself from Winston and Emily, and was prowling across the floor. Her eyes followed him. He came to a stop next to David, drew Paula's father to one side, began speaking to him intently. Shane is not himself today, Emma decided. He has a remote air. It occurred to her he might be suffering from ennui at this family function of hers, not to mention preoccupation with his impending trip to New York.

As for Sarah, her auburn-haired granddaughter appeared to be patently uninterested in Shane. Did Emily exaggerate? No, definitely not. Sarah, clinging to Jonathan like a barnacle to a hull, was, by her very actions, proving to Emma that she did indeed care greatly. If Shane no longer mattered to her she would not be huddled in a corner staying out of his way. Was Jonathan a handy convenience? Or had he and Sarah formed some kind of special alliance lately? If so, why? They had never been particularly close in the past.

Emma gave Jonathan a long hard stare, studying that bland and smiling face, noting his insouciant manner. How disarming he could be. He's clever, she thought, but not quite as clever as he believes he is. He has acquired the knack of dissembling, most likely from me. And because I'm better at dissimulation than he is, he doesn't deceive me one little bit. I have no hard evidence of his treachery, nothing concrete with which I can nail him, and yet I know he's up to no good.

When Emma had first arrived at Fairley Church, Jonathan had rushed over to her, and told her he would see her on Monday morning, would bring her his new evaluation of the Aire Communications building. She had merely nodded, kept her face inscrutable. But she had immediately wondered why he suddenly thought the evaluation of the building's worth was no longer urgent, that it could now wait until Monday. She had been stressing its urgency to him for some time. Emma had not had to think very hard to come up with the answer. Jonathan knew the evaluation was no longer pressing because he was aware that the Aire deal had collapsed. Neither she nor Paula had mentioned the failure of those negotiations, so he could only have acquired his information from Sebastian Cross, and in the last twenty-four hours.

This conversation at the church, coupled with Emily's revelation of the night before, had convinced Emma that Jonathan was somehow involved with the Crosses, in cahoots with them. But to what purpose?

She did not know. But she would soon find out. She had

no intention of confronting Jonathan on Monday morning. It was not her way to show her hand when that hand could be doling out rope, forming a noose. Instead she would go to London next week and start digging. Discreetly. Jonathan's behaviour today had only served to underscore the nagging suspicion that he was not trustworthy, a feeling that she had harboured for weeks. Without realizing it, he had alerted her further. If he were really smart he would have acted as though the Aire deal were still alive. He had made a small slip – but it was a fatal one in her eyes.

Jonathan happened to turn around at this moment. His glance met hers. He smiled broadly and loped across the room to her.

'Goodness, Grandy, why are you standing here all alone?' he asked showing concern for her. Not waiting for a reply he went on, 'Do you want anything? A glass of champagne, or a cup of tea maybe? And do come and sit down. You must be tired.' He took hold of her arm affectionately, and his posture was loving.

'I don't want anything, thank you,' Emma said. 'And I'm not a bit tired. In fact, I never felt better.' She gave him a smile as fraudulently sweet as his had been. Extracting her arm ever so gently, she remarked, 'I've been enjoying myself, standing here watching everyone. You'd be surprised what people reveal about themselves when they believe they're unobserved.' Her eyes were riveted to his face.

She waited.

He squirmed under her unflinching gaze, returned it, managed to keep his expression open and candid. But he laughed too quickly and too loudly as he said, 'You are a card, Grandy.'

And possibly you're the joker in the pack, Emma thought coldly. She said, 'What's wrong with Sarah? She's being rather aloof with everyone, apart from you, of course.'

'She's not feeling well,' he answered with swiftness. 'Fighting a bad cold.'

'She looks as fit as a fiddle to me,' Emma observed dryly, throwing a rapid glance in Sarah's direction.

Emma suddenly stepped back, moved away from Jonathan, and levelled her direct stare on him again. 'Did you come up here together? And when did you arrive in Yorkshire?'

'No, we came separately. Sarah by train last night. I drove up this morning.' This was said steadily enough, and he smiled down at her.

Emma saw the faintest flicker of deceit in his light eyes. She studied his face briefly. Arthur Ainsley's weak mouth, she thought. She said, 'I'm glad Sarah has you to look after her today, Jonathan. It's most kind of you.'

He said nothing, changed the subject by remarking, 'Are you sure you don't want to sit down, Grandmother?'

'I suppose I might as well.'

He steered her across the room towards Charlotte and Natalie, and Emma smothered a laugh. So that's where he thinks I belong, with the old ladies, she thought with some acerbity.

He saw her settled on the sofa, spoke briefly to his great-aunts, and disappeared, heading back to Sarah.

Emma watched him go, filled with sadness and disappointment. Too bad about Jonathan, she thought with resignation. He surely doesn't realize it, but he's as transparent as water. Just like his father. She had always seen right through Robin, and had been several jumps ahead of *him* all of his life, usually to his perpetual irritation and discomfort. Sighing, Emma pushed herself into the cushions and accepted a cup of tea offered by one of the waiters, then turned to her sisters-in-law. Natalie, Frank's widow, was unusually garrulous this afternoon, and she soon dominated the conversation, caught up in an endless recital about her only child, Rosamund, who lived in Italy

186

with her diplomat husband. Charlotte and Emma listened, eyeing each other with amusement from time to time, but Emma's interest rapidly waned. She soon fell into her myriad thoughts.

Emma would never know what prompted her to suddenly put down her cup of tea, stand up, and swing around at the precise moment that she did. And later, when she thought about it in private, she was to wish she had remained seated.

But she did go through these motions, and found Shane O'Neill in her direct line of vision. He did not see her. He stood alone, leaning against the wall in the shadow of a tall Regency cabinet. There was an expression of such unadulterated love and aching yearning on his handsome face Emma had to stifle a gasp of surprise. His face was naked, utterly vulnerable, and it revealed the strongest and most powerful emotions a man could feel for a woman.

And it was Paula whom Shane was staring at with such concentrated intensity and longing.

Oh my God, Emma thought, dismay flooding through her. Her heart missed a beat. How well she knew that look on a man's face. It signified passion and desire, the overwhelming urgency to possess absolutely. And forever.

But her granddaughter was oblivious to him. She was bending over the nursemaid who sat cradling Tessa, adjusting the child's christening robe, cooing to her. Paula's face was tender with a mother's love and she was completely absorbed in the baby.

Emma was so shocked by what she saw she could not move. She was rooted to the spot, staring at him transfixed, unable to tear her eyes away from Shane, who undoubtedly believed he was safe from prying eyes. Emma reached out blindly and gripped the back of the sofa, filled with a terrible shaking sensation.

To her immense relief the expression on Shane's face was fleeting. In a flash it vanished, was replaced by a studied expression of assumed nonchalance, one she knew so well. He moved out of the shadows without noticing her, and mingled with the crowd again. Distantly she heard his vibrant, throaty laugh, and then Randolph's voice in response to something he had said.

Endeavouring to marshal her thoughts, Emma shifted her stance, turned to face the room. Had anyone else witnessed this intensely private moment of Shane's when his guard was down? Where was Jim? Emma's quick alert eyes darted from side to side, came to rest on Emily, who stood motionless a few yards away, staring back at her appalled, anxiety clouding her pretty young face.

Emma frowned. She pinned Emily with a knowing look, then motioned to the door with a brief nod of her head. Emma went out of the drawing room slowly. She was filled with sorrow, and her heart ached for Shane O'Neill. And as she crossed the Stone Hall everything became crystal clear to her, and her sorrow deepened immeasurably.

Upon entering the library, Emma sat down heavily on the nearest chair. She was surprised her legs had carried her this far. She felt weak at the knees.

Emily came in a split second later, closed the door firmly behind her, and leaned against it speechlessly.

To Emma she looked as if she had seen a ghost. She was unnaturally pale and her face was tight, very strained.

Emma said, 'You saw it then? The way Shane was gazing at Paula?'

'Yes,' Emily whispered.

'He's very much in love with her,' Emma said, her voice husky. Her throat tightened. She paused, got a grip on herself, 'But then you knew that *before* today, Emily. In fact, you almost let it slip out yesterday. But you managed to stop yourself just in time. That is correct, isn't it?'

'Yes, Gran.'

'Don't look so scared, Emily. And come here and sit with me. I must talk to you about this. It's most disturbing.'

Emily ran across the room and took the adjoining chair. She gazed deeply into Emma's troubled face, which looked oddly fatigued and weary all of a sudden. She said, 'I'm truly sorry you had to find out. I never wanted you to know, Grandma. I knew it would pain you.'

'Yes, that's true, it does. But now that I do know, I've a couple of questions. First of all, how did you find out that Shane was in love with Paula in the first place?'

'Because I've seen that look on his face before. It was at Paula's wedding in London last year . . . when he thought no one was watching him. Much the same kind of situation as today. He was tucked away in a corner, at the reception at Claridge's, and his eyes never left her. And then there's his behaviour . . . let's face it, Grandy, he's been distant and peculiar with her for the longest time. Actually, to be honest, he's dropped her like a ton of bricks. Obviously he can't bear to be around her, knowing she's married to someone else.'

Emily bit her lip nervously. 'I suspect that's also one of the reasons he spends so much time abroad. I know he has to travel because of their hotel chain, but Merry recently said something to me about Shane constantly jumping on planes at the slightest excuse. She said he seemed to have ants in his pants these days.'

'I see,' Emma said. 'So Shane has never confided in you?'

'God no! He *wouldn't*. He's too proud.'

'Yes,' Emma said, 'I know what you mean.' She was reflective for a moment, then said almost to herself, 'That seems to be a family characteristic. And it's false pride, too. What a waste of time *that* is. So very foolish in the long run. It serves no good purpose.' She looked away, staring into the distance absently, seeing so much, understanding.

Emily patted her hand in her old-fashioned, motherly way, and urged, 'Try not to worry, Gran. I know you love

Shane like one of your own grandchildren, but there's nothing you can do about this.'

'I'm aware of that, darling. But getting back to the incident in the drawing room, do you think anyone else saw what we saw? Jim, for instance?'

'Jim had gone outside a few minutes before, Gran. I spoke to him as he followed Anthony and Sally out on to the terrace. Then Miranda joined them, and the twins.' Emily chewed her inner lip again. '*Sarah.* She has been sneaking looks at Shane all afternoon. She might have caught it, I'm just not sure.'

'I certainly hope she didn't!' Emma exclaimed worriedly.

'So do I.' Emily took a deep breath, volunteered in a low voice, 'There was one person who noticed . . .'

'Who?' Emma demanded, looking at her swiftly.

'Winston.'

'Well, thank God for small mercies. I'm glad it wasn't anyone else. Go and fetch him to me, Emily, and don't discuss a thing. Not in there. Too many nosy parkers around.'

'Yes, Grandmother.' Emily flew out of the room.

Emma rose and went to the windows, staring out at her beautiful gardens. How peaceful they look in the radiant sunlight . . . next door in the drawing room there is a young man who has everything except the woman he loves and who may never know genuine peace in his whole life because of that. Unless his love for Paula ceases to exist. Emma doubted this would happen. The kind of love she had seen etched on his face was everlasting. Its depth and intensity chilled her to the bone. She was absolutely convinced that a man like Shane O'Neill would not be content to worship from afar. His emotions could easily propel him to take more overt action in time. He might try to fight for Paula one day, in the future. And even if Paula was not interested in Shane, the situation still spelled trouble, in Emma's opinion. Triangles were not only uncomfortable, they were explosive.

Emma let out a tiny sigh. She had no answers, no solutions, and speculating was surely a big waste of time.

Her thoughts settled on Paula. She prayed her granddaughter would be happy with Jim Fairley for the rest of her life. If she was not, Shane might indeed make headway with her. Yet this first year of the marriage had been idyllic. On the other hand, there were things she herself had noticed, and which had given her food for thought and cause to wonder about Jim. Instinctively, she knew that he was no match for Paula when it came to inherent strength of character. Paula was inordinately stubborn, and she had a will of iron. And she was so much cleverer than Jim – on every level.

Emma admired Jim professionally – he was a brilliant newspaperman. Also, she was fond of him personally. It was difficult not to be. On the other hand, Emma had recognized for some time that his judgement was flawed in many areas, and most especially when it came to his assessment of people. He was not terribly discriminating. He liked everyone; furthermore, he wanted everyone to be happy, and all of the time, no less. He hated controversy and upset, bent over backward to keep the peace – and very often that was to his own detriment. In Emma's mind, one of Jim's main problems was his overwhelming need to be liked in return, to be popular with every member of the family, his friends, and those in his employment. This trait in him both dismayed and irritated Emma. It was lonely at the top. And it was generally not very wise to be overly familiar with employees. That quickly led to trouble. Loath though she was to admit it, Jim was simply not of the same calibre as Paula. Would he hold up over the years? Every marriage had its problems, its stresses, its emotional upheavals. If Jim caved in because of his lack of stamina and endurance under pressure, what would happen to that marriage? To Paula? To their children? She hated to contemplate the future in this dismal way, and instantly pushed all negative thoughts out of her mind. They did love each other very much, and perhaps their love would overcome any differences they may have.

Winston said, 'You wanted to see me Aunt Emma?' He sounded both nervous and concerned.

'Yes,' Emma said, pivoting. She walked over to a grouping of chairs, motioned Winston and Emily to join her.

They sat down opposite her, waiting.

Winston had been mystified when Emily had dragged him out of the drawing room, whispering that Emma had sent her to get him. He knew at once, from the girl's anxious demeanour, that something was wrong. Now his worried air intensified as he puffed rapidly on his cigarette. Out of the corner of his eye he saw that Emily's face was stark above her yellow suit, its bony pallor more pronounced.

Getting right to the point, Emma said, 'A few minutes ago I saw Shane looking at Paula in such a way that it left no doubt in my mind about his feelings for her. Emily tells me you also noticed.'

'Yes, I did,' Winston said, at once, realizing there was no point in denying it, or lying. He braced himself, wondering what she would say next. He studied her face which was severe and grave.

'Shane is in love with Paula,' Emma announced in a clipped tone.

'Yes. And desperately so,' Winston replied, shaking his head. He had wondered for a long time when this would come out in the open, and now that it had he decided it was wisest to be completely candid with Emma. In a way, he felt relieved that she finally knew. It had been a heavy burden for him to carry alone.

Desperately, Emma repeated under her breath. And her heart sank. Winston was underscoring her own suspicions,

192

confirming her conclusions. She said slowly, 'Has Shane discussed his feelings for her with you, Winston?'

'No, Aunt Emma, he hasn't. He's a very private man, and discreet. But I've picked up a few things lately, and I've known about his emotional involvement with Paula for a while now . . . through my own observations. After all, we do share the same house at weekends. To be honest, I have a feeling Shane *thinks* I know, but he's never brought the matter up. As I said, he's extremely discreet.'

Emma sat back, pursing her lips, her eyes more reflective than before. After a short silence, she said, 'They've been as close as two peas in a pod all of their lives, Winston. How could he have let her slip through his fingers?'

'I can only hazard a guess,' Winston muttered, eyeing her closely. He stubbed out his cigarette, the gesture filled with sudden anger. 'It's because they grew up together . . . I mean, I don't think he could see the wood for the trees, see what was under his nose. I'm positive Shane only realized the depth of his feelings for her when she became engaged to Jim. And they got married so quickly after their engagement was announced, Shane hardly had time to catch his breath. Or act. It all went very fast, as you know.'

Winston now lifted his shoulders in a weary shrug, and glanced away, thinking of Shane's abject misery. It had grown more intense and acute – and more noticeable – lately. He was glad Shane was going to the States – for Shane's own sake. He turned back to Emma, finished, 'That's my analysis of what happened, for what it's worth, Aunt Emma. I truly believe that it took another man in the picture to make Shane understand how much he loved Paula.'

'Yes, I think you're correct, Winston,' Emma said.

'Do you think Paula ever knew, or knows, that he cares about her in that way?' Emily asked Winston in a hushed voice, touching his arm lightly, looking up at him.

'I honestly can't answer that, Emily. But I – '

Emma interrupted with great firmness, 'I'm sure she didn't and doesn't have an inkling, dear.' She cleared her throat, continued in that same clear strong voice, 'This is a most tragic state of affairs for Shane, but there's nothing anyone can do, least of all me. Not any more. Also, it's really none of my business. Nor is it anyone else's, for that matter. The last thing I want is for Shane or Paula to become topics for the gossip mongers in this family, and we all know there are a few who would love to tittle-tattle, perhaps blow this matter out of proportion. I have implicit faith in the both of you, and in your discretion and loyalty. However, I must ask you both to promise me faithfully that you will never mention what you saw this afternoon to anyone, ever. Is that clearly understood?'

'Of course I promise, Grandma,' Emily cried in a shocked voice, looking at Emma aghast. 'You must know I would never talk about Paula, or do anything to hurt her. I feel the same way about Shane.'

'I wasn't doubting you, Emily. I simply felt compelled to stress the importance of your absolute silence on this matter.' She directed her attention at Winston.

He said, 'I promise, Aunt Emma. I care about Paula and Shane as much as Emily does. And I tend to agree with you about the gossips in our family. There's also a lot of free-floating jealousy about Paula. Shane too, in many ways. They're very special people, so obviously they'll always be targets. My lips are sealed, Aunt Emma. Please don't worry about *me*.'

'Thank you,' Emma said, and made a mental note of Winston's astute comments. She smiled thinly. 'I would prefer it if we ourselves never referred to this matter again. I believe it would be best forgotten by the three of us. Shane is going away for six months. Let's hope he will forget Paula – '

'He'll never let go of her!' Winston cut in fiercely,

194

heatedly. 'It's not in his nature to – ' Angrily he clamped his mouth shut, regretting that he had opened it in the first place.

But he had said enough for Emma to get a clear picture. Yes, she thought, that's what I'm afraid of, too. She said, as steadily as possible, 'Perhaps he *will* always care for her, Winston. But he's a young man, and virile. He has normal appetites and desires, I've no doubt. Let us hope that he'll eventually find someone who'll meet his needs, and come up to his standards, a woman who can help him to forget Paula. I sincerely hope he makes a rewarding life for himself, finds fulfilment and happiness.'

'I don't know about that,' Winston muttered, changing his mind yet again. He ought to be truthful with Emma. He owed her that, after all. He threw his aunt a gloom-filled glance. And then, because he had always been able to say anything to her without a shred of embarrassment, he added, in a blunt fashion, 'I'm sure he'll continue to have his brief, hit-and-run affairs, his sexual entanglements. He couldn't avoid them, not the way women throw themselves at him. Shane's no saint, you know. And he's hardly the type to lead a celibate life. After all, Aunt Emma, you don't have to be in love with a woman to sleep with her.'

'Quite,' Emma said, lifting a brow, glancing at Emily.

Winston noticed this, but Emily was a big girl. She knew what was what. Undeterred, he plunged on, 'I suppose you won't want to hear this, but I'm going to say it anyway. In my opinion, Shane O'Neill will never love anyone but Paula. You said a few minutes ago that this was a tragic thing for Shane. And it is. But it's also tragic for Paula, *I* think. She'd have been far better off and happier with a man like Shane than with Jim Fairley.'

Winston's harsh tone, not to mention his condemning words, brought Emma up with a start. She looked at him swiftly, in astonishment, noticing the grim expression ringing his mouth, the angry glint in his eyes. Why, he bears a grudge against Jim, she thought, that's what his suppressed rage and resentment are all about. Winston is against Jim Fairley because he won Paula, cut Shane out.

Emma nodded, made no comment whatsoever.

Emily, her face puckering up, said quietly, 'Poor Shane. Life's so unfair.'

'Come now, darling, you're only seeing Shane's side of this situation.' Emma clucked gently, reprovingly. 'Perhaps Paula doesn't think life is unfair. I'm sure she's happy with Jim. I know she loves him. And besides, Emily, whoever told you life is fair? It's most *unfair*, and it has always been damned hard, in my experience. How we cope with life, react to our hardships and suffering, and overcome them, that's what really counts in the end. We must all be strong, learn from our troubles, grow in stature and character. We can't ever let adversity get us down, Emily. Now, let us end this discussion. Run along the two of you. I want to be alone for a few minutes.'

Winston went over and kissed her. So did Emily. They left together in silence.

Emma sat by herself for a while.

She felt weary, bone tired. It seemed to her that she solved one problem only to encounter another. But then her life had never been any different. Dear, dear Shane, she murmured under her breath. My heart goes out to you. Life has dealt you a bad hand in this particular instance. But you'll survive. We all do.

Quite unexpectedly tears came into her eyes and trickled down her cheeks. She searched her pockets for a handkerchief and dabbed at her wrinkled old face. She felt like weeping buckets of tears. But that was not her way, giving in like that. And tears solved nothing. She blew her nose, pocketed her handkerchief, and stood up, smoothing down her dress as she did.

Emma walked over to the windows again, taking a few deep breaths, drawing on her great strength, her will power.

And slowly she pulled herself together. Her thoughts came back to Shane. Perhaps Winston was right in his assessment. Maybe Shane hadn't realized how he truly felt about Paula until it was too late. Then again, maybe he had believed he had all the time in the world to claim her for his own. We all think that time is endless when we're young, she sighed to herself. The years ahead seem to stretch out forever and indefinitely. But they don't . . . they disappear in a flash, in the wink of an eye. Blackie edged into her mind. She wondered what he would have to say about this situation. She decided, at once, not to tell him. It would upset him, cause him too much grief.

Last night Blackie had said that life was too damned short for dilly-dallying. There was a great deal of truth and wisdom in his words. Especially when it came to a couple of old warriors like themselves. Emma made another sudden decision. She was going to accept Blackie's invitation to go on that trip around the world after all. No more dilly-dallying for her.

Turning away from the window, Emma walked briskly across the floor and left the library. She went into the drawing room purposefully, seeking Blackie, picturing his expression when she told him to put his Plan with a capital P into operation immediately. And this she fully intended to do the minute she found him in the crowded room.

CHAPTER 12

'Do you think all families are like ours?'

'What do you mean – *exactly*?' Winston asked, turning to face Emily.

'We've always got a drama of one kind or another erupting. It seems to me there's never been a minute's peace for as long as I can remember. If it's not the awful aunts and uncles being beastly and scratching everyone's eyes out, it's our generation quarrelling and creating the most dreadful upsets. To tell you the truth, I feel as though I'm on a battlefield half the time, and I don't think I'm a very good combatant.'

Winston chuckled at her mournful tone, which reflected her dire expression. 'You manage all right, Emily. You're a good little scrapper – so I've noticed.'

The two of them sat together on an old stone garden seat at the bottom on the rolling lawns that sloped away from the wide terrace which fronted the Peach Drawing Room. Behind them, Pennistone Royal soared up into a sky of deepening blue, awesome in its grandeur and majestic beauty, the many windows glittering in the sunshine of late afternoon.

Now Winston said more thoughtfully, 'But to answer your question, I don't suppose other families are *quite* like ours. After all, how many have an Emma Harte as the matriarch?'

Emily drew away, looking up at him, a small frown puckering her smooth brow. Her eyes held his gravely as she said, 'Don't blame Grandma for the dramatics that are being endlessly enacted. I think she's an innocent by-stander, poor thing. I really get angry when I think of the heartache some members of this family cause her.'

Winston exclaimed, 'I wasn't being critical of her, if that's what you think. Or suggesting for one minute that she's responsible for these situations, Emily. I agree with you – she's not at fault. I was merely pointing out that as the most remarkable woman of our time, and an original, there's bound to be controversy surrounding her. Look, she's had a very complex and complicated life, and one she's certainly lived to the fullest. She has shoals of children and grandchildren, and if you include all of us Hartes, which you must, her family is *huge*. Bigger than most. And don't forget her other close attachments – the O'Neill and

Kallinski clans. Add up the numbers – and you've got an army, more or less.'

'Everything you say is true, Winston. Still, I do get awfully fed up with the infighting and bickering. I just wish we could all live peacefully together, and get *on* with it, for God's sake.'

'Yes . . . but there's another thing you must take into consideration, Emily. Immense wealth and power are vested in her, and in this family, so obviously there are going to be jealousies and competitiveness and all kinds of machinations. It strikes me that intrigues are inescapable, given the nature of people . . . they *can* be rotten, Emily. Selfish, greedy, self-serving and ruthless. I've discovered that some people will stop at nothing when their own interests are at stake.'

'Don't I know it!' Emily stared down into the murky depths of the pond, looking troubled. Finally she lifted her head, swung her eyes to Winston. 'When I mentioned dramas a few minutes ago, naturally I was referring to Shane. But, I must admit, I sensed things this afternoon, you know, *undercurrents*. As usual, the room was divided into camps. There was a lot of manoeuvring going on.'

'And who was doing what to whom?' Winston asked with some alertness, his curiosity aroused.

'Jonathan and Sarah are as thick as thieves, for one thing. That's very strange, because I know she never used to like him. I can't put my finger on it, yet I can't help feeling they're concocting something. Alexander is probably suspicious of that new liaison. Didn't you notice how he's steered clear of them today?'

'Now that you mention it, yes. Personally, I've never had much time for Jonathan Ainsley. He was a bully as a child, and like all bullies he's basically a coward. He projects a lot of charm these days, but I don't expect he's changed much over the years, not *inside*. I haven't forgotten the time he hit me over the head with a cricket bat. The nasty little bugger. He could have done me real damage.'

'I know he could, and he was always horrid to me when we were growing up. I still believe it was Master Jonathan who cut the tyres on that bicycle Grandy gave me when I was ten, even though he denied it when she challenged him. He came up with some sort of plausible alibi about his whereabouts that day, but I just *know* it was a total fib.' Emily scowled. 'As for Sarah, well, she's been a loner, and secretive, all of her life.'

'You know what they say – still waters run deep and the devil's at the bottom,' Winston remarked.

He bent down, picked up a pebble and idly threw it into the pond, watching the ripples eddying out from the pool's centre. 'There have been occasions when I've thought that Sarah has the hots for Shane.'

Emily started in surprise. 'You're not the only one,' she admitted quietly. 'Well, fat chance she's got . . .' She stopped, added swiftly, 'That sounded mean, and I didn't intend to be catty, Winston. I don't dislike Sarah. She can be very sweet, and I feel sorry for her really. Carrying a torch for a man like Shane O'Neill must be positively awful. Even heartbreaking, perhaps. She and I have never been all that close, but . . . well, I always thought she was true blue – until today. Now I'm not sure any more.'

'She might have been using Jonathan as a shield, and that's all. It was pretty obvious she was trying to disappear into the woodwork, because of Shane's presence, I've no doubt.'

'Maybe you're right.' Changing the subject, Emily remarked, 'Jim's very taken with Edwina and with Anthony, by the look of it. He's been glued to our young earl for the last hour or so. Maybe titles impress him. Anyway, what do you think about Anthony and Sally getting together?'

'Anthony's decent enough, but my father's not so happy

about Sally's involvement with him, mostly because of Edwina. If Sally does marry him, we're going to have that old battleaxe slap bang in our midst. Not a very pleasing prospect. She hates the Hartes for some reason.'

'It's because Grandma is a Harte!' Emily exclaimed. 'Edwina has always looked down her nose at her mother. What a stupid woman she is, I really can't bear her.' Emily looked away, pondering. After a short silence, she said in a casual tone, 'You don't like Jim Fairley, do you?'

Winston shook his head vehemently. 'No, no, you're wrong there. I *do* like him, and I certainly have a high regard for his professional abilities. It's just that – ' Winston shrugged, made a face, ' – well, I know Paula better than most people. Despite that quiet façade, she's very strong, as *you* know. She's also ambitious, driven, a work horse, and a brilliant businesswoman to boot. She's quite extraordinary for her age, and the older she gets the more like Emma she'll become, you mark my words. Actually she's been brought up and groomed to be exactly that – the next Emma Harte. By Emma Harte herself. So, because of this, and the differences in their personalities, I can't help thinking she and Jim are ill suited. But then I'm prejudiced I suppose . . . in Shane's favour. He's my best friend, and one hell of a man. But then – '

Emily broke in peremptorily, 'There's something I want to tell you about Jim, Winston. I believe he's got a lot more depth and strength than some people realize. Paula told me that he used to have the most terrible and agonizing fear of flying, because his parents were killed in a plane crash when he was a small boy. And that's why he took up flying and bought his own plane. He became a pilot to conquer his fear. I know Gran hates him tootling around in his little tin bird, as she calls it, but it's obviously important for him to do so, perhaps even essential to his well being.'

Winston looked surprised. He said, 'Then I've got to hand it to him, it takes guts and courage to overcome that kind of paralysing fear. I'm glad you told me, Emily. Anyway, I was about to say that I could be wrong about Paula and Jim. I'm not infallible. Maybe those two will make it together. I certainly don't wish any unhappiness on Paula, of whom I'm very fond. Or on Jim for that matter.'

He paused, gave Emily a cheeky grin, and finished, 'Besides, nobody knows what really goes on between two people, or what happens in the privacy of the bedroom. Jim could have hidden charms, you know.' He winked at her suggestively.

Emily could not help laughing. 'You are wicked, Winston.' Her eyes filled with mischief. 'You should have seen Grandy's face when you were rattling on about Shane and his hit-and-run affairs and sexual entanglements. It was a picture. And she kept giving me the most surreptitious and concerned glances, as if I wasn't supposed to know about sex.'

'And of course you *are* the lady of great experience, eh, Tiddler?'

Emily adopted a haughty expression and drew herself up on the bench. 'Have you forgotten that I'm now twenty-two years of age? *I* know exactly how many beans make five.'

They grinned at each other. She saw that Winston was highly amused.

Emily went on, 'Do you know, you haven't called me Tiddler since I was just that – a very little girl.'

'And you were, too. The tiniest of little tots for your age.'

'But I did sprout suddenly. I'll have you know I'm now five foot five inches tall, Winston Harte!'

'And a very grown up young woman, I'll wager,' he teased. 'We had fun as kids, though, didn't we, Tiddler? Do you remember that day we decided to play at being Early Britons, and I dubbed you Queen Boadicea?'

'How could I forget!' Emily shrieked. Her face flooded with merriment. 'You painted me blue. *All over.*'

'Not quite, since you insisted on keeping your knickers on, and your liberty bodice. You *were* a modest little thing, as I recall.'

'No, I wasn't! It was the dead of winter, and freezing in Grandy's garage. Besides, why would I be bashful *then*? I didn't have anything to show off when I was five years old.'

Winston gave her an appraising look, one full of speculation, seeing her through the eyes of a grown man. 'But you do now – ' He left the rest of his sentence unfinished, feeling self-conscious all of a sudden. Then he became intensely aware of her close proximity as he breathed in the scent of her floral perfume, the lemony tang of her newly-washed hair. Her face, at this moment upturned to his, was trusting, and it had lost its earlier pallor. She looked more like herself, so very pretty and delicate, and as sweet as a summer rose, dewy and fresh and innocent.

Winston cleared his throat, and could not resist drawing her closer to him, wanting and needing that closeness. He said tenderly, in a newly-gentle voice, 'It's a good thing you were a modest child, Emily. If you hadn't kept some of your clothes on, I *would* have painted you all over, and probably killed you in the process.'

'How were we to know, at our ages, that skin can't breathe through paint. It wasn't really your fault, Winston. I was just as bad, and after all I painted parts of you.' Emily relaxed against him. She was as conscious of Winston as he was of her, and she longed to prolong this unanticipated and unexpected moment of real physical contact.

He let out a deep chuckle. 'I'll never forget Aunt Emma's terrible fury when she found us in the garage. I thought she was going to give me the whipping of my life. Do you know, every time I smell turpentine I think of that day, of those gruesome turpentine baths she and Hilda gave us. I swear to God she scrubbed me twice as hard as she did you. Extra punishment for me, of course, the irresponsible ten-year-old boy, who should have known better. I was raw for days.'

Emily squeezed his arm. 'We were always getting into trouble, weren't we? You were the ring leader, I the devoted follower, faithfully trailing after you, doing your bidding. I did adore you so, Winston.'

He nodded, looking down into a pair of sparkling eyes that were extraordinary reflections of his own.

Winston caught his breath. He saw something flashing in those green depths, an intensity of feeling, the self-same adoration she had had for him when she had been a child. Unexpectedly his heart began to clatter, and before he could stop himself he bent forward and kissed her on the mouth.

Instantly Emily's arms went around his neck, and she returned his kiss so fervently he was momentarily taken aback. He gripped her tighter, and kissed her again, and then again, and with increasing passion. He felt an overwhelming desire for her flowing through him, rising in him. My God, he was suddenly as hard as a rock. He wanted Emily, and with every part of himself. His whole body was throbbing for her, and he was stunned, thrown off balance by this discovery.

Eventually they loosened their grip on each other and pulled apart breathlessly.

They stared at each other in amazement.

Emily's face was flushed, her eyes startlingly bright, and he saw, with sudden clarity, the love burning in them. Love for him. He touched her cheek and found it was red hot under his caress, burning like her eyes burned. Impatiently he dragged her into his arms again, and his mouth sought hers roughly. They kissed with mounting passion. Their tongues met tantalizingly. He probed her mouth, devoured it. They pressed closer, their bodies cleaving.

Vaguely, dimly, at the back of his swimming mind, Winston remembered how he had always had the urge to undress her when they had been children. In a rush he recalled the long-forgotten games they had played in the attics here . . . secret, intimate, exciting games when he had experienced his first arousals. He thought of how his clumsy boy's hands had explored her little girl's body . . . he wanted to explore it again with the sure hands of the experienced man he now was, to touch every part of her, woman that she now was, to plunge into her, to possess her completely. His erection was enormous and he thought he was going to explode. He struggled for control, knowing he ought to curtail their lovemaking at once, but he found he was unwilling to release her from his arms. He gave in to his feelings, kissing her face, her neck, her hair, touching her breasts, taut under the flimsy silk blouse.

It was Emily who finally broke the spell which held them enraptured with each other. She extricated herself from his forceful embrace, but ever so gently and with reluctance. She gazed up at him. Her expression was one of stupefaction.

'Oh Winston,' she whispered, and reached out to touch his sensual, trembling mouth with two fingers. She let them rest there for a moment, as if gentling him.

Winston was speechless.

He sat rigidly on the bench, waiting for his excitement to subside. Emily was motionless at his side, looking up into his face. His eyes bored into her, telegraphing so much to her.

At last he managed, in a strangled voice thick with emotion, 'Emily, I . . .'

'Please,' she whispered quaveringly, 'don't say anything. At least not now.' She glanced away, biting her inner lip, giving him a few moments to steady himself, to regain his composure. Then she stood up, held out her hand. 'Come on,' she said, 'we'd better go inside. It's getting ever so late.'

He said nothing, simply rose; and they walked up the steps in silence, holding hands tightly, each conscious of the other, whilst lost within themselves.

Emily was filled with euphoria.

He has noticed me again, she thought, her heart soaring. At last. Since I was sixteen I've been waiting for him to see me as a woman. I want him. I've never stopped wanting him since we were children. Oh Winston, please feel the same way as I do. Take me for yourself. I've always belonged to you. You made sure of that when I was a child.

Winston, for his part, was awash with all manner of conflicting emotions and turbulent feelings.

He was not only astonished at himself, but at Emily as well – staggered really. They had fallen into each other's arms a moment ago with such ardour and passion he knew that if they had been in more suitable surroundings they would have made love. Nothing would have stopped them. And they had come together without premeditation.

Self-analysis and self-appraisal now edged into his whirling thoughts, cooling him down considerably. He came to his senses, asking himself how this could have happened. She was his cousin, after all. Well, his third cousin. And he had known her for his entire life, although he had paid little attention to her over the past ten years. And inevitably he asked himself finally how he could feel so strongly about Emily when he was in love with Allison Ridley.

This thought nagged at him, and maddeningly so as they mounted the long flight of steps. But when they stepped out on to the circular driveway he let the thought go free as he saw Shane's red Ferrari hurtling around the corner. It slowed to a standstill with a screeching of brakes.

Shane rolled down the window and poked his head out,

grinning at them. 'Where have you two been?' he asked. 'I've been looking all over for you, to say goodbye.'

'Emily was feeling a bit bilious in that packed room, so we came out for a breath of fresh air,' Winston ad-libbed quickly. 'Where are you off to in such a tearing hurry, and at this early hour?'

'Like Emily, I was beginning to feel oppressed indoors. I thought I'd take a drive. To Harrogate. I have to say a few farewells . . . to a couple of chums.'

Winston's eyes narrowed imperceptibly. He's going to see Dorothea Mallet, he thought. Some good that'll do him. He said, 'Don't be late for Allison's dinner party. Eight sharp.'

'I'll be there on time, don't worry.'

Emily asked, 'Will you be around tomorrow, Shane?'

'I don't think so, Emily.' He opened the car door and got out. He took hold of her, hugged her tightly. 'I'll see you in six months, or so. Unless you come to New York first.' He smiled at her fondly. 'Aunt Emma just told me you're going to work for Genret. Congratulations, little one.'

'Thank you, Shane, I'm excited about it.' She stood on tiptoe and kissed his cheek. 'And perhaps I will get over to the States on my travels for Genret. You'll have to show me the town, you know!'

'That's a date,' he laughed. 'Take care of yourself, Emily.'

'And you too, Shane.'

'See you later, Winston,' Shane said, and got back into the car.

'Yes,' Winston answered laconically. He looked at Emily oddly as Shane drove off. 'You didn't tell me about Genret.' This was said fretfully, and he felt so unexpectedly gloomy that he was surprised at himself.

She said, 'I haven't had a chance, Winston.'

'Does it mean you'll be doing a great deal of travelling?' he probed, scowling at her.

'Eventually. Why?' Emily lifted a brow quizzically, secretly delighted by his reaction.

'Oh, I just wondered,' he muttered. He realized, with a small shock, that he did not relish the idea of her roaming the world by herself, trotting off on buying trips for Genret.

They fell silent again as they continued up the drive to the house, but just before they went inside, Emily ventured, in a hesitant voice, 'Is it serious? With you and Allison, I mean?'

'No, of course not,' Winston exclaimed swiftly, then asked himself why he had told such a bare-faced lie. He was on the verge of proposing to Allison.

Emily's face brightened. She said, 'I'm sorry you're busy tonight. I'd hoped you'd stay and have dinner with us.'

'I'm afraid I'm stuck.' Winston grimaced to himself, discovering, to his further astonishment, that he was no longer looking forward to the dinner party. He smiled with some wryness, then took hold of Emily's arm as she pushed open the back door, and swung her to face him. 'What are you doing tomorrow?'

'I have to take the girls back to Harrogate College after Sunday lunch here. I'm free in the evening,' she volunteered, and returned his steady gaze unblinkingly. Expectancy illuminated her face.

'How would you like to cook supper for a lonely bachelor? I could come over to your flat in Headingley, Emily,' he suggested.

The smile slipped off her face and she shook her head. 'It's not possible, Winston. I've just moved in here with Grandy. Yesterday, actually. I'm getting rid of the flat. Otherwise I'd have loved to cook for you.'

Winston stood staring down at her, his hands resting on her shoulders. He was swamped with mixed emotions. He was positive she wanted him. He certainly wanted her.

Urgently. Allison loomed up between them. Oh what the hell, he thought, making a decision he hoped he would have no reason to regret later.

Tilting her chin, he kissed her quickly on the mouth. He said, with a wide grin, 'Then we're neighbours. Come over to Beck House tomorrow night, and *I'll* cook for *you*. We'll have a nice evening, I promise. What do you say?'

'I think it's a super idea, Winston,' she said, filling with happiness and excitement. 'What time shall I come over?'

'As soon as you possibly can, darling.'

CHAPTER 13

The room was in total darkness.

Not even the merest sliver of light penetrated the tightly drawn curtains, and the lamps had been doused. He craved the darkness. It was like a balm to him. The darkness brought anonymity. He liked it that way. He could not bear to make love in the light any more.

He lay absolutely still, with his eyes closed, flat on his back, his long legs stretched out in front of him, his arms resting by his sides inertly. His shoulder barely touched hers. He could hear her breathing softly, in unison with himself.

It was not working between the two of them.

And it would not work, he knew that, and he wondered why he was here at all. He really ought to leave. Make a graceful exit. Immediately. He swallowed, fighting back the nausea, wishing he had not downed two glasses of whiskey on top of all that champagne. His head was swimming and he was dizzy, but he was not drunk. In a way, he regretted he was not.

She murmured his name, meltingly, pleadingly, repeating it several times, her fingers brushing up and down his arm.

He was motionless, saying nothing, endeavouring to find the energy to get up and dress and leave. He felt enervated, lethargic. The ghastly afternoon, with its extreme tensions and painful moments, plus the effort he had exerted to conceal his raw emotions, had vitiated him, undermined his stamina.

Now he felt an imperceptible movement close to him, but still he did not open his eyes.

She touched one of his nipples, tentatively at first, then more insistently, pinching it between her fingertips. Absently, he moved her hand away, without bothering to explain that his nipples were not as sensitive as she obviously believed they were. But he had told her that before, hadn't he? Her hand rested on his chest for a moment, then fluttered on to his stomach, making gentle circular movements, creeping down in the direction of his crotch. He knew what she had in mind, what she was about to do next, but he lacked the will to stop her, or to tell her he was leaving in a moment.

She began to stroke him. He hardly paid attention, drifting off into his thoughts. Vaguely he heard the rustle of sheets. She had slithered down the bed and was crouched over him. Her long hair brushed his thighs, and then her warm lips encircled him, enclosed him fully. She was a versatile lover. Despite his buzzing head, his queasy stomach and his lack of interest in her, slowly, steadily, with infinite care, and painstaking deliberation, she managed to arouse him. And in doing so she took him by surprise. When finally she lifted her head and moved her lips higher, on to his stomach, trailed them up over his chest to settle on his mouth, he found himself responding automatically. He returned her fervent kisses, his excitement mounting.

With suddenness, abruptness, he moved rapidly, holding

her tightly against him, rolling them both over so that he was lying on top of her. His hands went into the cloud of dark hair and he held her head in his hands, kissing her more deeply and thoroughly, their tongues grazing. He squeezed his eyes tightly shut, not wanting to look into her face pressed so close to his. His fingers left her hair, moved down to fondle her full, voluptuous breasts, her hardening nipples; he pushed his hands under her shoulder blades, then her buttocks, lifting her body, fitting it into the curve of his. He was hard enough to slide into her swiftly, easily, expertly. Together they found a rhythm, rising and falling, their movements growing swifter, more frenzied, gaining in momentum. Her legs went high around his back so that he could shaft deeper and deeper into the warmth of her.

The darkness . . . the blackness . . . welcoming him . . . enveloping him. He was falling . . . falling into that endless, bottomless, velvet pit. Paula. Paula. Paula. I love you. Take me. Take all of me. All of my essence. Brilliantly clear images of her exquisite face flashed behind his eyes, were trapped beneath his lids. Paula, my darling, he cried silently, oh Paula . . .

'Shane! You're hurting me.'

He heard the voice as if from a long distance, and it was like a knife slashing at his viscera.

It brought him down. Brought him back to this room. And back to her. And it killed the mood he had so carefully created for himself, and only for himself. His fantasy shattered around him.

He fell against her body and lay perfectly still. He was deflated, flaccid, all of his vitality draining away.

At last he said, in a low mumble, 'I'm sorry if I hurt you, Dorothea. It seems I don't know my own strength.' Perhaps you do, he added sardonically under his breath. Or rather, your want of it. Instantly he was embarrassed by his lack of staying power, his inability to bring the act of love to its proper culmination for them both. Act of sex, you mean, he thought, and he shuddered. Revulsion trickled through him, for himself, for her, although she was hardly to blame.

Dorothea said, 'Your watch strap was cutting into my back. But I suppose I shouldn't have said anything just then. You were on the edge, the verge of – '

He covered her mouth with his hand, gently but firmly, in order to stop the flow of words. He did not want to hear her apology. He did not say one single word, just lay against her for the longest moment, his heart slamming against his rib cage, his throat tight with a strangling sensation. Thankfully she, too, was silent. Finally, he lifted himself off her body, touched her shoulder lightly, and left the rumpled bed.

Shane went into the bathroom, locked the door and leaned against it, filled with considerable relief. He fumbled for the switch, snapped on the light, blinked rapidly in the sudden intense glare. The room swam in front of him, and the white-tiled floor appeared to tilt upward to hit him between the eyes. The vertigo and the nausea returned.

He stumbled to the wash basin, leaned over it, and vomited. Blindly he searched for the tap with one hand, and turned it on so that the sound of running water would drown out his retching. He retched and retched until he thought he had nothing left in his insides. When the nausea mercifully subsided he wiped his mouth with the flannel and drank several glasses of cold water, braced himself against the sink, staring down, his eyes closed.

Eventually Shane lifted his head and saw himself in the mirror and he did not like what he saw. His eyes were red-rimmed and bloodshot, his face puffy and congested, and his tousled black hair stood on end. He noticed a smudge of bright red lipstick on the side of his mouth and took the damp flannel and scrubbed at it furiously, angrily. But his anger was directed solely at himself. It had nothing to do

212

with Dorothea. This was not her fault. He was entirely to blame.

He could no longer make love to her successfully, or to any other woman, for that matter. Something always happened to bring him back to reality, and when he realized it was not Paula in his arms, as he had fantasized, he fell apart, could not reach fulfilment. Sometimes, stupefied by drink, his vision and his senses blurred, he could somehow manage, but even these rare occasions were becoming rarer.

He stared at his face in the mirror and without warning he was struck by panic and fear.

Was it always going to be like this? For the rest of his life? Would he never have a happy sexual relationship again? Was he doomed to lead an arid existence without a woman? Would he have to resort to celibacy to save face? To stave off that dreadful moment of embarrassment such as the one which had just occurred in Dorothea's bed?

He was not impotent. He knew he was not afflicted in that way. It was a simple matter really – if his partner intruded into his thoughts, made her presence felt, no longer remained anonymous, then he lost his erection. Try though he did, he could not hold it long enough to satisfy her or himself. The woman he idolized impinged, edged in between them, rendering him weak and ineffectual, he who had always been considered a good lover. What would he *do*, for Christ's sake? *How* would be cure himself? *Was* there a cure? Did he *need* to see a doctor?

The silence in the room pressed in on him. He had no ready answers for himself in his awful predicament.

His anguish flared. God damn it! God damn it to hell! he blasphemed silently, and unexpectedly his eyes filled with tears of helplessness, frustration and rage, startling him. And then instantaneously he was shocked and mortified by this shameful loss of control. For a split second he wanted to smash his fist into the mirror, to shatter that tearful

213

image of himself staring out to mock him. He wanted to smash those finely-tuned, crystalline images of Paula. Damn *her*. Destroy those indelible imprints of her that were stamped so strongly on his tormented, aching brain they seemed to control his life, affected everything he did. At times he felt hopelessly victimized by the vibrant inner vision of her face, the sound of her laughter and her gentle voice that echoed endlessly in his head. But all were locked so securely in his imagination he could not eradicate them, no matter how hard he tried.

But he did not move. He kept his hand clenched at his side, the knuckles white, protruding sharply. Then he closed his eyes convulsively, no longer able to look at himself in this moment of weakness. He leaned against the wall to steady himself, was immobilized like this until he grew calmer, got a grip on himself. Swinging around, he stepped into the shower stall, turned on the taps, let the water sluice down over him. And slowly, but with an iron-clad determination, he emptied his heart and his mind, threw out every vestige of emotion, all feeling.

Minutes later he emerged from the steaming shower, took a bath sheet and dried himself vigorously. He found a fresh towel, tied it around his waist, then searched the cupboard under the sink for the toilet kit he had left there weeks ago. He cleaned his teeth, ran the electric razor over his chin to remove his faint five o'clock shadow, splashed cologne on his face, and combed his damp hair.

He was refreshed, looked more like himself . . . coolly contained, smoothly in control once more. He stared at his reflection a fraction longer, wondering about himself. He was a strapping, healthy young man of twenty-seven, stood six foot three and had a muscular body that was strong and powerful. He had an equally powerful brain to go with his splendid physique. And yet . . . he was so fragile really. The mind is a peculiar thing, he thought, it has such a delicate balance. And who can explain the logic of the heart.

Turning away, he took a deep breath, prepared himself for the inevitable scene with Dorothea. Today he had come to her against his own volition – he could not wait to leave her.

He opened the bathroom door, blinked as he walked back into the shadow-filled bedroom, adjusting his eyes to the darkness. The room was silent, and he wondered if she had fallen asleep, prayed that she had. He groped around for his clothes on the chair where he had discarded them earlier, pulled on his underpants and socks, dispensed with the towel. He slipped on his shirt, buttoned it quickly, dragged his trousers up over his legs and zipped them.

At this moment the bedside lamp flared into life, flooding the room with chilly brightness.

'You're not leaving!' Dorothea exploded. She sounded aghast, furious.

He pivoted.

He could not look at her. Unable to meet her gaze, which he knew would be hurt and condemning, he stared at the far wall.

'I have to go,' he said after a short pause. He sat down on the chair and began to put on his shoes. He could feel her eyes on him.

'You've got a nerve!' she cried, sitting up violently, rattling the headboard as she did. She pulled the sheet around her body with an angry gesture. 'You stroll in here unannounced, help yourself to my booze, bed me, fumble *that*, and leave me high and dry whilst you disappear into the bathroom for half an hour.' She glared at him, added in the same harsh, accusatory tone, 'Then you creep back in here, and calmly proceed to dress in the dark as if you owe me nothing. You were obviously going to *sneak off* to your blasted dinner party!'

He winced. Sighing under his breath, he stood up, and

walked over to the bed. He sat down on the edge, took hold of her hand, wanting to be nice, to part with her in a friendly manner. She snatched her hand away, and pressed it to her trembling mouth, attempting to quell the tears glittering in her dark eyes.

Shane said, in his gentlest voice, 'Come on, don't get upset. I told you last week about the dinner tonight. And I reminded you about it when I first arrived this afternoon. It didn't seem to bother you a few hours ago, you were very welcoming.'

'Well, it bothers me now,' she gasped, choking on her words. 'I didn't think you'd leave me, not on your last evening in Yorkshire. Especially after we'd spent several hours in bed together. I thought we'd be having supper, we usually do, and that you would be sleeping here tonight, Shane.'

He was silent. He glanced away uncomfortably.

She misconstrued his reticence. 'I'm sorry I spoiled it for you, Shane. At the last minute, I mean,' she whispered, her voice softer, more cajoling. She adopted a most winning and conciliatory demeanour. 'Please say you forgive me. I love you so much. I can't bear it when you're angry.'

'I'm not angry, and there's nothing to forgive,' he muttered, striving for patience whilst longing to be gone. 'Don't start flagellating yourself, or donning a hair shirt. Look, it doesn't matter, honestly it doesn't, Dorothea.'

She caught something strange in his voice. She was not sure what it was exactly, but it riled her, nevertheless. 'It matters to me,' she snapped, her sweetness immediately evaporating. When there was no response from him, she cried heatedly, 'This afternoon finally *proves* it to me.'

'Proves what?' he asked, sounding bored.

'That you can't make it with *me* – because there's another woman. You're in love with someone else, Shane, and I think you're a bastard for using me the way you have.'

Stunned that she had unwittingly stumbled on the truth,

but trying to hide this, he stood up at once, his movements jerky. He edged away from the bed. 'I haven't used you,' he protested, his mouth tightening. He glanced at the door.

'I haven't used you,' she mimicked, her tone mocking, hard, her lip curling down with derision. 'Of course you have. *And*, by the way, I think your friend Winston Harte is as big a bastard as you are, for not inviting me to the dinner party tonight.'

'He's not giving it – Allison Ridley is, and she doesn't know you, or know about our relationship. You and I always agreed we would lead our own lives, with our own friends, and not become a special twosome,' he exclaimed, his voice rising. 'There've never been any strings attached to our relationship . . . that's the way *you* wanted it, if I'm not mistaken.'

Shane took a breath, curbed his increasing annoyance. 'Besides, you've never been interested in my chums before today,' he reminded her with a cool indifference now, wishing she would not colour everything with emotion.

'I've changed my mind. Please take me with you, Shane. I want to come. I really do. This *is* your last night. Please, darling,' she begged, offering him a wistfully-sweet smile, but it faltered in the face of his chilly expression, his rigid stance.

'You know that's not possible, not at this late hour. Anyway, it's a seated dinner. Look, don't try to make *me* wear a hair shirt – ' He moved wearily towards the door.

'I know *I'm* not welcome in *your* precious little clique!' she yelled, further losing her control. 'My God, you all make me want to puke! The O'Neills, the Hartes, the Kallinskis . . . what a tight, toffy-nosed group you are. No outsiders permitted to join *your* exclusive club, to become part of *your* charmed circle. No room for us common folk amongst *your* snooty lot. Anybody would think you're royalty the way you all behave, what with your airs and graces and pretensions. And your stinking money,' she scoffed irately, her face ringed with bitterness. 'You're just a bunch of rotten snobs – the lot of you. And bloody incestuous if you ask me, huddling together in the rarefied air of your posh compounds, shutting out the rest of the world. It's sick!'

Flabbergasted at her violence, he looked at her icily and with spiralling disdain. He was appalled at her words, her venom, but immediately held himself in check, deciding not to be provoked into retaliating.

There was an unpleasant silence.

'I've got to go. I'm extremely late.' This was said evenly enough, but Shane was seething inside. He strode across the room, his blood boiling at her insults, threw his tie around his neck, picked up his jacket, slung it over his shoulder.

'I'm sorry we're parting on such a bad note,' he said, giving her a glance of condemnation, 'but there seems to be nothing more to say.' He shrugged. 'I had hoped we could remain friends, at the very least.'

'*Friends!*' she repeated shrilly, her temper blazing. 'You must be crazy. Go on, get out! Go to your lady love. No doubt *she'll* be at your precious dinner!' She laughed hysterically through her blinding tears, then brushed her eyes, made an effort to cling to her last ounce of composure, without success. She swallowed a sob, cried, 'I must admit, I'm curious about one thing! What makes you come crawling back into *my* bed all the time, hot and bothered and raring to go, when someone else has a claim on your heart? Is she a crown princess from one of the clans? A young lady of such refinement – so chaste and virginal – you wouldn't dream of sullying her? What's wrong, Shane, don't you have the guts to sleep with *her* until you're well and truly married and have the blessings of your families? Or could it be that *she's* not interested in *you*? Don't your fatal charms have any effect on *her*? Are you less than irresistible – ' She bit off the end of her sentence when she saw the look of intense pain fly across his face, understanding that somehow she had struck the mark, albeit inadvertently.

'Shane, I'm sorry,' she apologized at once, instantly contrite. She was genuinely concerned, afraid she had gone too far this time.

She leaped out of bed, struggled into her robe. 'Shane, forgive me! I didn't mean it, didn't mean to be cruel, to hurt you. I love you, Shane. I have since the first day we met. Please, please forgive me. And forget what I just said.' She started to weep.

He did not answer. Nor did he look at her again.

He left. The door slammed with finality behind him.

Shane hurried across the hall, let himself out of her flat, and ran down the stairs at breakneck speed. His head was pounding, and his stomach lurched as the nausea rose in him again.

He sprinted across the lawn, wrenched open the door of his car and jumped in with agility. He drove off with a roar, his hands tightly gripping the wheel, his face set in angry lines, a muscle throbbing on his temple.

When he reached the Stray, the stretch of breezy open common ground in the centre of Harrogate, he slowed down and parked.

Shane sat smoking for a few minutes, pulling himself together, calming his frazzled nerves, a remote look in his troubled black eyes. He stubbed out the cigarette impatiently, suddenly hating the taste of the nicotine. His head ached, reverberated with Dorothea Mallet's vituperative words. Her attitude had been extreme, uncalled for under the circumstances, but then that was her usual pattern. She had displayed her jealousy before, and by now he ought to be accustomed to her tantrums, her temperamental outbursts.

Quite unexpectedly it struck him that he had no reason whatsoever to chastise himself about his behaviour towards her. He had always been considerate and kind to Dorothea. He was a decent man, and he had integrity and honour; furthermore, he would never willingly hurt her or any woman.

He considered the lousy things she had said. In particular her comment about another woman in his life had been like a punch in his stomach. But she was obviously stabbing in the dark, conjecturing, since she could not possibly know he loved Paula. No one knew. It was his secret.

Shane's heart tightened as reality hit him in the face with some force. There was no chance that Paula would ever be his. She was most obviously very much in love with Jim Fairley. He had seen it written all over her face earlier in the day. Not only that, she was a mother now . . . *they were a family*. She had been transparently delighted to see him at the christening, yet despite her loving warmth she had been preoccupied with her husband and her babies.

He squeezed his eyes tightly shut, his face twisting in a grimace of mental anguish. His love for her was a hopeless love without a future. It had nowhere to go. He had known this for the longest time, and yet a faint hope that something might happen to change things had lingered in his mind. Of course it would not. He must put Paula Fairley out of his heart, obliterate her from his consciousness, as he had decided on the moors yesterday. It was not going to be easy, he was well aware. On the other hand, it was imperative that he make the effort, draw on his inner reserves for strength. He had to make his sojourn in New York a new beginning . . . it was his chance to make some sort of worthwhile life for himself. His resolve intensified.

At last Shane opened his eyes, swung his head and gazed out of the window, shaking off the memories of Paula . . . his dearest love. And a married woman, a mother, he reminded himself.

Blinking, he became conscious of his surroundings.

He noticed the daffodils blowing in the breeze that had

lately sprung up – rafts of stinging yellow against the verdant green of the grass. I ought to have bought flowers for Allison, he thought absently, remembering the dinner party. He glanced at the clock on the dashboard. It read seven-thirty. The shops were closed . . . and he was going to be late. But if he kept his foot down on the accelerator he would make it in half an hour.

He switched on the radio, twiddled the knob to the BBC's classical station. The strains of the Pachelbel Canon filled the car as he swung it out on to the main road.

Within minutes the Ferrari was hurtling in the direction of the ancient cathedral town of Ripon where Allison Ridley lived. He gunned the engine forward, concentrating on the road ahead.

CHAPTER 14

There was something of the actor in Shane O'Neill.

It was a talent inherited from Blackie, and he was able to fall back on that skill whenever it suited him. It did now.

He pushed open the front door of Holly Tree Cottage, took several deep breaths, donned a mask of geniality, and headed down the stone-flagged passageway.

He paused at the entrance to the living room, drew his inbred self-assurance around him, and stepped over the threshold.

At this instant he became what they expected him to be – a man without the slightest care, and one who held the world in his arms.

Laughter sprang readily to his lips, a sparkle entered his brilliant eyes, and he exuded ebullience and bonhomie, strolling forward at a leisurely pace to join his closest male friends – Winston Harte, Alexander Barkstone, and Michael Kallinski. Allison and her women guests were nowhere in sight, and these three stood huddled in front of the window, next to the refectory table set up as a bar for the evening.

Meandering across the floor, Shane glanced about with interest, struck at once by the beauty of this main room in the cottage, which was really two dwellings knocked into one. He remembered that Allison had recently finished decorating it, and she had done wonders with the place. The low, beamed ceiling and wide stone fireplace – both Tudor – gave the setting its real character, but the colourful cretonnes covering the sofas and chairs, the old pine furniture, and Sally Harte's dreamlike watercolours on the white-washed walls contributed much to its intrinsic charm. It was a rustic country room, free of pretensions and fussiness, yet eminently comfortable and cosy, the kind he liked. He made a mental note to congratulate Allison the minute he saw her.

As soon as Shane drew to a standstill in front of his friends the banter started.

They joshed him unmercifully about being late, and made innumerable innuendos about the real reason behind his tardiness. He took it all with good humour, laughed good-naturedly, and shot back a few missiles of his own. The strain and tension eased out of his aching muscles and he started to relax at last, feeling comfortable and at home with the three men. And within minutes he was responding fully to their warmth, affection and friendship, and to the carefree mood, the jollity that prevailed here this evening.

At one moment he took a cigarette, brought his lighter to its tip, and as he did he thought fleetingly of Dorothea's virulent condemnation of his set, their world. Well, she had been correct in one sense – they were extremely clannish, he had to admit that. If they clung together, it was because they had been brought up with each other, had always been close and intimately involved on every level. Blackie, Emma and David Kallinski, Michael's grandfather, had seen to that. *They* had been through a lot together in the early days at the turn of the century, sharing their terrible struggles and later triumphs, and it was from them that the unbreakable bonds of friendship sprang. That extraordinary trio, founders of three powerful Yorkshire dynasties, had been tight most of their lives, from the day they had met in fact, and devoted thereafter, right up to David's untimely death in the early sixties. Because their children and grandchildren had been thrown together since birth, and in the ensuing years, it was only natural that a large number of them remained staunchly loyal, the dearest of friends and constant companions.

What the hell, Shane thought, filling with a spurt of impatience with himself. Why do I worry about *her* opinions of *us*? This is the way we are, the way we live; and what's more, we genuinely care about each other and deeply so. And we've always been there for each other in times of trouble and grief – just as our grandparents were before we were born.

Winston, misunderstanding Shane's sudden silence, said to the others, 'Okay, chaps, let's give him a breather. What would you like, Shane? A scotch?'

'No, thanks. Just soda water, please.'

'What's the matter with you tonight?' Winston asked, as he filled the glass. 'It's not like an Irishman to be imbibing this innocuous stuff.'

Shane grinned as he took the drink. 'Too much champagne earlier. But I must say, none of you seem the worse for wear and you were *all* knocking it back like sailors on shore leave.' Looking at Michael, he went on, 'I assume your parents are still in Hong Kong, since they weren't with you at the christening.'

'Yes. They get back in two weeks, and then I leave for New York. I hope we can get together, Shane. Where will you be staying?'

'At Aunt Emma's Fifth Avenue flat, until I find a place

of my own. And I'll be bloody furious if you don't phone me.' Shane now glanced past Winston. Valentine Stone, Michael's girlfriend, was coming back into the room from the garden, followed by Marguerite Reynolds and a blonde girl. He guessed she was Allison's American friend and the reason for the dinner party. He waved to them, then took Michael's arm. 'Do I notice a ring on Valentine's finger?'

'Yes, but it's on her right hand, not her left, you idiot!' Michael Kallinski made a face, chuckled. 'You'll be the first to know when I decide to take that ghastly step, Shane.'

Alexander cut in, 'Just listen to the man . . . we all know she's got you where she wants you, Mike.'

'You've got room to talk,' Michael shot back. 'Marguerite has you pinioned down in the same position, flat on your back in a stranglehold, gasping for air.'

They all laughed.

Alexander flushed, retorted, 'Don't be too sure.' He hesitated, then volunteered, 'One thing is certain though, Grandmother likes Maggie, approves of her. *She* thinks I should pop the question now, before some other fellow steals her away from under my nose. Some confidence Emma Harte has in her grandson, I must say.' Alexander shook his head, took refuge in his usual reserved shell, observing Maggie out of the corner of his eye. She looked stunning tonight in a scarlet pants suit, her light brown hair swept up in an old-fashioned pompadour. Perhaps he *should* take his grandmother's advice.

Shane, who had flinched inside at Alexander's words, said in a low voice, 'Don't let her escape. Aunt Emma's right, she's quite a catch, Sandy, and such a nice girl.'

Michael added, 'And the world *is* full of predatory males, as we all know, Alexander. You'd better do what E.H. says before it's too late.'

Shane swung to Winston. 'And where's *your* lady love hiding herself?'

224

'What?' Winston asked, pulling himself away from thoughts of Emily. He frowned. 'What are you talking about?'

'*Allison*. Where is she?' Shane stared at him, and went on, 'I haven't said hello to my hostess yet.'

'Oh! Yes, Allison. She dashed off to the kitchen just before you arrived,' Winston said quickly, trying to cover his lapse. 'She'll be back in a second. She went to see if the two local girls she hired for the evening are coping. In the meantime, I'd better take you over to the guest of honour, and introduce you, otherwise Allison'll have my guts for garters.' Winston gave Shane a knowing wink. 'Allison's friend lives in New York. If you behave yourself tonight she might even agree to go out with you.'

'I won't have time for women. I'll be far too busy with the hotel. Stop trying to fix me up, Winston,' Shane remonstrated, then thought to ask, 'Anyway, what makes you think I'd be interested?'

'Because she's rather nice,' Winston replied.

Shane made no comment, followed his friend down the long room to the fireplace where the three women stood chatting.

The tall, slender blonde watched them approaching, trying not to give the appearance of doing so, instantly struck by Shane O'Neill's undeniable presence even from this distance. In fact she had been aware of him the minute she had returned to the living room. Allison had told her who and what he was . . . the young scion of a famous Yorkshire family, the most eligible of bachelors, and one who had been born with a golden spoon in his mouth, the money to buy himself the world if he wanted. He also had the looks to take him wherever he wanted. And right into *any* woman's bed, if he so wished, she decided. Allison had not exaggerated.

Shane kissed Valentine and Marguerite, and Winston

said, 'Skye, I'd like you to meet Shane O'Neill. Shane, this is Skye Smith from New York.'

They shook hands, exchanged greetings.

Shane said pleasantly, with a friendly smile, 'I hear this is your first trip to Yorkshire. Are you enjoying it?'

'I'm loving every minute. It's so beautiful . . . the Dales are breathtaking. Allison's whizzed me all over this past week, buying antiques, so I've seen a lot of your glorious countryside.'

'Allison's the expert, so I'm sure she helped you find some really interesting things. You're in the same business, Winston tells me,' Shane remarked.

'Yes, I have a small antique shop on Lexington Avenue, in the Sixties. And fortunately a lot of good customers who are hungry for English antiques and silver.' She laughed lightly. 'I've bought up half of Yorkshire, and now I'm worrying about storing everything I'm having shipped home next week. My shop's going to be bursting at the seams.'

Valentine said, 'Allison told me you came across some beautiful old Victorian silver in Richmond. Surely you won't have a problem selling those pieces. And immediately.'

'No, I won't,' Skye said, and gave them a detailed description of every item of silver now in her possession. Winston excused himself, and ambled off. Shane lolled against the fireplace, bored with the subject of antiques and only vaguely listening to the women's chatter. He studied the American girl. She was charming; certainly she was good looking, personable, and obviously very bright. Still, he had known at once that she was not his type. Cool, pristine blondes who looked like Scandinavian ice maidens had never appealed to him much. He preferred dark exotic women. Like Paula. He crushed the thought of her.

After a polite interval had elapsed, he said, 'I really ought to go and find Allison. Please excuse me.' With a

226

brief nod he disappeared, went down the narrow hall, making for the kitchen. But as he passed the small intimate dining room he spotted Allison through the open door. She was surveying the table intently.

'There you are, Miss Ridley!' he exclaimed, striding inside, pulling her to him, enveloping her in a bear hug. 'Congratulations! The cottage looks lovely. Now, why are you hiding from me? I've begun to think you're punishing me for being so late.'

'Not you, Shane darling. You can do anything – I'd never be angry with you.'

'You'd better not let Winston hear you say things like that. You'll make him jealous.'

The merriment left Allison's face, and she said in a tight voice, 'I'm not so sure . . .'

Shane threw her a questioning look. 'What's that supposed to mean?'

Allison shrugged, bent over the table, and moved a small silver bird closer to its companion, averting her head.

Shane's face was a study in perplexity as he waited for her to finish fiddling with the table decorations, to respond to his question. When she did not, he took her arm gently, turned her to him. He immediately perceived she was upset.

'Hey, what's wrong?' he murmured softly, staring down into her bleak face.

'Nothing. Really and truly . . .' she began and broke off, wavering. Finally, she said in a great rush of words, 'Oh I'm not going to lie to *you*, Shane. Winston's been funny with me since he arrived tonight. Not himself. Distracted.' Her light grey eyes searched his face. 'Did something happen this afternoon . . . something that might have upset him?'

Shane shook his head. 'Not that I know of, Allison.'

'I think it must have. If it didn't, then his odd behaviour

must have something to do with me, with us. Perhaps he's lost interest in me.'

'I'm sure you're wrong.'

'I'm *not*, Shane. I know Winston almost as well as you do. Generally he is sunny tempered, and he's warm and affectionate. We've been getting on wonderfully these last few months. So much so, I had the feeling he might propose soon. He's been sending out signals . . . he told me how much his father liked me, and, perhaps more importantly, Emma Harte. When he arrived earlier I noticed a change in him . . . he was different, preoccupied. He got here late, when he'd promised to come before the other guests to help me move the refectory table and do a few other things – and you know he's never late. That didn't matter, of course. But he was cool, even a bit brusque, and naturally I was taken aback. He did soften during drinks, after Alexander and Maggie had arrived, but frankly he *is* distant. It's not like him in the least – being so moody, I mean.'

Shane was more baffled than ever. He ran the events of the afternoon through his head, wondering if something had occurred which had disturbed Winston. But nothing untoward had happened to his knowledge, and Winston had seemed untroubled to him.

He said, 'Listen, maybe it *is* something to do with business. That seems to be the most plausible explanation to me. Yes, it must be a business worry.' He offered her a reassuring smile. 'I'm convinced his attitude has nothing to do with your relationship. And he's certainly not lost interest in *you*. How could you think that?'

She looked at him for the longest moment, and smiled regretfully. 'A woman senses these things.'

Shane exclaimed, 'You're reading this the wrong way, imagining the worst.' He took her hand, tucked it through his arm and walked her to the door. 'Come on, let's go back to the sitting room and I'll buy you a good stiff drink.

I could use one myself.' His eyes were warm with affection. 'You'll see, Winston will be his old self with you.'

'You sound more certain of that than I feel,' she replied softly. But she brought a carefree expression to her face as she returned to her guests, clinging to Shane's arm, thankful to have his support.

Later in the evening, when they were at dinner, Shane decided that Allison had been right in one respect: Winston was not entirely himself.

He sat at the head of the table, and although he was pleasant and charming, played the good host to the hilt, Shane detected an abstracted look flickering behind his eyes, recognized the forced note in his laughter, the falseness behind his joviality.

To distract everyone's attention, and wanting to give Winston breathing space, Shane became the life and soul of the dinner party. He was gregarious, outgoing, witty and amusing. He was particularly attentive to Allison, on whose right he sat, was pleased that she responded in a positive way, and appeared to be more relaxed and at ease as the evening progressed.

But it was she who brought the meal finally to an end when, after dessert, she said, 'Let's have coffee and liqueurs in the sitting room, shall we?'

'That's a splendid idea,' Winston exclaimed, smiling at her more warmly than he had since his arrival. He was the first to rise, and ushered Allison and the other women out of the dining room. Shane followed with Michael and Alexander at his heels.

Winston went immediately to the refectory table, where he began to pour different liqueurs for the women guests. Shane strolled over to him, and striving to be casual, said, 'Make mine a Bonnie Prince Charlie, please.'

'Since when have you been drinking that awful stuff?' Winston asked, looking up. He grinned, turned back to his task of pouring white *crème de menthe* over the crushed ice he had spooned into a goblet.

'Don't sound so disapproving. You used to like it as much as I did when we were kids, gulping it down wholesale when Aunt Emma wasn't looking.'

'Yes, and if I remember correctly, we both used to get bloody sick on it. But okay, if that's what you want.' Winston filled a glass with the liqueur, handed it to Shane with another grin, finished pouring cognacs for Michael, Alexander, and himself.

Shane stood watching him. At last he asked in a low voice, 'Are you okay?'

Winston lifted his head sharply. 'Of course I am. Why do you ask?'

'You've seemed a bit out of it tonight.'

'It's been a long day, hectic. I am a bit weary, I'm afraid. Do me a favour, toddle over to Skye and ask her if she's changed her mind about an after-dinner drink, whilst I dutifully dispense these to the others. Allison will be back in a minute with the coffee.' Winston picked up the tray and walked across the room, whistling under his breath.

Shane's eyes followed him, narrowing thoughtfully. Winston seemed normal enough now, and perhaps he had spoken the truth when he had claimed fatigue. Shane sauntered over to Skye Smith who sat on the wide stone hearth by herself. 'You're not drinking. Try this,' he said in a commanding tone, handing her the glass.

She took it, sniffed it delicately, looked up at him questioningly.

'It's a Bonnie Prince Charlie,' Shane explained.

'What's that?'

He laughed. 'Drambuie. Go on, take a sip, it won't poison you.'

She did as he said, and nodded her approval. 'It has an unusual taste. I like it. Thank you, Shane.'

'Don't move. I'll be right back.' He returned a moment later with a Drambuie for himself, sat down next to her, and clinked her glass with his. 'Cheers.'

'Cheers.' Skye glanced at him out of the corner of her eye. He *was* handsome. Perhaps too handsome. Men who looked like Shane O'Neill terrified her. They were usually untrustworthy . . . too much temptation fell into their paths.

Shane savoured his drink for a minute, then put his glass on the hearth, asked: 'Do you mind if I smoke a cigar?'

'No, not at all. And tell me something – why is Drambuie called Bonnie Prince Charlie?'

'Because when Bonnie Prince Charlie went to Scotland, in 1745, trying to regain the throne of his ancestors, he was aided by a Mackinnon of Skye. In gratitude, Prince Charlie gave the man his own recipe for his personal liqueur. Ever since then the secret for its preparation has remained with the Mackinnons, and Drambuie gets its nickname from the legend. And speaking of the Isle of Skye, is that how you spell your name . . . sky with an *e* at the end?'

'Yes, but my name is really Schuyler. It's Dutch. A family name. I have a feeling my Mom thought plain old Smith needed jazzing up a bit.' She smiled at him slowly.

'It's a very pretty name. It suits you,' he said with a show of gallantry.

'Why, thank you kindly, sir.'

They fell silent.

Skye Smith was trying to decide whether she could suggest he call her in New York without appearing forward. She was not interested in him as a lover, on the other hand she had found herself drawn to him during dinner, almost against her will. He was entertaining, good company, and a delightful man, if a little vain and too sure of himself. But perhaps they could be friends.

Shane was still dwelling on Winston, discreetly observing him. He lounged on a sofa at the other side of the room, nursing his brandy, looking relaxed. Whatever problem had been bothering him earlier had apparently been resolved, or dismissed as unimportant. He was laughing suddenly and in a natural manner, and teasing Allison. Shane noticed that her face was radiant. So much for all that, he thought, it was a storm about nothing. He filled with relief. He was going away tomorrow and he did not like to think he was leaving when his dearest friend had troubles.

Skye finally spoke, interrupting Shane's contemplations. She said, 'I hope this doesn't sound pushy or anything like that, but if I can be of help in New York, do feel free to call me.' She added quickly, wanting to sound more businesslike, 'The shop is listed under Brandt-Smith Antiques.'

'That's very kind of you. I will,' Shane said, and startled himself with his ready acquiescence to her suggestion. He puffed on his cigar for a second, then feeling the need to explain, he went on, 'I don't know many people in New York. Just a couple of lawyers who work for our company. Oh, and I have an introduction to a man called Ross Nelson. A banker.'

'Oh,' she exclaimed.

Shane glanced at her, saw the surprise in her eyes. Or was it shock that had registered? 'So you know Ross,' he said, his curiosity flaring.

'No. No, I don't,' she replied too swiftly. 'I've heard of him, read about him in the newspapers, but that's all.'

Shane nodded, and for a reason he could not fathom, he immediately changed the subject. But as they talked about other things he could not help thinking that Skye Smith was much better acquainted with the notorious Mr Nelson than she wanted him to believe. And he asked himself why she had felt the need to lie about this.

Shane O'Neill left Yorkshire the following morning.

It was dawn. The mist had rolled down from the moors

and the higher fells to spread across the meadows like a mantle of grey lace, partially obscuring the trees and the drystone walls and the cottages nestling in the folds of the fields. And all were inchoate images, spectral and illusory under the remote and bitter sky. Dew dripped from the overhanging branches, glistened on the white wildflowers gleaming in the hedgerows, ran in little rivulets down the grassy banks at the sides of the lane. Nothing stirred in the drifting vaporous mists and there was an unearthly quiescence, an unmoving stillness lying over the whole of the countryside and it was a dreamlike landscape . . . the landscape of his childhood dreams.

Gradually, from behind the rim of the dim horizon, the early sun began to rise, its streaming corridors of slanting light piercing outward to illuminate the bowl of that cold and fading sky with a sudden breathtaking radiance. And through the tops of the leafy domes of trees, caught in the distant shimmer of sunlight like a mirage, glittered the chimneys of Pennistone Royal. House of his childhood dreams . . . but there was another house in his childhood dreams . . . a villa by the sea where they had laughed and played and dreamed away the careless carefree days of their childhood summers . . . where nothing had ever changed . . . and time had been an eternity.

And she was always there . . . with him . . . at that villa high on the cliffs above the sunlit sea . . . laughter in her eyes the colour of the summer sky and gentleness in her smile that had truly been only for him . . . dreamlike landscapes . . . dreamlike houses . . . dreamlike child of his childhood dreams . . . locked in his heart and mind for all of time . . . haunting him always . . . dim shadows on his Celtic soul.

He was going away now . . . so far away . . . leaving them behind . . . but he never left them behind . . . he carried them with him wherever he went . . . and they would never change . . . they were his childhood dreams

. . . Paula and Pennistone Royal and the villa by the sunlit sea . . .

The car sped on, down the narrow winding country lanes, past the great iron gates of Pennistone Royal, on through the village of the same name, out now on to the main road. Shane glimpsed the familiar signs flying by . . . South Stainley, Ripley, Harrogate, Alwoodley.

He slowed down as he roared into Leeds, although there was no traffic, no one abroad, deserted as it was at this hour and without a sign of life. Grey, grimy, vital Leeds, great industrial city of the North, the seat of Emma's power and his grandfather's and David Kallinski's family.

Circling City Square, where the statue of the Black Prince dominated, he drove on, down the short hill near City Station, heading towards the M1, the road leading south to London. Shane picked up speed the moment he rolled on to the motorway, and he did not reduce it until he was nosing the car over the county boundary . . . leaving Yorkshire behind.

CHAPTER 15

The garden was her magical place.

It never failed to give Paula a sense of accomplishment and satisfaction and it was therapeutic when she was frustrated or needed a release from the stresses and tensions of business.

When she began to plan a garden, whether large or small, she gave free rein to her imagination, and every plot of ground that fell into her sure and talented hands was miraculously transformed, became a breathtaking testament to her instinctive understanding of nature.

In fact, she was an inspired gardener. Flowers, plants,

trees and shrubs were woven into a tapestry of living colour and design by her, one that stunned the eye with its compelling beauty. Yet despite her careful planning, none of her gardens ever looked in the least contrived.

Indeed there was a genuine old-world air about them, for she planted them with an abundance of old-fashioned flowers and shrubs, that were typically English in character. The garden she now called her own, and which she had been working on for almost a year, was beginning to take on this particular look.

But for once she was hardly aware of the garden.

She stood poised at the edge of the terrace, gazing down the long green stretch of lawn, yet not really seeing it, an abstracted expression on her face. She was thinking of Jim. Their quarrel of last night had been dreadful, and although they had eventually made up – in bed where they usually managed to put aside their mutual anger – she was still shaken. They had quarrelled about Edwina. Again. And in the end he had won, since she was hopelessly weak where he was concerned, loving him the way she did. And so she had finally agreed to entertain Edwina tonight, to show her the house and the grounds, offer her cocktails before they went out to dinner. But Paula wished now that she had been more resolute with him. In the early hours of the morning, after he had made love to her, he had cajoled, teased and laughed her into agreeing to do as he wished. He had cleverly twisted her around his little finger, and she resented it suddenly.

Sighing, she walked purposefully over to the rockery she was creating, trying to shake off the remnants of the violent quarrel. I refuse to harbour a grudge, she told herself firmly. I've got to let go of my anger before he comes home tonight. She knelt down, continuing the work that she had started earlier that day, hell bent on bringing order to that intractable pile of stone, filled with the intense desire to make this rockery as beautiful as the one at Grandy's seaside house.

As usually happened, Paula soon lost herself entirely in gardening, concentrating totally on the work, allowing the tranquillity of nature to lap over her until she was enfolded by its soothing gentleness, at peace within herself.

It was as a child that Paula had discovered her love of the earth and all growing things. She had been eight years old.

The same year Emma had bought a house to use during her grandchildren's spring and summer holidays from school. It was called Heron's Nest and it stood on the high cliffs at Scarborough, overlooking the pale sands and the lead-coloured bay beyond, a piece of Victorian gingerbread with its intricately-wrought wood portico, wide porch, large sunny rooms, and sprawling garden that was a veritable wilderness when Emma had first taken title to the property.

Aside from wanting a place where she could spend the holidays with her young brood and enjoy their company, Emma had had another valid reason for purchasing Heron's Nest. She had long felt the urgent need to have her grandchildren under her complete control and influence for uninterrupted periods. Her objective was simple. She wanted to teach them a few of the essentials of life, the practicalities of everyday living, and to make sure that they understood the true value of money. Emma had for years found it intolerable that most of her children had grown accustomed to living in luxury without giving one thought to the cost of their pampered existences, and that they were overly dependent on armies of servants to take care of even their simplest needs.

And so, in her inimitable way, she had devised a scheme when she had decided that her grandchildren must be brought up to be less spoiled, more self-reliant, and certainly down-to-earth where matters of money were concerned. 'There's an old Yorkshire saying and it goes like

236

this – ' she had remarked to her investment banker, Henry Rossiter, one day, ' – from clogs to clogs in three generations. Well, you can be damned sure that that's not going to hold true for my lot!' Immediately afterwards she had signed the cheque for the house.

Heron's Nest was the answer to many things, in her mind. And it would become her school. To this end, Emma had seen fit to engage only one maid, a local woman from the town who would come every day. And she had told the rather jolly, plump Mrs Bonnyface that her main task would be to take care of the seaside villa when the family were not in residence. Emma had gone on to outline her rather unorthodox plans, had explained how she fully intended to run the house herself – with the help of her numerous grandchildren. Whatever Mrs Bonnyface had thought of this unusual state of affairs, she had never said. She had accepted Emma's scheme and with enthusiasm, and had obviously felt privileged to work for the famous Mrs Harte, if her general demeanour was anything to judge by.

Being clever and a dissembler of the highest order, Emma had not confided her intentions or motives in anyone else, least of all her grandchildren. Only after she had made the acquisition and hired Mrs Bonnyface, had she told them about Heron's Nest, but she had given glowing details, cloaked it with such an aura of glamour they had been agog with excitement. They regarded the whole idea of a house by the sea as a great adventure, since they would be alone with Emma and far away from their parents.

Emma had realized almost immediately that the regime she had instituted had come as something of a shock, and she had smiled inwardly as she had watched them floundering around with mops and buckets, carpet sweepers and brooms, furniture polish and dusters, and unmanageable ironing boards. There had been huge disasters in the kitchen . . . demolished frying pans, pots charred to cinders, and vile, unpalatable meals. They had grumbled about burnt fingers, blisters, headaches, housemaid's knee, and other minor ailments, real and imaginary, some of which had sounded extremely farfetched to Emma.

But it was Jonathan who had come up with the most inventive and imaginative excuse for wriggling out of his allocated chores, on the day he had told her that he had strained his Achilles tendons mowing the lawn, and was far too crippled to do any more work for days. Emma had been both startled and impressed by his cleverness. She had nodded most sympathetically. And to prove to this canny little boy that she was so much smarter than he believed she was, she had explained to him, and in diabolically graphic terms, exactly how strained Achilles tendons were treated. 'And so, since you're in such dreadful agony, I'd better drive you down to the doctor's surgery so that he can get to work on you immediately,' she had said, reaching for her handbag and the car keys. Jonathan had swiftly suggested they wait for a few hours, just in case the pain went away. Seemingly it did. He had made a stunningly rapid recovery, apparently not relishing the prospect of spending the remainder of the spring uncomfortably encased in a plaster of Paris cast reaching from the tips of his toes to his waist. Or of being left behind with Mrs Bonnyface when his cousins returned to their respective schools and his grandmother to Pennistone Royal.

During those first few weeks at the holiday house in Scarborough they soon settled down to a steady routine. The girls quickly began to show a certain proficiency in their housework and cooking, and the boys readily learned to cope with the heavier household work, weeding the garden and mowing the lawns. Not one of them was ever permitted to shirk his or her duties. Emma was not the type to stand any nonsense for long, and she was relatively strict, showed no favouritism whatsoever.

'I've never heard of anyone dying from scrubbing a floor or polishing the silver,' she was fond of saying if one of them dared to complain or invent an imaginary illness as Jonathan had done. The recalcitrant child who had screwed up enough nerve to protest or fib would instantly blanch under her steely green gaze, remembering Jonathan's narrow escape.

And when the time came for them all to pack up and leave the seaside house Emma had congratulated herself, had admitted that they had been real troopers indeed. They had put on good faces and had truly pulled together to please her. As far as she was concerned, the experiment had proved to be an unconditional success. Every year thereafter, when the harsh Yorkshire winters gave way to the warmer weather, she had gathered them up and carted them off to Scarborough.

Eventually the Harte cousins and the O'Neill and Kallinski grandchildren became regular visitors. Even they were given their fair share of chores, and they had had no choice but to pitch in cheerfully when they arrived to spend July and August by the sea. They quickly came to understand that they would not be invited back if they did not comply with Emma's wishes and pull their weight.

The children had called Emma 'The General' behind her back, and indeed they had often felt as though they were living in an army camp because of her stringent rules and regulations. On the other hand, they had truly enjoyed themselves during those happy, carefree years, and they had ended up having such enormous fun together that even the chores were regarded as games. Much to their parents' astonishment, and Emma's immense satisfaction, each one had come to so look forward to those sojourns in the little seaside town they vociferously declined any other holiday invitations. They had insisted on returning to Heron's Nest the minute Emma opened up the house.

Despite her own terrible addiction to work and little

else, Emma had been shrewd enough to recognize that her 'small band of brigands', as she called them, needed plenty of opportunities to let off steam and lots of pleasurable pursuits to fill the long summer days. 'All work and no play makes Jack a dull boy, you know,' she would constantly repeat to Mrs Bonnyface, and then proceed to invent exciting projects in which she and the children could participate together.

She took them on interesting expeditions up and down the coast, to Whitby, Robin Hood's Bay and Flamborough Head, and gave them numerous other rewards for their strenuous endeavours. There were visits to the local picture house and the town's little theatre; they went for leisurely picnics on the cliffs; sailed in the bay and had swimming parties on the beach. Frequently they went fishing with the local fishermen and were thrilled when they were allowed to keep some of the catch. On those propitious days they would return in triumph to Heron's Nest, where they would cook their small and meagre fish for Emma's supper, and she had eaten them as if they had been prepared by the French chef at the Ritz. When the weather was overcast and the seas rough, Emma had organized egg-and-spoon races and treasure hunts in the garden, and, since she truly understood the acquisitive nature of children, she made certain that the treasure was extra special and worth finding. And she had always provided more than enough items for each child, had usually dropped blatant clues to those who were coming up empty-handed and wearing tearful or disappointed expressions. On rainy days when they had to stay indoors they had played charades or put on their own plays.

One year the boys formed their own band. They called themselves The Herons, and Shane and Winston were the chief instigators and organizers. Shane appointed himself the band leader. He was also the piano player and the vocalist. Alexander sat at the drums and cymbals, Philip blew the flute, Jonathan scraped the violin and Michael Kallinski warbled the harmonica. But it was Winston who thought he was the most important and talented member of the ensemble. He adopted the trumpet as his own and fervently insisted he was the new Bix Beiderbecke, inspired no doubt by a film Emma had taken them to see called *Young Man With A Horn.* Sarah wondered out loud where he had learned to play and Emma smiled thinly and said that he hadn't, and that was the trouble. And at times she thought her eardrums would burst when the cacophony of sound filled the house during practice times, which seemed eternal and never ending to her.

Eventually, when they believed themselves to be polished enough to perform before a live audience, The Herons invited Emma and the girls to a concert in the garden. Emma watched them in amazement, secretly amused by their elaborate and endless preparations. They put out deck chairs, set up a small stage made of planks balanced on bricks, and rolled out the piano to stand next to it. And they took great pains dressing themselves in what they called their 'rig-outs' – their new white cricket flannels worn with brilliant scarlet satin shirts, made, no doubt, at one of the Kallinski factories, Emma decided. Purple satin kerchiefs were tied around their necks and debonair straw boaters were rakishly angled on top of their heads.

Having caught a glimpse of them assembling on the stage, from her bedroom window, Emma immediately changed into a silk afternoon dress and hurried down the corridor to the girls' rooms. She insisted they wear their best cotton frocks in honour of the auspicious occasion, and they had all trooped out just after four o'clock dressed in their finery, curiosity and expectancy written on their pretty young faces.

As Emma listened to The Herons give their renditions of current popular songs and a couple of old ballads, she found herself enjoying the concert, and was rather surprised to discover that they really weren't such bad musicians after all. At the end of their recital she praised the boys, laughing with merriment as she showed her delight in them. The boys laughed too, and taking her lavish accolades to heart they had gone on playing relentlessly all that summer, much to the horror of the girls. Whenever they heard them rehearsing they made snide remarks, sniggered loudly and declared that The Herons stank to high heaven.

Shane, like Winston, was exceptionally vain about his musical accomplishments, and most especially his voice. He soon made certain that the critical young females were suitably intimidated. One night all of them found a foul-smelling object in their beds, ranging from frogs and dead fish with glassy eyes, to raw onions and bags of sulphur. Shane's retaliatory measure worked. After that dreadful night of changing sheets, opening the windows wide and shaking Emma's good perfumes all over their rooms, none of the girls dared to use the word stinking for the rest of the holidays. At least certainly not in reference to The Herons.

And slowly but very deliberately over these years, Emma had strived to instil in every child the importance of the team spirit, playing the game, being a good sport and abiding by the rules. Duty and responsibility were words forever on her lips, for she was resolute in her determination to arm each and every one of them with sound principles, and the proper precepts for the future when they became adults. She taught them the meaning of honour, integrity, honesty and truthfulness, amongst so many other things. But her frequently strong and tough pronouncements were always spoken with an underlying kindness, and she gave them a great deal of love and understanding, not to mention genuine friendship. And it was a friendship most of them were never to forget for the rest of their lives. Deep in her heart, Emma regretted that she had neglected her own children at certain times in her life, when they were in their formative years and growing up. She wanted her grandchildren to benefit from the mistakes she had made in the past, and if some of this washed off on her great-nephews and nieces, and the grandchildren of her closest friends, then so much the better.

But of all the years they had spent in the tall old villa on the cliffs, that very first spring of 1952 had been the most special and memorable to Paula, and it would live in her heart and her mind always. That particular year she became aware of her affinity with nature and her overwhelming desire – the need in her really – to make things grow.

One blustery Saturday in April she wandered out into the garden with little Emily whom Emma had put in her charge that day. Paula glanced around, her eager young eyes keenly observing, newly perceptive. The undergrowth had been cut away, the hedges neatly trimmed, and the lawns mowed to such perfection by the boys they resembled bolts of smooth emerald velvet rolled out to touch the perimeters of the high stone walls. The piece of land behind the house was now uncommonly immaculate – and totally lacking in character.

She was amazed at herself when she unexpectedly realized how the garden *could* look if it was correctly planted. The eight-year-old girl had a vision, saw reflected in her child's imagination an array of textures and shapes and great bursts of colour . . . luscious pinks and mauves, blazing reds and blues, brilliant yellows, warm ambers, oranges and golds, and cool clear whites. She instantly envisioned dazzling mixtures of flowers and shrubs . . . plump bushes of rhododendrons with their delicately-formed petals and dark polished leaves . . . pale peonies, wax-like in their perfection . . . splayed branches of azaleas laden down with heavy bright blossoms . . . masses of stately foxgloves brushing up against merry tulips and daffodils . . . and hugging cosily to the ground, dainty

243

beds of pansies, primroses and violets, and the icy little snowdrop scattered randomly under the trees.

And as she saw all this in her mind's eye, she knew what she must do. She must create the most beautiful garden – a garden for her Grandy. And it would be filled with every flower imaginable, except roses, of course. For some unknown reason her grandmother hated roses, detested the smell of them, said they made her feel nauseous, and she could not stand to have them in her houses or her gardens. She rushed into the house, bursting with excitement, her young face flushed, her eyes sparkling.

Paula raided her money box, hurriedly breaking it open with her embroidery scissors.

As the pennies and threepenny bits and half crowns and shillings came tumbling out, Emily cried fretfully, 'You'll get into trouble when Grandma finds out you've smashed your new money box and stolen the money.'

Paula shook her head. 'No I won't. And I'm not stealing it. All this is mine. I saved it from my weekly pocket money.' Armed with her precious hoard, and with Emily trotting faithfully after her, she walked purposefully into the town.

As it turned out, Emily became something of a nuisance in Scarborough and Paula soon began to regret bringing her along. Emily wanted to stop for mussels and winkles at the shellfish stand, then for lemonade at a nearby café, claiming she was hungry and thirsty, and in a burst of wilfulness she stamped her foot.

Paula gave her a stern look. 'How can you be hungry? We've just had lunch. And you ate more than anybody. You're growing more like a fat little porky pig every day.' She hurried on, leaving Emily trailing behind, pouting.

'You're mean!' Emily yelled and she increased her pace, endeavouring to keep up with her cousin's longer strides.

Paula glanced back over her shoulder, and said, 'I think you must have a tape worm.'

This was announced so suddenly and so fiercely Emily stopped dead in her tracks. After a moment's shocked silence, she began to run after Paula as fast as her little legs would carry her. 'What a horrid thing to say!' Emily shouted at the top of her lungs. She was terrified by Paula's words, and the mere thought of some huge worm growing inside her propelled her forward, and with urgency. 'I don't have a worm! I don't!' She caught her breath, and gasped, '*Do* I, Paula? Oh please, please tell me I don't. Can Grandma fish It out of me?'

'Oh don't be so silly!' Paula snapped with growing irritation, intent on her purpose, anxious to find a flower shop selling bulbs and plants.

'I don't feel well, Paula. I'm going to be sick!'

'It's all that bread-and-butter pudding.'

'No, it isn't,' Emily wailed. 'It's thinking about my worm. I feel awful. I'm going to throw up,' the child threatened. Emily turned ashen, and her huge eyes swam with tears.

Paula was instantly filled with chagrin. She did love little Emily and she was rarely unkind to her. She put her arm around the five-year-old's heaving shoulders and stroked her soft blonde hair. 'There, there, don't cry, Emily. I'm sure you don't have a tape worm, really I am. Cross my heart and hope to die.'

Eventually Emily stopped crying and searched the pocket of her cardigan for a handkerchief. She blew her nose loudly, then put her hand trustingly in Paula's and trotted along next to her quietly, tamed and subdued as they walked along the sea front past the many quaint old shops. At last she plucked up her courage and ventured timidly, in a whisper, 'But just suppose I do have It? What will I do about my – '

'I forbid you to discuss your nasty worm, you horrid little girl!' Paula exclaimed, her impatience returning. 'You know what, Emily Barkstone, you're a pest. A *terrible* pest. I may send you to Coventry, if you don't shut up.'

Emily was crushed. 'But you always say I'm your *favourite*. Do you mean I'm your favourite pest?' Emily asked, hurrying to stay in step, gazing longingly at her older cousin, whom she worshipped.

Paula started to laugh. She pulled Emily into her arms and hugged the small round child. 'Yes, you're my favourite pest, Apple Dumpling. And because I know you're going to be a good girl and stop behaving like a spoiled baby, I'm going to tell you a very, very special secret.'

Emily was so flattered her tears ceased, and her green eyes widened. 'What kind of secret?'

'I'm going to make a garden for Grandy, a most beautiful garden. That's why we came to Scarborough, to buy the seeds and the things I need. But you mustn't say anything to her. It's a big, big secret.'

'I promise, I promise!' Emily was excited.

For the next half-hour, as the two little girls roamed from florist to florist, Paula kept Emily completely enthralled. She was articulate as she spoke about the wonderful things she was going to plant in her garden. She described the colours and the petals and the leaves and the scents of the flowers in detail, and Emily was so utterly enchanted and delighted to be part of such a grown-up enterprise she soon forgot about the tape worm. Slowly, and with painstaking care, Paula finally settled on her grandmother's favourite flowers and made her purchases. They left the last flower shop with a bag brimming with bulbs and packets of seeds and gardening catalogues.

When they reached the top of the street, Emily looked up at Paula and smiled with great sweetness, her round little face dimpling. 'Can we go to the winkle stand now then?'

'Emily! You're being a pest again! You'd better behave yourself.'

Emily paid no attention to this remonstration. 'I've got a better idea. Let's go to the Grand for tea. I'd like that. We can have cream puffs and cucumber sandwiches and scones with strawberry jam and clotted cream and – '

'I don't have any money left,' Paula announced with firmness, hoping to demolish this idea immediately.

'Scribble on the bill like Grandma does,' Emily suggested.

'We're not going to the Grand, and that's final. So shut up. And look, Emily, stop dawdling . . . it's getting late. We'd better hurry now.'

By the time the two little girls arrived at Heron's Nest they had become firm friends again. Emily immediately volunteered to help, wishing to ingratiate herself with her cousin, as always seeking Paula's approbation and her love. She crouched on the ground, offering unsolicited advice in her piping child's voice. After watching Paula for a while, Emily said, 'I bet you've got green fingers, if anybody does, Paula.'

'It's a green thumb,' Paula corrected, without looking up, intent on her work. And she continued digging into the rich soil, planting her first flowers with supreme self-confidence, never doubting for a moment that they would flourish and grow. She was gathering up the garden tools when Emily startled her as she leaped up and let out a wild scream of terror.

'Oh! Oh!' Emily screeched, jumping up and down and brushing her skirt in a frantic fashion. 'Oh! Oh!'

'What's wrong with you, you silly thing? You'll have Grandy out here in a minute and then the garden won't be a surprise.'

'It was a worm! Look, there near your foot! It was crawling on my skirt. Ugh! All slimy and wriggly.' Emily had gone as white as chalk and she was trembling.

Paula was struck by her second inspired idea that day, and she cleverly seized the opportunity. She grabbed the trowel and jabbed at the worm, cutting it in half. She piled soil over it and gave Emily a cheerful and triumphant grin. 'It must have been your tape worm. I expect It left you of its own accord. And I've killed It, so now everything's all right.'

Paula picked up the small box of tools and beckoning Emily to follow, she hurried up the garden path to the potting shed. She stopped suddenly, and after a minute's rapid thought, she said, 'But you'd better not mention anything about It to Grandy, or she might make you take some medicine just to be sure you don't get another.'

Emily shuddered at the very idea.

Later that same summer, when Paula and Emily came back to the villa by the sea, they could hardly contain themselves when they saw the garden in full bloom. A profusion of flowers had sprouted up during their absence, and the many different species Paula had selected splashed the dark earth with their brilliant paintbox hues.

Emma was touched when, on their first day at Heron's Nest, the two girls led her through the garden, showing her everything that Paula had planted, looking up at her expectantly, watching her face for her reactions. Emily told her all about their trip into Scarborough although she was careful to omit any mention of worms. Emma had been aware of the little expedition on that Saturday in the spring, but she pretended to be surprised. She praised them both for being so clever, and, recognizing Paula's potential as a budding horticulturist, she had encouraged her to pursue her hobby.

And so Paula's long and passionate love affair with gardening began that year. She had not stopped planting, weeding, pruning and hoeing since then.

With Emma's approval she had cultivated vegetable and herb gardens on her grandmother's Yorkshire estate, and eventually she had created the now famous Rhododendron Walk. The Walk took her years to plan, plant and grow, and it was another example of her determination to excel at whatever she did, and in this instance it was a rather spectacular example at that.

But of all the gardens Paula had created, the one at Heron's Nest remained the dearest.

She was reminded of it this afternoon, seventeen years after she had started it, as she stood up and stretched. She pulled off her gardening gloves, placed them on the wheelbarrow, stepped back to regard the rockery.

Finally it's beginning to take shape, she thought. Making Edwin Fairley's garden beautiful was giving her as much pleasure as her first garden had done.

After Edwin Fairley's death, Jim had inherited his house in Harrogate called Long Meadow. It was here that Paula had come to live as a bride almost a year ago. Although the house was sound and in good repair, it was badly in need of remodelling as well as redecorating. Conversely, Edwin Fairley had seen to it that his gardener had tended the grounds religiously. Nevertheless, they were bereft of colour since little replenishing had been done as flowers and flowering shrubs had died. Paula had seen these deficiencies the moment it became hers, and had itched to start working on it. However, the house took precedence; yet somehow she managed to cope with both at the same time, bringing wholly new aspects and fresh dimensions to both.

Glancing at the herbaceous borders she decided that her dogged toil over the last eleven months *had* been worthwhile. The garden was her private world, and here she found escape and emotional enrichment as her business and personal problems fled.

Well, for a short while. For the last hour or so she had not given one thought to their quarrel of the night before. Now the memory of their heated words edged back. The problem was that Jim could be so stubborn. But then, so could she, and very often to her own annoyance. We both have to be more flexible, she thought, otherwise we're always going to be at loggerheads about certain matters. The funny thing was they hadn't really had any disagreements before their marriage, and no serious quarrels until the problem of Edwina had arisen. They had certainly locked horns about her. She loathed her aunt; Jim was much taken with her. Therein lay the problem.

Quite unexpectedly, Paula remembered something her grandmother had said to her last year, words spoken with love immediately prior to her wedding. They echoed with great clarity in her mind.

'Love is a handful of seeds, marriage the garden,' Emma had said softly. 'And like your gardens, Paula, marriage requires total commitment, hard work, and a great deal of love and care. Be ruthless with the weeds. Pull them out before they take hold. Bring the same dedication to your marriage that you do to your gardens and everything will be all right. Remember that a marriage has to be constantly replenished too, if you want it to flourish . . .'

Such wise words, Paula thought, turning them over in her mind. She leaned back in the chair and closed her eyes. Their quarrel was a weed, wasn't it? So she must uproot it. At once. Yes, she must toss it aside before it took hold. The only way to do that was to dismiss their differences about Edwina.

Paula opened her eyes and smiled to herself. She felt better all of a sudden. She pulled off her muddy Wellington boots, and put on her shoes, and went into the house. She loved Jim. He loved her. Surely that was all that really mattered. Her heart felt lighter as she flew up the stairs to the nursery and their children.

CHAPTER 16

Nora, the nursemaid who looked after the Fairley twins, sat sewing in a rocking chair in the nursery. As Paula's smiling face appeared around the door, she brought her finger to her lips and made a soft shushing sound.

Paula immediately nodded her understanding, mouthed silently, 'I'll be back in a while. I'm going to take a bath.'

After luxuriating in a hot tub for fifteen minutes, Paula felt rejuvenated. But as she dried herself vigorously she had to admit that although the warm water had eased her tired body, this lovely sense of well being sprang from the decision she had just made in the garden to be more understanding about Jim's feelings for Edwina. Yes, it was the only attitude she could take, she saw that clearer than ever. To adopt any other stance would be utterly self-defeating. She would simply rise above it all, as Grandy would do in similar circumstances. Her grandmother was too big a woman to succumb to pettiness, and she would try her level best to act exactly in the same way.

Paula put on a towelling robe and went back into the bedroom. This was spacious, with a high ceiling and a bay window overlooking the gardens, and it bore no resemblance to the way it had looked when Edwin Fairley had been alive. The first day Paula had seen the room her heart sank as she had stood staring in horror at the dark blue flocked wallpaper and the heavy, ponderous mahogany furniture crammed into the space. The bedroom had reflected the rest of the Victorian house, which was a dubious monument to a bygone age. All of the rooms had been old-fashioned, dark, lifeless and depressing. The house had oppressed her with its gloomy, shadow-filled rooms and antiquated furniture and ornate festooned draperies and ugly lamps. She had wondered dismally how she could ever live at Long Meadow with any degree of comfort or happiness, or bring up children in such a bleak and dreary ambience.

But Jim had insisted they move in, and he had refused point blank to take even one look at the lovely old farmhouse which Winston had found for her at West Tanfield. And so she had been obliged to acquiesce to keep the peace, but only with the understanding that Jim allowed her *carte blanche* to renovate and redecorate the entire house. Fortunately he had agreed, and this she had done immediately, before he had a chance to change his mind. Or tried to persuade her to live in the midst of the hopeless muddle of nondescript furnishings which his grandfather had so assiduously accumulated during his lifetime. The refurbishing of the house had been her parents' wedding gift to them, and her mother had helped her create a totally new look, and with such efficiency, boldness and speed even Emma had been surprised, and somewhat amused by their ruthlessness. They threw out everything except a few good pieces of furniture, including Edwin's desk, a Venetian mirror and a French Provincial armoire of light oak, as well as several relatively valuable oil paintings. The pale pastel colours she and Daisy had selected for the rooms instantly brought an airy lightness to the house and opened it up to introduce a feeling of great spaciousness and freedom. Pretty fabrics, porcelain and jade lamps, and the charming country antiques her mother had found added charm, liveliness, understated elegance and comfort.

The dark blue bedroom was transformed into a bower of yellow, white, peach and pale green, with these clear colours repeated throughout in the floral wallpaper and matching fabrics and in the Chinese lamps. Although Jim had voiced the opinion that the white carpeting was rather impractical, he had afterwards acknowledged that the room was lovely and in perfect taste. And to Paula's relief he had liked the rest of the house.

Their bedroom looked sunny and restful this afternoon as she padded across the floor to the dressing table which took pride of place in the wide and curving bay window. She sat down, and, after brushing her hair, she applied her makeup in readiness for the evening ahead. Her thoughts lingered on her grandmother. How lovely she had looked at the christening, and she had been so charming and gracious, so alive with energy and spirit, everyone had paled in comparison. Jim had said the same things about her grandmother over dinner on Saturday night at the Red Lion in South Stainley, where they had gone to dine alone. And then he had lapsed into one of his strange silences for a few minutes and she had known he was thinking of his grandfather.

Paula put down her lipstick, and swivelled in the chair, and sat staring into space, remembering the night Jim had first brought her to this house to meet Sir Edwin Fairley KC.

The scene played for her again, vividly alive in her mind.

He had been dozing in front of the fire in the small, pine-panelled library, and he had roused himself when they arrived, had walked across the floor, smiling warmly, his hand outstretched, a frail, white-haired old man, and lovely in his gentleness and courtesy. When he had been only a few feet away from her his step had faltered as he had seen her more clearly in the dimming light. Shock struck his face and he had looked as if he had seen a ghost as Jim had introduced them. And of course he had. He had seen a reflection of Emma Harte in *her*, although she and Jim had not understood this at that time. But he must have dismissed the resemblance as mere coincidence because he had recovered himself almost immediately. And then during drinks he had asked her what she did, and she had said she worked for her grandmother, Emma Harte, as Jim did, but that she was employed at the stores. He had started violently in the chair and stifled a gasp, and stared at her more intently. His eyes were suddenly alive with burgeoning interest and an unveiled and avid curiosity. He had asked her about her parents, and her life, and she had answered him frankly, and he had smiled and nodded and patted her hand and told her she was a lovely young woman, that he approved of this match. She had met him several times after that first occasion, and he had never been anything but welcoming, obviously overjoyed to see her. After she and Jim had broken up he had apparently been disconsolate, and extremely distressed as their rift had widened, Jim had told her.

Sir Edwin had died before they were reconciled. And then married, with Emma's blessing.

She had asked her grandmother innumerable questions about Edwin, once *their* old story was out in the open and no longer relegated to the closet along with the other skeletons Emma had hidden there.

Emma, who had hitherto glossed over certain aspects of her early life, had suddenly been quite willing to talk, and she had been surprisingly candid. She had told Paula how she had become involved with Edwin when she had been a servant at Fairley Hall, how they had drawn together after both of their mothers had died. She spoke of the moors and the Top of the World and the cave where they had sheltered from the raging storm and where Edwin had seduced her. 'Oh, but Edwin Fairley wasn't a bad person,' Grandy had said to her only a few weeks ago, when they had been discussing things again. 'Just terribly, *terribly* weak, and afraid of his father, and hidebound to his class. Naturally. That was the way it was in those days. We're going back over sixty years, you know. Still, I've often wished that he hadn't been so cowardly, that he had made some sort of effort to help me when I was carrying his child. Then perhaps I wouldn't have hated him so much.'

Emma had shrugged. 'But there you are, that's the way it happened. I survived, didn't I. I was sixteen and about to have an illegitimate child, and because I didn't want to bring shame to my father, I ran away to Leeds. To Blackie. He was my only friend in my dreadful predicament. And Laura, of course, though Blackie wasn't married to my lovely Laura at the time. I had the baby, obviously. You know the rest.'

Paula had asked her why she had called the child Edwina. 'A peculiar, rather unfortunate, slip of the tongue,' Emma had replied with a dry laugh. 'When I wasn't thinking. Or rather, perhaps I should say when I was thinking about Edwin.'

'But how on earth did you manage, Grandma?' Paula had next asked, her eyes full and her heart aching as she had pictured the young Emma's awful ordeal, one she had had to face alone and penniless and without her family.

'Ah well, I had a couple of things going for me,' Emma had remarked with an odd smile. 'And they pulled me through.' Paula had quietly insisted she elaborate further, and Emma had said, 'Well, let's see. I had my strength of character, my physical stamina, a few brains, not such bad looks, and most importantly an implacable will to succeed. Plus, a hell of a lot of courage, now that I think about it. But that's enough of my life story today.' And at this point Emma had brought the conversation to an abrupt halt.

Now Paula thought: Edwin Fairley was not only weak, he was unconscionable in the way he treated her. She shifted her thoughts to her grandmother and was overwhelmed with pride, and enormous love for her. Emma Harte had been strong, and because of her great strength and her immense courage she had conquered the whole damned world. She had stood tall, and she still stood tall. Edwina suddenly flashed through her mind. That child born a Fairley had caused Emma nothing but heartache from the day she had been born. And that's one of the reasons I can't bear being near her, Paula muttered. Why doesn't Jim understand? she asked herself, and squashed this question instantly. Edwina had caused *her* problems recently, but only because she herself had allowed that to happen. Edwina is insignificant in the scheme of things. Grandy said so weeks ago, and as usual she is absolutely right.

The clock struck the half-hour and Paula glanced at it, saw that it was four-thirty. She had no more time to waste, she realized, pulling herself away from her reflections. Jumping up she went to her clothes closet, found a pair of grey flannel trousers and a white silk shirt, dressed in them swiftly. And her step had a ring of decisiveness as she walked across the upstairs hall and into the nursery.

Nora peered out of the tiny kitchen, once a large cupboard that Paula had had remodelled into a nursery pantry. She was holding a baby's milk bottle and said, 'I was about to feed them, Mrs Fairley.'

'Then I'm just in time to help you, Nora.' Paula bent over the cot nearest to her. Tessa was now wide awake, gazing up at her through eyes as stunningly green as her great-grandmother's, and she suddenly began to gurgle and kick her little fat legs in the air. Paula picked up her daughter, holding her tightly, kissing the child's fuzzy head and soft downy cheek, her heart clenching with love and she held Tessa for a second longer before returning her to the cot. Immediately the baby girl began to cry.

Paula glanced down at Tessa and there was joyful laughter in her voice as she said, 'Well, my goodness, aren't you the rumbustious little one, Miss Fairley? But we don't play favourites in this family. I have to give your brother a few kisses too, you know, and a little bit of attention as well.'

Almost as if she had understood the baby girl stopped her wailing.

Paula stepped over to the other cot to see Lorne staring at her solemnly. She lifted him out, hugging him as fiercely as she had his sister, experiencing the same profound emotions of protectiveness and tender love.

'Oh you darling,' she whispered against his cheek, so warm, and wet with slaver, 'Your father is right, you're a little poppet.' She kissed Lorne, held him away from her, and shook her head, grinning broadly at him. 'But you're always so serious, Lorne. You remind me of a little old man. Goodness me, you have such ancient worldly eyes, and you gaze at me as if there's nothing you don't know.'

Paula walked over to the small loveseat in front of the windows and sat down. She bounced Lorne up and down on her knees and the baby seemed to enjoy this, since he at once started to chortle and waved his clenched fists as if he was happy and glad to be alive.

'I'll feed Lorne, since I have him, Nora, and you can take care of his more vocal sister,' Paula said.

'Yes, Mrs Fairley.' Nora smiled at her, glanced over at Tessa's cot. 'She is a little minx, I must admit. She certainly wants to make sure we all know she's here.'

Paula and Nora chatted desultorily about the babies and matters pertaining to their care as they fed the twins. At one moment Paula explained that she had adjusted her timetable and office hours again, so that she could fit in with the schedule the twins were currently following and went on: 'So I'll be home early every day, to help you feed and bathe them. But I won't be able to spend bath time with you tonight, I'm afraid, Nora. We're having guests for drinks, before we go out to dinner.'

'Yes, I understand, Mrs Fairley.' Nora brought Tessa upright in her arms. She laid the baby against her shoulder and patted her back. The little girl burped loudly, and several times.

This brought a smile to Paula's face.

Nora said, 'Isn't she a pickle! She'll find a way to make herself heard, no matter what. But she's a good baby, so is Lorne.'

Paula nodded. 'Let's be thankful for that. But, you know, both my mother and my grandmother seem to think that Tessa's going to be the maverick in the family.' She smiled to herself, mulling this over and leaned back against the cushions, concentrating on Lorne.

Paula cherished these quiet times with her children, away from the bustle and frantic pace of her hectic working life. All was peace and gentleness in the large yet cosy nursery, with its white-painted walls and furniture, blue-and-pink accents and nursery-rhyme paintings hanging on the walls. Golden sunlight filtered in through the filmy curtains blowing gently in the light breeze and there were the mingled smells of babies and talcum powder and boiled milk and freshly-ironed clothes permeating the air. She looked down at her son, so contentedly sucking on his bottle, and she stroked his small fair head. How lucky I am, she mused. I have so much to be thankful for . . . these adorable healthy beautiful babies . . . Grandy and my parents . . . a job that excites me, and, most important of all, the most wonderful husband. Quite suddenly she couldn't wait for Jim to get home from the newspaper so that she could tell him how much she loved him and how much she regretted their ridiculous quarrels about their aunt.

'I'm glad everything's gone well on your first day, Emily, but don't overdo it this week. You sound awfully tired,' Paula said. 'Please try and pace yourself properly.' She sat back in the chair, dragging the telephone across the white wicker desk as she did.

'Oh yes, I will, don't worry,' Emily exclaimed, her voice rising slightly as it came over the wire. 'Grandy's already told me to keep regular office hours, not to try and gulp everything down all at once. But it's so exciting here at Genret, Paula, and I've so much to absorb and learn. Len Harvey is a super person, we're going to get on fine together. He says we'll probably go to Hong Kong next month. On a buying trip. We may even go into Mainland China. Something to do with purchasing pigs' bristles or whiskers.'

Paula's laugh rang out. 'What on earth are you talking about?'

'*Brushes*. Made of pig's bristles. They're the best, so I understand. Paula . . . it's quite amazing here. I hadn't realized how much merchandise we bought abroad. Genret is the biggest importing company in England. Well, *one* of the biggest. We stock everything . . . false eyelashes, wigs, cosmetics, silks and satins, pots and pans – '

'Not to mention pigs' whiskers,' Paula teased. 'Yes, I knew that, Emily, and I think this job is going to be marvellous for you. A lot of responsibility – but I know you can handle it. To tell you the truth, Apple Dumpling, I miss you already, and this is only your first day over there.'

'I feel the same way. I shall miss working with you, too. Still, it's not as if we're disappearing from each other's lives. What made you call me Apple Dumpling just then? You haven't for years.'

Paula smiled into the phone. 'I've been gardening today, making a rockery, and I kept thinking about the first garden I planted . . . at Heron's Nest. Do you remember that day I took you into Scarborough – '

'How could I ever forget it. I've been terrified of worms ever since,' Emily cut in with a light laugh. 'And I *was* an apple dumpling then, wasn't I? More like a roly-poly butterball.'

'But not any more, little one. Listen, would you like to join us for dinner tonight? We're going to the Granby . . . at least I think that's where Jim's decided to take us.'

'I'd love to, but I can't, I'm afraid. Anyway, who's *us*?'

'Sally, Anthony and Aunt Edwina.'

'Oh God, I don't envy you, Paula,' Emily groaned. 'I

would come if I could, just to give *you* moral support. However – ' she broke off and giggled. 'I have a rather special date.'

'*Oh!* Who with?'

'My secret lover.'

'And who's that?' Paula asked quickly, her curiosity aroused.

'If I told you he'd no longer be my secret lover, now would he?' Emily replied mysteriously. 'He's someone extra special and gorgeous, and when the time comes – if it comes, that is – you'll be the first to know.' Laughter shaded her voice.

'Have I met him?' Paula probed, as usual feeling protective of Emily.

'I refuse to say one more word about him.' Wanting to change the subject, Emily asked in a more sober tone, 'By the way, why did Grandy go to London this afternoon?'

'She said something about pulling a new wardrobe together, for her trip with Blackie to far-flung places. Why do you ask?'

'That's what she said to me, but I just wondered if there was another reason. She always tells *you* everything.'

'What other reason *could* there be?' Paula asked, sounding baffled.

'Well . . . she popped in to see me a little while ago, and she looked as if she was on the war path. You know that expression she gets on her face when she's about to do battle. *Implacable* is the best way to describe it, I suppose.'

Paula was thoughtful at the other end of the phone. She stared out at the garden, a frown marring her smooth brow. 'I'm sure she doesn't have any business in London, Emily,' she said after a short pause, and laughed dismissively. 'Besides, you ought to know by now that Grandy always looks implacable. It's become her normal expression. Also, she was probably in a hurry when you saw her. Mummy and Daddy were driving back with her, and she wouldn't have wanted to keep them waiting in the car. I know the clothes are preoccupying her. She told me yesterday that they're going to be hitting a lot of different climates, and that they'll be gone for three months. Let's face it, Emily, she has quite a task ahead of her selecting the appropriate things.'

'Perhaps you're right,' Emily conceded slowly, not entirely convinced. 'She's very excited by the trip, Paula. She's done nothing but talk about it to me all weekend.'

'It'll do her good, since it's the first real holiday she's had in years. And she can't wait to see Philip, and visit Dunoon. She always had such wonderful times there with my grandfather. And listen, Dumpling darling, talking of my baby brother, I'm going to have to hang up. When he telephoned from Sydney yesterday I promised I'd write to him today, and tell him all about the christening. I must get the letter out of the way before Jim gets home.'

'I understand. Thanks for ringing, Paula, and I'll see you later in the week. Give Philip my love. Bye.'

Paula murmured her goodbye, replaced the receiver, and immediately started her letter to Philip. Her young brother was recuperating from a bout of pneumonia, and she and her parents and her grandmother had all agreed it was unfair and unnecessary to drag him from Australia just for one day. As she wrote, Paula relived the weekend, filling the letter with details about the church ceremony, the reception afterwards, along with news of the entire family and their mutual friends, especially the O'Neills and the Kallinskis.

She stopped after three pages in her small neat script and looked up, thinking about Philip. They had always been close and were good friends, and she missed him. She was aware that Philip missed her too, and their parents and Grandy, and that he was sometimes awfully homesick for England. On the other hand, Dunoon, their sheep station at Coonamble in New South Wales, had fired his imagination since his childhood, and she believed it now held his complete affection. Also, running their vast Australian holdings, which their grandfather, Paul McGill, had left Emma, was a tremendous challenge. She knew Philip more than relished his job. He had settled down at last in this past year, and had started to make a full and complete life for himself out there, and she was glad of that. She finished the letter, addressed and sealed the envelope, then stood up, walked to the far end of the room. She bent down and picked up several blossoms which had dropped off a bright pink azalea, laid them in an ashtray on a ceramic drum table and then glanced around, wondering whether to serve drinks in here or in the drawing room.

Although Paula thought of this favourite room as her very own private spot in the house, it had fallen into general use lately. She often found Jim reading here, and most of their guests automatically gravitated to it. In actuality the room was a conservatory, typical of those built on to Victorian mansions in the second half of the nineteenth century, after Joseph Paxton had pioneered the use of iron girders as supports for glass houses. Paula considered the large conservatory, like the garden, one of the few real assets at Long Meadow. It was Gothic in design, and she had filled it with tropical green plants, small trees, and exotic orchids, plus a lovely array of small and colourful flowering shrubs. The fir green carpeting, and the green-and-white ivy print she had chosen for the wicker furniture and skirted tables produced a cool restful ambience, and the conservatory appeared to flow out into the grounds beyond the glass walls. Since Paula's redecoration it provided an extra sitting room as well as a study for her in the refreshing environment of a garden that grew the year round.

Turning around, her eyes fell on one of her prized hydrangeas and she was concerned to see that it had developed discoloured edges. She continued to examine it thoughtfully until the shrilling telephone forced her to return to her desk. She answered it with a bright 'Hello?'

'And how's the little mother?' Miranda O'Neill asked in her lovely, lilting voice.

'I'm fine, Merry, how're you, lovey?'

'Exhausted, if you want to know the truth. I've had my nose to the grindstone all day, and I was in the office most of yesterday, developing my idea for the Harte boutiques in our hotels. I believe I've formulated some really workable plans. I want to show them to my father tomorrow, and then I thought we might get together later in the week, if you have time.'

'Of course I do, and I must say you've been awfully fast, and extremely diligent.'

'Thanks. Aunt Emma was most enthusiastic when I spoke to her on Saturday, and I didn't want to lose any time. As your grandmother always says, time is money. Besides, if we're going to do it, the areas for the boutiques must be included in the new architectural blueprints, and those will be on the drawing board soon.'

'I realize there's a time element involved here, because of your building and remodelling programme, Merry. So let's meet on Wednesday. About two o'clock?'

'That's perfect for me, and let's do it in my office.' Miranda chuckled, said, 'Isn't it fabulous news about Aunt Emma going off on a world tour with Grandpops? We're all thrilled at home.'

'So are we . . . it'll do them both good.'

Merry said: 'You should have seen him this morning. I couldn't believe it when he showed up at the office bright and early. There he was behind his desk, where he hadn't been for months, making phone calls, hustling and bustling, and driving that poor old secretary of his crazy. He kept saying to her, "First Class, *First Class*, and all the way, Gertie! This has to be a de luxe trip." Aunt Emma

263

agreeing to go with him has given him a new lease on life, not that he really needed one, actually, since he's always so *up*, and bubbly. But do you know, he got quite miffed with me when I mentioned my idea about the boutiques. He actually bellowed at me to keep Emma out of it, said that he didn't want my piddling bit of business interfering with his plan with a capital P. It took me ages to calm him down.'

'How did you manage to do that?' Paula asked, laughing under her breath, trying to envisage Blackie in a rage, which was rather difficult to do.

'When I finally got a word in edgeways, I said Aunt Emma wasn't involved, that you were, and that *we* could cope very well without *either* of them. Then he beamed and said I was his clever darling girl, but just to be sure to keep out of his way for the next few days, because he was very preoccupied and extremely busy. Anybody would think they were going off on a honeymoon.'

'Well, he did give her the ring, you know, Merry.'

'Isn't it *sweet*. They're a couple of lovely old dears, aren't they?'

Paula burst out laughing. 'I'd hardly characterize *my* grandmother and *your* grandfather as a couple of *old dears*. Blackie and Emma are more like firecrackers, in my opinion. And weren't you the one who told me only the other day that they were incorrigible when they got together?' Paula reminded Miranda.

Merry had the good grace to laugh with Paula, and she admitted, 'That's true, I did, and you're right. And by the way, talking of Aunt Emma, I don't know what to buy her for her eightieth birthday. I've been racking my brains for days. Any suggestions?'

'You've got to be joking! We all have the same problem. Mummy and Daddy were discussing it with me over lunch today. And Emily's been nagging me to think of something she can get. Frankly, I'm at a loss, like you and everyone else.'

'Well, let's compare notes again on Wednesday,' Merry said. 'I'd better go, Paula. My father's waiting for me. We have to go over some of my rough drafts for the press release – about the acquisition of the hotel in New York. I hope to God he likes *one* of the versions, otherwise I'm going to be at my desk until midnight. Not that that would be anything unusual,' Miranda grumbled. 'I seem to have become a work horse lately. No wonder I don't have any private life these days.'

'I just told Emily to take it easy at Genret. And you'd better do the same, Merry,' Paula cautioned.

'Listen who's talking!' Miranda said, and laughed hollowly.

CHAPTER 17

Since the conservatory opened directly off the marble-floored entrance hall, Paula heard Jim's footsteps the moment he entered the house. She was standing near the fading hydrangea plant, holding the discoloured leaf in her hand, and she turned, expectancy and warmth filling her face.

'Hello, darling,' she said, as he came down the two steps, and moved swiftly towards him, her eagerness to see him most apparent.

'Hello,' he replied.

They met in the centre of the room. He gave her a light kiss, then lowered himself into a chair without saying another word.

Paula stood staring down at him, puzzlement in her eyes. He had sounded so apathetic and the kiss was so

265

perfunctory she knew he was not himself. She said instantly, 'Is there something the matter, Jim?'

He shook his head. 'Just tired,' he said, smiling that bland, dismissive smile she had come to know so well. 'There was an accident on the Harrogate road, quite a pile up of cars because of it, and it slowed the traffic. We crawled along for miles. Frustrating . . . exhausting, actually.'

'How awful. I'm sorry. That's all you needed. Let me fix you a drink,' she suggested, not entirely satisfied with this explanation but making up her mind not to press too hard for the moment.

'That's a good idea,' he exclaimed in a stronger tone. 'Thanks, a gin-and-tonic should hit the spot.'

'I'll just go for some ice,' she said, and made to leave the conservatory.

'Ring for Meg. She can bring it.' He frowned. 'The bell's not broken again, is it?'

'No, but it'll be quicker if I go,' Paula said, pausing with one foot on the step, glancing over her shoulder.

'I wonder, sometimes, why we have a maid,' he said with a hint of irritation, looking up, levelling his pale greyish-blue eyes on her.

She stared back at him, detecting criticism in his tone and manner, but she remarked with evenness, 'She's awfully busy right now, and anyway Grandy brought us up not to be overly dependent on servants, as I've told you so many times.' Not waiting for a response she hurried out, but she heard his pained sigh as she went into the hall. Maybe it *is* only weariness, a hard day at the paper, the difficult drive home, plus the hectic weekend, Paula thought, endeavouring to persuade herself these were the real reasons for his peculiar mood. He wasn't often moody, at least not exactly like this. As she pushed open the kitchen door she noticed she was still holding the leaf. It was mangled in her hand. Relax, she instructed herself, his moodiness means nothing. He'll be more like himself after a drink.

Meg said, 'Do you think I've made enough canapés, Mrs Fairley?' She indicated the silver tray, pausing in her work.

'Yes, that's plenty, Meg, and they look delicious. Thank you. Could you fill the ice bucket please?' Whilst the maid busied herself at the refrigerator Paula threw the leaf in the rubbish bin and washed her hands at the kitchen sink.

Jim had risen in her absence and he was standing looking out into the garden when Paula went back to the conservatory with the ice. His face was in profile, nonetheless she could not fail to miss the morose curve of his mouth, and when he swung around his eyes were vague.

Questions flew to her tongue, but she bit them back and hurried to the skirted table which held bottles and a tray of glasses. Pouring his gin-and-tonic, she said without turning around, 'I thought we'd have drinks in here later, or do you prefer the drawing room?'

'Wherever you wish,' he replied in an uninterested voice.

Striving for a normal manner, she continued steadily, 'Did you book at the Granby after all, Jim?'

'Yes. We have a table reserved for eight-thirty. Anthony called earlier today and said they wouldn't be able to get here until seven-fifteen. That gives us an hour to relax.'

'Yes.' Anxiety was rising in her. He *was* strange, there were no two ways about it, and she wondered if their quarrel of the previous evening still lingered in the back of his mind, rankled perhaps. But why would it? He had won, and anyway he had been chatty and pleasant at breakfast. But she resolved to get to the root of whatever was bothering him. She also decided to have a vodka-and-tonic, even though she hardly ever drank hard liquor.

Jim seemed to visibly cheer up as he sipped his drink. He lit a cigarette, asked casually, 'Heard from anybody today?'

'Emily, Merry O'Neill. And Grandy, of course. She rang

me just after you left this morning to let me know she was going to London for a few days.' Paula now looked directly at him, took a deep breath. 'Why are we making small talk, Jim, when you're troubled? I know something's wrong. Please tell me what it is, darling.'

He was silent.

She leaned forward intently, her unwavering eyes holding his. 'Look, I want to know what's bothering you,' she insisted.

Jim sighed heavily. 'I suppose there's no point putting it off . . . I had a bit of a set-to with Winston today, and – '

Paula laughed with relief. 'Is that all! Well, you've had clashes with him before, and they always blow over. So will this – '

'I've resigned,' Jim announced flatly.

She looked at him uncomprehendingly, totally at a loss for words. Slowly she put down her drink. Her dark brows drew together in a frown. '*Resigned?*'

'As managing director of the company, that is,' he added quickly. 'Effective immediately.'

Thunderstruck, she continued to gape at him. She found her voice and it rose slightly as she asked, 'But *why*? And why didn't you mention it to me, tell me what was on your mind? I simply don't understand . . .' She did not finish her sentence, sat tensely in the chair.

'There was nothing to discuss. You see, I didn't know I was going to resign – until I did.'

'Jim, this is perfectly ridiculous,' she said, attempting a laugh. 'Just because you had a little row with Winston doesn't mean you have to do something as drastic as this . . . after all, Grandy has the final word, you know that. She appointed you, she'll reinstate you at once. She'll put Winston straight, deal with him. Look, I'll speak to her tomorrow, ring her first thing in the morning.' She gave him an encouraging smile, but it faltered as he held up his hand with an abrupt movement that was uncharacteristic.

'I'm afraid you're misunderstanding me. Winston didn't force me to resign, or anything like that, if that's what you're thinking. I did so of my own accord. I wanted to, and rather badly, although I must admit, in all truthfulness, that I didn't realize this until the opportunity presented itself. So I certainly don't want to be reinstated.'

'But why not, for heaven's sake?' she cried, her perplexity and concern mounting, rising to the surface to cloud her face.

'Because I don't like the job. Never have. When Winston came to see me this morning, he asked me point blank if I wished to continue as managing director, and as he was speaking I knew – really *knew*, Paula – that I didn't. I've never been particularly good at administrative work, or interested in it, and I told Winston so, and he said he'd sensed this for some time. He pointed out that perhaps it would be better if I stuck to journalism, ran the papers but not the company. I thoroughly agree with him, so I stepped down. That's all there is to it, actually,' he shrugged, smiled faintly.

'*All there is to it,*' she echoed incredulously. She was aghast at what he had done, and at his attitude. 'I don't believe I'm hearing *you* say these things. You're acting as if it didn't matter, as if this wasn't serious, when it's terribly serious. And you're being so cavalier, so dismissive, I'm absolutely staggered.'

'Don't get so het up. Frankly, *I'm* filled with relief.'

'Relief should be the last thing on your mind,' she said in a small dismayed voice. 'What about duty? Responsibility? Grandy showed a great deal of faith in you, put her trust in you when she appointed you managing director last year. *I* think you've let her down, and rather badly.'

'I'm sorry you feel that way, Paula, because I must disagree with you. I haven't let Grandy down,' he protested. 'I'm still going to be managing editor in charge of two of the most important newspapers in the Consolidated group.

I'll be doing what I do best, being a newspaperman, and a damned good one at that.' He sat back, crossed his legs, and returned her penetrating stare with an unblinking gaze. His expression was adamant.

'And who's going to run the company, now that you've stepped down?'

'Winston, of course.'

'You know very well he doesn't want that job.'

'Neither do I.'

Paula's lips drew together in aggravation. Another thought struck her and she exclaimed fiercely, 'I hope this sudden and rather extraordinary decision of yours doesn't mean that Grandy will have to cancel her trip with Blackie. She really needs that holiday. What did she say? I presume you've told her.'

'Naturally I've told her. Winston and I walked over to the store at lunch time for a meeting with her. Your grandmother accepted my resignation, Winston's agreed to take the job, and he didn't seem very perturbed about the idea either. Grandy isn't going to cancel her holiday, rest assured of that.' He leaned forward and clasped her hand in his. 'Come on, relax. You're the one who's more upset than anyone. Grandy and Winston respect my decision. They didn't quibble. In fact, there was very little discussion . . . it was rather cut and dried, actually.'

'You've simply misunderstood their reactions,' she murmured filled with misery.

Jim laughed. 'Now *you're* being ridiculous, Paula. I know them both very well and I can assure you that everything is all right.'

Paula could think of no easy reply to this statement. She was astonished at his lack of insight, and his assumption that things were on an even keel showed extremely flawed judgement on his part. Jim obviously had no conception of what made her grandmother and Winston tick. *She* didn't have to think twice to know that they had accepted the

270

situation because they had had no alternative. They would pull together to keep the company running smoothly. That's *our* way she thought. We do our duty, accept responsibility, no matter how difficult that is. Things were far from *all right*, as he so glibly put it.

Jim was watching her, trying to ascertain what she was thinking but her violet eyes were veiled, unreadable. He said anxiously, 'Please try to see my point of view, understand my feelings about the situation. Your grandmother and Winston do. And don't let's argue about my resignation. Since it's a *fait accompli* this is all rather silly, wouldn't you say?'

Paula said nothing. She leaned back in her chair, extracted her hand quietly, and reached for her drink. She took a quick sip. There was a protracted silence before she said, 'Jim, I do wish you'd reconsider . . . there are other things involved here. Grandy was going to tell you this herself later in the week, but I know she won't mind if *I* tell you *now*. She's going to change her will. At the moment her shares in the newspaper company are part of the assets of Harte Enterprises, which as you know my cousins are to inherit. But she's decided to leave the newspaper shares to the twins – our children – so I know it's important to her that you're totally involved with the newspaper company and on every level. I don't care what she said to you this morning, I'm absolutely convinced she's terribly disappointed deep down because you've chosen to step away from the managerial side – '

Jim's brief laugh stopped her short. She looked at him, searched his face, wondering if she had imagined the edge to that laugh.

He said patiently in a soft, smooth voice, 'Paula, whether I'm managing director, managing editor or both, or neither, for that matter, your grandmother will still change her will. She'll leave those shares to our children no matter what and for several good reasons.'

'What reasons?'

'They're Fairleys, for one thing, and then there's her guilt.'

Paula blinked, for a second not understanding what he was getting at, then quite suddenly she had a flash of insight, and she stared at him intently. She hoped she had misunderstood the implication behind his words. She took a deep breath to steady herself, and asked very slowly, 'Her guilt about *what* exactly?'

'Wresting the *Yorkshire Morning Gazette* away from my grandfather, grabbing control of the company,' he said off-handedly, lighting a cigarette.

'You make it sound as if she stole it!' Paula tersely exclaimed. 'You know very well that your grandfather ran that newspaper into the ground, and that certainly had nothing to do with Grandy. You've said often enough that he was a brilliant barrister but a lousy businessman. Surely I don't have to remind you that the other shareholders begged Grandy to take over. She bailed them out – and your grandfather, for that matter. He made a lot of money on his shares.'

'Yes, you're correct – especially about him mismanaging the paper, but I suppose he would have muddled through, limped along somehow and retained control, if your grandmother hadn't swooped down and scooped it up.' He gulped some of his drink, drew on his cigarette.

'The paper would have gone bankrupt! Then where would your grandfather have been?' She glared at him. 'In a mess, that's where!'

'Look here, Paula, don't sound so shocked. I'm only reminding you of the facts. We both know that Grandy ruined the Fairleys.' He gave her an easy lopsided smile. 'We're both adults, so we'd be rather silly if we tried to sweep all that under the rug, just because you and I are married. What happened did *actually* happen, you know. You and I are not going to change it, and it's certainly

272

nonsensical for us to quarrel about it now, so long after the event.'

Paula recoiled, gaping at him. Dismay had lodged like a rock in the pit of her stomach and she was shaking inside. As his words echoed in her head, her patience evaporated, the tension of the last few weeks rose up in her, and something snapped all of a sudden. 'She no more ruined the Fairleys than I did! It just so happens that Adam Fairley and that eldest son of his, Gerald, did it all by themselves. Whether you want to believe it or not, your great-grandfather and great-uncle were negligent, stupid, self-indulgent and very poor businessmen. And besides, even if she had ruined them, I for one wouldn't blame her. I'd applaud her for settling the score. The Fairleys treated my grandmother abominably. And as for your sainted grandfather, what he did to her was . . . was unspeakable!' she gasped. 'Unconscionable, do you hear! Fine upstanding young man Edwin was, wasn't he? Getting her pregnant at sixteen and then leaving her to fend for herself. He didn't even lift a finger to help her. As for – '

'I know all that – ' Jim began, wondering how to placate her, stop this flow of angry words.

She cut him off peremptorily. 'What you don't know perhaps is that your great-uncle Gerald tried to rape her, and believe you me, no woman ever forgets the man who has attempted *rape* on her! So don't start presenting a case for the Fairleys to me. And how dare you point a finger at my grandmother, after all she's done for you! Could it be that you're trying to gloss over your abdication of your duty to her – ' Paula stopped herself from saying any more. Her emotions were running high and she was so furious she was shaking like a leaf.

A sudden chill settled in the room.

They stared at each other. Both of them were appalled. Paula's face was so white her deep blue eyes seemed more startling than ever, and Jim's face was taut with shock.

273

His distress prevented him from speaking for a few seconds. He was stunned by her outburst and dismayed that she had chosen to totally misconstrue his words, uttered idly, and rather carelessly, he now had to admit.

He finally exclaimed with great fervency, 'Paula, please believe me, I wasn't making a case for the Fairleys, or pointing a finger at Emma. How can you possibly think I would do anything like that. I've always respected and honoured her, since the first day I worked for her. And I've grown to love her since we've been married. She's a wonderful woman, and I'm the first to appreciate everything she's done for me.'

'That's nice to know.'

Jim caught his breath, cringed at her sarcastic tone. 'Please, Paula, don't look at me like that. You've misunderstood me completely.'

She did not reply, averted her face, stared at the mass of plants lining the glass walls of the conservatory.

Jim jumped up. He grabbed her hands and pulled her out of the chair, took her in his arms. 'Darling, please listen to me. I love you. The past doesn't matter, Grandy's the first person to say so. I was wrong to even bring it up. What *they* all did to each other half a century ago has nothing to do with *us*. Somehow we've gone off the rails because of this . . . this discussion about my resignation. Everything has been blown out of proportion. You're overly upset about nothing. Please, please calm yourself.' As he spoke he led her to a loveseat and pressed her down, seated himself next to her, and took her hand, looked deeply into her face.

He said, 'Look, I agree with you, Paula, what my grandfather did *was* unspeakable. And he knew that himself. He lived with a guilty conscience for the rest of his life. In fact, his actions as a young man *ruined* his life in many ways. He confided that in me before he died. He never stopped regretting losing Emma and their child, nor

274

did he stop loving her, and at the end all he wanted was your grandmother's forgiveness. When he was dying he implored me to go to Emma and beg her forgiveness for everything the Fairleys had done to her, himself most of all. Don't you remember I told you this? I spoke to Grandy about it the night she announced our engagement.'

'Yes,' Paula said.

'I repeated everything to Grandy – his last words just before he slipped away. He said, "Jim, it will be an unquiet grave I lie in if Emma does not forgive me. Implore her to do so, Jim, so that my tortured soul can rest in peace." And when I told Emma she wept a little, and she said, "I think perhaps your grandfather suffered more than I did, after all." And Paula, Emma forgave him. She forgave all of the Fairleys. Why can't you?'

She lifted her head sharply, startled by the question. 'Oh Jim, I – ' There was a short pause before she finished, 'There's nothing for *me* to forgive. I think *you've* misunderstood *me*.'

'Perhaps. But you were so angry, shouting at me, going on about the Fairleys . . .'

'Yes, I did lose my temper, but you riled me when you said Grandy had guilty feelings. I know her, and far better than you, Jim, and I'm convinced she doesn't feel guilty about anything.'

'Then I was wrong,' he said with a weak smile. 'I apologize.' He was relieved she sounded more normal.

'You're wrong about something else too.'

'What's that?'

'The past. You just said that the past doesn't matter, but I can't agree with you. The past is always coming back to haunt us, and we can never escape it. It makes prisoners of us all. Grandy might give lip service to the idea that the past is no longer important, but she doesn't really believe this. She's often said to me that the past is immutable and it most certainly is, in my opinion.'

'The sins of the fathers and all that – is that what you mean?' he asked quietly.

'Yes.'

Jim exhaled, shook his head.

Paula looked at him carefully. 'I have a question. You might not like it, but I feel compelled to ask it.' She waited, watching him closely.

He stared back at her. 'Paula, I'm your husband, and I love you, and there should never be anything but complete honesty and directness between us. Obviously you can ask me anything. What's the question?'

She took a breath, plunged. 'Do you resent Grandy? I mean because she's the owner of the *Gazette* and not you? If your grandfather had managed to retain control you would have inherited the paper.'

Jim's jaw dropped in astonishment and he gaped at her, then he laughed. 'If I had any resentment – or bitterness or jealousy – I'd hardly be resigning as managing director. I'd be scheming to get the paper for myself – at least, to get as much power as I possibly could. And I'd have been dropping hints to you long ago to influence Grandy to leave the newspaper shares to our children . . . so I could get absolute control through their holdings. With that kind of clout at my fingertips I would be kingpin in the company, after Emma was dead. Actually, it would be mine in a manner of speaking, since I would be handling their business affairs until they came of age.' He shook his head, still laughing. 'Now wouldn't I have done that?'

'Yes, I suppose so,' Paula admitted in a drained voice, feeling suddenly debilitated.

Jim said, 'Paula, surely you realize by now that I'm not money hungry, nor particularly ambitious for power. I like running the papers, being managing editor, I admit that, but I don't want to be involved in business and administration.'

'Not even when you know that the newspaper company will be your children's one day?'

'I trust Winston. He'll do a good job. After all, he does have rather a big stake in the Consolidated group when you consider that he and the Hartes own half the company. He controls forty-eight per cent of the shares, don't forget.'

Paula knew there was no point arguing with him any further about his resignation, at least not now. She stood up. 'I think I've got to go outside . . . I need some fresh air.'

Jim also rose, looking at her with concern. 'Are you all right? You're awfully pale.'

'Yes, really. Why don't you spend a few minutes with the babies before you change? I'll be up in a short while – I just need to take a stroll around the garden.'

He caught her arm as she moved towards the door, swung her to face him. 'Friends again, darling?' he asked softly.

'Yes, of course,' she reassured him, conscious of the anxiety reflected in his eyes and recognizing the plea in his voice.

Paula walked slowly through the garden, circumvented the plantation of trees and took the narrow path leading to the second lawn that sloped down towards the grove of laburnum trees and the pond.

She was considerably shaken by their quarrel and her senses were swimming. She sat down on the steps of the white-painted summerhouse, relieved to be alone, to regain her equilibrium. She deplored the fact that she had lost control, flown into a temper, and her only excuse was the extreme provocation. Jim's remark that her grandmother was guilt-ridden about the Fairleys had been so inflammatory it had made her blood boil. The suggestion was ridiculous. Just as his resignation was ludicrous.

Although she was desperately troubled by that impulsive

and irresponsible move on his part, her dismay about it had been jostled to one side by the impact of their collision. This last row was a lot more serious than one of their quarrels about Edwina. It had struck an important fundamental in any marriage – trust; and it raised questions in her mind about Jim, his innermost feelings for her grandmother and his loyalty to Emma. Her head was teeming with questions. Did he bear a grudge against Emma Harte because she now owned everything the Fairleys had once owned? Perhaps subconsciously, without really understanding that he did? It struck her, and very sharply, that this was not beyond the realms of possibility. After all, he had been the one to launch into the past, not she, and if the past didn't matter, as he had claimed, then why had he brought it up in the first place?

Were resentment and bitterness at the root of his statement after all? She trembled at this thought. Those were the most dangerous emotions in the world, for like cancer they gnawed away at a person's insides, and they were destructive, coloured everything a person did. Yet when she had asked Jim bluntly if he resented Grandy he had obviously been flabbergasted by the idea, and his answer had been immediate, direct, and totally without guile. He had been genuine, she had seen that instantly. She had always found Jim relatively easy to read. He was not a devious man, quite the reverse really, in that he was not constitutionally cut out to dissemble.

Paula leaned against the railings and closed her eyes, her mind working at its rapid and most intelligent best, assessing and analysing. She had always believed she knew Jim inside out, but did she really? Perhaps it was arrogant of her to think she had such great insight into him. After all, how well did anyone know another person when one got right down to it? There had been times when she had found those who were closest to her, with whom she had grown up, difficult and even impossible to comprehend on occasions. If members of her immediate family and her oldest friends were frequently baffling, how could she possibly understand a man she had known for a brief two years, a man who might easily be termed a stranger even though he was her husband? She had come to realize that people could not always be taken on face value . . . most people were highly complex. Sometimes they themselves did not recognize what motivated them to do the things they did. How well did James Arthur Fairley actually know himself? And, come to think of it, how well did he know *her*?

These nagging questions hung in the air, and she finally let go of them, sighing, understanding that she had no ready answers for herself. She opened her eyes and looked down at her hands, so relaxed, curled in her lap. The tension had gone, and now that her anger had all but dissipated entirely she was able to think objectively and with a cool head. She acknowledged that she had leaped down Jim's throat. Of course he had been awfully provocative, but that was no doubt unintentional on his part. They were both at fault, and if he had a few imperfections then most assuredly so did she. They were both human. As he had defended himself against her strong verbal onslaught she had heard the ring of truth and sincerity in his voice, had noted the genuine love written all over his face. It suddenly seemed inconceivable to her that Jim could harbour ill feelings for her grandmother. Furthermore, she owed it to her husband to believe that he did not. Yes, she must trust him, give him the benefit of the doubt. If she was not capable of doing that then their relationship would be threatened. Besides, he had made a very salient point, one she could not now ignore. He had said he would hardly be resigning as managing director if he was embittered and felt that the *Gazette* was his by rights, that instead he would be making sure he grabbed all the power for himself. She could not deny that his words made sense. Anybody who was goaded on by resentment to get even, to win, would hardly be quitting the arena. He would be planning the *coup-de-grâce*.

Thoughts of his resignation intruded more sharply, but she clamped down on them with resoluteness. Wisely, she decided she had better shelve that sensitive issue for the time being. It was hardly the time to start tackling him about that again when their guests were due to arrive shortly. And especially since Edwina was one of those guests. She most certainly wasn't going to let *her* see a chink in the armour.

Jim stood at the window where, from this angle, he could see Paula sitting on the steps of the summerhouse. His eyes remained riveted on her and he wished she would come back inside. It was imperative that he smooth things over between them.

He had not meant any harm when he had mentioned that old worn out story about Emma Harte ruining the Fairleys. But he had been tactless, no use denying it, and a bloody fool for not realizing that Paula would react fiercely. Jim exhaled wearily. She had overreacted in his opinion; after all, facts were facts and quite inescapable. But then his wife was irrational about her grandmother, worshipping her the way she did. She wielded a club on anyone who dared to even hint that Emma was less than perfect. Not that he ever said a wrong word about her . . . he had no reason to criticize or condemn Emma Harte. Just the opposite, actually.

Paula's revelation about Gerald Fairley attempting to rape the young Emma edged to the front of his mind. It was undoubtedly true, and the very idea of it was so repellent to him he shivered involuntarily. On the rare occasions Gerald's name had cropped up in conversation, he had divined a look of immense distaste and contempt on his grandfather's face, and now he understood why. Jim shook his head wonderingly, thinking how entangled the lives of the Fairleys and the Hartes had been at the turn of the century; still the actions of his antecedents were hardly his fault or his responsibility. He had not known any of them, except for his grandfather, and so they were shadowy figures at best, and anyway the present was the only thing that mattered, that counted for anything.

This thought brought his eyes back to the window. He moved the curtain slightly. Paula was a motionless figure on the steps of the old summerhouse, lost in her contemplations. Once she had returned to the bedroom to change her clothes, he would sit her down, talk to her, do his damnedest to make up to her, apologize again if necessary. He was beginning to loathe these quarrels, which had become so frequent of late.

He ran his hand through his fair hair absently, a meditative look settling on his finely-drawn, rather sensitive face. Paula could be right – maybe Emma was not in the least troubled by her past deeds. Now that he considered it objectively, in a rational manner, it suddenly struck him that she was far too pragmatic a woman to worry about matters that could not be altered. And yet he could not dismiss the sense of guilt he had detected in her from time to time. Perhaps her guilt was centred solely on him, had nothing to do with those long-dead Fairleys. There was no question in his mind that Emma worried about him. This was the reason he had not been in the least surprised when Paula had mentioned the will, since he had always expected Emma to change it, to favour his children. He did not crave the shares for himself, nor could Emma leave him her interest in the papers without causing a stink in the family. And so Emma, being fair minded and scrupulous, was doing her level best to make amends, to make things right and proper in the only way she knew how. She was giving Lorne and Tessa their birthright . . . the inheritance he himself would have willed to his children if his family had retained control of the newspaper.

Jim was completely convinced that genuine emotion motivated Emma. She had once loved his grandfather, and, in consequence, she cared deeply about him. There was not the slightest doubt in his mind about that. He might even have been her grandson if circumstances had been slightly different.

Yes, Grandy had shown her true feelings for him in an infinite variety of ways – he had hard evidence. He ran all of the instances through his head . . . she had given him the job as managing editor when there had been other candidates just as well qualified; she had ended her vendetta against the Fairleys because of him; she had blessed his marriage to her favourite grandchild. In fact, Emma Harte was always bending over backward to please him, and she was on his side – her actions more than proved this. Grandy had persuaded Paula to live here at Long Meadow because he so wished it. She had acknowledged that the twins must be christened at Fairley Church and, moreover, she had not objected when he had invited Edwina. It was only ever Paula who made a fuss about that unfortunate woman who had never done anybody any harm.

Jim shifted his stance impatiently, wondering how long Paula intended to sit out there. He glanced at his watch with irritation. If she did not come in within the next few minutes he would go out and talk to her in the garden. He did want to make sure she understood one thing . . . Emma was not disappointed in him. That morning, when he had told her he wanted to resign, Grandy had agreed, said that she appreciated his honesty. 'If that's what you want, then that's what you must do,' Emma had said with a little smile. 'I'd be the last person to stop you.' Emma was compassionate and full of humanity, and she loved him in her own way. And he was loyal to her, devoted. There was a special bond between them. It was never mentioned but it existed, nevertheless.

Much to his relief Jim now saw Paula walking up the path. Thank God she was coming back to the house. His tension lessened, even though it was impossible from this distance to gauge her state of mind, or ascertain what her attitude would be. But then he always had trouble doing that. It seemed to him that she constantly had him on the edge, kept him guessing. She was temperamental, even difficult at times, but no woman had captivated him, ensnared him as she had. And she had done so without even trying. There was enormous chemistry between them and their sexual attraction for each other was so strong it was overpowering. Paula was so intense, so serious, so complex she often left him floundering and baffled. Yet he found her depth and sincerity gratifying; equally he was thrilled by her passion, her desire for him in bed. The women he had been involved with before her had often complained about his sex drive. They seemed to think it was abnormal, were unable to cope, balked at his staying power. But not Paula . . . she never complained, always welcomed him with open arms, as ready as he to abandon herself to their lovemaking, and he could never get enough of her. He knew she felt the same.

Paula was the best thing in the world that had ever happened to him, and he was struck by this realization more and more every day. How lucky he had been to meet her on that plane journey from Paris.

He thought back to it now, remembering clearly every little detail of their first meeting. Her name had sounded familiar and her lovely face had touched a chord in his memory, but he had not been able to place her. But later that night, restless, unable to sleep, haunted by her, everything had suddenly clicked into place. It had dawned on him that she was the daughter of David Amory, who ran the Harte stores, and that she was therefore the granddaughter of Emma Harte, his employer. He had been at once intimidated and dismayed, had not closed his eyes all night, worrying about the situation and the ramifications it involved.

The following morning, confused, disturbed and ambivalent, he had wavered, had wondered whether to cancel their dinner date planned for that evening. In the end he had been unable to resist seeing her again, had gone to the Mirabelle in a troubled state. He had been keyed up, anxious, and his heart had been in his mouth. After one of the waiters had made a remark about her grandmother, he had seen his chance. He had the perfect opening gambit, had asked her who her prestigious grandparent was, and Paula had told him without hesitation. She had made light of this, had made it easy for him, and surprisingly her relationship to Emma Harte had suddenly not mattered. His extraordinary feelings for Paula swept everything to one side, and he had fallen in love with her over dinner at the Mirabelle, had made up his mind to marry her – even if Emma sacked him and disinherited her heiress.

Jim recalled the night, a month after their first date, when he had finally succeeded in getting Paula into bed. Unexpectedly, erotic images of them together began to dance around in his head, made the heat rush through him. He knew what he was going to do the minute she walked in, knew how to put everything right between them. Words and long explanations were meaningless, inconsequential, now that he thought about it. Actions counted. Yes, his was the best way, the only way to demolish the residue of their quarrel completely.

Now, as Paula entered the bedroom, Jim saw that she was calmer, that her colour was perfectly normal. He went to her, took her hands in his. 'I can't bear these awful rows,' he said.

'Neither can I.'

Without saying anything else, he took her face between

his hands and kissed her, his mouth working sensually on hers. His passion soared. He was at full arousal. His arms went around her and he brought her closer, so that she was positioned into the curve of his body. His hands slid down her back on to her buttocks, and he pressed her into him with impatience. She must understand the extent of his excitement, understand that he intended to possess her immediately.

Paula accepted his kisses, and then quickly but gently pushed him away. 'Jim, please. They'll be here in a few minutes. We don't have time – '

He silenced her with another kiss, then breaking away from her, he led her to the bed. He pushed her down on to it purposefully, lay next to her, wrapped his long legs around her. In a voice thickened by desire, he said against her neck, 'I must have you. *Now*. Quickly, before they arrive. We do have time. And you know we always make up, once we've made love. Come on, take your clothes off for me, darling.'

Paula started to protest, not wanting this, wary of him, sensing she was being manipulated again. But he was already fumbling with the buttons on her shirt and so she swallowed her words. It was far easier if she was compliant, as she had so quickly come to realize in the last year. Jim believed that sex solved every one of their problems. But of course it did not.

CHAPTER 18

At six-thirty the following morning Paula left Long Meadow for the office, looking coolly elegant in a smartly tailored black linen suit and a crisp white silk shirt.

After a restless night of tossing and turning and worrying, she had risen earlier than usual. Only Nora had been astir at that hour, preparing the babies' bottles, and after she had showered and dressed Paula had spent fifteen tranquil minutes with her and the twins in the nursery, before going downstairs to the kitchen. As she had drunk a quick cup of tea she had scribbled a note to Jim, explaining that she was facing a hectic day at the store and wanted to get a head start.

This was only partially true. Paula had the most urgent need to unscramble her jumbled thoughts and take stock of the situation. She could only do that when she was alone – and the only time she was not surrounded by people was either when she was gardening or driving.

As she pointed the car down the gravel driveway she realized she was relieved to be escaping from the house. It seemed more suffocating than ever to her today. Although she enjoyed the grounds and the conservatory, Long Meadow would never really be her favourite place, despite the more attractive ambience she and her mother had created. As Grandy had said, 'You've both done your best but you can't make a silk purse out of a sow's ear.'

And whatever Jim believed, the house *was* oppressive. Her grandmother felt the same way as she did, and rarely came, preferring instead to have them over to Pennistone Royal. This aside, it was extremely difficult to run efficiently. It was poorly designed, had endless staircases, winding corridors and dark landings. Meg and the daily char, Mrs Coe, were constantly complaining, and even Nora, who was younger than they, had taken to grumbling about her aching legs lately. Jim made light of their complaints. He loved Long Meadow, and she knew he would not consider moving, so there was no point in dreaming about another house, one which was more practical and suitable for their needs.

He was selfish.

So jolted was Paula by this unexpected thought she stiffened and gripped the steering wheel tighter. She stared ahead at the road, her eyes momentarily glazed by her troubles. What an unkind and disloyal thing to think, she chided herself. But try though she did to convince herself she was wrong about Jim, she did not succeed. It was the truth. For months she had tried to ignore this unfortunate and dismaying characteristic in him, had made perpetual excuses for him. Suddenly this was no longer possible. She had to stop deluding herself about Jim, look at the facts unflinchingly, accept that he only ever did what he *wanted* to do. He was deceptive in that he gave the impression of trying to please, especially with colleagues and friends, and when small irrelevant matters were involved. Then he bent over backward to be obliging. When it came to major issues he dug his feet in and always strove to get his own way, regardless of anyone else's wishes. That was the dichotomy in his nature and it had begun to worry her.

Paula sighed to herself. They were both stubborn, but at least she was not inflexible. With a start, Paula recognized that Jim was absolutely rigid. This trait had been staring her glaringly in the face for months, yet she had been reluctant, perhaps even afraid, to acknowledge it.

She began to scrutinize the pattern of their life together for the past year, and now discovered that she could remember innumerable examples of that ingrained rigidity. There had been his refusal point blank to accept a new plane from Grandy, not to mention the fuss about their wedding plans. He had been adamant when her grandmother had asked him to get rid of his rickety old four-seater plane, and suggested he buy a more up-to-date jet at her expense. Being conscious of his pride, Grandy had handled it diplomatically, had pointed out that she felt she should have a company plane at her immediate disposal, and who better to select the best piece of equipment and make the purchase than he. But he would not budge from his position, and Emma had thrown up her hands in exasperation at his intractability.

Almost immediately afterwards he had told her parents and Grandy that he wanted to have their marriage ceremony at Fairley Church. They had all three been staggered by this suggestion, and so had she. Apart from the fact that the village church was far too small to accommodate some three hundred guests, her parents and Emma had wanted the wedding to be held in London, to be followed by a reception at Claridge's Hotel. It had been especially important to her grandmother that she have a lovely, elegant and glamorous wedding. It was her mother who had scotched Jim's idea. Daisy had told him that the marriage arrangements were hardly his concern, since they were always the prerogative of the bride's parents. Clever clever Daisy. She had won by simply pointing out the correct etiquette, the proper form. In this instance he had had no option but to back down.

But he had made a swift recovery, and the next battle had been about Long Meadow. Jim had been the winner that time, but in a sense by default. She had only agreed to live there to keep the peace, and also because her grandmother had told her to be accommodating. 'Jim's ego and his masculinity are on the line,' her grandmother had remarked. 'I agree the house is a monstrosity, but he has a genuine need to be the provider, to give you a home on his own terms. You'd better accept the situation for now.'

For this same reason she and Grandy had gone along with his wish to have the twins christened at Fairley Church, even though Emma had initially balked at this idea, had hardly been overjoyed to trek all the way to Fairley, of all places. She rarely went *there* these days.

Paula slowed down and stopped at a traffic light, mulling over this first year of marriage. People said it was the most difficult year and perhaps it *was* inevitable that there would be a few unpleasant revelations. Whizzing up the short hill, she cruised past the Stray and turned on to the main road to Leeds. I suppose I might as well accept that the honeymoon is now definitely *over*, she muttered under her breath, then laughed ironically. He had even been contrary about their actual honeymoon, had whisked her off to the Lake District instead of to the sunny South of France. Wanting to please him, in love and feeling euphoric, she had accepted his decision, even though France had been more appealing to her. They had been greeted by inclement weather and thunderstorms when they had reached Windermere, and had spent a week shivering in front of the fire in their hotel suite, or in bed making love.

Her thoughts automatically settled on their sex life. She was in love with Jim, and wanted him physically, had normal desires and a healthy attitude about sex. But lately it was growing more and more apparent to her that Jim was abnormally driven. His marathons were becoming tiring, even tedious. There were other things in a marriage as well as sex. He was insatiable, and endless, mindless sex was not particularly fulfilling to her. Sometimes she found herself wishing he had more finesse, a better understanding of a woman's body – *her* body, *her* needs. Loath though she was to admit it, she knew deep within herself that Jim was just as selfish in bed as he was out of it, always pleasing himself, never giving a thought to her. It was growing harder and harder for her to cope with his need to make love all the time. Her work was demanding and she craved sleep, but he was seemingly tireless.

Sudden anger flared in Paula as she considered the way he used sex as an antidote for their rows. Her resentment was increasing, because it was manipulative. It seemed incredible to her that he believed their problems evaporated into thin air once they were locked in a tight embrace. Of course that didn't happen, their difficulties were still there afterwards. And naturally they remained unsolved.

Oh God, if only he would *talk* to me, Paula thought. He should communicate. Instead he retreats behind his charm and his jokes, and whenever I try to explain my feelings he laughs me off. Yes, Jim had a childish tendency to pretend their differences did not exist. She could never get him to open up, try though she did. It occurred to her that she had reached an impasse. She had come to a turning point in her marriage. And after only one year, she said to herself wonderingly. Had she made a terrible mistake? Was divorce the only solution?

Horror trickled through her at the mere idea of breaking up, and was quickly replaced by a rush of panic. Beads of sweat broke out on her forehead, and she began to tremble inside. Slowing the car to a crawl she pulled into the first side road she saw and parked. Leaning forward, she rested her head on the steering wheel and closed her eyes. Divorce was unthinkable. She was stunned that it had even crossed her mind a moment ago. She loved him . . . truly, truly loved him. And in spite of their problems they were compatible in so many important ways. And there were the twins . . . Lorne and Tessa needed a father, needed Jim as much as she needed him.

Instantly, it struck her that she had been unfair to her husband, adding to his faults, mentally compiling lists of grudges against him when he was not present to defend himself. He was a nice man, a good man, and he had so many lovely qualities. She owed it to him to be scrupulously honest with herself about his manifold attributes.

Silently she began to tick them off in her head. He understood about her work. He appreciated her desire to be out there in the marketplace. Certainly he never interfered with her career; he did not grumble about her preoccupation with the stores, the late hours she kept. At least he's an enlightened man in that respect, she acknowledged swiftly, and he allows me to be myself. He's not threatened by me either. Furthermore, he was obviously cut out to be a marvellous father, that was already evident. There was no question that he adored her, was devoted to her. Jim would never be a philanderer who played around with other women. He was strictly a one-woman man and totally geared to his family, and family life, and she was thankful of that.

Straightening up, Paula smoothed her hair into place. I've got to make a go of this relationship, she told herself. It's vitally important to me, and I know it's essential to Jim. She remembered something her grandmother had once said . . . that it was always the woman who made a marriage work. Paula believed this. Her grandmother was wise and experienced, she had lived it all, seen it all. No one knew better about marriage than Emma Harte.

Paula resolved to be as understanding of Jim as she possibly could. She would put extra effort and time into their relationship. She would be loving and tolerant. It would be immature of her if she did not. After all, everybody had faults, and you didn't stop loving a man simply because he had a few imperfections. You loved him in spite of them.

Turning the ignition key, Paula started the car and backed out of the side road. Her mind began to revolve around her grandmother and Jim's resignation as she sped down the road heading in the direction of Alwoodley. Convinced though she was that Jim had totally misjudged Emma's reaction to his decision, she nevertheless hoped that her grandmother was not angry with him. She did not want Grandy to think badly of Jim.

Less than half an hour later Paula sat behind her desk in her office at the Harte store in Leeds, talking to her grandmother whom she had reached at the flat in Belgrave Square.

'I'm sorry to wake you up,' Paula apologized, although she strongly suspected she had not done so.

Emma's warm and vibrant voice flowed over the wire and confirmed this, as she said, 'I was having my morning

291

tea and waiting for your call. You want to talk to me about Jim, his resignation, don't you?'

'Yes, Gran. I was a bit floored last night when he told me what he'd done, and naturally rather upset. I feel he's let you down, and at the worst time, when you're about to go away. I can't help thinking that you must be disappointed in him.'

'A little,' Emma said. 'However, I decided not to persuade Jim to retain the managing directorship . . . not under the circumstances. His heart's not in the job, Paula, and that's not good. It's better he steps down.'

'Yes,' Paula agreed quietly. 'What about Winston? Is he frightfully annoyed?'

'Well, he was at first, and I thought for a moment he was going to explode when I told him he would have to take on the job. But he agreed, almost at once. There's no one else, as you well know.'

'I feel awful about this situation, Grandy. There's not much I can say, except that I'm sorry. Jim shouldn't have done this in my opinion. I think it was irresponsible. *He* doesn't agree with me, of course.' There was a fractional pause, and then Paula added, 'I'm not trying to make excuses for him, Gran, but I've come to realize that Jim isn't like *us*, you know as far as duty is concerned. We've all done jobs we haven't really liked during the years we've all worked for you. Those jobs never killed us, and we learned a lot from the experience. I know I shouldn't make comparisons, but last night when Jim was talking I kept thinking of little Emily – her example. She's been a brick, the way she's gone into Genret and with the best will in the world.'

'That's true,' Emma agreed, then added swiftly, in a kinder tone, 'You mustn't be too hard on Jim, Paula dear. People do have their limitations, and remember, he wasn't brought up in the same way as you and your cousins. Anyway, let's be grateful for his talent as a managing

292

editor. He's brilliant, the best in the business, and that's why I gave him the job years ago. Now, if he'd resigned from that position we *would* have a major tragedy on our hands.'

'I realize that. He does love the newspaper business, and that's why he's been so successful as a journalist.' Paula was beginning to feel easier in her mind, and she went on, 'I have to defend Jim in one respect . . . he's been honest with you, and we must give him credit for that. He's as straight as a die, Grandy.'

'You don't have to tell me, Paula. Jim's not duplicitous. Far from it, and I told him yesterday morning that I appreciated his truthfulness. Half-hearted, unenthusiastic executives spell disaster to me.'

'Then you're not too angry with him?' Paula asked, clutching the phone tensely, holding her breath.

'That was only a passing feeling yesterday. It quickly dissipated,' Emma said. 'We can't let emotions take charge of us in business, we must always deal from intelligence, but then I've told you that all of your life. Sorry to keep repeating myself.'

'That's all right, and I must admit I'm relieved you're taking this so well, Grandma. He'd never *intentionally* do anything to hurt or upset you.'

Brushing this remark aside, considering it unimportant, Emma said, 'I want you to relax, Paula. This is not really your problem. Anyway, we do have everything under control. Actually, when I was talking to Winston after Jim had left, it occurred to me – and rather forcibly – that things are not going to be much *different* at Consolidated. Winston was sitting there, grousing away, going on and on *ad infinitum* about being overworked, listing his present duties, demanding to know how I expected him to cope with everything. And as he talked his head off I began to realize that he's actually been carrying the administrative and business load at Consolidated for the longest time. He's been functioning as managing director without knowing it. I told him so, told him he was now getting the title to go with his tremendous responsibilities, plus a large raise in salary. You know Winston has a great sense of humour, and he began to laugh. He said, "Damn it, Aunt Emma, we both think we're so smart, so why haven't we realized before today how brilliant *I* am?" So, darling, you don't have to be concerned about me, Consolidated, or Winston either.'

'I'm glad to hear that, Grandy. Look, can I ask you something? It's about the shares in Consolidated. Why are you changing your will and leaving your interest to the twins?'

'What a funny question. I thought I'd made it clear, thought that you'd understood me. Surely it's obvious – I'm leaving my shares in the newspaper company to the twins because they are *your* children, Paula. What other reason could there be?' Emma murmured, sounding extremely perplexed.

'None, I just wondered, that's all,' Paula answered. 'However, it struck me the other day that your decision might have something to do with Jim. You know, because he's a Fairley. I mean, if his grandfather had hung on to the *Gazette* it would have been his today, wouldn't it?'

Emma burst into peals of laughter. 'I very much doubt that,' she gasped. Immediately recovering herself, she said, 'Edwin Fairley would have lost the paper eventually, as I've told you before. Besides, the Fairleys owned only the *Yorkshire Morning Gazette*, none of the other papers in the Consolidated chain. You know I acquired those myself, and with the help of my brothers.' Her incredulous laughter reverberated down the wire again. 'You can't possibly think that I feel *guilty* about the Fairleys,' she spluttered, obviously highly entertained by this idea.

'Of course I don't,' Paula exclaimed heatedly, wishing

she had never brought the subject up, realizing that she had been right, and Jim wrong, all along.

'I should hope not, my darling girl,' Emma said, stifling her merriment. 'I've always admitted that I gave the Fairleys a few nudges, and very sharp ones at that, as they waltzed down the path to folly which they had chosen for themselves. But I can assure you that I never once lost a wink of sleep about any of my actions. I was delighted I was able to turn the tables on them, come out the big winner. So don't think for one minute that I'm troubled by any guilty feelings about a lot of dead Fairleys, or Jim for that matter. And if he has suggested such a thing to you, you can tell him from me that he's wrong, quite wrong.'

'Oh no, he didn't bring it up,' Paula lied smoothly, knowing such an admission would annoy her grandmother. 'It was merely a thought that flitted through my active brain.'

Emma chuckled under her breath at Paula's hurried response, uncertain of its veracity. She said, 'I hope you feel better now that we've cleared the air about Jim's resignation.'

'Yes, Gran, you always help me to get everything in its right perspective.'

CHAPTER 19

Ten days later Emma could not conceive how she had managed to do all that she had since she had been in London. But she had worked miracles, accomplished more in that brief span of time than in the last six months. Or so it seemed to her this afternoon as she glanced at her check list on the yellow legal pad.

She had reviewed her various business enterprises, to be certain everything was in perfect order and to reassure herself that there would be no snags during her long absence. She had met with her solicitors several times, and with her banker Henry Rossiter, and she and Henry had even been able to spend a couple of pleasant social evenings together. There had been long sessions with Winston and Alexander respectively; she had conferred with Sarah, approved all of the designs for the 1970 Spring Collection of Lady Hamilton clothes and had gone over the new advertising campaign with her. And as she had worked late at the store, rushed hither and yon, switching mental gears as she went from one meeting to the next, she had found time to pull together that all-important wardrobe for her round-the-world trip with Blackie.

Emma felt settled in her mind about everything – except Jonathan. He was her enemy. She did not know the reason why, nor could she prove it. Nonetheless, Emma was filled with the growing conviction that he was the one grandchild she could not trust.

Opening the folder on her desk, her shrewd eyes scanned the report from private investigators she had engaged to check on Jonathan's activities in his business and personal life. They had turned up nothing untoward, but this did not convince her that he was innocent of any wrongdoing. The firm of Graves and Saunderson would have to dig deeper, look farther afield. She was positive there was something – somewhere.

All of her life Emma Harte had been able to see through everyone, had the gift of second-guessing her family and friends and adversaries alike. It was almost as if she had a demon telling her things. She also possessed that highly sensitive built-in antenna which born survivors are usually blessed with, a sort of sixth sense that enabled her to pick up vibrations – both good and bad, but especially bad. And then of course there was her gut instinct which she had come to trust, to rely on without questioning it, knowing it would never mislead her. For some time now, all of her faculties of acute perception had combined to alert her to trouble brewing, yet so far she had not put her hand on anything concrete. Still, it was there, as if hovering in the dark, and just beyond her reach.

Her gaze now settled on the few brief paragraphs about Sebastian Cross. They were good friends, he and Jonathan, real intimates, in fact, but that was the extent of it. When she had first learned of their close relationship, which dated back to their school days at Eton, she had wondered whether or not there was a homosexual involvement here. But apparently not, quite to the contrary, according to Mr Graves. She closed the folder with a decisive slap. There was no point in reading it over and over again. That was a waste of time. Besides, she had gone through it with a small-tooth comb already, searching for one single clue, a small lead, and had come up empty-handed. Emma slipped the folder in the desk and locked the drawer, not wanting to dwell any longer on the possibility of treachery.

A dismal feeling trickled through her. It had been painful and sad for her to resort to these awful and chilling measures – to put detectives on one of her own kin. But she had not known what else to do. And she had only ever taken such a dreadful step – spied on someone – once in her life before, and then, like now, it had been repugnant, had gone against her nature. Some forty years ago she had seen fit to have the activities of her second husband monitored . . . to protect herself and her children. She was suddenly struck by the bitter irony of the present situation. Her second husband, Arthur Ainsley, had been Jonathan's grandfather.

Sitting back in the chair, Emma wrestled with another pressing problem – whether or not to discuss her suspicions about Jonathan with Alexander and Paula. Maybe it would be wisest to confide in them. What if something happened to her when she was abroad? What if she fell sick? Or dropped dead? She did not think there was much chance of either. She was in good health and she felt strong and vital, and certainly she was more energetic than ever. On the other hand, she *would* be eighty years old in a couple of days. Perhaps, to be on the safe side, she ought to tell them. They were her chief heirs. Her empire would be under their control one day in the future . . .

There was a knock on the door and as she said, 'Come in', Gaye Sloane's face appeared around it. 'Do you need anything else, Mrs Harte?' her private secretary asked.

Emma shook her head. 'No, Gaye, thanks very much. I'm waiting for Paula. We're going out to dinner. But there's no need for you to hang around. You might as well get off.'

'Thanks, Mrs Harte, I will. See you tomorrow, and good night.'

'Good night, Gaye dear.'

Ten minutes later Paula walked in, and Emma looked up from the papers on her desk, her face softening. 'Paula, you look awfully tired!' she exclaimed, her worry resounding audibly. 'You've got dark shadows and you're very pale. Are you sure you're all right?'

'Yes,' Paula reassured her, and gave her a small rueful smile as she flopped down into the chair opposite the desk. 'It's been one of those beastly days. Interminable problems with the French Week planned for July.'

'What kind of problems?' Emma asked, straightening up and then leaning over the desk, resting her chin in her hands.

'People problems mostly. You know, temperaments, ruffled feathers, noses out of joint. But I've managed to get things moving smoothly again. I really miss Emily, though, Grandy. She was always so good at pulling our special events together, and she was certainly a soothing influence on everybody.'

'That's part of Emily's talent, I've always thought. I know she used to make the store managers tremble in their

298

boots, but she usually had them eating out of her hand in the long run, charming them all the way. Perhaps you ought to consider getting an assistant – someone to replace Emily.' Emma's brows lifted. 'Why not?'

'Oh I don't know – ' Paula shrugged. 'I think I can cope, anyway, let's not worry about that now. The French Week is finally under control and I don't foresee any more major difficulties cropping up. God forbid! In the meantime, did you get a chance to look at the boutique plans? And did you speak to Merry?'

'Yes, I did. This afternoon. I spent an hour poring over the plans and then I phoned her, told her you both had my blessing. You were right, Paula, the scheme is excellent, and we should do very well with the boutiques.'

'Oh I'm so glad you agree, Grandy.' Paula looked pleased as she added, 'Merry worked so hard, and *she* deserves all the credit, not I. Incidentally, I mentioned our new venture to Emily yesterday. Since she's going to Hong Kong early next month, I thought she might keep her eyes open for special merchandise for the boutiques. You know, straw hats and bags, sandals, pretty shawls, summer jewellery, *anything* really that would be suitable for holiday and resort wear.'

Emma nodded her approval. 'Very good thought, and Emily does have a penchant for spotting fashionable goods.' She paused, placed a pile of papers in a blue folder, then glanced up, gave her granddaughter a careful look. 'Did Emily tell you anything special? I mean, confide anything in you?'

Paula began to laugh. 'I suppose you're referring to her new boyfriend. I must admit, she's being awfully cagey with me, and that's not like Emily. We've always shared our secrets, as you well know. However, she hasn't shared a thing about her new love, other than to drop hints that he's gorgeous, and special. She calls him her mysterious lover, no, *secret* lover. Mind you, I'm sure he's not *actually* her *lover*,' Paula suddenly thought to add, being protective of Emily, not wanting her grandmother to get the wrong impression about the young girl's morals. 'You know how she tends to exaggerate.'

Emma bit back a smile, filling with understanding. 'You don't have to defend Emily to me, Paula dear. I know she's not promiscuous . . . she hasn't followed in her mother's footsteps, that's one thing I'm absolutely certain of. However, he *is* her lover.'

Paula said, very startled, 'How do you know that?'

'Why I got it from the horse's mouth,' Emma announced, mischief sparking her tired eyes with sudden life. She sat back and grinned at Paula.

'You're looking like the cat that's swallowed the canary, Grandy,' Paula laughed. 'Which horse?'

'*Emily*. She told me all about him herself. And the so-called secret lover is no longer a *secret*, neither is he very mysterious.' Emma's mouth twitched with amusement as she watched Paula, noted the surprised expression settling on her face.

'Oh,' was all Paula could manage.

Emma's light laugh rang out. 'Emily came to see me the night before last, and she was rather blunt – in her usual fashion. She said, "Gran, I'm terribly in love, and it's very serious. I'm sleeping with him, but I don't want you to worry. I won't get pregnant. I'm taking birth control pills." That didn't surprise me, after all she was always a rather practical girl . . . Emily does have her head screwed on the right way, like you. In fact, Elizabeth could take a few lessons from the two of you. Well, I *was* taken aback, I don't mind admitting *that*, but not shocked, though I suspect Emily had anticipated that I would be. I wonder occasionally if that girl thinks I'm the Virgin Mary. Anyway, she was very honest, endearingly so.' Emma paused, then smiled her very special smile that filled her face with radiance. 'Our little Emily has stars in her eyes right now, darling. She's genuinely in love. Very much so.'

'But who *is* he?' Paula pressed. 'You said he's not mysterious, so it must be somebody I know.'

'Oh yes, it is.' Emma chuckled and her eyes twinkled brightly. She was suddenly enjoying herself, enjoying teasing Paula, glad to turn away from the unpleasantness surrounding Jonathan, which she found so appalling.

'Come on, don't be so mean,' Paula admonished, smiling herself, picking up on her grandmother's gaiety which was infectious. 'Tell me his *name*, for heaven's sake! I'm dying to know.'

'Winston.'

'*Winston*,' Paula gasped, and her violet eyes widened. 'I don't believe it!'

'Oh but you must, because it's absolutely true. Don't look so shocked, darling. Winston's very eligible, and let's face it, he has lots of charm, a lot going for him. He's also rather good looking. He's a lot like me, you know.'

Paula hooted with laughter, tickled by this small show of personal vanity on her grandmother's part. She said, 'Yes, Grandma, I have noticed the resemblance from time to time.' She then continued, 'The *only* reason I'm thunderstruck is because this news is so unexpected. And rather startling, I mean, Winston and Emily . . . goodness me, when did they become romantically entangled? When did all this start?' Paula's black brows drew together in a sudden frown. 'Oh dear, what about nice Allison Ridley?'

'Yes, nice Allison indeed. That part is sad – I always rather liked that young woman. But I'm afraid it's off with her. Winston spoke to me yesterday about Allison, explained that he went to see her, told her as kindly and as gently as possible that it's over between them. As to the first part of your question, I believe Emily and Winston realized the depth of their feelings for each other on the day of the christening. Winston asked me if I minded about his involvement with Emily and I told him I didn't, that I was delighted.' Emma once again leaned across the desk, the expression of deeply-felt happiness flashing on her face. She confided, 'I had a business meeting with Winston this morning, and after we'd finished, he brought out the ring he's bought for Emily. It's an emerald.' Emma paused, then announced, 'Winston asked my permission to marry Emily. I gave it, and they're going to announce their engagement this week, before I leave for New York.'

'Oh Gran, this is going a bit fast isn't it?' Paula asked softly, and with a hint of concern, staring at Emma.

'I wouldn't say that, dear,' Emma remarked. 'They're hardly strangers, Paula. They grew up together, and I should think they know each other pretty well by now. They won't have any unpleasant surprises about each other after they're married. Of course the wedding can't take place until *next* summer, what with my trip to Australia and their travelling. But frankly, I'm relieved to know Emily has someone to look after her . . . I won't be around forever, you know. Yes, I find it most satisfying that those two are settling down together, most satisfying indeed. It gives me a lovely warm feeling here.' She patted her chest, continuing to smile.

'If you're happy and Emily is happy then I am too,' Paula said. 'And come to think of it, she and Winston were extremely close when they were little . . . they're admirably suited. Shouldn't I call her, Gran, to congratulate her?' Paula half rose, made to reach for the telephone on Emma's desk.

Emma said, 'I don't think you'll find her at Belgrave Square. She was going to the theatre with Winston, and she's probably left the flat by now.' Glancing at her watch, Emma nodded. 'Yes, it's already turned seven. You'll have to ring her late tonight. In the meantime, I really think I've got to get out of this place, I've been here since eight this morning. I've had it – and you look as if you have too.'

Emma stood up, frowning at Paula as she did. 'Are you sure you're quite well?'

Paula summoned a smile. 'Never better, Gran,' she fibbed, not wanting to worry her grandmother.

Privately Emma thought that Paula looked completely exhausted, worn down. She had never seen the girl like this and it concerned her. But she made no further comment, and turning away she picked up her handbag. Her mouth tightened imperceptibly. She had a sneaking suspicion that for all his easy grace and lighthearted charm and boyish manner, Jim Fairley was a difficult man. But she would not pry, nor would she try to live her granddaughter's life for her.

As they left the office, Emma said, 'I've booked a table at Cunningham's – I hope you fancy fish.'

'Yes, and I'm not very hungry anyway, Gran.'

Later, over dinner at the Mayfair oyster bar and fish restaurant, Paula's appearance underwent a change, one which pleased Emma. Her alabaster complexion took on a soft shell-pink cast, and her eyes lost their haunted expression as she visibly relaxed. By the time coffee was served Paula seemed so much more like her normal self, Emma made a decision: She would take Paula into her confidence. Before they left Cunningham's this evening she would make brief mention of her suspicions about Jonathan, but casually so, and in passing. She felt it was necessary to warn Paula; on the other hand she did not wish to alarm her unduly. And tomorrow, when she had dinner with Alexander, she would apprise *him* of the situation. In one sense it was more important that he was alerted, put on his guard, since Jonathan Ainsley worked for Harte Enterprises.

CHAPTER 20

It was 30 April and today she was eighty years old.

She awakened early, as was usual, and as she lay in her bed, shaking off the residues of sleep, she thought: Today is a special day, isn't it? And then instantly she remembered why this day was different from others. *It was her birthday*.

Emma had an aversion to lying in bed once she was awake, and she pushed herself up and brought her feet to the floor, half smiling to herself as she padded across the carpet to the windows. *She had made it*. She had never imagined she would live so long. Why, she was eleven years older than this century. In 1889, in that small cottage in Top Fold in Fairley village, her mother Elizabeth Harte had brought her into the world.

Drawing the draperies, she peered out. Her smile widened. It was a gorgeous day, full of sunshine and a startling brilliance. The sky was a crystalline blue and cloudless, and the trees below her in Belgrave Square were full blown and brightly green, their heavily-laden branches undulating with shimmering light under the breeze. She had been born on such a day as this, a balmy spring day, her mother had once told her, a day that was unusually warm for this time of year, especially in the cool Northern climes of Yorkshire.

Emma stretched. She felt alert and refreshed after a good night's rest, and as vigorous as she had ever been. Full of piss and vinegar, she thought, and immediately an image of her brother Winston flashed into her mind. That had been his favourite expression to describe her, when she had been revved up and bubbling over with enthusiasm, energy and drive. She wished he was still alive, and her younger brother, Frank. Sudden sadness streamed through her, but it was fleeting. Today was not a day for feeling sorry for herself, for missing those whom she had so dearly loved and who had departed this world. Today was a day for positive thoughts. A day for celebration. A day for looking to the future, concentrating on the younger generation . . . her grandchildren.

If all of her children except Daisy were lost to her, at least she had the immense satisfaction of knowing that their offspring would carry her bright banner forward, continue the great dynasty she had created, preserve her mighty business empire.

She stopped abruptly, paused in her progress across the room, and asked herself if it was a ferocious personal vanity that had fostered the dynastic impulse in her. *A desire for immortality perhaps?* She was not certain. But she did comprehend one thing – to produce a dynasty such as she had done, it was absolutely necessary to view ambition on the grandest of scales, to imbue it in others.

Emma laughed out loud. It was just conceivable that she had always envisioned herself as being larger than life, different, and so truly indomitable she was not mortal at all. Egotism, she thought, and once more her rippling laughter filled the silent bedroom. Her enemies had frequently labelled her the total and supreme egotist. But why not? It was the truth, indeed it was. And without her enormous ego surely she would never have done the things she had done, accomplished all that she had. That ego, that belief in herself, had given her courage and self-confidence, had propelled her forward and upward, right to the top. To the glittering pinnacle of success.

Well, she didn't have time to waste this morning, contemplating her motives, analysing the internal forces that had driven her all the days of her life. She had done what she felt had to be done, and, very simply, that was that. She walked purposefully into the bathroom to prepare herself

305

for the day facing her, shoving to one side these thoughts, deeming them unimportant.

An hour later, after she had bathed, dressed and breakfasted, Emma hurried downstairs to the second floor of her maisonette. She looked fresh and vitally alive, dressed in a crisply tailored light-wool dress in a shade of delphinium blue. She wore splendid jewellery with it – sapphire earrings and a matching brooch pinned on to one shoulder, a double strand of pearls, Paul's wedding ring and Blackie's large diamond. Not one hair of her immaculate, gleaming silver head was out of place, her makeup was perfect, and the bounce in her step belied her great age.

Emma still lived in Belgrave Square in the elegant, beautifully appointed mansion which Paul McGill had purchased for them in the late summer of 1925, soon after the birth of their daughter Daisy. At the time, catering to Emma's fear of vicious gossip, her reluctance to flaunt their relationship and her overwhelming need to be discreet and circumspect, he had had the house remodelled into two flats. And he had spared no expense in the process. The noted architect he had engaged had designed small bachelor quarters on the ground floor for Paul; the three floors which soared above were transformed into the luxurious triplex flat for Emma, Daisy, the nanny, and the rest of the staff. To the outside observer, the bachelor apartment and the large airy flat spanning three floors were entirely separate, were two distinct, self-contained dwellings, each having its own entrance. However, the two were ingeniously linked by a private interior elevator, which ran between the small hall in Paul's bachelor quarters to the larger and more elegant foyer in Emma's flat on the next floor. Because of this lift, the dwellings operated efficiently as one house.

During the war years, immediately following Paul's crippling accident and tragic suicide in Australia in 1939, Emma had closed up his bachelor flat. Unable to enter it without breaking down with uncontrollable grief and searing despair, she had turned her back on these rooms, ignoring them except for having them regularly cleaned. In 1948, when she was finally able to confront his possessions, she had had some of the rooms modernized and redecorated. Since then she had utilized the smaller downstairs flat as guest quarters for visiting friends or her grandchildren.

Parker, her butler, was busy sorting the morning post when Emma walked into her study. This was a pleasant, airy room of medium size, comfortably furnished with country antiques.

'Happy birthday, Mrs Harte,' said Parker, looking up and smiling. 'Quite a heavy post this morning, madam.'

'Oh my goodness, I see what you mean!' Emma exclaimed. The butler had stacked a staggering amount of mail on the chintz-covered sofa, and was methodically opening envelopes with a paper knife, removing the birthday cards, and throwing the envelopes into the wastepaper basket.

Emma joined him in this task, but soon she had to keep breaking off to answer the phone, and then, not long afterwards, the door bell began ringing as flowers and gifts arrived in a steady and continuing stream. Parker and Mrs Ramsey, the housekeeper, had their hands full, and Emma was left alone to cope with the post.

At about eleven-thirty, when the activity was at its height Daisy McGill Amory walked in, unexpected and unannounced.

Emma's youngest daughter would be forty-four in May, but she did not look her age. She had a slender figure, softly curling black hair that framed her tranquil, unlined face, and luminous blue eyes that mirrored her lovely disposition and gentle nature. Unlike her daughter Paula, who favoured a hard-edged chic and was extremely fashion conscious, Daisy was more like Emma in her taste in clothes. She always chose soft, rather feminine outfits, and this morning she wore a simple lilac wool suit and a matching blouse with a frilly jabot which fell down the front, gold jewellery, and black patent pumps and handbag.

'Happy happy birthday, Mother,' Daisy said from the doorway, her expression loving, her eyes awash with tenderness.

Emma looked up from the pile of envelopes and broke into smiles. She was delighted to see Daisy, welcomed her calm presence. Springing up from behind the desk, Emma went to greet her with affection and warmth.

'This is from us . . . David and I do hope you like it, Mummy.' She laughed. 'You're awfully hard to buy for, you know. You *do* have everything.' She thrust a package at Emma.

'Thank you, Daisy, and since you have the best taste in the world I'm sure it's going to be something quite lovely.'

Sinking on to the sofa, Emma began to unwrap Daisy's gift. 'All this fuss! And at my age!'

Daisy knew that her mother was enjoying every minute, despite her protestations. She joined her on the sofa and said, 'But Mummy, that's just the point. This is an important day . . . you must sit back, relax, and savour every minute of it.'

'Perhaps you're right. But it certainly looks as if I'll never get to the store this morning.'

Daisy stared at her, her bright blue eyes aghast. 'You can't go to work this morning, darling, it – '

'Why ever not?' Emma interrupted. 'I *always* go to work.'

'Not today you're not! It wouldn't be appropriate.' Daisy shook her head vigorously. 'Besides,' she paused, glanced at her watch and went on, 'in a short while I'm going to take you off to lunch.'

'But I – '

'No buts, my darling Mamma,' Daisy said, her tone amused yet firm. 'I'm not your daughter, *and* Paul McGill's, for nothing. I can be just as tough as he *was*, and as you *are*, when I want to be. And this is one of those days when I'm putting my foot down. *Hard*. We haven't had lunch together for the longest time, and in a few days you'll be leaving with Uncle Blackie – and you'll be gone for months, from what *I* hear. Please don't disappoint me, I've been so looking forward to it, and I've already reserved a table at the Mirabelle.'

Emma smiled at Daisy, her favourite, her best-loved child. She had always found it hard to refuse her anything. 'All right,' she said, relenting. 'We'll have lunch together, and then I'll go to the store this afternoon. Oh Daisy, this is lovely!' Emma now exclaimed, staring at the solid gold, handmade evening bag she held in her hands. 'Why, darling, it's simply beautiful.' Her pleasure was apparent as she turned the bag around, opening it, looked inside, closed it. After examining it for a few seconds longer, she returned it to its protective black leather case, leaned over and kissed her daughter. 'Thank you, Daisy, this is stunning. And perfect for my trip, since it'll go with all my evening clothes.'

Daisy nodded, pleased and relieved that the gift was a success. 'That's what David and I thought, and we really racked our brains to come up with an unusual present. Are you sure you like the style? If you don't, Asprey's will be happy to send a salesperson over with two or three others for you to look at.'

'No, no, I don't want to see anything else, I like this one,' Emma assured her. 'Actually, I shall carry it tonight.'

The phone rang. 'Shall I get that for you, Mummy?'

'Would you, darling, please?'

Daisy leaned over the desk, took the phone, answered crisply. There was a brief exchange of pleasantries and after a moment Daisy said, 'I'll see if she can come to the phone. It's a little hectic here this morning. Just a minute, please.' Depressing the hold button, Daisy glanced at her mother. 'It's Elizabeth. She's back in London. Do you want to speak to her? I think perhaps you should.'

'Of course I'll speak to her.' Emma crossed to the desk. If she was surprised she did not show it, and she said steadily, 'Hello, Elizabeth.' Sitting down, she leaned back in the chair and cradled the receiver on her shoulder, toying with the pen in the onyx inkstand.

'Thank you,' she responded shortly, 'yes, it *is* a grand age, but I don't feel eighty. More like fifty-eight! And I'm as fit as a fiddle.' There was another pause. Emma focused her eyes on the wall opposite. They narrowed slightly and suddenly she cut in peremptorily, 'I think Winston was simply being courteous when he asked my permission. It wasn't really necessary. I don't think I have to remind you that Emily is of age. She can do anything she wants. And *no*, I didn't speak to Tony. I thought it was up to Emily to break the news to her father.'

Emma fell silent as her middle daughter talked incessantly at the other end of the phone. She looked across at Daisy, and made a face, rolled her eyes heavenward. Her patience began to dwindle and she interrupted again. 'I thought you phoned to wish me a happy birthday, Elizabeth, not to complain about Emily's engagement.'

An ironic smile flitted across Emma's face as she listened to Elizabeth's protests that she was not complaining.

'I'm glad to hear you say so,' Emma said into the receiver, 'because that would be a waste of breath. Now, how was your trip to Haiti? And how's your new boyfriend – Marc Deboyne?'

Elizabeth gurgled ecstatically into Emma's ear for a few more minutes, and finally Emma brought their conversation to a close with a brisk, 'Well, I'm glad you're happy, and thank you for calling, and for the birthday present. I'm sure it will arrive here any minute. Goodbye, Elizabeth.' She hung up.

Daisy asked, 'Is she upset about Emily and Winston?'

Emma laughed with some acerbity. 'Of course not. She's just making appropriate noises because she wasn't informed first, before me. You know Elizabeth as well as I do, she's very self-involved. But it was nice of her to ring up for my birthday.' Emma walked back to the couch and sat down. She gave Daisy an odd look, and half shrugged. 'Edwina phoned earlier, and so did Robin and Kit . . . I must say, I was very surprised to hear from my sons. I haven't heard a peep out of them, since that debacle over the will last year. Then today they're as nice as pie, and tell me they've sent me gifts too. Can you believe it?'

'Perhaps they're sorry, Mother, regret their plotting – '

'I doubt it!' Emma exclaimed softly. 'I'm far too cynical to think that either of *them* would have a change of heart. No, I'm sure their wives were behind the calls. June and Valerie have always been decent women. I can't imagine how they've managed to put up with my sons all these years. Kit plots. Robin schemes. Oh well – ' Emma reached out now and took Daisy's hand in hers. 'There's something I've been meaning to ask you, darling. It's about this house . . . are you sure you don't want it?'

Daisy was startled, and she said in a surprised voice, "But you've left this house to Sarah, haven't you?"

'Yes. However, I only bequeathed it to her because you indicated that you weren't interested in owning it, when we discussed the matter last year. But it should be yours or your children's. After all, your father did buy it for *us*.'

'I know, and I've always adored this house. It holds so many special memories for me . . . of my years growing up, of Daddy and you, and the lovely times the three of us had here. It is a little big though, and – '

Emma held up a silencing hand. 'Not if you think of it as two flats rather than one house. He did that for me, as you know. I did so want to keep up appearances . . .' Emma broke off and started to laugh. 'Goodness, Daisy, how times have *changed*. People think nothing of living together quite openly these days. Anyway, getting back to the disposition of this house, I thought you might want to reconsider. You have grandchildren now. Philip's bound to marry one day and in the not too distant future, I expect. He'll have children, he may even want to send them to school in England. Two self-contained flats under one unifying roof is awfully useful.'

'I'm not sure what to say, Mother. Your points are well taken, though.'

'Think about it. I can always change my will.'

'But you've left me so much . . . more than I'll ever need. It seems greedy, accepting this house.'

'That's a load of codswallop, Daisy. By rights it should be yours. If you decline, then I think that perhaps I'd better leave it to Paula or Philip.'

'But what about Sarah?'

'She's not a McGill.'

Daisy pursed her lips thoughtfully. 'All right, I'll do as you say – think about it. Look here, Mother, I know a woman of your immense wealth has to have her affairs in proper order at all times, but to tell you the truth, I do hate these discussions about your will and your death. They really make my stomach churn. Your death is certainly something I can't bear to think about, never mind discuss in this off-handed way. I get very upset.'

Emma looked at Daisy, said nothing. She squeezed her hand, sat back, continuing to stare at her intently.

Daisy took a deep breath, exhaled, forced a weak smile. 'Sorry, I didn't mean to speak to you so harshly. However, I do especially dislike talking about such things today, of *all* days. It's your birthday, remember.'

'I understand.' There was a tiny silence, and eventually Emma said in the quietest voice, 'I have been a good mother to you, haven't I, Daisy darling?'

'How could you ever think otherwise!' Daisy cried, her face ringed with concern. Her large and brilliant eyes of the deepest cornflower blue widened considerably, unexpectedly filled. 'You've been the most wonderful mother anyone could ever have wished for, always so loving and understanding.' Daisy returned Emma's steadfast gaze unblinkingly, and as she looked deeply into that wrinkled face her heart clenched with the most profound love for this remarkable woman who had borne her. She knew that the forbidding demeanour and the permanently stern expression were only surface characteristics, camouflage for a vast reservoir of emotion, and compassion. Emma Harte was a complex, many-faceted person, and contrary to what some believed, she was much more vulnerable and sensitive than most.

Daisy's gentle face underwent another change as her adoration and loyalty to her mother rose up in her. 'You're so very special, Mummy.' Daisy stopped, searched Emma's face, and shook her head wonderingly. 'You're the most honourable and loving person I've ever known. I've been so very lucky to have you all these years. Really blessed.'

Emma was deeply moved. 'Thank you, Daisy, for saying those beautiful things.' She looked into the distance, then murmured in a saddened voice, 'I've failed miserably with your half-brothers and half-sisters. I couldn't bear to think that I'd also failed with you. Or that I'd ever let you down in any way, not given you my best and dearest love.'

'You've given me everything . . . why, I couldn't begin to tell you what I owe you. And I don't believe you've failed the others. Not in the slightest. Didn't my father say once that each of us is the author of our own lives? That we are responsible for what we are? For the deeds, both good and bad, that we do?'

'He did.'

'Then *believe* it, Mother. It's true!'

'If you say so, darling.'

Emma fell into momentary silence, reflecting on her daughter's words. She was proud of Daisy, or the woman

313

she had become. For all her sweetness, her soft manners and her intrinsic charm, Daisy had a strong, even tough, inner core and immense resilience and fortitude. Emma knew that when she chose to be, her Daisy was as immovable as a mountain and unwavering in her resoluteness. This was especially true if her convictions and principles were involved. Daisy, so young looking, was also inordinately youthful in her attitudes. She had a gaiety, a joyousness about life that was infectious, and she was of that rare breed of women who are liked by their own sex as well as by men. In fact, Emma was well aware that most people found it difficult, if not indeed impossible, to dislike Daisy. She was so full of integrity, so honourable, so beyond reproach, yet so truly human and caring, she towered above everyone. If her half-brothers and half-sisters were jealous of her, even resented her slightly, they were nevertheless rendered helpless under the force of her warm personality and extraordinary sincerity. It was her goodness, purity, and sense of fair play that also kept them off balance and at bay. She was the conscience of the family.

'You've got a faraway look on your face, Mother. Are you daydreaming? You seem so intense all of a sudden, what are you thinking about?' Daisy leaned closer to Emma, searching her face, and touching her cheek lightly.

'Oh nothing much.' Emma shook off her introspection, gave Daisy's clothes an appraising glance. 'Perhaps I ought to go and change, since we're going to the Mirabelle for lunch.'

'You don't have to, darling. Don't bother struggling into something else.'

'All right, I won't. But what about tonight. Blackie tells me he's wearing a dinner jacket. You don't think he actually wants me to wear a *long* frock, do you? I mean, after all, we're only going to be eight.'

Oh my God, Daisy thought, wait until she finds out it's

closer to sixty. She wondered if her mother would be annoyed with them for giving the surprise party. Clearing her throat, praying that she sounded off-hand, Daisy remarked, 'But Uncle Blackie wants this to be a festive evening, extra special. As he said to me the other day, "How often is your mother going to be eighty?" So naturally I agreed with him that we should dress. Still, you don't have to be that grand, wearing a long frock, I mean. I've decided on a peacock-blue faille cocktail dress myself. Look, I'd wear one of those lovely chiffons of yours, if I were you.'

'That's a relief. I have the green chiffon, it'll do quite nicely. Oh dear, there's the door bell *again*! I do hope it's not more flowers. This place is beginning to resemble a funeral parlour.'

'Mother! What an awful analogy!'

Daisy sprang up, moved swiftly across the floor, said over her shoulder, 'Perhaps it's the gift Elizabeth sent, or the ones from Kit and Robin. I'll go and ask Parker.'

Before Emma had a chance to blink, Daisy returned. 'It *is* a gift, Mother.' She glanced into the foyer, nodded, then took up a position near the fireplace, standing under the portrait in oils of Paul McGill.

Emma, acute as ever, peered at her suspiciously. 'What's going on? You looked exactly like your father did when he had something up his sleeve.' Her eyes strayed to Paul's portrait and then back to Daisy. There was no doubt whose daughter she was. Her likeness to him was more pronounced than ever today . . . the same bright blue eyes, the black hair, the cleft in the chin. 'Come on, what are you hiding?'

Daisy looked expectantly at the door and beckoned.

On cue, Amanda and Francesca walked in, doing their level best to be sedate and grown up. They came to a halt in the centre of the floor, focused on Emma.

'Happy birthday to you, dear Grandma, happy birthday

to you,' they chorused, sounding enthusiastic if slightly off-key.

Sarah, Emily and Paula had followed them into the study, stood behind their young cousins. They echoed, 'Happy birthday, Grandma,' gazing at her lovingly.

'Good heavens, what's all this!' Emma cried, truly taken by surprise. She gaped at her granddaughters, then addressing the twins, asked, 'And what are *you* two doing here? It's not half-term, is it?'

Daisy cut in, '*I* took them out of school for a couple of days, Mother. They're staying with me and David. After all, it *is* your birthday.'

'I knew somebody was cooking up *something*,' Emma said, giving Daisy a sharp penetrating look. 'To tell you the truth, I thought you and Blackie were conniving together, Daisy. I suspected that you'd planned some sort of celebration for tonight.'

Daisy managed to keep her face neutral. But before she got the opportunity to say anything, Emily came forward purposefully. She handed a beautifully-wrapped package to Francesca, and touched Amanda's shoulder lightly. 'You haven't forgotten your speech have you?'

'Course not,' Amanda hissed back indignantly, reached for Francesca's hand and gave her twin a little tug, drew them both nearer to Emma.

Taking a deep breath, the fifteen-year-old said carefully, enunciating each word clearly, 'Grandy, this gift is from all your grandchildren – from Philip, Anthony, Alexander, Jonathan, Paula, Sarah, Emily, Francesca and me. Each one of us has contributed to it, so that we could present you with something special on this your eightieth birthday. We give it to you with our very dearest love always.'

Amanda went to Emma, bent down and kissed her; Francesca followed suit, then handed her the present.

'Thank you, girls,' Emma said to the twins. 'And your little speech was very nicely rendered, Amanda. Well done.'

She looked over at their sister and cousins. 'My thanks to *all* of you.'

Emma sat for a moment without moving, holding the present on her lap. She let her eyes rest on each one of her elder granddaughters who were grouped together, and she smiled at them individually, nodding to herself, thinking how pretty and charming they looked. Tears welled unexpectedly, and she blinked them back, glanced down at the package, endeavouring to conceal her emotional reaction to this unexpected family scene. To her astonishment her hands shook as she untied the purple ribbon and lifted the object from its box.

The gift was a clock in the shape of an egg, made of the most translucent blue enamel she had ever set eyes on. A miniature cockerel, enamelled and delicately worked, was mounted on top of the egg, heavily jewelled with diamonds, rubies and sapphires. Emma marvelled at the design and craftsmanship, which were exquisite, and she recognized the clock for the precious work of art it truly was.

'It's by Fabergé, isn't it?' she managed at last, her voice hardly audible.

'Yes,' Emily said. 'Actually, Gran, it's an Imperial Easter egg which Fabergé made for the Empress Marie Fedorovna of Russia. Her son, Nicholas II, the last Tsar, ordered it for her.'

'How on earth did you manage to find something as rare and valuable as this?' Emma asked, awed. As an art collector of discernment she was aware that such pieces by Fabergé were becoming increasingly scarce.

'Paula heard about the clock through Henry Rossiter,' Emily volunteered. 'He had learned it was going to be auctioned last week at Sotheby's.'

'And Henry went to the auction for you?'

'No, Grandy. We all went *en masse*, except for the twins, who were at school, of course. Henry did come with us, though. Paula had called us, and we got together for a confab. We each agreed at once that we should try to buy the clock for you – as a collective gift from us. It was terribly exciting!'

'We almost lost it several times, but we just kept on going, topping other bids. And suddenly we had it. We were so thrilled, Grandma!'

'And so am I, my darlings.' Her eyes encompassed them all.

Parker suddenly appeared, also on cue from Daisy, bringing in a tray of glasses brimming with sparkling champagne. When each of them had a drink they clustered around Emma, wished her a happy birthday again, and toasted her health.

Once things had calmed down, Emma turned to Daisy and said, 'Are we really going to lunch at the Mirabelle? Or was that a ruse to prevent me from going to the store?'

Daisy grinned. 'Of course we're going to lunch – all of us who are present, in fact. Anthony, Alexander, Jonathan and David will be joining us. So, you can forget about going to work today, Mother.'

Emma was about to assert herself on this point, but she recognized the look on Daisy's face. Since it forbade argument, she held her tongue.

It was dusk.

Emma walked across the entrance foyer, so bosky and still at this hour, her step light as she entered her study.

She was dressed for the dinner party Blackie was giving at the Ritz, wearing a short dress made of layers and layers of pale and dark green chiffon, simply cut with long floating Mandarin sleeves. The magnificent McGill emeralds, blazing at her throat, on her ears, arms and hand, looked stunning against the mingled greens of the delicate fabric, the fire, depth and brilliance of the gems intensified by the repetition of their colour.

Yes, it was a good choice, Emma decided, as she passed

the one mirror in the room and caught a fleeting glimpse of herself. She did not stop, but continued across the floor, the only sound the swishing of her dress as she moved with her usual briskness.

When she reached the console where some of her many birthday presents were stacked, she picked up the Imperial Easter egg and carried it back to the drawing room.

Placing it on an antique occasional table near the fireplace, she stood back, admiring it again. It was undoubtedly one of the loveliest things she had ever been given, and she could not wait to show it to Blackie.

The sharp trilling of the bell made her start, and in rapid succession she heard Parker's footsteps resounding in the foyer, the front door banging and muffled voices.

A moment later Blackie was striding into the room, splendidly attired in a superbly-cut tuxedo, the wide grin on his face competing with the sparkle in his black eyes, and he was obviously buoyed up with excitement.

'Happy birthday, me darlin',' he boomed, and drawing to a standstill he swept her up into his arms. Then he released his grip, stepped away and caught her hands in his, looked down into her face, repeating the gestures practised on her for years. 'You look bonnier than ever tonight, Emma,' he said, beaming, and bent to kiss her.

'Thank you, Blackie.' Emma returned his smile, and moved towards the sofa. 'Did you tell Parker what you wanted to drink?'

'Sure and I did. My usual.' He lowered himself into the chair opposite her, his large frame filling it completely. 'I don't want you to think I've come empty handed – your birthday present is outside. I'll go and get it – '

The butler's discreet knock interrupted him, and Parker came in with a tumbler of neat Irish whiskey for Blackie and a goblet of white wine for Emma.

As soon as they were alone, Blackie raised his glass.

'Here's to you, mavourneen. And may we celebrate many, many more of our birthdays together.'

'I know we will,' Emma laughed. 'And here's to our trip, Blackie dear.'

'To the trip.' After only one sip, Blackie sprang up. 'Don't move,' he instructed, 'and when I tell you to close your eyes, I want you to do just that, and no cheating, mind you.'

She sat waiting for him to come back, guessed he had enlisted Parker's help when she heard the low murmur of the butler's voice, Blackie's response, then the sound of paper being ripped.

'Close your eyes,' Blackie ordered from the doorway several seconds later. 'Remember what I said, no peeking, Emma!'

'I won't,' she reassured him, laughter bringing a lilt to her voice. She sat perfectly still, her hands clasped in her lap, and she suddenly felt like a young girl again; like the little starveling girl who had received her first real present wrapped in silver paper and tied with silver ribbon. It had been from him – had been that cheap little green glass brooch which she had cherished all of her life. She still had it tucked away in her jewel case, alongside the fine replica he had eventually had made in emeralds. And once, long ago, that bit of green glass had been her most treasured and valuable possession.

'Now!' Blackie cried.

Slowly Emma opened her eyes, and as she looked at the painting he was holding in front of her she instantly recognized the work of her great-niece, Sally Harte. Emma gasped in astonished delight, and then she filled with a swift and piercing pain of poignant nostalgia as haunting memories rippled through her. Her throat tightened. She focused her eyes, took in every detail, every brushstroke, and she could only gaze at the painting's evocative beauty, unable to say a word.

'Oh Blackie,' she said at last, 'it's perfectly lovely . . . the moors above Fairley. My moors, where we first met.'

'Look a bit closer, me darlin'.'

'I don't have to, I can see it's the Top of the World.' She raised her eyes and shook her head in wonderment. 'What a truly meaningful gift this is, my dear old friend. The painting is extraordinary. Why I feel as though I can reach out and pick a bunch of that heather, as I used to do for my mother.' She let one finger rest lightly against the canvas, barely touching it. 'I can hear the tinkle of this little beck, here in the corner, and the sound of its crystal water tumbling down over the polished stones. It's so . . . so real, I can even smell the scent of bilberry and bracken and the heather. Oh Blackie darling . . .'

Emma looked up at him and smiled her incomparable smile, then swiftly brought her gaze back to the painting. 'It's a real Yorkshire sky, isn't it? So full of clarity and shimmering radiance. What immense talent that girl has, and only Turner and Van Gogh have ever been able to capture the true quality of light on canvas in such a way. Yes, Sally has surpassed herself with this.'

Gratification and pleasure shone on his craggy, expressive face. 'I took Sally over there myself, showed her the exact spot. And she kept going back, time and time again. She wanted perfection for you, Emma, as I did, and I think she got the painting just right in the end.'

'She most certainly did. Thank you, thank you so much for thinking of such an unusual present.'

Blackie said softly, 'I had her write this on the back. In paint.' He turned the painting around, indicated the neat lettering. 'You won't be able to read what it says without your glasses, so I shall tell you what I asked her to put. It says, "To Emma Harte on reaching her eightieth birthday with love from her life-long friend, Blackie O'Neill." Then there's the date underneath.'

For the second time that day, Emma was greatly moved.

She could not speak, and she turned away quickly so that he would not see her misty eyes. She sat down, took a sip of her drink, composed herself, and finally murmured, 'That's lovely, just lovely, darling.'

After propping the painting against a console table, and making sure it was in her direct line of vision, he returned to his seat and lifted his own glass. 'And it *is* a lifetime, too, Emma. Sixty-six years to be precise.' He nodded at the painting. 'Aye, the Top of the World – your mother's name for Ramsden Crags. I'll never forget the day you found me lost on the moors, and we came up out of the Ghyll and I saw the Crags for the first time.'

Emma followed the direction of his eyes. Over six decades dropped away and she saw herself as she had been at fourteen. A poor little servant girl . . . trudging across the moors at dawn in her broken-down button boots and the old patched coat Cook had given her. That coat had been a treasured item too, even though it had been small and tight and threadbare. It had hardly protected her from the rain and snow and bitter North wind.

Now she stared fully at Blackie, seeing him as he was tonight, but remembering how he had looked in his rough, drab workman's clothes and his cheap cloth cap worn at such a cheeky angle, carrying his sack of tools slung over his broad shoulder. *Disreputable*, Cook had called the dirty old burlap bag that contained *his* most treasured possessions – his hammers and trowels and mortar board.

Emma said slowly: 'Who would have thought that we would both live to such great ages . . . that we would acquire so much in our lifetimes . . . immense power, immeasurable wealth . . . that we would become what we are today.'

Blackie gave her an odd look, then chuckled, at the amazement ringing in her voice. 'I for one never doubted our rosy futures,' he announced, his voice underscored by a bubbling merriment. 'I told you I was going to be a toff,

322

a real millionaire, and that you would be a grand lady. Mind you, me darlin', I'll be confessing to you now that I never suspected you'd be quite as *grand* as you are.'

They both smiled, their wise old eyes holding, secure in their love and friendship, revelling in the knowledge that they truly understood each other, and as no other person alive did. So many years . . . so many experiences shared welded them. The bonds between them were like steel, and so strong they were unbreakable.

The silence drifted for a while.

Eventually Blackie roused himself. 'Now, mavourneen mine, tell me about your busy day.'

'One thing surprised me, Blackie. *They* called. *The plotters*. I was startled to hear from my sons and Elizabeth, I don't mind telling you. She's back in London of course. No doubt with the French boyfriend. Edwina gave me a ring this morning, and she was pleasant, believe it or not. Perhaps *she's* mended her ways finally. And I had two other most wonderful calls . . . they really touched me.' Her eyes lit up. 'Philip rang from Sydney, and your Shane from New York. Wasn't that nice?' He nodded, smiling, and she continued, 'It seems that your grandson and mine are planning birthday parties for me when we arrive in their cities, so be prepared. As for my day, well you can see for yourself what it's brought.' Emma waved her hand around, her eyes sweeping the room. 'Flowers, cards and so many gifts. And I had lunch with Daisy, David and my grandchildren at the Mirabelle.'

She proceeded to recount every detail of the luncheon party, then told him how they had whisked her away from the restaurant at three-thirty and taken her to her store in Knightsbridge. Marched by her grandchildren into her board room, she had been greeted by her top executives who were anxiously awaiting her arrival at the special reception they had arranged for her.

When she had finished this somewhat breathless recital,

Emma rose and picked up the Imperial Easter egg, said confidingly, 'This is what my grandchildren gave me, and like your painting it is a most meaningful gift. I shall treasure them both always.'

'So you had a lovely day – I'm glad. That's the way it should always be.' Blackie stood up. 'Come along, I think we'd better be on our way. We're meeting in Bryan's suite at the Ritz for a drop of bubbly before we go down to dinner.'

Ten minutes later when they arrived at the Ritz Hotel in Piccadilly, Blackie ushered Emma up the steps. He paused briefly at the reception desk, asked the young man behind it to announce his arrival to his son, Mr Bryan O'Neill, and gave the number of the suite.

'Of course, Mr O'Neill.' The young assistant manager smiled at Emma. 'Good evening, Mrs Harte.'

Emma acknowledged his greeting pleasantly, and after Blackie had expressed his thanks they proceeded along the lobby unaware how striking they looked and of the heads turned to watch them.

Emma remained silent as they rode up in the lift, and Blackie stole several surreptitious looks at her, wondering if she had any inkling about the party which had been planned with such secrecy. He could not hazard a guess. Her face, as always, was inscrutable. He believed Emma would not be angry, despite Daisy's prediction that her mother might easily react adversely. He knew his Emma, understood that she was like a child at times. She enjoyed surprises and gifts and special occasions, particularly when those occasions revolved around her.

That's because of the deprivations of her youth, he said to himself. In those days she had had nothing, nothing of any real value. No, that wasn't strictly true. She had had her startling looks, her brains, her stamina and her extraordinary health, and her enormous courage. Not to mention that terrible pride of hers. Oh that pride, and oh the shame she had experienced because of that pride and because she was poor. 'But poverty's not a crime, even though people who're better off always try to make you feel like a criminal,' she had once cried to him, her anger bringing a fierce dark gleam to her young eyes. Ah yes, he remembered everything . . . Emma had had more than her fair share of pain and sorrow and grief in her life. But she would not suffer again, nor ever be deprived again, and there would be no more pain. They were both far too old for tragedies . . . tragedies were for the young.

Finally they drew to a stop in front of the door to the suite. Blackie smiled inwardly. The phone call from reception had been the alert signal for Bryan and Daisy to keep the guests absolutely quiet. Obviously they had succeeded admirably. A pin dropping would have sounded like a gun going off in the silence permeating the corridor.

Giving Emma a final rapid glance, Blackie raised his hand and rapped. The door was opened almost at once by Daisy. 'There you are, Mother, Uncle Blackie. We've been waiting for you. Do come in.'

Blackie propelled Emma forward and stepped inside after her.

'*Happy birthday!*' fifty-eight people shrieked in unison.

That Emma was thunderstruck was immediately evident to everyone present. She stared at the crowd made up of relatives and friends who had gathered together to celebrate her birthday, her expression startled, and she coloured slightly, the blush rising from her neck to suffuse her face. Her eyes immediately swivelled to Blackie's, and she whispered, 'You devil! Why didn't you give me a hint, some warning at least?'

He grinned, gratified that the secret had obviously been well and truly kept. 'I didn't dare. Daisy said she'd kill me. And don't start telling me you're annoyed, because I can see from your face that you're not!'

325

'That's true,' she admitted and finally permitted herself to smile.

She swung her head, faced the packed room, and was momentarily rooted to the spot. The lingering smile slowly grew wider and wider as she noted the familiar faces smiling back at her in welcome.

Her two sons, Kit Lowther and Robin Ainsley, were there with their wives, June and Valerie; her daughters Edwina and Elizabeth flanked a distinguished-looking man who was outrageously handsome. She supposed this was the notorious Marc Deboyne – International White Trash, Emily had so succinctly labelled him. Still, he did have a rather fascinating smile and a glamorous aura. Elizabeth always went for the pretty ones, of course. Well, *she* was hardly the one to criticize. The men who had tenanted her life had had their fair share of good looks.

Daisy had slipped across the room, stood with her arm linked through David's, and he, in turn, was positioned next to her sisters-in-law, the two old ladies, Charlotte and Natalie, who were dressed to the nines and dripping with jewels. Paula and Jim hovered next to them; Winston was shepherding Emily, Amanda and Francesca, and was apparently enjoying his role of protector. Emma's eyes automatically dropped to Emily's left hand and she winked at her granddaughter when she spotted the glittering emerald engagement ring.

She stared beyond them into the adjoining suite, saw Sarah, Jonathan, Alexander and his girlfriend Maggie Reynolds crowded together in the entrance. On their left was the entire Kallinski family, and edging up to them were Bryan, Geraldine and Merry O'Neill. Positioned next to the latter were the rest of the Hartes. Randolph's beaming face peered out at her, just visible above the shoulders of his two daughters, Vivienne and Sally. Anthony, her grandson, smiled back at her from Sally's side.

Henry Rossiter was leaning against the fireplace at the far end of the second suite. He looks better than ever, Emma thought, and eyed his current girlfriend, the noted model Jennifer Glenn. She was at least forty years younger. That's one way to ensure a heart attack, dear Henry, Emma thought to herself, her eyes amused. Gaye Sloane, her private secretary, graced Henry's right, and the remainder of the guests were made up of old friends, as well as close business associates such as Len Harvey, who ran Genret, and his wife Monica.

Emma's initial stunned surprise had completely dissipated in the few minutes she had stood motionless surveying the gathering. Now she was again totally in command of herself, all those present, and this occasion. Looking autocratic, proud, dignified, and supremely elegant she took a step forward and inclined her head.

'Well,' she exclaimed, her strong clear voice ringing out as she broke the silence at last, 'I never realized I knew so many people who were capable of keeping a secret. At least, from *me*.' Their laughter rippled around her as she glided forward into their midst, accepting their affectionate greetings and good wishes with a graciousness that few could match.

Blackie edged over to Daisy, stood watching Emma circulating, dispensing her inimitable charm. And by the ladleful, he muttered under his breath. A huge grin suddenly illuminated his face and his eyes crinkled with humour. He exclaimed to Daisy, 'And you worried yourself to death, thinking she was going to be upset! Just *look* at her . . . she's in her element, handling them all with aplomb and behaving as if she's Royalty.'

CHAPTER 21

An hour later, at eight o'clock, Blackie escorted Emma into the private dining room farther along the corridor where the birthday celebration dinner was to be held.

Bending towards her, he whispered, 'Daisy didn't want anybody's feelings to be hurt, nor did she wish to be accused of favouritism, so none of your children or grandchildren will be sitting at our table.'

'That was smart of her,' Emma murmured, her mouth twitching with hidden laughter. Well, Daisy *was* the one true diplomat in the family; on the other hand, she knew her sons would not exactly be clamouring to sit with her. Emma was still astonished that they had deigned to come at all. Elizabeth's presence did not surprise her. It was just conceivable that her daughter wanted to make friends again, since she always had her eye on the main chance. No doubt she thought she could ingratiate herself, probably with the hopes of extracting more money. Her other motivations would be a desire to see her children and show off her new boyfriend. As for Edwina, she was currying favour with Anthony, who would have disapproved if his mother had declined the invitation.

Slowly she and Blackie crossed to the main table, which was flanked on either side by two other tables. All were arranged in a semi-circle around the small dance floor, and at the opposite side of this square of polished parquet a band was already playing a selection of popular music.

Emma's all-encompassing glance took in everything. In the flickering candlelight emanating from the five round tables, the room resembled a charming summer garden, with masses of flowers banked on every side, and small colourful bouquets decorating the tables. The latter were

328

covered in shell-pink tablecloths and gleamed brightly with the sparkle of crystal, silver and fine china.

Nodding with pleasure and smiling with approval, Emma turned to Blackie as they came to a standstill, and said, 'What a lovely setting Daisy has created . . . it's so very festive.'

Blackie beamed. 'Yes, she worked hard with the banqueting manager, and supervised everything herself.' He pulled out a chair for her, but remained standing himself.

Once she was seated Emma squinted at the place cards on either side of her, and said, 'I see you're on my right, Henry on my left, but who else will be joining us?'

'Charlotte and Natalie of course, Len and Monica Harvey, and Henry's girlfriend Jennifer. We've also got Mark and Ronnie Kallinski and their wives with us, which makes twelve altogether.'

'Oh I *am* glad some of the Kallinskis will be sitting with us. I couldn't help thinking of David tonight, wishing he were here. Although Ronnie doesn't look as much like David as Mark, he does remind me of his father. He has many of his mannerisms. Don't you agree?'

'I do indeed, me darlin'. Ah, here comes Randolph with his mother and his aunt.'

Emma half turned, welcomed Charlotte and Natalie, and with his usual flourish and show of old-world gallantry, Blackie ushered Emma's sisters-in-law to their seats.

Randolph, bluff and hearty as always, squeezed Emma's shoulder and boomed, 'I'm sitting at Bryan's table, over there. But I'll be back, Aunt Emma.' He winked at her. 'I intend to claim at least one dance.'

Laughing, Emma said, 'A foxtrot, Randolph, nothing more energetic than that.'

'You're on.'

His mother leaned over to Emma and confided, 'Emily's the best thing that has happened to that grandson of mine. I couldn't be more delighted about the engagement.'

'Oh so am I, Charlotte, and that was a sweet gesture of yours, giving Emily the strand of pearls as an engagement present. I remember when Winston gave them to you.'

Charlotte beamed. 'Yes, when we became engaged in 1919. Now, about the wedding. I do hope they'll get married in Yorkshire, Emma. Elizabeth was talking to me earlier, and she seems to think the wedding should be in London.'

'Does she now,' Emma said with dryness. 'I wouldn't worry about it for one moment. Elizabeth's always had grand ideas, and usually they're self-serving. Under the circumstances, I think it's for Emily and Winston to decide, and they've indicated to me that they want to get married in Ripon Cathedral. I think that's a lovely idea, and then we can have the reception at the house.'

The three women talked about Emily's wedding, planned for the following summer, for a few minutes longer and then Emma started to tell them about her impending trip with Blackie and the places they would visit on their journey to Australia.

Blackie continued to direct traffic, and within a few minutes the room had filled up, everyone was seated, and the waiters were gliding between the five tables, filling glasses with white wine. There was a feeling of conviviality and gaiety in the air. Laughter reverberated, the cacophony of voices rose to a crescendo, the hubbub of noise balanced by the strains of the light music playing in the background.

Emma, her mind as razor-sharp as always, her eyes everywhere, soon discerned that her family and friends were enjoying themselves wholeheartedly, appeared to be having the best of times. After the first course of smoked salmon had been served, some of the younger guests immediately took to the dance floor, and Emma watched them, filled with pride, thinking how attractive they looked . . . the girls in their pretty dresses, the young men in their smart dinner jackets. They whirled around the dance floor,

330

their clear young faces shining with happiness, their eyes bright with hope and limitless expectations for the future, their lives ahead of them, offering so much.

Jonathan's bland and smiling face came into her line of vision as he guided young Amanda around the perimeters of the floor, and for a split second she wondered if she had been wrong about him. She clamped down on this thought, not wanting to dwell on problems tonight, and swung her eyes to his father. Robin was dancing with his half-sister, Daisy, and oozing charm. Dark, exotic-looking Robin, once her favourite son, the dashing Member of Parliament, currently politically secure after a few rocky rides. Well, he *was* shrewd and smart when it came to his own career. He had always been the dyed-in-the-wool politician, the consummate deal maker, and, she had to admit, popular in the Labour Party, not to mention with his constituents in Leeds.

Blackie cut into her thoughts when he touched her arm lightly, pushed back his chair, and said, 'Come on, Emma, you owe me the first dance.'

He led her proudly on to the floor, took her in his arms, and they glided away, smoothly in step to the strains of the Cole Porter medley the band had begun to play.

Blackie was well aware that they cut quite a swathe together, and towering above Emma as he did, he was conscious that they were the centre of attraction, knew that all eyes were on them. He caught sight of Kit scrutinizing them and he inclined his head, smiled, and peered around, seeking Robin. There he was, swinging Daisy across the floor, so smooth, so sleek . . . and so slippery. Blackie despised her sons for their treachery towards Emma, and now he wondered if either of them had enough sense to realize how foolish they had been, pitting themselves against this brilliant woman, trying to outsmart her. They had had as much chance as a snowball in hell. Of course she had won hands down. She always won.

Emma whispered against his chest, 'Everybody's looking at us, talking about us, Blackie.'

'Nothing's changed much then.'

Emma simply smiled and they finished their dance in silence.

The evening continued to progress without a hitch. Everyone ate the delicious food, partook of the excellent wines, talked, joked, laughed and danced, and with a carefreeness that surprised Emma. It seemed to her that for once there were no undercurrents. It was as if an unspoken truce had been automatically declared between the various factions, as if animosities, rivalries, hatreds and jealousies had been temporarily buried. Tomorrow they might well be at each other's throats, but tonight they were friendly, and apparently at ease with each other. Perhaps this was only on the surface, but nonetheless it pleased her to see them behaving with a decorum that befitted the occasion.

Emma, too, was enjoying herself, but as the hours sped by she realizing the evening was inducing mixed emotions in her. Memories came unbidden . . . memories that were both joyous and heartrending. Bits of her life kept rushing back to her, and even the location had a profound effect on her at one moment. The Ritz Hotel was so bound up with Paul and their early years together, for here they had snatched shreds of happiness during the First World War before he had gone back to the trenches in France. For a second or two Paul McGill dominated her mind, and she sank back into herself, looking inward, her eyes momentarily glazed as she drifted into the past. But then she heard Daisy's vivid laughter at the next table, and looked up sharply as the present intruded forcefully. She shook off the wistfulness that had briefly enveloped her, sternly reminded herself that she had recently resolved to look only to the future.

Blackie, who had become conscious of her periodic lapses

into silence, drew her into conversation, and had her laughing in a matter of minutes. Suddenly, he interrupted himself in the middle of a story he was recounting and exclaimed, 'Brace yourself, me love, here comes Randolph to claim his dance.'

'Then dance I shall,' Emma said, and allowed herself to be swept off by her beaming nephew. They had circled the floor once when Jonathan cut in, who in turn had to give way to Winston after only a few minutes. Anthony was the next to steal his grandmother away, and soon Alexander was tapping his cousin on the shoulder, so that he could complete the waltz with her.

When the music stopped Alexander did not release her, but stood looking down at her as they lingered in the middle of the floor, an unreadable expression in his eyes.

Emma searched his face inquiringly. 'What is it Sandy? You look as if you're about to say something important.'

'I am, Grandy.' He bent closer and whispered.

'Of course,' Emma said, smiling. She whispered something back to him as he escorted her to her table.

Sitting down, Emma turned to Blackie, fanned herself with her hand. 'Phew! That was a *marathon*. To tell you the truth, I think I'm getting too old to be gallivanting around dance floors.'

'What, a spring chicken like you? *Never*. Anyway, you seem to be thoroughly enjoying yourself,' Blackie laughed.

'I am, darling. It's a lovely party, and everyone's so very friendly with each other.' When he did not answer, she stared hard at him. 'They really are, you know.'

'Aye,' he said at last, laconic, very non-committal, 'perhaps you're right.' But Blackie was not so certain she *was* right, found her children's unexpected chumminess suspect. On the other hand, they were behaving themselves, and that was all that mattered to him. In a few days the two of them would be winging their way to New York, and when Emma was gone from their midst her family could start murdering each other for all he cared.

Suddenly the din ceased and everyone glanced at each other as the wall candelabras and ceiling chandelier were dimmed. There was a deafening drum roll. A waiter came forward pushing a trolley on which there reposed an enormous birthday cake topped with eighty candles flickering brightly in the muted light. The moment the waiter came to a halt in the middle of the dance floor the band struck up the 'Happy Birthday' refrain, and the majority of the guests followed Blackie's lead as he began to sing, joining in exuberantly. When the music finished Blackie assisted Emma to her feet and walked her over to the cake, and together they blew out the candles. Emma picked up the knife and cut the first slice, and smiling and nodding to the guests she returned with Blackie to their table.

Champagne was poured, the cake passed around by the waiters, and once each person had been served, Daisy rose and tapped her glass with a spoon. 'Can I have your attention! *Please!*' Conversation ceased and all eyes settled on her.

'Thank you,' Daisy said, 'and thank you very much for coming tonight, to celebrate my mother's birthday. Blackie and I are delighted you managed to keep our secret. We knew from Mother's face when she arrived that she was truly surprised.'

Daisy gave them her warmest smile, continued: 'In the past few weeks Blackie and I have been approached by various members of the family, and friends, who wanted to say a few words, to pay tribute to Emma Harte this evening. It was quite a dilemma for us – knowing who to choose, and inevitably we realized that the great lady we are honouring would soon become impatient if she had to sit through a lot of speeches. Especially since she herself would be the subject of those speeches. It was Blackie who came up with the best solution, but before I announce the first speaker, I would like my mother and all of you to know that we had requests from the following.'

Daisy picked up a piece of paper, glanced at it, lifted her head and focused her eyes on Emma. 'All of your grandchildren wanted to propose a toast to you, Mother, to be the representative of the third generation. Robin and Elizabeth both wished to say something on behalf of us, your children. Henry, Jim, Len and Bryan all asked to be the one to offer you the very best wishes of your many friends and business associates.'

Emma inclined her head graciously, looking first to her right, then to her left, acknowledging those whom Daisy had mentioned.

Daisy proceeded, 'As I told you, Blackie solved our little problem, and most appropriately, in my opinion. Now I would like to introduce our first speaker – Mr Ronald Kallinski.'

Ronnie rose. He was a man of dominating presence, tall, slender, with a saturnine face and black wavy hair tinged with grey. He had inherited the eyes of his father and his grandmother Janessa Kallinski. These were of the brightest blue and seemed all that more startling because he had a weatherbeaten complexion.

'Daisy, Emma, Blackie, ladies and gentlemen,' he began, his generous smile revealing flashing white teeth. Ronnie had a considerable amount of charm and savoir faire, and as chairman of the board of Kallinski Industries, he was used to public speaking. 'There are many of Emma's friends and business associates present, however I feel certain that they will not be offended if I term this evening a gathering of the clans. Three clans to be precise . . . the Hartes, the O'Neills and the Kallinskis. Well over half a century ago three young people became bosom friends. Emma, Blackie and David, my father. From what I've been told, this friendship apparently seemed startling, even peculiar to many people, who could not understand what a

335

Gentile, an Irish Catholic and a Jew could possibly have in common. But those three young people knew. They recognized their own likeness in each other, saw qualities that *were* common denominators. They were warm, loving, outgoing and filled with hope. They shared ambition, drive, a determination to succeed at all costs, yet without sacrificing honour, honesty or integrity. And they believed in charity to others. The trio were soon bound together by bonds of love and respect, and they remained loyal, and devoted throughout their lives, until my father's death a few years ago.'

Ronnie shifted his stance slightly as he paused for breath. 'Some of you may not know this,' he remarked after a moment, 'but the trio dubbed themselves the Three Musketeers, and when Blackie asked me to speak to you tonight, to pay homage to Emma, he said I would be standing in for that third Musketeer who is no longer with us. *My father.*'

After a quick sip of water, Ronnie levelled his eyes at the main table. 'Emma Harte is the most remarkable of women, and her attributes are manifold. So it is hard, if not downright impossible, to know which one to single out as being extra special. However, if David Kallinski were present tonight I know that he would choose to speak to you about the immense and extraordinary *courage* of Emma Harte. This quality first manifested itself to the Kallinski family in 1905 when Emma was sixteen. Let me tell you about this. One day, as she wandered in the North Street area of Leeds seeking work, she came across a group of ruffians attacking a middle-aged man. He was in need of help, since he had fallen to the ground and lay huddled near a wall trying to protect himself as they continued to stone him. Without giving a thought to her condition – Emma was pregnant at the time – this young girl on the deserted street instantly rushed to his aid. She was fearless as she drove the attackers away. After helping the man to his feet and checking his injuries, she retrieved his scattered packages and insisted on escorting him to his home in the Leylands. The name of that man was Abraham Kallinski. He was my grandfather. As Emma guided him to the safety of his simple abode, she asked Abraham why the ruffians had been stoning him. Abraham told her: *Because I am a Jew.* The young Emma was baffled by this statement, and Abraham went on to explain to her that the Jews in Leeds were persecuted because their religion, dietary laws and customs appeared foreign to the local people. He told her of the terrible brutalities the Jews suffered at the hands of marauding bands of hooligans who entered the Leylands, which was a ghetto, and attacked them and their homes. Emma was disgusted and outraged to hear such things. And she at once condemned these persecutors as cruel, stupid and ignorant.'

Ronnie Kallinski nodded to himself, then looked directly at Emma, his face reflecting his love and admiration for her. He said slowly, 'From that day to the present, this most extraordinary woman has fought stupidity, ignorance, and every kind of inequity, has always condemned the wicked traits she recognized in some at such a tender age. She has continued to loathe religious and ethnic prejudice, any kind of prejudice, in fact. Her courage has never diminished. It has only grown in strength. She has remained consistent in her belief in justice, truth and fair play.'

Henry Rossiter began to clap, and others followed suit, and Ronnie eventually had to call out for them to be quiet.

'My father once told me that Emma, Blackie and he had helped to create a city's greatness as they had lifted themselves out of the grinding poverty of their youth, but that it was Emma most of all who had put her indelible stamp on the city of Leeds. Indeed he spoke the truth, and her contributions to industry and her philanthropy are renowned. However, I would like to add a comment of my own, and it is this: Emma has also put her inimitable imprimatur on each one of us present . . . not only on every member of the three closely-knit clans, but on her friends and business associates. We must be proud of that, for we are better people for knowing her, for being part of her circle. Emma Harte honours us with her devoted friendship, her love and depth of understanding. And she does us the greatest honour by her presence tonight. And so, in my late father's name, and in the name of all the Kallinskis absent and present, I ask you to raise your glasses to Emma Harte. A woman of outstanding courage and indomitability who has never been defeated, and who has always stood tall . . . so tall she towers above all of us.'

Ronnie raised his glass. 'To Emma Harte.'

After the toast had been repeated, Ronnie said: 'And now Blackie will say a few words.'

Blackie pushed himself to his feet. 'Thank you, Ronnie. David could not have said it better, and your own tribute to Emma was fitting and most moving. As Daisy told you, we knew Emma would not sit still for a lot of laudatory talk. Also, since I'm aware she regards the shortest of speeches as humbug, I'm going to be brief.' Blackie chuckled. 'Well, as brief as I can be. Obviously on this special occasion of Emma's eightieth birthday I do feel the need to say a few kind words about her.'

As Blackie launched himself into a recital about her strength of character, her ability to conquer against all odds, and her great business achievements, Emma sat back. She was only partially listening. During Ronnie's speech, she had begun to ruminate on her early beginnings. She thought of the place she had started out from, the great distance she had travelled and she marvelled at herself, wondering how she had accomplished all that she had, and for the most part entirely by herself.

But after a short while she became aware that many pairs of eyes were on her as well as Blackie, and she roused herself from her reflections. Her old friend was moving away from bygone eras, talking of the present. And Emma's thoughts instantly settled on her life as it was today.

Well, she thought, whatever my life has been about my grandchildren are proof positive to me that it has been worthwhile. Quite unexpectedly, as she experienced a flash of clarity, everything became clear to Emma. So clear she was startled for a moment. And she knew what she must do tonight, what her course of action must be.

Blackie was drawing to a close. 'It has been the greatest privilege of my life to be her friend. So please join in my toast to Emma, which comes from my heart.' Blackie leaned forward, grasped hold of his glass.

Lifting it high, Blackie smiled down at her. 'Emma, you truly are a woman of substance in the finest sense of that phrase. May you long be with us. To you, Emma.'

Emma felt the heat rush to her face as the roomful of smiling friends and relatives toasted her and her throat tightened with sudden emotion.

Once everyone was seated, Blackie, who had continued to stand, said: 'I give you our guest of honour, Emma Harte.'

Emma rose, stepped around her chair and pushed it under the table. She stood with her hands resting on its back, her eyes slowing roving around the room, her glance touching each one of them briefly.

Finally, she said, 'Thank you for joining me on my birthday, and for the lovely gifts and flowers you sent me today. I was very touched. I must also express my thanks to Blackie and Daisy, for giving this party, and for being such wonderful hosts.'

She let her gaze linger on Ronnie Kallinski, her eyes very bright, glittering with moisture under the wrinkled lids. 'I am so glad you and your family are here with me tonight, Ronnie. And I thank you for your eloquent words, for standing in for your father. David is sorely missed.' She turned her attention to Blackie. 'You said some beautiful things about me too . . . thank you, Blackie.'

Then in a crisper tone Emma said, 'As many of you know, Emily and Winston are to be married next year. However, they did want me to formally announce their engagement to you all this evening. It seems that romance is in the air in the Harte clan. Alexander also asked me to announce his engagement to Marguerite Reynolds. So, let us drink to the future happiness of these four young people.'

The toast was given amidst a ripple of excited whispers, exclamations.

Emma stood waiting, gripping the back of the chair more tightly than ever. Her expression was benign but her narrowed green eyes were watchful. She knew exactly what she would say, even though she had decided to make this announcement only ten minutes before.

Paula, scrutinizing Emma, took note of the friendly expression on her face. But her grandmother did not fool her for one moment. She recognized that implacable glint in her eyes. It signalled something . . . Emma was about to drop one of her bombshells. Paula instantly tensed, wondering what this could be. She could not hazard a guess. Her eyes remained riveted on Emma. How imperious Grandy looks at this moment, she thought, standing there so erect and proud, totally in command of herself, and this audience.

Emma moved slightly and in the soft light emanating from the many candles the emeralds blazed more brilliantly, and there was a shimmer, a luminosity about Emma at this moment. Power, Paula thought. My grandmother exudes immense power.

A hush had fallen over everyone and, like Paula, they stared at Emma, filled with unexpected anticipation.

Finally Emma spoke. Her voice rang out clear and strong, dominating the room. 'In everybody's life there comes a time when it is appropriate to step aside, to permit younger voices to be heard, greater visions to be perceived. *Tonight is that time for me.*' Emma paused, letting her words sink in.

There was a collective gasp.

'*I am going.* And going willingly. It struck me tonight that I've earned the right to rest these tired old bones at last, to relax for the first time in my life, and who knows I might even get around to having a little fun.'

Her light laugh reverberated as she scanned their faces. Their shock was unconcealed. 'How surprised you're looking,' she remarked, almost off-handedly. 'Well, perhaps I've even surprised myself. But I came to a decision during the speeches. As I sat there listening to my life being recounted it suddenly occurred to me that now is the right time for me to retire. And to retire gracefully. Everyone knows that Blackie and I are about to leave on a trip around the world. I am happy to announce to you that I've decided to spend the rest of the days left to me on this earth with my oldest, dearest and most trusted friend.'

Half turning, Emma lifted one hand and let it rest easily on Blackie's broad shoulder. She said, in a more confiding tone, 'Blackie said to me the other day, "Grow old with me, the best is yet to be," and you know, he might just be right.'

No one moved or spoke. Each guest continued to regard her intently, understanding that this slender, silver-haired woman who wielded enormous power had something more to say to them.

Emma stepped away from her chair and walked with swiftness to one of the other tables. She came to a halt next to Alexander, who jumped up immediately. His eyes were brilliant in his white face. Recognizing that he too was reeling from shock, she touched his arm lightly, as if to reassure him.

Glancing around at the expectant faces, Emma said

briskly, 'My grandson Alexander has just become the head of Harte Enterprises.' She thrust out her hand. He took it, staring at her speechlessly. 'Congratulations, Alexander.' He stammered his thanks.

Moving at a dignified pace to the table diagonally opposite, Emma was aware of the tension and the sheathed excitement permeating the air. She drew to a standstill next to Paula. Pushing back her chair, Paula was on her feet as speedily as Alexander had been.

Taking the young woman's hand in hers, Emma held on to it tightly. How icy it is, she thought absently, and squeezed it, endeavouring to impart some of her own great strength to Paula, who had begun to tremble.

Once again, Emma's piercing green gaze swept the entire room. 'The Harte department store chain will, as of tonight, be run by my granddaughter, Paula McGill Amory Fairley.'

She pivoted to face Paula and gazed long and hard into her violet eyes. And then Emma smiled her incomparable smile that filled her face with radiance.

'I charge you to hold my dream,' Emma said.

Heiress

'Passions spin the plot; We are betrayed
by what is false within.'

GEORGE MEREDITH

'I am not made or unmade by the things which
happen to me but by my reactions to them.
That is all God cares about.'

ST JOHN OF THE CROSS

CHAPTER 22

She had been alone for two weeks and had drawn strength and a sense of renewal from her solitude.

But now on this warm and pleasant Sunday Paula suddenly experienced a little spurt of pleasure at the thought of seeing Emily. Her cousin was driving over from Pennistone Royal for tea, and she was really looking forward to her company.

After she had finished setting the wrought-iron table on the terrace, Paula hurried down the steps and on to the lawn, to check on the twins. Lorne and Tessa lay in the double pram, sleeping peacefully in the shade. They looked so contented she could not help smiling before turning away and going back to the terrace to wait for Emily.

It was one of those afternoons in the middle of September which frequently occur in Yorkshire and rival the most beautiful days in midsummer. The arc of the sky was a light periwinkle blue, clear and radiant, with a few scattered cotton-ball clouds scudding intermittently across the sun which had blazed down since the late morning. The gardens at Long Meadow were riotous with colour and the warm air was filled with the pervasive scents of the flowers and shrubs.

Paula stretched out on the garden chaise, basking in the golden light, thinking of nothing very special as she relaxed. The tranquillity soothed her, was like a balm after her particularly hectic week, during which she had been on the go nonstop. They had been holding their annual Autumn Fashion Fair for five days; models had paraded through the Birdcage at lunch time wearing the latest ready-to-wear winter styles; every afternoon at three o'clock there had been a fashion show of designer clothes in the couture salon. Fashion aside, Harte's had had other special events during the past week, including the opening of a cooking school in the basement; daily appearances by a famous makeup artist in the cosmetic department; on Thursday evening there had been a cocktail party for the unveiling of the new art gallery in the store and the exhibition of oils and watercolours by Sally Harte. The *vernissage* had been a huge success and most of Sally's paintings of the Yorkshire Dales and the Lake District had already been sold. Whilst coping with these in-store promotions, Paula had had to handle her normal work load and it seemed to her now that every department had needed her complete attention. Much to her dismay, two buyers had resigned on Tuesday and she had had to start interviewing replacements immediately; she had also found it necessary to dismiss the jewellery buyer for incompetence late on Friday and this had proved to be a most unpleasant scene. But continuing daily problems and constant activity of this nature were par for the course, part of the daily routine of a large and successful department store such as theirs. Still, Paula knew she had been pushing herself harder than ever since Jim had been abroad, rising at five in the morning to get to the store by six-thirty so that she could leave early on most days in order to arrive home in time to bath the twins.

She had eaten dinner alone every night, had not done any socializing whatsoever, and, apart from Sally Harte, the only other people she had seen were her staff at the house, her business colleagues, the few friends who had attended the art gallery opening. During these two weeks of solitariness in her private life Paula had come to realize more fully how vital it was for her to have these stretches of absolute peace and rest at the end of each frantic day. Working as intensely as she did, in a job that required her total concentration, frequently left her frazzled. It was essential for her well being to have periods entirely alone so that she could recoup her sapped strength. She had the need to think, to review her schedule, to plan ahead as she pottered around in the garden, played with the babies, read or simply listened to classical music in the cool greenness of the conservatory.

With a wry smile Paula had to admit that even if she had wanted to gad about, lead a gay life during Jim's absence in Canada, there was no one available to play with. Winston had flown off a week ago to join Jim in Toronto where they were attending a world conference of newspaper editors, publishers and proprietors. But the real reason for Winston's trip was to start negotiations with a Canadian paper mill which was up for sale. He hoped to acquire it for the Yorkshire Consolidated Newspaper Company. Miranda O'Neill was in Barbados for the opening of their new hotel and the launching of the Harte boutique. Sarah was with her, acting as fashion adviser, supervising the interior displays and the dressing of the windows. Alexander was taking a holiday in the South of France with Maggie Reynolds, and they were staying at Emma's house in Cap Martin. Until last night Emily had been in Paris on a buying trip for Genret.

Jonathan was the only member of the family who was not travelling somewhere, but *their* paths rarely crossed. This was the chief reason Paula had been surprised when he had dropped in to see her at the store on Wednesday. Before she had even asked him what he was doing in Yorkshire, he had volunteered, and rather defensively she thought, that he was in Leeds on real estate business for Harte Enterprises. He had wasted an hour of her precious time chatting about absolutely nothing, although he had asked her, and several times during the course of their aimless conversation, when Grandy was returning from Australia. She had said she had no idea, which was the truth, and had been non-committal about matters in general. Cautious by nature, Paula had never been overly-fond of Jonathan Ainsley, always wary of him. This feeling had only intensified since Emma had alerted her to him, confided her worries about his loyalty.

After her grandmother's unexpected retirement and her departure on her world tour – almost five months ago – she and Alexander had met in London to discuss the situation in general. They had agreed they should continue to confer regularly once a month, in order to review matters pertaining to the business empires they were running, had even acknowledged they might well need each other as a sounding board.

At their first get-together they had come to the conclusion that Emily should be told about Emma's suspicions regarding Jonathan. They had invited her to lunch the following day, and had taken her into their confidence, had suggested that she attend their monthly brainstorming sessions. All three had concurred that they must watch Jonathan like a hawk. By mutual agreement they had also made the decision to exclude Sarah from their confabs, feeling that her sudden closeness to Jonathan was suspicious. Paula, Emily and Alexander had thus become the self-appointed triumvirate who were resolved in their determination to run Emma's companies in the way she wanted, whilst guarding her great legacy.

The French doors leading to the drawing room were open and dimly, in the background, Paula heard the grandfather clock in the hall striking four. She roused herself and went inside, hurrying through into the kitchen. She put the babies' bottles in a pan of water to be warmed up later, loaded the tray with sandwiches, scones, strawberry jam, and a cream cake, then went to the cupboard for the tea caddy. Ten minutes later, as she completed her tasks, she heard a car in the driveway and

348

looked out of the window to see Emily alighting from her battered white Jaguar.

Emily bounced into the kitchen with her usual *joie de vivre*, wearing a happy grin. She ran to Paula and hugged her. 'Sorry I'm late,' Emily said as they drew apart, 'but that pile of old junk has been acting up all the way from Pennistone Royal. I really think I'll have to splurge and buy myself a new car.'

Paula laughed. 'You're not late, and I think you're right about the Jag, it *has* seen better days. Anyway welcome back, Emily.'

'It's good to be home, although I did enjoy Paris. It's still my favourite city.' Emily perched on the edge of a kitchen chair as Paula hovered near the stove. 'Have you heard from anybody? Grandy to be specific?'

'Yes.' Paula swung around, the kettle in her hand. 'She rang me up at midnight on Thursday. She wanted to hear about the *vernissage* and how the opening of the art gallery went – you know that's been her pet project for the last year. She said she and Blackie were going to Coonamble with Philip for four or five days. She sends you her love.'

'I'm beginning to think she'll never come back. Did Gran indicate what their plans were?'

'Yes she did, as a matter of fact. She and Blackie intend to leave Sydney in the middle of October, wend their way back to New York before returning here sometime in late November. She promised to be home in time for Christmas at Pennistone Royal.'

'My God, that's a long way off! I can't wait to see her. It's not the same without Grandma is it?'

'No.' Paula stared at Emily, scowled. 'You've got a face like a wet week, Emily. Do you have problems with Genret?'

Emily shook her head negatively. 'No, no, everything's fine. I miss Gran, that's all, and even though she *has* retired, it's awfully reassuring to know she's in the background. And right now she seems so far away, sitting over there at the other side of the world.'

'I know what you mean,' Paula said slowly, having sorely missed Emma's presence herself. She dreaded to think what it would be like, how they would manage, when her grandmother was gone from them forever. She instantly squashed this morbid and distressing thought, and forced a bright smile. 'Come on, Emily, let's go out to the terrace. I thought we'd have tea in the garden, it's such a gorgeous day. But we have to feed the babies first. Nora asked to change her day off this week, and Meg is never here on Sundays, so I've been coping alone today. I've enjoyed it actually.'

Emily followed her outside to the terrace. She ran down the steps to the pram. 'They're both wide awake,' she called over her shoulder, and began making cooing noises to the twins, leaning into the pram and touching their downy cheeks.

'Upsidaisy,' Paula murmured, lifting Lorne into her arms, 'time for your bottle, little boy.'

Emily scooped up Tessa and the two young women returned to sit at the table on the terrace. Half an hour later, after the children had been slowly fed, dutifully burped and then returned to their perambulator, Paula went inside. Not long after she came back carrying the tea tray.

As she poured, she said, 'Any news from Winston?'

'Yes, he phoned me last night. He's gone up to Vancouver. He's already in negotiations with the directors of that paper mill, and he thinks he's going to make the deal. There are a few more details to iron out, but he says they'll be able to conclude everything in a matter of days. He was very optimistic, and the mill will be a wonderful acquisition for Consolidated. Anyway, he's going to stop off in New York to spend a few days with Shane. Apparently *he's* in

Barbados for the opening of the hotel, and won't be in New York until the middle of this coming week.'

'I'm glad to hear the deal is going through!' Paula exclaimed. 'When I spoke to Jim a few days ago he sounded uncertain about its outcome, and said Winston was down in the dumps. Obviously he was wrong, or things have changed radically overnight.' She sipped her tea and continued, 'Talking of Barbados . . . Sarah flew out there ten days ago to help Merry supervise the unpacking of the Lady Hamilton clothes and get the merchandise on the racks. I expect they're all having a whale of a time – '

Emily exclaimed, 'Sarah went to Barbados! Why ever was that necessary?' She banged the cup down with such an angry clatter Paula was taken aback.

She threw Emily a baffled look. 'Goodness, you *do* sound fierce. Sarah seemed to think it was her *duty* to go out there. In fact, she was hell bent on going. Since she *is* running our fashion division, and since the boutiques are mostly stocking Lady Hamilton beach clothes and resort wear I suppose she has a point. Besides I couldn't very well interfere. She doesn't have to answer to me . . . only to your brother. You know Sarah, she considers herself her own boss.'

'Oh well.' Emily shrugged, trying to act as if Sarah was of no consequence. But her fertile brain whirled and two and two suddenly made more than four. She was convinced the only interest Sarah Lowther had in Barbados and the Harte boutique was Shane O'Neill. Sarah must have found out from Miranda that he was going to be in the Caribbean for the opening of the hotel. Sarah was probably making a fool of herself at this very moment – throwing herself at Shane.

Emily, changing the subject, said with a rueful smile, 'Poor Alexander. I called him yesterday before I left Paris and found out that Mummy's descended on him with Marc Deboyne in tow. She's installed them at Grandy's villa,

351

claims she has a right to be there and to visit with her darling daughters. Sandy says she's being a pain in the neck. Very bossy. I think Amanda and Francesca are anxious to fly home immediately. They haven't had much time for Mummy, not for ages.'

'Oh what a shame he's having to cope with problems on holiday – he was so looking forward to going away. Won't your little sisters have to be back here very soon anyway?'

'Yes. They're due at Harrogate College on the last day of this month. I'm glad Gran agreed to let them stay there for another term before packing them off to Switzerland. I don't think those two relish the idea of being far away from her, and – ' Emily stopped, cocked her bright blonde head, listening. 'Isn't that the phone?'

'Yes. I'll be back in a second.' Paula dashed through the drawing room into the hall to answer it, snatching at the receiver.

Before she had a chance to say a word, the caller was exclaiming, 'Jim? Is that you?'

'Oh hello, Aunt Edwina,' she said, surprised. 'It's Paula. Jim's not here. He's in Canada on business.'

'*Canada*. Oh my God!'

Instantly recognizing the anxiety in the high-pitched voice, Paula asked, 'Is there something wrong?'

Edwina began to babble so hysterically Paula was unable to make sense of her aunt's words. She was incoherent, obviously distraught. Paula listened for a few seconds longer, filling with increasing alarm. Finally she cut in. 'Aunt Edwina, I can't understand a thing you're saying. Please speak a little more clearly, and slower.'

Paula heard Edwina sucking in her breath. There was a drawn-out moment of silence.

'It's poor Min,' Edwina gasped at last. 'Anthony's wife . . . she's . . . she's . . . *dead*. She's been found . . . drowned . . .' Though she had choked on these words, Edwina managed to add, 'In the lake at Clonloughlin. And

352

'. . . and . . .' Edwina was unable to continue and began to weep.

Paula went cold from head to toe. Innumerable questions leaped into her mind. How had she drowned? Accident? Suicide? And why had Min been at Clonloughlin in the first place when she and Anthony were estranged? Aware suddenly that her aunt's sobbing had lessened, if only a fraction, Paula said sympathetically, 'I'm so sorry, so very sorry. This must be a terrible shock for you.'

Edwina gasped, 'It's not only Min. It's poor Anthony. Paula – the police are here. They're questioning Anthony again. Oh my poor boy! I don't know what to do! I wish I could talk to Jim. It's also a pity Mother isn't in England. She'd know how to handle this ghastly mess. Oh dear God, what am I going to do?'

Paula stiffened. Her mind worked swiftly, striving to comprehend what Edwina was intimating. 'What do you mean about the police? You're not trying to tell me they think Anthony is somehow involved in Min's death are you?'

There was an awful stillness at Edwina's end. Her voice was a terrified whisper when she spoke. '*Yes,*' she said.

Paula sat down heavily on the hall chair. She felt prickles of goose flesh on her arms and her heartbeat accelerated against her rib cage. Horror was trickling through her but instantly this gave way to a burst of anger. 'How ridiculous! Your local police force must be bonkers. Anthony under suspicion of murd – ' Paula bit off the remainder of the word, reluctant to say it. Again she exclaimed, 'This is *preposterous.*'

'They think he ki – ' Edwina faltered, for like Paula she was unable to voice the unthinkable.

Striving to take hold of herself, Paula said in her firmest manner, 'Aunt Edwina, please start at the beginning and tell me everything. Grandy and Jim may not be here, but I am, and I will do everything I can to help, but you must be

353

absolutely honest with me so that I can make the proper decisions.'

'Yes. Yes. All right.' Edwina sounded slightly calmer, and although she stumbled a few times she was able to give Paula the essential details about the discovery of Min's body early that morning, the arrival of the police, who had been summoned by Anthony, their departure and their subsequent return two hours ago. After poking around the estate they had ensconced themselves with Anthony in the library at Clonloughlin and were still with him.

When Edwina finished, Paula said, 'It sounds very cut and dried to me. Min obviously had an accident.' She hesitated. 'Look,' she went one, 'I think this is merely routine . . . I mean the police coming back this afternoon.'

'No! No!' Edwina cried. 'It isn't routine. Min's been creating problems lately. She changed her mind several weeks ago – about the divorce. She refused to go ahead with it. Other things have been happening. Dreadful things.' Then Edwina added rapidly, in a voice so quiet Paula had to strain to hear, 'That's why the police are here.'

'You'd better tell me everything,' Paula said as steadily as she could, even though her sense of dread was mounting by the second.

Edwina gulped. 'Yes, I think I must. The trouble started a month ago actually. Min came down here – she's been living in Waterford – and started to make a nuisance of herself, caused the most horrendous scenes. Sometimes she was really sloshed, reeling from drink. She and Anthony had fierce quarrels and there were some unfortunate scenes in front of the staff, the estate workers, and even a nasty confrontation one afternoon in the village, when she accosted Anthony. All the rows, the violence, have inevitably caused gossip, and Sally Harte's presence here earlier this summer hasn't done anything to help the situation. You know what people are like in a small place, Paula.

Gossip is their way of life. There's been an awful lot of talk – distressing talk – about *the other woman*.'

Paula groaned inwardly. 'Let's go back for a moment. What did you mean when you referred to *violence*?'

'Oh violent words mostly. Shouting and screaming on Min's part, but Anthony did become enraged last weekend when she showed up on Saturday. At dinner time. He had guests. I was there. They had a fight, a verbal fight that is, and she hit Anthony with a golf club. He pushed her away from him, a natural reaction, I suppose. She fell though, in the hall. Min wasn't really hurt, but she pretended she was. She was overly dramatic about it, screamed something about Anthony wanting her – '

'Yes, Aunt Edwina, go on,' Paula encouraged as the silence lengthened.

There was a sound of harsh breathing before Edwina told Paula, with a sob, 'Min shouted something about Anthony wanting her dead and buried and that she wouldn't be surprised if she was found murdered. And very soon. Several people heard her say this. I did myself.'

'Oh my God!' Paula's heart sank and her apprehension spiralled into genuine fear. She did not think for a single moment that her cousin had killed his wife, but it was suddenly apparent to her why the police harboured suspicions about Anthony. Her mind momentarily floundered, then rallied, as she told herself she had to come to grips with this dilemma. But where to begin? Who to enlist?

Paula said in a strong, calm voice that belied her inner nervousness, 'All the gossip, the scenes are meaningless in the long run. The police need hard evidence before they can do anything – arrest Anthony, accuse him of killing her. When did she drown? What about an alibi? Surely Anthony has one.'

'They're not sure about the time of death . . . at least that's what they say. I think they're doing an autopsy,'

Edwina went on miserably. 'Alibi? No, that's the terrible part, Anthony doesn't have one.'

'Where was he yesterday? *Last night?* Those must be the crucial hours.'

'Last night,' Edwina repeated as if she was confused. Then she said quickly, 'Yes, yes, I see what you mean. Min arrived at Clonloughlin at about five o'clock yesterday. I saw her driving up – from my bedroom window in the Dower House. I phoned Anthony to warn him. He was annoyed. He told me he was going to hop into his old land rover and drive out to the lake – in the hopes of avoiding her.'

'And he did that? Went out to the lake?' Paula asked.

'Yes. But she must have seen him driving off in that direction or she simply second guessed where he had gone . . . it was one of his favourite spots. She followed him out there. And – '

'They had a quarrel at the lake?' Paula cut in.

'Oh no. He never even spoke to her!' Edwina cried. 'You see, he saw her mini in the distance – the land is flat around the far side of the lake. He simply got back into the land rover and was going to return to the house the long way around. But he hadn't driven very far when the land rover conked out. Anthony left it parked and started to walk home. He wanted to avoid Min . . . don't you understand?'

'Yes. And he left the land rover near the lake, is that what you're saying?' Paula demanded, wondering if this was incriminating or not.

'Of course he left it there, it wouldn't start,' Edwina was saying, her high-pitched voice trembling again.

'Please don't cry, Aunt Edwina,' Paula pleaded. 'It's essential that you control yourself. *Please.*'

'Yes. Yes. I'll try.' she sniffed.

Paula heard her blowing her nose and then her aunt resumed, 'You don't know Clonloughlin, Paula, it's vast.

It took Anthony an hour to walk back. He had to go up the hill, through the wood and several fields to get to the road that cuts across the estate and leads to the village. He – '

'Road!' Paula exclaimed, seizing on this fact immediately. 'Didn't he see anyone?'

'No, he didn't. At least he never mentioned that. Anyway Anthony got back to the house around six-thirty. He phoned me, told me about the land rover breaking down. Then he said he would change for dinner, see me later. I went up to the house around seven. We had drinks and ate, but Anthony was very nervous, not himself. You see, he thought Min would show up and start behaving offensively again.'

'But she didn't, did she?'

'No, we were alone all evening. As I said, Anthony was out of sorts and he walked me back to the Dower House around nine-thirty, perhaps nine forty-five, then he returned to Clonloughlin.'

'And who found Min's body?'

'The estate manager. He was driving past the lake very early this morning and saw the land rover, also the mini. Then he found – ' Edwina broke down, sobbing as if her heart would break.

Paula tried to soothe her aunt, reassure her, and said, 'Please, Aunt Edwina, be brave. I'm sure everything is going to be all right.' She prayed she was right.

'But I'm frightened for him,' Edwina mumbled in a tear-filled tone, 'truly frightened – '

'Now listen to me and please do as I tell you,' Paula instructed peremptorily, taking charge. 'Don't make any more phone calls, and if you receive any, hang up as quickly as possible. I want you to keep this line open. I shall ring you back very shortly. I presume you're calling from the Dower House?'

'Yes.' Edwina hesitated, asked, 'But what are you going to do?'

'I think I'd better get my mother over there to stay with you for the next few days. You shouldn't be alone at a time like this. I assume there's going to be an inquest. The main thing is I don't want you to worry. Fretting won't help anyone. I know it won't be easy, but you *must* try. I'll ring you back within the hour.'

'Th-th-th-thank you, P-P-Paula,' Edwina stammered.

They said goodbye and hung up. Paula immediately lifted the phone and dialled her parents' flat in London. The line was busy. She flung the receiver back into the cradle with impatience and leaped up, realizing she had better go and talk to Emily.

As Paula raced through the drawing room she almost fell over an occasional table in her haste. Righting it, she stumbled out on to the terrace, blinking as she came out in the bright sunlight.

Having heard the crash Emily swung her head and grinned. 'You are a clumsy clot – ' She stopped, her eyes opening widely. 'What's happened?' Emily asked. 'You're as white as a sheet.'

Paula leaned against a chair. 'We have some trouble, really *serious* trouble, Emily. I'm going to have to deal with it – and you'll have to help me. Please come inside. I must reach my mother. It'll save time if you listen whilst I explain everything to her.'

CHAPTER 23

'You don't think he could have done it, do you?'

Paula lifted her head sharply. 'Of course not!' She stared at Emily, who sat opposite her on the sofa in the conservatory. Her stare intensified and she frowned, 'Why, do you?'

Without hesitation, Emily exclaimed, 'No. I don't think

he would be capable of it.' There was a pause, and Emily bit her lip. She said in a rush, 'On the other hand, you said something – '

'*I* did? What do you mean? When?'

'Oh not today, Paula, months ago, when you and Alexander took me to lunch just after Gran left. You know the day we discussed Jonathan. We also spoke about Sarah. You made an interesting remark and it's stuck in my mind ever since. You said we never *really* know about other people, not even those who are closest to us, and that we know very little about what goes on in people's private lives. I was struck by the essential truth in your words at the time, and let's face it, we don't know Anthony all that well. We've never spent a lot of time with him.'

'You're right. But I've got to go with my gut instinct on this, Emily, I just know he didn't have anything to do with Min's death. Admittedly the circumstances *sound* peculiar, but no . . .' Paula shook her head vehemently, 'I don't believe he killed her. I'm convinced it was an accident. Or suicide. Look here, Emily, Grandy is the shrewdest person we know, and she is brilliant at reading people, spotting character flaws. She thinks the world of Anthony and – '

'Even the nicest people can commit murder,' Emily interrupted quietly. 'If they're under pressure, pushed hard enough. What about crimes of passion, for instance?'

'We must presume Anthony's innocence! That is British law, after all – innocent until proven guilty.'

'Please don't think I was implying that he *did* kill her, because I wasn't. I was just speculating that's all. To be honest, I'm inclined to go along with you on the suicide theory. Still, I hope she didn't kill herself. Think how hard that would be on Sally and Anthony – having to live with the knowledge that Min took her own life because of them.'

'Yes, that had crossed my mind earlier. It would affect them in the worst way,' Paula said, her eyes darkening with worry. She glanced at her watch. 'I wish my mother would call back. I hope she's not having a problem getting a plane to Ireland.'

Emily also checked her watch. 'She's only had fifteen minutes, Paula. Give her a chance. In the meantime, let's go over your list again, check your plan.'

'Right,' Paula replied, aware positive action would help to subdue her nagging anxiety. Lifting the pad, she scanned it, said, '*One*. We get Mummy over to Ireland as soon as possible, so that she can hold the fort. She's already working on that so – ' Paula picked up her pen, ticked it off, ' – *Two*. My father has to put a call through to Philip at Coonamble between nine and ten tonight, to alert Philip. God forbid Grandy reads about this trouble in the papers first. Daddy understands he must do this once Mother is on the plane.' Again this item was checked off, and she went on reading aloud: '*Three*. Put a lid on this mess as far as the newspapers are concerned. I'll call Sam Fellowes at the *Yorkshire Morning Gazette* and Pete Smythe on our evening paper. Actually, I'll have to call all of the papers in our chain. I can't control the national press but I can certainly make sure those we own don't carry a single line. *Four*. Talk to Henry Rossiter about legal advice. We might have to send John Crawford. As the family lawyer he would represent Anthony if necessary. *Five*. Get hold of Winston, Jim, or both, to let them know what's happened.' She lifted her eyes. 'Maybe you can make *that* phone call, Emily, but not until *we* have everything under control. I don't want either of them flying back here. *Six*. Ring Edwina to reassure her and talk to Anthony, tell him what we've done. *Seven*. Locate Sally Harte. You can do that as well.'

'Okay.' Emily peered through the door of the conservatory and out into the hall. The telephone was in her direct line of vision. 'I think you should work at your desk here, and I'll use the phone in the hall. That way we can see each other, talk easily between calls.'

'Good idea. Look, I had better speak to Fellowes and get that out of the way.'

'Yes, and I'll start trying to find Sally. Did she tell you on Thursday where exactly she was going in the Lake District?'

'No, and I didn't think to ask, but Uncle Randolph will know. Don't mention a thing about this – not yet,' Paula warned.

'Not on your life. He'd go into a flat spin.' Emily jumped up. 'If the other line rings while you're talking to Fellowes I'll pick it up. It'll probably be your mother.'

As Emily ran out, Paula lifted the receiver and dialled the editor's private line at the *Yorkshire Morning Gazette*. He answered on the second ring, and Paula quickly cut through the usual pleasantries. 'Sam, I'm calling about a family matter. My cousin, the Earl of Dunvale, has had a terrible tragedy. His wife has been drowned in the lake on his estate in Ireland.'

'That is indeed tragic,' Fellowes said. 'I'll get one of my top writers on to the obituary immediately.'

'No, no, Sam. The reason I'm calling is to let you know I don't want anything in the paper. I'm pretty sure the wire services will be carrying something later tonight, or tomorrow. In any event, I want the story killed. No obituary either.'

'But why not?' he demanded. 'If the story's on the wires, the national press will be running it. We'll look ridiculous if we don't mention – '

'*Sam*,' Paula cut in quietly, 'you should know by now that Emma Harte does not wish to read anything – *anything at all* – about *her* family in *her* newspapers.'

'I know that,' he snapped. 'But surely this is different. How's it going to look if every paper in the country but ours has it? What kind of newspaper are we anyway? I definitely do not like suppressing news.'

'Then perhaps you're working on the wrong newspaper,

Sam. Because believe you me, Emma Harte makes the rules around here, and you'd better respect them.'

'I'm going to call Jim and Winston in Canada. *They* run the papers, and it seems to me that it's their decision – about what we print and what we don't print.'

'In their absence, and in the absence of my grandmother, it is my decision and mine alone. *I* have told you what to do. *No* story. *No* obituary.'

'If you say so,' he said, his anger ill-concealed.

'I *do* say so. Thank you, Sam, and goodbye.'

Paula hung up, bristling. She pulled her address book towards her, looking up Pete Smythe's home number, since the evening paper was closed on Sundays. She hoped she would not get the same arguments from Smythe. She was about to dial when Emily flew down the steps, and she swung around in the chair. 'Was that my mother?'

'Yes, or rather, Uncle David. Aer Lingus has a flight out early this evening, but he doesn't think Auntie Daisy will make the airport in time. So he's arranged for your mother to be flown over by private plane. Uncle David's going to phone Edwina right now, to let her know Auntie Daisy's virtually on her way. Your mother's packing. She'll call before she leaves the flat.'

'That's a relief. Did you speak to Uncle Randolph?'

'No, he was out. But Vivienne told me Sally's due back in Middleham shortly. It's been raining in the Lake District, so she packed her painting gear and is driving home. I told Vivienne to have her call here the minute she arrives.'

'Was she curious?'

'Not really. I said you wanted to speak to Sally, and got off the phone quickly.'

'I dread having to tell her about this – ' Paula murmured, her face grim, her eyes reflecting her deep concern.

'Yes, it's going to be awful for her, but she'll *have* to be told. In person, I think, don't you?'

'*Absolutely*. Well, let's not waste time. We'd better get on, Emily.'

'What shall I do next?'

'Could you bring the babies into the house, please? You can park the pram in here for a while. I must call those other editors.'

'Yes, do it, and I'll be back in a jiffy.'

Paula reached Pete Smythe, editor of the *Yorkshire Evening Standard* at his home in Knaresborough. She repeated the story she had told Sam Fellowes. After sympathizing with her about the accident, Pete concurred with her decision and gave her no arguments.

'I wouldn't have run anything anyway, Paula,' Pete told her, 'I know how Mrs Harte feels. She'd skin me alive if a single line appeared about any of you, regardless of the circumstances.'

'Sam Fellowes was a bit difficult,' Paula volunteered. 'I hope I'm not going to meet any similar resistance from our other editors.'

'You won't – Sam's a special case. Not the easiest person to deal with. If you want I'll make the calls to our Doncaster, Sheffield, Bradford and Darlington papers.'

'Oh would you, Pete? That'd be marvellous. I really appreciate your help. Thanks a lot.' The phone shrilled the moment Paula had put it down. It was her mother.

'Hello, darling,' Daisy said with her usual calm control. 'I'm about to leave. I'm taking a cab to the airport, so that your father can be here at the flat, just in case you need him. He spoke to Edwina a few minutes ago. She's relieved I'm on my way. He said she sounded less agitated. The police have left. Anthony's with her. They're waiting for your call.'

'I know. I'll ring them when we hang up. Thanks for going over to Ireland, Mother. You're the only one who can handle this. Edwina does trust you, and you'll deal with everyone diplomatically, which is more than she could manage.'

'Heavens, Paula, I don't mind. We are a family and we must stick together. But what an appalling situation. I can't understand the police over there . . . it seems very straight-forward to me. Your father agrees. Anyway talking about it endlessly won't solve a thing. I must rush. Goodbye, dear.'

'Bye, Mummy, and have a safe journey. We'll speak tomorrow.'

Emily was pushing the pram down the two low steps into the conservatory when Paula glanced up from her pad. 'I'm going to make a fast call to Henry, and then I'll talk to Ireland.' As she dialled Henry's number Paula quickly gave Emily details about her conversations with Pete Smythe and her mother.

It was Henry Rossiter's housekeeper who answered at his Gloucestershire house. Paula spoke to her briefly, replaced the receiver, said to Emily, 'I just missed him. He's driving back to London. Apparently he should be arriving around eight-thirty. Do you think I should call Gran's solicitors or wait to speak to Henry?'

'I'm not sure . . . what do you think Grandy would *do*?' She answered herself instantly. 'She'd talk to Henry first.'

'That's my feeling,' Paula agreed, her hand resting on the telephone. She took a deep breath, preparing herself to make the call to Edwina at Clonloughlin. Picking up the receiver, she instantly put it back in the cradle, swung around. 'Sally may be in touch any minute. You'll have to talk to her, Emily, so let's decide what you'll say.'

The two young women stared at each other worriedly for the longest moment.

Finally Paula said, 'It seems to me that the wisest thing would be to tell her that *I* have a problem, that I want to see her, talk to her, and will she please drive over immediately.'

'She'll want to know what's wrong on the phone!' Emily cried, her eyes flaring. 'I know I said we should tell her face to face, but now I'm wondering what explanation to give.'

'You'll manage. Wriggle out of it, don't say anything concrete. You're very good at being evasive, Emily.'

'I *am*?' Emily gave Paula a doubtful stare. 'If you say so.' She shrugged, then ran over to the pram as Tessa began wailing.

Paula sprung up and followed her cousin. 'They're probably *both* damp and need changing. Let's take them upstairs anyway, and maybe you could then start preparing their bottles.'

'Nora would be off today, wouldn't she?' Emily moaned.

'It's always the way,' Paula murmured, rocking her baby daughter in her arms, making soft hushing sounds.

'Dower house, Clonloughlin,' a quiet male voice announced when Paula got through to Ireland fifteen minutes later.

She gave her name, asked to speak to the earl, and a split second later Anthony was on the line.

'*Paula* . . . hello. Thanks for everything, for taking charge the way you have. I'm very grateful. My mother was panicked earlier, quite at her wits' end, and she fell apart when the police came back.'

'I realize that, and it was nothing, really. I'm glad to help in any way I can. How are you feeling?'

'Fine. Very fine,' he asserted. 'I'm holding up pretty well under the circumstances. This is extremely unpleasant, of course, but I know it's going to be all right.'

'Yes,' Paula said, thinking he did not sound fine. Not in the least. His voice was weary, drained. Hoping she sounded more positive than she felt, she added, 'Everything will be over and done with in the next twenty-four hours, you'll see. Try not to worry in the meantime. I'd like to know what's been happening, but first I must tell you that

Emily spoke to Sally a few minutes ago. She's coming over here. She thinks *I* have some sort of crisis. We thought it was wiser not to tell her about this on the telephone.'

'I'm relieved to hear you've contacted her, Paula, I've been worried about Sally. I didn't know where to reach her in the Lake District. When we spoke on Friday Sally said she'd call me on Monday or Tuesday. Perhaps you would ask her to ring me, once you've explained this dreadful situation.'

'Of course. What are the latest developments? I know from my mother that the police have left . . . obviously they haven't charged you – '

'How could they!' he interrupted heatedly. 'I haven't done anything *wrong*, Paula! I wasn't involved in Min's death – ' His voice cracked and there was a pause as he struggled for control. After a moment he spoke more steadily, apologized, 'Sorry for breaking down. It's been such a terrible shock. Min and I have been having bitter quarrels, and she *was* being impossible, but I didn't wish anything like this to happen.' He lapsed into silence.

Paula heard his harsh breathing as he tried to compose himself. She said gently, 'You must be strong. We'll get you through this safely, Anthony, I promise.'

Eventually he said, 'You've been awfully good, Paula, awfully helpful. Well' – he sighed, added wearily,' – they've established the time of death. The local doctor did an examination. He thinks it was between ten-thirty and midnight.'

Paula's mouth went dry. From what Edwina had said, Anthony had taken her back to the Dower House around nine forty-five, then returned home. To go to bed? If so it was most unlikely that he had an alibi for his whereabouts during those key hours. But she made no comment, not wanting to alarm him further. 'Your mother said something about an autopsy.'

'Oh yes. I hope that'll be tomorrow. The inquest and

Coroner's Court will be on Wednesday or Thursday. Everything's so tediously slow here.' There was another heavy sigh, then dropping his voice, Anthony confided, 'It's that damnable land rover. I'm not certain the police believe me – about it breaking down in the afternoon.'

'Yes,' Paula acknowledged. 'But are you sure no one saw the land rover out there in the late afternoon, when it really *did* break down? Perhaps one of the estate workers? That would prove to the police that you're speaking the truth.'

'No one has come forward, and it's very deserted in that area of the estate – miles away from the house. I doubt anyone was around. However, there has been *one* positive development. A bit of news. The police have information that should exonerate me. They've been interviewing everyone here for the past few hours . . . the staff, the estate workers. Bridget – my housekeeper – told them that she saw me in the house between eleven and midnight.'

'Why didn't you tell me this before! Then you have an alibi!' Paula was flooded with relief.

'Yes, I do. I only hope the police believe her story.'

'Why wouldn't they?' she demanded, tensing.

'Don't misunderstand me, Paula, I've no reason to think they don't believe her, but Bridget has worked at Clonloughlin all of her life. Her mother was the housekeeper here before her, and she and I – well, we sort of grew up together. I'm praying the police don't get the idea she's lying to protect me. Mind you, she's unshakable in her story.'

Puzzled, Paula asked nervously, 'Why didn't *you* mention this to the police before? If you were with her last night after your mother left, surely –'

'I wasn't with her,' Anthony interjected. 'Actually, I didn't even see her. Bridget suffers from migraines, and apparently she had one all last evening. She was cleaning the kitchen after dinner when the migraine became unbearable. She passed the library on her way upstairs to her room. The light was on, the door was open, and she glanced in, saw me reading. However, she didn't call out to me because of her blinding pain. She ran upstairs, found her pills, and returned to the kitchen. She made herself a pot of tea, rested in the chair for half an hour, finished her work, set the dining room table for breakfast, and just after midnight she went to bed. Again she glanced through the open library door. I was by then working on the estate books, doing the accounting, and not wishing to interrupt me, she simply went on up to bed without even saying goodnight. It was her day off today and she wasn't here when the police first came.'

'Oh Anthony, this is the best news I've heard today!'

'I think it is. Still, she is the only person who saw me during those crucial hours. The two maids who work here had already gone home to the village – they come in daily. So . . . there's no one to corroborate her story, and it's well known around these parts that she's devoted to me, and is extraordinarily loyal to our family. The police might – and remember I'm only saying *might* – doubt her word, think she and I concocted the alibi.'

Paula's heart plummeted, her relief of a moment ago evaporating entirely. 'Oh God, don't say that.'

'I have to look at the worst, view this situation objectively,' Anthony said. 'On the other hand, I don't see how the police can dismiss her, say she's lying without being absolutely certain that she *is* making it up, and I know she'll stick to her guns.'

Pulling herself upright in the chair, Paula said slowly, 'Yes, that's true. However, when I talk to Henry Rossiter later, about getting legal advice, I'm also going to suggest we retain a criminal lawyer.'

'Hang on a minute!' Anthony exclaimed. 'That's jumping the gun isn't it!' He sounded aghast at this idea. 'I haven't done anything *wrong*, I've told you that, Paula. *A criminal lawyer*. Christ, that's going to make me look as guilty as hell.'

'Of course it isn't,' Paula shot back sternly, determined to stand her ground. 'And let's wait to hear what Henry has to say. I trust his judgement, as Grandy has for many years. He won't steer us in the wrong direction. Please, Anthony, don't make swift decisions out of hand.'

'Very well, get Henry's opinion,' he agreed, although somewhat grudgingly.

After they had concluded their conversation Paula sat at her desk in the conservatory. She ran a hand through her hair, rubbed her eyes, stretched. Then eyeing the pad in front of her on the desk she dragged her thoughts back to her list. Three people still had to be called . . . Jim, Winston, Henry Rossiter. Looking at her watch she saw that it was now seven-thirty. Henry would not be available for another hour at least, and obviously Emily had not had a chance to reach Jim or Winston in Canada, since she was preparing the babies' bottles in the nursery. Paula went to join her there.

Once they were settled comfortably, each cradling a child, Paula recounted her conversation with Anthony.

Emily listened carefully as she adjusted the feeding bottle, glancing at Paula several times, nodding her understanding.

'That's the gist of it then . . . Bridget has given Anthony an alibi.'

A silence fell between them as they concentrated on the babies. Then very quietly, but in a voice of steel, Paula said, 'No grandson of Emma Harte's is going to be in the dock standing trial for murder. *I promise you that.*'

CHAPTER 24

'I hope you really *do* understand why we had to lie to you, Sally,' Paula said gently.

'Yes. And it's just as well that you did.' Sally Harte swallowed and cleared her throat nervously. Her voice shook as she added, 'I don't think I could have driven over here without having an accident if Emily had told me the truth on the phone.'

Paula nodded, continued to survey her cousin intently, filled with anxiousness for her.

For the last fifteen minutes, all through Paula's account of the events in Ireland, Sally had managed to cling to her self-control. Paula admired her for taking the terrible news without flinching. I ought to have known she would be brave, Paula thought. She always was stoical even as a child. The Harte backbone, her grandmother called it. Yet despite this extraordinary show of strength, Paula knew Sally was shattered. It showed in her cornflower eyes, now so devastated, and in her lovely face which was stark with shock.

Sally was holding herself so rigidly in the chair she looked as if she had been paralysed by Paula's recital, and leaning forward Paula took hold of Sally's hand. She was alarmed at its deathly coldness, said, 'Sally, you're frozen! Let me get you a brandy, or make you a cup of tea. You need something to warm you up.'

'No, no, really. Thanks anyway.' Sally attempted to bring a smile to her face without success, and as she continued to meet Paula's worried gaze her eyes suddenly filled. 'Anthony must be under the most dreadful strain,' she began unsteadily and stopped. Now the tears came, spilling out of her wide blue eyes, rolling down her ashen cheeks. Still she did not stir, nor did she utter a sound.

Paula got up and went and knelt in front of Sally, encircling her cousin with her arms. 'Oh darling, it's going to be all right,' Paula murmured with the utmost gentleness, full of compassion. 'Don't fight the tears. It's much better to cry really, to get the pain out, and crying does help a bit. It's a release.'

Sally clung to Paula, heaving with silent, racking sobs, and Paula stroked her black hair, gentled her, and eventually the awful quiet heaving lessened. Soon Sally straightened up, brushing her wet face with her strong painter's hands.

'I'm sorry,' she gasped, her voice strangling in her throat. She strove hard to get a hold of herself, blinking the tears away. 'I love him so much, Paula. I can hardly stand it, knowing what he's going through . . . he's so *alone* over there. I'm sure Aunt Edwina is no help at all. She's probably blaming all this on me.' She shook her head desperately. 'Oh God!' She pressed her hands to her contorted face which expressed her anguished thoughts. 'He needs me . . .'

Paula, who had returned to her chair, stiffened at these words. She held her breath, willing herself to be silent. She knew what must be said, but she was also aware that it would be wiser and kinder to wait until Sally had calmed herself further.

Emily, hovering in the doorway of the drawing room, flashed Paula a warning look and began to move her head violently from side to side. Silently Emily mouthed, *'Don't let her go over there.'*

Paula nodded, motioned for Emily to come into the room. This she did at once, seating herself in a nearby chair. In a half-whisper, Emily said to Paula, 'No luck, I'm afraid. There's no reply from Jim's room or Winston's either. I've left messages for them to call here the minute they get back to their hotels.'

Although Emily had spoken softly, Sally had heard her, and at the mention of her brother's name her hands fell away from her face. She jerked her head, looked directly at Emily. 'I wish Winston were here. I feel so . . . *helpless* . . .'

'I wish he were here too,' Emily replied and patted Sally's arm in her motherly way. 'But you're not helpless, since you've got us. It's going to be fine, honestly it is. Paula's been super, and she's in full control, on top of everything. Try not to worry.'

'I'll do my best.' Sally's eyes swivelled to Paula. 'I haven't thanked you – you've been wonderful. So have you, Emily, and I'm very grateful to you both.'

Discerning that Sally was a little more composed, Paula said, 'There is one thing I must say to you – please don't go to Ireland to be with Anthony. I know you're sick at heart, dreadfully concerned about him, but you really mustn't go over there. You can't do anything constructive, and, very frankly, your presence would be highly inflammatory.'

Sally was startled. 'I've no intention of going to *Clonloughlin*! I know there's been a lot of nasty gossip, Anthony told me about *that* weeks ago – he tells me everything. Obviously I don't want to add fuel to the fire. But Paula, I do think I ought to go to Ireland, either to Waterford or, better still, Dublin. I'll go tomorrow. I can leave in the morning, from Manchester Airport, and be there in several hours. At least I'll be closer to him than I am here in Yorkshire – '

'No!' Paula exclaimed with unusual sharpness. 'You can't go. You're staying here – even if I have to put you under lock and key!'

Sally began, 'But I – '

'*I'm not going to let you go to Ireland.*' Paula threw her

372

cousin a stern look and her mouth settled into resolute lines.

Sally stared back at Paula defiantly, and her pellucid blue eyes filled with stubbornness. Asserting herself, she said with equal firmness, 'I understand your reasoning. On the other hand, what harm is there in my being in Dublin?' When Paula remained silent Sally went on, 'It's hundreds of miles away from Clonloughlin.' She stopped again, frowned. 'If I'm in Dublin, Anthony will at least know I'm within easy reach, and we can be together once the inquest is over,' she finished shakily, sounding less sure of herself. The trembling started anew, and Sally clenched her hands together in her lap, striving to curb this, and then her eyes unexpectedly welled. 'He needs me, Paula. Don't you understand that? Understand that I have to be with him?'

Paula commanded: 'Now listen to me, and listen very, very carefully. You cannot help Anthony in any way whatsoever in this trying situation. In fact, you could easily do him irrevocable damage by showing up in Ireland. If Anthony were suspected of murder, you could be his motive. In Grandy's absence I am in charge in this family, and you'd better understand that I'm making *all* the rules. Therefore, Sally, I must insist that you stay here.'

Sally had shrunk back in the chair, momentarily stunned by Paula's vehemence. She had not realized how formidable her cousin could be.

Paula and Emily were watching Sally and now they exchanged knowing glances. It was Emily who broke the silence. She touched Sally's arm, said, 'Please take Paula's advice, Sal.'

Emotionally, Sally had the desire to be with Anthony because she believed he needed her during this dreadful time; intellectually, she was beginning to accept that going to him would be the wrong move to make. Paula *was* right in everything she had been saying. Listen to your head, not your heart, she cautioned herself.

'I'll stay here,' Sally whispered finally, leaning back in the chair, passing her hands over the aching muscles in her face.

Paula let out a sigh of relief. 'Thank God for that. Are you feeling up to ringing Anthony now? He's anxious to speak to you and you'll set his mind at rest, once he knows how well you're coping.'

Sally jumped up. 'Yes, yes, I must talk to him at once.'

'Why don't you go to my bedroom where it's quiet – private,' Paula suggested kindly.

'Thanks, I will.' Sally paused at the door, swung her head. She stared at Paula. 'You're the most daunting person I know,' she said and disappeared down the hall.

Paula gazed after her, then looked at Emily speechlessly.

Emily said, 'I'd better get to the phone too – don't you want to reach Henry Rossiter? It's well past eight-thirty, you know.'

Together they sat on the terrace, enjoying the gentle stillness of the gardens, cloaked now by a dark-blue sky peppered with brightly twinkling stars. It was a clear night, cloudless, with a full moon, and its silvered rim was just visible above the tops of the distant trees swaying and rustling under the soft evening breeze.

'I don't know about you, but I'm wiped out,' Emily said, breaking the long silence at last, peering across at Paula in the dusky, shadowy light.

Paula turned her face, and quite suddenly it was clearly illuminated in the bright glow emanating from the lamps in the drawing room immediately behind them. Emily noticed at once that the stern veil had been lifted, and a lovely softness dwelt there again and there was warmth in her cousin's expression.

Finally Paula answered. 'Yes, I'm a bit done in too, I must admit. But at least all the important phone calls are out of the way.' She lifted the goblet of white wine and took a long swallow. 'This *was* a good idea of yours, Emily. Sitting waiting for Jim or Winston to ring us was getting awfully wearisome and frustrating.'

'Yes, it was. I wonder if your father has managed to get hold of Philip yet? It must be nine-thirty by now.'

Squinting at her watch, Paula nodded. 'Almost. We have to give him time to get through to Australia. He'll be in touch soon.' Paula cleared her throat, continued, 'I do wish Sally had stayed longer. Do you think she was really all right when she left?'

'She was certainly calmer when she came downstairs, but awfully subdued.'

'Well, that's understandable.'

Emily made no response. Shifting her position in her chair, she picked up her drink, sipped it. 'Did you notice anything different about Sally?' There was a moment's hesitation on Emily's part before she added, 'I don't mean when she left, but in general.'

'She's put on weight.'

Emily's fingers tightened around her glass and dropping her voice, she whispered, 'I have a horrible feeling . . . well, I might as well say it, I think Sally's pregnant.'

Paula sighed. Her worst fears had been confirmed. 'That's what I was afraid you'd say, Emily. Actually, so do I.'

'Oh bloody hell!' Emily exploded, her voice rising. 'That's all we need. I'm surprised you didn't spot her condition at the *vernissage*. Or did you?'

'No, I didn't. Mind you, she was wearing a sort of loose, tenty dress. Anyway I was harassed, surrounded by people. But when she walked in tonight I was struck by her heaviness, especially across her bustline. Still, I was so concerned about the news I had to break I didn't dwell on her figure. I noticed her weight gain when she was standing near the fireplace, just before she left. It was most pronounced.'

'That's when it occurred to me. Oh my God, Paula, the balloon's going to go up when Uncle Randolph finds out!' Emily groaned loudly. 'I can't help wishing Gran were here.'

'So do I, but she isn't, and I don't want her dragged back needlessly. We'll have to cope the best way we can.' Paula rubbed her weary face and exhaled heavily. 'Oh God, what a ghastly mess this is, and poor Sally . . .' She shook her head sadly. 'I do feel sorry for her . . .' Paula left the rest of her sentence unfinished, sat staring into the shadows, filled with terrible misgivings about the situation in Ireland.

Emily said suddenly, 'Well, if she is pregnant there's no problem. At least they'll be able to get married now that –'

'Emily!' Paula swung her head, glared at her cousin horror struck. *'Don't say it,'* she warned.

'Oh sorry,' Emily apologized swiftly, but could not resist adding with her typical unnerving bluntness, 'Nevertheless, it *is* true.'

Paula gave her a withering look.

Lifting the wine bottle out of the ice bucket, Emily refilled their glasses, and remarked, 'I don't think I'd better mention the possibility of Sally being pregnant to Winston.'

'Don't you dare! In fact, we're not going to say anything to anyone, not even Grandy. I don't want *her* to have that kind of worry. As for the rest of the family . . . you know how gossipy they're inclined to be. To even hint that Sally's pregnant would be like throwing a can of petrol on a bonfire. Besides, let's face it, Emily, we don't *know* that she is expecting. She might have merely gained weight lately.'

'Yes,' Emily said, 'there is that possibility, and we don't want to give certain people room to talk.' She fell silent, sank back into the chair, gazing out at the garden. It had acquired a magical almost ethereal quality and the trees had turned to shimmering silver in the moonlight which now bathed everything in its extraordinary radiance. 'It's so peaceful, so beautiful,' Emily murmured. 'I could sit here forever. But I suppose I ought to drive over to Pennistone Royal to get my clothes for the office tomorrow, if I'm going to stay here with you tonight. I told Hilda what to pack for me, and she'll have my suitcase ready, so I won't be very long.'

Paula roused herself from her own reverie. 'Perhaps you should pop back there, but take my car, Emily. The Jag *is* ready for the scrap heap, and I don't want you stranded in the middle of nowhere.' Paula stood up. 'I'll look in on the babies, and then start supper. Do you really want bubble and squeak?' she asked, reaching for the ice bucket and moving into the drawing room.

'Yes, it's sort of *comforting*, it takes me back to the summers at Heron's Nest. We always had bubble and squeak on Sunday nights with Gran when we were little. Oh for the good old days. Besides, you've a lot of left-over vegetables in your fridge. We might as well use them up. And I'm ravenous.'

Paula looked over her shoulder and shook her head wonderingly. 'Doesn't anything ever affect your appetite, Apple Dumpling?'

Emily, following her inside, grinned somewhat self-consciously. 'I suppose not, Beanstalk,' she shot back, using Paula's childhood nickname. 'But listen, I'm going to scoot. I'll be back as quickly as I can, and if Winston happens to ring give him lots of love from me.'

As was usual on Sunday night, Harrogate was deserted and virtually free of traffic, and within minutes Emily was on the main Ripon road, speeding steadily along towards Pennistone Royal.

Since Paula had said she could take either of the two cars in the garage, Emily had elected to drive Jim's Aston Martin. For a while she concentrated on getting the feel of the powerful piece of machinery under her hands, enjoying

377

its smoothness and the sense of security she felt in the well-built and beautifully designed car. It was certainly a pleasant change from her rickety Jaguar which was so decrepit it was practically useless and probably unsafe.

Emily had clung to the old Jag for sentimental reasons in a way, inasmuch as it had once belonged to Winston. He had sold it to her four years ago and, until their fraternal relationship had blossomed into a love affair, driving his car had somehow seemed to bring him closer to her. It no longer held any significance because Winston himself was completely hers now that they were engaged. And the Jaguar had become a nuisance really, always breaking down at the most inopportune times. Grandy had been after her to get rid of it for ages and she decided she had better do so next week. She wondered what car to buy. An Aston Martin perhaps? Why not, it was a solid car, constructed like a tank. Emily began to ponder cars, but after a short while her thoughts not unnaturally turned to events in Ireland.

The land rover breaking down was a rotten piece of luck for Anthony, Emily thought. If it hadn't he would be totally in the clear. This would be an open-and-shut case. Pity he didn't go back for it before dinner, but no doubt he was trying to avoid Min. That poor woman . . . dying like that . . . drowning is the worst death . . . terrifying.

Emily shivered involuntarily as she contemplated the accident, endeavoured to push away the image of cold black water eddying and swirling, dragging Min down into its murky depths. Emily swallowed, held the steering wheel more tightly. She had inherited her grandmother's fear of water, and like Emma she was a poor swimmer, assiduously avoided boats, the sea, lakes and even the most innocuous of swimming pools. All terrified her.

In an effort to dispel the vivid mental picture of Min Standish's death, she turned on the car radio, twiddled the knob, but unable to find the station she liked she instantly switched it off. Through the car window she noticed the sign post which indicated she was approaching Ripley, and slowed down as she went through the small village, picking up speed as she left it behind, heading for South Stainley.

Unexpectedly, Emily felt her face tensing as a thought so distressing suddenly flashed through her mind, and she swerved, caught in the grip of apprehension. Righting the car immediately, she brought her full attention to the road, telling herself she would have an accident if she didn't concentrate.

Nonetheless, the thought would not go away. It was a question really, and it hovered over her in the most maddening way, and she wondered why it had not reared up before now. Finally she faced it head on: What *had* Min actually been *doing* out at the lake for some *five hours* before she drowned?

All through those summers they had spent at Heron's Nest, Emma Harte had instilled many things in her grandchildren. Chief amongst these was the importance of analysing a problem down to the last detail, examining every single aspect of it. Now Emily's brain began to turn with rapidity in the way it had been trained by Emma.

One possible answer to the question struck her instantly – Min had not spent five hours at the lake, because she had not been there in the afternoon. It had been late at night when she had gone there for the first time yesterday. Oh my God, Emily thought, shuddering uncontrollably, that would mean Anthony is lying. That can't be so, and even if he *was* responsible for her death, why didn't he remove the land rover? Why did he leave it at the lake?

Start at the beginning, Emily instructed herself. Think it through logically, and first of all work on the premise that he *could* be lying. She ran a possible sequence of events through her head.

Anthony has dinner with Edwina. He takes her home to the Dower House afterwards. He returns to Clonloughlin House

379

*around ten. Min arrives unexpectedly soon after. They quarrel.
He rushes out, jumps into the land rover and drives off. Min
follows, accosts him at the lake. They row again, she becomes
violent, following her pattern of the past few weeks. He fends
her off. They struggle. He accidentally kills her. He dumps the
body in the lake so that it will look like an accident. Then the
land rover won't start, or it conks out. He has no alternative
but to walk back to the house.*

It could have happened that way, Emily told herself
reluctantly. But *if* it did, why didn't he return to the lake
later to get the land rover? The last thing he would do is
leave it there.

Her mind raced as she took her original thought to its
conclusion.

*Anthony decides it's risky trying to tow the land rover by
himself late at night. He resolves to remove it early the next
morning. But the estate manager is up and about at the crack of
dawn and finds it first. Anthony concocts a plausible story with
Edwina about Min arriving in the afternoon, explains the land
rover broke down at that time. He cleverly bluffs his way
through, counting on everyone to conclude, as I myself did, that
only an innocent man would leave such damning evidence at
the scene. On the other hand, Anthony does have an alibi for
those crucial hours late at night. The housekeeper saw him. But
is Bridget to be believed?*

Was Anthony's story a huge pack of lies? Was this an
immensely daring and brilliant bluff?

As Emily passed through Pennistone village and turned
into the gates of her grandmother's estate she told herself
that a man would have to be awfully cold-blooded and
ruthless, would have to have nerves of steel to carry off
such a scheme so successfully. Was Anthony such a man?
No. How do you know that, Emily Barkstone? Only a few
hours ago you told Paula that neither of you knew him all
that *well.*

Appalled at her thoughts, Emily did her best to shake them off as she parked and climbed out of the car.

Hilda, her grandmother's housekeeper, was coming out of the door leading to the kitchen and the servants' quarters at the back of the house.

A broad smile flew on to Hilda's face at the sight of her. 'There you are, Miss Emily,' she said, and peered through her glasses worriedly. She clucked, 'You're looking a bit poorly. You'd best come to the kitchen for a cup of tea.'

'Thanks, Hilda, but I have to get back to Miss Paula's immediately. I'm fine, honestly, just a bit tired.' Emily managed to produce a smile, then glanced around, looking for her suitcase.

'Your overnight bag's here,' Hilda said, producing it from behind one of the heavy Tudor hall chairs. She carried it to her saying, 'What terrible news, just awful. It gave me a right turn, that it did. I had to sit down and have a drop of brandy after your phone call. His poor lordship . . . oh deary me what a tragedy for him. But then life's so unpredictable, isn't it.' She nodded, her face mournful, then took hold of Emily's arm with a show of affection. Accompanying her across the hall, she said, 'Does Mrs Harte know yet? Have you spoken to her?'

'No, Hilda. Mr David is trying to reach Mr Philip in Australia. Don't worry, Grandma will be all right.'

'Oh I've no doubts about that, none at all, Miss Emily. But it does seem so unfair. Just when she gets a chance for a little rest, a nice holiday, a dreadful thing like this accident has to happen. Your poor grandmother's life has been full of troubles . . . I'd hoped that by now she'd be free of them.'

'Yes, Hilda, I second that. But you said it yourself – unexpected things happen and we can't control life.'

Emily began edging her way to the front door, looking about her as she did, savouring the beauty of the Stone Hall, but also suddenly acutely conscious of its normality.

It was filled with lovely warm light, the fire in the huge hearth blazed as it always did through the autumn and winter, and pots of gold and bronze chrysanthemums were clustered in the well of the great staircase. Yes, this hall looked exactly the way it had all of her life, even to the brass urn filled with copper beech on the refectory table.

Its unchanging appearance engendered an enormous sense of security in Emily, and she felt Emma's presence so powerfully, so forcefully at this precise moment she was reassured, and her fears began to ebb away. Her grandmother was a brilliant woman with a shrewd and penetrating understanding of people. She loved and trusted Anthony . . . not because he was her grandson but because of his character and his qualities as a man.

Swinging around, Emily gave Hilda a dimpling smile and although her green eyes were serious her voice was strong as she said, 'Don't worry, Hilda, Gran will take this in her stride. And thanks for packing my bag.'

'It was no trouble, Miss Emily, and you drive carefully, do you hear.'

Taking her leave of Hilda, Emily ran outside to the Aston Martin, threw her bag on the back seat and within seconds she had reversed the car and was spinning down the driveway, heading back the way she had come.

On her return trip to Harrogate she kept a firm hold on the positive feelings she had experienced at Pennistone Royal, and she kept telling herself that Anthony had been truthful and that Min's death was an accident.

In fact Emily had so brainwashed herself she was in exceptionally good spirits when she drove into the garage at Long Meadow. Although she had made the journey to Pennistone and back in record time, it had taken her a good hour, and she was beginning to feel faint with hunger. She was looking forward to a pleasant supper and her mouth watered as she thought of cold lamb, bubble and squeak and a glass of icy white wine.

But all such thoughts were swept out of her head as she went into the kitchen. She could not fail to see the disarray at once. Food lay abandoned on the counter top. The lamb was only half carved, the bubble and squeak had congealed in the frying pan on top of the stove and cupboard doors swung open.

Paula sat inertly at the kitchen table and there was such a stricken look on her face Emily's worries sprang to life.

'What is it?' she cried from the doorway. 'Something awful's happened at Clonloughlin. They haven't arrested — '

'No, no, nothing like that,' Paula assured her, lifting her eyes. 'I haven't even heard a peep out of them.' Her voice was exhausted.

'Then what is it?' Emily demanded, joining her at the table, scanning her troubled face.

Paula exhaled, remained mute.

Emily suspected her cousin had been crying, and leaning forward she took hold of her slender, tapering hand and patted it. 'Please tell me,' she said softly.

'I've had a terrible row with Jim. He phoned a little while ago and he was so snotty with me I can't get over it.'

'But *why*?'

'*Sam Fellowes*. He ignored my warning and called Jim. He left three urgent messages at the hotel in Toronto. When Jim got in he rang him back, and Fellowes told him about the accident, and my instructions not to run a story, or an obituary. Fellowes said I'd treated him in a most rude and high-handed manner, that I'd even threatened to give him the sack. Jim was obviously furious, yelled at me, *chastised* me. He thinks I handled things most undiplomatically. He said he'd had to spend twenty minutes placating Fellowes, and had finally convinced him not to resign.' Paula reached for a handkerchief and blew her nose.

383

'I can't believe it!' Emily was aghast. 'Surely Jim apologized once he understood your reasons for putting a lid on the story, when you explained about Anthony being under suspicion.'

'Oh he did ease off a bit,' Paula told her morosely, 'but his nose was definitely out of joint. And no, he didn't apologize. He was more concerned about whether he could get a flight to Ireland tomorrow. He thinks he should be with Edwina and Anthony to give them moral support.'

Emily made a disagreeable face. 'He would.' She shook her head slowly. 'What's wrong with Jim? Has he forgotten Grandy's rule about the family not being mentioned in our newspapers?'

'No. At the outset of our conversation he said this was different, that since reports of Min's death would probably appear in the nationals, we'd look ridiculous if we didn't carry an obituary. Once he was fully aware of the facts he sort of calmed down, but he still insisted I had handled Fellowes in the wrong way.'

'What the hell did he expect you to do?'

Paula smiled thinly. 'He said I should have told Fellowes not to run anything in the early editions, but to have the obituary prepared, and then to hold it until either Winston or he had been contacted in Canada. He told me it was their decision – his and Winston's – not *mine*.'

Emily's jaw dropped and she gave Paula a hard and baffled stare. 'Doesn't he *know* that you have Grandy's power of attorney, and Winston's, to act on their behalf in an emergency?'

'I didn't see any reason to say anything before he left,' Paula murmured. 'I didn't want to hurt his feelings. I'd have had to break the news that I'm the trustee, with Winston and Alexander, of our children's shares in Consolidated, not him.' When Emily said nothing, Paula insisted, 'How could I tell him *that*, Emily?'

'Well, you should have,' Emily retorted crossly.

'Perhaps,' Paula admitted, ignoring her tone.

I bet she still hasn't told him, Emily thought, but said, 'Is Jim *really* going to rush to Ireland?'

'I'm not certain. He was anxious to talk to Winston. Jim had been trying to reach him in Vancouver before he called here.'

'You mean we were the *last* on his list and after all the urgent messages I left?' Emily was flabbergasted.

Paula nodded. The two cousins exchanged long, very knowing looks, remembering their grandmother's strictest rule, one that had been drilled into them continually. Emma had told them to always check with at least one member of the family in any emergency before acting, to resist talking to strangers, to be supportive of each other, and most importantly to close ranks to protect the family.

Paula said hesitantly, 'I suppose he thought there was something wrong at the paper – '

'He might not have been brought up by Grandy, but he sure as hell knows her rules!' Emily exploded. 'He ought to have called us *first*, then he would have had the facts. It might have prevented the row you two had if nothing else.' She sat back jerkily, her annoyance with Jim apparent.

'That's true. Oh, never mind, Emily, it doesn't matter. Look, I should have told you this the moment you arrived . . . Winston rang.' Paula gave her a smile, determined to forget about Jim's unreasonable behaviour.

'When?' Emily asked eagerly, then added pithily, 'I bet *he* didn't have long dialogues with the whole world first!'

Paula laughed for the first time in hours. 'You're absolutely right, darling. And he reached me just a few minutes after I'd hung up on Jim.'

'Tell me everything Winston said, and please don't miss out on one single word.'

Paula looked across at Emily with fond indulgence, her expression warm and caring. 'Winston had been having lunch with the chairman of the board of the paper mill, at the latter's home. When he finally got back to the hotel late this afternoon, afternoon in Canada that is, he found a pile of messages. Sam Fellowes had called – *naturally* – so had Sally, Jim and you. Since you'd left *this* number, and since Fellowes had said it was urgent they speak, Winston immediately suspected there was some sort of crisis at the paper. Naturally he wanted to talk to me or you before anyone else. Grandy's golden rule is not something any of *us* is likely to forget. Winston was really thrown off balance when I told him Min was dead, and he was particularly concerned about Sally. "Keep that sister of mine as far away from Clonloughlin as you can," he repeated quite a few times. I set his mind at rest, of course, and he was awfully relieved I'd been tough with her. He asked a lot of pertinent questions, which I was able to answer, and he said I'd done the right things, and that between the two of us we'd made all the right moves, too. He was also glad you're staying here tonight.'

'Does he plan to fly home?' Emily asked.

'No, not unless the situation at Clonloughlin changes – for the worse. He reminded me that we'd all been trained in the same army camp by the same general, and pointed out that he couldn't contribute anything more than you or I could, and so therefore he intended to go about his business in a normal manner.'

'He's right of course.' Emily paused for a fraction of a second, before asking, 'Did you say anything about the row, Jim's attitude towards you?'

'Only in passing, Emily. I didn't want to make a big thing about it, but I'm afraid Winston was fit to be tied. He was very down on Jim. He also said Fellowes was a fool, that his job had been in the balance for a long time. And then he sort of wondered aloud why Jim hadn't spoken to me before calling Fellowes back.' Paula shrugged. 'I told him his guess was as good as mine. In any event, he's going to talk to Jim about Fellowes, and also about going to Ireland. He thinks Jim should stay in Canada, but I got the feeling Winston wouldn't interfere if Jim insisted on leaving for Dublin tomorrow. That's about it, but he asked for you, of course, and he sends his love.'

'I do wish I hadn't missed him. I was longing to talk to him,' Emily said a little wistfully.

'Oh you can do that, any time after midnight – our time,' Paula immediately volunteered. 'Winston's not going out this evening. He told me he would order something up to the suite, and he indicated he was going to ring Sally and Jim, and I suspect he's going to give Sam Fellowes an earful.'

'I'm sure he is, and I'll give him a buzz a bit later.' Emily rose, slipped out of her cardigan and hung it on the back of the chair. 'What about your father . . . did he reach Philip?'

'Yes, about an hour ago, only a few minutes after you'd left for Pennistone. It was breakfast time at Dunoon and Grandy was up, having her morning tea and toast with Philip. She knows. Daddy spoke to her as well.' Paula eyed Emily carefully. 'What do you bet we'll hear from her before very long?'

'Everything I have,' Emily laughed. 'It's a certainty Grandy'll ring us as soon as she's had time to think up a few penetrating questions which are bound to catch us off guard.'

Paula could not help laughing with Emily. 'That's a bit naughty.'

'Well, you know as well as I do that Emma Harte is always testing her grandchildren, to see if they're on their toes. Why should tonight be any different?'

Throwing her a thoughtful glance, Paula said, 'I don't suppose it is, and let's be thankful she brought us up the way she did . . . at least we're capable of handling any emergency.'

'Yes,' Emily agreed. 'And in the meantime, I'm going to revive the bubble and squeak and make us a lovely supper.'

CHAPTER 25

'I'm beginning to think that Jim and I are always going to be at cross purposes, Daddy,' Paula said.

David Amory, who was standing at the bar cabinet in the drawing room of his Regent's Park flat, swung around. The remark had startled him inasmuch as he had caught a most discernible hint of irritation in his daughter's voice. A dark brow lifted. 'In what sense, darling?'

'He sees things quite differently than I do. Of course, that's all right, because everyone has their own vision of the world, of life, and each of us handles problems, people and situations in our individual way, as best we can. But Jim will never admit he's wrong about anything, and he's continually accusing me of over-reacting.'

David made no response. A wry smile flickered and his cool intelligent eyes held his daughter's for a split second before he turned back to the bar and refilled their glasses. Carrying them over to the seating arrangement in front of the tall windows, he handed her the vodka and tonic, seated himself opposite her.

Settling back in the chair, David took a swallow of his scotch and soda, and asked, 'Does he think you've reacted too strongly to the mess in Ireland? Is that it?'

'Yes.'

David nodded thoughtfully. 'Do *you* think you have?'

'No, I don't.'

'Good girl. I've always rather admired your decisiveness, your unwavering attitude, and you're one of the few women I know who isn't forever changing her mind. So stick to your guns, and don't let Jim upset you, especially when you're certain you've made the proper moves. We can't please everyone in life, Paula, and so the important thing is to be true to oneself. That's *your* priority.'

'I know it is.' Paula leaned forward, said now with some intensity, 'I have enough common sense to admit it when I'm wrong, but in this instance I'm convinced I was wise to take the precautions I did, to clap a lid on everything, to cover us for *any* eventuality. It may be a status quo in Ireland, and the national papers may have treated the story in a routine way – so far. But that doesn't mean we're out of the woods yet.'

'Naturally we're not, and we won't be until after the autopsy and the inquest.' David gazed down into his drink reflectively. 'I didn't particularly like the wire service story that ran today in some of the papers . . . about the police investigating the mysterious circumstances surrounding Min's death. On the other hand, there was no mention of Anthony. Thank God for the rather stringent libel laws in this country.' He looked up, frowned. 'I'm just praying that none of the more sensational dailies don't blow the investigation out of proportion. Well – ' He gave her a kindly smile, finished, 'We're just going to have to sit this one out, darling. And getting back to Jim, I don't wish to sound critical, but if you ask me he's the one who has over-reacted. It was quite unnecessary for him to fly to Ireland. Your mother is coping nicely.'

'Yes she is, and I'm proud of her.'

Reaching for a cigarette and lighting it, David remarked, 'For what it's worth, you did exactly what Grandy would have done had she been here. Throughout the twenty-seven years I've known her, Emma has constantly told me she doesn't like unpleasant surprises, and that in her lexicon prevention is infinitely better than any kind of cure. Jim may not concur with your decisions, your actions, but Grandy, Henry and I do, and we've all told you so in the last twenty-four hours.'

'You've been very supportive, and when Gran called me again this afternoon, just before I left Leeds, she reiterated her confidence in me and in all of us, actually.'

'So you said – and that's the reason she's decided not to come back. Look Paula, this may sound silly, when we're under such a great deal of tension, but please do try to relax. *I* certainly shall. And don't worry about Jim's attitude. Whilst I'm fully aware you want his approval, you'd be wise to recognize you're not going to get it, because he doesn't understand – ' David stopped short, regretting this slip, not wishing to criticize his son-in-law. He had long been disappointed in Jim, but he had managed to keep his feelings to himself thus far. He had not even voiced them to Daisy.

Paula, quick as ever, said, 'Were you going to say he doesn't understand my reasoning, or that he doesn't understand me?'

There was an awkward silence.

Paula stared at her father. David met her questioning gaze unblinkingly. He was convinced Jim Fairley did not have the slightest conception of his daughter's character nor her business ethos, but electing to go with the lesser of two evils, he said, 'Your reasoning.'

She nodded. 'I've known that for some time now. Jim can be very naïve, which is especially surprising to me, since he's a newspaperman accustomed to seeing so many of the worst aspects of people, of life. Yet his judgement is way off more often than not, and it seems to me that he looks at the world through rose-coloured glasses.' She let out a tiny sigh. 'And to be honest, I'm also starting to think he doesn't understand the first thing about me, or the way my mind works, or why I do the things I do.'

David was conscious of the misery in her tone and he looked across at her, filling with concern at the sight of her forlorn expression and her confirmation of his own suspicions about Jim. 'You can tell me to mind my own business if you want – but look here, Paula, is your marriage in trouble?'

'No, I don't think so, even though we do have our differences. I love Jim very much, Daddy.'

'I'm sure you do and that he feels the same way, but love isn't always enough, Paula. You've got to be able to live with someone twenty-four hours a day, year in and year out, and comfortably so on that continuing basis. And you can only do that if there is true understanding between the two of you.'

'Yes,' she agreed with a faint, hesitant smile, wondering whether to pour out her troubles to her father. She decided against it. Tonight was not the right moment. Adopting a more confident tone, she assured him, 'We'll work it out, I'm certain of that, because we really do care for each other. Please don't worry, and don't say anything to Mummy, will you? Promise?'

'I promise, and I'm not going to pry, but I do want you to remember that you can confide in me any time you wish, darling. I love you very much and naturally your happiness is important to me.' David drained his glass, continued, 'As it is to your mother too. However, you're right, she'd be disturbed if she thought your relationship with Jim was anything less than perfect.'

'You've been so happy with Mummy, haven't you, Daddy?'

'Yes. *Very.* Mind you, we've had our ups and downs.' David chuckled, noticing the look of genuine astonishment registering in Paula's eyes. 'It's nice to know you were never aware of our rough patches, and we *did* have a few. But then any marriage worth its salt is never all sweetness and light. There's a marvellous line in *David Copperfield* which I've always been partial to, and it's very apt when I think of my marriage to Daisy . . . *the strongest steel goes through the hottest fire.* Yes, my dear, we had our troubles just like most people do. Nevertheless, we overcame them.'

Paula, still surprised at his revelation said, '*Troubles*. Were they really serious?'

Shaking his head and chuckling again, David told her, 'Now, when I look back, they were very piddling, but when we were suffering through them they seemed quite monumental. Which is why I'm inclined to agree with you when you say you'll work things out with Jim. I'm sure you will, and the marriage will be all that much better. But if it isn't – ' He gave her a long hard stare. 'Then don't be afraid to let go, to end it whilst you're still young and can find someone else. And don't fall into the trap of staying together for the children's sake if the marriage *is* seriously damaged. That kind of reasoning is cockeyed in my opinion. In the long run, everyone's miserably unhappy, including the children. Self-sacrifice of that nature is for martyrs, and *they* usually end up being a pain in the rear end,' he finished, deciding he had said enough, if not far too much perhaps. Still, Paula was strong, sound of judgement, and determined to lead her own life. He knew she would brook no interference. And neither he nor anyone else would have much, if any, influence on her decisions. Not now or in the future.

'Thanks, Daddy, for being such a good friend,' Paula said, 'and for not pontificating as some fathers would. I see you've finished your drink, and I don't really want mine, so let's go to dinner, shall we?'

'Splendid idea.' He glanced at the clock on the mantelpiece. 'Why yes, we ought to get a move on. I have a table for eight-thirty at Ziegi's.'

They went out into the hall together and as David helped her on with her coat he bent and kissed the top of her head, making a sudden gesture of affection. She pivoted to face him, stood on tiptoe to kiss his cheek in return. 'You're a truly special man, Daddy.'

His eyes, usually so cool and appraising, filled with great warmth. 'So are you, Daughter.'

Out on the street, David found a taxi at once, and after whizzing across town to Charles Street in Mayfair, they were being seated in the upstairs dining room of the famous club fifteen minutes after leaving the flat.

David brushed aside Paula's announcement that she was not very hungry, as he had so often done when she was a child. He took matters into his own hands, ordered Colchester oysters, steak Diane and puréed vegetables for them both, perused the impressive wine list with a knowledgeable eye, finally selected a vintage Mouton Rothschild, then insisted Paula share half a bottle of champagne with him whilst they waited for the meal.

By unspoken agreement neither mentioned the difficult situation at Clonloughlin, wanting a respite from their worry. For a while Paula did most of the talking, discussing matters pertaining to the stores, of which her father was now chairman of the board since Emma's retirement. Paula had stepped into his shoes automatically, held the title of managing director, and in consequence it was she who bore the brunt of running the chain on a day-to-day basis.

He was content to sit back and listen, enjoying her company, her wit and her charm, not to mention her indisputably brilliant mind. But then his daughter had always intrigued him. When she had been growing up she had seemed, at times, more like Emma's child than Daisy's and his, in that Emma had made Paula her very own. He had vaguely resented this, but had never been able to combat Emma's influence over her. Then when she was ten or thereabouts he began to understand that the child loved the three of them equally, played no one as a favourite, for with a wisdom that was remarkable, almost frightening, in one so young, she had made this perfectly clear to him, her mother and Emma. David was amused when some members of the family implied that Emma had brainwashed Paula to such an extent she had turned her into a clone. He knew his daughter had far too strong and stubborn a mind to follow the leader blindly, to permit herself to become something she was not, to accept indoctrination without question. The truth was much simpler. Emma had indeed trained Paula in her ways, but his daughter was already so much like Emma this had hardly been necessary. The similarities of their characters aside, they had always been on the same wave length and over the years this had become so finely tuned they appeared to read each other's thoughts, and frequently finished sentences for each other, much to everyone's amazement, including his own. But of all the qualities they shared, the one which truly impressed David was their ability to bring the most intense concentration and single-mindedness to the matter at hand. He was aware of the amount of mental and physical energy this took, and he considered it a great virtue in both women, a mark of their extraordinary genius. For genius it was.

Sometimes David had to remind himself that Paula was not yet twenty-five, as he did at this moment, struck as he was by her maturity and her keen understanding of complex business matters. As he absorbed her words he observed her closely, noting for the second time in the last hour her elegance and refinement. He never thought of Paula as being beautiful, and she was not, at least not in the accepted sense, because of her somewhat angular features, broad forehead and strong jawline. Rather, she was arrestingly attractive with her vividness of colouring, her translucent complexion and her superb grooming. Yes, it's her immense elegance, he thought, that's undoubtedly what draws all eyes to her. For the half-hour they had been in Ziegi's he had not failed to miss the discreet glances directed at them from time to time. He wondered, with a small flicker of amusement, if they thought she was his young mistress.

Detecting the laughter playing around his eyes, Paula

abandoned the point she was making and leaned forward. 'What's so funny, Daddy?'

He flashed a wide grin. 'I'm the envy of the men in this room . . . they most probably think you're my girlfriend.'

She shrugged, smiled, eyeing him objectively. If the other diners did harbour such a thought it was not so far-fetched really. At fifty-one her father was a good-looking man whom women found attractive and appealing. He had a strong, well-bred face, fine clear eyes, and a head of dark wavy hair tinged at the sides with grey that did nothing to age him. He was athletically inclined, skied and played squash in winter, took to the tennis courts in summer, and in consequence he was in excellent physical shape. Fastidious about his appearance, he was always beautifully dressed, a characteristic she knew she had inherited from him.

David was saying, 'You do look lovely tonight, Paula. The dress has great style. Black has always suited you, of course. Still, few women could carry it off as well as you do. It is rather severe, and – '

'Don't you like it?'

'Very much so.' He studied the Egyptian-style gold collar that encircled her long neck and partially filled out the squared neckline of the long-sleeved wool dress. Nefertiti, he said under his breath. Aloud he remarked, 'I've never seen you wearing the collar before. It's beautiful, rather striking, in fact. Is it new? A gift from Jim?'

Paula smiled mischievously, dropped her voice. 'Don't tell anyone, but it's a piece of costume jewellery. From Harte's. I'm sure it's not even brass, and it'll probably turn colour in no time at all. But when I saw it I knew it was perfect for this dress. It gives it a bit of a dash, wouldn't you say?'

'I would indeed.' He made a mental note to talk to the jewellery buyer tomorrow, decided to have the collar copied for Paula for her Christmas gift. He was usually at a loss to know what to give her for anniversaries and special occasions. She was not overly fond of jewels or other baubles and because of her highly individual taste it was difficult to shop for her successfully.

As the dinner progressed David and Paula touched on many topics of mutual interest, but eventually Paula brought the conversation back to business. Slowly, but with her usual self-assurance, she began to outline an idea she had for the stores.

David sat up straighter in the chair, listening alertly, intrigued by her concept, which showed an intuitive understanding of the buying public. And like so many really clever ideas it was rooted in simplicity. He wondered why no other retailer had ever thought of it.

Paula said, 'You've got a peculiar look on your face. Don't you think it will work?'

'On the contrary, I think it will be a tremendous hit. Expand on it further for me please, Paula.'

She did so, finished, 'But it would have to be a completely self-contained shop within the store.'

'You'd need a whole floor?'

'Not necessarily. Half a floor should work very well. I thought there could be three separate salons. One selling suits, plus shirts and blouses, another for coats and dresses, and a third salon offering shoes, boots and handbags. The key, of course, is having the individual salons adjoining each other, so that a woman can co-ordinate a complete outfit quickly and easily without having to trundle up and down to other floors searching for different items. It will save mistakes, not to mention time, for the shopper. And with an imaginative advertising campaign and some clever promotion I think we can do tremendous business.' She sat back, watching him through keenly attentive eyes.

'It's excellent. Yes, I'm enthusiastic. Any ideas about a name for this total shop of yours?'

'There are several very obvious ones, Daddy, such as

Working Woman or *Career Woman*. However, I've already dismissed those as being far too prosaic. We need a name that expresses exactly what we are about. We must put over the concept that we are selling clothes – good, well-designed clothes – to working women with business and professional careers, that we are offering a special service since we're making their task of putting a wardrobe together so much easier.'

'What about *Career Cachet*?' David suggested.

'Not bad.' Paula frowned. 'Is it too much in the other direction? Too fancy perhaps?' she asked, thinking aloud, and before he had a chance to reply went on, 'I thought of *Career Club* when I was driving to London this afternoon. But I'm not sure if that says what I want to say. Well, right now the name doesn't really matter. The main thing is to get the career shop into work. So . . . do I have your blessing?'

'Naturally you do, although you don't really need it.' David's eyes twinkled as he reminded her, 'The Harte chain is yours, Paula, lock, stock and barrel, and you *are* managing director.'

'But you're the chairman of the board,' she shot back. 'And therefore you're still my boss.'

'You always did have to have the last word, didn't you?' he murmured, and could not help thinking: as Emma always does.

'Sorry I'm late getting back,' Paula apologized as she hurried into the executive offices at the Knightsbridge store on Wednesday afternoon at five minutes to three.

'How was your meeting with Henry Rossiter?' Gaye asked, rising, following Paula into the palatial Georgian-style office that bore Emma's inimitable stamp.

'No problems. We spent most of the time reviewing Grandy's other holdings. We hardly touched on the Irish mess, gave it only a few minutes after our business session.

When we were having lunch, actually. Any further news from over there, by the way?' Paula threw her handbag on a chair, sat down behind the huge partners' desk that had once been her grandmother's.

'Yes. Your mother rang again. She wanted you to know she won't stay on after the inquest in Cork tomorrow as she had planned. She's decided to fly back to London immediately,' Gaye explained, taking the chair opposite the desk.

'I'm glad she's changed her mind. Once the inquest is out of the way we'll be able to breathe a little easier . . . I sincerely hope.'

'Since the police haven't made any moves I'm positive the hearing will be quite routine,' Gaye volunteered in a quiet tone.

'Let us pray.' Paula attempted a smile, then noticing Gaye's gloomy demeanour for the first time, she asked, '*You're* not looking too happy. What's been happening since I walked out of here at eleven o'clock?'

Gaye cleared her throat. 'Sorry to greet you with problems, Paula . . . but I'm afraid that's all we've got this afternoon.'

'Par for the course this week, or so it seems. All right, Gaye, let's have the bad news.'

'I'll start with what I feel are the real priorities,' Gaye said, lifting her head. 'Dale Stevens rang you about twenty minutes ago. Not from Texas though. He's in New York. At the Pierre Hotel. He sounded odd, worried, in my opinion. Certainly he wasn't his usual ebullient self.'

Trouble at Sitex, Paula thought. Stifling her apprehension, she said, 'Did he give you any indication why he wanted to speak to me?'

Gaye shook her head. 'But he did ask me when you plan to visit Harte's in New York. I said probably not before November, and this seemed to upset him. He sort of bit back a four-letter word and asked, "Are you sure she won't be over in the States earlier than that?" I said you wouldn't, not unless there was something urgent that needed your attention. I was fishing when I made that remark, but he didn't rise to the bait.'

'I'd better ring him back.' Paula reached for the phone.

Gaye said, 'He's not there. He went to a meeting. The message was to call him at six our time.'

'That's *all* he said?'

'Not one word more. Very cagey, our Mr Stevens was. I can tell from your expression that you're worried, think the worst, suspect that there's something amiss at Sitex Oil. I have to agree. He did sound awfully tense, even morose.'

'As you said before, that's very unusual. Dale's always so relaxed and cheerful. But there's no use speculating. Okay. Sitex at six. What's next?'

'Winston checked in from Vancouver over lunch time. *He* was also anxiety ridden. He has unexpected problems with the Canadian paper mill. They erupted late yesterday, after you and he had already spoken. The negotiations have stalled. He's withdrawing the offer today, as you both agreed he should if any difficulties developed. He's going to give them twenty-four hours, and if it's not back on the tracks by then he's flying to New York on Friday. He doesn't want you to bother ringing him. He said he'd be in touch – either way. But he doesn't hold out much hope of making the deal. He has a feeling it's kaput.'

'Damnation, that *is* annoying! It would have been such a good acquisition for Consolidated. We'll just have to hope he can turn the situation around. Go on, Gaye.'

'Sally Harte's disappeared,' Gaye murmured, giving Paula a sympathetic look.

'The fool! The silly little fool!' Paula cried sitting bolt upright. 'I told her not to go rushing off to Ireland, and I bet that's exactly where she's gone. Who called? Uncle Randolph?'

'No, Emily. Your Uncle Randolph spoke to her a couple of hours ago. Emily was on her way out when she received the call. She's on her way to town right now. As you know, she has a meeting at the London office of Genret tomorrow. Anyway, apparently your Uncle Randolph is in quite a rage, although Emily says she did her best to calm him down. Emily thinks Vivienne is hiding something, knows where Sally's gone but won't talk. She suggested you tackle Vivienne when you have a moment.'

Paula groaned. 'I do so love Emily's advice. Why the hell didn't she speak to Vivienne when she was still in Yorkshire! This is all I need today.'

'I did ask Emily to take a minute to talk to Vivienne before setting off, but she demurred, explained that it wouldn't do any good. She said, "Tell Paula I'm not as daunting as she is," and she hung up before I could say another word.'

'I see.' The two women exchanged concerned glances. Paula looked away, focusing on the fireplace, her face reflective, and then her mouth curved down in a stern and resolute line and her eyes narrowed.

Watching her closely, Gaye could not help thinking how much Paula resembled her grandmother at this moment and she thought: I hope to God she really is as strong as Emma Harte – as we have all come to believe.

Paula brought her gaze back to her assistant. 'I'll get to Vivienne later. Wherever Sally is, I can't very well remove her bodily, or force her to do as I say. Right now, business comes first. Anything else?'

'John Cross telephoned. He's in London. He asked for an appointment. Tomorrow morning, if convenient.'

'Oh!' Paula exclaimed, but she was not as surprised as she appeared to be. She had been expecting to hear from the head of Aire Communications for weeks. She and her grandmother had agreed he would come crawling back eventually.

Gaye stared at her, trying to fathom her expression which was quite unreadable. 'Cross left a number, Paula,' she said at last, breaking the silence. 'What do you want to do? You've a fairly clear calendar tomorrow.'

Pursing her lips and shaking her head, Paula admitted, 'To be truthful, I'm not sure . . . there doesn't seem to be much point in seeing him. I've nothing to say to that particular gentleman. I'll let you know before the end of the day.'

'Your cousin Sarah's back from Barbados, and she wants to see you. At four o'clock today. She says she has to come over to the store to see the ready-to-wear buyer, and could pop up for a few minutes. She was rather insistent.'

'She's back sooner than I expected. I'd better see her. It can't be anything important, so it shouldn't take very long. Sarah most likely wants to tell me about the opening of the boutique and the new hotel this past weekend. Is that all of it, Gaye?'

'It's enough, isn't it?' Gaye replied dourly.

Paula sat back, surveying her. 'Do you really like being my assistant? Or would you prefer to be my secretary after all? I can demote you, Gaye, if that's what you want. I aim to please in all things,' Paula teased, and laughed in spite of her many worries.

Gaye had the good grace to laugh too. 'Sorry I sounded so glum. And I'm relishing the new job, honestly I am. Besides, Sheila would be hurt and affronted if she was relegated to being the junior secretary again. She's so proud she works for you personally. She's very efficient, isn't she?'

'Yes, thanks to your assiduous training over the last few years.'

The telephone rang. Paula glared at it, shook her head.

Lifting the receiver, Gaye said crisply: 'Mrs Fairley's office.' There was a slight pause before she added, 'She's

401

right here.' Handing her the phone, Gaye mouthed, 'It's okay – it's only Alexander.' Gaye hurried out of the room.

'How do you like being back at the old grindstone?' Paula said into the phone.

'Bloody awful after two weeks of sunshine and indolence in the South of France. But it's a relief in one sense – I don't have to cope with my mother,' Alexander answered in a sarcastic voice, rushed on, 'Can you have supper with me tonight? There's a few things I'd like to discuss with you.'

'Serious?'

'No. Interesting, though.'

'Why don't you tell me now?' Paula pressed, her curiosity flaring.

'Too involved. Also, I'm due to start a meeting in exactly ten minutes. Since you and I are both in town and alone, I thought it was a good opportunity to get together. Fancy dining at the White Elephant?'

'That sounds like a nice change. Thanks for the invitation, and I'd love to see you, as long as we can make it around nine. I have to work late.'

'Who doesn't, and nine's fine. I'll pick you up at Belgrave Square, shall I? Around eight-thirty?'

'Perfect. Oh, and Sandy, you'd better make the reservation for three. Your sister's on her way up to London, and I'm sure Emily'll insist on joining us.'

'Too true. Miss Nosey Parker has to be in on everything,' he responded with a dry laugh. 'See you later.'

Paula rose and walked over to stand with her back to the fireplace. The weather had turned cold in the last few days and as soon as there was the slightest hint of an autumn nip in the air the fire was automatically lit every morning as it had been for years. Paula was glad that Emma's long tradition continued unchanged. She suddenly felt chilled to the bone and the bright blaze was warming, also brought a cheerful aspect to the handsome room.

She scowled to herself as her thoughts settled on Dale Stevens. It was not unusual for him to be in constant contact with her, since she was her grandmother's representative at Sitex. Emma, who with forty-two per cent of the stock was the largest single stockholder, had always been a power in the oil company and a member of the board. Now that she filled this role Dale conferred with her several times a month. On the other hand, this afternoon's call had apparently not been routine. Gaye had discerned a troubled note in his voice, and she trusted Gaye's judgement. After all, it had been the redoubtable Sloane who had discovered the plot against Grandy last year. Dale is probably having trouble with the Harry Marriott faction on the board, Paula suddenly thought. He had been her grandfather's partner when Paul McGill had founded Sydney-Texas Oil in the twenties, and he had always been difficult. Emma had managed to get him kicked upstairs as chairman of the board in January of 1968, and had manipulated the board to do her will. They had voted with her, and had hired Dale Stevens, Emma's protégé, as the new president. Still, some of the board members who were Marriott's cronies resented Dale, and Paula decided that they were most likely creating an untenable situation for him.

Damn, she cursed under her breath. I wish I could reach him before six. Paula glanced at her watch. It was three-thirty. Two-and-a-half hours to wait. Well, at least she had time to sign her letters, go over the inter-office memos piled on her desk, and speak to Vivienne Harte before Sarah Lowther appeared on the scene.

Returning to her desk, Paula flipped through the memos, saw that some of them raised questions which were too complicated to deal with quickly, and these she placed on one side. After signing the morning's correspondence, she put through a call to Allington Hall in Middleham.

'Hello, Vivienne,' Paula said when her cousin answered. 'How are you?'

'Oh, Paula! Hello. I'm pretty good, and you?'

'Worried, Vivienne. I just heard that – '

'If you're phoning about Sally I won't tell you where she is! *I promised her*. Daddy can't get it out of me, and neither will you.'

Paula said with firmness, 'Now, Vivienne, I'm sure Sally wouldn't be upset if you told me. I'm the – '

'Oh yes she would,' Vivienne interrupted heatedly. 'She doesn't want anybody to know where she's gone. Not even you. Please don't badger me, put me in this terrible position.'

'You *can* tell me . . . Listen, I won't say a thing to your father, or another soul, not even Winston when he calls me later. You must know I won't break my word.'

'No, I don't know that . . . you're expecting *me* to break *mine*,' Vivienne retorted. 'My poor sister is like a wounded bird, worn out too, and she needs to have a little peace and quiet. Daddy hasn't stopped ranting and raving at her since Sunday night.'

'I'm sorry to hear that. Look here, you don't have to tell me where she is, but would you agree to tell me where she's *not*?'

'What do you mean?' Vivienne asked warily.

'If I name a place where Sally has *not* gone, will you tell me? All you have to say is *no*.'

Vivienne laughed hollowly. 'You're trying to trap me, Paula. If I'm silent when I hear a particular name you'll know immediately that's where she's staying.' Vivienne laughed again, her incredulity echoing down the wire. 'Do you think I'm daft? Or green? I haven't fallen off a banana boat, you know.'

'I need to know where your sister is hiding herself,' Paula snapped, growing exasperated, 'and for a variety of reasons which I don't propose to go into with you.'

'Don't talk to me as if I'm a little kid. I'm nineteen,' Vivienne cried, her own temper flaring.

Paula sighed. 'Let's not argue, Viv, and I can only add this . . . if Sally's gone dashing off to Ireland she's a bigger fool than I thought, because she will only be creating problems for herself, and for Anthony.'

'Sally's hardly a *fool*! Obviously she wouldn't be stupid enough to go to Ireland – ' Vivienne stopped abruptly.

Success, Paula thought with a faint smile. Her ruse had worked. She said, 'If Sally happens to phone you, tell her I'm having dinner with Alexander and Emily at the White Elephant tonight. Just in case she wants to join us.'

'I've got to go, Paula,' Vivienne said hurriedly after a short pause. 'Daddy needs me in the stables. So I'll say goodbye now.'

'Tell Sally to get in touch with me if she needs anything. Goodbye, Vivienne dear.'

Paula stared at the phone for a long moment, reflecting on their conversation. Well, Sally was not in Ireland. More than likely she was not in London either, since it was not her favourite place. Could she still be in Yorkshire? If so, where? A phrase Vivienne had used echoed into her mind. She had referred to her sister as a *wounded bird*. A figure of speech to describe Sally's state? Or had it perhaps been an unconscious association in the girl's mind? Wounded birds tried to get back to their nests . . . Heron's Nest? *Of course*. Sally loved Scarborough and many of her paintings were of the spots where they had spent so much time as children. That's where *I* would go if I wanted to hide, Paula said to herself. It's accessible, comfortable, the larder is always fully stocked, and old Mrs Bonnyface has a set of keys.

Lifting the receiver, Paula started to dial Heron's Nest and then changed her mind. It would be infinitely kinder to leave Sally alone for the time being. Whether she was in Scarborough or not was irrelevant really. The important thing was that she was nowhere near Clonloughlin, and this knowledge now eased Paula's anxiety about Sally Harte, of whom she was extremely fond.

'Paula?'

'Yes, Gaye?' Paula asked leaning closer to the intercom.

'Sarah's arrived.'

'Have her come in, Gaye, please.'

A moment later Sarah Lowther was walking across the floor, the expression on her pale freckled face as purposeful as her step. She wore a bottle-green gabardine suit so beautifully cut it did wonders for her somewhat plumpish figure. Also, the colour was a flattering contrast to her russet-red hair which framed her face in luxuriant waves and softened her broad but not unattractive features.

'Hello, Paula,' she said briskly, coming to a halt in the centre of the room. 'You're looking well. Thinner than ever. I don't know how you do it . . . it's a struggle for me to lose an ounce.'

Paula half smiled, and brushing aside the personal comment, said, 'Welcome back, Sarah.' She stepped around the desk, kissed her cousin on the cheek. 'Let's sit over there by the fire,' she went on. 'Would you like a cup of tea?'

'No, thanks anyway.' Sarah turned smartly on her high heels and moved in the direction of the sofa. Seating herself in the corner nearest the fireplace, she leaned back, crossed her legs and smoothed her skirt. She let her eyes rove over Paula, admiring the simplicity and elegance of the deep purple wool dress. It was a marvel, and as head of the fashion division of Harte Enterprises Sarah knew it was by Yves Saint-Laurent. Biting back the compliment which had sprung to her lips, she said, 'Jonathan tells me the Irish lot are killing each other off . . . I'm surprised Grandmother hasn't hot-footed it back here.'

'That's not a very nice thing to say about Anthony, Sarah,' Paula gently reproved, seating herself in a chair, frowning. 'Min's death was an accident, and *why* should

Gran come back? The whole thing's going to be over and done with by tomorrow at this time.'

Sarah gave Paula an odd look, raised an auburn brow. 'Let's hope you're right.'

'Tell me about the opening of the new hotel and our first boutique,' Paula said, neatly changing the subject.

Sarah remained silent.

Paula insisted, 'Come on, I'm longing to hear all about it.'

'It went off well,' Sarah said at last. 'But then why wouldn't it? I've worked very hard for months to ensure that it would. To tell you the truth, the whole trip was a hard grind. I was on my feet twenty-four hours a day. Miranda was tied up with the hotel, so I had to really buckle down, supervise the unpacking and pressing of the dresses, get the windows dressed, create eye-catching interior displays,' she grumbled. 'But the merchandise I selected turned out to be perfect, even though I do say so myself. My Lady Hamilton dresses and resort wear appealed to everyone. They said the colours were fantastic, the fabrics superior, the designs bang on. We were jammed the day we opened, so we should do record business right through the season.'

'Oh I am pleased,' Paula said with enthusiasm, deciding to ignore Sarah's remarks about her contribution to the boutique which, in all truth, had been negligible. She asked, 'How's Merry?'

'All right, I suppose. I didn't see much of her. The O'Neills invited a plane load of celebrities to the hotel's gala opening weekend. So naturally she was busy rubbing noses with the famous.'

Paula's back went up at this remark, which she deemed bitchy and uncalled for, but she wisely let it pass. 'Did Shane fly down from New York?'

'Yes.'

'And?'

407

'And *what*?' Sarah asked, her voice turning huffy all of a sudden. She gave Paula a challenging stare and her face settled in cold lines.

Instantly struck by the dislike in Sarah's expression, Paula recoiled in surprise. Thrown though she was, she managed to say, 'Surely you saw something of Shane and Uncle Bryan? Merry may have been rushed off her feet as head of public relations, but I can't believe the O'Neills ignored you. After all they're family, and they're not like that.'

'Oh yes, I was invited to the gala evenings. But I was generally to exhausted too enjoy them. I didn't have much fun at all. That side of it was a complete bust.'

Sarah glanced into the fire, remembering her mortifying weekend of embarrassment, acute disappointment. Shane had been cruel, ignoring her much of the time. And when he had deigned to notice her he had been off-hand, patently uninterested in her as a woman. He wouldn't have treated Paula in such a rotten way, she thought miserably, sinking back into herself. An image of his face leaped out at her from the flames, his expression one of immense passion and love. She blinked, wanting to expunge this from her mind. That look had not been for her, but for Paula . . . that terrible day of the christening . . . she would never forget that look or that occasion. It was only then she had realized, to her horror and distress, that Shane O'Neill loved Paula Fairley. That's the real reason he has no time for me, she said silently. Damn Paula. I detest her. Jealousy rose up in Sarah so unexpectedly and with such force she kept her face averted, willing the emotion to go away, feeling faint and sick inside.

'Well, I'm sorry you didn't have a good time,' Paula murmured, attempting to be gracious yet asking herself what she had done to engender such sudden dislike in Sarah. Paula sat back and her eyes narrowed thoughtfully. She had no reason to think that Sarah was lying about the gala weekend, but somehow she did. She considered Sarah's self-congratulatory remarks, her pleased tone when she had spoken of her hard work. How she exaggerated.

Paula could not resist adding, 'So the work was gruelling – that's retailing, you know, Sarah. And let's face it, *you* were the one who insisted on going to Barbados. If I – '

'And it's a jolly good thing I did, isn't it?' Sarah interjected peremptorily, tearing her gaze from the fire, swinging her head to glare at Paula. 'Somebody had to be there to organize things. We'd have been in a nice mess if we'd relied on Merry, in view of her abdication of her duties. Or if we'd left things to chance as you wanted us to do.'

Paula was further astonished by this criticism and the belligerence underlying the comment. Unwilling to let Sarah get away with it, she said with some sharpness, 'That's most unfair of you. I had no intention of leaving anything to chance. I had intended to fly out there myself, until you made such a song and dance about going. Anyway, you don't have to worry about the other boutiques. I've hired Melanie Redfern from Harvey Nichols. She starts next week. She will be in charge of the Harte shops in all the O'Neill hotels, and she'll be working closely with me. And Merry, of course.'

'I see.' Sarah shifted her position and cleared her throat. 'Actually, the main reason I came to see you today is to make you an offer.'

'An *offer?*' Paula stiffened, wondering what Sarah was about to spring on her.

'Yes. I'd like to buy the boutiques for my division. There won't be any problem about money. We have stacks of spare cash. You see, in view of my considerable involvement with the boutiques, I'd like to have them under my aegis, make them part of Lady Hamilton Clothes. So just name your price – I'll meet it.'

Flabbergasted though she was at Sarah's ridiculous proposition, Paula retorted swiftly. 'Even if I wanted to, I couldn't do that, as you well know. The boutiques belong to the Harte department store chain.'

Sarah stared Paula down. Her expression hardened. 'So what – I'm offering you an easy way to make a fast profit. And a big one. That should please you, since your eyes are eternally glued to the bottom of a balance sheet.'

'I'd like to remind you that the Harte chain is a public company,' Paula exclaimed, thinking that her cousin had taken leave of her senses. 'I do have shareholders and a board of directors to answer to, in case this has escaped your notice.'

Sarah smiled narrowly. 'Don't talk to me about the board at Harte's. We all know about the board, my dear. It consists of Grandmother, you, your parents, Alexander and a handful of old codgers who'll do anything you say. If you wanted to, you could easily sell me the boutiques. It's your decision. Don't expect me to believe otherwise. That board will acquiesce to your wishes no matter what, as they always did what Grandmother wanted in the past. She had them in her pocket, and so do you.'

Paula fixed a pair of immensely cold eyes on her cousin, and her voice was equally icy, as she said, 'Harte's have invested a great deal of money in the new shops, and I have personally devoted an incredible amount of time and effort to the project for many months. I therefore have no intention of selling them to you, or to anyone else, even if the board sanctioned such a sale, which believe me, they wouldn't, not at this stage. You see, Sarah, I want the boutiques for Harte's, they're part of our growth and expansion programme. Also, I – '

'*Your* effort!' Sarah cried, seizing on this particular point. 'That's a laugh. I've worked much harder than you, and I selected all of the merchandise. Under the circumstances, it's only fair that – '

'Stop right there!' Paula warned, her face revealing her growing annoyance and impatience. 'I'm not sitting still for this nonsense, Sarah. Why you're bloody preposterous. You walk in here, commence to criticize me, then try to take credit for the success of the Barbados shop . . . and at the moment that's a moot point. Only time will tell us how successful it really is. But getting back to *your* efforts, I think you have a real nerve. It just so happens that Emily has done a lot more for us than you. She purchased every single accessory, which was no mean feat, and I recall that *I* picked out every bit of beach wear. Furthermore, Merry and I selected all of the clothing from your company – not *you*. I'll concede that you made the best lines available at Lady Hamilton, and designed the special evening wear, and perhaps you have worked conscientiously for the past ten days. However, your contribution to the first boutique was minor, very *minor* indeed.'

Paula rose and walked over to her desk, and sat down behind it. She finished quietly, 'As for trying to buy the boutiques from Harte's –' She shook her head wonderingly. 'I can only add that that's the most foolish thing I've ever heard, especially coming from you, when you of all people know how Grandy has structured things. Look, if you want to get involved in a new project, maybe we can put our heads together –' Paula stopped, immediately regretted her conciliatory gesture. Sarah's coldness was more pronounced than ever.

Sarah stood up without saying a thing. She made a beeline for the desk, stood facing Paula.

In a soft and uncommonly steady tone, Sarah said, 'Grandmother might have other ideas about the boutiques. She may well like the idea of selling them to me – has that occurred to you?' Not giving Paula a chance to reply, she continued in her oddly calm way, 'Grandy's not dead yet, and if I know her, I bet she hasn't signed over her seventy per cent of the shares in Harte's to you. Oh no, she's hanging on to those, I'm *quite* certain, wily as *she* is. And so, as far as I'm concerned, she's still the boss lady around here. I want you to understand one thing . . . I'm not letting the matter rest here. With you. Oh no, not by a long shot. I fully intend to telex Grandy. *Today*, Paula. I shall apprise her of our meeting, my offer and your rejection of it. We'll see who really runs Harte stores, won't we?'

Paula gave her a regretful look through saddened eyes. 'Send a telex. Send ten if you wish. You won't accomplish anything – '

'You're not the only grandchild Emma Harte has,' Sarah cut in, her voice biting. 'Although anyone would think it, the way you behave.'

'Sarah, don't let's quarrel like this. You're being childish, and you've always known Harte's is a public – ' Paula's sentence was left dangling in mid-air. Sarah had walked out. The door closed softly behind her.

Paula stared after her, shaking her head again, not yet fully recovered from her astonishment, Sarah's preposterous proposition and irrational attitude. She sighed under her breath. Only two weeks ago she had remarked to Emily that tranquillity had reigned supreme since their grandmother's departure in May.

I spoke too soon, Paula now thought, and she discovered that the most disturbing part of the meeting had been Sarah's blatant dislike of her. As Paula continued to contemplate her cousin's unexpected hostility she asked herself if it signalled the beginning of open warfare.

CHAPTER 26

Emily was awed.

'Just look at this evening gown. It's absolutely exquisite,' she said in hushed tones, lifting the garment out of the large box lined with layers and layers of tissue paper.

Alexander, lolling on the bed in one of the guest rooms in Emma's Belgrave Square flat, nodded in agreement. 'It also looks as if it's in perfect condition.' A fond smile glanced across his serious face as Emily glided into the middle of the floor and held it against herself, carefully.

The gown was a long slender sheath of turquoise silk, entirely encrusted with thousands of tiny bugle beads in shades of pale blue and emerald green. Emily moved slightly and the dress undulated, the beads instantly changing colour as they caught and held the light. The effect was dazzling.

Cocking his head to one side, continuing to regard his sister intently, Alexander said, 'You know, it contains all the colours of a summer sea in the South of France, and it certainly matches your eyes, Emily. What a pity you can't keep it, have it for yourself. It's not a bit outdated.'

'Oh I know, and I'd love it, but it's far too valuable really. Anyway, I couldn't do that to Paula. She needs the dress for her fashion exhibition next January.'

'Has she found a name for that yet?'

'She's considering calling it Fashion Fantasia, with the subheading Fifty Years of Elegance and Style. I rather like it, don't you?'

'Yes.' He watched Emily as she expertly folded the gown into the box and covered it with the tissue, remarking, 'Imagine Gran keeping the evening dress all these years. It's easily forty-five years old, and it really pongs of moth

413

balls.' He curled his nose in distaste, then added, 'But I bet our Gran looked smashing in it, with her red-gold hair and green eyes.'

Emily lifted her blonde head. 'To say the least, and you're right about its age. Just before Gran left she said we'd find it in one of her cedar closets on the top floor, along with the other clothes. Gran told us she'd first worn it at the supper dance she gave Uncle Frank and Aunt Natalie when they got engaged.' Emily put the lid on to the box, patted it down, glanced over at her brother. 'Do you know, there's even a pair of emerald satin slippers from Pinet to go with it, and they're in mint condition too. They look as if they've been worn once or twice and that's all.'

'Yes, everything's been so carefully preserved,' Alexander observed, thinking of his canny grandmother's sense of thrift which was legendary. Swinging his legs off the bed, he ambled over to the long metal clothes rack positioned near the window, ran his hand along the rack. Peering at the labels on the suits, dresses and evening gowns, he read out loud, 'Chanel, Vionet, Balenciaga, Molyneaux . . . these are all as good as new, Emily, and they *must* date back to the twenties and thirties.'

'They do, and that's why they're essential for the exhi-. bition. Several other women who are noted for their elegance – Best Dressed List ladies – are loaning similar designer clothes to Paula, and they've all accepted her invitation to come to the cocktail party at the store the night she opens the exhibition to the public.'

Emily now crossed to the dressing table, picked up a typed sheet, made a notation, slipped the sheet into its folder and said, 'Thanks for keeping me company, Sandy, while I checked everything off. Well, let's go downstairs, that's all I have time to do tonight. I promised to help Paula organize the rest of the clothes this weekend, since she's snowed under at the moment.'

'Where is she, by the way?' Alexander asked, following Emily out of the guest room on to the second floor landing. 'Don't tell me she's still at the store.'

'Oh no, she's here,' Emily said over her shoulder, tripping down the staircase. 'After we'd unpacked the clothes and hung them up to be checked for any minor repairs, she went to change her dress. She's probably popped into the old nursery.'

Alexander pushed open the drawing room door for Emily, stepped inside after her. 'Are the babies here too?' he asked, surprised.

'Yes, and Nora. Paula brought them to town with her on Monday afternoon. Oh look, Sandy, good old Parker's put out a bottle of white wine for us. Shall we have a glass now?' She rushed over to the console.

'Why not? Thanks, Emily.' He took a chair near the fireplace, crossed his long legs and lit a cigarette, studying his sister as she poured the wine. Although she was of average height he generally thought of her as being small, perhaps because she was so delicately made, so daintily proportioned. He nodded to himself. Emily had turned into a very pretty young woman in the last few years. How mean he and his male cousins had been to little Emily when they were children, teasing her about her enormous appetite and her totally spherical body, calling her Apple Dumpling. She was no longer anything like a dumpling – tonight she resembled a pert china doll in the flattering pink wool dress. Some china doll, he added under his breath, ruminating on her tremendous physical and mental energy, wondering, as he so often did, where it came from. Their grandmother. Certainly it was not something she had inherited from their parents. Their mother was an indolent, bored, spoiled socialite without a serious thought in her head. Their father was a has-been who had never really made it in the first place, forever the failure. Poor Dad, he thought, he's without doubt the nicest, kindest chap I know. Alexander reminded himself to ring his father tomorrow to make a date for lunch or dinner. They didn't really see enough of each other these days.

'Gosh, Sandy, I didn't notice your lovely tan when we were upstairs,' Emily remarked, bringing him the glass of wine, scrutinizing him closely. She flopped on to the chair opposite. 'You really look super. You should sit in the sun more often.'

'What, and let Harte Enterprises go to rack and ruin? Not on your life.' He raised his glass. '*Santé*.'

'Cheers,' said Emily, and after taking a sip, she asked, 'Where's old Mag?'

'She went to Scotland this morning to look at a shooting lodge that's going up for sale. The owner wants the real estate firm she works for to handle it, so Maggie's about to be given the grand tour. If she likes it, it'll go on their books. God knows who'll buy it, though. Who on earth wants a shooting lodge in this day and age I ask you?'

'A rich American,' Emily suggested. 'Have you set a date for your wedding?'

'June . . . possibly.'

'That's not fair!' Emily wailed, her eyes flashing. 'You know Winston and I are getting married in June. You'd better make sure Maggie checks with me before you set a firm date.'

'We could have a double wedding,' he said, and burst out laughing at her expression. 'Why are you looking at me like that?'

'If you don't know then I'm not going to tell you,' she retorted huffily. 'On the other hand, perhaps I should.'

'Forget that I said it. Anyway, I wasn't really serious.'

'Yes, you were, and I *shall* tell you,' Emily announced. 'There are three good reasons. One . . . every bride wants to be the centre of attraction on *her* special day and she certainly can't be if there's *another bride loitering around*. Two . . . Gran would have a fit because she'd consider it icky, bad form. Three . . . we can't disappoint our grandmother who's looking forward to giving *two* big super-duper extra special weddings with all the trimmings next summer.'

'You've convinced me, Emily – a double wedding is out of the question,' he replied in a teasing voice. He sobered almost at once, drew on his cigarette, quickly stubbed it out, his gestures unexpectedly nervous.

Emily, forever the acute observer, exclaimed, 'Is something the matter?'

'Paula might have managed to nip one scandal in the bud – over in Ireland – but I'm afraid we have another one about to explode. It's – '

'*Scandal,*' Paula repeated quietly, entering the room. She closed the door behind her and stood staring at Alexander and Emily with a worried expression.

'Paula,' Alexander said, rising and going to greet her affectionately. 'Let me get you a glass of wine, and then we'll have a little pow-pow before we go to the White Elephant.'

Paula sat down on the sofa and her gaze followed him across the room. With a scowl she asked him, 'What kind of scandal, Sandy?'

He brought her the drink, returned to the chair. 'It's Mother again – I'm sorry to have to tell you both.' His concerned eyes swung from Paula to Emily. 'She rang me this morning from Paris sounding quite hysterical. Apparently Gianni Ravioli – '

'Don't be mean,' Emily remonstrated. 'How many times do I have to tell you his name's Ravello and Gianni's very sweet.'

' – Has started divorce proceedings,' Alexander continued in a stronger tone, after throwing a chastising frown in Emily's direction, 'and she's on the verge of nervous collapse, or so she says – '

'What the hell does she expect,' Emily broke in again. '*She's* the one who did a bolt with the detestable Frog.'

'If you keep interrupting me, we're never going to get to dinner,' Alexander pointed out, sternly wagging a finger at his sister. 'In any event, our Mother's distressed because of Gianni's intractability. You see, even though she's given him the evidence, he refuses to name Marc Deboyne.'

'*Why?*' Emily asked, her curiosity piqued.

Paula said, 'Who *is* he naming? Obviously that's at the root of your mother's upset.'

Alexander gave her a sharp look. 'Smart girl, that's it exactly.' There was a slight pause before he went on with the utmost quiet, 'It seems he's going to cite a number of . . . Ministers of the Crown as the co-respondents. Darling Mummy must've gone through the Cabinet like a dose of salts.'

'You've got to be joking,' Paula cried, staring at him in astonishment and alarm.

'I wish I were,' Alexander said, his gloominess mounting as he thought of the consequences of his mother's adultery, the embarrassment to the family, particularly his grandmother. *She would be mortified.*

Emily was all agog. Her eyes widened and she shrieked, 'Uncle Robin's cronies I'll wager!' Groaning theatrically she rolled her eyes at the ceiling. 'I can just see the banner headline in the *Daily Mirror* – Italian count cites entire British Government in society divorce. Or what about this one in the *News of the World* – Socialite lays all her eggs in Government basket. The papers are going to have a field day with this one!' She leered at them wickedly.

Paula's mouth twitched involuntarily and she could not help laughing despite her annoyance with her aunt and the seriousness of the situation. 'Stop it, Emily, you're impossible.' Paula attempted to swallow her rising laughter, which she knew partially sprang from her nervousness tonight.

Alexander, who was not amused, glared at both women. 'It's not funny, you know . . .' He broke off, shaking his head, suddenly at a loss for words. He had been seething ever since his mother had telephoned him that morning. Like Emma, he was constantly maddened by her outrageous behaviour, and being conservative her morals were offensive to him.

In a rush, Emily said, 'I'd love to know who Mummy's lovers were.' A speculative gleam flashed across her face and she wrinkled her nose. 'No, I can't picture the beauteous Elizabeth in bed with Fat Dabs.'

'Fat Dabs?' Paula echoed in perplexity.

'Really, Emily!' Alexander exploded.

Quite undaunted by Alexander's reprimand, and adopting an exaggerated Yorkshire accent, Emily informed Paula, 'Aye, Fat Dabs. That's wot t'lads at Genret call our 'Arold from 'Uddersfield.' Another thought instantly occurred to Emily, and, reverting to her normal cultivated tone, she pointed out, 'Robin's going to have apoplexy. Let's not forget that our charming uncle, Member of Parliament for South-East Leeds, is also one of Harold Wilson's Cabinet Ministers. He's expecting to be appointed Chancellor of the Exchequer, you know, if Labour gets in again at the next election. Gosh, Sandy, you're right, there's going to be a huge scandal . . . shades of Profumo, do you think? We'll never be able to nip this one in the bud.'

'I'm not going to worry· myself about Uncle Robin's precious political career,' Alexander retorted with acerbity. 'Oh no, not at all. Besides, he's such an opportunist he'll find a way to get mileage out of this, if I'm not mistaken. Anyway, it's probably all his fault. You put your finger on it, Emily, I'm sure Mother met the gentlemen in question through him. She was constantly dashing over to his fancy parties in Eaton Square.' He shot Paula a worried glance. 'Once the divorce papers are filed with the law courts the press will be on to it in no time, and Emily's not too far off the mark about those banner headlines.'

Paula sat reflecting, said at last, 'How much? To buy him off?'

'Not sure,' Alexander said.

Emily cried, 'Oh I don't think he wants anything.'

Paula pinned her cousin with her cool knowing gaze. 'I'm surprised at your naïveté, Emily. We've been raised by a woman who has continually told us that everyone has a price, and that it's only ever a question of how much. Of course he wants money – *then* he'll do the gentlemanly thing and name Marc Deboyne.'

Emily protested with fierceness, 'I know him better than either of you and I don't think he's like that.'

'Gran is also fond of saying that the price isn't necessarily money,' Alexander was quick to remind them. 'And now that I think about it, I'm inclined to agree with you, Emily. I honestly don't believe he wants lots of cash. But he does want something. *Revenge.* I'm certain he still loves our mother – although God knows why in view of her treatment of him – and he's badly hurt. So . . . he has the need to strike back, hurt her in return and the only way he knows is to embarrass her publicly.'

'Maybe,' Paula admitted, seeing the sense in Alexander's theory. 'Apparently he has all the evidence he needs?' This came out sounding like a question.

'Oh yes,' Alexander told her, 'Mother was quite clear that he has the goods on her. He's not making idle threats.'

'Are you sure she didn't tell you who the ministers were?' Emily probed with her usual inquisitiveness.

Alexander looked at her pityingly. 'Come *on*, she may be a foolish, misguided woman, but deep down she's quite crafty. Of course she didn't volunteer any names.'

Paula said, 'Did your mother tell you what she wanted you to do, Sandy?'

'Yes, she wants me to go and see Gianni, to persuade

420

him to name Marc Deboyne in the suit. She seems to believe I can influence him, but she's up a bloody gum tree there. I don't know him that well, and anyway, it's Emily he likes the most.'

'Oh no,' Emily shrieked, 'not me!'

Alexander and Paula exchanged conspiratorial looks, and Paula said, 'You might be the best person to deal with him, darling.'

Emily moaned, fell back in the chair. She found the idea of talking to Gianni about her mother's infidelity quite repugnant. On the other hand, she liked the man, and Alexander might be tactless with him. She said firmly, as she straightened up, 'I simply refuse to offer Gianni money, and that's flat!'

'What will your approach be?' Alexander asked, filling with profound relief that she'd apparently agreed to take on this unpleasant task.

'I shall – ' Emily thought hard and her face brightened. She said, 'Why I shall appeal to his better nature, explain that he will be hurting Amanda and Francesca more than Mummy, and he's very fond of the girls. He wouldn't want them to suffer.'

Paula said with a degree of hesitation, 'Very well . . . Handle it that way – however, you'd better have something up your sleeve, just in case his better nature fails him.'

'You do sound cynical at times,' Emily declared, pursing her lips reprovingly. 'I will not insult that poor betrayed man by offering him money.'

Paying no attention to Emily's irate manner Paula shrugged, said, 'You could always offer him a job – if he's adamant, if he insists on naming half the damned Government.'

'A job? Where? Who with?'

'With Harte's, Emily. I've been looking for someone to run Trade Winds, the new antique accessory shop I'm planning to open in the near future. Since Gianni's an

421

expert in that area perhaps he'd prefer working for the family rather than that antique importing company where he's currently employed. We'd be killing several birds with one stone in a sense – ensuring he's on *our* side, if not your mother's especially, and he wouldn't really be under our feet since he'd have to do a lot of travelling. Also, I might get myself a good man for Trade Winds. And he'll certainly earn more at Harte's.'

'What a marvellous solution!' Alexander exclaimed, immediately cheering up, relaxing in his chair.

Emily bit her lip. 'I shall only mention the job at Harte's if he's difficult,' she warned, convinced that Gianni was not an opportunist. She added quickly, 'I *know* he won't be, that he'll do the right thing. I just do.'

'We'll see,' Paula murmured.

Alexander stood up, strode across the room. 'Now that we've dealt with Mother's love life there's another matter I must discuss.' He paused at the door. 'Won't be a minute . . . I left my briefcase in the hall when I arrived.'

In his absence, Emily leaned towards Paula, confided, 'Gianni really is a lovely person, you just don't know him very well.'

'I'm sure he is, under normal circumstances. But it's wiser to be prepared for the worst.'

Emily said nothing, and a moment later Alexander returned, sat down, took a folder out of his briefcase. He handed it to Paula.

'What's this?' she asked, taking it from him.

'A report from Mr Graves of Graves and Sanderson. But there's no need to read it now.'

'Is it about Jonathan?' Paula ventured, turning the folder over, fingering it, her breath catching in her throat with apprehension.

'No. The report concerns Sebastian Cross.'

'*Oh*.' Paula put one hand to her mouth, remembering

that day in the board room at Aire, wondering why she had a sudden sense of foreboding.

Alexander explained, 'I think it'll be quicker if I give you the information in a few short sentences. The report *is* rather long, tedious in parts, which is why I suggest you peruse it at your leisure.'

'Hurry up then, tell us, Sandy,' Emily ordered. 'We ought to be leaving for dinner in a few minutes. I'm starved.'

'Mr Graves has been digging for months, trying to find something on Sebastian, as you're both aware,' Alexander commenced. 'His inquiries were business-oriented at first, since he was following Grandy's instructions. When he came up empty-handed yet again, he decided to investigate Sebastian's private life. After a number of false leads, interviews with different people in London, he went up to Yorkshire. And he stumbled on some information that's not very pleasant, I don't mind telling you. Knowing that a lot of the chaps from Aire Communications congregate at Polly's Bar in Leeds he started hanging around there. One lunch time he struck up a conversation with a young chap who'd once worked at Aire. Graves and the fellow eventually became very chummy, got to meeting for drinks regularly over a three-week period. One night Tommy Charwood – that's the fellow's name – told Graves that Sebastian was a nasty piece of work, said he'd like to get him in a dark alley one night and give him the thrashing of his life.' Alexander stopped to light a cigarette, then continued, 'When Graves asked the reason, Tommy Charwood told him that he'd been courting a girl who had also worked at Aire, and that Sebastian had taken her away from him. Now, it seems that the girl, Alice Peele – '

'I've met Alice – ' Paula interjected quickly, her face quickening with interest. 'She's in public relations, and she once came to see me about a job at Harte's.'

'What's she like?' Alexander asked curiously.

'Talented in her field, rather pleasant. I remember her quite distinctly because she was well turned out and very striking. Tall, dark, with an unusually pretty face.'

Alexander cleared his throat, pinned his grave eyes on Paula. 'I'm not too sure how pretty she is these days. According to Tommy Charwood, Sebastian Cross beat her up a number of times. And so badly the last time, Alice Peele had to see a plastic surgeon. Charwood told Graves that she would have been disfigured for life without the prompt emergency treatment she received at Leeds General Infirmary. You see, Cross beat her with such a vengeance her jaw was broken, also one cheekbone, and her face was a bloody pulp.'

'Oh my God!' Paula cried. 'How appalling, what a horrible thing to happen.'

Emily had also blanched. Shuddering, she looked across at Paula, then whispered, 'Your instincts were right about Sebastian Cross.' Emily swallowed, turned to her brother. 'Didn't the girl bring charges? Go to the police? Prosecute?'

'No, seemingly not. Charwood told Graves that she was terrified of Cross. Her father had wanted to go to the police, but Alice begged him not to do so, insisted it would only stir up more trouble. That's when Mr Peele confided in Tommy, whom he'd remained friendly with. Tommy tried to talk Peele into going to Leeds CID – he knows a number of detectives on the force – but Peele kept wavering. In the end he decided against it. About a month after this last terrible beating, John Cross paid a visit to the Peele family, offered Mr Peele money. Peele, who sounds like the salt of the earth, threw the money in John Cross's face. As soon as Alice was sufficiently recovered, he shipped her off to live with her married brother in Gibraltar. The brother's in the Royal Navy, helicopters I think, and is stationed permanently in Gib. Tommy Charwood believes she's still out there.'

'What a ghastly story,' Paula said, continuing to shiver.

'I'm not surprised Alice Peele is terrified of Cross . . .' She faltered, stopped, turned away, filled with revulsion for the man.

Emily gasped, 'He must be a maniac! That girl's family should have prosecuted him, regardless of what *she* said.'

Alexander nodded, and his expression, reflecting Paula's, was one of immense distaste. He said with harshness, 'And that's not all . . . Charwood gave Graves some additional information, after our wily private eye ingratiated himself further. Charwood swears Sebastian is into *drugs*, quite aside from being a heavy drinker, and is a congenital gambler who has suffered some big losses at the tables. At Crockford's, and God knows where else.'

'And this is the man who is Jonathan Ainsley's best friend,' Paula said. 'This is just awful.'

'Yes, it is,' Alexander concurred. 'And whilst the information about Cross doesn't really do *us* any good, it does reflect rather badly on Jonathan, in that he's Cross's bosom chum. Wouldn't you say?'

Paula nodded.

Emily looked from Paula to her brother. 'Do you think Jonathan's also on drugs? That he gambles?'

'He'd better not be on drugs,' Alexander snapped. 'Not if he wants to continue running the real estate division of Harte Enterprises. Let's not forget he handles a great deal of money, and also has to make some very important decisions at times.' Alexander stood up, walked over to the console, poured a glass of wine, muttered, 'I'm going to have to monitor *everything* he does from now on – watch him even more closely than before. I simply can't afford to have him make any mistakes whatsoever. As for gambling – ' Alexander shrugged, shook his head. 'I can't hazard a guess about that. But he might be playing the tables, and that's another reason why I'm going to take a bigger interest in the real estate division. As I said, there's an awful lot of cash going through that company.'

'Presumably you've instructed Mr Graves to keep at it, Sandy. To dig deeper?' Paula said.

'Naturally.'

'Oddly enough,' Paula went on thoughtfully, 'John Cross rang the store today. He wanted an appointment.'

'Are you going to see him?' Alexander asked, returning to the chair.

'I don't know – probably not. Gaye tried to reach him at his hotel late this afternoon but he'd gone out. I expect he'll phone again in the morning.'

'In one sense, I'd be curious to know what he has to say. He can't possibly imagine we'd be interested in Aire. Not now, after he's sold the building, which was the main asset of the company.'

Paula lifted her shoulders in a shrug, and instantly changed the subject. She said, 'Sarah came to see me this afternoon.' She proceeded to recount the meeting, not missing out on a single detail. When she had finished she sat back, waiting for their reactions.

Emily had been all eyes and ears throughout Paula's recital. She exclaimed, 'I'd like to hear Miranda's version of the weekend, not to mention the whole ten days Sarah spent in Barbados. I have a feeling their stories will vary considerably. Sarah was always rather good at taking the credit when it wasn't due her.'

'Yes, I know.' Paula immediately thought of their childhood days at Heron's Nest. She and Emily had been aware of Sarah's craftiness even then. Their cousin had forever tried to curry favour with their grandmother, paint herself in the best possible light, frequently at their expense.

Alexander spoke up. 'Sarah's not stupid. She knows you can't sell the boutiques, not without first going to the board. She's also well aware that she can't spend the fashion division's money willy-nilly unless she has my permission. Therefore she must have convinced herself she can bypass us, succeed in her aims by going to Grandy

426

directly. I'm certain she sent the telex, as she threatened to do.'

'I am too,' Emily muttered, condemning Sarah under her breath. Paula had far too many worries and problems to contend with at the moment, without Sarah creating difficulties.

'I won't argue with either of you.' Paula smiled faintly. 'However, I can assure you that the telex ended up in the wastepaper basket. What Sarah doesn't know is that Grandy really came to believe in the boutiques before she left in May. At the last minute she suddenly saw them as a clever means to expand and in a relatively easy way for our organization. She's convinced the boutiques will increase the value of the Harte shares, and of course they will, so she has no more intention of selling off the boutiques than I do.'

'Yes, but you just said Sarah doesn't realize that,' Emily pointed out quietly. 'And anyway, I've always thought she was infuriated because you got the Harte chain and not her. After all, she *is* the eldest granddaughter, and she has quite an opinion of herself as a businesswoman.'

'Emily's taken the words out of my mouth,' Alexander said, turning swiftly to Paula. 'Sarah's visit this afternoon may have been a nasty little exercise – one specifically designed to upset you, Paula, to unnerve you, throw you off balance.' As he was speaking another thought struck him. 'I say, could this be the beginning of the guerrilla war we've talked about, and have been anticipating?'

'That had crossed my mind earlier,' Paula told him.

'If it is, what does Sarah hope to gain, Sandy?' Emily demanded.

'The satisfaction of knowing Paula's aggravated, under additional pressure. Also, a person who has been thrown off balance is not always thinking clearly or coolly, and frequently concentration is damaged.' Alexander gave them both a very pointed look. 'Sarah's been hand-in-glove

427

with Jonathan for a long time. She bears watching as closely as he does.'

Paula stood up. 'Enough of *them*, for tonight at least. Let's go to dinner. It's been a difficult day, and a terrible week so far.' She sighed wearily. 'I'm not going to burden either of you with my problems at Sitex Oil, but I've had those to cope with today as well. I think I've just run out of steam. I need a little light relief, such as an amusing evening at the White Elephant.'

'Are they serious problems?' Alexander asked as the three of them went out into the entrance foyer to get their coats. He squeezed Paula's shoulder affectionately. 'Can I be of help?'

Paula gave him a grateful smile. 'Thanks, Sandy, it's sweet of you to offer. I've got things under control – ' She hesitated before adding, 'Dale Stevens was determined to resign as president this afternoon. I spent over an hour on the phone with him, convinced him to stay on. He has a number of enemies on the board, unmitigated trouble-makers who try to tie his hands whenever they can.' She shook her head ruefully. 'What I should have said a moment ago is that he's agreed to stay on as president until the end of the year. All I've done really is buy myself a little time.'

CHAPTER 27

'John Crawford offered to explain the procedure in a coroner's court,' Daisy said, looking from Edwina to Anthony. 'He feels it will help us to be more relaxed about the inquest.'

Anthony said, 'It certainly would, Aunty Daisy.' He stood up. 'I'll go and fetch Bridget. I think she ought to hear what your family solicitor has to say. Excuse me, I won't be a moment.'

As he left the library, Daisy rose and joined Edwina on the sofa. She took her half-sister's hand in hers and squeezed it, looking deeply into her care-worn face. 'Try not to worry, Edwina. In a few hours this tragedy will be behind us. We must go on, you know, endeavour to get on with our lives as best we can.'

'Yes, Daisy, and thank you for your concern. I'll be all right,' Edwina murmured in a tired voice. The last few days of anxiety and strain had taken their toll, and she looked exhausted, near total collapse. The black dress she had chosen to wear, stark and unrelieved by jewellery or any accent colour, did nothing to enhance her appearance. It appeared to drain what bit of colour she had from her face, emphasizing her pallor more than ever. She looked ill, and her age showed pronouncedly this morning.

Gratitude suddenly flickered in Edwina's silvery-grey eyes as she added quietly, 'I don't know what I would have done without you and Jim. Where is he, Daisy?'

'Right now he's on the phone to Paula, and I believe he has a few calls to make to people on the paper. But he'll join us as soon as he's finished. It's not really essential for him to be briefed. He knows the inner working of a coroner's court since he used to cover inquests in his early days as a reporter.'

'Oh yes, of course, he would understand about those things.' Edwina shifted her glance to the clock on the mantelpiece at the other side of the handsome panelled room. 'It's almost eight-thirty. We'll have to leave soon to drive into Cork. It'll take us well over an hour, perhaps an hour and a half, you know.'

Detecting the nervousness and panic in Edwina's voice, Daisy said reassuringly, 'We've plenty of time. The inquest is set for eleven, and this session with John won't take very long. He said he could cover the important points in about

429

ten minutes. After that we can start out, drive in at a leisurely pace. Do stay calm, my dear.'

'I'm fine, really. Just a little tired. I didn't sleep very well.'

'I don't think any of us did,' Daisy said with a slight smile. 'I'm going to have another cup of coffee. Would you like one?'

'No, thank you, Daisy.' Edwina sat rigidly on the sofa, twisting her hands in her lap, her chest tight with apprehension. For four days and nights she had lived with this terrible fear for her son. She could not wait to go to the county court, to get the inquest over and done with, so that the cloud surrounding him would be lifted finally. Only then would she be able to relax. She would willingly give her life for Anthony. He was the only person who mattered to her, and once the inquiry into the cause of Min's death was over, she would support him in anything he wished to do. Even if that meant accepting Sally Harte, of whom she did not approve. Until the day she died she would regret her passive role in the trouble that had developed between Min and Anthony in the past few weeks. Anthony had asked her to intercede, to reason with her, insisting she could influence his estranged wife to proceed with the divorce as originally agreed. And perhaps she could have, but she would never know, for she had refused. Now poor Min was dead. She would still be alive if I had spoken to her, Edwina thought for the umpteenth time. The pain in her heart intensified. Her guilt soared.

Daisy brought her cup of coffee and sat down in the chair opposite. She said, 'Have you decided what you want to do? Will you come to London for a few days' rest after the funeral?'

'Perhaps I should get away from here,' Edwina began and stopped, looking at the door as Anthony came in with Bridget O'Donnell, the housekeeper at Clonloughlin.

430

'M'lady, Mrs Amory,' Bridget said, inclining her head, taking the chair Anthony indicated.

Daisy, always gracious, smiled at her. 'As you know, Mr Crawford is our solicitor and he came over to help in any way he can. He is going to explain a few things to us, Bridget, as I'm sure Lord Dunvale has told you. However, I just want to add that there's nothing to be alarmed about.'

'Oh I'm not worried, Mrs Amory, not at all,' Bridget answered quickly, in a clipped tone that partially obscured the lilting burr, meeting Daisy's gaze unblinkingly. 'It's a very simple matter, telling the truth. And that's what I aim to do.' A small smug smile flicked across her narrow pale mouth and she sat back, crossed her legs. Her red hair gleamed in the sunlight, its fiery hue contrasting markedly with her icy cold blue eyes.

Daisy's opinion that Bridget O'Donnell was a cool customer, calculating and sure of herself, was reaffirmed. She did not particularly like this woman, whom she guessed was about thirty-five or thereabouts, even though she did not look it.

Glancing away, Daisy turned to Anthony, but before she had a chance to say anything the door opened to admit John Crawford, the son of Emma's solicitor of many years and now a senior partner in the firm of Crawford, Creighton, Phipps and Crawford. Of medium height and build, he was nevertheless ramrod straight and had a military bearing which combined with his forceful personality to give him an aura of presence. At forty-six he had sandy hair peppered with grey, bright informed brown eyes in a pleasant face that was oddly bland, and did nothing to reveal a razor-sharp legal brain of great brilliance.

'Good morning. Sorry to keep you waiting,' he said briskly, striding forward to join them at the windowed end of the long book-filled room. Daisy offered him coffee but he declined. He remained standing behind a chair, his hands resting lightly on its back. He looked completely

431

relaxed and untroubled, and as he always did with his clients, he endeavoured to convey a feeling of supreme confidence whatever his private thoughts and opinions were.

Crawford said, 'I realize this is going to be quite an ordeal for you this morning, and so I thought I might help if I gave you a run down on the manner in which a coroner's court is conducted. Understanding something about the proceedings may lessen everyone's nervousness, I hope.' His eyes swept over the four of them. 'Feel free to ask any questions as I go along. Since none of you have attended an inquest before, let me first say that the coroner's court is conducted in a rather *informal* way. However – ' He paused, looked at them keenly, and speaking slowly, as if to give added emphasis to his words, went on, 'I must stress that the informality in no way lessens its *importance*. It is one of the *highest* courts in the land, and it is ruled by the *law of evidence*. Any questions?' A sandy brow lifted. 'All right, on to the next – '

'Excuse me, John,' Daisy said, 'could you please clarify what you mean by *informal*. I don't quite understand.'

'Ah yes, of course. By informal I mean that the coroner is not wearing robes. He is dressed in a business suit, also the manner of speaking is less formal than other courts. The coroner chats informally with the interested parties before evidence is given on the witness stand under oath.'

'Thank you, John. One other question. The coroner is usually a solicitor, a barrister, or a doctor with legal training, isn't he?'

'That is quite correct, Daisy. The coroner is not a judge, even though he is in fact making the ruling. He also has a very wide latitude in his conduct of an inquiry. If there are no other questions, I shall continue. I now come to a most important point, and it is this. The coroner will accept *hearsay* in this court, which is not common practice in other courts of law under British justice, where hearsay is *inadmissible* evidence.'

Anthony leaned forward. 'What does that mean?' He shook his head. 'It can't mean what I think it does!' he went on to exclaim, his voice more high-pitched than normal.

'Yes, Lord Dunvale, it does. A coroner will listen to something a person has heard but does not know to be true . . . rumour, gossip, if you will.'

'I see,' Anthony said in a more composed voice, even though he was experiencing inner alarm at the thought of the gossip which had been rife in the village for months.

Edwina and Daisy exchanged worried glances. Neither said one word.

John Crawford, aware of their uneasiness, cleared his throat, continued, 'Let me qualify hearsay more fully, as it applies in the coroner's court. In this instance, hearsay might be words spoken by the deceased, immediately prior to his or her death, to a member of the family, a friend, a doctor or a solicitor. A witness might say that the deceased has threatened to commit suicide on one or numerous occasions. Or may venture the opinion that said deceased was depressed. The coroner will take note of these points. Perhaps another example would be useful, a good illustration – a policeman could pass the opinion to the coroner that he believes the deceased has committed suicide based on the evidence he has gathered. Or then again, a policeman might say his findings lead him to believe that death was accidental. The coroner does take such opinions into account. I would also like to stress that hearsay of this nature *does* have a bearing on the case and indeed on the rest of the questions posed by the coroner.'

'Do the police question any of the witnesses?' Anthony asked.

'No, no. Never. That is not permissible in a coroner's

court. Only the coroner is empowered to ask the questions.'
Crawford swung around as the door opened.

Michael Lamont, the estate manager at Clonloughlin, entered swiftly, closed the door behind him. Tall and heavy-set, he had a shock of dark curly hair and a merry weather-beaten face that matched a jovial manner. As he hurried across the floor he apologized profusely.

Anthony said quickly, 'I'll fill you in later, Michael. John's been explaining the procedure . . . the way in which an inquest is conducted.'

Nodding his understanding, Lamont sat down next to Edwina on the sofa, acknowledged the other women with a quick smile. He said, 'I did attend an inquest once before, so I'm vaguely aware of the form.'

'Good, good,' Crawford exclaimed with a brief nod. 'I shall get on with this as quickly as possible. There may or may not be a jury of six or eight people. Either way, the coroner imposes his will, if necessary talks the jury around to his way of thinking and what he feels is right. But it *is* the coroner who decides and pronounces the verdict – of misadventure, suicide, accidental death, natural causes or – ' He paused, added quietly, ' – or murder.'

There was a deathly silence as this word hung in the air.

It was Anthony who broke it. 'What if the coroner is uncertain? What if he can't decide whether it was suicide, an accident, or murder?'

'Ah yes, well, in that instance the coroner would have to leave an open verdict . . . he might pronounce that a person or persons unknown could be responsible for the death of the deceased and that they could be brought to justice at a later date.'

Edwina, watching her son intently, gasped and turned ashen. Michael Lamont reached out and took her hand, whispered something to her.

Crawford glanced at them, then brought his attention back to Anthony. 'The pathologist's report, the findings of his post-mortem, usually clarify cause of death and without any question of doubt.'

'I understand,' Anthony said in a low voice.

Crawford announced, 'I've covered the most important points, I believe. I would like to add that I am most confident that the inquest will progress in a normal manner.' His eyes rested on Michael Lamont. 'You will probably be the first witness, since you were the one who found Lady Dunvale's body. The Clonloughlin police sergeant will give evidence after you. Then we will hear medical testimony – from the local doctor who did the initial examination and from the pathologist who conducted the second examination and performed the post-mortem. Does anyone need further clarification on any specific point?'

'Yes,' Anthony said. 'Just a couple – I presume I will be questioned. But what about my mother? And Bridget?'

'I see no reason for Lady Dunvale to be called to the witness stand, since she really cannot contribute anything. You will have to give evidence, and, most probably, so will Miss O'Donnell. It's very likely that the coroner will chat to all of you in an informal way, before the main witnesses are called, as I explained earlier. Nothing to worry about.' Crawford glanced at his watch. 'I suggest we leave here in the next ten minutes or so.' Turning to Daisy who had risen, he asked, 'Where's Jim? Perhaps you ought to let him know we're going to leave shortly to drive into Cork.'

'Yes,' Daisy said. 'I'll tell him right away. I've got to go upstairs for my things.'

Fifteen minutes later the small group left Clonloughlin House.

Edwina, Anthony, Bridget O'Donnell and Michael Lamont travelled in the first car, with Michael at the wheel.

Jim Fairley drove the second car, and followed closely behind. He was accompanied by Daisy and John Crawford.

No one spoke for the first ten minutes or so. Finally, Jim said, 'Explaining the formalities was a good idea, John.' He glanced out of the corner of his eye at Crawford, who sat next to him on the front seat, swung his eyes back to the road, went on to remark, 'I'm sure it helped my aunt. She's a bundle of nerves. Anthony seems calm enough, though. Rather self-contained, totally in control. But he looks dreadful. This ghastly mess has aged him quite a lot.'

'Yes,' Crawford said laconically. He rolled down the window, peered over his shoulder at Daisy, said, 'Do you mind if I smoke?'

'No, not at all.' Daisy leaned forward, resting her hand on the back of the front seat, and addressed Jim. 'How was Paula?'

'She's fine and sends her love.' Jim's grip on the steering wheel tightened as he wondered whether to repeat Paula's final comments, which she had voiced with such anxiety he himself had become alarmed. Uncertain of what to do he remarked, 'She kept insisting we phone her immediately the inquest is over, as if we wouldn't have done that anyway.'

'She'll be anxious to get in touch with Mother at once,' Daisy murmured. She settled back in the corner, smoothed the skirt of her understated and restrained dark grey suit, thinking of Emma sitting in suspense at their sheep station in Australia, worrying about the outcome and about her grandson Anthony. The fact that her mother was under such strain worried Daisy. After all, she *was* eighty. Reassuring herself that Emma Harte was invincible, was really taking this in her stride as she kept insisting when she telephoned, Daisy attempted to relax. Eventually she said, 'Have you decided what you're going to do, Jim?'

'Yes, I'll stay on here, for the funeral tomorrow. I think they'll appreciate the support and it's the least I can do. I'll fly back on Saturday. I hope to persuade Anthony to come with me. He has to get away from this place for a while.'

'Of course,' Daisy said. 'And I'm sure he'll want to see Sally.' She swung her eyes to John Crawford. 'I assume the inquest will be over in a couple of hours . . . David has arranged for his friend's private jet to be at Cork Airport at noon, waiting for us. You will be coming back to London with me, won't you, John?'

'Yes, thanks a lot. I appreciate the ride. And yes, all being well we should be through in a couple of hours. I just hope we don't have to recess for lunch. In the event that this happens the inquest will unfortunately drag on into the afternoon.'

Jim said, 'You don't have any reason to believe it won't be routine, do you?'

'No, not really,' Crawford replied, but there was a strange hesitancy in his voice.

Jim picked this up at once. 'You don't sound as confident as you did last night, John. Is there something Daisy and I ought to know?'

'No, no, of course not,' Crawford murmured.

This response did nothing to convince Jim. He decided to plunge in, confide Emily's worries, which Paula had relayed to him during their phone conversation earlier. He said, 'Paula's a bit anxious. Emily's raised something . . . apparently she woke Paula during the night, and told her that ever since Sunday she has been concerned . . . about those five or six hours Min spent at the lake, after she arrived in the afternoon and before she died late at night. Emily thinks – '

'I don't understand why those hours are important,' Daisy interjected.

John Crawford pondered for a second, elected to be honest and swung around in the front seat to face Daisy. 'I must now confess that I myself have been troubled about the self same thing, my dear. And if *I* find that elapse of time strange, not to mention young Emily, don't you think an experienced coroner will ask himself what the deceased was doing for that extraordinary length of time.'

'Yes.' Daisy frowned. 'But *why* do those hours matter anyway? Look, maybe she went away and came back again.'

'Or maybe she was never at Clonloughlin in the afternoon,' Crawford said softly. 'That possibility might easily occur to the coroner, as it has to me, and probably to young Emily too. Don't you see, Daisy, those unexplained hours raise questions . . . in regard to Lord Dunvale's story about the time his wife arrived, a story which, I might add, is only corroborated by his mother.'

'You mean the coroner could think Anthony is lying, that Min came there late at night.' Daisy caught her breath. 'Oh good Lord, yes, I see what you mean! The coroner might jump to the conclusion that Anthony was also at the lake late at night – ' She broke off, and began to tremble, feeling suddenly nervous for the first time since her arrival in Ireland.

'Perhaps. But Daisy, my dear, I do say *perhaps*. It would ease my mind considerably if we had a witness who saw the late Lady Dunvale driving into the grounds of Clonloughlin in the afternoon, or leaving around that time. Unfortunately, we apparently don't have such a witness.' Crawford threw Daisy a sympathetic look. He had adored her for years, wanted always to protect her. 'Please don't distress yourself needlessly, my dear. I haven't mentioned my worries to you before, for the simple reason I knew I would upset you if I did.' Giving her a reassuring and confident smile, he finished, 'The post-mortem is usually the key in this type of case. It *will* prove conclusively how she died.' Crawford gave Jim a pointed look. 'I'm quite certain the pathologist will pronounce it death by accidental drowning.' As long as he had found water in her lungs, Crawford added to himself, praying that the pathologist had done so. If he hadn't, they were in trouble. The gravest trouble

438

imaginable. Lack of water in the deceased's lungs would prove she had died before her body entered the water. In which case a murder charge would be levelled at somebody . . . or persons unknown.

Jim, understanding that John wished to allay his mother-in-law's nervousness, said in a strong firm voice, 'I agree with you wholeheartedly, John. I'm sure Min's death was accidental. Now, Daisy, stay calm and cool, as you have been all through this ordeal. Edwina will fall to pieces if she detects the slightest sign of distress in you.'

Daisy said, 'I'm all right, you've nothing to be concerned about, and I agree, I think we should all three of us be as positive as possible. Anthony and Edwina are going to find the inquest exceedingly trying, no matter what, so we must be supportive and cheerful.'

Once again, Daisy McGill Amory settled back into the corner of the seat, and for the rest of the journey into Cork she remained silent, left the talking to Jim and John Crawford. She had her own troubling thoughts to pre-occupy her.

Mr Liam O'Connor, a local solicitor, was the coroner presiding at the judicial inquiry into the cause of death in the case of Minerva Gwendolyn Standish, the late Countess of Dunvale.

The inquest was being held in the small coroner's court within the County Law Courts in the city of Cork, county seat of Cork County.

A jury of six people sat to his right. They were all local residents of the city who had been passing the courts that morning, and had been gathered together by an official of the coroner's court. This was the custom under British law in regard to inquests. Whatever their engagements planned for that day, they had had no option but to do as bidden and enter the coroner's court to be sworn in as jurors.

The coroner said, 'And now Lord Dunvale, before

I hear testimony from Police Sergeant McNamara, the pathologist, and others present, perhaps you could give the court some idea of the deceased's state of mind, prior to her tragic death. You may speak from where you are sitting. You do not have to stand in the witness box at this moment.'

Anthony said in a clear and remarkably strong voice, 'My wife and I were séparated and were about to divorce. In consequence of this, she had moved out of Clonloughlin House and was living in Waterford. Lately she had been in the habit of visiting Clonloughlin, and in the past month I began to realize that her disposition had changed radically. She was somewhat irrational, even quite violent both verbally and physically. I became increasingly concerned about her mental stability.'

The coroner nodded. 'Did the deceased ever mention suicide? Did she ever threaten to take her own life during these spells of irrationality?'

'No, she did not,' Anthony replied in an even firmer tone. 'Furthermore, I would like to state categorically that I do not believe my wife would kill herself whatever her state of mind. She was not a suicidal type of person. I am convinced her death was an accident.'

The coroner asked for further details about the deceased's behaviour, and as Anthony answered, Daisy watched the coroner closely, listening with great attentiveness. Liam O'Connor was a small, spry man, with a deeply lined face. His expression was somewhat dour, but she noticed that he had wise and kindly eyes and a reflective manner, and these characteristics filled Daisy with a degree of relief. She was confident Liam O'Connor would brook no nonsense in his court, that he would stick to the letter of the law most scrupulously, yet she also sensed he would be eminently fair.

As the coroner continued his informal questioning of Anthony, Daisy stole a surreptitious look at Edwina. Her tension was so acute Daisy feared she would collapse any minute. She reached for Edwina's hand, held on to it tightly, wanting to give her strength and confidence.

'Thank you, Lord Dunvale,' the coroner was saying. 'Lady Dunvale, I wonder if you have anything you can add pertaining to your daughter-in-law's unusual behaviour immediately before her death?'

Edwina was evidently surprised to hear her name mentioned and she started in her seat, literally gaped at the coroner speechlessly. She began to shake.

Daisy tightened her grip on her hand, whispered, 'Edwina, don't be afraid. And do answer the coroner, my dear.'

Clearing her throat numerous times, Edwina finally spoke in a low voice that trembled excessively. 'Min . . . my daughter-in-law, that is, was . . . *was* distressed in recent weeks. Yes, that is quite true.' Edwina stopped abruptly, choking on her words, and tears sprang into her eyes as she thought of the dead young woman, whom she had loved like a daughter. There was a long and painful hesitation before Edwina whispered, 'I'm afraid she was – was – drinking heavily lately. At least she arrived at Clonloughlin in an inebriated state numerous times over the last month. Bridget, er . . . er . . . Miss O'Donnell, my son's . . . Lord Dunvale's housekeeper – ' Edwina stopped again, glanced at Bridget, then resumed, 'Quite recently Miss O'Donnell had to put my daughter-in-law to bed in a guest room at Clonloughlin. I remember the occasion very clearly. Miss O'Donnell told me she was afraid Lady Dunvale would have an accident if she was allowed to drive back to Waterford in her . . . debilitated condition.'

Edwina swallowed. Her mouth had gone dry and she was unable to continue. Also, the effort to speak coherently and to hang on to a semblance of control had depleted her. She fell back against the seat, her face chalky and filmed with perspiration.

'Thank you, Lady Dunvale,' the coroner said, sounding sympathetic. He put on his glasses, referred to the papers in front of him, looked up, removed his spectacles and surveyed those gathered before him. 'Miss O'Donnell, would you give me a few more details about the particular occasion to which Lady Dunvale has just referred, please?'

'Yes, sir, indeed I will.' Bridget leaned forward slightly, and in her usual clipped, precise way she confirmed Edwina's story and also the various incidents of irrationality referred to by Anthony.

Listening to her, Daisy thought that never had a better witness been heard. The woman was quite remarkable, especially in her attention to the smallest detail, and she obviously had a prodigious if not indeed photographic memory.

'And did the deceased ever suggest to *you*, Miss O'Donnell, that she might do anything at all to harm herself?' The coroner steepled his fingers, peered out over them, fixing his keen eyes on the housekeeper.

Apparently Bridget O'Donnell did not have to think twice about this question. 'Oh yes, sir, her ladyship did. Not once, but several times lately.'

There were audible gasps in the courtroom.

Anthony, stiffening in his chair, exclaimed, 'That can't be so – ' He made to rise, but was restrained by John Crawford, who hushed him into silence, aware of the stern eyes of the coroner.

The latter motioned for silence in the court, and the hurried whisperings which had broken out ceased. 'Please recount those incidents, Miss O'Donnell,' he ordered.

'Yes, sir,' she said without hesitation, but she did cast a swift glance at Anthony before continuing.

Daisy, whose eyes had not left Bridget's face, thought she saw an apology signalled to him silently, but she was not sure.

Bridget O'Donnell, directing herself to the coroner, said,

'The late Lady Dunvale was a changed woman in the last few weeks of her life, as his lordship mentioned. She was hysterical in my presence on numerous occasions, and privately she said to me that she had nothing to live for, that she wished she were dead. The last time she threatened to put an end to her life was about a week before her death. She drove to Clonloughlin one afternoon, but I was the only person who saw her. His lordship was out on the estate with Mr Lamont, and the Dowager Countess was in Dublin. In any event, sir, her ladyship was very despondent, and she repeated over and over again that she wanted to escape the misery and unhappiness of her life by – by dying. She cried uncontrollably that afternoon, and although I tried to calm her, give her sympathy, she was beyond help really. At one moment, when I tried to soothe her by putting my arm around her, comforting her, she struck me across the face. The minute she had done this she seemed to come to her senses, and apologized over and over again. I made a pot of tea and we sat and talked in the kitchen for a while. It was then that her ladyship confided in me about something else. She told me that the greatest tragedy of her life was that she had not had any children.' Bridget paused, took a breath, resumed: 'Lady Dunvale began to weep again, but quietly, sort of desperately, and added that she was barren, that she couldn't bear children. Again I attempted to comfort her ladyship. I told her she was a young woman, had a lot to live for, and that she could make a new life for herself. This helped to calm her, and I thought she seemed more hopeful about things when she left a little later.'

Bridget sat back. She glanced down at her hands. Raising her eyes she stared at the coroner, and enunciated in the clearest voice, 'I think her ladyship did take her life, sir, because of the failure of her marriage and because she knew she could never have children.'

The coroner inclined his head, brought his gaze back to the papers spread before him.

The court was deathly quiet. No one stirred and not one single whisper was heard.

Daisy, glancing around discreetly, saw that the jurors wore thoughtful expressions and there was no doubt in her mind that everyone had been affected by Bridget O'Donnell's story. In its full context it left little to the imagination regarding the late woman's mental state, her unhappiness and despair. Stealing a quick look at Anthony she was struck by his extreme pallor and a pulse beating rapidly on his temple. His face was devastated.

The coroner's voice brought an end to the extraordinary stillness. Glancing at Michael Lamont, he said, 'Since you are employed by Lord Dunvale to run the estate at Clonloughlin, Mr Lamont, you obviously came into contact with the deceased in the last few weeks. Do you have anything to add to Miss O'Donnell's comments?'

Lamont cleared his throat, said in a subdued tone, 'Not really, sir. I never heard her ladyship mention suicide, and I would be inclined to agree with Lord Dunvale that she was not the sort of woman to harm herself. However – ' There was a moment's hesitation before he added, 'I can attest to her ladyship's despondency . . . Miss O'Donnell is correct in that assertion. I spoke to Lady Dunvale about two weeks ago, and she *was* in a very depressed state.' He cleared his throat nervously. 'She had also been drinking. Quite heavily, I thought that day. But what struck me the most was the deep, deep depression. She seemed burdened down by it. But that is all I can tell you. Lady Dunvale did not indicate why she was depressed, nor did I refer to it.' Another pause, and then he finished softly, 'I didn't think it was my place to intrude on her ladyship's privacy. As an employee of Lord Dunvale's that would have been a presumption on my part.'

'Thank you, Mr Lamont.' The coroner swivelled in his

seat, focused his attention on the police sergeant. 'Sergeant McNamara, can you shed any light on the disposition and mental state of Lady Dunvale?'

'Well, sir, I'm afraid that I can't be telling you anything I've observed personally,' McNamara began, rubbing his chin, and shaking his head somewhat mournfully. 'I haven't had the occasion to speak to her ladyship in the past few weeks. Mind you, sir, I knew she'd been visiting Clonloughlin House. Oh yes, that she had. I'd seen her little red car going through the village. And there has been talk in the village about her very weird behaviour from time to time in recent weeks, which sort of confirms the things Miss O'Donnell and Lord Dunvale have said about her stability not being what it usually was.'

'Have you formed any opinion about the cause of death?' the coroner asked.

'Well now, sir, I've had several opinions,' McNamara said, straightening up a trifle importantly. 'At first I believed her ladyship's death was an accident. Then later I must admit I thought of suicide. I've also wondered if foul play was involved, since her ladyship did die in mysterious circumstances.' McNamara pulled out a notebook, opened it.

'You will be able to elaborate on your findings, from the witness stand a little later in the proceedings, Sergeant McNamara,' the coroner said.

'Yes, sir,' the police sergeant replied, closing the notebook with a slap.

The coroner sat back, clasped his hands together, and directed his next words to the entire court. He said, 'It is the duty and burden of this court to establish the manner, cause and circumstances of the death of Minerva Gwendolyn Standish, the Countess of Dunvale. After hearing the evidence, the court must decide if death was from natural or unnatural causes, whether it was an accident, suicide, or a murder committed by persons known or unknown.'

Anthony was now called to the stand, and was asked to recall, to the best of his ability, the events of the previous Saturday. Speaking quietly, Anthony told the court: 'Late that afternoon my mother telephoned me from the Dower House. She had seen my wife's car entering the grounds and driving up to the main house. In view of the distressing scenes between my wife and myself in the preceding weeks I decided to leave Clonloughlin House. I thought that once she realized I was not at home my wife would leave, that we would therefore avoid any further unpleasantness and disturbances. I drove out to the lake in my land rover. I had not been there very long when I saw my wife's red Austin mini approaching in the distance. I was standing under a tree near the lake and I went back to the land rover, intending to drive away. It would not start, the battery seemed to be dead, so I set out to walk back to Clonloughlin House, taking the long way around the estate to avoid my wife. I spoke to my mother on the telephone once I got home, and she arrived to have dinner with me a little later. Around nine-thirty I walked my mother back to the Dower House, returned home and spent several hours working on the estate account books in the library. I then went to bed. I did not know my wife had remained on the estate at Clonloughlin until I was awakened the following morning by Mr Lamont, who told me he had found my wife's – ' Anthony's voice trembled, as he finished, 'my wife's body in the lake.' He stopped again, took a deep breath and his eyes were moist and despairing when he said with overwhelming sadness. 'I should have waited at the lake – spoken to my wife. She might still be alive if I had.'

After thanking Anthony, the coroner asked Bridget O'Donnell to take the oath, to give her evidence. He commenced to question her about her activities on the day of the death.

'No, sir, I did not see Lady Dunvale's car that afternoon,

nor did I know his lordship had left the house,' Bridget said. 'I was making dinner in the kitchen. Later on I served his lordship and the Dowager Countess, and after dinner I worked between the kitchen and the dining room for half an hour, clearing up.' She then spoke about her migraine, told how she had walked past the library around eleven o'clock on her way upstairs to get her pills, had noticed the earl at his desk in the library, and had seen him again around midnight when she had retired for the night.

'I was up very early on Sunday morning, sir,' Bridget O'Donnell continued. 'After drinking a cup of tea in the kitchen I drove to Waterford to attend first mass with my sister. I stayed in Waterford for lunch, and in the middle of the afternoon I returned to Clonloughlin village to see my mother. It was only then that I learned of her ladyship's death, and naturally I drove back to the estate, where I was interviewed by Sergeant McNamara.'

The next person to take the witness stand was the estate manager. Michael Lamont also said that he had not seen Lady Dunvale on Saturday afternoon, and explained his movements the following morning. 'I too was up and about quite early last Sunday. I was driving to my office at Clonloughlin House to retrieve some papers I had left there, which I needed to work on that day. I saw his lordship's land rover parked near the lake, and I got out to investigate.' Lamont swallowed. 'I thought Lord Dunvale was in the vicinity. When I realized he wasn't, I turned around to go back into my jeep. It was then that I saw her ladyship's car at the far side of the lake. Before I reached the Austin mini I saw a body floating in the lake.' Lamont suddenly looked discomfited, and he bit his underlip, appeared upset. Gaining control of himself almost immediately, he went on, 'I jumped out of the jeep for a closer look. The body, or rather a piece of clothing, had caught on a large log near the edge of the lake. I saw at once that it

447

was Lady Dunvale in the lake. I went immediately to Clonloughlin House to inform the earl.'

'And after you informed Lord Dunvale, you telephoned the police presumably?'

'That is correct, sir, and Sergeant McNamara arrived promptly, and we, that is Lord Dunvale and myself, accompanied the sergeant to the lake.'

The coroner now called on Sergeant McNamara to report his findings. After confirming the details of Lamont's story, McNamara launched into a recital of the investigation he had conducted on the Sunday morning after the discovery of the body.

'Mr Lamont and I retrieved the body, his lordship being too distressed by far to help. I then removed the deceased to Doctor Brennan's surgery in the village, for examination and to establish possible time of death. From there I put through a phone call to forensic in Cork, knowing there would have to be a post-mortem, and to arrange for immediate transportation of the body to the forensic laboratory in Cork. I went back to Clonloughlin House, where I took a statement from his lordship, the Dowager Countess and Mr Lamont. I then searched the area around the lake, also Lady Dunvale's Austin. There was a silver hip flask, empty, but smelling of whiskey, in the glove compartment. Her handbag was on the seat and its contents did not look as if they had been tampered with. There was a considerable amount of money in the wallet. In the afternoon I thought I'd better return this to the estate. You see, sir, it was like this . . . I was baffled . . . and about several things: Doctor Brennan had told me he believed death had occurred around eleven-thirty at night. I couldn't help wondering what her ladyship had been doing *out at the lake alone for five hours or more*. There was something else odd. I couldn't imagine how anybody could accidentally *fall* into the lake. There is no high ground, in fact the land is rather flat, and to get into Clonloughlin Lake a person would have to *walk* or *wade* into it. It was during this second search that I found an empty whiskey bottle thrown into a clump of bushes. Now that got me to thinking, it did indeed, sir. I asked meself if death had really been accidental, as everyone was thinking. The more I pondered the more I came around to thinking it could have been suicide, perhaps even murder.' Sergeant McNamara nodded to himself. 'Yes, I must admit I did wonder if her ladyship had been the victim of foul play.'

'Foul play by whom, Sergeant McNamara?' The coroner stared intently at the police officer, his face more dolorous than ever.

'By persons unknown, sir. A tramp, a stray gypsy, perhaps a stranger in these parts, up to no good, who her ladyship might have surprised out there in that lonely, deserted spot. But there were no signs of any kind of struggle, or a scuffle. No trampled bushes, no marks in the grass near the lake, marks like a body being dragged would cause for instance. No, no, nothing like that at all, sir. The Mini was carefully parked, and as I said her handbag was lying there on the seat.' McNamara rubbed the side of his large red nose. 'Nor am I suggesting that Lord Dunvale had anything to do with his wife's death. Miss O'Donnell's statement that he was in the library at the time the deceased drowned removes any suspicion about his lordship. I had to interrogate him a second time on Sunday afternoon, mind you, sir. That was in my line of duty.' McNamara gave Anthony a careful look, as if to exonerate himself in his eyes. 'Anyway, it's those five or six hours. What her ladyship was doing out there during that long period remains the greatest mystery to me, sir.'

The coroner pondered, said thoughtfully, 'Of course, Sergeant McNamara, Lady Dunvale could have left the grounds of Clonloughlin House, driven back to Waterford and returned to Clonloughlin later – on the evening in question, perhaps hoping to speak to the earl at that time.'

'Oh yes, sir, that is true. Very true, indeed it is. *But she didn't*. I made inquiries in the village, sure and I did, and not one solitary soul saw her during those *mysterious* five hours. And she would have had to drive through the village to get to the main road leading to Waterford.'

Daisy, who had been holding herself very still, hardly dared to breathe. She looked worriedly at John Crawford, who gave her a reassuring smile. But she guessed he was as concerned as she was at this moment. Drat Sergeant McNamara, she thought.

'Thank you, Sergeant McNamara.' The coroner nodded his dismissal and called the village doctor, Patrick Brennan, to give evidence.

Doctor Brennan's testimony was brief. 'I examined the body of the deceased late on Sunday morning, after receiving a telephone call from Sergeant McNamara, and the arrival of said body at my surgery. I saw at once that rigor mortis was present throughout the entire body. I established death to be in the proximity of eleven-thirty to midnight.'

'Were there any visible marks on the body of the deceased?' the coroner said.

'Nothing other than a diagonal bruise on the deceased's left cheek, which could have been caused by the log mentioned by Mr Lamont.'

The coroner thanked the doctor and summoned the Cork pathologist, Doctor Stephen Kenmarr.

Daisy moved to the edge of her seat, scrutinizing the pathologist intently. His would be the most crucial testimony, as she and the rest of the family were aware. She felt the tension of the Dunvales and Jim enveloping her as though this were a palpable thing. The court was deathly quiet once again, so quiet, in fact, Daisy could hear her own heart thudding.

Doctor Stephen Kenmarr was as precise a witness as Bridget O'Donnell had been. He got straight to the point.

'I concur with Doctor Brennan's theory about the abrasion on the deceased's left cheek. It could have been caused by an object in the lake, which the deceased struck when entering the water, most probably the aforementioned log. On Lady Dunvale's left cheek and cheekbone was an area of ecchymosis, that is, a dark bruise, reddish-blue in colour. I determined that it was a fresh ecchymosis, and not an old one, because of its colour. For the benefit of the laymen present, a bruise changes colour in stages, goes from reddish blue or dark purple to brown, then paler brown, lightens to a yellowish green and yellow in its last healing stages. Therefore, because of its dark colour, I knew the abrasion was recent. I found no traumatic wounds to the skull or other injuries to the head area of the body. There were no outward visible marks on any area of the body, no sign of a struggle, nor any evidence to suggest that the deceased had been attacked physically in a violent manner, or killed prior to the body entering the water. After the external examination I performed an autopsy on the deceased.'

Kenmarr paused, peered at his sheaf of notes. He said, 'I discovered that the deceased's bloodstream contained a large amount of alcohol and barbiturates. The lungs held a quantity of water. I therefore concluded that death was by drowning due to the excessive amount of water taken into the lungs. Death occurred at approximately eleven-forty in the evening.'

'Thank you, Doctor Kenmarr,' the coroner said. He slipped on his glasses and looked down at the papers before him. After a few minutes he settled back in his chair and, turning to his right, he addressed the six jurors.

'From testimony we have heard in this court today we must all be fully and most sadly cognizant of the fact that the deceased was a troubled woman who was under severe mental strain, whose normal stable disposition had been affected by acute depression, owing to the failure of her marriage, and her inability to bear children.' He leaned forward. 'I put great store in the testimony of Miss Bridget O'Donnell, a clear, coherent and unemotional witness, who was perhaps far more able to see the deceased in an objective light than her husband. Miss O'Donnell was most convincing, and I trust her judgement when she says that the deceased was, only days before her death, in a frame of mind that could induce her to do harm to herself. We have heard the testimony of Doctor Kenmarr, the pathologist. He has told us there were no signs of a struggle, nor any visible marks on the body, other than the abrasion, which he has explained was recent, caused by the log. We have heard his toxicology report, his findings of alcohol and barbiturates in the bloodstream. The excessive amount of water in the lungs proved conclusively to Doctor Kenmarr that death was by drowning.'

The coroner's direct gaze rested for a split second on each juror. He resumed, 'Sergeant McNamara has drawn our attention to the curious elapse of time between the deceased's arrival at the lake and her death some five hours later. Sergeant McNamara referred to them as *mysterious hours* – but are they really? Let us now try to reconstruct those crucial hours when the deceased was alone at the lake – and we must presume she did remain there, since no one saw her leave the grounds of Clonloughlin House or pass through the village. Let us also consider the deceased herself – a troubled, depressed woman who was in a state of irrationality, that irrationality obviously inflamed by alcohol. She may well have been drinking before her arrival, but undoubtedly she consumed a large quantity of alcohol after she arrived. It was found in her bloodstream, and Sergeant McNamara testified that he not only discovered an empty *flask* smelling of *whiskey*, but an empty *whiskey bottle* thrown into the bushes. We have the deceased sitting at the lake, drinking, possibly hoping, indeed perhaps *expecting*, her husband to return to the lake within a short span of time. Let us not forget that his land rover was parked on the other side of the water, and was quite visible to her. Is it not then within the realm of possibility that she did indeed remain there? That she hoped to discuss her problems with him, to find some surcease from her pain? Let me propose the following to you . . . hours pass . . . it Grows dark . . . as she continues to linger, could not the alcohol have blurred her sense of time? Or even rendered her unconscious. Then again, could it not have induced in her the conviction that her husband would indeed come back to retrieve the land rover? But finally, in the end, realizing her hopes were groundless, could she not have come to a most terrible and tragic decision? The decision to put an end to her life? We have been told she was unusually despondent, filled with a feeling of hopelessness about her future, and by *two* witnesses. It is quite conceivable to me that the deceased swallowed barbiturates at this most dreadful moment in time, either in a misguided attempt to ease her mental anguish – or perhaps to numb her senses before walking into that lake. Yes, I believe that the events on that evening could have progressed in exactly this way and as I have so outlined to you. There is no other feasible explanation. Medical testimony has ruled out the possibility of foul play – murder. Sergeant McNamara has pointed out that it would be difficult for a person to accidentally fall into the lake at Clonloughlin even if a person was in a drunken stupor, befuddled and disoriented by alcohol, because of the nature of the topography of the area. There is no high ground surrounding that particular body of water.' There was a split second's pause, before the coroner finished, 'And so, after giving due consideration to all of the evidence presented today, I must draw the conclusion that this is a clear case of suicide.' The coroner scanned the jurors for one final time. 'Are there any questions?'

The jurors turned to each other, spoke together in low

tones for a few seconds, and finally a clean-cut young man addressed the coroner with the apparent approval of the others. 'We are all in agreement, sir. We believe as you do and that it happened the way you say.'

Straightening himself up to his full height in the chair, the coroner now addressed the entire court.

'As coroner presiding in this Coroner's Court of the County of Cork I must now pronounce a verdict that Minerva Gwendolyn Standish, the Countess of Dunvale, did die by her own hand whilst the balance of her mind was disturbed, and whilst she was under the influence of alcohol and barbiturates.'

There was a moment of complete silence and then a buzz began, rippling through the court. Daisy patted Edwina's hand, leaned forward and glanced at John Crawford, who smiled very faintly and nodded. Daisy's eyes rested momentarily on Anthony, who sat as unmoving as a statue on the seat. He looked stricken, disbelieving. Daisy filled with sadness and pity for him. He had so wanted Min's death to be proven an accident.

Daisy rose and helped the weeping Edwina to her feet, escorted her out into the corridor. Bridget O'Donnell caught up with them.

'I'm sorry, your ladyship,' Bridget murmured.

Edwina turned, stared at her, shook her head vehemently without speaking.

Bridget went on, 'I had to say what I said about Lady Dunvale because – ' There was the merest fraction of a pause before she finished sullenly, 'Because it was the truth.'

Daisy, observing her, thought: Oh no, it wasn't. Startled at herself, she wondered what had prompted her to assume such a thing, and instantly dismissed the curious idea that Bridget O'Donnell had been lying. But the thought was to recur often and the housekeeper's testimony would trouble Daisy for the longest time.

Edwina swayed against her, and Daisy turned her attention to her half-sister. 'Come, Edwina dear, sit down,' she murmured with great gentleness and led her to a bench.

Bridget rushed to help. 'I'll go and fetch you a drink of water, your ladyship.'

'No!' Edwina exclaimed. 'I don't want you to get me anything.'

The sharpness of Edwina's tone seemed to stun Bridget, and she stepped back uncertainly. 'But your ladyship – ' she began and faltered.

Ignoring her, Edwina opened her handbag and took out a compact, patted her red nose and tear-stained face with the powder puff. Bridget continued to gape at Edwina, her icy blue eyes filling with perplexity and then she edged nearer to the door leading into the coroner's court. When she saw Michael Lamont emerging she hurried to his side.

'Are you all right now, Edwina?' Daisy asked, bending over the other woman, filled with concern.

Edwina made no response. She rose and looked Daisy fully in the face. To Daisy it seemed as though an immense change had been wrought in her during the passing of only a few seconds. A veil of dignity had fallen over Edwina's face and her bearing was suddenly regal, almost imperious.

Finally she spoke, and her voice was clear, unusually strong. 'I have just remembered who I am – I am Emma Harte's daughter and my son is her grandson, and therefore we are made of sterner stuff than most people might think. It's about time I made them realize that, and I also think it's time that I stopped feeling sorry for myself.'

A warm smile swept across Daisy's astonished face. She reached out and grasped Edwina's arm. 'Welcome to the family,' she said.

CHAPTER 28

Miranda O'Neill was laughing with such merriment tears sprang into her eyes.

Recovering herself after a few seconds, she flicked the tears away with her fingertips. 'Honestly, Paula, I've never heard such a load of nonsense in my life.'

Paula said, 'You're confirming my suspicions . . . I thought Sarah was lying to me.'

Searching her handbag for a tissue, Merry blew her nose, said, 'Lying is rather a strong word – let's just say that she fudged the facts. Or, to use one of Grandpop's favourite phrases, she bent the truth to suit her purpose.'

'So what really happened in Barbados?' Paula probed. 'She made it sound as if she worked like a galley slave.'

'Oh rubbish! She had lots of help from the two local girls I'd engaged and the young woman who's going to manage the boutique for us.' Merry stood up, drifted over to the sofa positioned near the window in Paula's office at the Leeds store.

Watching her progress across the room Paula decided she had not seen Miranda looking so well for a long time. She had caught the sun in the Caribbean and her freckled face, usually so pale, had a soft tan that was most flattering to her, gave her an extra-special glow. She wore a full-skirted wool dress of an unusual ginger shade that enhanced the colour of her burnished copper hair, and her tawny eyes seemed more golden than hazel today. Paula could not help thinking of the autumn foliage in her garden at Long Meadow. Merry's natural colouring and the clothes she had chosen echoed its russet hues perfectly.

Draping herself on the sofa, Miranda explained: 'The minute Sarah arrived she was obviously in that take charge

456

mood of hers, very superior, bossy, even demanding. I volunteered to help in any way I could, but she practically ordered me out of the shop, said she could manage, thank you very much. Frankly, I was taken aback since she's not really involved with us in the boutiques. But I decided to let her have her way.' The auburn brows met in a deep frown and her expressive face signalled her irritation. 'She didn't want me around, Paula, that's the long and short of it. I *was* rather busy with other things in the hotel, but not too busy to check in several times a day by phone. And I went down every evening to see how the boutique was shaping up.' Miranda's wide-set eyes rested on Paula, grew quizzical. 'Surely you knew I'd be on top of things?'

'Naturally I did, silly. I'm only mentioning it because Sarah made such a fuss about the hard work she *said* she'd done. She also told me that she hadn't enjoyed herself, implied that the O'Neills ostracized her.'

'Now that *is* a downright lie!' Miranda exclaimed, her annoyance more apparent than ever. 'Both my father and Shane paid numerous visits to the shop, and she was invited to every single one of our special events.' Miranda glanced at her hands thoughtfully, nodded to herself and looked up at Paula. 'Well, perhaps she didn't have any fun actually. She was certainly bizarre in the way she behaved. She seemed to think it was Shane's duty to be her permanent escort, to drag her around with him wherever he went, *and* to pay constant court to her. Shane was awfully pleasant and patient under the circumstances – after all he was preoccupied with the hotel. We were all *working*, for God's sake.'

'I know you were,' Paula answered. 'And I didn't really pay attention to the things she said . . . but I must admit I was a bit thunderstruck at first. And why would she lie to me? Surely she knew I'd find out from you what actually transpired.'

'Sarah's strange, lives in her own world.' Miranda leaned

forward, gave Paula a knowing stare. 'Consider some of the rotten little things she did when we were children. And she's always been full of her own importance. Smug. Self-satisfied. Look, I don't think she merits this long discussion, do you? Let's – '

'There's something I haven't told you. The real reason she came to see me two weeks ago was to make me an offer . . . she wanted to buy the boutiques.' Paula sat back, waiting for Merry's reaction, aware that she would be angrier than ever. But she had to be told.

'What a bloody cheek! *Our boutiques!* I've never heard of anything so outrageous in my life . . . where was her head? I mean, you're a public company. I presume you sent *her* on her merry way and with a few choice words ringing in her ears. I hope you did!'

'Yes, of course. But she wasn't taking my *no* for an answer. She threatened to telex Grandy in Australia.'

'And did she?'

'No. She telephoned her at Dunoon. Can you imagine, bothering Gran like that? Anyway, Grandy made short shrift of her.' Paula's mouth worked with sudden amusement as she thought of her recent conversation with her grandmother. 'When Sarah told Gran that she thought she should be allowed to buy the boutiques for her division, because of all her hard work, effort, brilliance, etcetera, Gran told me she said, "Oh really, Sarah, so that's what you think, is it? Well, remember what thought did – followed a muck cart and thought it was a wedding." Then Grandy told her that her suggestion was ill-conceived, ridiculous, and out of the question. She added that it would *always* be out of the question, advised Sarah never to dare to mention such a thing again.'

'There's nobody quite as pithy and scathing as Aunt Emma when she wants to be,' Miranda said, and leaned back. 'I assume dear Sarah got the message?'

'I haven't heard a whisper from her since.'

'Well, that doesn't mean anything, she's busy with the summer line right now.' A look of comprehension flitted on to Miranda's face. 'What you've just told me probably explains something – Sarah was awfully funny with me when I went up to Lady Hamilton Clothes the other day. I can't say she was rude, because she's always well mannered, but she was unusually standoffish, even for her. Not to digress, but it's a lovely line by the way, and I hope you'll see it when you're in London next week. We ought to place our order soon, Paula.'

'Yes, I know, and Gaye has made an appointment for me to go to the showroom. And whatever else she is, Sarah is a marvellous designer. The Lady Hamilton Collection has never been anything but stunning.'

'Yes,' Miranda said, thinking how generous and fairminded Paula was, and she constantly strove to find something positive in everyone. 'Incidentally, Allison Ridley was at the fashion show, and *she* was strange with me as well, treated me as if I had a social disease.'

'Probably because of Winston and Emily.'

'What's that got to do with *me*?'

'You're very close to Emily, and I hear that Allison's extremely cut up about Winston. Quite broken-hearted, according to Michael Kallinski, who came in to see me yesterday. He told me she and Sarah have become very thick lately, and no doubt Allison regards you as a member of the enemy camp. Anyway, Michael said Allison's thinking of moving to New York. *Permanently*.'

Miranda was surprised. 'Well, well, well . . . maybe she's contemplating going into partnership with that friend of hers – Skye Smith.'

There was such a disparaging note in Merry's voice Paula glanced at her quickly. 'Don't you like Skye Smith?'

'Not particularly,' Merry answered, as usual being completely open and honest with her dearest friend. 'I have to admit that she has been very nice to Shane since he's been

459

in New York. She's given a few dinner parties for him and has introduced him to some of her friends, and he seems to like her. But – ' Merry's voice trailed off, and she made a face. 'She's too good to be true, in my opinion, so sweet all the time, too sweet if the truth be known. She acts as if butter wouldn't melt in her mouth, plays the innocent, but I can't help feeling she's quite experienced – where men are concerned. I said so to Shane, but he just laughed, thought it was very amusing. Winston tended to agree with me. I'm sure he's told you that Shane had a small dinner party for us both at Twenty One when we were in New York last week. Well, it was actually for Winston – to celebrate the deal he made with the Canadian paper mill.'

'I thought he hadn't missed out one detail,' Paula said slowly, 'but obviously he did, since he made no mention of Skye Smith.'

'Oh,' Merry said, thinking this omission was odd. She hurried on, 'But Skye *was* there. With Shane. And I had a chance to get to know her a bit better, observe her more closely. I came away from that dinner with the most peculiar feeling. I think she has something to hide – you know, about her past.'

'What a strange thing for you to think, Merry.'

'Isn't it,' Merry agreed. 'And don't ask me *why* I think it, because I can't offer you a proper explanation. Instinct, perhaps, intuition on my part.' Merry gave a tiny shrug. 'Still, on the plane coming back to London with Winston, he and I had a long discussion about her, and we both decided she has a devious nature. He's not very keen on her any more, even though he quite liked her when he and Shane first met her at Allison's in the spring.'

'Is it serious? I mean between Shane and her?' Paula was surprised how tight her voice sounded and as her stomach lurched she realized that the idea of Skye and her old friend being involved troubled her. Her eyes did not leave Merry's face.

'I sincerely hope it isn't! I don't like the idea of *her* being around on a permanent basis. Winston thinks it's only platonic, and he ought to know. By the way, talking of Winston, how's Sally?'

'Oh she's much better. Anthony came over from Ireland about ten days ago and went immediately to Heron's Nest, where Sally's been staying. I spoke to them on the phone yesterday, and they're benefiting from the peace and quiet, are glad to be alone together. Actually Anthony's coming to see me this afternoon.'

'What an awful time you must have had because of his wife's death. I would have to be out of the country, wouldn't I? I wish I'd been here, to give you moral support, Paula.'

'Oh Merry, that's sweet of you. But fortunately Emily was back from Paris, and she and I managed to keep each other going. We got through it, which is the main thing.'

'Yes. But you do look tired,' Merry ventured, using the mildest word she could find. From the moment she had arrived at the store she had been struck by Paula's white, drained face, the dark shadows. Her friend looked quite ill to her. 'Can't you take a few days off? Get away somewhere for a rest?'

'You've got to be joking! Look at this desk.'

Merry made no further comment, deciding it would be wiser not to voice her worries about Paula's health. She averted her face to conceal her anxiousness. Her eyes fell on the collection of family photographs on Emma's large mahogany side table. A number of familiar faces gazed back at her – her grandparents, Blackie and Laura on their wedding day, her father as a baby lying on a fur rug, she and Shane when they were toddlers, her parents on the day of their marriage, and Emma's children in various stages of growing up.

Reaching for the largest photograph of the handsome man in an officer's uniform, she studied it for a moment, then remarked, 'Your mother looks a lot like Paul McGill. Yes, Aunt Daisy has her father's eyes. But then, so do you.' Glad she had found a way to change the subject, she added, 'But the frame's dented, Paula. You ought to get it fixed for Aunt Emma. It's such a shame. Why, this is a really lovely piece of silver. An antique.' Merry held up the frame, pointed to the damage.

'Grandy doesn't want it repaired,' Paula told her with a faint half-smile. 'When I said the same thing a couple of years ago, she laughed and told me the *dent* was part of her memories.'

'What did she mean?' Merry asked.

'My grandfather didn't return to England after the end of the First World War. He stayed in Australia. The story is a bit involved, but one day, in a moment of rage and frustration, Gran threw his picture across the room – that particular picture in that very frame. The glass shattered, the frame was dented, but she kept it nevertheless. She told me that ever since then, whenever she looked at his photograph, she reminded herself to trust love. She thinks that if she had trusted Paul when he disappeared – *trusted his love for her* – she would have had absolute faith in him, would have waited for him to come back. She believes she would have saved herself the terrible years of heartache she suffered during her dreadfully unhappy marriage to Arthur Ainsley.'

'But Paul and she did get back together in the end, had years of happiness,' Merry said softly, her expression suddenly disconsolate.

'You do sound unhappy, Merry. Love problems yourself? None of your old boyfriends around, is that it?' Paula looked sympathetic.

Merry nodded. 'No new ones either. I seem to have nothing but bad luck in that department these days. Most of the men I've gone out with in the last few months can't seem to see beyond the O'Neill money, my looks and my so-called sexuality. I'm getting more leery by the minute.' Merry grimaced. *'I'll* probably end up being an old maid. Emily's lucky, snagging Winston the way she did. At least she knows he's in love with *her* and not her bank balance. Especially since he's got a pretty hefty one of his own.'

'Oh Merry, not every man is after money –' Paula began and stopped, recognizing there was a grain of truth in Merry's statement. Being an heiress *did* have its manifold disadvantages, although money was only one of them.

Miranda was silent. After a moment she said, *'Perhaps.* The trouble is that the men *I* meet are simply not able to see beyond their noses, past the externals, to the person I am, to the real me. I'm not a fairy tale princess, for heaven's sake. I work jolly hard and carry quite a load of responsibility at O'Neill Hotels International. And I have very real values, as you're aware. Shane and I were brought up to understand the value of a pound note, just as you were. And my father and grandfather aside, they all instilled, Aunt Emma certainly drilled enough sense into me during those summers at Heron's Nest.'

Paula said, 'Yes, I understand what you're trying to say. People do have funny ideas about us, don't they? But nothing is ever the way it seems – to outsiders anyway.'

Walking over to Paula's desk, Merry sat down in the chair opposite, her sadness mirrored in her tawny eyes. Her face became more downcast. 'I'll tell you something else, Paula, I'd much prefer to marry a man I've known all my life, who loves me for *myself*, for what I am as a person, and not for what he *imagines* me to be. The other day I came to the conclusion that I don't want to get seriously involved with a fascinating stranger. To hell with fascinating strangers, they spell trouble and are frequently full of nasty surprises. If it's not the money, then it's the power they crave. Then there are the sex maniacs, the chaps who're only interested in hopping into bed.' She smiled wryly. 'As Shane keeps saying, sex is easy to come by but love is hard to find. That brother of mine happens to be right in this instance.'

Anthony said, 'It's awfully good of you to spend all this time with me this afternoon, Paula. I really appreciate it, and I'd just like to say again that you've been wonderful through this most difficult period. I can't tha – '

Paula held up her hand. 'If you say thank you to me once more I'll turf you out of my office.' She lifted the teapot and poured him a second cup of tea. 'I'm glad to be of help when I can, and let's not lose sight of the fact that you're a member of this family.' She gave him a small but warm smile. 'Besides,' she added quickly, 'I'm not all that busy this afternoon,' resorting to the white lie in order to make him feel better. 'Now, to answer your question, I think Grandy *would* be upset – very upset actually – if you and Sally got married before she returns from Australia.'

'You do really,' he murmured, his face crestfallen. He lit a cigarette, sat back in the chair and crossed his legs. He stared past her into space, focusing on the painting above the antique chest on the far wall. He seemed momentarily distracted, as if trying to work something out in his head. 'And when do you think she will be getting back, in fact?' he asked eventually, bringing his attention to Paula again.

'She promised me she'd be home in time to have our traditional family Christmas at Pennistone Royal – ' Paula stopped in mid-sentence, struck by a sudden, and appealing, idea. Leaning forward over the butler's tray table between them, she exclaimed, 'That's when you should marry Sally. At Christmas. Gran will love it, and you can stay with her at Pennistone Royal through the holidays.'

He made no response.

Paula said in a rush, 'It's a marvellous idea, Anthony. Why are you hesitating?'

Still he was mute, and as she watched him closely Paula saw a pained look cross his sensitive face, which was grey and lined with fatigue. His eyes became anxious, even alarmed. He has eyes like Jim, like Aunt Edwina. Fairley eyes, Paula thought idly. She pushed aside this inconsequential observation, and wanting to pin him down, said, 'Yes, Christmas *would* be perfect, ideal. Do say yes. We can try and reach Grandy in Sydney. No, it's too late now,' she muttered, thinking aloud about the time difference, glancing at her watch. It was four o'clock. Two in the morning in Australia. 'Well, we can send her a telex,' she announced decisively.

'I suppose Christmas will be all right,' Anthony said slowly, reluctantly. 'It *will* have to be a quiet wedding, Paula. Very quiet. Because by then – ' His voice wavered slightly, became a low mumble as he told her, 'Sally's pregnant, and her condition will be noticeable by then.'

Aware at once of his discomfort, Paula adopted a cheerful, matter-of-fact tone. 'I imagine Sally will be about six months along in December, so we'll have to make her a really lovely wedding dress that conceals her awkward figure.'

Startled, Anthony said, '*You knew?*'

'No, guessed. Both Emily and I thought she had put on weight when we saw her in September, and we came to the conclusion she might be expecting. Don't worry, no one else knows, except Winston.'

'Her father and Vivienne are also aware – '

'I'm talking about the rest of the family, Anthony. And as you said it should be quiet . . . only a handful of people. The Hartes, of course, Gran, Jim and myself, your mother, and Emily. She'd be hurt if she didn't come.'

'Yes,' he said. 'I'm very fond of Emily, and she was such a help . . .' He stopped, swallowed. 'Under the circumstances, do you think it's indecent – my getting married again? I mean, so soon after Min's death?'

'No, of course I don't.'

Anthony looked at Paula uncertainly.

She looked back, her gaze direct and penetrating.

She saw a man under great strain, and this showed in his haggard face, was echoed by his bleak manner, and the apathy she had divined in him the moment he had arrived. That he had aged in the past few weeks was transparent. He was not the same person he had been at her grandmother's birthday celebration. His fair colouring and very blond, rather English good looks had been most pronounced, and he had appeared more striking than ever in the well-tailored tuxedo, which he had worn with the same kind of panache Jim possessed. That night he had laughed a lot, been so carefree and gay, unusually outgoing, charming them all. Now he was a shattered wreck.

Paula made a snap decision. She leaned forward, pinning him down with her eyes. 'Listen to me, Anthony. You were unhappily married to Min, separated from her and about to divorce. You've been devastated by her death, the circumstances of it, and understandably so. However, it was not your fault. You must put it out of your mind, otherwise it's going to come between you and your happiness with Sally, affect your future, perhaps even ruin your life.' Recognizing she had spoken harshly, she softened her tone. 'You must think about Sally and the baby from this moment on . . . they are your priorities.'

'Oh yes, what you say is true,' he acknowledged. 'I'm not a hypocrite. Please don't think I'm mourning excessively for her.' A quiver entered his voice when he said, 'But I never wished her dead, Paula. That she had to die in such a terrible way is more than I – '

Paula stood up, joined him on the sofa. She took his hand, looked into his face, her own filled with immense compassion. 'I know, I know, Anthony. And please believe me, I'm not being cold hearted, not in the least. And whatever *you* think, you *weren't* responsible. My grandmother, *our grandmother*, says we are each one of us responsible for our own lives, that we write our own scripts and then live them out to the bitter end. That *is* true, you know. Min was responsible for herself, her life, not you. Try and draw strength and courage from Grandy's philosophy.'

'Yes,' he said. 'But it *is* hard, so very hard.'

Paula was more convinced than ever that her cousin was in grave emotional trouble, and she racked her brain, wondering what to say, how to jostle him out of his present troubled state. She was not insensitive to his feelings. But she also knew that if he allowed Min's death to dominate his life he was cutting off his chance of making that brand new life with Sally.

Speaking so quietly, so gently that her voice was hardly audible, Paula said, 'It may be difficult for you to believe me when I say that I can comprehend your feelings, but truly I can. You must put this tragedy behind you. If you don't it will cripple you. You will also be committing a terrible sin – against your own child.' Purposely she stopped with suddenness, abruptness, sat waiting, watching him.

He blinked, his eyes wide with shock. 'What on earth do you mean by that?' he managed in a strangled voice. 'I don't understand . . . *committing a sin against my own child*,' he repeated. He was horrified.

'Yes. If you permit Min's memory, her suicide, to haunt you, to fill you with guilt, you will not be able to love that child as you should – with all your heart and soul and mind. Because Min will be there, creating a wedge between you, and, let me add, between you and Sally. Also, remember that you and Sally created this baby out of your love for each other . . . it didn't ask to be born . . . it's an innocent little thing. Don't cheat it because of *your* problems. He or she is going to need the very best of you, Anthony. To give the child anything less . . . well, yes, that would be a sin.'

He stared at her for the longest moment, blinking, striving to curb his emotions so dangerously near the

467

surface. He leaped up, strode to the window, stood peering absently into the street below. But he saw only the death mask of Min's face as it had looked when they had brought her back from the lake. He closed his eyes convulsively, needing to expunge the image. Anthony groped for his handkerchief, blew his nose, ruminated on Paula's words. And then Sally's voice echoed in his throbbing head. *Life is for the living*, she had said last night. *We can't change what has happened. We can't spend the rest of our lives flagellating ourselves. If we do then Min will have won. And won from the grave.* The things Sally had said had been rooted in fundamental truths, he might as well admit it. Something else occurred to him, brought his head up with a swift jerk. The woman Min had become in the last few years bore no resemblance to the girl he had fallen in love with. Min had turned sour, bitter and vindictive, and her bitterness and resentment had only served to erode his love. Sally had not broken up his marriage, as Min had so violently asserted. Only bad marriages could be shattered by another person. Those unions that were strong remained inviolate against all outside forces. Now he thought: it was Min who broke up our marriage. For a split second he believed this was a sudden revelation, but then acknowledged that he had always been aware of this in the back of his mind. He had been so busy blaming himself he had not let this fact rise to the surface. The pain in his chest began to ease, and slowly he gathered his self-possession to him. Eventually he turned and went back to the sofa and Paula.

Anthony's pellucid eyes held hers, and it was his turn to reach out, to take her hand in his. He said, 'You're a very special woman, Paula. Wise, and so very compassionate, such a good and loving person. Thank you for bringing me to my senses. I shall give Sally and our child every ounce of love that I have. They will have the very best of me. I promise you that.'

After Anthony had left, Paula plunged into her work with a vengeance. She was still hard at it when Agnes poked her head around the door at six-thirty.

'How late are we going to be here tonight, Mrs Fairley?'

Paula raised her eyes, put down her pen and sat back in the chair. 'Come in, Agnes.' She rubbed her aching face, picked up the cup of tea, and, realizing it had gone cold hours before, immediately put it down with a grimace. 'I'll be about another half-hour, that's all, but you can leave if you want.'

'Oh no, I wouldn't dream,' Agnes said. Conscious of Paula's drawn white face, she eyed the cup, volunteered, 'Let me make you a nice cup of hot tea, Mrs Fairley. You look dead beat.'

'Yes, thanks a lot, Agnes. No, wait a minute, let's have a drink. I could use one tonight, and I'm sure you could too.'

'That'll be very nice, Mrs Fairley. But what have we got?'

Paula let out her first genuine laugh that day. 'Sorry,' she apologized, observing the hurt and baffled expression on her secretary's face. 'You did sound droll just then. And you're right, what *do* we have . . . very little that's palatable, I suspect. There was a bottle of sherry in the coat closet. Why don't you see if it's still there.'

Agnes hurried to the walk-in closet and Paula started to shuffle her papers, slipping items into the different coloured folders spread before her, quickly bringing order to her desk.

A second later Agnes emerged from the closet, smiling triumphantly. 'Bristol Cream, Mrs Fairley.' She held up the bottle with a flourish.

'Oh good, let's have a glass, and we can kill two birds with one stone, go over a few final things since it's Saturday tomorrow. I've decided not to come in, Agnes. I want to spend the day with my babies. And you don't have to be here either, you know.'

'Thank you, Mrs Fairley.' Agnes beamed at her.

Ten minutes later, between sips of sherry, Paula had reduced the pile of folders on her desk. Most of them now sat on the floor at Agnes's feet.

'You can send these last three to Gaye Sloane in London. The blue folder contains all the final details for the career clothes shop. Incidentally, I've decided to use the name Emily came up with, after all. I think it's the best . . . *The Total Woman* says exactly what I want it to say. Do you like it?'

'I do, very much. I told Miss Emily so the other day. She was, well, sort of taking a poll around the executive offices, asking the other secretaries and typists what they thought.'

'Was she now,' Paula murmured, smiling to herself as she thought affectionately of Emily, her busy little bee forever trying to be of help. 'The red folder has all the information for the fashion exhibition in January, and this green one has my notes for Trade Winds, plus a list of merchants we'll be buying from in Hong Kong, India and Japan. Do you have your pad?' Paula nodded as Agnes lifted it up. 'Drop a line to Gaye and ask her to make duplicates of the lists. Also, send a memo to – '

The private phone on Paula's desk began to ring and Agnes, rising and reaching over, answered it. 'Yes, just a minute please,' she said, depressing the hold button. She handed the receiver to Paula. 'It's Mr Stevens calling from Odessa, Texas.'

'Hello, Dale,' Paula said. 'How are – '

He cut her off abruptly. 'Paula, I'm sorry, but I have bad news.'

'What's wrong, Dale?'

'The worst, I'm afraid. One of our oil tankers is in trouble. It was loading crude oil off the coast of Texas this

470

morning, Galveston, and there was an explosion in the engine room. A very bad explosion.'

Gripping the phone tightly, striving to hear him through the abnormally bad static, Paula said, with rising apprehension, 'No casualties, I hope, Dale?'

There was a moment of silence. 'Yes, I'm afraid we've lost six of the crew . . . four other crew members badly injured – '

'Oh Dale, this is horrendous!' Paula exclaimed. 'How did it happen, for God's sake?'

'We don't know. We're investigating. Blaze ripped through the vessel. It's under control now. She's not gone down. I stress *not* gone down . . .'

There was a bad echo on the line and Paula cried, 'I'm having difficulty hearing you.'

'I'm here,' he shouted back. 'Static sure is high today. I said we don't know what caused the explosion, but there'll be an inquiry. We've lost one and a quarter million gallons of crude, and we're facing a massive clean up job. The crude's drifting into Galveston Bay already. Seabirds and wildlife threatened by it, also the shrimp breeding grounds. God knows how much oil spill will wash ashore.'

'This is a disaster,' Paula said unsteadily.

'I can't hear *you*, Paula,' Dale Stevens bellowed.

'I said it's a catastrophe. We're going to have everybody on our backs from ecology people to – I dread to think who else. The families of the crew members – those poor people must be taken care of, Dale, as I'm sure you know without me telling you. Small comfort financial compensation will be. Listen, do you want me to fly over? I don't know what I could do, though, except give you moral support.'

'No, no, Paula, there's hardly any point in that. I'm handling everything. I've been in touch with the insurance company. It's going to cost us millions of dollars to do a concentrated clean up.'

'How much?'

'Don't know. Depends on the spill, the damage it does. It could be anywhere between five to ten million dollars to do a proper job.'

Paula caught her breath, aghast at the figure, then said, 'To hell with what it costs. We have to do it. Stay in touch, Dale. I want to know how such an explosion could possibly happen. We've had such a good safety record.'

'Nobody's immune. That's the oil business. I'll call you tomorrow, perhaps even later tonight if I have any further news.' The line was clearer now, his voice coming over as if he was speaking from around the corner.

'I'll be home all evening,' Paula said. 'And Dale, do everything you can for those bereaved families.'

'It's already in the works.'

'This is going to be a stain on our record.'

'I know, honey. I'm going to have to hang up. Situation is pressing here.'

'Dale, one more thing . . . you haven't told me which tanker it was.'

'Sorry, Paula, but it's the *Emeremm III*. I'm very sorry, honey.'

Paula put down the phone and fell back against the chair, feeling sick inside. Her face was grim.

Agnes said worriedly, 'I got the gist of your conversation, Mrs Fairley. One of the Sitex oil tankers sank.' This assertion came out sounding more like a question.

Paula shook her head, gave her secretary the details, then explained, 'The *Emeremm III* was named for my grandmother. She once owned a company called Emeremm and my grandfather loved the name – it's a contraction of emeralds and Emma. His favourite stone and his favourite lady.' She attempted a smile unsuccessfully. 'It was he who launched the first Emeremm, and then the *Emeremm II*. Ever since then it's been a tradition to have a vessel in the Sitex fleet bearing that name . . . that very special name.'

'I am sorry, Mrs Fairley,' Agnes sympathized. 'I know

how proud you are of the company's safety record. This is just awful.'

'Thank you, Agnes,' Paula murmured. 'It's a dreadful blow, especially since there has been loss of lives.' Pulling herself together, she exhaled, drew her pad towards her. 'I'd better draft a telex to my grandmother.' As she picked up her pen Paula shivered, felt a quiver run up her spine. Although she was not superstitious by nature she had a strange presentiment that disaster loomed. The explosion in the *Emeremm III* was a bad omen.

CHAPTER 29

'Didn't you enjoy yourself, Winston?' Emily asked, squinting at him in the muted glow emanating from the dying fire in the living room at Beck House.

Winston put down his brandy balloon and gaped at her, genuine astonishment invading his face. He shook his head in wonderment. 'Paula sits there looking as if she's at death's door, hardly opening her mouth all night. Jim manages to get stewed to the gills between cocktails and the main course. My sister is so pregnant she seems about ready to drop *triplets* right there at the dinner table. Merry doesn't stop bemoaning the fact that she's on the shelf at twenty-three because all of the men she's grown up with are otherwise involved. Alexander is in a raging snit because of your mother's sexual antics with half the bloody Government. Maggie Reynolds bores me senseless, droning on about some dilapidated shooting lodge in the Outer Hebrides, and you ask a question like that. Oh yes, Emily, I enjoyed myself thoroughly. I had a wonderful time. It was one of the most exciting, entertaining evenings of my life.' He began to laugh, suddenly seeing the humorous side.

Emily laughed with him. She snuggled into the corner of

the sofa, tucked her feet under her and said, 'But Anthony was on good form.'

'Amazingly so. Well, he seems to have *his* feet on the ground these days and is coping extremely well.'

'Thanks to Paula. She told me she had a long talk with him a few weeks ago, sort of gave him a lecture, advised him to put the past behind him and get on with his life.'

'She's very good at that,' Winston muttered, swirling the cognac around in his glass, his face thoughtful.

'What do you mean?'

'Giving advice. Mind you, she's usually right about everything she says. If only she'd take some of her own advice.'

Emily's face sobered instantly. 'Yes.'

Winston leaned back against the cushions, put his feet up on the coffee table, and let himself drift into his thoughts. The evening at Long Meadow had been a disaster and he had been relieved to escape with Emily relatively early, to come back here to the comfort and tranquillity of Beck House. But one dreary dinner party was meaningless, of no consequence. What troubled him was Paula's physical appearance and her state of mind. For some weeks now, since his return from Vancouver via New York, he had been vaguely conscious of her misery. The last few hours had confirmed his feelings. She was an unhappy woman. He was convinced her marriage to Jim was at the root of her pain.

Emily said, 'You're very quiet, Winston, you're worrying about Paula, aren't you?'

'I'm afraid so, darling. Apart from the fact that she looked so dreadful tonight, she spoke in monosyllables. I know she's a bit reserved at times, not a chatterbox like you, but she's normally much more communicative, especially with the family group.'

'It's not the work that's getting her down,' Emily exclaimed, 'she's used to pressure, long hours, carrying tremendous responsibilities. Anyway, she has the stamina of a bull – like Grandma.'

'I'm aware of that, Emily. I know Paula almost as well as you do. I meant it just now when I said she looks as if she's at death's door; however I realize she's not actually physically ill. She's emotionally disturbed at the moment.' He swung his feet to the floor, searched the pocket of his robe for the packet of cigarettes. 'There are a lot of problems in that marriage. Want to bet?' he asked, lighting a cigarette.

'Oh you're so right, Winston. I've tried to bring the subject up several times lately, but she just gives me funny looks and retreats into herself, or talks about something else.'

'But you two have always been so close. Hasn't she said anything at all?' he asked, his voice rising an octave, registering his surprise.

'No, not really. I told you before, she was upset on that awful Sunday in September. You know, because of Jim's attitude, the way he spoke to her in regard to her problems with Sam Fellowes. And I knew she'd been crying when I got back from Pennistone Royal. The weekend Jim returned from Ireland, when the three of us were in London, she murmured something about Jim being irritable, even irascible with her. I started to probe a bit, and she sort of . . . shrugged it off, became as uncommunicative as she was tonight. But I've noticed that tendency a lot in the last few months, and she *is* burying herself in work. That's all she does actually, except for spending any free time she has with the babies. She adores the twins. Actually, *I* think they've become her whole life, aside from business of course.'

'That's no good. Aunt Emma's going to be miffed, not too thrilled, when she gets back next month – seeing Paula like this.' Winston shifted his position on the sofa, immediately saw the concern ringing Emily's face. He took her hand, 'Hey, poppet, come on, don't look so miserable. It'll all work out. Life has a funny way of taking care of itself.'

'I suppose so,' Emily murmured, wondering if it would, deciding that it wouldn't, because of Paula's basic nature. She would cling to her marriage no matter what, because of the children and her extraordinary sense of duty to them, as well as her determination not to be defeated.

'Would you like me to talk to Paula,' Winston ventured. 'I could – '

'God no!' Emily cried fiercely, sitting up with a jerk. 'She'd resent it, consider it an intrusion into her privacy, and anyway, you'd only get a flea in your ear for your trouble.'

Winston sighed. 'I suspect that's true. Listen, if you want my opinion, I think she and Jim ought to get a divorce.'

'She'd never do that! She thinks as I do about divorce.'

'*Oh*. And how's that?' he asked, pricking up his ears. He gave her a long hard stare.

'Well,' Emily said slowly, 'we sort of disapprove really. I mean after all, we've had a lovely example with my mother. She's had so many husbands and so many divorces I've lost count.'

'Your mother's the exception to the rule, Emily.'

Ignoring this comment, Emily hurried on, 'Paula believes that if there are problems in a marriage they've got to be worked out. She says that people can't keep getting divorced at the drop of a hat, just because they meet a few snags along the way, that this is no solution. She thinks marriage requires a great deal of effort – '

'It takes two to tango, you know.'

A reflective look washed over Emily's face as she nodded, said, 'You're implying Jim might not make the effort . . . Is that actually what you mean?'

Winston hesitated. 'Perhaps. But I could be wrong, and

anyway who really knows about other people's private lives. That's why this conversation should be terminated right now. It's rather futile, Dumpling.'

'Yes,' she said. 'Winston, don't call me Dumpling. I'm very svelte these days.'

He laughed. 'I meant it affectionately, not critically, you silly goose.' He put down his drink, moved over to her side of the sofa. Putting his arm around her, he whispered against her cheek, 'So I'm stuck with you for the rest of my life it seems, in view of your opinions about divorce.'

'Yes,' she whispered back, 'we're stuck with each other. Thank God!'

'I second that.' He pulled away slightly, looked down into Emily's innocent young face. How pretty she was, and there *was* an innocence about her and she was very young, and yet she had a depth of wisdom that at times took him by surprise. He said softly, 'I could never be happy with anyone else, Dumpling, not now after I've had you.'

'Why?' She returned his gaze through flirtatious eyes.

'Always fishing, aren't you?'

'Tell me why . . .'

'Because I know you so thoroughly and understand you, my love, and because we're so compatible sexually.'

'Are you really sure we are?' she teased.

'Now that you mention it . . . well, perhaps we ought to give it another try.' He smiled, loving her with his eyes. Standing up, he held out his hand. 'Let's go to bed, darling, and experiment some more, just to make quite certain.' He led her upstairs.

'It's a good thing you put central heating in this house, otherwise we'd be freezing. It's very cold tonight,' Emily said half an hour later, wrapping part of the sheet around herself.

'Oh, I don't know about that, I think we're pretty hot stuff together.' Winston winked, pushing a pillow behind

477

his head and reached for the glass of brandy he had brought upstairs with him. He offered it to Emily. 'Like a sip?'

'No thanks, I don't want any more. It gives me heart palpitations.'

'Oh damn! And I thought I was the one who caused those.' He grinned, asked, 'Shall I light the fire anyway?'

'Aren't we going to sleep?'

'That wasn't part of my present plan,' he said, leering at her. 'Are you tired already?'

She shook her head, laughing, and her gaze followed him as he leaped out of bed, pulled on his dressing gown and strode to the fireplace directly opposite the old-fashioned four poster. He struck a match, ignited the paper and wood already arranged in the grate, then worked the pair of old bellows to get the blaze properly going. Emily liked watching Winston doing things. He was so clever and competent with his hands, forever repairing things in the house and on the grounds. She thought of the little bridge he had built across the pond at Heron's Nest when they were children. It had been charming, and a masterpiece of intricate design and clever engineering. Yes, he had been excellent at carpentry. She still had the small jewellery box he had made for her tenth birthday, so prettily painted and lined inside with red velvet. But he had given up his woodworking for music when he and Shane had formed The Herons.

Smiling to herself, she said suddenly, 'Winston, whatever happened to your trumpet?'

He was in a crouching position in front of the fire and he swung his head, taken aback by this question which had come out of the blue. 'Whatever made you think of my trumpet, for God's sake?'

'I was lying here remembering . . . you know, remembering bits of our childhood.'

'Funnily enough, Sally came across it a few weeks ago, when she was poking around in one of the cupboards at

Heron's Nest.' He returned to the bed, threw off his robe and climbed in next to her. 'Wasn't I awful in those days? Really fancied myself on the old horn, thought I was the bee's knees.'

'*I* thought you were *wonderful*. Not the trumpet though . . . you did stink. Gosh, I bet it was *you* who put the dead fish in *my* bed!' She thumped him on the arm. 'You rotten thing. I'll never forget that fishy smell. Ugh!' He grabbed her, wrestled her back against the pillows, pinned her down with his hands. 'You deserved it, you were a precocious little wretch.' He bent into her, kissed her on the mouth, let his tongue linger on hers. As he drew away finally, he whispered, 'If I'd had any sense I should have put myself in your bed – '

'You'd never have dared, Winston Harte, so don't pretend you would! Grandma had eyes in the back of her head.'

'She still does,' he quipped. He moved away from her, amusement dancing in his eyes. He picked up the brandy balloon, nursed it in both hands, then savoured a mouthful. He felt so good, was enjoying this friendly bit of idle banter with Emily, this relaxed break in their arduous but exciting lovemaking. He always did with her. She was so easy to be with afterwards. There was never any tension between them when their passion was spent, only during their loving. Then her intensity, her endless desire for him inflamed and thrilled him. He reached for her hand lying on top of the sheet, held on to it tightly, thinking of his narrow escape. He knew now that it would never have worked with Allison Ridley. He hadn't loved her, not really, not in the way he loved Emily.

Winston closed his eyes, reliving that special Sunday night in April, when she had driven over to have the supper he was supposedly going to cook. He never did cook it. The moment Emily had arrived they had looked knowingly and longingly into each other's eyes. And they had ended up, a fast ten minutes later, in the middle of this bed, where he had proceeded to surprise himself by making love to her three times in quick succession. His cousin, third cousin he corrected himself, had astonished him with her lack of inhibitions, her willingness to give pleasure and receive it, her unstinting generosity and joyousness in bed. At eleven-thirty, wrapped in bath towels, sitting in front of the living room fire, they had made an al fresco picnic of the odds and ends in his bachelor refrigerator, washing everything down with a bottle of Shane's vintage champagne. It had been the most wonderful evening . . .

Emily said, 'Winston, please don't get cross with me, but there's something I want to tell you. It's really important.'

Dragging himself away from his erotic meanderings about her, he lifted his lids, glanced out of the corner of his eye. 'Why should I get angry. Go on, tell me, Dumps.'

'That's even worse than Dumpling,' she groused, pulling a face, pretending to be annoyed. 'Why is it that the English have this ridiculous predilection for silly nicknames?'

'Because nicknames are pet names, and they express warmth, affection, familiarity, intimacy, caring. Are you going to tell me this *really important thing*, or not, Dumps?'

'Yes, I am.' She pushed herself up and half turned to face him, propping herself on her elbow, staring into his face intently. 'It's about Min's death . . . the inquest.'

'Oh no, Emily, not again!' He groaned and rolled his eyes in an exaggerated fashion. 'You've driven Paula crazy, now you're starting on me.'

'Please listen to me, just for a minute.'

'Okay, but you'd better make it quick. I think I've got myself into quite a state again.'

'Winston, you're insatiable.'

'Only with you, my sweet seductive passionate little thing.'

'I'm not so little,' she countered. 'Listen – Sally told me

480

Anthony is still unconvinced that Min killed herself. He thinks it was an accident, and I – '

'This is a terrible waste of time, darling,' Winston interjected impatiently, wanting her desperately. 'Aunt Daisy and Jim have each given us detailed accounts of the inquest. It couldn't have been an accident from what I understand. No chance.'

'I agree. I mean about it *not* being an accident. However, *I* don't believe it was suicide either.'

Winston laughed disbelievingly. 'Are you trying to tell me you think it was murder? Oh come on, Emily.'

'I'm afraid I *do* think so, Winston.'

'*Then who did it?* Certainly you can't possibly harbour the idea that it was poor old Anthony, who wouldn't say boo to a goose?'

'No. And I don't *know* who. But her death bothers me a lot . . . I can't seem to forget it. You see Winston, it's those five hours. They've always seemed odd to me, and even that Irish policeman called them mysterious, Aunty Daisy told me so. I happen to agree with him, they are, and they're also most peculiar.'

'You've missed your calling, poppet. You should have been a mystery writer,' he retorted, chortling. 'Maybe she just passed out from the booze.'

'Laugh if you want, Winston, but I bet it'll come out one day, you wait and see,' Emily shot back. Her voice was grave.

Winston sat up, paying attention. For as long as he could remember he had always thought Emily was exceptional – bright, smart, clever, and a lot shrewder than some of the family realized. This belief had been considerably re-inforced since he had become seriously involved with her. She made sense in so many ways, and he had grown accustomed to listening to her, trusting her judgement. Certainly it was she who had pushed him to go after the Canadian paper mill, insisted he persist when the talks had faltered. Lately, even some of her drive and ambition had washed off on him, and she had convinced him it was his duty to make a bigger contribution to the newspaper chain. So much so, he had actually abandoned the idea of leading the life of a country gentleman.

For all these reasons he had to take her seriously now. Slowly, he said, 'You say you don't know who could have killed her, and that is a tough nut, I admit. On the other hand, you've obviously thought a great deal about Min's death, so you must have some theories about what *might* have happened. Tell me, I'm all ears. Honestly, Dumps, I'm not laughing at you any more.'

Emily gave him a small gratified smile. 'Nothing will ever convince *me* that Min hung around the lake for all that length of time. I think she left, *went to see someone*, where she proceeded to get horribly drunk. Whoever she was with probably helped her along, might also have given her the pills – you know, Winston, to dull her senses. Then, once she was out cold, unconscious, she was put in the lake to make it look like suicide or an accident.'

'Look, I'm not ridiculing you, honestly I'm not, but this is a bit far-fetched. Besides, from all the accounts we've heard, she never left the estate.'

'I know, but that's a presumption. And she *might* have. She could have *walked* somewhere, left her Mini at the lake.'

'Oh Emily, Emily.' He shook his head, looking at her helplessly. 'This doesn't make any sense. Who would want to kill Min? And why? What was the motive? I have lots of questions, and I could shoot lots of holes in your theory. I'm sure Paula did. What did she say?'

'She more or less said the same thing as you . . . then she told me to forget it, that the case was closed, that everyone had come out of it relatively unscathed. She used some terrible cliché like "let sleeping dogs lie", and brushed me off. But what about Anthony and Sally having to live with the knowledge that Min killed herself because of them? And there's another thing, Winston, think of Min. If she was murdered in cold blood, which I think she was, the person who did it should be brought to justice.'

Winston was silent, mulling over her words. He said quietly, 'Oh darling, don't be a crusader. There's nothing you can do really, and Paula's right, the case *is* closed, finished with. You'd only be opening a tin of worms, putting Sally and Anthony through more unpleasantness. I could talk to you for hours about this matter, Dumps, but – ' He sighed. 'I just don't have the inclination or the strength at the moment.'

Emily bit her lip. 'I'm sorry. I shouldn't have brought it up tonight.'

'Well, let's face it, darling, you did pick a most inopportune time.' He touched her cheek lightly with one finger, traced a line down on to her neck, ran it diagonally across her bare chest to the edge of the sheet tucked around her. 'Emily, in case you didn't realize it, I do have other things on my mind.'

She smiled winningly, shoving aside her worry about the inquest. 'I said I was sorry. Let's drop it.'

'Your wish is my command.' He turned, put the brandy glass on the side table, then swivelled his head quickly, 'I'd prefer you not to mention any of this . . . your theory . . . to Sally.'

'Of course I won't. I'm not a dunce.'

'Far from it. Come here. I want you.' He switched off the lamp.

Emily did the same, slithered across the bed, nestled into his arms opened to her, wrapped her legs around his body, fitting herself into him.

He said, 'See what's happened. Your lurid murder theory has rendered me incapable of performing my duty as a devoted fiancé.' He stroked her hair which simmered brightly gold in the firelight blazing up the chimney.

'Not for long, if I know you,' she murmured, pulling his head down to hers, seeking his mouth, kissing him passionately.

Responding to her ardent kisses, he ran his hand over her body, touching her breasts, her stomach, her inner thigh, enjoying the feel of her silky skin. He brought his hand up swiftly, cupped one breast, lowered his mouth, let it linger around the nipple. Her hand went into his hair and he felt her strong fingers on the nape of his neck, heard the faint moan in her throat as the tip of his tongue touched the tip of her hardened nipple.

Emily held herself very still, her breathing strangled as Winston moved down and away from her breast. He began to kiss her stomach, and his hand stroked down her outer thigh again, then her inner thigh, his touch sensuous, thrilling her. He knew exactly how to arouse her. But then he always had. He had acquired more expertise, more finesse, had a better understanding of a woman's body since their childhood days. His hand fluttered between her thighs, then probed, enveloped her fully. In a swift, sudden movement that momentarily startled her he pulled his hand away, dragged himself on top of her. He slipped his hands under her back, lifting her forward as he went into her and took possession of her. His mouth found hers, they locked together, her body arching to his. Emily gripped his shoulder blades, let herself be carried along by his rhythmic movements and the growing momentum of their bodies rising and falling in unison.

Some time later, as they lay exhausted in each other's arms, Emily said with a small smile, 'I wonder who passed around that nasty and most erroneous story about Englishmen being terrible lovers?'

There was a contented sigh from Winston, followed by a deep chuckle. 'Foreigners, who else,' he said.

CHAPTER 30

It was a blustery day.

The leaves swirled around her feet as Paula walked down the path and across the lawn to the wheelbarrow, which she had left there yesterday. The sun came out from behind the bank of leaden clouds that piled the bitter sky with sombre grey, its brilliance shafting through the autumn foliage. Suddenly the trees shimmered in the refulgence of light as they fluttered in the wind and they looked as if they had been draped with shreds of gold and copper.

She stopped in her tracks and lifted her head, her eyes scanning the garden. How beautiful it is, even in November, she thought. Her glance travelled the length of the lawn and this too looked as if it had been spread with a cloth of gold or perhaps an ancient tapestry woven with skeins of russet and copper, burnt ochre and chrome yellow.

Moving forward, she reached for the rake and began to scrape the leaves towards her, making a large heap, working doggedly, glad to be out of the house for a short while. Her mind was numb from worry and fatigue, and she hoped that an hour in the garden would revive her, enable her to shake off the sense of desperation which was slowly turning into a feeling of depression, an unfamiliar state of being for her. She stopped after only a few minutes, leaned the rake against the wheelbarrow and took off her gardening gloves. She tightened her scarf, pulled her wool cap over her ears and turned up the collar of her old tweed coat, feeling the bite of the Northern wind. There was a nip of frost in the air, a hint of snow. She slipped on her gloves, started raking again, then stopped to shovel the leaves into the wheelbarrow. About half an hour had passed when she heard the crunch of footsteps behind her on the path. She went on raking, knowing it was Jim.

'Morning, darling,' he called, endeavouring to sound cheerful. 'You're out here bright and early.'

Not wanting to look at him until she had arranged a neutral expression on her face, she continued to rake, said, 'I thought I ought to clear up some of the leaves before I left for London. Anyway the fresh air and the exercise do me good.'

His footsteps finally stopped. 'Yes, I suppose so, but you don't have to kill yourself. Fred can do it tomorrow. That's what he's paid for.'

'It's too much for one gardener.' Paula straightened up, swung around, planted the rake in the ground and leaned her weight on it, her eyes finally meeting his.

His smile was sheepish, embarrassed. 'You're angry with me.'

'No, I'm not, Jim.'

'You should be. I got awfully drunk last night.'

'It doesn't happen often,' she said, then asked herself why she was making excuses for him, giving him a way out. He had been intoxicated a number of times in the last few weeks, but last night his condition and his behaviour at his own dinner party had been inexcusable.

Relief flooded across his face and he stepped closer, eyeing her nervously. He placed his hands on top of hers on the rake. 'Come on, let's really make up,' he said shakily. 'After all, what's one drink too many amongst friends.' When she was silent he leaned forward and kissed her on the cheek. 'I apologize. It won't happen again.'

'It's all right, really it is.' She pushed a smile on to her face. 'It was a pretty ghastly evening anyway. Everyone was acting strangely, and I'm not a bit surprised Winston and Emily left early.'

'Those two have better fish to fry.' He laughed, the nervousness echoing noticeably. 'I say, I hope I didn't

486

insult Winston, or anyone else for that matter.' He seemed concerned, contrite.

'No, you didn't. You were very cordial if very drunk.'

'I'm paying for my bacchanalia this morning, if that's any consolation. I feel lousy.' He hunched into his overcoat, stuck his hands in his pocket, shivering. 'It's bloody cold out here. I don't know how you can stand it.'

She said nothing, examined his face closely. He was pale, a little drawn around the eyes. The wind whipped his hair and as it blew about in the sunshine it was shot through with silvery-gold. He lifted his hand and brushed it away from his forehead, squinting at her in the brilliant light. 'Well, darling, I think I'll push off. Just came out to tell you how sorry I am about last night, give you a hug and a kiss, wish you *bon voyage*.'

Paula frowned, asked in a surprised tone, 'Where are you going?'

'Yeadon.'

'Surely you're not going flying in this awful wind and with that hangover.'

'The hangover will evaporate once I'm up there – ' he said, raising his head to the sky, ' – in the bright blue yonder.' He dropped his eyes to hers, half smiled. 'It's nice of you to worry about me, comforting really, but please don't, I'll be fine. I phoned the airport a little while ago and they told me the weather forecast is good. The wind is supposed to drop in an hour.'

'Jim, please don't go to Yeadon, at least not yet, not until I've left for London. Let's go inside and have a cup of coffee. I'm going to be in New York for two or three weeks and I don't want to leave with things the way they are between us. I must talk to you.'

'*I* must be a bit dense,' he remarked lightly, but his eyes narrowed, turned wary. 'I'm not really following you. What do you want to talk about?'

'About us, Jim. Our marriage, our problems, this awful strain between us.'

'*Strain?*' He looked at her blankly. 'There isn't any that I know of . . . we're both tired, that's all. And *if* we have problems, they're unimportant ones, very normal, actually. We both work hard and we're under a great deal of pressure, and there's been that dreadful fuss in Ireland to plague us. So . . . it's not unnatural that there are tensions at times. But they'll pass, Paula. They generally blow over. I know – '

'Why do you always do this?' she cried, her eyes blazing. 'You're like an ostrich, sticking your head in the sand. We have *problems*, Jim, and I for one can't continue like this.'

'Hey, steady on, don't get so excited,' he said, smiling weakly. He sought a way to placate her. He was growing weary of her constant attempts to discuss and dissect their marriage, to delve into areas that were best left alone. He wondered how to forestall this impromptu chat. He wanted to flee immediately, to go flying, to lose himself up there for a while. Only then, as he soared higher and higher above the clouds, did he feel free, at peace and able to escape his mundane worries, his internal strife. Yes, those were the very best moments of his life . . . *and* being with his children . . . *and* making love to her.

Leaning forward, he took hold of Paula's arm. 'Oh come on, darling, don't let's quarrel like this immediately before you go off on a trip. Everything's fine. I love you. You love me, and that's all that counts. Being away for a while will do you good. You'll come home refreshed, and we'll work out our little differences.' He grinned, looking suddenly boyish. 'They'll probably have worked themselves out before you even return.'

'I don't think so, not unless you start talking to me, discussing our difficulties in an intelligent and mature manner. That's one of the problems – perhaps the worst –

this perpetual reluctance on your part to engage in a little verbal give and take.'

'If we have problems, Paula, as you insist, it's because of your tendency to over-react to every situation, to blow small, inconsequential incidents out of proportion. And there's another thing, you're too sensitive by far.'

She gaped at him. 'Oh Jim, don't try to throw the blame on me. Why won't you admit you have trouble communicating with me?'

'Because I don't . . . that's something in your imagination. In any event, making love is the best way two people can communicate, and we have no problems in that area, none whatsoever.'

'I think we do,' she whispered so softly he barely heard her.

It was Jim's turn to look astonished. 'How can you say that! We're ideally matched sexually. You know you like it as much as I do.'

Paula winced, recognizing once more that he had no comprehension of what she was as a person, or any idea what she was getting at. 'I have normal desires, Jim, after all I'm a young woman, and I do love you. But sometimes you're – ' She stopped, seeking the right expression, knowing she was treading on dangerous and sensitive ground.

'I'm what?' he pressed, leaning into her, fixing her with his light transparent eyes, his interest fully engaged.

'You're a little too . . . overenthusiastic, that's the best way to put it, I think. I'm frequently exhausted when I get home from the office and not up to midnight marathons in bed.' She hesitated, meeting his gaze directly, asking herself if she had been wise to embark on such a touchy subject. She now wished she had not responded initially.

He said slowly, 'I've been telling you for months that you're working too hard these days. You're just going to have to slow down. It's not necessary for you to be on this foolish treadmill. My God, you're going to be one of the richest women in the world one day.'

Irritated though she was by this last statement, she said as steadily as she could, 'I work because I enjoy it, and because I have a great sense of responsibility, not only to Grandy because of the legacy she's leaving me, but to our employees.'

'Nevertheless, if you didn't work as obsessively as you do, you wouldn't be so tired all the time.' He blinked, shading his eyes against the sun with his hand. Another thought flickered in the back of his mind. He asked, and with sudden urgency, 'Are you saying that I don't satisfy you in bed?'

She shook her head. 'No, I'm not.' There was a brief hesitation, then, against her better judgement, she added, 'But my needs are a little different from yours, Jim. Women are not made exactly the same way as men physically. Women . . . we . . . *I* need to be led into . . . well, into the final act, and gradually. You see, it's . . .' she did not finish, noticing the change in his expression. He looked as if some basic truth had just dawned on him.

In point of fact, Jim was not certain whether he was annoyed or amused. So that's it, he thought. *Sex*. The root of all evil, or so they say. He gave her a quick glance, his eyes roving over her. 'Paula . . . darling . . . I'm sorry, especially if I've been selfish, thinking only of myself. I didn't realize, really I didn't. Actually, it's your fault in one sense – because of the way you make me feel. Perhaps I'm inclined to get carried away by my own desires and drives. I'll be different in the future, I promise you.' He gave a little laugh, 'I must admit I've never been much of a man for the . . . er . . . er . . . the preliminaries in bed. They've always struck me as being rather unmanly. However, I will try to help you along, be less impatient, wait for you to be – ' He cleared his throat. 'I believe *ready for me* is the correct phrase.'

Paula felt the colour flooding her face. His voice had been slightly sarcastic with a patronizing undertone, and she was mortified. *Help me along*, she thought, he makes me sound like a cripple. All I want is a little understanding in every area of our marriage. Unfortunately he had seized on their sex life, sidetracking her, and she regretted rising to the bait. And there was another thing. Why were they standing out here having such a vital and serious talk? In the middle of the garden, for God's sake. Because he would feel pinned down indoors, she answered herself. He doesn't want to talk. If the truth be known he wishes he could wriggle out of it yet again, slide off to go flying or occupy himself with one of his other hobbies. He's only humouring me. Paula shivered, feeling chilled now that the sun had dipped behind the clouds in the darkening sky that presaged rain.

'You're cold,' he observed, swiftly taking her arm. 'Maybe we should go indoors after all.' He smiled a slow and somewhat suggestive smile. 'I have a wonderful idea, darling. Why don't we hop into bed right now. I'll prove to you that I can be the most considerate lover in the world and – '

'Jim, how can you!' she exclaimed, shaking his hand off, drawing away from him, glaring. 'You think sex solves all of our differences!'

'You just implied we have sexual problems. I'd like to show you that that isn't true.'

'I did not imply any such thing. I said I wasn't up to making love endlessly.' She almost added *mindlessly*, but managed to restrain herself.

He said, 'Come on,' and hurried her up the garden path.

She did not protest, allowed herself to be led into the house. He turned to her in the hall, remarked quietly, 'I'll get us two mugs of coffee.'

'Thanks, I'm freezing.' She shrugged out of her coat. 'I'll be in the study.' She knew her voice was clipped, but

491

she couldn't help it. Her exasperation was running high. He said nothing, disappeared in the direction of the kitchen, and she pushed open the door to his private domain. Here a log fire blazed cheerfully in the grate, throwing off tremendous heat in the small room, one of the more cosy areas in Long Meadow.

Seating herself in a wing chair in front of the fire, she tried to relax, but when he came in a moment later carrying the mugs of coffee she noticed at once that his face was cold and closed. Her heart sank.

'All right,' he said briskly, handing her one of the mugs and taking the other wing chair, 'let's talk.'

Although his tone did little to encourage her, she said, 'Jim, I do love you, and I want our marriage to work . . . but very frankly, I don't think that it is. Not at the moment anyway.'

'What's wrong with it?' he demanded.

She saw the bafflement on his face, and wondered if he was genuinely puzzled or faking it. 'There's that lack of communication I've just mentioned,' she began. 'Every time I try to broach something that troubles me, you reject me out of hand, turn away from me, behave as if my thoughts and feelings don't matter.' She gazed at him miserably. 'Yet I know you love me. On the other hand, I feel shut out. It's as if you've built a wall around yourself. I can't seem to reach you any more. And whenever something flares up between us, your solution is to make love. You think once we've done so all of our difficulties will disappear but they don't, they're still there afterwards.'

He sighed. 'I'm sorry. Unfortunately I wasn't brought up surrounded by a huge family like you were. I was a solitary little boy, with only my grandfather – an old man – for company. Perhaps I do have trouble articulating things to you . . . but I did think I listened to what you have to say. As far as sex is concerned, it's the only way I know

492

how to patch things up between us. I thought you enjoyed it as much as I do, but if I'm forcing myself on you then – '

'Jim, no! Stop right there!' she exclaimed. 'You're misunderstanding me. Of course I want a normal sexual relationship with you, you're my husband, and I do desire you. But I can't bear it when you use sex to manipulate me. It's exploitative and unfair.'

He sucked in his breath in amazement. 'You see, there you go *again*! Exaggerating, imagining things. I never *manipulate* you.'

Paula swallowed. She decided to take a different approach, wanting to force him into being honest with her if she could. 'I probably sound as if I'm criticizing you, and I'm not. I'm only pointing out a few things that disturb me a bit. Look – I'm sure I can be annoying at times. So . . . fair's fair. It's your turn, air your views about me. Ventilate your feelings, and let's have an intelligent exchange like two mature adults.'

Jim began to laugh. 'Oh Paula you're so intense, so irate this morning. Quite frankly, I think you're being rather silly, creating a situation where one doesn't exist. As for my views about you, why darling, I can only say that I think you're wonderful and that I love you. If I've any complaints or criticisms . . . well . . . they're very minor ones, of no consequence.'

'They are to me. Tell me what they are, Jim. *Please*.'

With obvious reluctance, he said slowly, 'I do think you tend to be hard on yourself, where your work is concerned. Your hours are crippling and they don't have to be. Just because your grandmother worked like a drudge all of her life doesn't mean that you have to do the same. Also, it seems to me that you're taking on too many unnecessary projects.'

Ignoring the remark about Emma, she said, 'Do you mean the new departments at Harte's, and the fashion exhibition?'

'Yes. After all, Harte's is a thriving success, and it has been for donkey's years. You don't need to – '

'Jim,' she interjected impatiently, 'the secret of retailing *is* constant change and growth. We need innovation and on a continuing basis, and we have to meet the public's buying needs, second-guess new trends, have the vision to know exactly when and how to expand for the future. No business can stand still, particularly a department store chain.'

'If you say so, darling, you know best.' Privately he believed she was absolutely wrong, killing herself with work the way she did, but he did not have the interest, energy or desire to engage in a long discussion about her business. That would be pointless since she always did as she wished. Instead he felt the pressing need to curtail any further carping and probing into their relationship on her part. He was bored to death already, growing more anxious than ever to leave. He glanced at the clock surreptitiously.

Paula noticed, said swiftly, 'This is so important, Jim. We're beginning to make a good start. I think we ought to continue, thrash – '

'And *I* think you have to relax, Paula, learn to curb this compulsion of yours to turn minor problems into stupendous dramas. If you want my opinion, this discussion is really rather stupid. I can't imagine why you thought it was necessary in the first place, and especially *today* when you're leaving for almost a month. We're very happy together, yet you insist on borrowing trouble by trying to convince me we're not.'

'Oh Jim, I only want to save – '

'Hush, darling. Hush,' he said softly, smiling engagingly, taking her hand in his. 'When I look around at our friends and acquaintances I know we have the most marvellous of marriages. We're very lucky, Paula, and I congratulate myself every day, knowing how compatible we are.'

Dismay lodged in her stomach like a heavy stone. Observing the stubbornness settling on his face she acknowledged there was no reason to continue. She was talking to a brick wall.

Jim said, 'You *are* looking thoughtful all of a sudden. And do you know something, you think too much and far too hard.' He laughed lightly, dismissively, taking the sting out of his words. 'Analysing every tiny thing the way you are prone to do isn't very smart. I discovered that years ago. Whenever one puts something under a microscope, seeking flaws, one inevitably finds them. There's nothing wrong with our relationship, Paula. Do try to take it easy, darling.' He bent forward, kissed her on the cheek, then rose purposefully. 'Now that we've had our chat, settled matters, I'll be going, if you don't mind.' He squeezed her shoulder. 'Drive carefully and phone me tonight before you go to sleep.' He winked. 'That's always when I miss you the most.'

Paula sat staring at him, stupefied, unable to speak. Finally she managed a nod. When he turned away her eyes followed him. There was a void in her heart as she watched him walk across the room.

The study door clicked behind him. She heard the echo of his footsteps crossing the hall, the front door slamming, and a few seconds later the sound of his car as he revved the engine. She sat very still in the chair for a long time after he had left, filled with despair and an overwhelming sense of defeat.

Finally she roused herself from her troubled thoughts, pushed herself up out of the chair and left the room. Slowly, wearily, she climbed the stairs to the nursery and her children. They had always been the joy of her existence. They were her whole existence now.

CHAPTER 31

Paula looked from Dale Stevens to Ross Nelson. 'My grandmother would never consider selling her stock in Sitex Oil. Never.'

Ross Nelson smiled, his expression sanguine. '*Never* is a word I've learned to distrust. It has a way of coming back to haunt one, and that's why I hardly ever use it.'

'I understand the point you're trying to make,' Paula said, 'but, nevertheless, I know what my grandmother's feelings are about Sitex, and she wouldn't be interested in your proposal. She promised my grandfather – ' Paula cut herself short, shrugged off-handedly. 'However, that's another story, and this conversation is really a waste of time – Dale's, yours and mine.'

Dale Stevens said, 'Maybe you ought to broach it to Emma when she gets back from Australia next month, test the water, see what she has to say. She might like the idea. Times have changed, and let's not lose sight of the fact that she stands to make millions if she sells out.'

'I don't think money comes into play here,' Paula answered.

'Harry Marriott and his cronies on the board are a tough bunch, Paula,' Dale remarked, giving her a pointed look, levelling his alert dark eyes at her. 'They've wanted Emma out for years, resent her influence, and the situation can only worsen, get harder for you in the future. When she's no longer around you'll find yourself – '

'My grandmother's not dead yet,' Paula interjected, meeting his fixed stare with a cool glance. 'And I refuse to speculate about the future and eventualities that are a long way off. I deal with business the only way I know how – on a day to day basis. I'm certainly not going to seek out trouble, and I'd like to remind you that Marriott is a very old man. He won't last for ever, and, therefore, neither will his influence.'

'There's that nephew of his,' Dale pointed out quietly. 'Marriott Watson's a nasty son of a bitch, a troublemaker.'

'Oh don't talk to me about nephews,' Paula began and stopped, biting her inner lip. She turned to Ross, remembering that he was the nephew of Daniel P. Nelson and his heir. She laughed lightly, and apologized, 'Sorry, Ross, I didn't mean to sound disparaging about nephews in general. I wasn't getting at you.'

He laughed with her and there was a hint of humour surfacing in his hazel eyes. 'Don't worry, I don't take offence that easily.' He leaned forward, his face growing serious. 'What Dale is trying to say is that those members of the board who have strained under Emma's yoke are going to be awfully rough with you, for the simple reason that you're a –'

Paula held up her hand. 'You don't have to say it, Ross, I know the reason – I'm a *woman* and a young one at that. I realize they've only listened to my grandmother all these years because they've had no option. She *is* the single largest stockholder, and my grandfather *was* the founder of the company, and obviously certain people have always hated her because of her enormous power, and, of course, because she is a woman.' Paula paused. 'Still, Emma Harte has managed, and managed very well indeed. She has always outsmarted that board, and so will I. I'm not without intelligence and inventiveness – I'll find a way to make them listen, take notice of me.'

Ross and Dale were silent, exchanged knowing glances.

Ross spoke first. 'I wouldn't want you to think I'm bigoted, a male chauvinist pig like some of those idiots on the board of Sitex, but despite the inroads women have been making in business lately, of which I totally approve I

497

might add, I'm afraid we have to face the facts. It's still a man's – '

Paula broke into laughter, instantly cutting him off. 'I know it's still a man's world, you don't have to rub it in. And it always will be until the day women can go into the men's room.'

Ross Nelson's smile was slow, amused. He appreciated her sense of humour as well as her inherent toughness and courage. She was one hell of a woman. His eyes lingered on her appraisingly. He was strongly attracted to her, fascinated by her self-control, her sharp mind, her extraordinary self-confidence. He wanted her for himself. He wondered what approach to take, the best tactics to use, how long it would take him to get her into his bed. He fully intended to do that – and the sooner the better.

He disengaged his eyes from hers, conscious of the prolonged silence. He said, with a strangled laugh, 'Not all deals are made in the men's room, Paula.'

'Most of them are,' she shot back, throwing him that challenging look again. 'Or the equivalent of the men's room,' she added, making a moue with her mouth.

This further inflamed him, and he could only grin, suddenly feeling asinine, like an inexperienced schoolboy. He had the compelling urge to fasten his mouth on hers and he would have done so if Dale had not been present.

Dale coughed behind his hand, said quickly, 'Marriott Watson has been gunning for me for a long time, Paula, because I'm Emma's protégé. Don't think he won't make strong moves against me when I'm no longer under her protection. He can't wait.'

'I'm well aware of that,' Paula replied, her tone as sober as his. 'But right now you do have her protection, and mine, for what it's worth. Also, let's not overlook those board members who are on our side. Together we wield a lot of power. In September you promised me you'd stay on as president until Christmas. Last month you agreed to continue until your contract runs out, in spite of the present harassment from certain quarters within the company. You're not changing your mind, reneging on me, are you?'

'No, honey, no way. I'll be right in there with you, fighting the good fight,' Dale insisted with firmness. 'However, I would like you to mention Ross's idea to Emma when she's back in England.'

'I've every intention of doing so, and she has a right to know. Don't be concerned, she'll get a full report of this meeting.' She swung her head to face Ross. 'She *will* ask me who your client is, Ross. Naturally she'll want to know who's interested in buying her stock. You haven't given me the name yet.' She sat back in the chair, eyeing him speculatively.

Ross Nelson, in full control again, shook his head. 'I can't tell you, Paula. At least not yet. Once you express a genuine interest in selling the Sitex stock I will, of course, do so at once. Until then the name must remain confidential. At the specific request of our client. And I would like to repeat what I said at the outset of this meeting – that the interested party has been a client of the bank for a long time and is highly respected.'

Paula was amused at his insistence on secrecy but she kept her face neutral. 'It's obviously another oil company, and I doubt that it's one of the really huge ones like Getty or Standard. It must be a medium-sized company – a company such as International Petroleum perhaps?' There was a shrewd glint in her knowing violet eyes.

Ross was impressed. His admiration for her went up another notch. She had stabbed in the dark most probably, but hit the bull's eye nonetheless. 'No, it isn't International Petroleum,' he lied smoothly. 'And please don't start a guessing game, because it won't do you any good.' He flashed her one of his deep warm smiles. 'The name cannot be revealed until our client gives permission, and it may interest you to know that not even Dale has an inkling of who it is.'

But you haven't denied it's an oil company, Paula thought. She said, 'Then I suppose I may never know, since my grandmother won't be interested in selling.' Paula crossed her legs, adopting a more relaxed posture, wondering if Ross had told her the truth when he had denied it was International Petroleum. She was not sure, neither was she sure of her feelings about the man himself. Her attitude towards him had always been ambivalent. She had never been able to decide whether she liked him or not. On the surface Ross Nelson was charming, courteous, sure of himself, forever ready to oblige. A handsome man in his late thirties, he was about five feet nine, well built, fair of colouring with an open almost guileless face and the friendliest of smiles that flashed relentlessly to reveal his big white perfect teeth. His appearance was sleek and polished, his clothes impeccable, as were his manners.

And yet all of this was deceptive, or so it seemed to Paula. She could not help thinking that there was something concealed and predatory about him. Quietly observing Ross now, it suddenly struck her that the beautiful clothes and the insouciance he projected were mere façades to camouflage unpleasant characteristics that only came to light behind the closed doors of the bank's board room. As Emma had divined before her, Paula scented a cold and calculating ruthlessness in him, a grim hardness behind the charm, the smiles, and the golden boy image.

Dale and Ross had been chatting about the explosion in the engine room of the *Emeremm III*, and Paula gave the two men her entire attention.

Dale was saying, 'Of course sabotage crossed my mind, Ross, but it's been ruled out. There was that recent inquiry and nothing untoward was discovered. Nothing at all. Anyway, who would do such a thing?' He shook his head rapidly, frowned. 'No, no, it was definitely an accident, even though we haven't been able to discover exactly what caused the explosion.'

Paula thought: the disaster to the *Emeremm III* was a harbinger of bad luck, but she said, 'So it remains a mystery it seems, and a terrible stain on our safety record.'

''Fraid so, honey.' Dale's grin was rueful and his brown eyes crinkled at the corners in his leathery, weatherbeaten face. 'Hate to keep repeating myself, but the oil game is a high risk business in more ways than one. However, the *Emeremm III* is a sturdy vessel and I just heard this morning that she's seaworthy again and back in the fleet.'

'Well, that's a bit of good news!' Paula exclaimed, looking pleased, giving Dale a warm smile. The president of Sitex was a man she liked and trusted and whom she never had any qualms about. He was smart, tough, exceedingly ambitious for himself, but he was honest, and exactly what he seemed, not given to dissembling or craftiness. Studying him surreptitiously, she thought that even his clothes reflected the man himself, were good but conservative, lacked the expensive elegance of the other man's. She asked herself then what this wily, hard-grinding, fifty-three-year-old Texan who had risen the hard way could possibly have in common with the smooth Eastern Seaboard banker sitting next to him. The latter reeked of the old guard, pots and pots of inherited money and a privileged heritage. Yet close friends they were. Ross Nelson had introduced Dale Stevens to Emma two years ago, and it was through the investment banker that Dale was now president of the oil company.

Watching *her* watching *him*, Dale suddenly said, 'I hope you don't think I lack confidence in you, because that's not true, honey.'

'But I am an unknown quantity, right?' she retorted swiftly, and continued in the same mild voice, 'I understand your motives, Dale, and I can't say I blame you. You're looking to the future, and you've decided that things will

501

operate much more smoothly at Sitex if our big block of preferred stock is controlled by someone else, someone whom you believe *might* be better equipped to handle the disruptive faction on the Sitex board.'

Continuing to scrutinize her closely, forever conscious of her astuteness and perception, and never one to underestimate this clever young woman, Dale decided to be truthful. 'Yes,' he said, giving her a direct and open look, 'that's part of my reasoning, I admit that. But it's not all of it. In one sense I'm also thinking of you, your heavy burdens. It seems to me that you have your hands full with the Harte chain and your considerable business interests in England and Australia. And of course, you *are* based in England, honey.'

Paula said pithily, 'Telephones work, telex machines transmit, planes fly.'

'But Sitex is still an additional pressure for you,' he said, paying no attention to her sarcastic tone. 'And do you really need it?' Dale shook his head, as if making up her mind for her. 'I don't think you do, and if it were me, why I'd persuade Emma to sell out and make a huge profit. You could reinvest the millions you make from the stock in something else – something that's less of a headache.'

She said nothing.

'I concur with Dale,' Ross stated, his tone flat. He cleared his throat. 'Obviously I've long been aware of the difficulties at Sitex, not only through Dale, but because of Emma's confidences over the last few years. And so, when the bank's client professed an interest in buying up Sitex stock, I immediately thought of Emma's vast holdings in the company. I spoke to Dale and he agreed we should raise the matter with you immediately. The bank's client has already invested in Sitex's common stock. And with your forty-two per cent – ' He stopped, offered her one of his perpetual all-embracing smiles. 'Why, Paula, that would give our client real clout.'

'*Anybody* who owns that forty-two per cent has *clout*,' Paula said crisply. 'Whether it's us or your client is quite beside the point. You know as well as I do that it's the actual stock, not the owner of it, that counts. And anyway, your client's common stock doesn't come into play since it's not voting stock and has no power attached to it. Obviously this client of yours – whether an individual or a company – needs my grandmother's stock to give him, or them, a voice in the running of the company. *Control* is what they're after. I understand everything perfectly.'

Neither men responded, both acknowledging to themselves that there was no point in making denials and in so doing looking foolish.

Paula stood up, and adopting her most gracious manner, went on, 'I'm afraid I have to bring our informal little get-together to a close, gentlemen. I think we've covered as much ground as we can today. I will talk to my grandmother in December, and I'm sure you'll be hearing from her personally. And it really is up to her – her decision.' Paula laughed softly, murmured, 'And who knows, she might surprise even me and decide to sell after all.'

Dale and Ross had risen when she had, and as Paula walked them to the door, Dale said, 'I'm flying back to Odessa tonight, but just give me a holler if you need me, or need anything at all. In any event I'll be calling you next week to touch base.'

'Thanks, Dale, I appreciate that,' Paula said, taking his outstretched hand.

'Are you sure you won't join us for lunch?' Ross asked.

'Thank you again, but I can't. I have a date with the fashion director of Harte's USA, and since we're going to be planning the French Designer Week promotion over lunch it's not possible for me to cancel.'

'Our loss,' he said, sounding disappointed, keeping his eyes focused on her, still clasping her hand tightly in his. 'Unlike Dale, *I'm* not flying off anywhere, Paula. I'm

503

staying right here in little old Manhattan. Let me know if *I* can help you with anything – anything whatsoever. And I hope I can take you to dinner one evening this week.'

Extracting her hand, Paula said, 'How kind of you, Ross. I'm afraid I'm rather busy this week. Every night actually.' This was untrue but she had no desire to see him socially.

'Not next week I sincerely hope!' He leaned into her, squeezed her arm. 'I'll call you on Monday and I won't take no for an answer,' he warned with a hearty laugh.

Once they had left, Paula walked slowly across the room to the desk, a great slab of glass supported by a simple base of polished steel. It was the dramatic focal point in Emma's highly dramatic office at Harte Enterprises, where Paula always based herself when she was in New York. The room was furnished with modern pieces and washed throughout with a melange of misty greys and blues. The soft muted colours were enlivened by some of Emma's priceless French Impressionist paintings, while sculptures by Henry Moore and Brancusi, and rare temple heads from Angkor Wat, were displayed on black marble pedestals around the room. All made a strong definitive statement, and evidenced Emma's great love of art.

Seating herself at the desk, Paula placed her elbows on it, cupped her face in her hands, thinking about the meeting she had just finished. At the back of her mind a germ of an idea flickered, began to take shape, and as it did a slow smile spread across her face. Quite unwittingly Ross Nelson and Dale Stevens had shown her a way to resolve some of her problems at Sitex, if not, in fact, all of them. But not now, she thought. Later, when I really need to make everyone keep in step to the beat of *my* drum.

As she straightened up she laughed out loud. It was not a very nice idea, indeed it was rather diabolical – Machiavellian – but it would be effective, and it bore Emma Harte's inimitable stamp. Still laughing quietly, she thought: I must be growing more like Grandy every day. The possibility that this was true pleased her. In a sense it helped to alleviate some of the depression and frustration she had been experiencing since her abortive attempt to talk to Jim before she had left England.

If her marriage was in a shambles, her personal life grounded in aridity, then she was going to make certain she had a fruitful career, her own successes in business to compensate for her other losses. Work had been Emma's strong citadel when *her* private life had been wrecked, and so it would become Paula's, sustaining her at all times. With her business to occupy her thoughts, and her abiding love for her children to give her emotional nourishment, she would survive, and survive well, perhaps even with style as her grandmother had done. Her thoughts jumped to Jim, but they were neither rancorous nor condemning. She felt only a terrible sadness for him. He did not know what he had lost, and that was the pity, the tragedy of it all.

Shane O'Neill was in a quandary this afternoon.

He strode up Park Avenue at a rapid pace dodging in and out between the other pedestrians, his thoughts twisting and turning at a similar accelerated rate. He was unable to make up his mind about Paula. Should he phone her or not? The knowledge that she was in New York, sitting only a few blocks away from him at this very moment, had so unnerved him he couldn't imagine what being in her presence would do to him. And if he did call her he would have no alternative but to see her, invite her out, take her to lunch or dinner, at the very least have drinks with her.

Earlier that day, when he had been talking to their London office, he had been taken aback when his father had mentioned in passing that Paula had flown to New York yesterday. 'Merry and I had supper with her in London on Sunday night,' his father had gone on to explain

505

before reverting to their discussion about current business matters. And before they had hung up, his father had exclaimed, 'Oh Shane, just a minute, here comes Merry now. She wants to say hello to you.'

But Merry had given him more than a greeting. She had issued instructions. 'Please ring Paula,' Merry had urged. 'I gave her your numbers the other night, but I know she won't call you. She'd be too intimidated.' When he asked her for clarification, his sister had told him that Paula had long been acutely conscious of his aloofness, as she had herself. 'She'll be scared of being rebuffed,' Merry had pointed out. 'So it's really up to you. Be nice, Shane, she's such an old friend. And she doesn't look very well.' This last statement had been announced in a grave and worried voice, and Merry had rushed on, 'She seems weighted down, troubled, morose even, and that's not the Paula *we* know. Please take her out, give her a good time. Have some fun together, Shane, make her laugh again, like you used to do when we were all children.' His sister's comments had alarmed him; he had pressed for more information about Paula's state of mind and health. Merry had not really been able to enlighten him any further, and before they had said goodbye he had faithfully promised his sister he would get in touch with Paula.

But he was wavering again. Whilst he longed to see her, he knew that by succumbing to his yearning he would only be inflicting punishment on himself. She was another man's wife. Lost to him forever. To spend time with her would open up all the old wounds . . . wounds which had not exactly healed but *had* scabbed over at least, and were therefore much less painful. It will be unsettling, he thought, reflecting on the life he had built for himself in New York over the past eight months. It was not an exciting life; rather it was dull and uneventful, with no great highs but no debilitating lows either. He was neither happy nor sad, in limbo in a sense, but he did have peace and quiet. There were no women around any more. Two sorties in that direction had foundered miserably and rendered him helpless, despairing. And he had decided, yet again, that celibacy was infinitely preferable to disastrous scenes in the bedroom which ended in embarrassment, left him shaken and filled with mortification at his own inadequacies. And so he scrupulously avoided all female entanglements, and spent most of his time working. More often than not he remained at the new offices of O'Neill Hotels International until eight or nine at night, and then went home to a dreary supper in front of the television set. From time to time he made a date with Ross Nelson or with one of the other two men he had become friendly with; occasionally he took Skye Smith to a movie or the theatre and then on to dinner afterwards. But for the most part he led a solitary existence, with books and music as his sole companions. He was not happy, but there was no pain to deal with. He was dead inside.

As all of this ran through his head Shane had a sudden change of heart. He really ought to see Paula, if only for appearances' sake. Should any of his other childhood friends happen to visit the city, he would wine and dine them automatically. To avoid Paula would look peculiar, pointed actually, especially to Emma and his grandfather, who would undoubtedly ask him about her when they passed through New York next month. Besides that, Merry had said Paula was not looking well. Yes, he had better invite her to dinner, just to satisfy himself she was really all right. But she's not your responsibility, he cautioned himself, thinking of Jim Fairley. *Her husband*. Unexpectedly, a savage feeling of jealousy seized him, and he had to make a strenuous effort to fling this emotion off as he crossed Fifty-Ninth Street and continued on up Park, making for the mid-sixties.

In a few minutes he would be arriving at the site of their new hotel. The construction company had almost finished

507

rebuilding the old-fashioned interiors and momentarily he would be surrounded by the crews, the foremen, the architects and the interior designers. All would be demanding his attention. *I must make a decision about Paula. Now.* No more procrastinating. Oh, to hell with Jim Fairley! *She's my oldest and dearest friend. I grew up with her. Of course I'm going to see her. No, you can't. It will be too hurtful.* Once again Shane reversed himself.

And he was paralysed into inaction by the knowledge that he was vulnerable to her. If he so much as set eyes on the only woman he loved he would be exposing himself to pain and suffering from which he might never fully recover.

Skye Smith looked at Ross Nelson nervously, and her voice quavered slightly as she said, 'But your divorce has been final for weeks now. I don't understand. I always thought we were going to get married.'

'I'm afraid that has been wishful thinking on your part, Skye,' Ross said, endeavouring to keep his voice level, to be courteous if nothing else.

'But what about Jennifer?'

'What about her?'

'She's your child, Ross!'

For a moment he said nothing. He had been furious when he had arrived home from Wall Street ten minutes earlier to find Skye Smith, his former mistress, sitting in his living room so coolly composed and obviously determined to fight with him yet again. He was growing exasperated with her and the constant pressuring. The moment she left he was going to fire his housekeeper for being stupid enough to allow her into the apartment.

Skye sat twisting her hands together, her face white, her eyes filled with mute appeal.

Ross Nelson stared at her, his implacability increasing as he noted her agitation. Her apparent distress did nothing to engender sympathy or compassion in him. It only served to annoy him further. 'You say she's my child. But is she really?' he asked cruelly. 'I've never been too sure . . . about her paternity.'

Skye gasped, drew back on the sofa. 'How can you say that! You know you're her father. She's the spitting image of you, Ross, and there's the blood test. And anyway you kept me virtually under lock and key for four years. I never so much as looked at another man.'

He smiled ironically. 'But you're looking at one these days, and very lovingly so, aren't you, Skye? Shane O'Neill to be precise. And since you're sleeping with him I suggest you use your considerable sexual wiles to ensnare him. You'd better lead *him* by the nose to the altar, and as quickly as possible.'

'I'm not sleeping with him,' she protested fiercely, her apathy dropping away, her eyes flashing angrily with sudden life.

'Do you really expect me to believe *that*,' he exclaimed with a cynical laugh. 'I know everything there is to know about you, Skye, and then some.' His eyes hardened as they swept over her and his mouth lifted at the corner in a scornful smile. 'You can't resist tall husky handsome studs, they've always been your terrible weakness, my dear. As we both know only too well. You'd be wise to marry one of them while you still have your beautiful blonde looks and that extraordinarily athletic sexual ability. Shane's definitely the most likely prospect. He's getting it from you in bed, so why don't you get him to make it legal, while the romance is still in that first euphoric flush. He's your type, no two ways about it. He's also a rich man, and he's certainly available.'

'Ross, I'm telling you the truth. I'm not having an affair with Shane O'Neill,' she insisted.

Ross laughed in her face, reached for the silver cigarette box on the antique Chinese coffee table, slowly put a flame to the cigarette he held between his fingers.

Skye's eyes rested on him. She wondered why she had ever let herself become embroiled with him, and so foolishly, years ago, asked herself why it was her misfortune to love this man in the way in which she did. The trouble was he knew exactly how she felt, and that was why he had lately begun to cool towards her. Ross only wanted the things in life which he could not possess, and especially women who showed no interest in him whatsoever. He's perverse, she thought, but oh God how I love him. She knew she had to make him believe her about Shane for the child's sake as well as her own. Suddenly realizing that the only way to convince him was to be open and explicit, she said quietly. 'All right, I admit it. I did go to bed with Shane. *Once.* It was when I discovered you'd taken Denise Hodgson to South America with you, when I found out about your affair with her. Retaliation, I suppose. But it didn't work between us. We never made love. And we've never been near each other since, not in that way, Ross. We're friends, that's all. Chums.'

'*Chums*,' Ross spluttered, shaking his head. 'Come on, Skye, it's me you're talking to, remember. I haven't known you for five years not to understand exactly how you can make a man feel, especially in the beginning, when he's not yet slept with you.' He laughed derisively. 'Didn't work between you, eh?' he muttered, his expression one of total disbelief.

Skye swallowed, knowing she had to continue talking, give him a full explanation if she was to make any headway, ingratiate herself with him again, somehow win him back. 'Yes, that's correct, I promise you, Ross. Shane and I are simply good friends.' She swallowed again. 'He couldn't . . . well, the night we went to bed . . . he wasn't able to . . . you know, do anything.'

Ross slapped his knee, raucous laughter rippling through him. 'Do you expect me to believe Shane O'Neill couldn't get it up with you? Oh no, Skye, I'll never accept that one from you.'

'But it's the truth,' she whispered, remembering so clearly that miserable night, Shane's dreadful embarrassment, her own confusion. 'It's the God's truth.' She leaned across the coffee table, finished in a much stronger tone, 'I swear it on Jennifer's head, on my child – on our child.'

His laughter ceased and his eyes narrowed, observed her thoughtfully. Instantly he knew she was not lying, not when she brought the child into it. He said, 'So . . . Shane's got a little problem, has he?'

She nodded. 'With me at least.' She hesitated. 'I have a feeling he's in love with someone.'

'I wonder who that could be, who the woman in question is? Do you know?'

'That's a silly thing to ask. How could I possibly know. He hasn't confided anything. Don't you see, Ross, that's why he's not available as a husband for me.'

'Neither am I.'

'Why?'

'I have no desire to get married again,' he said almost chattily, 'not with my track record. I've had enough of grasping wives and the divorce court. Besides I'm paying too much alimony as it is. Hundreds of thousands of dollars a year. But if I *were* ever demented enough to take that suicidal plunge I can assure you my bride would have to be a rich one.'

'Oh come off it! Money doesn't interest you, Ross,' she scoffed. 'You couldn't spend your millions if you lived to be a hundred.'

He said nothing.

Skye said slowly, her face growing soft, almost tender, 'We've had so much together. We have a child, and I love you very much.'

'You don't seem to understand – I don't love you.'

She flinched, but kept her hurt to herself. He had a

penchant for being cruel, and his moods changed like the wind. In five minutes he might easily do a turn about and sweep her off to bed. That had happened so many times before. A thought came to her, and she stood up, went and sat down next to him on the other sofa, laid her hand on his knee. She drew closer, whispered, 'You don't really mean that, Ross darling, you know it's not true. You do love me. There's a special kind of magic between us, and there always has been.' She smiled into his cold face, her eyes enticing. 'Let's go to bed. I'll show you just how strong the bonds are between us.'

He lifted her hand from his knee and placed it in her lap. 'I didn't think you were a masochist, that you'd want a repetition of your misadventure with Shane O'Neill. It must be very humiliating for a woman like you to realize that her sexual expertise has lost its power.'

She pulled away from him, gaping, and her eyes filled with tears.

Wanting to be rid of her, he went in for the kill, said in the quietest but hardest of voices, 'You see, Skye, you don't turn me on any more.'

Rising, she blundered across the room to the window, flicking the tears off her cheeks, trying to stem their flow, her shoulders heaving. She knew she had lost him. Her life was in shreds.

Ross also rose and crossed to the small Regency writing table. He opened the drawer, took out his chequebook, picked up the pen and wrote. As he ripped the cheque out of the book she turned around, stood staring at him, puzzlement replacing the anguish on her strained face.

'What are you doing?' she asked, beginning to tremble.

'This is for you, for the child,' he said, pushing himself up out of the chair, walking to her. 'I will make arrangements with my accountants for you to receive the same amount every month. It should be more than enough.' He stopped in front of her, held out the cheque.

Skye shook her head wildly. 'I don't want it, Ross. *I* can support *our* child. I'm not interested in your money, and I never have been. It's only you I want. As a husband, as a father for Jennifer.'

'That's too high a price for me.' He tried to force the cheque into her hands but she refused to take it, balling her fists, backing away from him.

He shrugged, turned, walked back to the sofas in front of the fireplace. He opened her handbag, slipped the cheque inside, then carried her bag to her, put it in her hands. 'I think it's time for you to leave, Skye. I'm expecting guests. It's over between us. There's nothing more to say.'

Lifting her head, she gathered some of her shattered pride around her, and she was surprisingly cool and steady as she said, 'Oh yes, there *is* something more to say, Ross, and it's this . . .' She paused, looked deeply into his face. 'Things are *not* over between us and they never will be, whether we see each other again or not. And one day you're going to need me. I don't know for what reason, or why, but need me you will.' She opened her bag, took out the cheque and tore it in half without looking at it. She let it flutter to the floor. And then she pivoted and walked away from him without a backward glance, her pace measured and controlled.

Ross picked up the torn cheque and pocketed it, his face expressionless. He would write another one tomorrow and mail it to her. He ambled over to the window and parted the curtain, looked down on to Park Avenue. In a few minutes she would leave the building and cross the street as she always did, heading in the direction of Lexington. He sighed. It was a pity about the child. His face softened a fraction. There was no way he could have his three-year-old daughter without the mother, and the mother he neither wanted nor needed. She was far too troublesome in far too many ways. He felt a sudden twinge about Shane and the manner in which he had manoeuvred him, had tried to throw Skye into his arms. Funny coincidence, he thought, the way Skye and Shane were introduced in Yorkshire and then a week later he phoned me at the bank with an introduction from Emma Harte. The minute he had met Shane he had thought of Skye, realizing he might have found a solution to his problems with her. He had manipulated Skye, had augmented the beginning of the affair, if one could call it that. Oh well, they say all's fair in love and war. Skye's unexpected revelation about Shane's impotency *had* surprised him though. Shocked him. Shane O'Neill of all people. Poor son of a bitch, Ross muttered, wondering for the second time what woman had so got her hooks into O'Neill he couldn't perform with anyone else.

Ross pressed his face to the glass, saw Skye hurrying across Park, lingering on the centre island, waiting for the lights to change. She was wearing the mink coat he had given her. He supposed he had loved her once. Now she bored him. He let the curtain drop, and she was instantly dismissed as he turned his mind to his present plans.

Moving towards the fireplace, Ross Nelson stood for a few minutes with his hand on the mantelshelf, staring into space, lost in his reverie, pondering Paula Fairley. He had known her for years, paid little attention to her in the past. But this morning, in her office, he had been intrigued by her. He had to have her. He was going to have her. Nobody, nothing, would stop him. Now there is a powder keg of suppressed sexuality, he decided. He had spotted that at once. It was apparent in the way she held her body, from the hunger he had detected in those unusual violet-tinted eyes, so long-lashed and seductive. He would put the match to the powder keg, explode it, then lie back and let the flames of her sexuality consume them both. He began to realize that just thinking about her excited him inordinately, in a way he had not been excited for some time, jaded as he had become. He itched to get his hands

514

on that slender body, so willowy and graceful, yet curiously boyish except for the beautiful breasts. He closed his eyes, holding his breath, recalling how taut and firm they had looked under the white silk shirt she had been wearing. He lusted for her right now, this very minute. Her image was suddenly so vividly alive in his mind he snapped his eyes open swiftly, lowered himself on to the sofa, knowing he must dispel the tantalizing picture of them in bed together. He would have a miserable evening if he did not do so immediately.

But Ross Nelson discovered she was difficult to forget, so potent was her sexual appeal to him. And then of course there was her money. He began to contemplate her great fortune, Emma's fortune, which she would inherit one day. To his astonishment the idea of matrimony was suddenly most appealing after all. There was a husband in the background somewhere, wasn't there? He would soon dispense with Fairley. Once he had bedded Paula she would be his completely. They always were, particularly those who came inexperienced and breathless with anticipation into his arms. He felt the old familiar ache in his groin. To take his mind off sex he endeavoured to concentrate on Paula Fairley's huge fortune. The ache only intensified. He crossed his legs, growing uncomfortably hot. He began to laugh at himself. How fortunate it was that he had not indulged himself in his erotic imaginings about Paula earlier. Otherwise he would have been forced to take Skye to bed – for one last time.

He glanced at the phone on the writing desk, wondering why it had not yet rung. He had been expecting to hear from Paula the moment he had arrived home.

CHAPTER 32

'Where on earth did those ghastly vermilion roses come from, Ann?' Paula asked, staring through the open door of the drawing room and then turning to look at her grandmother's American housekeeper.

Ann Donovan, standing next to Paula in the large entrance foyer of Emma's Fifth Avenue apartment, shook her head. 'I don't know, Miss Paula. I left the card on the console, next to the vase.'

She followed Paula into the room, continuing, 'I wasn't sure where to put them, to be honest, the bouquet is so huge. I even wondered if I ought to leave them out here. In all the years I've worked for Mrs Harte we've never had roses in the apartment. Don't you like them either?'

'They don't really bother me, Ann, at least not in the way they disturb my grandmother. I'm just not accustomed to seeing roses around, that's all. I never plant them, or buy them for that matter.' She wrinkled her nose, indicating her distaste, remarked off-handedly, 'And that colour, it's such a violent red, and the whole arrangement is overwhelming. Very pretentious.'

She reached for the envelope, ripped it open, looked at the card. It had been signed by Ross Nelson. His writing was small, neat, cramped almost, and he was inviting her to his country house for the weekend. What a cheek he's got, Paula thought. And what makes him think I'd want to spend the weekend with him. I hope *he's* not going to become a pest. She tore up the card, dropped it into a nearby ashtray, said to the housekeeper, 'I really can't stand the roses, Ann, would you mind taking them out to the back, please?'

'No, of course not, Miss Paula.' Ann picked up the

offending vase and headed out of the drawing room, saying over her shoulder, 'You received some other flowers – not very long ago. I popped them in the den.'

'*Oh.* Well, I suppose I'd better go and look at them,' Paula murmured, walking out after the housekeeper who was already hurrying across the foyer in the direction of her own rooms.

Paula's face lit up the minute she saw the lovely little basket of African violets in the centre of the mahogany coffee table near the fireplace. She bent over them, touched the glossy dark green leaves, then the velvet-textured petals of the deep purple flowers. How delicate, how tender they are, she thought and picked up the envelope. It was blank and she wondered who the violets were from as she opened it. She stiffened in surprise. The name *Shane* was scrawled across the front of the card in his familiar bold handwriting. There was no message, simply his first name.

Still holding the card, Paula sat down on the nearest chair, frowning to herself, not quite certain what to make of the flowers. For the first time in almost two years he had done something sweet and thoughtful, the kind of thing he used to do in the past. And she was at a loss, not sure how to deal with it. She pondered. Was the basket of violets a signal that he wanted to be friends with her again? Or merely a polite gesture, one made out of a sense of family obligation and duty? Certainly sending her flowers was a way of saying welcome to New York without him actually having to speak to her.

Paula glanced into the fire, her expression abstracted. She was positive that Merry would have told him she was in the city, after all they were brother and sister and business colleagues, and they chatted back and forth across the Atlantic on a weekly, sometimes daily, basis. Perhaps her friend had put pressure on Shane to make an effort, to be nice to her. His aloofness and remoteness still perplexed Paula. How many times had she asked herself what she had done to hurt or upset him, and how many times had the answer been a negative one. She had done nothing wrong. Yet he continued to hold himself apart, barely acknowledging her existence. And when he did do so, she knew it was because he had no alternative, considering the long and intimate involvement of their two families.

Pulling her eyes away from the fire, Paula stared at the card again and for the longest time. The simple signature without one other word was not very encouraging. In a way it was intimidating. If only he had suggested that she phone him, or hinted that they might get together before she returned to England.

Damn, she muttered under her breath, and suddenly stood up abruptly, unexpectedly filled with anger with him. Shane O'Neill had been her dearest friend for as long as she could remember, since she could first walk and talk. They had grown up together . . . shared so much . . . become so very close over those formative and meaningful years . . . their lives had been so deeply intertwined. And then he had dropped her, turned away from her, and without any kind of proper explanation. It was not logical.

I've had enough of this. I'm sick and tired of people behaving as if *my* feelings don't matter, she thought, still bridling with anger. She rushed out of the den to find her briefcase. It was on a bench in the foyer where she had left it when she had walked in from the office. Grabbing it, she sped back to the den and sat down at the desk. Snapping open the locks, she pulled out her address book, turned to Shane's New York numbers, then sat back in the chair, eyeing the phone.

I'm going to have it out with him once and for all, she decided, whether it's tonight, next week, or the very day I leave. I don't care when it is, as long as I pin him down finally. I want to know why he ended our long friendship so cruelly. *I'm entitled to an explanation.* She reached for the receiver, then let her hand fall away, realizing it would be prudent to calm herself first. Yes, it *would* be most unwise to confront him now. She had not seen Shane since April. He had just sent her flowers. Therefore it would appear odd, even irrational, if she tackled him about their relationship out of the blue. Also, she abhorred telephone confrontations, preferred to look people right in the eye when she was thrashing out something of crucial importance, needing to observe their reactions. I ought to have insisted on a frank talk long ago, she added under her breath. I've been spineless. It suddenly occurred to her that she was not so much angry with Shane as she was with herself. She should never have permitted the breach to continue as she had. Her annoyance began to dissipate.

Sitting up straighter, she lifted the receiver, then hesitated. How would she begin the conversation? You are befuddled, really jet-lagged tonight, she told herself with a rueful smile. Obviously you'll thank him for the flowers. What else? It's the perfect opening gambit. She dialled his apartment. The phone rang and rang. There was no reply. Disappointed, she replaced the receiver. Then something his father had said to her on Sunday night flashed through her mind. Uncle Bryan had made a remark about Shane being as addicted to work as she was these days. Paula looked at her watch. It was a few minutes before seven. Could he still be at the office? Miranda had given her two numbers for O'Neill Hotels International, and one of them was Shane's private line.

Once again she dialled.

The phone was picked up on the second ring. 'Hello,' a very masculine voice said.

'Shane?'

There was a pause before he answered. 'Hello, Paula,' he finally said.

'Why Shane, how clever of you to recognize my voice and at once,' she exclaimed with assumed flippancy. 'I'm so glad I caught you. I just got back here and found your violets. They're lovely, so springlike, and it was such a dear thought. Thank you.'

'I'm glad you like them,' he said.

His neutral, unenthusiastic tone was so off-putting it chilled her, but nevertheless, she hurried on, 'It's been ages since we've seen each other, at least eight months, and now here we both are, far away from Yorkshire, a couple of Tykes in New York City. The least we can do is get together – ' She stopped, then taking a deep breath said, very rapidly, ' – for dinner.'

There was an even longer pause at his end of the phone. 'I . . . er . . . well . . . I'm not sure when I could do that actually. When were you thinking of, Paula? Which night?'

'Tonight seems as good a time as any,' she said determinedly. 'If you're not already busy, that is.'

'I am a bit, I'm afraid. I'd planned to work late. I have an awful lot of paperwork to catch up with this week.'

'You've got to eat sometime,' she pointed out in her most persuasive voice. She laughed gaily. 'Remember what Grandy was forever saying to Mrs Bonnyface at Heron's Nest. All work and no play, etcetera. And you never used to argue with that sentiment.'

He was silent. .

Softly she said, 'I'm so sorry, I shouldn't be pushing you like this. I know what it's like to be overburdened by work. Perhaps another night. I'm going to be here for about three weeks. I'll leave it up to you, call me if you have a free evening. Thanks again for the flowers, Shane. 'Bye.' She hung up immediately, not giving him an opportunity to respond.

Pushing herself out of the chair, Paula walked over to the coffee table, picked up the card and threw it into the fire, watched it burn. He had been cold, unbending, only marginally civil.

Why? Why? Why?

What ever had she done to Shane O'Neill to make him

behave in such an unfriendly and unkind manner? She ran her hand through her hair distractedly, then shrugged as she returned to the desk. I am a stupid fool, she thought. He's probably heavily involved with Skye Smith and can't be bothered to entertain a childhood friend, especially one he no longer cares about. He might even be living with her. Merry and Winston think their relationship is platonic, but how can they really know. They're always saying he's close mouthed. Funny, though, he never was with me, nor I with him, for that matter. We never had secrets, we told each other everything.

The phone shrilled. She glanced at it, picked it up. Before she said hello he spoke.

'I couldn't make it for at least an hour, maybe a bit longer,' Shane said hurriedly, sounding breathless. 'I'll have to go back to my flat to change, and it's turned seven already.'

'You know you don't have to bother doing that for me, of all people, for heaven's sake,' she exclaimed softly, surprised but gratified that he had rung back. 'After all, we're family.' She laughed under her breath. He was vain about his appearance, but she didn't mind. She rather liked that trait in him. 'Anyway,' she went on, 'you can freshen up here if you want, and listen, we don't have to go to a fancy restaurant, a simple place will do nicely.'

'All right. I'll be there around seven-thirty,' he said. 'See you then.' He hung up as swiftly as she had done a few minutes before.

Paula sat back, staring at the phone. She felt curiously light headed and wondered why.

Shane O'Neill sighed heavily, crushed out the cigarette he had lit before calling Paula.

Reaching for the phone again, he dialled a small French bistro he liked, made a reservation for nine o'clock and then stood up. Hurriedly rolling down his sleeves, he fastened the buttons on the cuffs, knotted his tie which he had loosened earlier, then walked over to the closet to get his jacket and overcoat.

You're a bloody fool, he chastised himself, allowing her to get to you in the way she did. You threw your resolve not to see her out of the window and all because she sounded so wistful when she said goodbye. And disappointed. And lonely. Desperately lonely. He had lived in that solitary and isolated state far too long not to detect it in her immediately. Besides, he knew and understood Paula much better than anyone else did, and he had always been able to accurately gauge her moods. Even when she was putting up a front. Like her grandmother she was adroit at doing that, and exceptionally deceptive. She could don that inscrutable expression at will, affect a gaiety when she spoke that did nothing to betray her real feelings. Except to him, of course. She had adopted a fraudulent lightness with him a few moments ago, he was well aware. Her laughter and flippancy had been forced. So his sister *had* been right. Paula was troubled, disturbed. But about what exactly? Business? Her marriage? Well, he wasn't going to contemplate *that* relationship.

Slipping into his sports jacket, he pulled his overcoat off the hanger and left the offices, locking the door behind him. Several seconds later, stepping out of the building on to Park Avenue, he was relieved to see that the traffic had eased. He spotted a cab, hailed it, jumped in and gave the address on Fifth Avenue. Settling back, he fished around in his pocket for cigarettes and his lighter.

As he smoked a sardonic smile struck his wide Celtic mouth. You're putting a noose around your neck, O'Neill, he warned himself. But then you knew that when you sent her the flowers. You expected her to call you when she received them, be honest, you did. You simply lobbed the ball over into her court. Yes, this was the truth – and yet only partially so.

That afternoon, on his way back to the office from the hotel site, he had noticed the violets as he had passed the flower shop, instantly thinking of her eyes. And then, as he had hovered uncertainly outside, gazing through the window, he had been transported back in time . . . back to the house by the sea . . . and she had been there in that dreamlike villa high on the soaring cliffs . . . dreamlike child of his childhood dreams . . . the tender young girl with the garden hoe . . .

He had gone in and bought the violets, knowing how much she would love them, not giving it a second thought, swept along by the tide of his nostalgia. Only later had he questioned his motives.

Oh what the hell, it's too late now, he thought, impatiently stubbing out his cigarette. I've invited her out. I've got to go through with it. After all, I'm a grown man, I'm well able to handle the situation. Besides, I'm simply taking her to dinner. Surely there is no harm in that.

CHAPTER 33

Some ten minutes later Shane was alighting on Fifth Avenue at Seventy-Seventh Street.

Since he had lived in Emma's apartment for the first three months he had been in New York the doorman on duty knew him, and they exchanged greetings before the man turned to the intercom to announce him.

Riding up in the elevator to the tenth floor, Shane discovered he had a tight knot of apprehension – or was it anticipation? – in his chest. He cautioned himself to watch his step with Paula, took a firm grip on his emotions and arranged a pleasant smile on his face. When he reached the duplex he hesitated for a split second before ringing the bell. As he lifted his hand to do so the door suddenly opened and he found himself staring into Ann Donovan's pleasant Irish face.

'Good evening, Mr O'Neill,' she said, stepping back to let him enter. 'It's nice to see you.'

'Hello, Ann, it's nice to see you too.' He walked in, closed the door behind him, shrugged out of his overcoat. 'You're looking well.'

Ann took his coat. 'Thank you, and so are you, Mr O'Neill.' She turned to the coat closet, and added, 'Miss Paula's waiting for you in the den.'

But she wasn't. She was walking across the spacious hall towards him, a bright smile of welcome on her face.

The impact of seeing her hit him in the pit of his stomach, and the shock sped down to his legs. For a moment he was rooted to the spot, unable to move or speak. He recovered himself swiftly, stepped forward, the smile on his face growing wider.

'Paula!' he exclaimed, and he was surprised that his voice was steady and perfectly normal.

'You got here in record time, Shane,' Paula said, 'it's just seven-thirty.'

'Not much traffic tonight.' His eyes were riveted on her as she drew to a standstill in front of him.

Paula looked up at him, her eyes glowing.

He bent forward to kiss her proffered cheek, took hold of her arm with one hand, drawing her closer, then he let his hand fall away quickly, afraid of even the merest close contact with her.

She began to laugh, staring at him.

'What is it?'

'You've grown a moustache!' She eyed it critically, her head on one side.

'Oh. Yes . . .' His hand went to his mouth automatically. 'Of course, you haven't seen it.'

'How could I. I haven't set eyes on you since April.'

'Don't you like it?'

'Yes . . . I think so,' she said haltingly, then linked her arm through his, led him into the den, continuing to talk. '*You* certainly look as fit as a fiddle. My God, that tan! And all *I* hear is how hard you're working in New York. I bet if the truth were known you're really leading an idle life on the golden sandy beaches of the Caribbean.'

'Fat chance of that. The old man's a slave driver.'

He was glad when she let go of his arm finally and moved away from him, putting distance between them. She walked over to the small chest at the far side of the room. He hovered near the coffee table, watching her as she plopped ice into the glass. He noticed that she poured scotch, added soda, without asking him what he wanted. But why would she ask? She knew what he drank. He caught sight of the basket of violets and smiled and then suddenly she was beside him, offering the drink.

He took it, thanked her, asked, 'Aren't you having anything?'

'Yes, a glass of white wine. It's over there. I'd just poured it when you arrived.' As she spoke she sat down in the armchair near the fireplace, lifted the goblet. 'Cheers, Shane.'

'Cheers.' He lowered himself into the chair opposite, relieved to be sitting down. He still felt shaken, unsteady, and so extremely conscious of her he was slightly alarmed. You'd better be careful, he thought, and put down his glass on the end table. He lit a cigarette to hide his nervousness, and discovered, as he puffed on it, that he was unexpectedly tongue-tied. He glanced around, admiring the room as he usually did. He felt comfortable here. Emma had used a mixture of light and dark greens, a colourful floral chintz on the sofa and chairs, and some rather handsome English Regency antiques. The ambience gave him a sense of home, evoked nostalgic feelings in him. He said, at last, 'I practically lived in this den when I was staying here.'

525

'Funny you should say that, so do I.' Paula leaned back in the chair, crossed her long legs. 'It reminds me of the upstairs parlour at Pennistone Royal, although it's smaller of course, but it's cosy, warm and lived in.'

'Yes.' He cleared his throat. 'I've booked a table at Le Veau D'Or. Have you ever been there?'

'No, I haven't.'

'I think you'll like it – like the atmosphere. It's a small French bistro, very lively and gay, and the food's excellent. I took Aunt Emma and Grandpops there one night, when they were in New York. They really enjoyed themselves.'

'It sounds lovely. And talking of our grandparents, they'll be here again in a few weeks, on their way back to England, won't they? Are you coming home with them? For Christmas?'

'No, afraid not, Paula. Dad wants me to go down to Barbados for the holidays. It's a big season for the hotel.'

'Everybody'll be disappointed not to see you in Yorkshire,' Paula murmured, looking across at him, trying to get used to the moustache. It changed his appearance, made him seem different, a bit older than his twenty-eight years, and more dashing. If that was possible. He had always been the kind of man people looked at twice, because of his height and build, his dark good looks, the sense of presence he exuded.

'You're staring at me,' he said. A black brow arched and his expression was questioning.

'I could say the same about you.'

'You've lost weight,' he began, stopped, reached for his drink.

Paula's brow wrinkled worriedly. 'Yes, I have. And I haven't been dieting, you know I never do that. Am I too thin?'

'Yes, a little. What you need is fattening up, my girl, and since we're on the subject, you also – '

'You've been saying that to me all of your life, and *mine*,' she interrupted, pursing her lips. 'At least for as long as I can remember.'

'True enough. I started to say you also look tired, in need of a good rest, a holiday.' He brought his drink to his mouth, his gaze levelled at her over the rim of the glass, studying her. After taking a swallow, he set it on the table, leaned forward avidly. 'You've done a good job with the makeup, but then you always do. However, cosmetics don't fool me. Your face is gaunt and you've got faint purple smudges under your eyes,' he remarked with his usual unnerving forthrightness. 'No wonder my sister and Winston are worried about you.'

This comment took Paula by surprise, and she exclaimed rapidly, 'I didn't know they were. Neither of them has said anything to me!'

'I'm sure they haven't. In fact I don't suppose anybody has – they're all afraid of you, afraid of upsetting you. But not me, Beanstalk, we've always been blunt with each other, and honest. That'll never change, I hope.'

'So do I.' She could not help thinking about his behaviour lately, the break he had created in their relationship. He had been less than honest with her about that, she was quite sure. She wondered whether to take him to task about it, then decided not to do so. Another time would be more appropriate perhaps. She did not want to put him on the defensive, create trouble on their first evening. She wanted to relax with him, enjoy his company. She had truly missed Shane, now wanted him back in her life on the old footing, needed to rekindle their childhood friendship. It was vital to her. And so she said, 'It's lovely to see you and I'm so glad we're having dinner together, Shane. It'll be like old times.'

She gave him such a warm and loving smile and there was such eagerness in her fine, intelligent eyes, his heart missed a beat. He smiled back at her. 'It already is,' he said, and realized that this was the truth. His tension.

slipped away and he began to laugh. 'I'm not very nice, or very gallant, am I? Picking on you the minute I arrive. And despite what I've just said, you do look lovely, Paula, and as elegant as always.'

His eyes swept over her approvingly, took in the scarlet silk shirt and the white wool trousers. A smile of amusement tugged at the corner of his mouth. 'Now, if you'd only thought to add a purple kerchief, you'd look absolutely bang on, perfectly smashing.'

Perplexity flashed on to her face. She glanced down at her shirt and then started to laugh with him. 'The Herons! It never occurred to me when I was dressing, but of course, these were your colours.'

He nodded, his black eyes merry, and then he stood up. He took his glass to the chest, added more soda water and ice to dilute the scotch. She had fixed the drink exactly right, the way he liked it, but he wanted to be especially careful tonight. Returning to the fireplace, he said in a more sober voice, 'Winston told me Sally stayed at Heron's Nest during all that fuss in Ireland, and I understand everything's back to normal. But how is Sally *really*?'

'She's marvellous. Very well. Anthony is living at Allington Hall for the moment. I expect you know she's pregnant.'

'Yes, Winston told me – ' He broke off, looked at her alertly. 'No wonder you're done in, worn out – all *you've* had to cope with.' He was suddenly sympathetic, and it showed on his face.

'I managed.' Wanting to keep the conversation light-hearted, and long weary of family problems, Paula changed the subject by launching into a recital about Emma, Blackie and their travels. She regaled Shane with snippets she remembered from her grandmother's long letters, titbits chosen at random from their weekly phone conversations. She spiced up her stories with comments of her own, peals

528

of laughter and merriment punctuating these small asides as she warmed to her subject.

Shane's laughter echoed hers, and he nodded from time to time, listening attentively, content to sit back and let her do the talking. It gave him a chance to observe her more closely, to fully enjoy her. The familiar vivacity was there, spilling out of her, and she was humorous, pithy, and gentle by turn, displaying her love for Emma and his grandfather with every word she uttered.

If her gaiety had been forced, fraudulent, on the telephone earlier, it no longer was. He had to acknowledge that she was her natural self, open, outgoing, the girl he had grown up with and whom he knew as well as he knew himself. There was an easiness between them now, after the first few strained moments, and he felt as though he had seen her only yesterday. The rift he had created in their friendship might never have happened.

As he continued to listen to her soft musical voice, a tranquillity settled over Shane. He was at peace with himself, and in a way he had not been for the longest time. But then he was generally at peace when he was with Paula. They never played silly games. There were no false barriers, no affectations, no phoney attitudes. They were entirely themselves, and they were completely attuned to each other as they had been since they were children.

He studied her face quite openly, no longer bothering to hide his interest in her. Its angularity and gauntness had been softened by the warm light from the lamp behind her. It was mobile, expressive, and it articulated much about her thoughts and feelings. There were those who said Paula was not beautiful. She was to him. Her colouring was startling in its vividness, exotic really. The shiny black hair coming to a dramatic widow's peak above her smooth wide brow, the translucent ivory complexion unstained by colour, the violet eyes set wide apart, large and thickly lashed – all these features combined to create a unique kind of beauty. If he had to equate her with any of the flowers she loved to grow, he would have had to liken her to an orchid or a gardenia – and yet he would never send her either, only ever violets. He thought of her basic nature then . . . she *was* retiring, reserved and gentle. But, conversely, she was also intense, ardent, passionate about her likes and dislikes, and quick, intelligent, fair minded and honourable. He smiled to himself. She could be devious when it came to business, but that was a family trait, inherited from the redoubtable E.H. Now, as he pondered Paula, Shane had to admit she was the most complex of women, more complicated than any female he had ever met. Yet he loved that very complexity in her which others might easily find so baffling, even disturbing. Perhaps that was because he knew exactly where she was coming from, knew the elements and forces that had made her all the things she was.

He sat back trying to see her objectively, as another man might. His gaze lingered, then he dropped his eyes. His own emotions were intruding, blinding him, making it impossible to view her with any kind of objectivity. How could he do that? He loved her. Loved her desperately. He would always love her. If he could not have her, and he knew he could not, then he would have no other woman. Second best was worse than nothing at all. Also, without another woman in his life he would not be forced into making comparisons as he yearned for Paula. And he *would* continue to yearn for her. You mustn't think of that, he told himself sharply. She is your oldest, dearest friend. You've missed her. So settle for friendship – if that's all you can have. And enjoy this evening for what it is, not what you think it could be in your imagination.

Paula was saying, 'Anyway, that's all of my news about our indefatigable, globe-trotting grandparents. They're apparently having a whale of a time.'

'Yes, it sounds like it,' Shane agreed. 'And Emma's

a much more diligent correspondent than Blackie. All Grandpops does is send each one of us a weekly picture postcard with an obtuse message scribbled on the back. I have three I'll prize forever. One from Hong Kong, showing Chinese junks in an orange sunset, with a single word on the other side – *Cheers*. Another from Bora Bora on which he'd written, *Drinking your health in coconut juice*.' Shane grinned at her. '*That's* a likely story, as we both know.'

Paula giggled, asked, 'And the third card?'

'One from Sydney which said, *Off to the outback today*. What a character he is, and I must say I've enjoyed hearing your news about the two of them, their activities. It brings them closer somehow.'

'Yes, it does, but now it's your turn to do the talking,' Paula announced. 'Tell me all about your life in New York.'

'There's not much to tell, Paula,' he said, thinking of his lonely existence, the barrenness of his life. 'I race between the office and the hotel site six, sometimes seven, days a week, fly down to Jamaica and Barbados about once a month, to make sure the hotels are running smoothly. It's the usual grind, and the truth is, I *do* work like a dog.'

She nodded. 'I thought you were only staying in New York for six months. It's been eight already.'

'Dad and I decided it would be more practical if I remained here until the hotel is finished and open, operating properly. It's a lot more practical than flying backward and forward between New York and London, also the islands are closer. Now Dad has indicated he wants me to stay on in the States indefinitely.'

'Well, I can understand his reasoning,' she acknowledged softly. Swirling the drink around, she stared down into the glass, her face thoughtful. The idea of Shane being in New York permanently filled her with sudden and inexplicable anxiety. Then unexpectedly she thought of Skye Smith, experienced the same twinge of discomfort she had felt when Merry had mentioned her name weeks ago.

Before she could stop herself, Paula said, with a faint smile, 'I suppose New York is a wonderful place to be – for a fun-loving bachelor like you, Shane. I bet the girls are falling all over you, queuing up for dates.'

Astonishment crossed his face. 'I'm not interested in other women,' he exclaimed, and halted, recognizing his slip, instantly cursing himself. He decided to let the remark slide by, aware that the less said the better.

Not understanding that he had been referring to her, Paula nodded. 'Oh yes, of course, you have a girlfriend now. Merry mentioned Skye Smith to me.'

Irritated though he was with his sister and her big mouth, he nevertheless managed to grin, relieved that his gaffe had gone over Paula's head. 'Oh, Skye Smith's only a friend, whatever Merry has said to you. I'm not involved with her – or anyone else for that matter.' He gave Paula a hard stare. 'I told you, Dad's very practised at cracking the whip these days, and I'm devoting my time to business. I don't enjoy much of a social life. I stay at the offices until all hours, stagger back to my apartment and fall into bed exhausted.'

'It seems we're all on a treadmill these days,' Paula said. Shane had obviously changed a great deal. He and Winston had been a couple of Don Juans, playboys, wild and reckless, according to the family gossip she had heard. But Winston had settled down. Perhaps Shane had done so as well. She was pleased he was not having an affair with Skye. Why did that woman bother her? Probably because Merry had been so scathing about her.

'Penny for your thoughts,' Shane said.

She laughed. 'They're not worth a farthing. Merry told me you have an apartment on Sutton Place South,' she went on, 'what's it like?'

'Not bad actually. I rent it furnished, and the owner's

taste is not mine exactly. But it's the penthouse and the views are spectacular, especially at night. The whole of Manhattan is stretched out at my feet, and as far as the eye can see. I find myself sitting and enjoying those glittering vistas for hours on end. This is an exciting city, Paula, and challenging. I also happen to think it's beautiful, and the architecture never ceases to astonish me.'

'I can tell from your voice that you like it here, but sometimes I wonder about the States – ' She shook her head, her face growing serious, reflective.

'What do you mean?'

'I can't help thinking that it's a violent country. All those dreadful, mind-boggling assassinations – Martin Luther King, President Kennedy, and then Bobby Kennedy only last year. And this past August the ghastly Manson murders in California.' She shuddered. 'And the hippies and the drugs and the crime and the protests.'

Shane looked across at her, said slowly, 'There's a lot of truth in what you say. But it's a young country in a sense, and still going through its growing pains. Things will be all right here, they'll level off, I guarantee you that. Besides, we have hippies, drugs, crime and protests in England, everywhere in the world. The sixties *have* been turbulent, but we'll soon be in a new decade. Perhaps the seventies will be more tranquil.'

'I hope so. Anyway, I do hope you'll invite me over to see your apartment before I leave.'

'Any time you want. And talking of leaving, I think we'd better make tracks to the restaurant. I don't want to lose the table.'

'Fine, I'll just go and get my things.' She was halfway across the room when she stopped, pivoted to him. 'I'm not very thoughtful, am I? I said on the phone you could freshen up here and then immediately forgot all about it. Would you like to use my bathroom?'

'No, no, thanks anyway. The one down here is okay.'
Rising, he followed her out.

'See you in a minute then,' she said, running lightly up
the stairs.

Shane strode across the foyer to the guest bathroom. He
washed his hands and face, combed his curly black hair,
stared at himself in the mirror. He wondered whether to
shave off his moustache tomorrow morning. No. He liked
it. He grimaced at his reflection, wishing he had gone
home to change his clothes after all. Oh what the hell, I'm
not trying to impress Paula, he thought, and went out.

She stood waiting for him in the foyer.

She had put on a white wool jacket that matched the
trousers, and had flung a white mohair cape over her
shoulders. She looked impossibly beautiful to him.

He turned to get his overcoat out of the closet, gritted
his teeth as the familiar longing for her surged through
him. He clamped down on the feeling, knowing that the
situation was useless, hopeless. She was married to Jim
Fairley and very much in love with him.

All you can be is her friend, as you've always been,
Shane reminded himself as they left the apartment and
went down in the lift.

Le Veau D'Or was busy, jammed with people, as Shane
had known it would be.

Gerard came forward to greet them, smiling, as usual the
genial host. He promised them that their table would be
ready in ten minutes, suggested they have a drink at the
small bar while they waited to be seated.

Shane ushered Paula forward, pulled out a stool for her,
and without asking her what she wanted he ordered two *kir
royales*. He lit a cigarette, watched the bartender pour the
cassis into the large wine goblets, then fill both to the brim
with sparkling champagne.

Once they had their drinks, Shane turned to Paula,

clinked glasses with her. 'To old friendships,' he said, and looked down at her, his eyes warm.

'Old friendships, Shane.'

'Do you know, the last time I had one of these was at La Reserve in the South of France . . . with you.'

She gave him a quick glance, and a smile of recollection glanced across her mouth. 'I remember . . . you'd been so unkind to Emily, driving the boat at a crazy speed and with such wildness. She was terrified, poor thing. Then to make amends, you dragged us both off, pouring *kir royales* into us with a vengeance.' She shook her head, laughing. 'It was about four years ago, that summer we all went down to Gran's villa at the Cap.'

'But the drinks had no effect, if I remember correctly. My escapade with the speedboat cost me dearly . . . an expensive silk scarf was the price I had to pay for my lack of thought and recklessness. Still, it was worth it, just to bring the smile back to Emily's face.'

'She's petrified of water – so is Gran.'

'But you're not afraid of anything, are you?'

'What makes you say that?' She frowned at him.

'You were intrepid as a child, tagging along after me, doing all the things I did. You were such a tomboy, quite fearless, and you never flinched, whatever the obstacle, or its danger.'

'But I trusted you. I knew you wouldn't let anything happen to me, and you never did.'

And I never will, my darling, he thought, filled with love for her. A lump came into his throat, surprising him. He took a long gulp of his drink, momentarily averted his face as he placed the glass on the bar, not wishing her to see his eyes. They would reveal too much.

Paula began to chat about Emily's engagement to Winston, and once more Shane was happy to let her do the talking. It gave him a chance to marshal his feelings, get a hold on them again before they overwhelmed him. Eventually he was able to join in the conversation in a normal way, and they covered a wide range of topics. They gossiped about their mutual friends, discussed the Harte boutiques in the O'Neill hotels, wondered about Emerald Bow's chances at the Grand National. And they were still dissecting the difficulties of the Aintree course and the greatest steeplechase in the world when they were finally seated.

Settling back comfortably on the red banquette, Shane said, 'All I had for lunch was a sandwich at my desk, so I'm ravenous. Knowing you, you're going to say you're not hungry, but I think we should order immediately.'

'But I am hungry,' she protested truthfully. For the first time in months she was looking forward to dinner. Her violet eyes, resting on him, welled with humour. 'However, I'll let you order for both of us. I'll have the same as you – it's safer, don't you think?'

His mouth twitched. 'I believe so. Otherwise you'll want what I have, as you always did when we were kids, end up eating off my plate and leave me starving.' He winked. 'Don't think I've forgotten your bad habits, because I haven't.'

After perusing the menu, Shane motioned to their waiter, selected *saucisson chaud* to be followed by *tripes à la mode de Caen* and asked for a bottle of burgundy.

It was the custom at Le Veau D'Or for appetizers to be placed before the diners, to tide them over while they waited for dinner to be served. Two plates instantly materialized in front of them, and Shane exclaimed, 'Oh good, mussels tonight. They're delicious. Try them, Paula.' Dipping his fork into the mound of shellfish, he continued, 'Will you be going to Texas while you're in the States?'

'I don't think so – gosh, you're right, these are good.' She munched on a forkful of the mussels, before adding, 'I hope I don't have to go to Odessa. I met with Dale Stevens

536

this morning, and fortunately things are relatively quiet at Sitex. Naturally, Harry Marriott is being his usual obstreperous self. That man is singularly without vision. He forever tried to block my grandfather, hated expansion and innovation, and he's constantly trying to do the same with us. He's still grousing about Sitex going into North Sea oil. But it's working extremely well, as you know. The off-shore drilling paid off, and we were one of the first companies to strike oil this year. Once again, Emma Harte has proved that man totally wrong.'

Shane smiled, nodded, went on eating.

Paula said, 'I know Grandy gave you an introduction to Ross Nelson. What do you think of him?'

'Ross is okay. We get on quite well, actually. I suspect he's a bit of a sod when it comes to women, though. As for business,' Shane shrugged, 'he's above board. Very sharp, mind you, but honest. Obviously he's always looking out for the bank, that's only natural. He's been very helpful, useful to me in a variety of ways.' He eyed her. 'And what's your opinion of Mr Nelson?'

'The same as yours, Shane.' Paula told him about the meeting with Dale and Ross earlier in the day, confiding all of the details.

'Emma would never sell her shares in Sitex!' Shane exclaimed, when she had finished. His black brows knitted together. 'I can't imagine how Ross could think that or why he is so keen for you to sell out. He can't make a profit from insider information about stock transactions, trading, it's against the law. And as a private investment banker of his standing and reputation he would be a stickler about legalities, staying within the law, toeing the line drawn by the Securities Exchange Commission. No, financial gain has nothing to do with this, and anyway he's as rich as Croesus. Of course, if Ross helped to steer that kind of deal through for one of the bank's clients, he'd be a big man with that client, now wouldn't he?' Not waiting for a response, Shane rushed on, 'Yes, that's why he's interested in Sitex. From all you've just told me, his client wants control, or so it seems. Then again, if he's such a chum of Dale's, he's probably looking out for his buddy. He's trying to kill two birds with one stone.'

'Yes, I reasoned things out the same way as you earlier, after they'd left. Ross Nelson can pester me as much as he wants – I've no intention of talking Grandy into selling, which is what he hopes I'll do, in my estimation.'

Shane gave her a cool and piercing look. 'You'd better watch old Ross – he's bound to make a pass at you.'

Paula was about to tell him about the roses, the invitation to spend the weekend at Ross's country home, but for a reason she could not immediately fathom she changed her mind. She said, with a dry laugh, 'He wouldn't dare. I'm married. Also, he wouldn't want to upset Gran.'

'Don't be so naïve, Paula,' Shane retorted swiftly. 'Your marital status and your grandmother's displeasure would not influence Ross Nelson. Not one iota. He's bloody unscrupulous, if one is to believe the gossip one hears, and I'm afraid I do.' Shane did not particularly like the idea of the banker hovering anywhere near Paula, and he brought the conversation around to another subject. He began to speak about their New York hotel, and continued to do so through the first course and as they waited for their main dish.

She listened with growing interest, enjoying being at the receiving end of his confidences. Earlier, before Shane had arrived at the apartment, it had crossed Paula's mind that they might feel awkward, perhaps shy with each other, discomfited and restrained even. They had not been alone or spent any time together for ages. But this had not been the case, nor was it now. It *was* like old times, as she had predicted it would be over drinks. It had not taken them long to get back on their former footing. There was warmth and affection flowing between them, and the camaraderie of their youth was much in evidence.

'So I'd like you to come over to the hotel, take a look round,' Shane said, 'whenever you have a spare hour this week. Some of the floors are finished and I can show you a few of the suites. I'd appreciate your opinion about the decorative schemes – I just received the renderings from the interior design firm this afternoon. You have such good taste, I'd like your opinion.'

Paula's face lit up with pleasure. 'Why I'd love to see the hotel. I've heard quite a lot about it from Uncle Bryan and Merry. Actually, tomorrow's an easy day for me. I could meet you there in the late afternoon.' She leaned closer, looked up into his face, hers full of eagerness. 'And perhaps you'd come back with me for dinner at the apartment. Ann told me she wants to cook for you. She said something about your favourite Irish stew. And why not tomorrow evening?'

Because the more I see of you, the more I'll want you, he thought.

He said, 'Thanks a lot, that'll be nice.' He was startled that he had accepted her invitation so readily. Then suddenly, with a small shock, he knew that he intended to spend as much time with her as he could during her sojourn in New York.

He walked her back to the apartment.

It was a clear, bright evening, cool, but not particularly cold for November. After the warmth and noisiness of the bistro the air was refreshing, their companionable silence restful.

They were on Madison Avenue, drawing closer to Seventy-Second Street, when Shane said, 'Would you like to go riding on Sunday?'

'I'd love to,' Paula cried, turning to glance up at him.

'It's ages since I've been on a horse. I don't have my riding togs with me, obviously. But I suppose I could wear jeans.'

'Yes, or you could go to Kauffman's. They're down town and they have everything you'd need.'

'Then that's what I'll do. Where do you ride?'

'In Connecticut – a country town called New Milford. Actually I own a place up there. An old barn. I've been renovating it, remodelling it for the past few months and – '

'Shane O'Neill! How secretive and mean of you! Why didn't you tell me about the barn before?'

'I haven't had a chance so far. We've had such a lot of other things to talk about over dinner. More important things, such as your business affairs, our new hotel.' His laugh was deep, throaty. He went on, 'Would you like to see it?'

'That's a ridiculous question. Of course I would. But I will, won't I? On Sunday, I mean.'

'Yes.'

'If you like I can fix a picnic lunch, and we can take it up with us. What time would we leave on Sunday?' Paula asked.

'You ought to leave fairly early. You see, I'll be there already. I've arranged for a couple of our carpenters to be there on Friday to work with me. I'm driving up on Thursday night. I plan to spend the weekend at the barn.'

'Oh. Then how will I get there on Sunday?'

'No problem, I'll arrange for a car and driver to bring you. Unless – ' he paused, exclaimed, 'I have a great idea, Paula. Why don't you drive up with me on Thursday night, stay for the weekend? Surely you can take Friday off.' He gave her a quick look out of the corner of his eye, added in a jocular tone, 'I'll buy you a spade. You can dig to your heart's content, make a garden for me.'

She laughed. 'In this weather! The ground's probably as

hard as iron. But I'd love to come up for the weekend, Shane.'

'Terrific.' He smiled to himself.

She linked her arm through his, fell into step with him. They walked on in silence. She was thinking of their childhood days at Heron's Nest and, although she had no way of knowing it, so was he.

CHAPTER 34

Paula awakened on Friday morning to the sound of raised masculine voices and raucous laughter echoing outside.

She sat up in bed with a start and rubbed her eyes, blinking in the faint light, for a moment disoriented and wondering where she was. Then she remembered. Of course, she was at Shane's barn in New Milford. Glancing at her small travelling clock on the white wicker bedside table she saw to her surprise that it was almost ten. She found it hard to believe she had overslept and by four hours. Normally she was up and dressed by six o'clock every day.

Bounding out of bed, feeling rested and filled with energy, she padded over to the window, parted the red cotton twill curtains, looked down into the yard. Just below her, two men stood talking near a pile of lumber.

Shane was out of her line of vision, but she knew he was there when she heard him say, 'Listen, you guys, keep the noise down, will you please. My lady friend is still asleep. And when I say lady I do mean *lady* – so watch your language.'

Half smiling, she turned away and looked around the bedroom with interest. She had been too tired last night to pay much attention, but now she realized how charming it was, small and quaint, with white walls that stopped at a floor painted bright red. The few pieces of furniture were of white wicker, but it was the brass bed covered with patchwork quilt that dominated the space.

Gliding into the adjoining minuscule of bathroom, Paula took a quick shower, brushed her hair, put on lipstick and mascara, went back into the bedroom. She dressed in a pair of blue jeans, a pink cotton shirt and a heavy purple sweater, then pulled a pair of knee-high red leather boots on over the jeans. After strapping on her watch, she ran downstairs to the kitchen.

This was large, country in feeling, with rustic beams and wall-hung copper utensils, but there was every modern appliance, and it was spotless. It looked to her as if it had just been freshly cleaned. The white cabinets and counter tops, encircling the white walls, gleamed brightly in the sunshine that filtered in through two small windows where blue-and-white checked curtains hung in crisp, starched folds. She peered out. Shane and the men were nowhere in sight.

Paula sniffed. There was a lovely aroma of coffee in the air, and spotting the bubbling percolator, she began opening cupboards, looking for a mug. She found one, filled it, then strolled through into the main living area of the barn.

She came to a halt halfway down the long expanse of space, her eyes sweeping around, trying to take in everything at once, knowing this was virtually impossible. She needed days to absorb everything Shane had accomplished here. It had looked lovely last night; this morning, filled with sunlight, it was breathtaking.

Only one room, he had said, as they were driving up from Manhattan. But what a room it was – huge, spectacular in its dimensions, with a high ceiling of exposed rafters intersected by cross beams, a picture window on a long wall, and a gargantuan stone fireplace. A fire already blazed up the chimney, the big logs hissing and spitting in the silence.

She stepped over to the baby grand and sat down on the stool, sipping the coffee, continuing to glance up and down. He had positioned the piano in the exact centre of the room and she understood why. It created a natural demarcation between the seating arrangement next to the fireplace and the dining area near the kitchen. The colour scheme was primarily white, the coolness warmed by dark wood tones. The walls had been whitewashed; two huge Chesterfield sofas and the big armchairs were upholstered in heavy white twill; the draperies matched; there were white area rugs on the polished wood floor. But pictures, prints, books and plants added splashes of livelier colour against the white background.

Shane had told her he had gone antiquing in the area, had stumbled on some genuinely good pieces. Now her eyes rested on two handsome chests she had not really noticed last night, moved on to regard a Coromandel screen that was obviously very old and rare. Its decorative panels made a striking backdrop for the mahogany dining table. I bet that screen cost a fortune, she thought.

A feeling of dismay trickled through her.

It was quite apparent that he had spent a great deal of money on the barn, not to mention time and effort. Shane had explained that most of the basic remodelling had been done by Sonny and Elaine Vickers, from whom he had bought the barn. 'All I did was put in the cantilevered staircase and the plate glass window, and add a few other finishing touches to the basic shell before I furnished,' he had said.

Nevertheless, in the last few minutes something had registered and it troubled her. The place had the look of permanence, had been made into a real home for someone who intended to live in it for a long time. Not only that, he was somewhere outside right now with the carpenters, sawing wood for shelves and cupboards. They were intended for the tiny spare room he had shown her and which he had said he was turning into a den for himself.

Did he plan to stay in America for ever? Was he never coming back to England? And why did that matter to her?

Paula jumped up abruptly and hurried to the fire. She seated herself in an overstuffed armchair and placed the mug on the hearth. Her eyes fell on his cigarettes and lighter and, although she rarely smoked, she took one, lit it, sat smoking, thinking hard about the previous evening. They had arrived at nine o'clock, just as the thunderstorm had hit the area. They had been drenched after making several trips to the car to collect the bag of groceries and their suitcases, and he had insisted she change into dry clothes, immediately shooing her upstairs.

Twenty minutes later she had come back down and had stood hovering on the threshold of this room, admiring it. In her absence he had turned on all the lamps, lit the fire. The baronial expanse seemed more intimate, suffused in a warm and welcoming glow and reverberating with the strains of Bob Dylan's *Blowin' In The Wind*. Wandering over to the fireplace, she had swung around to stand with her back to it, an old habit. At that very moment she had been surprised to see him emerge from the kitchen, carrying two drinks, looking spruced up and fresh in a pristine white shirt and blue jeans.

'You've been quick, doing all this and changing as well,' she had exclaimed. He had given her a cheeky grin. 'Training will out, as they say, and I was trained by a hard-assed general in a tough army camp, remember.' She had retorted in mock reproof, 'Emma Harte hard-assed! That's not a very nice thing to say about my distinguished grandmother.' Handing her the vodka and tonic, Shane had clinked his glass against hers, then asserted, 'Emma would appreciate my description of her, even if you don't.'

They had begun to reminisce about Heron's Nest then, laughing a lot and teasing each other, and later he had brought out a huge platter of smoked salmon and a tray of cheeses. They had sat on the floor, eating off the coffee table in front of the fire, washing down their light supper with ice-cold Pouilly Fumé. And they had talked endlessly, late into the night, and about so many varied things, content to be together, at ease and comfortable in their companionship.

Towards the end of the evening Shane had noticed that she kept rubbing her neck, and in answer to his concerned glance, she had volunteered, 'It's stiff – from sitting long hours at my desk, I've no doubt. It's nothing. Really.' Without saying a word, he had knelt behind her, massaged her shoulders, her nape, and the base of her skull.

Recalling the scene, Paula remembered the pleasure she had felt as Shane's strong hard fingers had kneaded her aching muscles, drawn the tension out of her. She had not wanted him to stop. And later, when he had given her a chaste goodnight peck on the cheek outside her bedroom door, she had felt a compulsion to put her arms around his neck. She had gone in swiftly, closed the door, her cheeks flaming.

Paula sat up in the chair with a jerk. Last night she had been baffled at herself. Now she understood. She had *wanted* Shane to touch her, to kiss her. Face it. Your so-called sisterly feelings towards him aren't very fraternal. Not any more. *They're sexual. You're sexually attracted to him.*

This last thought so startled and shocked Paula, she leaped to her feet, threw the cigarette into the fire, and almost ran across to the picture window.

She stood staring out at the landscape, hardly aware of its beauty as she tried to calm herself. She *must* put aside these new and extraordinary feelings he had aroused in her. They shook her up, distressed her. And she had no right to be interested in Shane O'Neill – she was married.

Besides, she was only his childhood friend, nothing more in his eyes.

Endeavouring to nudge thoughts of him out of her mind she discovered that they refused to budge. They nagged at her, and then the image of Shane as he had looked last night danced before her eyes. He had seemed different, and yet his appearance and manner were exactly the same as they always were. Then it dawned on her. It was she who was different – and she had been looking at him through newly objective, newly perceptive eyes.

Why am I suddenly so aware of Shane? Because he is handsome, virile, amusing and charming? Or because he exudes such sex appeal? But he always has, he hasn't changed. Besides blatant sex appeal makes no impression on me. His sexuality isn't blatant, though. It simply exists as an integral part of him. My God, I must be insane, thinking in this way about Shane. Anyway, I'm not interested in sex. It turns me off. Jim has seen to that.

A little shiver ran through Paula. Jim loomed up in front of her. Merry had an expression she used to describe certain men. She called them, 'the wham, bang and the thank you, ma'am chaps'. How apt. Paula sighed heavily, blinked in the sunlight as it pierced through the window, a blinding cataract of brilliant light. Her thoughts remained on Jim. Shane's image was demolished.

Yesterday afternoon, around two o'clock, she had telephoned Long Meadow. It had been seven in the evening in England. She had spoken to Jim. But only briefly. He had been pleasant, bland as always, but hurried, on his way out to dinner, he had informed her. He had quickly passed her over to Nora, so that she could chat to the nurse about her babies, get all the news. She missed Lorne and Tessa terribly. When she had asked Nora to put her husband back on the line, Nora had said that he had already left the house. Paula could hardly believe that he had not waited to say goodbye to her. Furious with him, she had hung up.

Then the depression had set in. Seemingly Jim had forgotten their confrontation last Sunday – and what it had been about.

My God, that's less than a week ago, she thought, as the picture of them standing in the garden flashed through her head with startling clarity. Something had died in her that day. It would never be reborn. Jim had been dense, dismissive, cavalier in his attitude. And yes, irresponsible and indifferent to her, almost callous, now that she thought about it again. He simply didn't care about her emotions, her thoughts, her needs. Once more she acknowledged that he and she were incompatible. And on every possible level, not only sexually. If sex were their only problem she would be able to cope. His attitude on the phone had only reinforced her sense of despair about him. The last vestiges of her commitment to her marriage had been swept away, and she had turned to the papers on her desk, thankful that she had so much business to occupy her.

My work and the children . . . that's where I shall direct all of my energies from now on, she reminded herself for the umpteenth time. Hurrying back to the hearth, she picked up the mug, headed for the kitchen. It was high time she went outside to find Shane, to wish him good morning and ask about their plans for the rest of the day.

But he was already in the kitchen, pouring himself a mug of coffee. 'So there you are!' he exclaimed. 'I bet my chaps woke you up, rowdy devils!'

Paula gaped at him, instantly conscious of his rough clothing. He was wearing shapeless, baggy corduroys, heavy work boots, a bulky fisherman's sweater and a cloth cap set at a rakish angle on his black curls. She began to laugh, shaking her head.

'What's the matter?' he demanded, frowning, his eyes clouding.

'Your clothes!' she spluttered. 'You look like an Irish navvy!'

547

'My dear girl, hasn't anybody told you that that's exactly what I am. Just like my grandfather.'

Later in the morning they drove into New Milford.

On their way down the hill, Shane pointed out the farm where his friends Sonny and Elaine Vickers lived, told her in passing that he had invited them over for dinner that night. 'He's a musician, she's a writer. They're lots of fun, you'll like them,' he said, and then went on to discuss the menu with her.

By the time they were parking the car they had agreed on what she would cook – an old-fashioned North Country dinner with all the trimmings. They would start with Yorkshire pudding, have a leg of lamb, roast potatoes and brussel sprouts for the main course, finish with an English trifle.

They went to the farm stands and various markets, bought fresh vegetables, fruit and lamb and various other meats for the weekend, and spices, fancy candles and armfuls of bronze and gold chrysanthemums. They staggered down Main Street, their arms laden, laughing and joking, their hilarity high.

On the return journey, Paula realized that she was being her normal self with Shane, as he was with her. But then why wouldn't he be? He couldn't read her mind, and even if he could, there was now nothing unusual to read – except friendly, affectionate thoughts, happy remembrances of their youthful past. Fortunately those strange and disturbing feelings he had evoked in her last night had entirely disappeared in the last few hours. Shane was just her old chum, her good friend, and part of the family. Everything was normal again. She felt weak with the relief.

Once they were back at the barn, Shane unpacked their purchases and put them away, while she arranged the flowers in two large stone pots. As they worked, he said,

'I'm afraid it's another picnic for lunch. Is that okay with you, Beanstalk?'

'Of course. But what about your carpenters? Don't you have to feed them?'

'No. They brought their own sandwiches and they told me they were going to eat at noon, while we were out shopping. But I wonder where they are? They were supposed to start putting up some of the shelves – it's awfully silent.' He began to laugh as the sound of hammering floated down from the upper floor. 'I spoke too soon, it seems. They're obviously hard at it.'

Lunch, eaten in front of the fire in the main room, consisted of ripe brie cheese, thick chunks of French bread, fruit and a bottle of red wine. At one moment Paula looked across at Shane and said, 'Are you planning to live in the States for the rest of your life?'

'Why do you ask that?' He wondered why it mattered to her.

Glancing around, she said, 'This place has the look of a permanent residence, and you've obviously put a lot of care and money into it.'

'Yes, and it's been very therapeutic for me, coming up here whenever I could, working on the place. It's given me something to do at weekends, in my spare time. I don't have many friends, no real social life to speak of. Besides, you know I've always enjoyed rebuilding old places.' He lolled back in the chair, his eyes resting on her thoughtfully. 'Winston and I turned a tidy profit when we sold those old cottages we renovated in Yorkshire, and I know I'll do the same here, when the time comes for me to sell the barn.' He continued to observe her. Was that relief in her eyes, or was he imagining things?

'What's going to happen to Beck House? I mean now that Winston and Emily are getting married?' Paula asked curiously.

'When Winston was in New York he said he and Emily

wanted to live there for a while, to see if Emily liked it. If she does, he'll buy me out, if she doesn't – ' Shane shrugged. 'There's no problem, we'll probably continue to share it as a weekend place. Or we'll put it up for sale.'

'Winston told me he's asked you to be his best man.'

Shane nodded.

'And I'm going to be Emily's matron of honour.'

'Yes, I know.'

'Won't you be in England before then, Shane?'

There it was again, that peculiar concerned expression in her eyes. He said, 'I've no idea, Paula. As I explained the other day, Dad wants me to spend the Christmas season in Jamaica and Barbados, and I might just have to go to Australia next February or March.'

'Australia!' She sat up straighter on the sofa, looking puzzled.

'Yes. Blackie's taken a shine to Sydney, and several times, when he's spoken to Dad lately, he has urged him to build a hotel there. I spoke to the old man yesterday morning, and he's actually received a letter from Grandpops about that very thing. So – I may have to go over there, scout the place.'

'Blackie's as bad as Grandy. Don't those two ever stop thinking about business?'

'Do you? Or do I, for that matter?' He chuckled. 'We're a couple of chips off a couple of old blocks, wouldn't you say?'

'I suppose so.' She leaned forward, her face suddenly intent. 'Do you think I work too hard?'

'Of course I don't. Anyway, it's your nature to be a worker, Paula. It's also the way you were reared – as I was reared. I don't have much time for parasites. Frankly, I'd go crazy if I had lots of free time on my hands. I love being out in the marketplace, love the rough and tumble, the wheeling and dealing, and so do you. There's another thing, I get a lot of gratification knowing I'm continuing the family business started by Grandpops, and you have to feel exactly the same way.'

'I do.'

'It's expected of us both . . . duty has been beaten into us since our births, we wouldn't know any other way to live. Look, our respective grandparents devoted their lives to building two great business empires, strove to give us better lives than they had in the beginning, and financial security, and independence and power. How – '

'Jim says the pursuit of power leads to isolation, the death of human values and the death of the soul,' Paula interjected.

This was the first time she had mentioned Jim since she had arrived in New York and Shane was momentarily thrown. He cleared his throat. He had no desire to discuss her husband, but knew he had to make some sort of response. 'And you? Do you agree?'

'No, actually, I don't. Wasn't it Lord Acton who said power corrupts, absolute power corrupts absolutely? That's what Jim was getting at, I think. But to hell with Lord Acton, whoever *he* was. I prefer Emma Harte's philosophy. She says power only corrupts when those who have it will do anything to hang on to it. Grandy says that power can be ennobling, if one understands that power is a tremendous responsibility. And especially to others. I happen to agree with *her*, not Jim. I do feel responsible, Shane. To Gran, to our employees and shareholders. And to myself.'

Shane nodded. 'You're right, and so is Emma. I was going to say, a moment ago, how ungrateful and even unconscionable we would be if we were indifferent to our inheritances, turned away from them. It would be negating Blackie and Emma, and all their superhuman efforts.' He stood up, glanced at the clock. 'It's almost four, and since we're on the subject of responsibility I'd better go and find my chaps, pay them, tell them to knock off.'

Paula also rose, picked up the luncheon tray. 'The day's disappeared! I should start preparing the food for dinner.'

As they went out, Shane looked down at her, flashed his cheeky grin. 'And for your information, Beanstalk, Lord Acton was an English historian, a devout Catholic, a Liberal member of Parliament and close friend of Gladstone's.'

'That's nice to know,' she said, laughing, and walked into the kitchen.

After stacking the dishwasher, Paula peeled the potatoes, cleaned the sprouts, prepared the lamb, smearing it with butter, adding pepper and dried rosemary leaves. Once the trifle was made and had been placed in the refrigerator, she beat flour, eggs and milk into a batter for the Yorkshire pudding, humming happily to herself. Shane poked his head around the door several times during the hour she was working, volunteering to help, but she declined his offer, told him to scoot. She was enjoying herself in much the same way she took pleasure in gardening, using her hands instead of her brain for a change. Therapeutic, she thought, recalling his words about working on the barn.

When she eventually went back into the main room she noticed that he had laid the table for dinner, stacked piles of logs on one end of the hearth, put Beethoven's Ninth on the stereo. But he was nowhere in sight. Paula curled up on the sofa comfortably, listening to the symphony, feeling relaxed and even a little drowsy. She yawned. It's the wine. I'm not used to it at lunch time, she thought, closing her eyes. It had been a lovely day, the nicest she had spent in a long time, and free of tension, verbal fencing. It was a relief to be herself, not to be constantly on the defensive as she so often was with Jim.

Shane made her jump, when he said, 'Now, how about that walk?'

Sitting up, she covered her mouth with her hand, yawning repeatedly. '*Sorry.* I feel so sleepy. Do you mind if we scrap the walk for today?'

He stood near the sofa, hovering over her. 'No. I'm wacked myself, I was up at the crack of dawn.' He did not add that he'd hardly slept, knowing she was in the room opposite his, so near and yet so far removed from him. He had wanted her very much last night, had longed to hold her in his arms. He said, 'Why don't you have a nap?'

'I think I will. But what are you going to do?'

'I've a few more chores, a couple of phone calls to make, and then I'll probably do the same.'

She settled back against the cushions, smiling to herself as he went out, whistling under his breath. As she half dozed she remembered she had not yet tackled him about his behaviour over the last eighteen months. Oh there's plenty of time, all weekend, she thought. I'll do it another day. Something stirred at the back of her mind. It was an incomplete thought and it slid away before she could fully grasp it. She sighed contentedly, felt herself being enveloped by the music and the warmth. Within seconds she was fast asleep.

CHAPTER 35

It was one of those evenings which, right from the outset, was destined to be perfect.

A few minutes before seven, Paula came downstairs looking for Shane.

She was dressed in a light wool caftan which Emily had made for her. It was a deep violet colour, simply styled, loose and floating, with unusual butterfly-wing sleeves that buttoned tightly at the wrists. With it she wore a long strand of lavender jade beads, another gift from Emily, who had bought them for her in Hong Kong.

Paula found Shane in the main room. He stood by the huge window, looking out.

She noticed that he had lit the many candles they had scattered around earlier, and set up a bar on one of the small chests.

The fire blazed in the hearth like a huge bonfire, the few lamps he had turned on glowed rosily, and the voice of Ella Fitzgerald singing Cole Porter echoed softly in the background.

Walking forward, Paula said, 'I can see that there's nothing for me to do but sit down and have a drink.'

Shane swung around. His eyes swept over her.

As she drew closer he saw that she had stroked purple shadow on her lids, and because of this and the colour of her dress, those uncanny eyes appeared to be more violet than ever. Shining black hair, brushed back and curling under in a pageboy, framed the pale face, accentuated its translucency. The widow's peak made a sharp indentation on her wide brow. It was dramatic. She was dramatic.

The strain had gone out of her face. He thought she looked more beautiful than she had in years. He said, 'You look nice, Paula.'

'Thank you – so do you.'

He laughed dismissively. 'You mentioned a drink. What would you like?'

'White wine, please.'

Paula remained standing near the hearth, observing him as he opened the bottle.

He wore dark grey slacks, a lighter grey turtle-necked sweater and a black cashmere sports jacket. Studying him, she thought: he's the same old Shane, and yet somehow he's not. He *is* different. Maybe it's the moustache after all. Or is it me? She instantly squashed this possibility.

He brought her the drink. She caught the faint whiff of soap and cologne. He was freshly shaved, his hair well brushed, his nails newly manicured. Paula bit back a smile, remembering how his habit of looking at himself whenever he passed a mirror had driven her grandmother crazy.

Emma had even threatened to have all of the mirrors removed from Heron's Nest if he did not curb his vanity. He had been eighteen that particular year and very conscious of his astonishing looks, his husky, athletic build. She suspected he was still most aware of his physical appeal, although he no longer gazed at himself in mirrors. At least, not publicly. Perhaps he had learned to accept his striking appearance. She turned to the fire to hide another smile. He *was* vain, even a little conceited about some of his attributes and accomplishments, and so very sure of himself. Yet there was an inherent sweetness in him, a gentleness, and he was loving to the core with friends and family, and so very kind. How well she knew Shane Desmond Ingham O'Neill.

Shane, pouring himself a scotch and soda, called across to her, 'Don't be surprised if Sonny brings his guitar. He usually does. I may accompany him on the piano – give everyone a treat. We might even have a sing song later.'

'Oh God, shades of The Herons!' Paula laughed. 'You really did stink, you know.'

'On the contrary, I think we were rather good,' he retorted, also laughing. He joined her. 'You and the girls were jealous because we stole the show that summer, were the centre of attraction. And you were envious of our smashing rig-outs. I'm surprised you didn't start a girls' band just to compete with us.'

She laughed again. He touched his glass to hers.

Paula stared up at him towering above her, feeling dwarfed by his six feet four inches, and suddenly weak, defenceless and decidedly female. There definitely was something irresistible about him. The weird feelings he had aroused in her last night began to stir. Her skin tingled. Her heart missed a beat.

Their eyes held.

Paula wanted to look away but his dark and piercing gaze was hypnotic.

Shane broke the contact, swiftly turning, making a show of searching for his cigarettes as he stifled the urge to kiss her. You must be careful, he told himself. He wondered if he had been wrong inviting her for the weekend. He knew he was skating on thin ice. I won't see her again while she's in the States. Inwardly he laughed. He knew he would.

A series of cheery hellos rang out. To his immense relief Sonny and Elaine walked in.

Shane hurried across the room to greet them, a huge grin surfacing. He was glad he had invited them. His tension eased.

After propping the guitar case against a chair, Sonny grasped his hand, embraced him, said, 'Cognac . . . for after dinner.' He handed Shane a bottle wrapped in fancy paper.

Elaine thrust a basket at him. 'And here's some of my freshly baked bread for your breakfast,' she exclaimed as Shane bent to kiss her cheek.

Shane thanked them, put the gifts on a chest, and brought the Vickers over to be introduced to Paula.

The minute she met them, Paula knew she was going to like the couple. Sonny was tall, lean and fair, with a blond beard and merry brown eyes. Elaine, softly pretty and feminine, was one of those women whose genuine sweetness is instantly recognizable. She had an open, friendly face, and her eyes were vividly blue, her short, curly hair prematurely silver.

The three of them sat down, and Shane went to make drinks for the new arrivals. Paula was glad she had chosen the caftan, even though Shane had told her to dress casually. Elaine was wearing black velvet trousers with a Chinese jacket of blue brocade and looked elegant in an understated way.

Smiling at her, Elaine said, 'Shane told us you're Emma Harte's granddaughter, and that you run her business now.

I'm crazy about your London store. I can spend all day there – '

'She's not kidding either,' Sonny interrupted, grinning at Paula. 'My wife and your store are going to bankrupt me one day.'

'Oh don't pay any attention to my husband, *he's* the one who's kidding,' Elaine said, and continued to rave about Harte's in Knightsbridge.

But when Shane came back with glasses of wine for Sonny and Elaine, the conversation turned to country matters and local gossip. Paula leaned back in her chair, listening quietly, sipping her drink. As the talk ebbed and flowed between Shane and his friends, she soon became aware of his liking for them, recognized how relaxed he was in their company. But then, so was she. They were easy to be with – warm, outgoing, very real and down-to-earth people. Sonny's wit was as quick as Shane's, although not quite as brilliant and astringent, and the two men were soon bouncing funny lines back and forth. There was a great deal of laughter and jollity in the air, and a festive mood prevailed.

After the first half-hour, Paula felt as though she had known this engaging couple for years. Individually each of them drew her out, encouraged her to talk about her work, the stores, and both of them were particularly interested in hearing about her famous grandmother. And she, who was generally reserved with strangers, found herself chatting away. She and Sonny discussed music and his composing, and Paula discovered that he had written several Broadway musicals as well as the background music for numerous Hollywood films. Elaine, in turn, talked about her writing career and her books. And she did so in a manner that was not only informative but amusing, especially when she recounted funny incidents which had happened to her when she was on promotion tours. She told a good story, and entertainingly so, and there was a great deal of laughter and bonhomie among the four of them.

Occasionally Paula stole surreptitious glances at Shane. He was a wonderful host, constantly up and down, taking care of the drinks, changing the records on the stereo, throwing logs on the fire, and steering the conversation around to different subjects, involving them with each other. And he was obviously delighted with the way the Vickers had warmed to her. He kept smiling across at her, nodding as if in approval, and twice when he passed her chair to do a small chore he squeezed her shoulder affectionately.

Paula had been out to check on the food once, and the second time she rose, Elaine also stood up.

'I'm letting you do all the work,' Elaine said, 'and that's not fair. I'm coming to help you.'

'Things are under control,' Paula protested.

'No, no, I insist.' Elaine followed Paula out to the kitchen, and as she came through the doorway, she exclaimed, 'Everything smells so delicious – my mouth's beginning to water. Now, what can *I* do?'

'Nothing really.' Paula smiled at her, bent down and took the meat out of the oven, placed it on to a platter. 'Well, there is one thing. Could you cover this with silver foil, please?'

'Consider it done,' Elaine said, tearing off a large piece of the silver paper, tucking it around the leg of lamb. She stood watching Paula, and after a moment, she said, 'It's a lovely evening. I'm so glad you're here. And you certainly cheer Shane up.'

'Do I really?' Paula swung to face Elaine, gave her a curious puzzled look. 'You make it sound as if he's been down in the dumps.'

'We think he has. Sonny and I worry about him a lot. He's so nice, generous, very engaging, and pleasant and charming. Still . . .' She shrugged. 'To be truthful, he's

558

always up here alone, never brings . . . friends, and there are times when he seems despondent, melancholy.' She shrugged again. 'Of course England is a long way off and – '

'Yes, I do think he gets a bit homesick,' Paula volunteered, pivoting, turning her attention to the oven again.

Elaine stared at Paula's back, her brow puckering. 'Oh but I didn't mean it that way – ' She stopped abruptly as Shane walked in, swinging the corkscrew in one hand.

He said, 'I think I'd better open the wine, let it breathe for a while.' He proceeded to do so, remarking to Paula, 'I suppose the meat has to stand and bleed for fifteen minutes or so, before I carve it. Well, I might as well hang around, keep you company.'

Elaine slipped out quietly, leaving them alone.

'It was a wonderful dinner,' Elaine said, putting down her dessert fork and spoon, looking across the table at Paula. 'And I'd love to have the recipe for this trifle. It was yummy.'

'And the recipe for the Yorkshire pudding,' Sonny suggested. He flashed his wife a sly but loving grin, added, 'And I know Elaine won't take offence when I tell you that her puddings come out like great lumps of soggy dough.'

Everyone laughed.

Paula said, 'I'll write them out for you tomorrow.' A smile of pleasure tugged at her mouth. 'You're both very good for my ego. I've never had so many compliments about my cooking.'

'That's not true,' Shane exclaimed. 'I've been giving you praise for years. You never pay attention to anything I say, that's your trouble,' he groused, but there was laughter on his face.

'Oh yes I do,' Paula shot back. 'And I always have.'

Chuckling, Shane pushed back his chair. 'I'd better retreat to the kitchen, make the coffee.'

'I'll assist you,' Sonny said, springing up, walking out after him.

Elaine sat back in the chair, studying Paula. How arresting and unusual her looks were. She wondered how old she was. Earlier, Elaine had decided she must be in her late twenties, perhaps even thirty. But now, in the soft candlelight, Paula looked much younger than that; her face held the vulnerability of a little girl's, and she was most appealing. Conscious she was staring rudely, Elaine said, 'You're a beautiful woman, Paula, and so very accomplished. No wonder he's miserable most of the time.'

Paula instantly stiffened, put down her glass unsteadily. 'I'm afraid I'm not following you.'

Elaine blurted out, 'Shane . . . he's crazy about you! It's written all over his face, and reflected in everything he says. What a pity you're so far away in England. That's what I was getting at earlier – when we were in the kitchen.'

Paula was stunned. She managed, 'Oh but Elaine, we're just old friends, childhood friends.'

For a split second Elaine thought Paula was joking, continuing the banter which had punctuated the good talk during dinner. Then she saw the horrified expression on Paula's face. 'Oh my God, I've said the wrong thing obviously. I'm so sorry. I just assumed you and Shane were having . . .' Her voice trailed off miserably.

Paula pushed back her sense of dismay. 'Please don't look so stricken, Elaine. It's all right, really it is. I understand. You've simply mistaken Shane's brotherly affection for me, read it to mean something else, something entirely different. Anybody could make that error.'

There was an awkward silence as the two women regarded each other. Both were at a loss for words.

Elaine cleared her throat. 'Now I've gone and spoiled a lovely evening . . . me and my big mouth.' Her expression was chagrined, apologetic. 'Sonny says my mouth's always open and my foot's always in it. He's right.'

Wanting to make her feel comfortable, Paula murmured softly, 'Oh please, Elaine, don't be embarrassed. I'm not. I like you, and I do want us to be friends. And look here, why wouldn't you jump to conclusions. After all, I am staying here with him, living under the same roof, and we are rather free and easy with each other. But then we grew up together, and we've been around each other all of our lives. There's a certain kind of naturalness between us, and it could easily be misinterpreted. But our relationship is not what you think.' Paula attempted a laugh, glanced down at her hands. 'I've just realized I'm not wearing my rings tonight, and we haven't discussed my personal life, so you couldn't possibly know that I'm married.'

'Oh well, then that explains everything!' Elaine cried, immediately flushing. She shook her head. 'There I go again . . . forgive me, Paula, my apologies. I'm saying all the wrong things tonight. I've probably had far too much to drink.'

Paula summoned another light, dismissive laugh. 'I think we ought to talk about something else, don't you? Shane and Sonny will be back at any moment.'

'Agreed. And please don't say anything to Shane . . . about what I assumed. He'll think I'm a real busy body.'

'Of course I won't say anything,' Paula reassured her. She rose. 'Let's go and sit by the fire.'

As the two of them walked across the floor, Paula slipped her arm through Elaine's companionably, said in a low voice, 'Try not to look so upset, so worried. Shane'll spot that straight away. He's very intuitive. It's the Celt in him, I suppose. When I was little I actually believed he could read my mind . . . he was always second guessing me in the most maddening way.'

Elaine merely smiled at this remark as she lowered herself into a chair. Although she had recovered some of her composure, she was cursing herself under her breath. How stupid she had been to presume they were having an affair. But who wouldn't think that . . . there *was* an intimacy between them, a kind of bonding; and Shane devoured Paula with his eyes, hung on to her every word. It was transparent that he was in love with her, no matter what Paula believed. And who's *she* kidding? Only herself. Well, self-delusion is a very human trait, Elaine thought, and stole a look at Paula, who sat in the chair opposite. Whether she knows it or not, she adores him. And not just as an old friend would . . . it's much more than that, more complex and it runs deeper. Still, perhaps she hasn't realized the extent of her feelings for him. And *I* ought not to have said anything. Elaine chastised herself again.

But a few seconds later, when Shane brought the tray of coffee to the fireplace, Elaine saw Paula's eyes instantly fly to his face, detected curiosity and a new and avid interest glittering in them. Elaine thought: Who knows, maybe I wasn't so foolish . . . maybe I've done them both a big favour by speaking out of turn.

Shane served the coffee. Sonny poured cognac, and ten minutes later he fetched his guitar and began to play. He was a classical guitarist and immensely talented, and the others sat back, captivated by his playing and his music, entranced by the magic he created for them.

Paula was only half listening. She was thankful not to have to make conversation. Her mind was in a turmoil. Elaine had stunned her, and much more than she had permitted the other woman to see. But the shock was receding and she tried to sort out her troubled thoughts.

She was positive that Elaine had simply misunderstood Shane's attitude, his behaviour towards her. On the other hand, what if Elaine was correct? Elaine had asserted that her marriage explained everything – meaning, of course, that it explained Shane's unhappiness, which they had apparently detected. Paula suddenly remembered the incomplete thought she had had that afternoon when she had been dozing on the sofa. She had been dwelling on the past few days, thinking that Shane was his old self, the way he was before her marriage. Something had clicked in her head, but then she had fallen asleep. Now that thought became whole, fully formed. *Shane had changed, had dropped her, the moment her engagement to Jim had been announced.* Why? Because he was jealous. That was the obvious explanation. How stupid she had been not to recognize this before tonight. But why hadn't Shane made it clear to her that he cared for her? When she was still free. Perhaps he had not understood that . . . until it was too late. It all made sense suddenly.

Paula leaned back in the chair, shattered by her conclusions. She closed her eyes, letting the music lap over her. She thought of Shane. He sat only a few feet away from her. What were his thoughts and emotions at this moment? Was he really in love with her? Crazy about her, so Elaine had said. Paula's heart clenched. And what about me? How do I feel about Shane? Am I unconsciously responding to vibrations emanating from him? Or am *I* in love with *him*? . . . Have I always been in love with him without knowing it? She tried to examine her innermost emotions, take stock of her feelings. She floundered.

They left at eleven forty-five.

Shane saw them out.

She knew what she was going to do.

Rising, she walked over to the chest, retrieved the bottle of cognac, carried it back to the fireside. She refilled their brandy balloons, placed the bottle in the centre of the coffee table, threw a couple of logs on to the fire.

Then she sat down on the sofa to wait for him.

A few minutes later she heard his step, glanced around as he came in. She smiled across the room at him.

Shane faltered, surprised to see her sitting there, holding

another drink. He frowned. 'Are you planning to stay up all night? I would've thought you'd be half dead by now. It's been a long day, you worked so hard in the kitchen. Shouldn't we go – '

'I just got a second wind!' she cried, cutting him off before he suggested they go to sleep. 'I'm having a nightcap. I've poured one for you. Aren't you going to join me?' When he did not reply she laughed gaily. 'Oh don't be such an old spoil sport, Shane.'

He hesitated fractionally. He was afraid of being alone with her. He had been much too aware of her this evening. His desire for her had flared time and time again. His emotions were near the surface. He had sunk a lot of booze. He suddenly wasn't sure whether he could trust himself with her. This thought instantly annoyed him. He wasn't a callow youth, out on his first date, itching to make a conquest. He was a grown man. And he was with the girl he had known all his life. Yes, he loved her. But she trusted him. He was a gentleman. And he could handle himself. Still, I ought to put an end to the evening now, he thought. He said, 'Well, just one for the road. I'd planned for us to go riding tomorrow morning – bright and early.'

He strolled over to the fireplace, striving to appear offhand. He reached for the drink she had poured, stepped away from the coffee table, planning to sit in the chair next to the hearth.

Paula patted the sofa. 'No, sit here, Shane, next to me. I want to talk to you.'

He tensed, looked at her alertly, searching her face. Her expression was neutral, placid even. It baffled him. She was usually much more animated. 'Okay.' He sat as far away from her as possible, squashed himself in the opposite corner of the sofa.

'Cheers,' Paula said, leaning closer, knocking her glass against his.

'Cheers.' Their hands accidentally touched as they lifted

their glasses. He felt a spark of electricity shoot up his arm. He pushed himself even further into the corner, crossed his legs. 'What do you want to talk to me about?'

'I'd like to ask you a question.'

'Go on then . . .'

'Will you tell me the truth?'

He eyed her, suddenly wary. 'It depends on the question. If I don't like it I might be evasive in my answer.'

She gave him an odd look. 'You and I always told each other the truth when we were children. We never dealt in lies then . . . I'd like it to be like that between us again.'

'But it is!'

'Not really, Shane.' She saw the surprise registering in his eyes. 'Oh yes,' she said, 'it's been like old times this week, I admit, but there has been an estrangement between us for almost two years. Please don't even try to deny that.' There, it was out at last. 'In fact,' she went on quickly, 'you've been cold and distant with me for the longest time. When I asked you about your remoteness, your absence from my life, oh ages ago now, you brushed me off with silly excuses. Pressure of work, travel, you said.' Paula placed her drink on the coffee table and stared hard at him. 'I never really believed you in my heart of hearts, and that brings me to my question.' She paused, her eyes stayed on his face. 'And it's this: what awful thing did I do to you, to drive you out of my life? *You* – my oldest and dearest friend.'

He stared back at her, unable to make any kind of response. If he told her the truth he would reveal himself, his real feelings. If he lied he would hate himself for doing so. Anyway, she was clever. She would spot the lie immediately. He swallowed, put his drink down, looked ahead at the fire, his face reflective. Better to be silent.

Neither of them spoke for a while.

Paula, her eyes fixed on him, knew suddenly what his terrible dilemma was. Oh my darling, she thought, open

565

your heart to me, tell me everything. Her love for Shane flowed through her, sweeping all else aside. She caught her breath in astonishment as she finally acknowledged her feelings. She longed to put her arms around him, to expunge the sadness on his face with her kisses.

The silence lengthened.

Paula said softly, 'I realize how difficult it is for you to answer my question.' There was only the merest hesitation before she finished, 'And so I will do it for you. You dropped me because I became engaged to Jim and then married him shortly afterwards.'

Still he did not dare open his mouth, afraid of giving himself away. So she had guessed. But exactly how *much* had she guessed. He blinked, continuing to focus on the dancing flames. He knew he could not let her see his face until he had wiped it clean of all emotion.

Eventually he half turned to her, said slowly, in a voice that was strangely hoarse, 'Yes, that's the reason I put distance between us, Paula. Perhaps I was wrong to do that. But . . . you see . . . I thought . . . that Jim would resent me, yes, and that you would too. After all, why would either of you want an old chum like me loitering on your doorstep . . .' He left the sentence unfinished.

'Shane . . . you're not telling me the truth . . . you know you're not, and so do I.'

It was the inflection of her voice that caught his attention, prompted him to swing his head. In the bright glow of the firelight the pallor of her face had acquired a curious luminosity, a pearly sheen. The violet eyes had darkened, burned with an unfamiliar look he could not fathom. He noticed a vein pulsing rapidly in her neck. She parted her lips as if to say something, but remained silent. *That expression in her eyes.* Again it struck him with unusual force. His desire for her raged through him. His heart thudded, an internal shaking gripped him. It took all of his self-control to remain seated, to stay away from her. Then

566

he knew what he must do – he must get up, walk out, leave her. But he found he could not move.

They gazed at each other.

Paula saw his love, no longer concealed, leaping out from his brilliantly black eyes. Instantaneously Shane saw her love fully revealed, saw the yearning on her face, the longing and desire that hitherto had been only his to disguise, to withhold.

The shock of recognition transfixed him.

And then with sureness, absolute certainty, they moved at precisely the same moment.

They were in each other's arms. Their mouths met. Her lips were warm and soft and they parted slightly, welcomed him. Their tongues grazed, caressed, lay still. He pushed her down on to the mound of pillows, his left hand holding the nape of her neck, his right smoothing her hair away from her face, stroking her cheek, her long neck. Her hands pressed into his shoulder blades, then moved up into his hair, strong and firm on his scalp. He began to kiss her as he had wanted to kiss her for so long, with passion and force, his mouth hard and demanding on hers, his tongue thrusting, their breath, their saliva, mingling. But unexpectedly his kisses became gentle, tender, as he moved his hand on to her breast. He held it firmly, then slowly stroked it until the nipple sprang up hard under his fingers. His heart was slamming against hers.

They pulled apart at last, their breathing laboured. He looked down into her face. His eyes impaled hers. She reached up, touched his face, traced one finger across the line of his long upper lip under the moustache.

Shane stood up, undressed rapidly, flung his clothes on to the chair. Paula did the same, and they came together on the sofa with urgency, their hands clutching at each other. He took her in his arms and held her tightly against his chest, kissing her face, her hair, her shoulders. Then he pushed himself up on one elbow, bent over her. How well he knew this body. He had watched it grow from infant to child to young woman. But he had never seen it like this – entirely naked, every inch of it exposed to him, waiting for him. He let his hand slide down over her high, firm breasts, on to her flat stomach, along the edge of her outer thigh, then her inner thigh, smoothing, caressing, touching every part of her until they came to rest on that soft black vee of hair that concealed the core of her womanhood. He covered it with his entire hand, moved his body so that he could rest his face against her thigh. His fingers seemed to move of their own accord, gently seeking, probing, learning her. And finally he brought his mouth down to join with his fingers in their tender exploration.

Shane felt her immediately stiffen. He stopped, lifted his head, stared up along the slender stretch of her body, met her widening eyes. She was watching him intently, her expression baffled, alarmed. He smiled. So much for her marriage. His way of loving her, giving her pleasure, was seemingly new, and most transparently so. This sudden insight, the thought of her inexperience, delighted and thrilled him. At least no other man had touched her thus.

Her tenseness increased. She tried to raise herself on her elbows, opened her mouth to speak.

He murmured, 'Be still, let me love you.'

'But you, what about you?' she whispered.

'What's a few more minutes after all the years I've waited for you.'

Paula fell back against the cushions, sighing lightly. She closed her eyes, let her body go limp, allowed him to do as he wished with her. Her senses were beginning to reel, not only from the suddenness with which they had come together, but from his passion and sensuality. The way Shane was kissing and touching every part of her was unfamiliar, erotic. With his knowledge, expertise and sensitivity he knew exactly how to arouse her fully. He excited her as she had never been excited before, and she opened

568

up to him uninhibitedly. Quiver upon quiver ran through
her as his mouth and fingers loved her with delicacy, then
fervency and always with consummate skill. They seemed
to transmit a scorching heat, struck the core of her being
with an exquisite sensation that she had never known had
existed until this moment. The heat was spreading, searing
her body. 'Oh Shane, Shane, please don't stop,' she gasped,
unaware that she had spoken.

He could not answer unless he stopped, and he could
not stop now. He was being carried along by her mounting
excitement. It matched his own. He was aroused as he had
never been, and her desire for him was thrilling, a powerful
aphrodisiac. He intensified his concentration on her, savouring the warmth of her, bringing her to the pinnacle of
ecstasy. He knew that any moment she would spasm. She
did and he lifted himself on top of her, joined himself to
her with a power and force that made them both cry out.
She clung to him, screamed his name. He brought his
mouth down hard on hers. She cleaved to him, her body
arching. They began to move in unison, their mutual
passion rising.

Shane opened his eyes. The room was brilliant with
light. And he who had so recently craved darkness now
wanted that light . . . blinding glittering light. He wanted
to see her face, catch every flicker of emotion that crossed
it, needed to know that it truly was she whom he was
loving. He pushed himself up, his hands braced on each
side of her, and she lifted her lids, staring into his face. He
stared back. He began to move again and with rapidity and
she followed his lead and not once did his searching eyes
leave hers. Suddenly he slowed the rhythm, wanting to
prolong their joining.

He suddenly understood that this went far, far beyond
mere sexual possession. He was possessing her soul, her
heart, her mind, as she was possessing his. She was his
dreamlike child of his childhood dreams . . . in his arms at

last . . . truly his at last. She belonged to him now. He held the world in his arms. The pain he had lived with ceased abruptly. His old life fell away . . . down . . . down . . . into a dark void . . . a new life was beginning . . . he was someone entirely new. He was a complete man . . . made whole as he came up . . . up into the blinding, blinding light where she waited in the centre of the radiance.

They were mesmerized by each other. Their eyes locked, became wider as their scrutiny intensified. They looked deeper, deeper still, endeavouring to convey the extent and strength of their emotions, and they saw into infinity, saw their own souls and each other's. And everything was made clear.

She is my life, he thought. *And oh the blessed peace of it.*

She thought: *There is only Shane. There only ever has been Shane.*

He started to move against her, slowly at first and then more urgently and without restraint. She matched him, was as unrestrained as he. Their bodies entwined. Their mouths joined. They became one.

As he felt his life's essence flowing through him into her, he cried out, 'I love you, I have always loved you, I will love you until the day I die.'

Shane's bedroom was much larger and more spacious than the one he had given her, but it was warm because the entire barn was centrally heated.

As in her room, a huge brass bed dominated the space. Paula now lay propped up against the mound of snowy pillows, a down comforter tucked around her chest, only her bare shoulders revealed. She sighed, filled with contentment and an extraordinary feeling of inner peace, and of completeness. The physical release she had experienced with Shane was wholly new to her. She had never achieved satisfaction before, and she marvelled at him, at herself,

570

and at their lovemaking. How unselfish and tender he was, and oh how she had responded to his emotion, to his yearning desire for her. And because of his genuine understanding of her, his caring, their loving had been natural, uninhibited, full of exultation and joyousness, a true bonding in every way.

When they finally doused the lights in the main room and crept upstairs carrying their clothes, she had believed their mutual passion was entirely spent. Exhausted, they had lain here in this great bed, their bodies touching, holding hands under the sheet, and they had not stopped talking. And then quite suddenly their desire for each other had flared unexpectedly, and they had made love for the second time with the same urgent need and breathlessness.

Shane had turned on the lamp, thrown back the bed-clothes, telling her he must look at her, know that it was really she, must witness the emotions he was evoking in her. The kissing, the touching had been unhurried and voluptuous, and again he had brought her to that blissful state of fulfilment before taking her to him, and had led her into new regions, murmuring what he wanted, showing her how to excite him further, love him as he had loved her. And she had done so willingly, lovingly, taking pleasure from his pleasure. But he had stopped her when he was on the brink, and pulled her on top of him, his body thrusting upward to join with hers. And together they had reached greater heights of rapture than the first time.

Shane had finally switched off the lamp, and wrapped in each other's arms they had tried to sleep but it had eluded them both. They were too keyed up and conscious of each other, needed to prolong their new-found intimacy. And so they had begun to talk in the dark, and then a few minutes ago Shane had gone downstairs to make tea for them.

Paula leaned forward and glanced at the clock on the small campaign chest at his side of the bed. It was nearly four. We made love endlessly, she thought, but not mindlessly. Oh no, not mindlessly at all. She had not realized until tonight how beautiful the sexual union between a man and a woman could be. In fact she had always thought that sex was not what it was cracked up to be. How wrong she had been. But it has to be the right man with the right woman, she said under her breath. She sank into the pillows, another sigh escaping as she waited for Shane to come back.

He did so a moment or two later, carrying a laden tray and singing a popular song at the top of his voice.

'Who do you think you are? A pop star?' she cried, sitting up in bed, grinning at him.

His answer was to gyrate his body at her several times and leer in an exaggerated fashion.

He brought her the mug of tea and the plate of ginger biscuits she had requested, put his own tea and chocolate biscuits on his bedside chest. Continuing to hum the melody, he slipped off his robe, threw it across a nearby chair.

She looked at his broad back, massive shoulders and strong arms, and admiringly so. He was a big, well-built man, and she had seen him in swimming trunks for years. So why did his powerful physique seem so startling to her tonight? Because now she really *knew* him? Because she had learned about his body as he had hers and in the most intimate way?

As he swung around he noticed that she was staring at him.

'What's wrong?' he asked.

'Nothing. I was just thinking I've never seen you so brown.' She giggled. 'But you've got a white bottom.'

'And you too, madame, will have a brown back and a white bottom by this time next week.' He strode over to the bed, unself-conscious in his nakedness, and got in next to her, kissed her cheek. 'If I've got anything to do with it, that is.'

'Oh,' was all she said, gazing at him.

'Yes. I have to go to Barbados on Tuesday. Come with me, Paula.' His eyes appealed.

'Oh Shane, what a lovely idea. Of course I'll come with you.' Her face instantly dropped. 'But I couldn't get away until Wednesday.'

'That's all right.' He turned to get his mug of tea, took a sip. 'It'll give me a chance to do some of my work. Actually, I will have to spend some time every morning in the administrative offices. But we'll have the afternoons . . . and all those beautiful nights.' His smile was suggestive, his dancing black eyes wickedly teasing.

She said, with a small smile, 'I've been dying to go to Barbados – to see the Harte boutique.'

He lifted his brows. 'Ah ha, so that's why you agreed, and so readily. And I thought you were after my body again.'

Paula gave him a light playful punch on his arm. 'Oh you!' She drank her tea. It tasted good, hot and refreshing. And she felt good. No, wonderful. And filled with wonderment. She reached out, took a chocolate biscuit from the plate on his lap, munched it, then took another.

'I wonder what a psychiatrist would make of that?' Shane said.

'Make of what?'

'This constant desire of yours to eat off my plate. You've been doing it all of your life, and perhaps it has some hidden sexual meaning. Do you think it's a form of oral gratification, linked in some way to me and your feelings for me?'

She threw back her head and laughed, enjoying him, being with him. 'I don't know. And I'll try to stop doing it, but childhood habits are hard to break. As a matter of fact, very seriously, I've really got to curb my appetite. I haven't stopped eating since I've been with you. Anyone would think I've been on a starvation diet.'

Shane merely smiled, thought: You have, my darling, in more ways than you know.

They finished their tea and biscuits, continuing to chat about the trip to Barbados, and Shane was delighted she was so obviously thrilled and excited about the prospect of spending five days with him in the sun. At one moment Shane got out of bed, found his cigarettes and opened the window. 'You don't mind if I smoke do you?' he asked, climbing back into bed.

'Not at all.' Paula edged closer to him, so that their legs touched and their shoulders grazed, wanting the closeness of him.

'Happy, darling?' he asked, glancing at her through the corner of his eye.

'Very happy. Are you?'

'As never before.'

There was a short silence, then Paula confessed, 'I've never made love like that before.'

'I know you haven't.'

'Was it that obvious . . . my inexperience?'

He chuckled, squeezed her hand, said nothing.

She said, 'But you're *very* experienced, Shane.' She stole a look at his face. Jealousy, an unfamiliar feeling, trickled through her. 'You've had a lot of women.'

He was not certain if this last remark was a question or a statement. 'You've heard all the gossip about me and my romantic escapades over the years.'

'The stories were all true then?'

'Yes.'

'Why not me, Shane?'

'That's fairly obvious, easy to answer . . . because of Emma and Blackie, their relationship, the closeness and involvement of our two families. But even if I'd understood my true feelings for you, Paula, I wouldn't have dared come near you, tried to make love to you. I'd have been skinned alive, and you know I would.' He thought of Dorothea Mallet's words, added, 'Before your marriage, you were sort of — well, the crown princess of the three clans. And, therefore, inviolate. A man doesn't sleep with a woman like you, have an affair with her. He proposes marriage. Sadly, regrettably I didn't know that I wanted you desperately, or how I felt about you when you were available, unattached. I was too close to you, I suppose.'

'I understand.' She looked at his face. A feeling of possessiveness came over her, and the jealousy intensified. She asked softly, 'Those other women . . . did you make love with them the same way you made love with me tonight?'

He was momentarily startled by the question. He was on the verge of lying, not wishing to hurt or upset her, and then knew he should be honest. Opting for the cold truth, he said, 'Yes, sometimes, but not always, not with all of them. You and I made love in the most personal and intimate way there is, Paula. Most of my former girlfriends didn't arouse that kind of desire, that need in me — as you do. Oral sex is . . . well, *extremely* intimate, as I just said. I've got to be very emotionally committed to want that.' He half smiled. 'It's not something I have ever been able to do indiscriminately, Paula.'

She nodded. 'I think that it probably springs from the urge and the desire and the compulsion to totally possess the other person.'

'Oh yes, yes, it does.' He gave her a penetrating glance.

'Since you've been in New York — ' She paused, hating herself for prying, but she could not help it. She cleared her throat. 'Have you had a lot of affairs?'

'No.'

'Why not?'

'Because of you.' Shane drew on his cigarette, exhaled, said, 'My bedroom liaisons have been pretty disastrous ever since the day I understood that I loved you.' He turned his head, looked deeply into her eyes. 'Actually, I've had a lot of trouble in that direction . . . I've been impotent.'

He saw the surprise and dismay cross her face. She stiffened against him slightly, but she said not one word.

Shane went on, 'I managed to make it occasionally, if the room was dark and my partner did not shatter my fragile fantasy . . . my fantasy that it was you whom I was with. If I could hold the image of you in my mind, then it was all right. But for the most part it's been bloody difficult.'

Without mentioning names, he told her then about his experience in Harrogate the afternoon of the christening, and recounted other devastating incidents. He felt neither shame nor embarrassment talking to Paula in this most self-revealing manner. He was glad to unburden himself, and as he continued to speak he acknowledged that he was only following his old pattern of confiding in her, sharing his secrets with her as he had when they were children.

Once he had finished, Paula reached up, put her arms around his neck, held him close. 'Oh Shane, Shane darling, I'm so sorry I caused you such pain and heartache.'

He stroked her head, pressed it closer to his shoulder with one hand. 'It was hardly your fault.' He then asked softly, 'When did you discover how you felt about me?'

'I've been very conscious of you since I came to New York. Last night, then again this evening, the strangest feelings began to stir in me. I realized I desired you sexually, wanted you to make love to me, and I to you. Suddenly – when we were talking after Elaine and Sonny left – it dawned on me that I was in love with you.'

He did not speak for a few seconds, then he said, 'I didn't bring you up here to seduce you, Pau – '

'I know that!'

'I just wanted to be with you, spend time with you. I've

missed you very much.' There was a short pause. 'I've had a golden rule for years – no married women. I never wanted to take something that belonged to another man.'

'I believe I belong to myself,' she said.

Shane was silent. He was eaten up with curiosity about her marriage, and his jealousy of Jim was rife, but he was reluctant to embark on this subject, afraid of spoiling the mood that presently existed between them.

Paula remarked evenly, 'Surely you know I wouldn't be here with you like this, Shane, if I were happy in my marriage.'

'Jesus, Paula, of course I do! You're not promiscuous. I know you'd never play around just for the sake of it.' He scowled, eyed her closely through his narrowed gaze. 'It's not working then?'

'No. I've tried, Shane, God knows I've tried. I'm not blaming Jim. I think it takes two to create a disaster. I don't hate him, he's not a bad person. We're not right together, that's all there is to it. We're incompatible in every way.' She bit her inner lip. 'I'd like to leave it at that . . . for tonight anyway. All of a sudden I don't want to talk about my marriage.'

'I know, darling, I know.'

For a short while they were silent, lost in their own reflections. But eventually Paula murmured, 'Oh Shane, what a mess I've made. If only we could turn the clock back.'

'Ah but that's not possible . . . and time is not so important, you know. And you mustn't think about yesterday or tomorrow, only today. Anyway, time isn't portioned out and then encased in little capsules – time is like a river. The past, the present, the future all flow together to become one long continuing and never-ending stream. We get echoes of the past every day of our lives, and we see images of the future as we live in the present. Time gone and time yet to come is all around us, Paula, and time is a dimension unto itself.'

She looked up into his familiar and well-loved face, and in her mind's eye she saw the man as he had been as a boy, recalled his preoccupation with the Celt in himself and his Celtic forebears and Celtic legend. That old dreamy look born of his mysticism filled his eyes, and his deep introspection was evidenced in his expression and she knew that he was lost somewhere in the far, far distant past. And then he blinked, gave her a funny little lopsided smile, one she remembered so well. The man instantly became that small boy at Heron's Nest and their childhood was all around them, encompassing them, filling this room. And she knew that Shane was correct in the things he had said about time being like a flowing river, and she reached out and touched his arm and told him this.

He said slowly, thoughtfully, 'And there's another thing, Paula. Life has its own intricate pattern – there is a grand design, really. What has already happened in our lives was meant to happen, perhaps to show us the way, lead us to each other. And the future is already here with us, *now*, at this very moment, whether we're aware of it or not.' He put his hand under her chin, lifted her face to his, looked deeply into her eyes. 'And we're not going to think about anything except this weekend. We'll take each day after that as it comes.' He leaned into her, kissed her lightly, drew back. 'Don't look so serious. Life has a way of taking care of itself and I have a feeling that we are going to do just fine together.'

Her throat tightened with a rush of emotion. She clung to him, whispered, 'I love you so much, Shane. How could I have ever not known that!'

'You do now, and that's all that matters, isn't it?'

CHAPTER 36

She arrived in Barbados on Wednesday afternoon.

As she walked out of customs, carrying her suit jacket over her arm and clutching her travelling bag, she thought that he had not come to meet her after all. Disappointment replaced anticipation. She looked around seeking a chauffeur or someone wearing the uniform of the Coral Cove Hotel whom he may have sent in his place.

The porter trailing behind her, carrying her large case, asked if she wanted a taxi. She explained she was expecting to be met, then peered again at the blur of people crowding the busy airport entrance.

Paula saw Shane before he saw her.

He came barrelling through the main glass doors, looking anxious. She stood stock still, taut with excitement. Her heart began to clatter unreasonably. She had been with him on Monday night. Two days ago. But seeing him now was a shock. Every detail of his appearance leaped out at her, as though she was observing a total stranger, someone she did not know. His wavy hair, longish and curling down on to his neck, the well-defined brows and the distinctive moustache all appeared blacker and his brilliant eyes were like pieces of onyx in his tan face. Even the cleft in his chin seemed more pronounced. She saw that he wore a beautifully cut cream silk suit, a cream shirt with fine burgundy stripes and a burgundy tie. A silk handkerchief of the same wine colour flared in his breast pocket. His brown loafers gleamed. He was immaculate from head to toe. But he was the same old Shane. It was she who was new. The new Paula who was in love with him. He was the only man she wanted.

Finally he spotted her and pushed through the crowd,

purposeful, confident. He was there, towering above her, grinning, his eyes filled with laughter.

She felt weak at the knees.

'Darling,' he said, 'I'm sorry. I cut it fine, as usual.'

She could not speak, just stood there, smiling up at him inanely.

He bent to kiss her cheek, and then took her arm, motioned for the porter to follow them, bustled her outside.

A chauffeur leaning against the hood of a silver-grey Cadillac sprang forward, opened the passenger door, stowed the suitcase in the trunk. Shane tipped the porter, helped her into the car, climbed in after her. He pressed a button. The glass partition behind the driver's seat closed. As the car slid noiselessly away from the kerb he put his arm around her, tilted her face to his. He stared at her, as if he had not seen her for years. She stared back, saw her own reflection mirrored in his glistening black eyes. Her mouth went dry as he bent towards her. And as his tongue slid past her parched lips to touch hers, blood rushed through her. She felt dizzy. His grip on her tightened. Her arms went around his neck. Her hands slipped up into his thick hair. She knew he was terribly excited. But then, so was she.

Shane held her away from him, shaking his head, half laughing. 'I think I'd better exercise a bit of restraint here, otherwise I'll end up making love to you on the back seat and that *would* cause a scandal.' He held her eyes. He seemed unexpectedly amused at them both. 'You do get me hot and bothered, lady.'

'It works both ways, you know.'

Smiling, he lit a cigarette, asked her if she had had a good flight, and then began to talk effortlessly about the island, pointing out interesting landmarks, giving her a brief history of Barbados. For the next half-hour or so he talked incessantly, reached out to squeeze her hand from time to time.

'Coral Cove is on the west side of the island,' Shane was saying. 'It's not far from the Sandy Lane Hotel, which we'll be passing in a few seconds. I'll take you there to lunch one day – it's a lovely spot. Anyway, our place is located in the area known as the Platinum Coast, so called because of its sandy white beaches. I hope you're going to like it.'

'Oh Shane, I know I will, but I'd be happy anywhere with you, darling.'

His eyes instantly swivelled to hers. 'Would you really, Paula?'

'Yes, Shane.'

'Love me?'

'Madly.'

'You'd better.'

'And you?'

'I'm crazy about you, darling. So crazily, overwhelmingly in love with you I'll never let you go,' he replied, his voice light. And then he took hold of her hand tightly and his expression and his voice changed. 'I mean that, Paula. I won't let you go. *Never.*'

Startled, she swallowed, not knowing what to say. England and her life there, momentarily forgotten in her euphoria at being with him, loomed hideously. She met his piercing gaze, said haltingly, 'There're a lot of prob – '

He covered her mouth with his large, sunburnt hand, shook his head. 'Sorry, darling, I shouldn't have said that. At least, not now.' He gave her his cheeky, boyish grin. 'We're not going to even think about problems, never mind talk about them, for the next few days. There'll be plenty of time for that when we're back in New York.'

And before she could reply the car was slowing down. The chauffeur turned in through iron gates and as the Cadillac swept on she caught a glimpse of the name Coral Cove. A moment later, at the end of the short driveway, they came to a standstill in front of the hotel.

The intense heat hit her as Shane helped her out of the air-conditioned car. She looked around. Coral Cove was larger than she had expected, painted white and pale pink on the outside. She could see it was set in the middle of lush, exotic gardens. Just beyond the edge of the green lawns lay a stretch of silver sand and the turquoise ocean glittering in the sunshine.

'Oh Shane, it's beautiful,' she exclaimed as he looked at her expectantly, his eyes eager.

He nodded, took her elbow. 'I think so — and thanks. But come on, it's bloody hot outside at this time of day.'

He led her through the spacious, airy lobby, washed in white and furnished with rattan pieces and immense tropical plants in ceramic tubs. Ceiling fans whirred pleasantly, creating a gentle breeze and the ambience was cool, shady, welcoming.

Even though she wanted to stop and look around, Shane would not permit her to linger.

He whisked her smartly up to the suite, and once they were inside he pulled her into his arms roughly, began to kiss her, his hands hard on her body. Paula clung to him, returned his kisses. A loud rapping on the door interrupted this moment of intimacy, forced them apart.

Shane called, 'Come in, Albert,' and hurried forward to take her suitcase from the bellboy.

When they were alone, Shane said, 'All this kissing's going to lead to something else any minute. And since I don't want you to think I'm a sex maniac I'm going to show you around.' He drew her into the centre of the room. 'Listen, I've got a whole programme mapped out for you. Sun and sleep.' The impudent grin flashed, as he went on, 'And Shane. Lots and lots of Shane. Day and night, non-stop. How does that sound to you?'

'Scrumptious,' she said laughing. 'And so is this suite.'

'I knew you'd like this particular one, Paula.'

She glanced about with pleasure, noting the coral and

lime accents highlighting the cool whiteness of the room, the handsome wicker furniture, the comfortable sofas covered in a pretty floral fabric.

He had filled the room with masses of flowers. Bowls and bud vases held all manner of exotic blooms that were a blaze of stunning colour. 'Shane . . . the flowers . . . they're beautiful.' She smiled at him, reached out to touch a delicate purple spray. 'Just exquisite. Thank you.'

'Those are miniature orchids . . . wild orchids. But most likely you know that. They grow all over the island. Come on, let me show you the bedroom.'

He propelled her through the open door and she found herself standing in another large white room, this one accented with yellow and pale blue. The furniture was of white-lacquered wood; there was a big bed, curtained in white muslin, which faced out towards the terrace that ran the length of the suite. More flowers abounded here, but something was missing, and as her glance swept from wall to wall she realized that the bedroom, like the living room, looked curiously unoccupied. It had an unlived-in air.

She turned to him. 'Do you have another suite for yourself, Shane?'

'Yes, the adjoining one. I thought it was more discreet.' He smiled wryly. 'Not that anyone will be deceived – hotel staffs are notorious for knowing everything that's going on.' He took a key out of his pocket, opened a door, motioned her to follow him.

His suite was similar to her own, but here his possessions were strewn all over; his briefcase was on a table, a yellow sweater was thrown across the back of a chair; papers and his work littered the small desk; a bottle of scotch, an ice bucket and glasses were arranged on a tray on a white wicker console.

'Then why bother to have another suite, if that's the case,' she asked. 'I mean, our families would never be suspicious of us – we're supposed to be like brother and sister.'

'Then if this is incest, give me incest any time.'

She laughed.

He sobered, added, 'But you never know . . . I think it's wiser . . . just for appearances' sake, the switchboard, and the hotel register. Let's not borrow trouble unnecessarily. I've instructed the switchboard to monitor all calls. For both of us. That way we won't be taken off guard.' He put his arm around her, walked her through to her suite. 'Don't fret, I've every intention of staying in here with you. All the time. Now, do you want to freshen up, have a drink or a cup of tea? Or would you like to pop down to see the boutique?'

'Oh Shane, let's do that.' She gave him a studiously prim look. 'After all, that's the real reason I came to Barbados.'

'Rat.'

The Harte boutique was situated on the far side of the main garden nearest to the hotel. It was the central building in a semi-circle of five shops which looked out on to a grassy lawn. Here a fountain played in the centre. Flower beds added bright splashes of colour around the edge of the smooth clipped lawn.

A feeling of excitement trickled through Paula. There it was, the familiar and distinctive lettering that read *E. Harte*, staring out at her above the bright pink door. The large windows on either side were well-dressed, eye-catching, most professionally done.

She grabbed Shane's arm. 'I know it's only a boutique, and nothing like our large department stores, but I feel so proud, Shane. Here we are – in the Caribbean! Harte's has another branch. I do wish Grandy could see it, she'd be as thrilled as I am.'

'Yes, she would, and I know what you mean. It's a

combination of things — pride of ownership, gratification, a sense of tremendous satisfaction. And don't forget, this is *yours*, Paula, as the other boutiques in our hotel chain will be.'

'Merry thought of the idea, Shane, not I.'

'You did all the work.'

'Not according to Sarah.'

'I told you last week to forget Sarah Lowther. She's jealous of you.'

'Because I'm running the stores?'

'Yes. She's a nit-wit. She could never handle Emma's business, and Aunt Emma has always known that. She picked the best man she had . . . you.'

'If anybody else but you had said that, I'd accuse him of being a male chauvinist.'

'Sorry, you know I didn't mean it the way it came out. Just a figure of speech.' He gave her a pointed look. 'There's nothing masculine about you, my darling, let me assure you of that. Come on, let's go inside.'

He pushed open the door to the sound of tinkling bells.

Together they stepped inside and Paula caught her breath. The central area of the boutique was white with lots of chrome fixtures and the floor was made of white ceramic tiles. There was a paucity of clutter but this starkness made an ideal background for showing off the colourful clothes and accessories. A small cantilevered staircase led to an upper floor. It was cooled by the many ceiling fans.

'Oh Shane, you've outdone yourself,' Paula exclaimed.

He gave her a delighted grin, turned to introduce her to Marianna, the manager, and the three assistants who worked for Harte's. Paula chatted to them enthusiastically as she was given a tour. The young women were all pleasant, outgoing, well informed about fashion, and Paula found herself warming to them as they showed her the various displays, gave her a run down on current sales, showed her the latest sales figures.

At the end of an hour, she said to Shane, 'I have to buy a few things. I simply didn't get a chance to pick up everything I needed at the New York store. But look, you don't have to wait. I can meet you back at the hotel.'

'Oh I'm in no hurry,' he said with a nonchalant smile. 'I haven't seen you since Monday night. You're not getting rid of me that easily. Besides, I may have something to say about the things you're going to buy.'

After trying on swim suits and other beachwear, and having received a nod of approval from Shane, Paula began to look at cocktail dresses. She threw a number of casual summer evening outfits over one arm, and then Shane joined her, picked out several items he liked. Handing them to her, he gave her a conspiratorial wink. 'What about these?'

Paula made a face. 'I'm not sure they're really *me*.'

'Yes, they are. Trust my judgement.'

Not wishing to cause a fuss in the shop, she took them from him. As a child and a young girl Paula had always striven to please Shane, to cater to his wishes, and she found this desire surfacing. It overcame her objections to the outfits he had chosen. All of the dresses and evening wear bore the Lady Hamilton label, and as Paula went back into the dressing room she could not help thinking of Sarah again. Shane was correct about her cousin. Instantly she dismissed Sarah from her mind, not wanting to spoil her lighthearted mood by dwelling on unpleasant memories of *their* last encounter. She tried one of the outfits on, and returned to the main area of the boutique.

As she swung around she suddenly liked her reflection in the long mirrored wall. He obviously did. He was nodding emphatically. He told her she looked sensational.

Paula stood in front of the glass, studying the dress. It was short, made of the deepest blue chiffon and was simply

586

styled, with only one shoulder and a ruched effect over the bodice. If it lacked the hard-edged chic she usually favoured, it was flattering, feminine and curiously sexy in the way in which it clung to her body. It was a wholly new look for her, but the colour was glorious.

Shane enthused over a white silk trouser suit he had selected, but told her to forget the short red dress he had pulled off a rack. In the end she bought two of his choices, the blue and the white, and a long yellow shift made of silk jersey trimmed with violet ribbons. He waited patiently as she tried on sandals, settled on several pairs, and then picked up a couple of straw hats and added these to her purchases. After complimenting Marianna on the way she was running the boutique, Paula promised to visit them the following day.

They meandered around the semi-circle of boutiques, window shopping. Paula said, 'Our layout is stunning, Shane. Merry showed me the renderings, but one can never really tell from drawings. Thank you for making our boutique so special.'

'I'm notorious for pleasing those I love and adore,' he said.

Slowly they strolled back to the hotel. Shane could not help smiling as he noticed the way Paula's eyes swung from side to side, scrutinizing the many and varied tropical plants, flowering shrubs and unusual blooms indigenous to the island.

'Well,' he said, 'I'll know where to find you – if you're missing in the next few days. Did you pack a trowel?'

'No, and it's odd, Shane, I have no desire to do any gardening.' This was true and she was surprised at herself. She glanced up at him. 'All I want is to be with you.'

He put his arm around her shoulder, kissed the top of her head. 'So let's go up to the suite, shall we?'

She lay within the circle of his arms.

The bedroom was dusky, shadow filled. The filmy muslin curtains around the bed stirred gently in the soft breeze, and beyond the open louvered doors leading out to the terrace the sky had turned to a deep pavonne blue. The only sounds were the rustling of the palm trees and the faint distant roar of the ocean.

The bosky stillness was soothing after their frantic and impassioned lovemaking, and she luxuriated in it, and in her own sense of fulfilment. How surprising she was with him. Whenever they made love she felt completely satiated as they drew apart, exhausted, staring in astonishment. But the minute Shane was aroused again, so was she, and her feverishness echoed his. And each time he took her they reached a greater pitch of excitement and the ultimate in gratification.

A tiny sigh of contentment trickled through Paula. She could no longer recognize herself. Only a few days of loving Shane . . . being loved by him . . . and she would never be the same woman again. Shane had somehow helped her to shed her old self. He had recreated her. And in so doing he had made her his.

On Monday and Tuesday she had worked frantically to be able to leave for Barbados today. She had raced between the apartment, the store and Harte Enterprises, and had worked until three in the morning on Tuesday. He had rarely been out of her mind, and whatever she was doing he insinuated himself into her thoughts. Their relationship had reverted to what it had been when they were growing up. With added dimensions – sexual adoration and a deep abiding love, that of a man for a woman, a woman for a man.

There were no jarring notes or irritating habits to contend with. Shane was a communicator. He venerated the language, verbalized everything that came into his fertile, agile, searching mind. And he never shut her out. He shared, confided, never ever withheld. She did the same. His secrets were her secrets now. Hers had been conveyed to him and in explicit detail. His responses, his thoughts and his understanding were her great consolation. He made her feel whole, and completely female. A total woman.

She stole a look at his face. It was in repose. He drowsed. Her heart filled. What a mixture he was – impetuous, extravagant, and vain in some ways. Yet he was intelligent, tender, loving, thoughtful and passionate in everything he did. There was that strangely fey, mystical side to his nature which she knew sprang from the Celt in him, and he could be melancholy and brooding at times. And yes, he had a terrible temper. In the past they had had their violent quarrels. As a child she had often been the victim of his whims and moods and temperamental outbursts. But Shane was flexible, and he could disarm and enchant her with his self-deprecating humour, his dry wit, and his sweeping natural charm. As a man he was as complex as she was as a woman.

Suddenly she endeavoured to evaluate their relationship as it stood at this moment. It was so unusual she could think of no way to describe it to herself. And then she thought: Shane and I have an intimacy of the heart and mind as well as the body. Together we are complete. I feel more married to Shane than I do to Jim.

She held herself very still, appalled at this thought. Gradually she eased herself back into it, and acknowledged that it was the truth. Her mind swung to Jim.

Why did you marry him? Shane had asked her the other night in New York. *Because I was in love with him*, she had responded. Shane had admitted that she probably had been, but he had also suggested that Jim's fatal attraction might have been his name. *A Fairley was forbidden to you because of Emma's past*, Shane had ventured, and possibly he was right. She *had* believed herself to be in love with Jim, and yet now she understood that her feelings for him had never equalled her tremendous emotional bonding to Shane. She and Jim were totally different; she and Shane were incredibly alike. And she had never known what sex was all about, had never really enjoyed participating until Shane had made love to her. She had told him this. He had said nothing, had simply sighed and held her more tightly in his strong and loving arms.

Her life, her responsibilities, the complications of her business and family intruded. Suddenly the future glared her in the face like a terrible spectre. She was frightened. What was going to happen to them? What would she and Shane do? Release the fear, fling aside these distressing thoughts, she told herself. For God's sake don't dwell on your problems now. You'll spoil the next few days if you do. Enjoy this time with Shane, enjoy being free, unfettered.

She nestled closer to him, slipped her arm across his stomach, let her fingers curl against his side, bent herself into the shape of his body.

Shane stirred, opened his eyes, looked down at her. He smiled to himself, his heart full of love and tenderness for her. His dreamlike child of his childhood dreams had become his dreamlike woman. Except that she was no dream. Paula was reality. His reality. His life. She had extinguished all pain, all hurt, all of the anguish in his heart and mind. And with her he could truly be himself, expose himself, warts and all, and in a way he had never been able to do with any other woman. There had been legions of women until two years ago. Too many really, and of too little quality. Now he belonged to Paula – as he always had in his soul and heart and his imagination. He would belong to her for the rest of his life. She owned him.

She opened her eyes, looked up at him, smiled. He smiled back, bent to kiss her, stroked her rounded breast, moved his hand down to nestle between her thighs. She reached out to touch him, knowing how much he took pleasure from the feel of her hand on him. Within the space of a few minutes they were both aroused, craving each other. Shane rolled on top of her, slipped his arms under her back, took her to him. He began to move against her slowly, looked down into her unnaturally blue eyes, marvelled at the joy that lit her face. He whispered her name, spoke his love for her, his heart leaping at her swift and ardent responses. He closed his eyes, as did she, and they lost themselves in each other and their love.

The jangling telephone bell pierced the silence.

They stopped, startled, snapped open their eyes, gaped at each other. 'Oh Christ!' Shane groaned. He disentangled himself, switched on the light, shot another look at her as she clutched his arm fiercely.

Sitting up, Paula exclaimed, 'Maybe I'd better answer it, since we're in my suite.'

'It's all right, don't look so alarmed. I told you the switchboard's monitoring all of our calls.' He lifted the receiver on the fourth ring. 'Shane O'Neill.' He paused. 'Thanks, Louanne. Put him through.' He covered the mouthpiece with one hand. 'It's my father,' he said.

'Oh.' Paula tugged at the sheet, covered herself.

Shane began to chuckle. 'He can't see you lying here naked, you know.'

She had the good grace to laugh. 'But I feel funny. Exposed.'

'You'd better be – to me,' Shane said, then shouted into the phone, 'Dad! Hello! How are you? What's up?' As he began to listen, he cradled the phone between his ear and his shoulder, lit a cigarette, shuffled himself up against the pillows.

'Well, I have to admit I've been expecting it, Dad, and let's be honest, the idea does have a lot of merit. But look here, I can't go over there right now. Certainly not until January or February. I've got my hands full in New York. You know the hotel's at the most crucial stage. It would be disaster if I left. And I thought you wanted me down here in the islands over the holidays. Jesus, Dad, I can't be in two or three places at once.'

Shane flicked his cigarette ash, relaxed against the pillows, listening once more. 'Oh good,' he interrupted. 'Yes, yes, I agree. And you'll enjoy the trip. Why don't you take Mother with you?'

Paula slipped out of bed, found her dressing gown in the bathroom, slipped it on, returned to the bedroom. She began to pick up their clothes which were scattered all over the floor. We were in a terrible hurry when we first went to bed, she thought, then sat down on a chair, watching him.

Shane, silent again, winked at her, blew her a kiss, then again he interrupted his father. He exclaimed, 'I say, Dad, Paula's just this minute walked in and she wants to say hello.'

Paula shook her head. She felt ridiculously – and irrationally – self-conscious.

Shane put down the phone and his cigarette, leaped out of bed, grabbed her and dragged her to the phone, whispering, 'He doesn't know we've been making passionate love for the last two hours, you silly thing. It's only seven-thirty here. I'm sure he thinks we're having drinks before dinner.'

Paula had no option but to take the phone. 'Hello, Uncle Bryan,' she said in the most normal voice she could summon. Then she fell quiet, listening to Shane's father. 'Oh yes,' she said after a moment, 'I got in this afternoon. The hotel's simply beautiful, so is the boutique, Uncle Bryan. Shane's done a marvellous job. He's very talented. I'm most impressed.' She sat down on the bed, as Bryan commenced to relay his news from London.

Eventually, Paula had a chance to reply: 'Then you'll be seeing Grandy before me. And Uncle Blackie. Do give them both my love. And lots of love to Aunty Geraldine and Merry. See you soon, Uncle Bryan, and have a safe trip. Here's Shane again.'

He took the phone from her and she lolled across the end of the bed. Shane resumed his business conversation with his father, but after only a few minutes, he said, 'All right, Dad, that's it then. I'll be here until Monday morning, after that you can get me in New York. Love to Mother and Merry, kiss little Laura for me, and take care of yourself. And listen, don't forget to give my love to Grandpops and Aunt Emma. Bye, Dad.'

Shane hung up, looked at Paula, rolled his eyes. They burst out laughing. 'Come here, you witch, you,' he exclaimed, dragging her up from the end of the bed, wrapping his arms around her.

She struggled with him, still laughing and rumpling his hair. They rolled over and over on the bed, their merriment accelerating. He gasped, 'My father certainly picks the wrong time to call, doesn't he? Just as we were about to have another few minutes of lovely passion.'

'Few minutes!' she shrieked. 'More like an hour, you mean.'

'Are you complaining or is that a testimonial?' He kissed her ear, chuckled again, mimicked her, saying, 'Shane's done a marvellous job, Uncle Bryan. He's very talented. I'm most impressed.' Reverting to his own voice, he murmured against her neck, 'I sincerely hope Shane's done a marvellous job, that he's talented, and that you're truly impressed, sugar.'

'Oh you!' She beat her fists lightly against his chest. 'You vain conceited impossible gorgeous man!'

He caught her wrists, held them tightly in his hands, peered down into her face. 'But oh how that man loves you, darling.' He released her suddenly, sat up.

Paula did the same. She said, 'Imagine Blackie deciding to buy a hotel in Sydney. I'll bet you anything that that grandmother of mine was goading him on.' She gave him a long look. 'Uncle Bryan wanted you to go to Sydney, didn't he?'

'Yep. Grandfather hasn't actually bought the hotel yet. That's why he wants either Dad or me to fly there immediately, give it the once over. What I said's true, Paula, I can't get away. I'm jammed. And you don't think I'm going anywhere while you're still in New York, do you? It'll do Dad good to get away for a week or two. He said he might fly back to New York with Blackie and Emma early in December. But we'll see. I hope he takes my mother along, they'll have a good time.'

Shane kissed the tip of her nose. 'I'd better go and shower, get dressed, wander downstairs, check up on a few things.'

He sprang off the bed, pulled her to her feet. 'Would you mind meeting me downstairs when you're ready?'

'No, of course not. Where will I find you?'

'How long will it take you to dress?'

'About three-quarters of an hour.'

'By then I'll be waiting for you in the bar off the main lobby. You can't miss it – it's called The Aviary.' He chucked her lightly under the chin. 'I would've called it The Birdcage, but I didn't want to be accused of stealing someone else's idea.'

At Shane's twenty-fourth birthday party, early in June of 1965, Emma had made a comment to Paula. She had said that he had an intense glamour. Paula had not understood exactly what her grandmother had meant four years ago. She did now.

Paula was poised at the entrance to The Aviary, viewing him with unprecedented objectivity. He was at the far end, stood leaning with one elbow on the bar, one foot resting on the brass rail that encircled the base of the bar.

He was wearing black linen trousers, a black voile shirt and a jacket of silver-grey silk. Although he was tieless, he nevertheless looked extremely well dressed, as impeccably groomed as usual. But the aura of glamour her grandmother had spoken about had little to do with his clothes, as Paula was realizing as she continued to study him unobserved. It emanated from his height and build, his natural good looks, and the force of his personality. He was in command of himself – and this room. And he has abundant charisma, Paula thought. That's what it is, and it's the kind that every politician in the world would give his eye teeth to possess.

Shane was talking animatedly to a couple, obviously guests of the hotel, his face alive, expressive. The woman was entranced, hanging on to his every word. But then, seemingly so was the man who accompanied her.

Shane happened to swing his head. He saw Paula, straightened up, excused himself graciously.

The bar was fairly busy and as they walked towards each other Paula was aware that more than one pair of female eyes followed his progress.

'I'm glad you wore the blue dress,' he said, catching hold of her hand when he reached her side. He led her swiftly to a reserved table in the corner. 'It looks wonderful on you. You look wonderful.'

Her radiant smile, her shining eyes conveyed her pleasure and her thanks.

He said, 'I thought we'd have champagne, since it's a celebration.'

'What are we celebrating?'

'Finding each other again.'

'Oh Shane, that's a lovely sentiment.'

A waiter appeared, opened the bottle which already stood on the table in an ice bucket, poured a little into Shane's glass. He tasted it, nodded, 'It's perfect, Danny. Thank you.'

'You're welcome, Mr Shane.' The smiling waiter filled their glasses, quietly moved away.

'To us,' Shane said, raising his glass.

'To us, Shane.' After a few seconds Paula's eyes roamed around the bar discreetly, taking in the decor. 'I can see how this spot acquired its name . . . it looks exactly like the café in the Leeds store.' Her expression was teasing.

'Our birdcages aren't half as nice as yours though.' He grinned at her. 'Mind you, the artist did a good job with the murals. I must admit I do love exotic birds.' His eyes swept over her suggestively.

Paula laughed at the innuendo.

Shane moved in his chair, reached into his pocket for his cigarettes. His shirt was partially open down the front and she suddenly caught the gleam of gold against his suntanned chest. She peered at him. 'Goodness, is that the St Christopher medal I gave you?'

He looked down, fingered it. 'The very same.'

'You haven't been wearing it though – before tonight.'

'I haven't worn it for a couple of years. I found it in the flat on Monday night when I was packing. The catch was broken. I brought it with me, had it repaired in Holetown. They just delivered it back to me half an hour ago.'

'I'm glad you're wearing it again.'

'Do you remember when you gave it to me?'

'When you were twenty. For your birthday eight years ago.'

'And what did I give you when you were twenty?'

'A pair of antique earrings.' She frowned, then laughed lightly. 'Did you think I'd forgotten, Shane O'Neill?'

'I was sure you hadn't forgotten. However, I bet you don't remember what I gave you when you reached the ripe old age of five.'

'Oh yes I do. A bag of blue marbles.'

He sat back, looking pleased. 'Correct. Which you promptly began to lose one by one. You cried so much I had to promise to buy you another bag. But I never did, and so – ' He put his hand in his jacket pocket. ' – Here's

596

the replacement. Sorry it's taken me so long to fulfil a boyhood promise.' He dropped a small opaque plastic bag in front of her.

Laughing, enjoying his mood and flirting with him, Paula picked it up, opened the bag, dipped into it. 'You are a fool, but a most adorable one – ' She stopped. A pair of sapphire-and-diamond earrings, beautifully cut and of superb quality, lay glittering in her hands. 'Oh Shane, they're absolutely exquisite. Thank you, thank you so much.' She kissed his cheek, added, 'But you're awfully extravagant.'

'So I've been told. Like them?'

'Like them! I love them. And most especially because they're from you.' She pulled off the gold studs she was wearing, slipped them into her silk evening purse, took out a small mirror and put on the sapphires. She glanced at herself, admiring the earrings. 'Oh Shane, they *do* look lovely on me, don't they?'

'Almost as lovely as those uncanny eyes of yours.'

She squeezed his hand. She was touched by the unexpected present, overwhelmed really. Her throat tightened. She recalled the gifts he had given her when she had been a child. He had always been uncommonly generous, saving his pocket money for months to be able to buy something special. And he had had a knack of giving her exactly the right thing – like the earrings tonight. For a reason she could not comprehend her eyes filled with tears.

'What's the matter, darling?' he asked gently, leaning across the table.

She shook her head, blinking. 'I don't know, aren't I silly.' She groped in her bag, found a handkerchief, blew her nose, gave him a watery smile.

He watched her silently, waiting for her to compose herself.

'I was thinking of our childhood,' she commenced after a few seconds. 'At the time, it seemed as if it would never end – all those lovely summers at Heron's Nest. But it did come to an end, just as those summers did.' Before she could stop herself, she added, 'As this will come to an end too.'

He put his hand over hers. 'Oh darling, don't be sad.'

'Our days here in the sun, this magic time . . . it's just a brief sojourn really, Shane.'

Squeezing her hand, entwining his fingers with hers, he said slowly, '*You* talk of endings . . . *I* think of beginnings. That's what this is, Paula. A beginning. Remember what I said about time? Well, this *is* the future. It's here. Now. All around us. Part of the flowing river of time.'

She was silent, her eyes resting on him, searching his face.

'I hadn't wanted to get into a discussion about the mess we've found ourselves in, Paula, at least not down here. But perhaps we'd better have a talk. Would you like to do that?'

Paula nodded.

The smile settling on his face was confident, very sure. 'You know how much I love you. I said in the car, earlier today, that I'd never let you go, and I won't, Paula. Our feelings for each other are too strong to be ignored. We're meant to be together for the rest of our lives. Do you agree?'

'Yes,' she whispered.

'Then it's obvious what you're going to have to do. You'll have to get a divorce so that you can marry me. You do want to marry me, don't you?'

'Oh yes, Shane, very much.'

He saw that her face had paled, and that her very bright supernaturally blue eyes had darkened with apprehension. 'Tell me what's troubling you, Paula.'

'You said I was intrepid when I was a child – but as a grown woman I'm not. I'm frightened, Shane.'

'What about?' he asked, his gentleness increasing. 'Come

on, let's have it. If anyone can chase your fears away, surely it's me.'

'I'm afraid of losing my children and of losing you.'

'You know that will never happen. The three of us will be with you always.'

Paula took a deep breath, plunged in. She said, 'I don't think Jim will agree to a divorce.'

Shane pulled back slightly, eyeing her askance. 'I can't imagine him taking that attitude. Not once he knows you want to end a bad marriage.'

'You don't know Jim,' she interjected, her voice tense. 'He's stubborn, and he can be difficult. I have a horrible feeling he's going to adopt an inflexible stance. I told you, he doesn't think there's anything wrong with our marriage. He'll use the children as a wedge, and especially if he thinks there's another man.'

'He's *not* going to think there's another man in your life,' Shane said quietly. 'I'll be the only man you're seeing, and nobody is going to be suspicious of *me*.' He attempted to laugh. 'Me, your childhood playmate!' His brows shot up. 'Come on, darling, don't be so gloomy.'

Paula sighed heavily. 'Yes, perhaps I shouldn't anticipate.' She shook her head. 'Poor Jim. I feel sorry for him actually.'

'I know. But you can't build a relationship on pity, Paula. There's no reward in that for either party. You'll start regarding yourself as a martyr and he'll sink under his humiliation. You'll end up genuinely hating each other.'

'I suppose you're right,' she admitted, seeing the truth in his words.

'I *know* I'm right. And look here, don't start feeling guilty either. That's another wasted emotion.' He tightened his grip on her fingers. 'And anyway you don't have one single reason to feel guilty, Paula. You've given your marriage your best efforts, done your damnedest to hold it together, from what you've told me. It simply hasn't worked. And so you must end it – for Jim's sake as well as your own.'

Paula bit her inner lip. Her worry flared. Then she murmured, 'It may take me a while to work everything out, to get things settled properly.'

'I'm aware of that, these emotional situations are never easy. But I'll wait, I'll be a model of patience. I'll be there to give you moral support. And there's another thing, we're both young. We have all the time in the world.'

'Don't tempt providence, Shane!'

Shane shook his head, scoffed lightly, in amusement. 'I'm not, I'm merely stating facts.' Whilst he trusted her judgement, privately concurred with her assessment of Jim, he did not want to burden her further by acknowledging this. Not tonight. Instead he wanted to dispel her gloominess by making light of her worries. And so he produced his most assured smile, adopted his most engaging manner. He exclaimed, 'Let's make a pact – like we used to when we were kids.'

'All right. What kind of pact?'

'Let's agree not to discuss our problems, and they *are* mine as well as yours, for the next few weeks. Two days before you return to England we'll have a long session, thrash things out. Together we'll decide how you're going to proceed. What do you say?'

'Yes, it's a good idea. We mustn't let things get to us, must we? Otherwise we won't enjoy this precious time we have together.'

'That's my girl. Shall we drink to our pact? We've hardly touched this champagne.'

She nodded. He poured. They clinked glasses. Their hands automatically entwined.

His eyes were tender and warm as they rested on her. He said, after a while, 'You must trust me. Trust my love, Paula.'

She looked at him in surprise, remembering how her

grandmother had once said that it was important to trust love. As she met Shane O'Neill's dark and steadfast gaze, saw the depth and strength of his feelings for her, Paula's fears slowly began to evaporate. Her depression lifted.

'I do trust your love, and you must trust mine.' A small smile played around her mouth. 'Everything *is* going to be all right. It really is, Shane, because we have each other.'

But Paula was wrong. Her troubles were about to begin.

CHAPTER 37

Emma Harte stared hard at Paula, a frown knitting her brow. 'I'm not sure I'm following you,' she said. 'What exactly do you mean when you say Christmas is going to be difficult?'

Paula said quickly, 'Before I explain, I just want you to understand that he's all right actually – '

'Who's all right?'

'Jim, Grandy. I'm afraid he's had an accident. A rather bad accident, and he's – '

'Not in that plane of his?' Emma cried, and straightened up in the chair jerkily, her frown intensifying.

'Yes, he crashed. Two weeks ago. It happened a couple of days after I got back from New York, at the beginning of December,' Paula said in a rush. Wanting to allay her grandmother's worry, she hurried on, 'But he was lucky, in one sense at least, since the plane came down at Yeadon Airport. They were able to pull him out of the plane before it exploded in flames.'

'Oh my God!' Emma's hackles rose as she thought of Jim's narrow escape. He could so easily have been killed, and Paula might have been in the plane with him, might not have survived. Leaning forward, she asked in an urgent voice, 'How badly is he injured?'

601

'He's broken his right leg and his left shoulder, and his ribs are cracked. He's also badly bruised. But there are no injuries that are permanently disabling or life threatening. Obviously though, those he has sustained are serious enough.'

'No internal damage?'

'None, thank heavens, Grandy. Jim was rushed to Leeds Infirmary immediately, and he stayed there for five days, having all kinds of tests – neurological, what have you. Fortunately the doctors didn't find a thing. Every injury is external.' Paula paused, looked across at her grandmother. Worry ringed her face. She said, 'He's in two casts and his ribs are taped. I've had to hire a male nurse to look after him. You see, Jim can't dress himself and he finds it awkward, almost impossible, to do the most normal things.'

Emma exhaled, still reeling from the news. She exclaimed, 'Why on earth didn't you tell me about this when I was in New York? Or yesterday, when I arrived in London?'

'I didn't want to worry you when you were still on your holiday, and so far away. And last night you were so excited about being back I didn't want to spoil your homecoming and the little supper my mother had planned for you here. I'd intended to mention it on our way in from the airport but – '. Paula shrugged, gave her a small apologetic smile. 'I decided it could easily wait until today.'

'I see.' Emma sat back, shaking her head. 'I am sorry, Paula, this is just dreadful, simply dreadful. But we must be thankful it's not any worse, more serious than it is. He's going to be out of action for months, of course.'

'Yes,' Paula murmured. 'The casts have to be on at least six weeks. Then he'll have to have intensive physical therapy. The muscles will atrophy from lack of use. The doctor has explained that Jim won't be able to lift his arm or put weight on his leg until those dead muscles have been

602

built up again. It seems it'll be a good six months before he's back to normal.'

'Broken bones are a lot more serious than people realize,' Emma said quietly. She fixed Paula with a steely glance. 'And how did it happen?'

'The engine stalled. Jim tried to land as best he could, and thankfully he was on the approach to Yeadon airstrip. But – well, he couldn't control the plane. It plunged down, virtually broke in two when it hit the ground. He's been awfully lucky.'

'He has indeed.' Emma's mouth tightened. 'I always knew he'd have an accident in that damned plane one day, Paula. It's worried me to death.' She shook her head again, her dismay apparent. 'Whilst I'm upset and sorry that Jim's been hurt, I can't help feeling he's been somewhat irresponsible.' She gave Paula a long and careful look. Her eyes narrowed. 'He's a married man with two children, and he should not have been taking that kind of risk. Utter foolishness on his part. If only he'd given up that pile of junk when I asked him, this wouldn't have happened.'

'Well, Jim is inclined to be a bit stubborn.'

'That's the understatement of the year,' Emma snapped. 'I don't mean to sound callous or unsympathetic, but it strikes me he was putting himself in unnecessary physical danger. And why *I'll* never know. Perhaps that husband of yours will listen to me *now*. And I insist that we buy a corporate jet if we must have a plane in the family. I will not permit Jim to waltz around the skies in a flimsy light aircraft ever again. Oh no, not under any circumstances.' Emma leaned back in the chair, her face grimly set in its rigid determination.

'Yes, Grandy.' Paula glanced down at her hands, recognizing the implacability in that dear and familiar voice. Her grandmother was furious, and she could not blame her. Jim did lack a sense of responsibility and he had most wilfully ignored everyone's pleas to get a more stable, up-to-date plane.

Suddenly realizing she had sounded harsh, Emma said rapidly, in a softer tone, 'I expect poor Jim is in a lot of pain, isn't he, lovey?'

'Excruciating. The shoulder's driving him crazy. He says he's not sure which is the worst, the persistent nagging ache in the shoulder itself, or the cramp and stiffness from having his arm permanently bent in the cast. It's constricting, you know.' Paula winced, recalling the past ten days, knowing how much he was genuinely suffering. Once her initial shock and fright had subsided, exasperation with him had surfaced, only to be replaced by compassion. Being inherently kind, she was doing her utmost to make him as comfortable as possible. And she had shelved the discussion about a divorce. She would have to wait until he was in better physical condition to talk about her freedom.

Emma said, 'Surely the doctor has given him pain killers.'

'Yes and they help. But he says they make him feel doped up, woozy, a little out of it.'

'I hate pills myself. Still, if they ease the pain he ought to stay on them. I see what you mean about Christmas being difficult, Paula. Oh dear, this is such an added burden for you – on top of all of your work during one of our busiest seasons at the stores. Not only that, we have so many family things planned at Pennistone Royal . . . our traditional Christmas Eve with the O'Neills and the Kallinskis, lunch on Christmas Day, and Sally's wedding to Anthony – ' Emma cut herself short.

Her green eyes became thoughtful. An idea came to her and she made a snap decision. Taking command in her usual way, she exclaimed, 'Running back and forth between your house and mine is going to become the bane of your life, and transporting Jim hither and yon will prove tiring. I think you'd better move everyone in with me . . . Jim, the babies, Nora, and the male nurse. I've plenty of room and, in fact, I'd rather enjoy having you all with me after my eight-month absence.'

'Oh Gran, what a wonderful idea!' Paula cried, swamped with relief. 'And it's a marvellous solution.' A smile broke through as she confided, 'I've been panicky, wondering how I would ever cope.'

Emma laughed quietly, amusement flickering on her mouth. 'You'll always cope, my girl, that's your basic nature. But I don't see why your life shouldn't be made as easy as possible, since you carry enough responsibility to bury three people. Now that I'm back home, I aim to see to it that things run smoothly for you. You've had a rough few months, between business problems and all the family upsets.'

'Thank you, Gran. What a lovely thought, moving into Pennistone Royal, being with *you*. Why ever didn't I think of it?'

'I suspect you've had enough on your plate these past few weeks. I'm sure Jim is not a good patient . . . too active a man to be confined in this way. Is he getting around at all?'

'No. Ever since he came home from Leeds Infirmary he's been sleeping in his den, virtually living in it – he can't navigate the stairs, for one thing. He's awfully frustrated being disabled. Even more frustrated because he can't go to the paper. He misses it.'

'I'm sure he does. But he won't be able to go to work for a long time. No use fussing over that. Well, he certainly won't be able to manage the staircase at Pennistone Royal. It's too long and steep. But never mind. Hilda can turn the small parlour next to the dining room into a bedroom for him. Now, Paula, please try not to worry any more. What's done is done, we'll have to make the best of it.'

'You're right, Grandma, and moving in with you is going to make my life so much easier,' Paula said, thinking that

605

being surrounded by people was going to be a real blessing. Jim was becoming fractious because of the pain, his helplessness. He had started to complain about her work more vociferously than ever, forever grumbled about the hours she kept. And he was drinking more than he should.

Rising, Emma now walked across to the fireplace, stood with her back to it, warming herself. She and Paula were having coffee in the charming study of her Belgrave Square flat where they were both staying until they journeyed to Yorkshire the following day.

Paula glanced up at her grandmother, thinking how rested and well she looked this morning after yesterday's transatlantic flight. Emma wore a coral wool dress and pearls. Her silver hair was beautifully styled and immaculate and her makeup perfectly applied. There was a freshness and vitality about her. Paula thought: it doesn't seem possible that she is eighty years old. She looks ten years younger at least.

'You're scrutinizing me very intently,' Emma said. 'What's wrong with my appearance?'

'Nothing, Gran, and I was admiring you really. You're positively blooming this morning.'

'Thank you. I must admit to feeling marvellous. I'm not a bit jet-lagged.' She glanced at her watch. 'It's only ten o'clock. I'd better not ring Blackie just yet. He may still be sleeping. Bryan's driving him back to Harrogate later in the day, you know.'

'So Merry said last night at the airport.'

'It was nice having Bryan and Geraldine in Sydney for a couple of weeks,' Emma now volunteered with a smile of fond recollection. 'And they really enjoyed themselves. However, I was a bit disappointed that it wasn't Shane who came to negotiate the deal on the hotel they've bought.'

'From what Shane said to me, November was a difficult time for him.'

'Yes, Bryan mentioned it.' Flashing Paula a warm and

606

loving glance, Emma continued, 'I'm glad you were able to find time to pop down to Barbados to see our boutique when Shane was there. It did you good, seemingly. You're positively blooming yourself, Paula. You look better than I've seen you for years.'

'I enjoyed the trip, the little rest,' Paula said, keeping her voice very steady. 'I still have traces of my tan, so perhaps that's it.'

Emma nodded. She studied her favourite granddaughter. Paula has become as inscrutable as I am, she thought. I'm actually having difficulty reading her at this moment. Clearing her throat, Emma said, 'So . . . you and Shane are good friends again. I *am* happy about that.'

Paula made no comment.

Emma, riddled with curiosity, probed, 'And did he explain what it was all about finally?'

'Pressure of work, his schedule, his travelling, as he's always said, Gran. However, I do think he was afraid of intruding. . .' Paula met her grandmother's quizzical gaze with a cool, direct look of complete innocence. She added in a calm voice, 'You know what I mean – intruding on a couple of newlyweds. I think he was simply being diplomatic and considerate.'

'Really,' Emma said. A snowy brow arched. She did not believe his reasons, but she said nothing else, moved in the direction of the desk. Seating herself, she gave her attention to the three different folders Paula had arranged there earlier. Emma opened one, stared at the memorandum on top, but she was not actually reading it. Instead she was contemplating Paula and Shane. Ever since she had heard about their rapprochement, which was no great secret, she had wondered if Shane had finally made an overt move. She had never forgotten that look on his face at the christening. A man who loved a woman the way Shane O'Neill loved her granddaughter would be unable to repress his feelings indefinitely. He would have to come out in the

607

open. One day. He would not be able to help himself. Had he already done so? And if so, what had his reception been? She could not hazard a guess. Shane had been unreadable in New York, as Paula was now. She concentrated on Shane, whom she knew like one of her own, and thought of his nature. He was impetuous, impulsive, passionate. And what of Paula? Of course Paula would have spurned him. Would she? Yes, Emma answered herself. She is happily married. But is she?

Partially raising her eyes, Emma stole a look at Paula, surreptitiously, over the top of her glasses. There was something different about her granddaughter – she had noticed it last night. She seemed more womanly, more feminine than usual. Had there been a radical internal change? Or was it merely her outward appearance? The longer hair, the extra weight, the general air of softness she had acquired? Had a man's influence been at work? Shane's? Or was her current look simply a new style she had formulated for herself. I'm damned if I know, Emma thought. And I refuse to pry. Her life is her own. I will never interfere. I dare not. If she has anything to tell me she will do so . . . eventually.

Paula said, 'I asked Alexander and Emily to prepare those reports for you, Grandy, and I've written one myself. Each folder – '

'So I see,' Emma interrupted, glancing up. 'Are they simply summations of business matters over the past eight months? Or have you included anything I don't already know about?'

'Oh no, Grandy, we've simply recapped everything for you, the matters we telexed you about, or discussed on the phone. There's nothing new at the moment, but I thought you ought to have the reports just to refresh your memory. Later, at your leisure.'

'I don't have to refresh my memory,' Emma exclaimed dryly. 'I forget nothing. Thank you for going to all this trouble, though. I'm sure it goes without saying that I trust the three of you, and I'm very proud of you and your cousins. You've handled yourselves in the most exemplary manner, been extremely diligent, and, I might add, very smart in a number of instances.' Emma's eyes gleamed shrewdly under the hooded lids. 'And how's Gianni what's-his-name working out at Trade Winds?'

Paula could not help grinning at her grandmother's knowing expression. 'He's the best antique expert Harte's has ever had,' she said. 'And he's done a terrific job on his trips to the Orient recently. He's worth every penny we're paying him.'

'I sincerely hope so . . . presumably he's now giving Elizabeth the divorce without causing a scandal?'

'Yes, he is, Gran.'

'Alexander never did explain fully about that fuss and bother with his mother, when he rang me in Australia.' Emma's eyes sharpened. 'Who was Gianni going to cite instead of Marc Deboyne?'

'Oh some cabinet minister, I believe,' Paula said, striving to sound off-hand, not wanting to go into the outrageous details. 'Alexander was worried that a well-known politician being involved in the divorce would simply draw additional press attention to the case, to the family.'

'Good thinking.' Leaning over her desk, Emma now remarked, 'Talking of politicians, or rather a politician's son, have you anything to tell me about Jonathan?'

'Not one thing, Gran.' Paula hesitated. 'But Mr Graves of Graves and Sanderson dug up some unpleasant personal information about Sebastian Cross.' Paula grimaced. 'Alexander has the report. I'm sure you don't want to read it – it's rather disgusting. Alexander will explain it to you better than I.'

'I've lived with unpleasantness all of my life, Paula. However, obviously *you* prefer not to discuss it, so we'll let it go for now. I'll take it up with Alexander when he gets here later. And what about your cousin Sarah? Is she behaving herself?'

'I haven't seen her, but Emily tells me she's very snotty with her, and holding herself aloof. Apparently Sarah's become rather chummy with Allison Ridley, Winston's old girlfriend. Emily thinks that's the reason for Sarah's coldness towards her.'

'I'm rather surprised,' Emma muttered. 'Why would Sarah take umbrage at Emily?' She looked across at Paula, and began to laugh at herself. 'That's a pretty stupid comment on my part, when I think of the terrible things members of this family have done to each other.' She sat back in the chair, went on, 'Would you mind giving me another cup of coffee, please?'

'Of course not. Coming right up, Gran.' After filling the cup, adding milk and sugar, Paula brought the coffee to the desk, hovered. She said slowly, 'Look, this isn't a criticism of Emily, you know how much I love her, but she's got a ridiculous bee in her bonnet about the mess in Ireland. I'd like you to talk to her – '

'Oh she's already mentioned it to me, Paula,' Emma interrupted. 'Last night, when you were on the phone to Long Meadow.' Emma swallowed a smile as she observed Paula's serious expression. 'Murder most foul and all that nonsense, right?'

Paula nodded.

Emma said, 'I gave her a little lecture. I don't believe she'll ever bring it up again. However – ' Emma eyed her granddaughter closely. 'You know, your mother mentioned something about Ireland too last night. When you were out of the room. She doesn't believe the housekeeper was telling the truth . . . I mean about Min's craziness and drinking.'

Paula exclaimed fiercely, in irritation, 'Good God, the two of them are incorrigible! Honestly, Grandma, I hope you've nipped their imaginative chatter in the bud. It's a

610

load of tripe, and can only lead to further trouble. Loose tongues are dangerous.'

'Agreed. But whether it's tripe or not is beside the point, Paula. What matters, in reality, is that the case is closed. *Firmly closed*. Min's death was a suicide. That was the coroner's ruling and it's good enough for me. And for John Crawford. Don't worry, neither your mother nor Emily will mention anything about murder in the future. I've seen to that.'

'Thank heavens you have.' Paula came around the desk and hugged Emma tightly, kissed her cheek. 'Oh Gran darling, I'm so glad you're back. I've missed you so much. It's positively awful when you're not here.'

Emma smiled up at her, patted her hand. 'If you've said that once since I stepped off the plane, you've said it a hundred times, darling. But thank you, it's nice to hear. And I've missed you too – all of you. I've enjoyed myself, travelling the world with Blackie, seeing so many, many wonderful things. I've had a little fun for once. He was sweet. And he pampered me in a way I've not been pampered for years. Not since your grandfather died. But no more gallivanting off to foreign parts.'

'I didn't begrudge you the wonderful trip around the world, Gran, please don't think that . . . but you seemed to be so far away most of the time.'

'I was always here in spirit, Paula.'

'Yes, I know. but it's not quite the same as having you here in the flesh!'

'Alexander should be arriving in a few minutes.' Emma glanced at the carriage clock on the mantelpiece. 'Then Emily at noon. I thought we would lunch at one.' Her mouth twitched. 'I suggested to Parker that we have fish and chips – and from the local fish shop. That's the one thing I missed when I was away.'

Paula chortled. 'Oh Gran, you are lovely, and you haven't changed.'

'And it's hardly likely that I will, not at my age.'

'I'll just have time to dash across to Harte's, deal with a few things, and get back for lunch.'

'Yes, do run along, dear. I know what it's like . . . I used to feel exactly the same way when I was your age. I couldn't wait to get to the store.'

'See you later then.' Paula bent to kiss Emma's cheek.

'Yes. Oh and by the way, Paula, I had lunch with Ross Nelson the day before I left New York. I haven't had a chance to tell you – but I scotched that idea about selling my Sitex stock.'

'Good for you. He was getting to be a pest – in more ways than one, if you want the truth.'

Emma pursed her lips, staring at Paula with sudden alertness. 'Was he now,' she said. 'Well, yes, I must admit I did get the feeling he was rather keen on you. Tiresome man. Full of himself, and his so-called fatal charms, wouldn't you say?'

'He's the worst kind of bore. The deadliest really. And so transparent. I'm afraid I can't stand him.'

Paula walked to Harte's in Knightsbridge.

It was a frosty day. The etiolated sky was bloated with snow, but its bleached-out quality made the light seem curiously luminous despite the fugitive sun.

She was hardly conscious of the weather as she hurried along. She was thinking of Shane. She always thought of him. He was rarely out of her mind for very long. Today was 20 December. When she had spoken to him yesterday he had said he would ring her at seven New York time. Noon in London. Immediately afterwards he was taking a plane to Barbados, since it was the height of the season at the Coral Cove Hotel.

Paula sighed under her breath as she cut down a side street, heading for the main thoroughfare. Jim's accident had thrown all of their plans askew.

But this aside, he had nearly been killed and all because of his ingrained pigheadedness. Her mind leaped back to the dreadful weekend two weeks ago. She had arrived in London on Saturday, having taken an overnight flight from the States, and had been driven straight to Yorkshire by her grandmother's chauffeur.

When she got to Long Meadow in the early afternoon her first stop had been the nursery. To her distress the twins and Nora were suffering from streaming colds. At four o'clock, when Jim had walked in from the newspaper, he had muttered he was coming down with it himself, and had retired to bed immediately. She seized the opportunity to vacate their bedroom. That night she had slept in one of the guest rooms, explaining she could not afford to get sick, not with the whole household under siege and a business to run. He had not complained.

On Sunday Jim had been much better, certainly well enough to get up for lunch, eat a hearty meal and drink half a bottle of red wine. She had been aghast when he had insisted on going off to fly that dangerous little plane, had begged him to stay at home. Jim had laughed, told her she was being ridiculous, protested he was neither drunk nor sick. When the phone call had come through from the airport later that afternoon her heart had stopped beating for several seconds, and then she had leaped in the car and rushed to Leeds Infirmary to be with him. At odds with him though she was, and in love with Shane O'Neill, Paula still harboured affectionate feelings for her husband. She had once cared deeply for him, he was the father of her children, and she wished him no harm.

But later, when she could think clearly, she had realized there was no excuse for his behaviour. The crash need not have happened. He had been reckless. At heart Paula doubted his story about the engine stalling. He had been taking pills for his cold; he had demolished half a bottle of wine. If he had not been drugged or drunk exactly, he had hardly been in a fit condition to take the plane up.

When she had telephoned Shane in New Milford, later on that fated Sunday, he had been distressed for her. But he had been understanding of her dilemma, had agreed they could not make their moves until Jim was well enough to cope with her news. She was going to tell him she wanted a divorce.

As she swung into Knightsbridge, she prayed that Jim would agree. The worry that he might fight her nagged at the back of her head constantly.

Don't think about it, don't be so negative, she told herself firmly. All you have to do is get yourself through the next few months. She and Shane had made new plans this past week, changing their business commitments to accommodate each other. They needed to be together as often as they could. In January she would go to New York to be with him. During February and March he would visit Australia to start work on the rebuilding of the hotel the O'Neill chain had just purchased. He would stay with her brother Philip. Shane would come to England in April to see Emerald Bow run in the Grand National, but she would be with him in London before and after the race. At the end of April he would return to New York. They had decided that Jim ought to be on his feet again by then, and once Shane had left for the States she would tackle her husband. In May she would finally tell her grandmother everything, move herself and the twins into Pennistone Royal.

May, Paula repeated under her breath. Such a long way off. No, not really. And anyway, Shane and I have the rest of our lives ahead of us.

Her pace automatically quickened. She ached for the sound of his voice. Thank God for the telephone, she thought, as she went into the staff entrance at Harte's. At least we can talk every day.

CHAPTER 38

It snowed heavily for the next four days.

Yorkshire was quickly covered with a mantle of white. The countryside around Pennistone Royal looked particularly picturesque. Drystone walls disappeared under monstrous drifts, trees were weighted down by their laden branches, rivers and streams were glazed over with blue-tinted ice.

But the snowstorm ceased with abruptness on the afternoon of Christmas Eve. Suddenly the blindingly-white landscape had a crystalline beauty as the sun broke through. There was a diamond-bright dazzle to the sky, a sparkling crispness in the air.

By nightfall the fields and the fells and the rolling moors were ethereal under a clear winter moon that coated them with a silvery sheen.

Emma, standing at the window of her bedroom, was momentarily transfixed as she gazed down at her gardens. The snow and the ice had created the most magical effect, enveloping the land in a strange white silence, an overwhelming stillness that seemed like a palpable thing to her. But despite the breathtaking beauty spread before her, Emma knew that beyond the great iron gates of her house, the roads and country lanes were dangerous, very treacherous in this kind of weather.

As she turned away and walked through into the upstairs parlour, she could not help but worry, thinking of her family and friends who were currently driving on those roads. All were courageously braving the icy conditions in order to spend this special evening with her. It had been a tradition for many years, and none of them wanted to miss it. She hoped each one of them would arrive safely and without any mishaps.

Emma already had a full house.

Once they were back in Yorkshire, Paula had lost no time in moving her family into Pennistone Royal. Jim, the babies, the nanny and the male nurse were already ensconced. Emily had brought Amanda and Francesca home from Harrogate College earlier in the week. David and Daisy had taken the train from London yesterday, accompanied by Alexander and his fiancée, Maggie Reynolds. Edwina and Anthony had flown into Manchester Airport from Dublin that morning, had reached the ancient house in time for a late lunch.

Pausing at her desk, Emma picked up the guest list, scanned it quickly. Her sons and their wives had been invited, but she was quite certain they would not come. Well, it did not matter any more. She was adjusted to their absence from her life. Kit and Robin would avoid her again. She knew why. They were as guilty as hell about their treachery towards her. Elizabeth was not coming either, was remaining in Paris with Marc Deboyne, but at least her daughter had been gracious when she had phoned to decline and to wish her a happy Christmas. I hope this is the last husband *she's* going to have, Emma thought, her glance travelling on down the list.

Her eyes rested briefly on Jonathan's name. He had accepted. So had Sarah. They were driving over from Bramhope together. She could not help wondering about their current chumminess. Were they up to something? Now, Emma Harte, no bad thoughts tonight, she cautioned herself. It instantly struck her that she was unutterably weary of intrigue. It had dogged her all of her life. She was getting too old to pick up the sword again.

A thoughtful look settled on her face as she remained standing at the desk, clutching the guest list. *She was eighty.* She had paid her dues long ago. Her time was now far too precious to indulge in battles. Let them get on with it, she muttered. As I shall get on with my life – what's left of it. All I want is to have peace and quiet and to be with my dear old friend. We'll march on together into the future, Blackie and I . . . a couple of old war horses. She felt as if a great burden had been lifted as she suddenly acknowledged that she *had* abdicated eight months ago. She *was* out of the fray. She was determined to stay out.

Emma finished perusing the list. Blackie, who was spending Christmas with Bryan and Geraldine in Wetherby, was due to arrive with them and Miranda shortly. The entire Kallinski clan had also promised to come early. The Hartes would be out in full force tonight. Randolph, too, had a house full, since his mother, Charlotte, and his Aunt Natalie, were staying at Allington Hall with Sally, Vivienne and himself. Winston was a self-invited guest at Pennistone Royal, had walked in at four o'clock with his suitcase and three large shopping bags top-heavy with gifts. Only Philip and Shane are missing, Emma murmured to herself, putting down the list. But perhaps next year they will be here. We'll all be together. Then the three clans will really be complete.

The clock struck six.

The chimes roused her from her meandering thoughts. She gazed down at the one remaining present that lay on the desk. Earlier all of the others had been taken downstairs to the Stone Hall to be placed under the tree. Sitting down, Emma thought for a moment, then inscribed the card carefully.

There was a knock on the door. 'Cooee, Gran, it's me,' Emily called, floating in on a cloud of perfume.

Emma lifted her head, smiled at her granddaughter. 'And don't you look lovely!' she exclaimed, scrutinizing her intently. 'That's the dress tartan of the Seaforth Highlanders,' Emma remarked, referring to the long taffeta skirt Emily wore, immediately recognizing the plaid. 'My father's old regiment, and Joe's and Blackie's when they were in the First World War. It certainly looks smart with your white silk shirt.'

'Yes, I thought so too.' Emily planted a kiss on Emma's cheek, said quickly, 'You seemed a bit surprised when Winston arrived this afternoon. I could have sworn I'd told you he was coming to stay.'

'No, you didn't. But that's all right.' Sitting back, Emma pursed her lips, gave Emily a pointed look. 'I expect it's too much to ask you to behave yourselves, but *please*, do be discreet if you're bedroom hopping.'

Emily's face flushed. 'How can you think a thing like that, Grandma!'

'Because I was young once, believe it or not, and I know what it's like to be in love. But be careful, dear. After all, we do have a lot of house guests. I wouldn't want your reputation besmirched.'

'In this family! Good God, nobody can afford to throw any stones – ' Emily stopped. 'Sorry, I didn't mean to be rude, Grandma.'

'Don't apologize for speaking the truth, Emily. But remember what I've just said.'

Nodding and looking relieved, Emily drifted over to the fireplace, stood observing her grandmother. 'You should always wear dark green velvet. It's very becoming on you, especially with all your emeralds.'

'Goodness me, Emily, you make it sound as if they're dripping from every pore. I'm only wearing Paul's ring and earrings and Blackie's little bow. But thank you for the compliment, and tell me, what's happening downstairs?'

'Amanda and Francesca are finishing trimming the tree, at least the top half which I started earlier. Little monkeys, they haven't helped me one bit today. All they've done is loll around in their room, listening to the Beatles and shrieking their heads off, or alternately swooning and being silly. I routed them out an hour ago and set them to work.'

'Good for you. I'm going to have to take those two in hand during the holidays, put my foot down. There has to be a limit on the time they spend listening to those records. Apart from anything else, the racket was deafening this afternoon. Anyone else down yet?'

'Aunty Daisy, looking gorgeous in a red silk trouser suit and masses of rubies and diamonds – '

'Why do you always exaggerate?' Emma shook her head, faintly reprimanding, but her eyes were fond. 'She doesn't have masses of rubies and diamonds, to my knowledge.'

'Well, a pair of beautiful earrings,' Emily admitted, wrinkling her nose. 'She was helping to set up the bar. Jim's there, in the new wheelchair you got for him, having a drink and – '

'He's started a bit early, hasn't he?' Emma exclaimed, a silver brow lifting in surprise.

'What do you mean started early? He hasn't stopped since lunch.'

Emma was dismayed. 'Ought he to be drinking?' she asked. 'He's on pain killers – so Paula told me. That combination can be awfully dangerous.' Her eyes grew flinty with a mixture of concern and annoyance.

Emily nodded. 'I mentioned that to him a few minutes ago, so don't *you* say anything. He told me to mind my own business. He's awfully grouchy, I don't envy Paula one bit.'

'I've noticed his moodiness. Still, we have to make allowances, I suppose. Has Paula come home from the store yet?'

'No, but she should be here any minute.'

'Oh dear, the roads are so bad tonight . . .' Emma's voice faltered.

'Don't fret, Gran, she's a careful driver. Besides, she went over to the Harrogate store this afternoon. However, knowing Paula she'll probably stay until closing time. But at least her driving time has been cut in half.'

619

'I'll rest easier once she gets here. Well, continue, who else has made an appearance?'

'Maggie. She's sorting the Christmas tree decorations, helping the girls. Alexander and Uncle David are hanging mistletoe. Hilda and Joe are preparing the refectory table for the buffet, and Winston's stacking gifts under the tree.' Emily smirked. 'Oh yes, and Aunt Edwina is making herself useful for once – she's instructing Winston exactly *how* to arrange the packages for the best effect. As if it mattered.'

'At least she's talking to a Harte for a change. That's certainly a step in the right direction.' Emma motioned to Emily. 'Come here, dear, I want to show you something.'

As Emily joined her, Emma lifted the lid of an old leather jewellery case and then handed it to her granddaughter.

Emily gasped, staring down at the beautiful diamond necklace lying on the dark red velvet. It was a glittering lacy web of brilliant, perfectly cut and mounted stones. The diamonds had such fire, such life, such matchless beauty, Emily gasped again. 'This is extraordinary, Grandma, and obviously very old. Where did it come from? I don't think I've ever seen you wear it.'

'No, you haven't, because I never have. I haven't even tried it on since I've owned it.'

'I don't understand,' Emily said, her eyes perplexed.

'I've never wanted to wear it, and I only bought it when it was auctioned because – well, it was a sort of symbol to me. It represented everything I never had when I was a young girl – when I was a maid at Fairley Hall.' Emma took the case back from Emily, lifted out the necklace, held it up to the light. 'Yes, it's superb. Superb. It belonged to Adele Fairley, Jim's great-grandmother. I can still recall the night of a big dinner when I helped Adele to dress, fastened this around her throat. I was very bitter that night. The necklace, you see, represented the grinding toil and drudgery of the villagers, and my father, my brother

Frank, and I myself.' Emma shook her head. 'When the Fairleys went down the drain, after Adam died, Gerald put this up for sale.' Her shoulders lifted in a shrug. 'I outbid everyone,' she explained and placed the necklace in its case.

Emily said, 'But why have you never worn it, Grandy?'

'Because it was suddenly meaningless to me once I owned it . . . I preferred the things which had been given to me with love, by those who loved me.'

'What are you going to do with it?' Emily eyed the fancy wrapping paper and silver ribbon on the desk. 'Oh I know! You're going to give it to Paula because she's married to Jim.'

'No, not Paula.'

'Then who?'

'Edwina.'

'*Edwina*. Why her? She's always so awful to you!'

'So what. And just because she behaves badly doesn't mean I have to do the same. Anyway throughout my life I've tried to rise above that sort of thing. Always remember that it is far better to be gracious in difficult situations, Emily, than to sink to the levels of others. Anyway, Paula wouldn't want this. She might bear the name of Fairley, but I don't believe she considers herself to be one, no, not at all. On the other hand, Edwina *does*. The Fairley name is important to her, and I think she, above everyone in the family, would appreciate owning this and – '

'But Gran,' Emily began.

Emma held up her hand. 'Edwina was denied her birthright because she was illegitimate, and I know how much the circumstances of her birth troubled her, perhaps still do. I feel it is only proper that she has something that belonged to them – this kind of family heirloom. *I* don't want it, since it has no meaning for me. Neither am I trying to ingratiate myself with her, or redeem myself in her eyes. I simply want to give it to her, and that's all there

621

is to it. She will enjoy wearing it, of that I feel sure. Now, perhaps you would be kind enough to wrap it for me, Emily.'

'Of course I will. May I sit at the desk? It's easier to work there.'

'Yes.' Emma rose, walked across to the fireplace, stood with her back to it.

Emily glanced at the necklace again, closed the case, began to wrap it, thinking what an extraordinary woman her grandmother was. There was no one like her in the whole world. She was so generous and so very forgiving. Damn Edwina, she thought. I wish *she* would make just one gesture of love towards Gran. That would make *me* feel better.

There was a tap on the door. It opened and Paula looked in, exclaimed, 'Hello, you two! I'm frightfully late, I'm afraid. The Harrogate store was mobbed all day, like bedlam when we closed. Then the roads were ghastly. See you both in a while. I must pop in on the babies and Nora before I change.'

'Thank heaven you got here safely,' Emma was filled with relief at the sight of Paula's smiling face. 'And take your time, dear. Nobody's going anywhere.'

'I will.' Paula closed the door softly.

Emma said to Emily, 'Once you finish wrapping the necklace I think we'd better go downstairs. The O'Neills and the Kallinskis will be arriving any moment.'

'It's finished.' Emily clipped off the end of the silver ribbon, sat back to admire her handiwork. She lifted her dancing green eyes, focused them on her grandmother. 'I bet old Edwina has a heart attack when she opens this later, Gran!' she said, grinning mischievously.

'Really, Emily, sometimes – ' Emma shook her head, tried to look disapproving without much success.

The Stone Hall at Pennistone Royal derived its name from the local grey stone which had been used throughout – on the ceiling, the walls, the floor and the fireplace façade. But it was more than an entrance hall, had the overtones of a huge sitting room with its handsome Jacobean and Tudor furniture which partially underscored the architecture of the house.

Dark wood beams criss-crossed the stone ceiling, introduced a touch of warmth, as did the faded Aubusson carpets on the floor, the antique tapestries and oil paintings on the walls. The baronial overtones were further diminished by the blaze of rosy light from the chandelier and wall sconces, and the huge fire crackling up the chimney back. Pots of yellow, pink and purple chrysanthemums and deep-orange amaryllis sparked some of the wood surfaces, and tall brass urns filled with dark green holly, bright with red berries, graced several corners.

But taking pride of place and dominating the hall tonight was a giant Christmas tree. This was nine feet tall, with wide spreading branches and it towered up to touch the edge of the minstrels' gallery at the far end of the hall.

Emma, descending the staircase with Emily, paused half-way, stood for a moment admiring the scene. 'Oh, doesn't it look festive!' she cried. Not waiting for a response, she hurried down, glided across the floor to join the throng of family members, her eyes sparkling, her face wreathed in smiles.

'Hello, everyone,' she said. 'And well done. You've obviously worked hard to make the hall look beautiful tonight. Thank you.'

They came to greet her in turn, kissed her, told her she looked wonderful. Winston took the gift she handed him and put it under the tree. Jim, who had trouble manœuvring the wheelchair, could only wave.

Emma hurried over to him, rested her hand on his good shoulder, squeezed it, bent to kiss him. 'How are you feeling?' she asked, her concern for his well being apparent in her expression.

'Bloody awful, but I'll survive.' He gazed up at her through his light silvery eyes, then grimaced. 'What a rotten way to spend Christmas.'

'Yes, I know, dear, and you must be terribly uncomfortable. Can I get you anything?'

'No, thanks. Where's Paula? She should be home by now. It's almost six-thirty.' His voice was unexpectedly querulous, and he scowled at Emma, his mouth twisting into an angry line which he could not manage to conceal. Before she had a chance to answer, he exclaimed, 'I don't know why she had to go to the store today. It's ridiculous the way she works, and it is Christmas Eve. She ought to be here with her family. The babies need her, and furthermore, so do I – crippled as I am in this way. I think she's inconsiderate.'

Emma drew back, amazed at his words, his nasty tone, his sudden burst of petulance. She knew he was not feeling well, but she could not help thinking that he was overdoing it a bit. She said softly, 'It's because it *is* Christmas that she had to be at the stores today, Jim. You know this is her busiest period.'

'She should have left at noon,' he groused, 'come home to me. After all, the circumstances are a little exceptional, wouldn't you say?'

Emma bit back a sharp retort, knowing she must excuse him, blame his irascibility and immaturity on his condition. She said, more quietly than before, '*I* was never an absentee landlord and I doubt that Paula will ever be one either. And as a matter of fact, she just got back. She'll be down in a few minutes. She's changing into a cocktail dress. I see you have a drink and your cigarettes, Jim, so if you'll excuse me I'll go and deal with those two rowdy teenagers.'

Hurrying over to the tree, where Amanda and Francesca stood on two stepladders quarrelling furiously, Emma

624

exclaimed, 'Now, girls, stop that and come down. At once, do you hear!'

'Yes, Grandma,' Amanda said dutifully, quickly doing as she was bidden.

Francesca lingered. She placed a silver bell on the tip of a branch, craning her neck to study it.

Amanda, having reached the bottom of the ladder, took a step back, watching her sister. She shrieked, 'Not there, you clot! It's right next to a silver icicle. You need more colour on that branch. Put the red star you're holding in that spot instead of the bell.'

'Go to hell!' Francesca retorted. 'I'm sick of you tonight. You're a dimwit. And far too *bossy*.'

'That's enough!' Emma snapped. 'Get down, Francesca, and immediately. Otherwise you'll spend this evening in your room.'

'Yes, Grandy,' Francesca mumbled, clattering down the stepladder to join her sister who was standing next to Emma.

'Now upstairs, both of you.' Emma gave them a disapproving glance. 'You look like a couple of street urchins. I want you out of those disgusting jeans and grimy shirts and into more suitable clothes. *Instantly*. And wash your faces and brush your hair. I've never seen you both in such an appalling state. And please don't dress alike. I'm getting sick and tired of this twin-sister act of yours. You're like a music hall turn.'

'Yes, Grandmother,' Amanda murmured meekly.

'What do you want us to wear?' Francesca asked, eyeing Emma boldly, giving her a cheeky grin.

Quite unexpectedly, Emma wanted to laugh, but she controlled herself, said sternly, 'You can put on your red velvet frock, Francesca. And *you*, Amanda, had better wear your blue silk. That should do it. If nothing else, at least I'll be able to distinguish you from each other. Now run along.'

Emily, who had witnessed this little scene, laughed when her half-sisters were out of earshot. 'Thanks, Gran. They've been extremely bolshy these last few days. I almost threatened to send them to Paris to join our mother, but it would've been an idle threat. I wouldn't have the heart to do that to them – as tiresome as they are.'

'They're just trying the two of us on for size, you know, seeing how much they can get away with.' Emma chuckled.

'I know. Would you like a drink?'

'Why not, Emily. Perhaps you can ask Winston or your brother to open a bottle of champagne. I think I'd like a glass. And let's have some music.' Emma swung around as Emily hurried off to fetch the wine, and called across to David Amory, 'Please pop a record on, David dear, one of those selections of Christmas carols. No, not the carols just yet. I rather like that Bing Crosby . . . *White Christmas* I believe it's called.'

'Right away, Emma. And it's certainly appropriate this year.'

Emma turned to the box of tree decorations, started to dress the lower branches which were relatively bare and unfinished. She had been working only a few seconds when she felt a hand touch her arm tentatively. She swivelled, found herself face-to-face with Edwina.

'May I help, Mother?'

'Yes, I'd like that,' Emma said, camouflaging her surprise. 'Root around in the other box. Perhaps you'll find something sparkling and pretty for these low branches. It seems to me that the most beautiful ornaments generally end up on the top of the tree.' Emma's eyes roved over her eldest daughter. She nodded. 'Blue has always suited you, Edwina. You look lovely tonight, and that's a beautiful frock.'

'Thank you . . . Daisy talked me into buying it.' Edwina hesitated. 'You look very elegant, but then you always do,

626

Mother.' Edwina offered her a smile that was as tentative as her touch had been.

Emma smiled in return, wondering what to make of the unprecedented compliment, then reached for a gold *papier mâché* pear, hooked it on to a branch, frowning to herself. Edwina was certainly most cordial all of a sudden. Still, she had to admit she was pleased at this show of friendliness.

After a moment, Edwina tapped Emma's arm, held out a blue glass star. 'Here you are, Mother, would you like to hang this one? Maybe over there, next to the angel. Or wherever you think it would look right.'

Taking it from her, Emma searched her daughter's face.

For a split second she was transported back in time . . . to a Christmas long, long ago. *December of 1915.* Joe Lowther had still been alive. It was the year before he had been killed in the Battle of the Somme. They had lived in the avenue called the Towers in Armley. In her mind's eye the memory flashed so vividly Emma caught her breath. Edwina had been nine years old and exceptionally pretty with her long blonde hair, her silvery eyes so like Adele's, her delicate features inherited from Edwin Fairley, her father. But the little girl had believed Joe to be her father and she had adored him. Worshipped him really.

The three of them had stood in front of a giant fir, very similar to this one, and on a snowy Christmas Eve such as this. Dim echoes of their joyous laughter reverberated in Emma's head. But it had been the child and the man who had laughed, shared the delight and fun of dressing the splendid tree. She had been the interloper, unwanted by her daughter. Edwina had spurned her, slighted her every time she had offered that beautiful but disdainful child a pretty bauble to hang on the tree. And she had left the room, her heart almost breaking. She had put on her coat and run down the short avenue to Blackie's and Laura's house, and her dearest Laura had comforted her, helped to take the sting out of the child's spitefulness.

Edwina said, 'Are you feeling all right, Mother?'

Emma blinked. The memory dissolved. 'Yes,' she said, 'Oh yes, I'm fine. I was just remembering something.'

'What were you remembering?'

'Oh a Christmas . . . so long ago now you've surely forgotten it.' Emma smiled faintly. 'But I've never forgotten it – not really.'

'You were thinking about the Christmas of 1915, weren't you?' Edwina moved closer to Emma.

'Yes.'

'Mother . . .' Edwina looked deeply into Emma's old wise eyes. 'I've not forgotten that Christmas either.' She paused, seemed to consider and then reached out and took hold of Emma's hand impulsively. 'Forgive me, Mother, please, please forgive me for that terrible Christmas,' she whispered.

Emma stared back at her daughter in stupefaction. And then she instantly knew what Edwina was trying to say. She wanted to be forgiven for all of her transgressions over the years and not just that particular Christmas. Emma said slowly, 'You were such a little girl, so young. You didn't understand . . . understand how things were in an adult world. You had no conception of pain or heartbreak.'

'Please say you forgive me, Mother,' Edwina begged, her sincerity evident. 'It's become so very important to me.'

'Why of course I forgive you, Edwina. You are my daughter, my first born child. And I told you months ago that I've always loved you. My love has never wavered or changed, though you have doubted me.'

'I don't any more.' Tears swam in Edwina's pale eyes. 'Can we be friends at last – so late in our lives – do you think?'

'I know we can.' Emma smiled her incomparable smile that always filled her face with radiance. 'Why we already are, my dear,' she said, clasping Edwina's hand tightly.

Jonathan Ainsley was beginning to realize how dangerous the conditions were after he left the main Ripon road and manœuvred his Aston Martin down a narrow side lane, taking a short cut to the village of Pennistone Royal.

'You shouldn't have come this way,' Sarah complained. 'The lane twists and turns too much. We'll have an accident if you're not careful.'

'This is the fastest route,' Jonathan replied. A cold smile touched his mouth. 'I don't want to miss anything tonight, I think it's going to be – ' He broke off as he felt the wheels sliding on the ice. The car was going into a skid. He gripped the steering wheel tighter, turning the car into the skid in an effort to avert it, gently pressing his foot on the brake as he did.

Sarah, stiffening with fright, grabbed his arm.

Angrily Jonathan shook off her hand, managed to right the Aston in the nick of time, shouted, 'You'll have us in a bloody ditch!' He slowed his pace to a slow crawl. 'For God's sake don't ever do a thing like that again, Sarah. It's very dangerous.'

'I'm sorry. It *was* a silly reaction. Don't be angry with me. You know I can't bear it when you lose your temper.'

'Okay, okay, let's forget it,' he muttered, pushing his annoyance to one side. The last thing he wanted was to upset Sarah. He needed her too much to incur her disfavour. He peered ahead, watching for new ice patches in the glare of the headlights.

Neither of the cousins spoke for a while.

Sarah shrank into the corner of the seat, pulling her silver fox coat around her, hoping his good humour would soon be restored.

Jonathan concentrated on the road, driving now with the utmost care. The Aston Martin was new, not even paid for yet. A bashed up hood or a damaged fender would be costly. He relaxed a fraction as he hit a clear stretch, but still he did not increase his pace, determined to be cautious.

His mind swung to his cousin sitting next to him. He wondered how to persuade Sarah to put up more money, invest another few hundred thousand pounds in the company he secretly owned with Sebastian Cross. Sarah was their partner now. Her money was vital to them. Urgently needed. They had had a lot of bad luck lately. And Sebastian had made some disastrous deals, which negated the good ones he had closed. But they would pull out of it. One good deal would do the trick.

A grimness settled on his face as his duplicitous brain continued to turn at a rapid rate. Maybe he would have to steer one of the deals he was handling for Harte Enterprises into Stonewall Properties, his own company. *Why not?* The thought tickled him. Jonathan Ainsley was aware that he had larceny in his heart, accepted that he was avaricious, greedy for the good things in life, hungry for power. He also knew he was not a good sport, despite his grandmother's efforts to instil in him the importance of playing the game. Who wants to play the game? he now asked himself. He was a bad loser. He didn't care. But he would be damned if he would ever be the loser again. He was going to be the winner . . .

Sarah said, 'We're almost at the end of the lane, Jonny.'

'Yes, I know.' Jonathan began to ponder her. He had been manipulating Sarah for months, playing on her hatred for Paula, feeding her jealousy, envy and bitterness. But she had every reason to be bitter. Just as he did. Paula was the favourite. The Crown Princess. She was getting everything, damn her. And so was Alexander. A small tremor of fury shot through Jonathan. He instantly curbed it, warning himself to stay cool tonight. He had schooled himself not to show his hand to the family, and least of all to his grandmother. Bloody old witch, he thought. My father's right. She's never going to kick the bucket. We *will* have to shoot her in the end. Poor Dad. He was cheated out of his inheritance. But he's a great politician and one of the greatest men in England. He might even be Prime Minister one day. He's so smart. He thought my idea of starting my own business was brilliant. He gave me his blessing. Jonathan wondered if his grandmother suspected him. Never. She was too old, getting senile. Once Emma Harte was dead he would inherit the New York apartment. The bequest to him was in her will. It had to be worth five million dollars at least. And Sarah was to get the Belgrave Square house. I'll make her sell it, invest the cash with me. The mere thought of this enormous amount of money cheered him. He tingled with excitement. His mood became sanguine. He felt much better all of a sudden, and quite up to facing his boring family. He wished he could park and smoke a joint before they reached the house. He did not dare. Sarah would disapprove. She was such a bore. A pain really. Better cater to her. He needed her support, her continuing friendship. Sebastian had recently had the idea of marrying Sarah. Jonathan was not sure that he should encourage this. He despised Sarah, but Sebastian was a strange bird, and the gambling had grown worse – he was growing ever more reckless. Besides, Jonathan did not want to lose control of Sarah, or, more precisely, her money.

At the end of the lane Jonathan drew to a standstill, flicked his lights, then pulled out on to the main road. He said, 'That was a bumpy ride, but like all bumpy rides it was worth it. At least we won't be all that late.'

'Why are you so anxious to get to Grandy's early? What are you afraid of missing?' Sarah asked, filled with curiosity.

'*Family dramas.*' Jonathan chortled. 'And there are bound to be some, with that motley crew in attendance. There'll be our peer of the realm hovering over his pregnant mistress. Christ, Sarah, Anthony's been lucky. He's just missed standing trial for murder, and by the skin of his teeth. I hear Sally Harte's blown up like a helium balloon, got his bun in her oven all right, and for all the world to see.'

'Do you always have to be so crude?' Sarah said with her usual primness.

He glanced at her quickly out of the corner of his eye and, undeterred, said 'And there'll be our two lovebirds, billing and cooing inanely. I always knew Emily was itching to get into Winston's trousers when we were kids. She's a bloody little sex pot if you ask me, just like her randy mum.'

'Allison Ridley's devastated about Winston,' Sarah remarked as evenly as she could, brushing aside his vulgarity. 'She's moving to New York in a few weeks. I can't say I blame her. Our crowd is too close-knit . . . she'd always be running into Winston.'

'*He's* certainly riding high at the moment, got *his* hands on the newspaper company because of Jim's accident.' Instantly Jonathan saw a way to inflame Sarah, added swiftly, 'That plane crash was a bit odd, don't you think?'

'In what way?'

'It struck me at the time that Jim might have been trying to do himself in – you know, end it all in one dramatic moment.'

Sarah was shocked. 'Jonathan! That's a terrible thing to say! Why would Jim want to kill himself, for heaven's sake?'

'Who wouldn't – being married to the Ice Queen?'

'Yes,' Sarah muttered. 'She is a cold bitch. Probably frigid.'

'Oh, I wouldn't say *that* – ' Jonathan stopped, waiting for Sarah to take the bait.

'I thought you hated Paula as much as I do?'

'I haven't changed,' he reassured her.

'But you just implied that she's not cold, Jonny.'

'I heard something about her that leads me to think

632

otherwise – ' Again he broke off, wanting to further intrigue Sarah.

'Oh! Tell me the gossip.'

Jonathan sighed. 'I shouldn't have started this conversation with you, Sarah dear. The last thing I want to do is upset you on Christmas Eve.'

Sarah said, 'I won't be upset . . . come on, don't be mean, give me all the dirt on Paula. I'm certainly all ears.'

'No, I'm positive I oughtn't to continue.' He smothered a gleeful laugh, enjoying this cat and mouse game. He always did. It gave him a sense of power.

There was a small silence.

'On the other hand, you're a big girl – ' He patted her hand. 'And of course it might *not* be true at all.'

'For God's sake tell me . . . this is driving me crazy,' Sarah cried.

'Paula was in Barbados in November, as you know. But were you aware that Shane O'Neill was there at the same time?'

Sarah tensed. She sucked in her breath, obviously taken aback. 'So what?' she managed after a moment. 'He was down there when *I* went out to supervise the opening of the boutique. His presence on the island doesn't mean a thing.'

'Perhaps not – on the surface. But you were the one who told me you'd seen him ogling her, looking all hot eyed and turned on at the christening.'

'He was!'

'Well, Rodney Robinson, my old school chum from Eton, was in Barbados at the same time as Paula. He was staying at the Sandy Lane Hotel, and he told me he saw her having lunch at the hotel. She was with a man – '

'It may not have been Shane,' Sarah said swiftly. She could hardly bear to think of Shane with her cousin. It made her physically ill.

'It *was* Shane,' Jonathan said steadily. 'Rodney thought

he looked familiar. After they'd left, old Rod spoke to the head waiter, asked him if he knew the name of the man with the tall, dark, striking young woman. The head waiter told him it was a Mr O'Neill who owned the Coral Cove Hotel.'

'Having lunch together isn't anything unusual. They've always been close friends,' Sarah protested, willing the pain in her chest to go away.

'Oh I agree, love. Except for one thing. Rodney told me they were looking extremely cosy. Intimate, was his word. In fact, he said Shane was practically getting it off with her at the table.'

'P-p-please,' Sarah stammered, 'y-y-you know I loathe it when you're vulgar.'

'Oh sorry, love.' He patted her hand again. His glee spiralled. 'They were drooling all over each other and in the most disgusting way. So Rodney said. Obviously our Ice Queen isn't so icy after all, nor is she the little Miss Goody Two Shoes she pretends to be. Poor Jim. I'm not surprised he almost plunged to his death.'

Sarah swallowed. She was overwhelmed by jealousy, hardly able to breathe.

Jonathan, aware of her feelings for Shane O'Neill, continued relentlessly, 'Yes, methinks there's something rotten in the state of Denmark, to quote old Will Shakespeare. *Adultery* perhaps? Rocking the House of Fairley.' He chuckled sarcastically.

'They can't be having an affair,' Sarah moaned. 'Paula wouldn't dare. She'd be too scared that Grandy would find out. Anyway, she's in love with Jim.'

'A hundred to one that you're entirely wrong, Sarah, my poppet.'

'I don't think we should talk about this any more. I *am* getting upset after all. Actually, I feel rather queasy.'

'I do hope you're going to be all right,' Jonathan murmured softly, pretending to be concerned. 'I knew I shouldn't have told you. But you've always been able to twist me around your little finger. Thank God we have each other, Sarah. We'll fight those cousins of ours and to the bitter end. We'll come out on top, you'll see. Sebastian and I have the company really rolling now. You're going to make millions with us, and be as rich and powerful as Paula bloody Fairley.'

There was no response from Sarah, who sat hugging herself, fighting back the tears. She loved Shane so much it was painful hearing these things about him and Paula. She did not doubt Jonathan.

Jonathan said, 'Cheer up, love. And remember one thing – Shane is a Roman Catholic. He'd never marry a divorced woman. And *if* he is involved with the lady he's bound to tire of her soon. He's a real stu – ' Jonathan cleared his throat, quickly corrected himself by substituting, 'Ladies' man.' He continued, 'And he's still sowing his wild oats. That's what this affair with Paula is – Shane's bound to calm down soon. And *voilà*! You'll be there waiting for him. Rich, too, as you walk to the altar with him. By the way, I've been meaning to tell you, you're looking very beautiful these days, Sarah, since you lost so much weight. Shane won't be able to resist you. I'm going to help you, don't worry. I'm going to make certain you get the man you love.'

'Oh Jonny, you're always so nice to me,' Sarah said, instantly cheering. 'Everything you say is true, I just know it is. *I* will end up with Shane. And I am glad about our real estate company.' She peered at him in the dim light of the car. 'Am I really going to be as wealthy as Paula?'

'Absolutely. I guarantee it. Incidentally, after Christmas Sebastian and I want you to come to our first real board meeting. We'll show you the books, go over our various deals, explain the new ones that are pending. You may have to invest a little more money, but it'll be worth it. Think of the dowry you'll take to Shane. I realize that sounds old-fashioned, but don't let's be foolish enough to dismiss money in this instance. Shane O'Neill is bloody ambitious, and he'd never look twice at a poor woman. So . . . I'm going to make sure you are loaded, Sarah.'

'What would I do without you?' Sarah sighed, blissful at the prospect of her rosy future. 'I'm feeling tons better now.' She giggled. 'It must be the thought of lording it over Paula in the not too distant future, and snatching Shane out from under her nose.'

'That's the spirit, Sarah! When should I arrange for us to get together with Sebastian Cross?'

'Any time you like. And of course I'll put up some more money. I trust you, Jonny, you've always been on my side, been my best friend.'

'And as you have been mine, my pet.'

Within minutes Jonathan was turning into the gates of Pennistone Royal. As he parked he noticed the long line up of cars and realized they were probably the last to arrive. Secretly laughing up his sleeve at Sarah's gullibility, he nevertheless managed to keep his face straight as he helped her out of the car, ran around to the boot to collect their gifts for their grandmother.

Puffed-up with self-congratulation at his adroit handling of his cousin, he put his hand under her elbow, arranged a suitably insouciant smile and escorted her inside.

Joe, the houseman, was on duty, and he wished them a happy Christmas as he took their coats. They returned his greeting. Jonathan's sharp, ever-quick eyes darted around as he and Sarah went down the short flight of steps leading into the Stone Hall. The party was in full swing. Everyone was present. The air was filled with the sound of Christmas music playing on the stereo, and the high-pitched buzz of chatter intermingled with bursts of jolly laughter. The fire roared, the giant tree blazed with lights, and the familiar faces which turned to greet them were ringed with happy smiles.

Jonathan smiled back, nodded, but did not stop. He propelled Sarah on a steady course down the hall. He saw Paula sitting on the arm of Blackie's chair, talking to the old man very earnestly, her face tender. *If I exaggerated Rodney's story to goad Sarah, I know I wasn't far off the mark*, Jonathan commented silently. *I bet Shane O'Neill has got her where he wants her. In his bed. Good old Rodney. I owe him one.*

Now Jonathan noticed Jim, trapped in the wheelchair, talking to Anthony. They had a strong look of each other. *Fairley blood*, he thought. He felt the sardonic laughter rising in his throat, almost choking him. He swallowed, made sure his charming smile was intact. *As soon as Jim's alone I'll go over and talk to him, sow a few seeds of doubt in his mind about that holier-than-thou wife of his. In the meantime, I'd better find the old dragon, go over and genuflect.*

Jonathan's predictions to Sarah to the contrary, there were no dramas at Pennistone Royal that evening.

Emma's traditional Christmas Eve party progressed without a hitch. However, Emily's comment about Edwina being shocked to death when she saw the diamond necklace proved to be no exaggeration.

After the buffet supper had been served and eaten, and before the carol singing began, Emma distributed her generous tokens of her affection to her family and friends. They were thrilled and touched by their presents, recognizing the amount of time she had spent in selecting something extra special for each of them. Even the malcontents were pleased – Jonathan with his gold-and-jade cuff links, Sarah with the pearl-and-jade necklace she had received.

But it was Edwina who was genuinely stunned, momentarily rendered speechless as she gaped in amazement at the Fairley necklace. Observing her closely, Emma thought her daughter was indeed going to keel over from a heart attack. Instead Edwina collapsed in floods of tears.

After she had composed herself, Edwina began to realize that the Fairley heirloom she had been given was a gesture of unselfish love, that of a mother for a daughter, and she was more than thankful she had made the initial move to end her estrangement from her mother earlier. She remained at Emma's side for the rest of the evening.

The happy mood prevailed until midnight. Only Paula felt out of it at times, when her thoughts turned to Shane. She was attentive to Jim and his needs, and chatted with everyone, but she constantly found herself gravitating to the O'Neills, needing to be in the midst of Shane's family. Somehow it seemed to bring him closer.

Next year, she kept thinking. Next year. We'll be together next year.

CHAPTER 39

It was a rainy night in the middle of January.

Jim Fairley sat in the Peach Drawing Room, sipping a straight vodka, gazing at his favourite painting, the Sisley he loved so much and longed to possess for himself. So rapt was he in his contemplation of it, he did not realize that Emma had appeared in the doorway of her drawing room.

She stood observing him closely.

Her worry about Jim was increasing daily, and she could not help thinking now that she was watching the slow but steady disintegration of a man. He had changed so radically during her absence abroad and over the last six weeks, he was hardly recognizable as the personable young editor she had first employed. She had tried to talk to him, but her words seemed to flow over him, leaving him untouched. He continued on his downward slide.

He was drinking steadily. Ever since she had chastised him about this a few days after Christmas he had endeavoured to conceal his tippling. Still, she was aware he was consuming great quantities of liquor – day and night.

She thought of his family. Every single one of the Fairleys had been drinkers. His great-grandmother, Adele, had fallen down the staircase at Fairley Hall in a drunken stupor, breaking her neck. The shattered wine glass had been scatttered around her body, on that dreadful morning when Annie, the other maid, had found her.

Emma frowned to herself. She wondered if alcoholism was congenital. Jim was not yet an alcoholic, but she was convinced he was well on the way to becoming one. And then there were the pain killers. He had not really persuaded her he had stopped taking pills. And yet she could not for the life of her imagine where he was getting them from. Continuing to study his face in profile, thinking how good looking he was despite the ravages of drink, medication and his physical pain, a phrase Blackie had used recently leaped into her mind. They had been at Allington Hall stables, looking over his string of racehorses. 'The breeding's there, but no stamina,' Blackie had said, referring to one of his thoroughbreds. An appropriate analogy, Emma mused. Loath though she was to condemn Jim, it was apparent to her that he was weak, lacked strength of character. But had she not always suspected this?

Emma cleared her throat, said in a cheerful voice, 'Good evening, Jim.' She walked into the room purposefully.

She had startled him. He swung his head quickly. He gave her a half-smile. 'I wondered where you were,' he exclaimed, forcing a conviviality he did not feel. 'I hope you don't mind, but I didn't wait for you.' He glanced at the drink. 'But this *is* my first today, Grandy.'

That's a downright lie, she thought. She said, 'I was delayed on the telephone, but I'll now join you in a cocktail before dinner.'

Pouring herself a glass of white wine, Emma continued, 'I was just speaking to Daisy. She rang from Chamonix. They're so sorry you're not with them. David misses you on the slopes.' She brought her drink, and sat down near the fire. 'Daisy's not much of a skier, as you know, and David is feeling lonely without you, his boon companion. Well, never mind, you'll be able to go with them next year, Jim.'

'I sincerely hope so.' He moved his broken shoulder slightly, gave her a quirky little smile. 'It's a relief to have this in a sling, I can tell you that, and Doctor Hedley's going to take the cast off my leg tomorrow.'

She knew all about this, but faked surprise, not wanting him to know she was constantly consulting with the family doctor about him. 'That's *wonderful* news. You must start therapy immediately, get those muscles in shape again.'

'Try to stop me.' He gave her a long careful look. 'Did Paula call you from New York today?'

Emma's eyes flickered. 'No, she didn't, but I wasn't expecting to hear from her. Surely she told you last night, when she called, that she was flying to Texas today. Sitex business, you know.'

'Oh, that's right. I'd forgotten.'

Emma wondered if he really had, but let the comment pass. 'Emily just told me that Winston's coming to dinner after all. That'll be nice for you, Jim, a little male company should cheer you up. It must be very boring for you – surrounded by women.'

He laughed. 'You're all very attentive, but it'll be nice to see Winston, hear what's happening in the outside world. I feel so cut off, and weary of this inactivity. I hope I can get back to the paper in a couple of weeks. What do you think?'

It struck Emma that this would be a wise move, and she said swiftly, 'I'm all for it. I've always found that work is a wonderful cure for what ails *me*.'

Jim cleared his throat. 'Talking of the newspapers, Emma, there's something I've been meaning to ask you for the longest time.'

'Oh, and what's that, Jim?'

He hesitated briefly, then said in a low voice, 'When I came back from Canada in September, Paula and I had a bit of a quarrel about Sam Fellowes, and the instructions she had given him in my absence, you know, about suppressing the stories dealing with Min's death.'

'Yes, she mentioned something about it – her decision, not your quarrel.' Emma gave him a questioning look.

'Paula told me that she has your power of attorney, and Winston's, to act on your behalf or his, if the need comes up.'

'That's quite true.'

'I couldn't help wondering why you didn't give those powers of attorney to me?'

Emma sat very still, was silent for a second, and said gently, 'Jim, when you resigned as managing director of the Yorkshire Consolidated Newspaper Company you forfeited your right to any power in that company, other than the editorial power you have as managing editor, of course. Since you said you were not interested in the administrative side of the newspapers, it seemed patently obvious to me that those powers of attorney had to rest in the hands of someone who was ready, willing and able to act, to take charge, if the situation arose – *administratively* take control, I mean.'

'I see.'

Watching him closely, she saw his face stiffen in annoyance, his eyes cloud over with resentment. 'You did resign of your own accord, Jim,' she remarked evenly, in that same gentle voice.

'I know.' He took a long swallow of the vodka, placed the drink on the end table, stared into the fire. Finally he swung his eyes to hers. 'Paula is also the trustee of my children's shares in the newspaper company, isn't she?'

'She is.'

'Why, Grandy? Why didn't you make me the trustee for them? I am their father, after all.'

'It's not as simple as it seems, Jim. The shares which I am leaving to Lorne and Tessa are not in a separate trust, but in their overall trust fund into which I have placed many other shares from my different holdings. It seems clear to me that such a giant trust must be managed by one person. It would be ridiculous to have a number of different trusts, have each one handled by a different individual. Far too confusing.'

He nodded, made no comment.

Emma gave him a discerning look, recognizing that he was not only put out, but furious, even though he was doing his best to conceal this emotion from her. Whilst she knew she had no obligation to explain her actions to anyone, she nevertheless wanted to make him feel better about himself.

She said, 'My decision to appoint Paula is no reflection on you, or your ability. She – and she alone – would be the trustee of her children's trust fund whomever she was married to, Jim.'

'I understand,' he murmured, although deep down he did not. He felt he had been passed over. But then he had no one to blame but himself. He suddenly realized he should never have resigned as managing director of the newspaper company.

Ignoring his moody expression, his angry silence, Emma remarked, 'If Emily and Winston have children before I die, and if I created a trust fund for their offspring, which of course I *would*, Winston will be in the same position as

642

you are. So would Sarah's husband, should she marry whilst I'm still alive. I'm not singling you out.'

'I said I understand, and I do, Emma. Thanks for explaining things to me. I appreciate – '

There was a tap on the door, and Hilda came in, said, 'Excuse me, Mrs Harte, but Mr O'Neill is on the phone. He said that if you're busy you can ring him back. He's at Mr Bryan's, in Wetherby.'

'Thank you, Hilda, I'll take it.' She rose, smiled at Jim, 'Excuse me, dear, I won't be a moment.'

He nodded, and the minute he was alone he trundled himself over to the Regency sideboard and filled his glass with vodka, plopped in ice. He put the drink in his left hand which peeped out from the sling, then pushed his chair back to the fireplace with his right.

He drank half the vodka down quickly, so that Emma would not know he had refilled his glass, then sat pondering her words. Suddenly everything was clear to him. Emma was placing all of her power in the hands of her grandchildren. She was ensuring it stayed within the family. And absolutely so. He had thought he was family. He was an outsider after all.

Sighing, he lifted his eyes to the Sisley. The painting had always had a hypnotic effect on him. Again he wished it was his as he always did when he gazed on it. He wondered what exactly it was about this particular landscape that so enthralled him. There were other Sisleys in the room, and Monets. All were worth millions.

Suddenly, and with a small stab of acute horror, Jim understood. This painting represented wealth and power to him. That was the reason he coveted it – the *real* reason. That the Sisley was heartstopping, lyrical, a great piece of art which appealed to his sensibilities more than the others, was beside the point. His hand trembled and he put the drink on the table, closed his eyes, blocking out the painting.

I want the money. I want the power. I want it all back
. . . all that my great-grandfather and my great-uncle so
foolishly squandered or lost, and which Emma Harte took
from the Fairleys. Instantly Jim was appalled at these
thoughts and at himself. I've had too much to drink. I'm
getting maudlin. No, I'm not. I've not had that much
vodka today. I've been very careful about my intake.

The trembling seemed to seize his whole body, and he
opened his eyes, gripped the sides of his wheelchair to
steady himself. The image of Paula flashed through his
mind. He had married her because he was madly in love
with her. He had. He knew he had. *No.* There was another
reason. He had wanted her because she was Emma Harte's
granddaughter. Wrong again. Emma Harte's principal heir
to her vast fortune.

For a split second James Arthur Fairley saw himself as
he truly was. It was his epiphany. And he did not like what
he saw in that intense flash of clarity. *It was the truth.* He
did love his wife, but he craved her money and her power.
He groaned aloud and his eyes filled. This sudden self-
revelation was insupportable. He was not the man he had
believed himself to be all of his life. His grandfather had
brought him up to be a gentleman, to look to the higher
things in life, to be unconcerned about material wealth and
position. Edwin Fairley had brainwashed him. Yet secretly
he had always longed for the power, the glory and the
riches. There was a dichotomy in his nature. That was the
true cause of his internal strife. I've deluded myself for
years, he thought. I've lived a lie.

He groaned again and ran his hand through his hair. I
love Paula for herself, I really do.

The nagging pain in his shoulder intruded and so insistently he winced in agony. It was the rainy weather. His
shoulder was like a barometer. He groped around in his
pocket for a pill, washed it down with vodka.

'Blackie's so excited,' Emma said from the doorway,

hurrying in, laughing gaily. 'He's making such elaborate plans for the Grand National. He's taking *all* of us to Aintree for the steeplechase. It's the first Saturday in April.' Emma sat down, took a sip of her wine. 'And so you'll be able to come with us, Jim. You'll be as fit as a fiddle by then.'

CHAPTER 40

'What are we going to do, Shane?' Paula stared at him, her expression troubled.

'We're going to take this one step at a time, get through each day as best we can,' he said confidently. He gave her one of his reassuring smiles. 'And we're going to make it.'

They sat in her office in the Leeds store. It was an afternoon in the middle of April of 1970. Shane had just returned from a quick trip to Spain, where he had been to supervise the remodelling currently in progress at their Marbella hotel.

Now he edged closer to her on the sofa, put his arm around her, held her tightly in his arms. 'Try not to worry so much, darling.'

'I can't help it. The situation hasn't improved – it's just worsened. And everything's dragging on interminably. I'm beginning to think I'll never be free of my problems.'

'Yes, you will.' Moving away, he lifted her face, looked deeply into her eyes. 'We've both got innumerable business pressures right now, a load of responsibilities, and we're just going to have to concentrate on those, keep ourselves busy, knowing that ultimately we'll be together. And when we are it will be for always. Think of the future, Paula, keep your eyes trained on that.'

'I try, I do try, Shane, but – ' her voice wavered and stopped. Her eyes filled up.

'Hey, come on, love,' he said. 'No tears. We've got to keep moving ahead, and purposefully so. I keep telling you, time is on our side. We're both young, and we are going to win in the end.'

'Yes.' She brushed her eyes with her fingertips, forced a more cheerful expression on to her face. 'It's just that – oh Shane, I miss you so much.'

'I know, I know, and I miss you too. It's sheer hell being apart. But look here, I *would* have to go to New York next week, and then on to Sydney for two months, even if your situation was straightened out. There's no way I can change those circumstances. And it's not been so bad, has it? We were together in New York for part of January and we've managed to grab some time together these past few weeks. So – '

'I can't help feeling that it's not fair to you. I'm keeping you dangling and – '

His laughter obliterated her words. 'I love you, and only you. I'll wait for you, Paula.' He hugged her fiercely. 'What kind of a man do you think I am, you silly, silly girl. None of this is your fault. It's beyond your control. Life intrudes, that can't be helped. We're just going to have to battle it through.'

'I'm sorry, Shane. I *am* being mournful today, aren't I? Perhaps that's because you'll be leaving in a few days. I feel so desperately alone when you're not in England.'

'But you're *not* alone, Paula. You have me, my love and my support – *always*. I carry you in my heart wherever I go, and you're never out of my thoughts, not for a single moment. We talk on the telephone practically every day, and if you need me urgently I'll come to you as fast as I can. You know I'd be on the first plane out, whether I'm in Australia or the States.' He gazed at her, his black eyes quizzical all of a sudden. 'You *do* know that, don't you?'

'Yes, yes, of course I do.'

'Remember what I said to you in Barbados?'

'That I must trust your love for me.'

'That's right. *As I trust yours for me.* Now, are you going to change your mind and come to dinner at Beck House tonight? It'll do you good, and Emily was so disappointed when you declined her invitation.'

'Perhaps I will, after all.' Paula frowned. 'Do you think she and Winston suspect anything about us?'

'*No.* They believe we've become good friends again, and that's all.'

Paula was not entirely convinced he was correct. However she had no wish to implant troublesome ideas in his mind, and she said, 'I couldn't get there until eight. I want to go home to see Tessa and Lorne, and then I have to go to the nursing home to see Jim.'

'I understand.'

'You really *do*, don't you, Shane?'

'Of course, and I wouldn't expect anything less of you, Paula. You're far too good, and too compassionate a woman, to turn your back on Jim at a time like this. You said over lunch that he was a bit better. What's the general prognosis?'

'The doctor told me yesterday that he could be out of the nursing home in a few weeks, *if* he continued to improve the way he has. He's not as depressed as he was and he's responding well to treatment, to the psychiatric help.' She shook her head and her worry flared up in her. 'But you never know with a nervous breakdown. I mean, some people recover quickly, others take months, and it's not unusual for a person to have relapses.' She hesitated, murmured in a low almost inaudible tone, 'I can't bring myself to say anything to him just yet – about my freedom.'

'I'm aware of that, you don't have to keep repeating yourself,' Shane said rapidly but with gentleness. 'We agreed that we must wait until Jim's back to normal, truly capable of handling things, before you tell him you want a divorce. I'm not reneging on our agreement. What else *can*

647

we do? I'd like to be able to live with myself in the future, and I know you would, too.'

'Yes. Oh Shane, thank you, thank you so much for your understanding, and most of all for your love. I don't know what I'd do without you.'

He took her in his arms and kissed her, and they sat holding each other for a few minutes. Finally he released her. 'I've got to get back to the office. I've a couple of meetings scheduled, and with Dad in London at the international hotel conference I've got my hands full. Then I want to stop off and see Grandpops on my way home to Beck House.'

They rose and she walked him to the door. 'Give my love to Uncle Blackie,' Paula said, looking up at him. She offered him a brighter smile. 'I feel much better – now that I've seen you.'

Shane touched her face lightly. 'You'll be all right, darling, *we'll* be all right. Just so long as we stay cool and keep a positive attitude. We mustn't let anything rattle us or throw us off our course.'

Several hours later, when Shane pushed open the door of the library in his grandfather's house, he found Blackie standing in front of an antique chest. He had a soft yellow duster in his hand and was carefully rubbing away at the silver trophy which was now his pride and joy.

Shane smiled. If his grandfather polished it once a day, he did so at least half a dozen times. Of all the things Blackie owned it had become his proudest and most treasured possession. At the beginning of April, Blackie's eight-year-old mare, Emerald Bow, had run at Aintree and had won the Grand National. Winning the greatest steeplechase in the world had been the fulfilment of Blackie's lifelong dream. Curious though, Shane now thought, that of all the horses he owns it had to be the one Emma gave him which finally won the most coveted prize for him. There has to be something prophetic in that.

Moving forward, Shane said, 'Hello, Grandpops, sorry I'm late.'

Blackie turned around, his face lighting up. The sight of his handsome strapping grandson warmed his heart. 'Shane, me boy!' he cried and ambled across the floor.

The two men embraced. But as his arms went around his grandfather in a bear hug, Shane realized, with a small shock, that Blackie had lost weight since he had last seen him. My God, I can feel his bones through his suit. He's suddenly become so frail, Shane thought with a spurt of worry mingled with sadness. They drew apart and Shane looked into Blackie's face, his eyes scanning it swiftly. The weight loss was evident in the sunken cheeks, the scrawny neck. His shirt collar looked too big for him, and Blackie was unnaturally pale tonight. His ebony black eyes were cloudy, seemed to have a milky film.

'Are you feeling all right, Grandfather?' Shane asked, his scrutiny fixed on the old man.

'Never felt better.'

'That's good to hear,' Shane answered, but he reminded himself that his grandfather usually said this. Not wishing to press him further about his health, Shane eyed the cloth in Blackie's hand. 'If you're not careful you're going to rub a hole in that thing with your constant polishing, and then where will you be?'

Blackie snorted in amusement, followed Shane's glance, which was directed at the trophy. He lumbered over to the chest where it reposed, his pace as slow as before. Putting the cloth down, he rested his hand on top of the symbol of Emerald Bow's great triumph.

'I won't go so far as to say that winning this was the crowning moment of my life, but it was certainly the most thrilling.' Blackie nodded to himself. 'It truly was.'

Shane smiled across the room at his grandfather. 'And mine, too,' he asserted.

'Aye, lad, but you're going to have greater triumphs in your life than I've ever had. That's in the cards, sure and it is.' Stepping up to the small console, Blackie picked up a crystal decanter and poured whiskey in two glasses. 'Let's drink to that foregone conclusion with a drop of me good Irish.'

Shane joined him, took the tumbler, clinked it against Blackie's and said, 'To future triumphs – for us both, Grandpops.'

'Yes indeed. And to Emerald Bow and next year's Grand National. You never know, she could win again.' Blackie shot Shane a knowing look, went over to the fireplace and sat down in his favourite wing chair.

Shane followed him, struck once more by his grandfather's slow gait, which was almost a shuffle, and his fragility. Concern mounted in Shane, but he pressed down on it. Perhaps his grandfather was merely tired this evening. Also, the excitement of the Grand National, winning, and all the partying that had ensued might easily have taken its toll. And after all he was an old man, very old now. He was eighty-four years old.

Blackie sat musing to himself for a second or two, gazing into the flames, an abstracted look in his eyes, then he said to his grandson, 'I don't think I'll ever forget the finish.' Swinging his head, he leaned forward with a burst of energy and eagerness, his glass clasped tightly between his hands, his eyes shining brightly as he relived the race in his mind's eye.

He exclaimed excitedly: 'There they were, Shane, coming to the last fence! Emerald Bow with two other big horses alongside her! *Almost neck and neck*. Steve Larner, tough little sod that he is, going hell for leather. High in the stirrups, pushing her forward, a grim look on his face. Me heart was in me mouth, aye, it was that, Shane. I thought she wasn't going to make it. Sure and I believed one of the other two would beat her to it, if only by a hair's breadth. When Highland Boy went first, sailed up but hit the top of the fence, rolled over and was out of the race, just like that, well, I couldn't believe me eyes. And then King's Gold went the same way, catapulting over and landing on his back. I knew he'd taken it too close to the roots of the fence. Me old eyes were glued on Emerald Bow. And only a fraction of a second after the others had fallen, there she was, me valiant little mare, jumping the fence like a gazelle and finishing two hundred yards in front of the field. Aye, Shane, it was the most spectacular finish I've ever seen, and I've been to a hell of a lot of horse races during my long life.' Blackie's face was flushed, and he fell back against the chair. He was momentarily breathless, but recovered himself in a matter of moments.

'I was there, Grandpops. I saw it all, remember.'

Blackie winked at him. 'Sure you saw it, but I can't help reliving it with you, lad. It gets the blood flowing through me veins again, and you know your father doesn't understand how I feel – not really. It's you, Shane, who had inherited my love of horses, and you've got as good an eye as me when it comes to spotting a thoroughbred.'

Blackie paused, and his eyes danced merrily as another thought struck him. 'Poor Emma, how she suffered that day, in one way and another. Worrying because I was getting overly excited, concerning herself with thoughts of my disappointment if Emerald Bow lost, and she even got hurt in the process. I grabbed hold of her so hard at the finish she was bruised for days, at least so she tells me. Said I'd almost crushed some of her fragile old bones. Still, she did enjoy it, no two ways about that. And she was as excited as I was. As I still am, if the truth be known.'

'And why not, Grandpops, it was a wonderful victory for you, and so well deserved.'

Blackie sat back, took a sip of his whiskey. His face

sobered and he became reflective. After a moment he said, 'Randolph was always right about Emerald Bow, you know, from the day Emma gave her to me. He never stopped telling me she had the stamina required for the National. It's a hard race, bloody carnage too, when you consider that out of the forty horses that start, only about eight finish. If that. Thirty fences to jump, and twice over Beecher's Brook. So many horses are injured, and it's exhausting for those that last. The stuffing's knocked out of them by the time they're coming into the final stretch.'

'The National's also a hell of a *fast* race,' Shane volunteered. 'It's over in about ten minutes.'

'Aye, it is, it is.' Blackie peered at Shane. His expression was one of self-congratulation and gratification. 'The party I threw at the Adelphi Hotel after the race was one of the best ever given, so I've been told. It *was* a grand bash, wasn't it?'

'Smashing! And so was the welcome we received when we got back to Middleham on Sunday lunch time. The huge banner congratulating Emerald Bow stretched across the main street, the boys coming out of the pubs when you and Randolph paraded her around the town, and then the luncheon at Allington Hall – memorable, all of it, Grandfather. I was so pleased and proud for you, I wouldn't have missed it for anything.'

'I know you wouldn't, but still, I admit I was a bit worried when you got bogged down with work in Sydney, early in March. I held my breath, I did indeed. I thought you mightn't make it and that would have been a severe blow to me, my boy.' Blackie sighed and a look of true contentment crossed his face. 'It's been a wonderful twelve months when I look back now. The trip around the world with me darlin' Emma, and now this – ' He broke off, glanced at the trophy, the smile lingering on his face. 'Imagine *me* winning the greatest race in existence.'

'You're not still talking about the Grand National are

652

you?' Emma exclaimed sharply, walking into the library in her usual brisk way. 'We're never going to hear the end of it, I can see.'

Laughing, Blackie pushed himself, up, went to greet her, kissed her cheek. 'Now, mavourneen, don't spoil me bit of fun.' He held her away from him, and studied her closely. 'Bonny as always, and I see you're wearing my emerald bow.' His face filled with genuine pleasure as he gestured to the brooch pinned on to the white-silk shawl collar of her grey wool dress. 'I notice you haven't had this off since we won. Now if that's not an emblem of the National, I don't know what is, mavourneen.'

Emma laughed, squeezed his arm, turned to Shane as he walked across the floor to join them.

Shane said, 'Hello, Aunt Emma, and Grandfather's right, you do look lovely tonight.' He bent forward, kissed her cheek.

'Thank you, Shane. How was the trip to Spain? I see you're keeping that tan of yours going strong.'

'I try,' he said, grinning. 'And the trip was very successful.'

Returning to the chair by the fire and drawing Emma along with him, Blackie said, 'Shane will get you a drink. What would you like to have, Emma?'

'Sherry, thank you.'

'And where's Emily?' Blackie asked. 'I thought she was coming in for a drink. Is she parking the car?'

'No. She dropped me off and went on her way. She had to get over to Beck House early. She sends you her love, and her apologies. Apparently she's cooking dinner for Shane and Winston tonight.'

'Oh I am disappointed not to see her. I was looking forward to her visit – I've got a soft spot for young Emily. She always gives me a good chuckle, no one quite so pithy and blunt as Emily – except for you, of course.' Blackie reached for a cigar, clipped off the end.

Frowning at him, Emma exclaimed fiercely, 'Should you be smoking that thing? You promised me you were going to cut them out.' He gave a throaty chuckle, grinned at her. 'At my age!' Shrugging, he went on, 'I keep telling you, I'm living on borrowed time. I don't aim to deprive myself of me last few pleasures. *This* – ' He waved the cigar under her nose. 'And me drop of whiskey.'

Emma let out a long-suffering sigh, knowing there was no use arguing with him.

Shane carried the glass of sherry over to Emma, sat down on the sofa. His grandfather and she had begun to talk about Emily's wedding, which was to take place in two months. He sat back, lit a cigarette, listened, his mind straying to Paula. He worried about her constantly, and even though he presented a patient and understanding demeanour to her, he was extremely anxious for Jim to make a quick recovery from whatever ailed him. And what did ail Fairley? Booze and pills, Shane thought. He was convinced that this lethal combination had contributed to, if not caused, Jim's recent collapse. Emma, Winston and Emily tended to agree with him, and Paula had confided in January that she thought Jim was an alcoholic.

'Winston tells me you won't be able to be his best man after all,' Emma said, drawing Shane into the conversation. 'We're so disappointed.'

'No more than I am, Aunt Emma. But Dad wants me to go to Sydney again, after I've spent a couple of weeks in New York, and I'll have to remain there through the end of May into June. Nothing much I can do about it – somebody has to supervise the building of the new hotel.'

'Yes, so Winston explained.'

Shane said, 'Michael Kallinski's standing in for me, and I can't think of a better man for the job.'

'I hear his father's not been too well,' Blackie interjected worriedly. 'Have you spoken to Ronnie in the last few days, Emma?'

654

'Yes, and he's up and about. He's had a bout of pneumonia, but he's feeling much better. This April weather has been most treacherous. So sunny, but the wind has been awfully cold, hasn't it? I've felt nithered to death these last few days.'

'That's nothing new,' Blackie announced, sitting back, contemplating her fondly. 'You suffered from the cold even when you were a slip of a girl. I remember how you used to shiver and complain about being frozen stiff at Fairley Hall.'

The two of them were soon engaged in a discussion about the past, which Shane had noticed they were prone to do quite frequently these days. He listened for a while, but when the clock on the mantelpiece struck he glanced at it, saw that it was six-thirty. Stubbing out his cigarette and downing the last drops of his drink, he stood up. 'I'm going to push off, leave you two lovebirds to your own devices. Don't do anything I wouldn't do, Grandpops.'

'That gives me a lot of rope then,' Blackie retorted, winking broadly.

'Several hundred yards at least,' Shane answered, his tone jocular. He bent over the chair and kissed his grandfather in the tenderest way, touched his shoulder. 'Take it easy, and I'll come and see you tomorrow.'

'Yes, please do, my boy. I'll be looking forward to it, and have a nice evening.'

'Thanks, I will, Grandpops.' Shane stepped over to Emma. He thought how pretty she was despite her grand age. After kissing her, he said, 'Keep an eye on this old warrior for me, Aunt Emma. I know he's a handful — but then you've had his number for years.'

The look Emma gave Shane was full of love. 'I will.'

'Humph!' Blackie's eyes travelled from Emma to Shane. 'And don't think I haven't got *her* number. I've always had it!'

Their laughter followed Shane as he walked to the door.

He looked back over his shoulder as he went out, saw that they were already contentedly chatting away, retreating into their own private world, sharing their memories. He closed the door softly behind him.

Blackie glanced at the door, leaned forward and said in a conspiratorial whisper, 'Do you think Shane's still leading a wild life and chasing fast women, like he used to do, Emma?'

'No, I don't,' Emma reassured. 'I'm perfectly sure he doesn't have time for that, Blackie dear, not the way he works.'

'Everyone's getting married and he's still single. And at twenty-eight,' Blackie complained, sounding unusually fretful. 'I'd hoped to see him settled down before I died, but it doesn't look as if I will. No chance of bouncing *his* babies on my knee.'

Emma threw him a chastising look, clucked softly, said, 'Of course there is, you silly old thing. What's got into you tonight? You're the one who's forever telling me you're going to live to be ninety.'

'Ah, I've grave doubts about that, mavourneen.'

Ignoring this comment, Emma hurried on, 'Shane *will* settle down, but only when *he's* good and ready.'

'Aye, I suppose so.' Blackie moved his great white leonine head from side to side. A look of helplessness spread across his face. 'This generation – I don't know, Emma, they baffle me at times. They make such messes of their lives, or so it seems to me.'

Emma froze in her chair, watching him closely, her eyes growing sharper. Was he generalizing or was he referring to anyone in particular? Surely he had not guessed about Shane's feelings for Paula. She said: 'Were we any different? Our generation was just as bad, Blackie dear.'

He was silent.

'Think about it – you'll have to agree that I'm correct, you know that.' She smiled and her shrewd green eyes danced. 'Now who made a bigger mess than me at different times in her life?'

He had to laugh. 'That's true. And here I am, going on about Shane, and I haven't even asked you how Paula is faring. Is she all right?'

'Coping, poor girl. She does seem to have her hands full at the moment. However, Jim is on the mend, I think. I sincerely hope he is, for their sakes. She's been worried to death about him, and so have I.'

'I was about to ask you about Jim.' Blackie gave her an odd look and there was a small pause before he asked, 'How long is he going to have to stay in the mental asylum?'

'Psychiatric clinic,' Emma corrected. 'About another month, maybe six weeks.'

'That long! Oh dear, Emma, that is a terrible burden for Paula.' He rubbed his chin, gave her a piercing stare. 'He will get better, won't he?'

'Of course!' Emma said in her most positive voice, but she couldn't help asking herself if he would. Her mind strayed to his family's troubled history.

As if he had read her thoughts, Blackie reflected out loud, 'A funny family – the Fairleys.' He looked at her again and for the longest moment. 'Adele Fairley used to seem a shade demented to me . . . the way she wandered around Fairley Hall like an apparition. And then there was the dreadful way she died. Tragic. I can't help thinking that this illness of Jim's might be – '

'I'd prefer not to contemplate something like that, if you don't mind, dear,' Emma said firmly. 'It's all too depressing and worrying for everyone concerned.'

Leaning forward, Emma now smiled her most winning smile, and changed the subject. 'You and I agreed that we wouldn't go gallivanting off again, but I was wondering if you'd like to come and stay with me at my house in the South of France? This summer, Blackie, perhaps in the

657

middle of June, after Emily's wedding, and before Alexander's in July. What do you think?'

'That is a tempting idea. These old bones of mine could use a bit of warming sunshine. Like you, I've been feeling the bite of the Northern wind this past week or so. To tell you the truth, I thought I was coming down with the flu.'

'Aren't you feeling well?' Emma's quick darting glance betrayed her concern for him.

'Oh sure and I am, me darlin'. Don't be fussing over me, Emma, you know I've never been able to stand that.' His wide Celtic mouth curved up in a smile of tenderness. 'Let's face it, we're not spring chickens any more. We're both very old now.' He chuckled, eyeing her in amusement, his eyes suddenly teasing. 'Two bags of ancient bones, that's what we are, Emma.'

'Speak for yourself,' she retorted, but her expression was as loving as his.

They were interrupted by Mrs Padgett, Blackie's housekeeper, who came in to tell them that dinner was served.

As they walked across the library and out into the lovely circular entrance hall, Emma noticed, as Shane had done earlier, that Blackie's steps were belaboured this evening. She had to slow her own pace so that he could keep up with her, and this troubled her deeply.

During dinner she realized that he was picking at his food, not really eating. He seemed to have no appetite, and he hardly touched his glass of red wine, which was most unusual. But she made no comment, deciding instead that she would take matters into her own hands. Tomorrow she would telephone Doctor Hedley, ask him to drive over to give Blackie a thorough examination.

For a short while Blackie talked about the Grand National, and Emma let him ramble on, knowing how important winning had been to him. But at one moment he unexpectedly dropped this subject when he said, 'It's always seemed strange to me that Shane was never interested in one of your girls, Emma. There was a time, when they were growing up, that I thought he and Paula might end up marrying each other . . . one day.'

Emma held her breath. For a split second she was on the verge of confiding in him, and then instantly changed her mind. It would only distress him if he knew about Shane's love for her granddaughter. Particularly since she had now come to the conclusion that Paula did not reciprocate Shane's feelings. Blackie would not be able to bear the thought of Shane's heartache.

Emma leaned over and patted his hand lying on the table. 'I suppose being together all of their lives makes them feel like brother and sister.'

'Aye, most probably, but it would've been lovely if they'd married, wouldn't it, me darlin'?'

'Oh yes, Blackie, it would have been wonderful.'

As they left the dining room, Mrs Padgett reminded Blackie she was taking the rest of the evening off, and bid them good night. Slowly he and Emma walked back through the hall and went into the library. Emma poured a cognac for him, a liqueur glass of Bonnie Prince Charlie for herself.

They sat in silence for a while, sipping their drinks, lost in their own contemplations, as companionable tonight as they had been all of their lives. But eventually Blackie roused himself. 'Don't you think it would be nice to play some records, Emma? Listen to a few old tunes, the ones we used to love.'

'What a good idea.' Emma rose and went over to the small cabinet that housed the stereo, looked through the stack of records. 'My goodness, I didn't know you still had this . . . that John McCormack selection of old Irish ballads I gave you years ago. Shall I put it on?'

'Aye, why not.' Blackie gave her a small grin as she

returned to her chair, boasted, 'I still have a good voice, you know. I'll sing along with the music, if you like.'

'I always did love that rich baritone of yours.'

They listened to the selection and, true to his word, Blackie did sing a few snatches of the old songs now and then, but his voice was feeble and quavering, and so he mostly hummed the melodies.

When the record came to an end, Emma remarked, 'Those songs bring back a lot of memories . . . especially *Danny Boy*. I'll never forget that night I came looking for you, after I'd run away from Fairley Hall. I found you at the Mucky Duck, singing that ballad as if your life depended on it. Oh Blackie, you looked so marvellous, standing there next to the piano, and goodness me, you were *so* theatrical. A real ham.'

He smiled.

Emma's eyes rested on him affectionately, took in the wavy hair, still thick but white as driven snow now, the craggy features, the broad face marked by the signs of age, and suddenly, in her imagination, she saw him as he had been in his youth, as he had looked that night in the pub. Vibrant black curls rippling back from a tanned face, black eyes dancing, white teeth flashing between rosy lips, his superb looks prominently highlighted in the glare from the burning gas lamps.

Leaning forward, Emma asked, 'Do you remember that particular night, Blackie?'

'How could I ever forget it, Emma? We went and sat together in the Saloon Bar and you drank a lemonade. I had a pint of bitter. Ah, such a little snippet of a lass you were . . . and you told me you were pregnant . . . and I asked you to marry me. Perhaps you should have.'

'Yes, perhaps. But I didn't want to burden you . . .' Emma did not finish, and she picked up her liqueur, took a sip.

Blackie settled back in his chair, a faint smile playing

around his mouth, and then he nodded to himself, said, 'You do look bonny tonight, Emma. You're the most fetching colleen in the whole country.'

'You're prejudiced,' she murmured, returning his unwavering gaze, his gentle smile.

Blackie sat up a little straighter, peering across at her in the soft dim glow of the muted light in the room. 'I'll never be able to tell you what our holiday has meant to me, Emma. Those eight months with you have made up for all the bad things that ever happened to me in my entire life – the pain, the heartache, the sorrow. And I do thank you, me darlin'.'

'What a lovely thing to say, Blackie. But it is I who should thank you for making your Plan with a capital P.'

'It was a good plan – ' Blackie stopped short and grimaced.

Instantly Emma was on her feet, leaning over him. 'What's the matter? Are you ill?'

He shook his head. 'It's nothing . . . just a twinge of indigestion.'

'I'm going to ring the doctor, and then I'm going to get you upstairs to bed.' She turned away from him, made a movement towards the desk near the window.

'No, no.' He tried to restrain her but his hand fell away weakly. 'I won't make it, Emma.'

'Yes, you will,' she insisted. 'I'll help you.'

Blackie shook his head very slowly.

'I *am* going to telephone Doctor Hedley,' Emma announced with a show of her old firmness.

'Sit down here with me, Emma. *Please*,' he begged. 'Just for a minute or two.'

Emma pulled up a hassock, seated herself, took his hand in hers, searched his face. 'What is it, Blackie?'

He squeezed her fingers, then smiled at her. Suddenly his eyes opened very widely. 'All my life,' he whispered hoarsely, 'I've known you all my life. We've been through so much together, Emma.'

'Yes,' she said, 'we have and I don't know what I'd have done without you, Blackie.'

He sighed a very long slow sigh. 'I'm sorry to have to leave you alone. So very sorry, mavourneen.'

Emma could not speak. Tears rushed into her eyes, fell down her wrinkled cheeks, splashed over the white silk collar and the emerald bow, and on to their entwined hands.

Blackie's eyes widened again, and he stared at her more acutely, as if memorizing her face. And then he said in a surprisingly clear voice, 'I've always loved you, me darlin'.'

'And I have always loved you, Blackie '

A fleeting smile struck his pale mouth. His eyelids fluttered, closed, lay still. His head fell to one side. His hand went slack in her tenacious grip.

'Blackie,' she said. '*Blackie!*'

The silence overwhelmed her.

She held on to his hand tightly, closed her eyes. The tears seeped out from under her old lids, ran down her face in streaming rivulets. She lowered her head and rested it on their clasped hands, drenching them with her tears.

'Goodbye, my dearest friend, goodbye,' she said at last. She continued to weep quietly, unable to stem the tears, and she sat there for a long time, her aching heart full of love for him.

But eventually she lifted her head, let go of his hand and pushed herself up on to her feet. She bent over him, gently smoothed his snow-white hair back from his forehead, and kissed his icy lips. How cold he is, she thought.

Emma's pace was slow and her step faltering as she moved blindly towards his chair near the window, where he had so often sat lately looking out at his garden. She took the small wool blanket patterned with the tartan of the Seaforth Highlanders and brought it to him and covered his legs and tucked it around him.

And then at the same snail's crawl she went to his desk. She lifted the phone and with trembling hands she dialled Beck House.

It was Shane who answered. 'Hello?' he said.

On hearing his strong and vibrant tone her tears began to flow once more. 'It's Blackie,' Emma said through her tears in a voice that shook. 'He's gone . . . please come, Shane.'

Shane arrived within the hour, bringing Paula, Emily and Winston with him.

They found her sitting on the hassock next to Blackie, her hand resting on his knee, her silver head bowed. She did not turn nor did she move at all, merely went on sitting there, staring into the fire.

Shane hurried to her, put his hand on her shoulder lightly, brought his face to hers. 'I'm here, Aunt Emma,' he said in the kindest of voices.

She made no response.

Shane took her hands in his and brought her to her feet slowly, gentleness flowing out of him.

Emma finally lifted her face to look up into his and she began to weep and Shane took her in his arms and held her close, soothing her.

'I miss him already and he's only just died,' Emma said with a small heartbreaking sob. 'Whatever am I going to do without Blackie?'

'Hush, Aunt Emma, hush,' Shane murmured and then he led her over to the sofa, motioning with his eyes to Paula, who stood in the doorway white-faced and trembling. She came and sat with her grandmother, began to comfort her, and Emily joined them.

Shane stepped over to Blackie. His throat was thick with emotion and the sorrow rose in him and tears ran down his cheeks. He gazed at Blackie's face and saw how peaceful it was in death and then he leaned forward and kissed his withered cheek.

'God speed, Grandfather,' he said in a low and saddened voice. 'God speed.'

CHAPTER 41

Paula began cautiously, 'It's your birthday in two days, Grandy, and I thought we might have a –'

'Oh dear,' Emma interrupted softly, with a small frown. 'Don't bring that up. Blackie's only been dead a couple of weeks and I'm not in the mood for a celebration.'

'I know, and I wasn't talking about a big party. Just a small dinner here at Pennistone Royal. There would only be me, Emily, Winston and my parents. We thought it would cheer you up.'

'Cheer me up,' Emma repeated hollowly, and then reached out and patted Paula's hand. 'I don't think anything would cheer me right now. But I suppose I have to keep plodding on. All right then . . . just the five of you, though. Please don't invite anyone else. I'm not in much of a mood for people right now. They tire me.'

'I promise I won't invite another solitary single soul,' Paula assured her, pleased that the suggestion had met with success.

'And no presents, Paula. I don't want any presents. As far as I'm concerned reaching eighty-one is cause for lament, not receiving gifts and whooping it up.'

'Don't worry, Grandma, we'll keep it very simple and casual. And it'll be nice for you to have Mummy and Daddy here for a few days.'

'Yes,' Emma murmured. She glanced down at the album on her lap. She had been looking at it when Paula had arrived a short while ago. She stared at the old photographs absently, her thoughts drifting into the past for a few seconds. Then she lifted her head, pushed the album towards Paula, remarked, 'Look at us here – Blackie, Laura and me. We're standing outside my first shop in Armley. That's me – in the tam o'shanter.'

'Yes, I recognize you.' Paula had seen this picture many times before, knew the pages of the album by heart. But wanting to humour her grandmother, she said, 'Let's look at some of the others, and you can tell me a few of your lovely stories about your early days in business. You know how I like hearing them.'

Emma nodded and at once began to talk with sudden animation as they leafed through the book, and for the next twenty minutes the two of them sat side by side in the upstairs parlour, reliving parts of Emma Harte's life.

At one point Emma broke off, peered at Paula and said, 'How long do you think I'm going to live?'

Taken aback at this question, Paula stared at her grandmother askance, filling with sudden alarm. She cleared her throat, said firmly, 'A long time, darling.'

'You're very optimistic,' Emma said and turned away, looked out into space, a faraway expression settling on her face.

Paula exclaimed, 'You're extremely fit for your age, remarkable really, and not a bit forgetful. You have years ahead of you, Grandy, as long as you take care of yourself.'

Emma brought her ancient and wise green gaze to meet Paula's troubled face, and she smiled slowly. 'Yes, yes, you're quite right. I don't know what's got into me today – I'm being morbid, aren't I? Blackie's death has been such a terrible blow to me, but I suppose I must be positive.' She let out a chuckle. 'Anyway, I might be old and a trifle weary these days, but I don't want to leave this world yet.'

'That's the spirit, Grandy.'

Emma did not reply. She rose and walked over to the

oriel window, stood looking down at her gardens and the daffodils blowing in the breeze. It's such a beautiful afternoon, she thought. Another perfect spring day . . . just like the day of Blackie's funeral. How eternal the land is, constantly renewing itself. Yes, in death there is always life. Sighing again, Emma returned to the fireplace and sat down in the chair next to it. She said, 'It was lovely of you to come over to see me, Paula dear. But I think I'd like to be by myself for a while, to have a little rest before dinner.'

Paula came to her, kissed her cheek, her heart full of love for Emma. 'All right, Gran, and I'll pop in tomorrow with the babies.'

'That'll be very nice,' Emma answered, and settled back in the chair as her granddaughter left the room. Her mind turned inward. The young don't really understand, she thought. Paula tries, and tries very hard, but she doesn't know what it's like to be the sole survivor, the only one left of one's contemporaries. They've all gone now. They're all dead and buried. My dearest friends, my loved ones. Even my enemies are no longer around to get my goat and spark the will in me to fight. I'm so alone without Blackie. We kept each other going all these years – he and I. Rambling on together into our twilight years. We had so many memories to share, a lifetime of experiences, and so much love and friendship to give each other. Why, my whole life has been lived out with my sweet Irishman. I didn't expect him to go like that. Such a shock. I knew he was old, as I am old, but he seemed so strong, and indomitable, like me. Funny, I always thought I would die first. Whatever will I do? However will I manage without him?

Emma's grief and enormous sense of loss overcame her again, as it had done so frequently in the last two weeks since Blackie's sudden death. Tears came into her eyes and she choked back a sob, brought her hand to her trembling lips. I miss Blackie so much. Such a void without him. There are so many things I didn't tell him and now it's too

666

late. I ought to have told him about Shane and his love for Paula. I didn't want to upset Blackie. He would have worried. But I do wish I had told him after all.

Emma wiped her damp cheeks with her hand and rested her head against the chair. She was filled with an aching loneliness she could not endure. She closed her eyes and after a few minutes she began to drowse, drifting off into a gentle sleep.

After leaving her grandmother, Paula had gone downstairs in search of Emily. She had found her in the library and now they sat together discussing Emma.

'She's putting up a good front, of course,' Paula said, 'but she's really suffering inside.'

Emily frowned worriedly. 'I agree with you. She's absolutely lost without Blackie. I think all the fight's gone out of her. To tell you the truth, the other day I even wished we *had* found something on Jonathan. At least that might have captured her interest, made her angry enough to lift her out of this resigned mood.'

Paula said, 'She was very busy with the plans for your wedding before Blackie died. Can't you get her involved again?'

'Don't think I haven't tried, because I have. But she seems so distracted, almost absent-minded, which is not like her.'

'You know something, Emily, there's only one thing for it!' Paula leaned forward eagerly. 'Emma Harte has been a work horse all of her life, and her business was her strong citadel in times of grief and sorrow and trouble in the past. We've got to persuade her to come out of retirement . . . get her back in the harness again.'

Emily sat up with a jerk, her face brightening. 'That's the best idea I've heard in weeks. And Grandma used to say she intended to die with her boots on. Oh, let's do it, Paula.' Instantly Emily's face fell, and she bit her inner lip, shaking her blonde head. 'I'm not sure she'll agree. She might not want to intrude on us . . . she can be very funny, you know.'

'We have to make a stab at it – personally I think that it's her only salvation. She'll just fade away and die, if we don't encourage her to be active, come back to work.'

'Agreed, and you can count on me. There's another thing – ' Emily hesitated, gave Paula a careful look, then rushed on, 'Why don't you move back in here with Nora and the babies? At least until Jim comes out of the nursing home.'

'Oddly enough, I thought of that when I was with Gran a little while ago. There's nothing like a couple of babies to liven things up, and perhaps having her great-grandchildren with her will give Grandy a new lease on life.'

'Absolutely. And together you and I can jolly Gran out of her despondency, don't you think?'

'Oh God, I hope so, Emily.'

'When do you think you could move in to Pennistone Royal?'

Paula laughed. 'How does tomorrow sound?'

'Terrific. I'll come over and help you if you like.'

'I'd love it, and then on Monday morning I'm going to vacate Grandy's office at the Leeds store, move back into my old one. That evening when we have the dinner for her birthday, you and I can make our proposal to her. I'll alert my parents, and they might be able to add a few words of persuasion.' Paula stood. 'I'd better go, Emily. I want to stop off at the nursing home. I promised Jim I'd come by later today.'

The two cousins left the library and walked across the Stone Hall to the front door.

Emily caught hold of Paula's arm just before they reached the short flight of steps. She said in a low tone, 'Jim's been in there for ten weeks now. How much longer, Paula?'

'Another month to six weeks. If he continues to improve.

Otherwise – ' She shrugged wearily, added, 'Then it could be longer, of course.'

Emily stared at Paula, said swiftly, 'Look, I hope you don't mind me saying this, but I hope that Jim knows what drink does to him now. I mean, he won't be able to touch a drop ever again and – '

'He knows,' Paula interjected. 'And you can be damned sure *I* know. Thanks for being concerned, Emily. One step at a time right now. That's the only way I can live my life, get through each day without losing my sanity. And very frankly, our grandmother is my priority at the moment.'

'Yes,' Emily said. 'I understand, and she's mine too. You can rely on me to help you any way I can.'

They cajoled, pleaded, challenged and attempted to bully her, using every ruse they knew to get Emma Harte to return to work.

But consistently, and quite categorically, she refused to be budged. Her stance was inflexible. She would shake her head emphatically, repeat over and over again that she had retired and that was that.

Eventually Paula and Emily gave up, at least on the surface. But they were forever dropping pointed remarks and making asides at meal times. They continued to seek her advice, even when they did not really need it, using every opportunity to gain her interest, and induce in her the desire to take an active role in her business once more.

Emma was fully aware of their ploys, and she would smile to herself, touched by their love and concern for her, but she remained resolute in her determination to lead a quiet life at Pennistone Royal.

And then one morning in the middle of May, Emma awakened early. She discovered that she was filled with her old energy and restlessness and drive. This surprised her, and she lay in bed for a while pondering to herself.

'I'm bored silly,' she said to Hilda, when her housekeeper brought up her breakfast tray at eight o'clock.

Placing the tray on Emma's lap, Hilda clucked sympathetically. 'Of course you are, Mrs Harte. You've been such an active woman your entire life, this drifting along, doing nothing, doesn't sit well on you. Perhaps you ought to let Tilson drive you into Leeds today. You could have lunch with Miss Paula or Miss Emily. Getting out of this house would do you the world of good, I just know it.'

'I've got a better idea, Hilda,' Emma said thoughtfully. 'I think I'll start going to the office for a short while every day. I know I don't want to get involved with my business on a day-to-day basis, on the other hand, I would like to keep busy.' Emma shook her head, looking regretful. 'I ought to be helping Emily plan that wedding of hers. I've been awfully neglectful, a selfish old woman, now that I think about it . . . feeling sorry for myself because my old friends are dead.' A look of comprehension flitted across the wrinkled face. 'Why, Hilda, my grandchildren are my friends, aren't they?'

'You can be sure they are, Mrs Harte,' Hilda replied. 'And Miss Emily will be delighted to have your help with her wedding, what with her mother living in Paris and seemingly not all that interested. She's such a lot to do, and time is running out on her. June fifteenth is not so far off, you know, madame.' Hilda beamed. 'I shall go downstairs right now and ask Tilson to bring the car around at ten-thirty. How does that sound?'

'It sounds wonderful, Hilda. Thank you very much.'

It was ten minutes to twelve when Emma Harte walked into her large department store in Leeds. She looked smart in a tailored navy-blue dress and matching coat. Milky pearls encircled her throat. Diamonds glittered in her ears. Her silver hair was perfectly dressed and her makeup artfully applied.

Emma hurried through the cosmetic department on the

street level, her step purposeful and brisk, a wide smile ringing her mouth. And as she stopped to greet the various sales assistants she discovered she was almost moved to tears at the genuine welcome she received from them all.

She took the lift to the executive offices, and then hesitated for a moment outside the door leading into her own private suite. She could not help asking herself what Paula and Agnes would say. She turned the knob and stepped inside.

Paula and Agnes were standing next to the latter's desk deep in conversation. Both women automatically glanced at the door as it swung open. They were speechless at the sight of Emma, obviously completely taken by surprise.

'Well,' Emma said, 'I'm back. And I'm here to stay.' She began to laugh at their stunned expressions, and reverting to the vernacular of the North, she added, 'Don't stand there gaping at me like a couple of sucking ducks. Say something.'

Paula grinned with pleasure. 'Welcome, Grandy,' she said, moving forward, catching hold of Emma's arm. 'Come on, your office is waiting for you – it's been ready for weeks.'

It seemed to Emma that the next few months sped by before she hardly had a chance to catch her breath. Every day she arrived at the Leeds store at eleven and stayed until four o'clock. She was soon in the swing of things, and taking a renewed interest in her colossal business empire, although she left the daily running of it to her grandchildren. She strenuously refused to take back the reins, pointing out, yet again, that she had retired the previous year and had no intentions of resuming her role as head of her various enterprises. She did agree to be a sounding board whenever they needed one, and she was always available to them, offering astute advice. And she was as smart and as alert and as agile as she had ever been.

And so, whilst she kept a canny eye on the business, she devoted most of her time to planning the two weddings due to take place in June and July. Emily was vastly relieved to have her grandmother's help, as was Maggie Reynolds, Alexander's fiancée. Maggie's mother had been dead for a number of years, and her father, a retired army colonel, had not been in the best of health lately. Nor was he the type of man to embroil himself in such a feminine matter as his daughter's wedding, being gruff and taciturn by nature.

With her inimitable brand of efficiency, and her extraordinary ability to concentrate totally on the matter at hand, Emma ploughed ahead, making elaborate arrangements. She dealt with the invitations, the guest lists, the caterers, the florists, the dress designers and the musicians who were to play at the two receptions. Several times she visited the Dean of Ripon, the Very Reverend Edwin LeGrice, to discuss each marriage ceremony, which he was to personally perform in Ripon Cathedral. Emma spoke to the organist and to the choir master at great length, and she helped the two future brides and their grooms select the appropriate music for their nuptials.

Not even the slightest detail was left to chance. Emma Harte wanted perfection and she aimed to have it, whatever it cost in time, energy and money. Winston said to her one evening, 'Well, Aunt Emma, it's good to have you back in command, playing the general again, *and* cracking your whip like you used to at Heron's Nest. Whatever would we do without you?'

'Manage, I'm sure,' Emma said in her pithy way, but she laughed, pleased by Winston's remark. She wanted to be wanted, enjoyed feeling useful. And they help to keep me young and alive and cheerful, she thought later that same evening, as she was getting ready for bed. She also acknowledged that planning the weddings had helped to take her mind off Blackie's death, had eased her sorrow

672

and her sense of loneliness. Positive action, she muttered under her breath as she slipped on her nightdress. And happy occasions. That's what every old person needs to give them a reason to go on living.

It was with a heart bursting with love and pride and joyousness that Emma watched Emily walk down the great aisle of Ripon Cathedral on the arm of her father Tony Barkstone at noon on 15 June.

To Emma, her young granddaughter looked her most beautiful that day. She resembled a delicate Dresden figurine in her wedding gown made of white taffeta. It was styled like an old-fashioned crinoline, the overskirt lifted at the hem, draped and caught with tiny sprigs of forget-me-nots and lily-of-the-valley. A mixture of these same flowers, also made of silk, had been woven into a small coronet which held her flowing veil in place. Her only pieces of jewellery, other than her engagement ring, were the tear-drop diamond earrings Emma had given her in 1968, and Great-Aunt Charlotte's string of pearls which had been *her* engagement present from Emma's brother, Winston, immediately after the First World War. Emily's half-sisters Amanda and Francesca were her bridesmaids and were charming in blue taffeta gowns, wearing wreaths of honey-suckle in their hair.

The reception was held in the gardens of Pennistone Royal, and as Emma moved amongst her family, friends and the many guests she kept telling herself how fortunate she was to be here on this most special day in Emily's life and her own. The weather was glorious. The sky was a bright China blue, and the sun brilliant. Emma decided, as she glanced about, that her gardens had never been so stunning in their beauty, the many flowers a vivid blaze of riotous colour against the fresh greenness of the lawns and the trees. That afternoon she had an acute awareness of everything, and she saw nature's loveliness and the people present through eyes that were more penetrating than ever in their perception. The smallest things suddenly took on a new importance and significance, and at one moment Emma knew that she was filled with a contentment she had not hitherto felt.

As she sat drinking her tea, watching the young people dancing, she thought of her hard life, her struggles, the sorrow and pain she had endured, the defeats and losses she had suffered. Quite suddenly they were all quite meaningless. I've been so lucky, she commented to herself. Luckier than most, in fact. I've experienced a great love, had dear and loving friends, achieved enormous success, amassed colossal wealth, and enjoyed good health all of my life. And most important of all, I have grandchildren who love me, care about me now in my old age. Oh yes, I've been lucky to have all that I've had.

Five weeks later, at the end of July, Emma experienced similar emotions when her grandson was married to Marguerite Reynolds. Maggie made another lovely bride, was elegant and svelte in a simply-styled gown of heavy cream satin. It had a high neck, long tight sleeves and a slender skirt that extended out into a long train. With it Maggie wore a satin pillbox hat encrusted with seed pearls and a veil of Brussels lace. The glorious weather of June held for the July ceremony at Ripon Cathedral and for the reception, which was again held in the grounds of Emma's great old house.

One Sunday, about a week after the second wedding, Emma and Paula went for a walk through the gardens of Pennistone Royal. Emma said suddenly, 'Thank you for chivying me out of my despondency after Blackie died. If you hadn't I might not have been around to witness those two wonderful occasions, to see Emily settled with Winston and Sandy with Maggie.' She winked mischievously at Paula, and added, 'Now, with a little bit of luck, I might still be here to welcome a couple of new great-grandchildren into my family in the not too distant future.'

'You'll be here, Grandma!' Paula exclaimed, returning Emma's smile. 'I'm going to make damned sure of that.'

Emma linked her arm through Paula's as they continued to meander up the Rhododendron Walk. After a short while, Emma said quietly, 'I'm pleased Jim came out of the nursing home in time to attend Alexander's wedding, at least.'

'So am I, Grandy.' Paula turned to Emma, remarked evenly, 'And he's much better. Poor Jim – he's been down at the bottom of the pit. He can only go up from now on.'

'Yes, darling, let's hope so.' There was a slight hesitation on Emma's part before she murmured, 'I've tried to speak to him about the nervous breakdown because I wanted to understand what brought it on. But I'm afraid he's not very forthcoming, is he?'

'No. He doesn't seem able to talk about it, not even with me. I decided it was better not to press him. I'm sure he'll open up later.' Paula sighed. 'In some ways Jim's very introverted, Gran. Doctor Hedley told me that the psychiatrist at the nursing home has been somewhat baffled too. Apparently he hasn't really been able to get to the root of Jim's despondency.'

Emma made no comment and the two of them walked on in silence and finally sat down on the bench at the top of the hill. Emma stared ahead, still thinking of Jim. Her expression changed, became sad as she wondered why he was so bottled up inside and seemingly incapable of unburdening himself to the psychiatrist, a doctor who might well be able to help him.

Paula, watching her grandmother, said, 'What are you thinking about, darling? You look so pensive all of a sudden.'

'Nothing of any great importance,' Emma murmured. 'I'm glad Jim went to my house in the South of France with Daisy and David. I think the holiday will do him a lot of good. The sun, the fresh air, outdoor activities, plenty of good food and rest always seem to work wonders. When he comes back at the end of August he'll be able to go back to the newspaper.' When Paula was silent, Emma glanced at her curiously. 'He will, won't he? You're not hiding something from me, are you, dear?'

'No, no, of course I'm not,' Paula exclaimed, dragging herself out of her own worrying thoughts. 'And like you I'm happy he agreed to take the holiday with my parents.'

'I'm surprised he didn't insist you went with them,' Emma ventured, eyeing her with greater interest.

'I promised Jim I'd join them for a week in the middle of August, if that's all right with you. In fact, I was hoping you'd come too.'

'Oh no, I don't want to start gadding off again. I shall stay here, and keep my eye on those great-grandchildren of mine.' Emma paused, reflected, then remarked as casually as she could manage, 'It'll be nice for me if you'd stay on at Pennistone Royal, Paula. If Jim's agreeable and would like to live here, of course. The house is so big, and it's going to seem rather desolate without little Emily.' Emma burst out laughing. 'I'd better not call her that any more, had I? After all, she's a married woman now.'

'And very much aware of it,' Paula said, also laughing. 'I'd like us to live here with you, Grandy. I'll talk to Jim when I'm at the Cap.' Paula was on the verge of telling Emma that she also fully intended to talk to Jim about a divorce. She stole a look at her grandmother, and changed her mind. Why worry her. Far better to get everything settled with Jim first.

CHAPTER 42

It was a hot afternoon at the end of August.

Emma sat at her desk in her office at the Leeds store, checking a list of sales figures for Paula. Quite suddenly she had the feeling she was not alone. She looked up quickly and glanced at the open door leading into Paula's office, expecting to see her granddaughter standing there.

There was no sign of Paula.

'I'm beginning to imagine things,' Emma said out loud, and then laughed under her breath. I'm also talking to myself, she thought, I hope I'm not getting senile. That state of affairs I couldn't bear.

She put down her pen and stared at the sheet of figures on her desk. She was filled with distaste, found she no longer had any interest in them whatsoever. She peered at her watch. It was almost five. Paula usually slipped out on to one of the floors around this time, and perhaps she had gone to meet Emily in the Rayne-Delman shoe salon. Emily had said something about buying shoes when she had phoned from her office at Genret earlier in the day.

A smile of intense pleasure touched the corners of Emma's implacable mouth, softening its resoluteness. They were having a girls' evening at Pennistone Royal tonight, as they often did on Fridays. Just the three of them and Merry O'Neill.

Emma leaned back in her chair, ruminating on the evening ahead, looking forward to it, and then she blinked in the brilliant light which was streaming in through the windows. How bright the sun is all of a sudden, blinding really, she muttered to herself. Rising, Emma walked over to the sofa and sat down.

She closed her eyes, wanting to shut out that harsh light

which was flooding the room. But it seemed to penetrate through the thin skin of her old lids and she lifted them, stared out into that most extraordinary and unnatural radiance. Emma's eyes narrowed as she shaded them with her hand. How very dazzling it is, she thought again. I must tell Paula to get blinds for this office. It's quite unbearable in here on such a sunny day.

To avoid the intense glare Emma turned her head. Her gaze rested on the photograph frames on the table next to the sofa. The silver and the brass and the glass glittered sharply in the luminescence that now washed over her office, and there was a curious lustre to those well-loved faces that stared back at her and so hauntingly. Yes, they *had* been haunting her lately . . . Laura and Blackie, her brothers Winston and Frank, and Paul. Oh yes, always her dearest Paul. In the last few days their faces had been so vividly clear in her imagination, their voices so strong and vibrant in her mind. They were as real to her as when they had been alive.

It seemed to Emma that the past had started to acquire a greater and more pronounced reality than the present. She was constantly invaded by memories . . . memories of years gone by, and they rushed at her with a force and clarity that stunned. They engulfed her, led her into other regions of time and frequently she felt that time itself had been suspended at some juncture long ago when she had been a young woman. Yes, her dear, dead loved ones had begun to completely tenant her waking moments, encroach on her restless nights. For the past week she had dreamed so many strange dreams and *they* were there with her in those dreams.

Emma reached for Paul's picture, smiling to herself. She held it tightly between her hands, looking down into his face. How often she had picked up this particular photograph in the last forty-eight hours, irresistibly drawn to it, continually magnetized by his smile, his laughing eyes.

The intensity of the coruscating light sharpened so markedly Emma blinked again. Her whole office was glowing with a shimmering iridescence. It was as if thousands of lights had been turned on and were focused on the very centre of the room. She hugged Paul's picture close to her body and gazed wide-eyed into that supernatural light, no longer disturbed by its refulgence. It was glorious and it had an aura of splendour.

But after a few moments of gazing into it she leaned her head against the cushions and closed her eyes. Emma let out a tiny sigh of pleasure. She was filled with happiness, the kind of happiness she had never known before or believed existed. A feeling of warmth began to spread through her body. How lovely it is, she thought. And she, who had suffered from the cold all of her life, was suffused with that warmth and with a peacefulness that was perfection itself. She felt drowsy, enervated, without strength. And yet somehow Emma recognized she was stronger than she had ever been in her whole life. And gradually she became aware of something else. He was here. In this room with her. That was the presence she had felt a few minutes ago.

He walked through the light, coming towards her, growing closer and closer. But he was so young . . . he looked exactly the way he had that night when she had first set eyes on him at the Ritz Hotel during the First World War. He was wearing his army uniform. Major Paul McGill of the Australian Corps. He was standing over her, smiling that engaging smile of his, the blue eyes so wide and clear and spilling his love for her. 'I knew I'd find you here in the office, Emma,' Paul said. 'But it's time for you to stop. Your work on this earth is finished. You have accomplished all you had to accomplish, done everything you had to do. And now you must come with me. I've waited for you for over thirty years. Come, my Emma.' He smiled at her and held out his hand. Emma sighed through her smiles. 'Not yet, Paul,' she said. 'Don't take me yet. Let me see them again . . . Paula and Emily. They'll be here any minute. Let me say goodbye to my girls. Then I'll come with you and willingly so. I want to be with you now. I too know it is time for me to leave.' Paul smiled and moved away from the sofa, stepped into the core of the glorious shining light. 'Paul, wait for me, my darling,' Emma cried. He answered, 'Yes, I'm here. I'll never leave you again. You're safe now, Emma.' She reached out her arms to him, straining towards him.

The photograph fell out of her arms, crashed to the floor, the glass shattering. Emma felt so weak she did not have the strength to pick it up. She did not even have the strength to open her eyes.

Paula and Emily, entering the adjoining office, heard the sudden noise. They looked at each other in panic and ran into their grandmother's office.

Emma lay quite motionless against the cushions. In repose her face was so still, so quiet, they were both unnerved. Paula put a calming hand on Emily's arm and together they approached the sofa. They stood looking down at their grandmother in apprehension.

'She's just having one of her little snoozes,' Emily whispered, instantly filling with relief. She noticed the photograph on the floor, picked it up, returned it to its given place.

But Paula was regarding the still and gentle face more closely. She saw the pinched nose, so white around the nostrils, the pale lips, the chalky pallor of the cheeks. 'No, she's not dozing.' Paula's mouth began to tremble uncontrollably. 'She's dying, Grandy's dying.'

Emily's face paled and she went rigid with fear. Her green eyes, so like Emma's, welled, 'No, no, it can't be so. We must call Doctor Hedley immediately.'

Paula's throat tightened and tears sprang into her eyes. She flicked them away with a trembling hand. 'It's too late, Emily. I think she only has a few minutes.' Paula repressed a sob and knelt at Emma's feet, took one of her frail old hands in hers. 'Gran,' she said softly, 'It's me, Paula.'

Emma's lids lifted. Instantly her face lit up. 'I waited for you, darling, and for Emily. Where is she? I can't see her.' Emma's voice was feeble, fading.

'I'm here, Grandma,' Emily gasped, choking on her words. She too knelt down and took Emma's other hand in hers.

Emma saw her, half inclined her head. She closed her eyes but opened them at once. She straightened up with a small burst of energy and stared directly into Paula's tear-stained face. Her voice was very weak yet clear, almost youthful, as she said, 'I asked you to hold my dream . . . but you must also have your own dream, Paula, as well as mine. And you too, Emily. And you must both hold on to your dreams . . . always.' She lay back against the sofa as if exhausted and her eyelids drooped.

Her two granddaughters gazed at her speechlessly, clinging to her hands, seared by their grief, their strangled sobbing the only sound in the room.

All of a sudden Emma opened her eyes for a second time. She smiled at Paula and then at Emily before looking away. She directed her gaze into the far, far distance, as if she saw a place they could not see and someone who was visible only to her.

'Yes,' Emma said. 'I know it is time now.'

Her green eyes stretched, became very bright and shining and they glowed with the purest of inner light. And she smiled her incomparable smile which illuminated her face with radiance, and then her expression became one of rapture and perfect joy as she looked for the last time on her granddaughters. Her eyes closed.

'Gran, Gran, we love you so much.' Emily began to weep as if her heart would break.

'She's at peace,' Paula whispered, her mouth twisting in pain and sorrow. Tears were trickling down her face. After a m ent she stood up. Leaning over her grandmother, she kissed her on the lips, her tears dripping on to Emma's cheeks. 'You'll always be in my heart, Gran. All the days of my life. And you are the very best part of me.'

Emily had been kissing Emma's small hand over and over and over again, and now she too rose. Paula moved to one side so that her cousin could also bid Emma farewell.

Reaching out, Emily stroked her grandmother's cheek, then she kissed her on the lips. 'As long as I'm alive you'll be alive, Gran. I'll love you always. And I'll never forget you.'

Paula and Emily automatically drew together, put their arms around each other. The two young women clung together for a few minutes, weeping, sharing their grief, endeavouring to comfort each other. Gradually they became a little calmer.

Emily stared at Paula. Tremulously she said, 'I've always been afraid of death. But I'll never be afraid of it again. I'll never forget Grandy's face, the way it looked as she was dying. It was filled with such radiance, such luminosity, and her eyes were brimming with happiness. Whatever it was our grandmother saw, it was something beautiful, Paula.'

Paula's throat constricted. 'Yes,' she said shakily. 'She did see something beautiful, Emily. She saw Paul . . . and Winston and Frank . . . and Laura and Blackie. And she *was* happy because she was going to join them at last.'

CHAPTER 43

In death, as in life, Emma Harte was in full command.

After summoning Doctor Hedley to the store, telephoning members of the family, and then accompanying Emma's body to the undertaker's, Paula and Emily finally drove out to Pennistone Royal.

A tearful Hilda greeted them in the Stone Hall.

The housekeeper handed Paula a letter she was clutching. 'Mrs Harte gave this to me a few weeks ago. She asked me to hold it for you, Miss Paula, until her death.' Hilda, who had worked for Emma for over thirty years, burst into tears again. 'It doesn't seem possible that she's gone,' Hilda said, wiping her eyes. 'She looked so well this morning when she left for the store.'

'Yes, she did,' Paula murmured quietly. 'And let's be glad she had her faculties until the end, and that her death was so peaceful, quite beautiful really, Hilda.' Paula and Emily spent the next few minutes comforting the sorrowful housekeeper, and gave her the full details of Emma's passing, which seemed to soothe her.

Finally pulling herself together, Hilda said, 'I know you both must have a lot to do. I'll be in the kitchen if you need anything.'

'Thanks, Hilda,' Paula said. Slowly she walked across the Stone Hall and mounted the great staircase, clasping the letter to her chest. Emily trailed in her wake.

They went into Emma's upstairs parlour where a fire blazed and the lamps glowed. They sat down on the sofa together, and it was with shaking hands that Paula opened the sealed envelope and read the four pages covered with Emma's neat yet elegant handwriting. The letter was neither maudlin nor sad, but brisk and matter of fact and it contained Emma's instructions for her funeral. She wanted a short and simple service, only one prayer and two hymns, one of them to be sung by Shane O'Neill. She forbade eulogizing, but suggested that if Paula so wished there could be one. It had to be spoken by Randolph, her nephew, and no one else.

It was the very cheerfulness that brought the tears to Paula's eyes. Swallowing, she passed the letter to Emily.

'These are Grandy's last wishes. She doesn't want the funeral service to be long or drawn out, and it mustn't be overly religious. We must do as she asks, Emily.'

Emily also wept as she read the letter. After mopping her streaming eyes and blowing her nose, she asked in a quavering tone, 'Whatever are we going to do without Grandy, Paula?'

Paula put her arm around Emily and comforted her. After a while she said firmly, but with gentleness, 'We are going to do what she wants us to do, take charge, and bury her the way she requested. And from now on we are going to be strong, and very brave. She wouldn't expect less of us. After all, that's the way she raised us. She taught us to stand tall, as she did throughout her life, and so we *must*. We can't let her down. Not now. *Not ever.*'

'Yes, you're right.' Emily took a deep breath. 'Sorry, I don't mean to be a burden to you. I know it's just as hard for you as it is for me.' Emily frowned and then added, 'Did you notice the date on the letter?'

'Yes. She wrote it a few days after Alexander's wedding – only a month ago.'

'Do you think Grandy knew she was going to die soon?'

'Perhaps, but I can't be sure. Still, they say old people do see death approaching. Blackie going so suddenly shook her up, as you know, and it made her feel vulnerable, even more conscious of her own mortality.' Paula forced a watery smile. 'On the other hand, I'd like to believe that *our* Gran was just being her usual efficient self, thinking of every contingency when she wrote the letter. You know as well as I do that Emma Harte never left one single thing to chance.'

These comments seemed to cheer Emily. 'That's true. And at least Gran died the way she wanted to die – at the office, with her boots on.'

Both young women glanced around as the door opened suddenly.

Winston hurried into the parlour, his face grave, his eyes red-rimmed. 'Sorry I'm late. I've been on the phone for ages,' he said. He kissed his wife, squeezed her shoulder comfortingly, and then bent down and kissed Paula on the cheek. 'You both look as done in as I feel. How about a drink?'

'Thanks, Winston, I'll have a vodka and tonic,' Paula said.

'The same for me, darling,' Emily said.

He brought them their drinks, took a chair next to the fire and lit a cigarette.

Paula passed Emma's letter to him, explaining, 'These are Emma's last instructions, her final wishes.'

After reading it, he said, 'Emma's been very explicit and precise. Thank God. It'll save a lot of family discussions and arguments about her funeral, especially with Robin. You know what he's like, so vociferous about everything, too bloody opinionated.'

Paula looked across at him curiously. 'I hardly think he would volunteer an opinion about his mother's funeral – not under the circumstances. Surely he wouldn't dare.'

Winston grimaced. 'He might, knowing him. But her letter spells it out and that's that.'

'And you can be sure Grandy's funeral is going to be exactly the way she herself planned it,' Paula exclaimed.

Winston nodded, asked, 'What did Doctor Hedley say after he examined Aunt Emma?'

'Heart failure,' Emily volunteered. She gulped. 'Gran's poor old heart just gave out, stopped beating.'

Winston drew on his cigarette and looked away, his eyes suddenly swimming. There was a tremor in his voice as he remarked, 'Grandfather Winston always used to tell me that his sister had a heart as big as a paving stone, and Emma did, she surely did.' He sighed softly. 'At least she went peacefully, and for that we must all be grateful.' He

685

brought his eyes back to Paula. 'When is the funeral? Have you decided yet?'

'I'm afraid we can't have it until Tuesday at the earliest. Mainly because of Philip getting here from Australia,' Paula told him. 'Fortunately Pip was in Sydney, not out at the sheep station in Coonamble, when I rang him tonight. He said he'd leave first thing in the morning. Very early. He's chartering a private jet. He thinks it'll be quicker than taking a commercial flight. I also spoke to my mother. Naturally she was as devastated as we are, and she wants to get home as quickly as possible. So she, my father and Jim are flying from Nice directly to Manchester tomorrow morning. Alexander and Maggie will be arriving then, too.'

Emily said, 'I spoke to Mummy in Paris. I told her she didn't have to come until Sunday or Monday. I also talked to Robin and Kit. They're here in Yorkshire, so there's no problem. We managed to contact everyone on our list including Sarah and Jonathan. What about you, Winston?'

'I got hold of Dad at the hotel in London. He'll be on a train in the morning. Vivienne's at Middleham, of course. Sally and Anthony were both at Clonloughlin. But Aunt Edwina is in Dublin. Anthony told me he'll reach her later this evening. They'll fly over on Sunday. You're going to have a house full, Paula.'

'Yes, I know.'

Winston said reflectively, 'I think Emily and I ought to move in here with you for the next few days. What do – '

Paula interjected. 'Oh yes, please do. I'd appreciate it.'

Clearing his throat, Winston now asked in a muffled tone, 'When are they bringing her body – I mean, bringing Aunt Emma back to Pennistone Royal?'

Paula blinked rapidly as her eyes moistened. 'Tomorrow afternoon. I'm going to take the dress she wanted to wear to the undertaker in Leeds first thing in the morning.' Paula turned her head, pressing back her tears with her fingertips. After a second, she went on, 'Emily and I didn't want to leave her there all alone for the next few days. It may sound silly, but we didn't want – her to be lonely without us. And so her coffin will be brought here, to this house, her home, the one place she truly loved on this earth. We've decided to let the coffin stand in the Stone Hall. She liked the hall so much . . .' Her voice trailed off.

Emily said, with a little burst of anger, 'You wouldn't believe how stupid the undertaker was, Winston! So bureaucratic. He actually tried to argue with us earlier this evening, when we insisted on accompanying Gran to – his place.'

'Oh I know, darling,' Winston murmured sympathetically. 'There's always a lot of stupid red tape. But you got your way, which is the main thing.'

'You can bet your last shilling we did,' Paula asserted. 'By the way, Emily reached Merry just as she was leaving the office, to come to dinner here, and she went to tell Uncle Bryan about Emma. Apparently he was so heartbroken she had to drive him home to Wetherby.'

'I'm sure he was, and is,' Winston replied. 'Aunt Emma was like a mother to Bryan when he was a child growing up.'

'Merry rang us back at the office,' Emily said. 'The O'Neills are popping over at about nine o'clock to be with us.'

'Incidentally, I tried to get hold of Shane. He was due back from Spain this afternoon.' Winston fixed his eyes on Paula. 'But when I rang the London office at six forty-five there was no reply. I guess I missed him – '

'I caught him there,' Paula interrupted. 'At six. He'd just walked in from the airport. He's on his way to Yorkshire right now – driving. He'll come straight here, and he should arrive about eleven.'

There was a knock on the door and Hilda walked into the parlour. 'Excuse me, Miss Paula,' she said. 'But I'd already prepared the usual cold buffet for tonight, as I always do on Friday. You know, before you rang me about – ' The housekeeper stopped, covered her mouth with her hand. She took a breath, and her voice wobbled as she finished, 'About Mrs Harte passing away.' She stared at Paula helplessly, unable to utter another word.

'I'm sorry, Hilda, but I don't feel like eating.' Paula glanced at Emily and Winston. 'Do either of you?' They both shook their heads, and Paula added, 'I think we'd better skip dinner tonight, thanks anyway, Hilda.'

'Oh I understand, Miss Paula,' Hilda made a face. 'I can't eat either. To tell you the truth, I'd choke on the food,' she muttered and disappeared.

'Blunt as ever, Hilda is,' Winston said. 'But I know what she means. I feel the same way.' He rose and went to the console, where he poured himself another scotch and soda. He turned suddenly, looked first at his wife and then at Paula. He said thoughtfully, 'This may seem like a peculiar thing to say, rather far-fetched even, but now that Aunt Emma's dead I feel her presence more acutely than ever. I don't mean because I'm here in this room, which was her favourite, but in general. She's – well, she's just *with* me. I've felt her closeness ever since you called me at our Harrogate office to tell me that she'd died.'

Emily nodded and emphatically so. 'It's not far-fetched, Winston. Paula and I discussed that very thing when we were driving back here tonight.'

For a moment Paula sat silently reflecting and then she said in a quiet voice, 'We all feel her presence because she *is* here with us, Winston. She's all around us. And inside us. She made us what we are, gave us so much of herself that we're full of her.' A sudden and lovely warm smile spread across Paula's tired face. 'Grandy will be with each one of us for all of our days. And so, in a sense, she'll never really be dead. Emma Harte will live on forever through us.'

* * *

Emma Harte's funeral was held in Ripon Cathedral, as she had requested. It took place at one o'clock on the Tuesday following her death.

Her entire family was present, along with friends, colleagues, employees and most of the inhabitants of the village of Pennistone Royal, where she had lived for well over thirty years. The cathedral was packed to overflowing and if there were some present who were dry eyed, they were far outnumbered by those who were tearful and sorrowing.

Her coffin was borne down the central nave and through the great chancel to the altar by the six pallbearers she herself had chosen. Three of them were her grandsons: Philip McGill Amory, Alexander Barkstone and Anthony Standish, Earl of Dunvale. The other three were her great-nephew Winston Harte, Shane O'Neill and Michael Kallinski, the grandsons of her two dear friends from her youth.

Although her coffin was not heavy, the six young men walked at a slow, measured pace, their steps keeping time with the organ music that swelled to the rafters of the ancient cathedral. Finally the pallbearers came to a stop in front of the magnificent altar and it was here that they rested Emma's coffin amidst a profusion of exquisite floral bouquets and wreaths. The central area where the coffin stood was bathed in light from the many flickering candles and the sunlight pouring in through the jewel-coloured stained glass windows.

The family occupied all of the front pews. Paula sat between Jim and her mother. Her father was on Daisy's other side. He, in turn, had Emily on his right side. She was mothering Amanda and Francesca, who cried continuously into their damp handkerchiefs. Although Emily was as distressed as her sisters, she somehow managed to keep a firm grip on herself, endeavouring to comfort the heartbroken teenagers.

Once the pallbearers had been seated with the rest of the mourners, the Dean of Ripon, the Very Reverend Edwin LeGrice, began the short service. He spoke beautifully about Emma, his words eloquent and moving, and when he eventually stepped down from the pulpit ten minutes later, his place was taken by Emma's nephew Randolph Harte.

Randolph gave the sole eulogy. He had difficulty at times, his strong voice cracking with emotion and he choked on some of his sentences, his sorrow and sense of loss rising to the surface frequently. Randolph's words about his aunt were very simple and loving, spoken from the heart and with genuine feeling. His eulogizing of Emma was limited to a recital of her attributes as a human being. He made no mention of her business career as one of the world's greatest merchant princes. Instead he touched on her generosity of spirit, her kind nature, her understanding heart, her great acts of charity, her loyalty as a friend and relative, her extraordinary qualities as a woman of remarkable character and strength and indomitable will.

After the eulogy, which had caused many to weep, the Ripon Cathedral choir rose and gave their beautiful harmonized rendition of *Onward Christian Soldiers*, one of the two hymns Emma had learned as a child, and which she had wanted sung today.

As the choir sat down, the Dean of Ripon returned to the pulpit. He led the mourners in a single prayer, before offering up his own brief prayer for Emma Harte's soul and for her eternal life. When he brought this to a close he asked all of those present to say their own personal and private prayers for Emma during the next few minutes of absolute silence.

Paula, her head bowed, squeezed her eyes tightly shut, but the tears seeped out anyway and dripped on to her clasped hands. The cathedral was perfectly still now, its peacefulness enveloping them all. But occasionally the silent hallowed space echoed with a muffled sob, a small gasp of grief or a strangled cough.

And then suddenly his voice rang out, so true and clear and pure Paula thought her heart was going to burst. She had known Shane was going to sing *Jerusalem*, since this was one of Emma's last wishes, but nevertheless she was startled. She brought her handkerchief up to her face, wondering how she could ever bear this part of the service.

Shane O'Neill stood alone in a far corner of the cathedral and he sang William Blake's old hymn without accompaniment, his rich full baritone echoing to every corner of the church.

As he came to the end of the first verse and commenced the second Paula experienced a sudden and extraordinary feeling of peace and release as the words washed over her. He held her enthralled.

Shane's lilting voice reached out to touch everyone present as he now sang:

'Bring me my bow of burning gold!
Bring me my arrows of desire!
Bring me my spear! O clouds, unfold!
Bring me my chariot of fire!
I will not cease from mental fight,
Nor shall my sword sleep in my hand
Till we have built Jerusalem
In England's green and pleasant land.'

As Shane's voice faded away, Paula unexpectedly understood the need, the significance and the importance of the ritual and ceremony of death. Somehow they were helping her to endure her sorrow. The prayers, brief though they had been, the choir boys and then Shane singing so melodiously, the masses of flowers and the extraordinary beauty of this ancient cathedral had given her a degree of ease from her overwhelming pain. The presence of the Dean, whom she had known for years, was calming, comforting to her. It suddenly struck her that when grief could be shared in this way the burden of the heartbreak became slightly lighter to bear. She knew the service had been a shade more elaborate than her grandmother had intended, but somehow she felt it had been extremely consoling to those who genuinely cared about Emma and mourned her truly. We did her honour, we gave her a wonderful tribute as she leaves this earthly life, Paula thought. It has been our way of saying our loving goodbyes. Paula felt a new strength flowing through her as she lifted her head.

Instantly she became conscious of her mother's terrible anguish. Daisy was sobbing unrestrainedly against David's shoulder. Paula put her hand on her mother's arm, whispered, 'It's all right, Mummy. Draw comfort from knowing that she's safe at last. She's gone to your father, to Paul, and now they're together for all time, for eternity.'

'Yes,' Daisy gasped. 'I know, darling, I know. But I shall miss her so much. She was the best. The very, very best there is in this world.'

The organ music began again and rose to a crescendo as her coffin was lifted by the pallbearers. They brought it back through the chancel and down the nave and out of Ripon Cathedral. Emma's immediate family walked behind her coffin and then they stood outside, watching as it was placed in the hearse and covered with a blanket of flowers for her last journey.

Paula noticed that Edwina was as stricken and tearful as her mother and impulsively she went over, placed her hand on her aunt's arm. 'I'm glad you made your peace with Grandy,' Paula said in a shaky voice. 'Really glad, Aunt Edwina.'

Edwina turned to Paula, her light grey eyes brimming.

'It was too late. I should have done it years ago. I was wrong. So very wrong, Paula dear.'

Paula said, 'She understood. She always understood everything, that was the beauty of Emma Harte. And she was so pleased you and she became friends – overjoyed, if you want to know the truth.'

'That helps a little,' Edwina said softly. 'And you and I, Paula, we must be friends too. Can you forgive me?'

'Yes,' Paula said very simply, and bent forward and kissed Edwina's wet cheek.

A long line of cars followed the cortège out of Ripon and on to Harrogate. They soon left the bucolic Dales behind, passed through the city of Leeds, the seat of Emma's power, and travelled through the grimy industrial valleys of the West Riding. But eventually the procession came up on to the high moorland road that cut through the great Pennine chain of hills.

On this sunlit afternoon in early September those grim and savage Yorkshire moors had lost their blackened and daunting aspects that could so appal the eye. Dark and implacable for most of the year, they now blazed with sudden and glorious splendour. As it always did at the end of the summer, wave upon wave of purple and magenta heather undulated across the great sweep of wild, untenanted moors. It was as if a cloth of royal purple had been rolled out, and it rippled gently under the light breeze. High above floated a resplendent sky that was as blue as speedwells and brilliant with that incredible clarity of light so peculiar to the North of England. The air was pure and bracing. Larks and linnets wheeled and turned with a rush and fluttering of wings and their sweet trillings pierced the silence, and there was the fragrant scent of harebells and wild flowers and heather on the lucent air.

Finally the cortège began its downward descent, leaving the moorland behind, and several hours after its departure from Ripon it progressed slowly into the village of Fairley. The hearse came to a standstill outside the quaint Norman church where eighty-one years ago she had been christened.

Her six young pallbearers, representing the three clans, shouldered her coffin for the last time. Moving at a slow pace and with great care, they carried her through the lych-gate into the cemetery, where the vicar, the Reverend Huntley, was waiting at the graveside.

Against the drystone walls and under the blowing trees and along the winding paths stood the villagers of Fairley. They were silent and grieving, the men with their caps in their hands, the women and children holding sprays of wild flowers, and heather, for remembrance, and all had their heads bowed and most of them were weeping quietly. They had come out of love to pay their last respects, to say farewell to this woman who was one of their own, she who had risen so high in the world but had never once forgotten them.

After a brief ceremony under that wide and shimmering sky which she had believed to be unique, Emma Harte was buried in the benign earth which had for so long sheltered her loved ones. Her grave was between those of her mother and Winston, her final resting place overshadowed by the moors she had so loved and wandered over as a child, and where she had never felt lonely or alone in her solitude.

Tycoon

'Cease to ask what the morrow will bring forth, and set down as gain each day that Fortune grants.'

HORACE

CHAPTER 44

'I still think there's something fishy going on,' Alexander muttered, pacing the floor of Paula's office at the London store.

'So do I,' she agreed, her eyes following him as he progressed up and down between the fireplace and her desk. 'But having suspicions is simply not good enough. We need concrete evidence of some kind before we can make a move against Jonathan. And Sarah perhaps. I'm still not certain whether she is being treacherous or not.'

'Neither am I. But we do need to get the goods on him, you're quite right. Until then our hands are tied.' Alexander rubbed his chin, his expression thoughtful. He came to a stop in front of Paula's desk and levelled his gaze at her. 'My gut instinct tells me that Jonathan's double dealing is staring me in the face, and you can bet it's going to *hit* me in the face one day very soon.' He shook his head. 'And to borrow a phrase of Grandy's, I don't like unpleasant surprises.'

'Who does?' Paula sighed, her worrying growing more acute. She knew Alexander was the most conservative of men and not prone to exaggeration or flights of fancy. Besides, their grandmother had been convinced of Jonathan Ainsley's duplicity until the day of her death five weeks ago. But, like them, Emma had not had the proof. Settling back in her chair, Paula said, 'Whatever it *is* he's doing, he's obviously been very clever about it, since the accountants haven't found anything wrong after checking the books.'

'Naturally he is, and you know he's always been bloody

devious. He doesn't let his right hand know what his left is doing, for God's sake. He hasn't changed much over the years.' Alexander gave her a pained look. 'Don Littleton thinks I'm stark raving mad. If I've made him go over the books once, I've had him do it a dozen times.' Alexander lifted his shoulder in a helpless shrug. 'Don and two of the other accountants with his firm put the real estate division under a microscope. There's nothing untoward – not a single thing that seems suspicious. At least, not as far as money matters are concerned.'

Paula leaned forward, rested her elbows on her desk, propped her chin in her hands. 'He wouldn't be stupid enough to *steal*, Sandy, and he's smart. He'd cover his tracks wherever they led. I wish we could think of some way to lure him out into the open, get him to show his hand . . .' Her sentence remained unfinished as she considered this idea, racked her brains for likely possibilities.

Her brother Philip, who sat on the sofa at the other side of the room, had been listening intently for the last fifteen minutes. Finally breaking his silence, he said, 'The only way you'll ever trap our dear cousin is to set him up as a target.'

Alexander pivoted on his heels. 'How?' he asked.

Philip rose and strolled over to join them. Of all of Emma's grandsons, Philip McGill Amory was the most handsome. He was the spitting image of his grandfather and had the McGill colouring that his mother and his sister had inherited. His hair was the same glossy black, his eyes that uncanny blue which bordered on deep violet, and he was as tall, virile and dashing as Paul McGill had been. Although only twenty-four, Philip also happened to be the shrewdest of Emma's grandsons, since he had been blessed with Paul's extraordinary business acumen and financial genius, as well as a great deal of his grandmother's not inconsiderable brilliance. He had been diligently trained by

Emma since the age of seventeen and after taking over the vast McGill empire in Australia he had proved himself to be worthy of her trust many times over. He was known as a man to be reckoned with, and one who had a wisdom beyond his years.

Drawing to a stop next to Alexander, he put his hand on his cousin's shoulder and said, 'I'll tell you *how* in a minute, Sandy.' Lowering himself into one of the chairs facing his sister, he remarked, 'That detective Gran hired – Graves – hasn't been able to dig up a thing on Jonathan. However, *I* still believe that it's very probable he has his own company – one that is being run by straw men, and – '

'Don't think I've dismissed that possibility,' Alexander fiercely interrupted, 'because I haven't.'

Philip nodded. 'Okay, so let's start with the assumption that he *does* indeed have a real estate company, and that he's been funnelling deals into it. Big deals that by rights should be going to Harte Enterprises. That in itself is enough to hang him.' Philip sat forward urgently, looked first at his sister and then at Alexander. 'I propose that *we* put the noose around his neck. And I'll tell you how. It's very simple really. We have to get someone to present a deal to Jonathan as head of the real estate division of Harte Enterprises. Now, here's the twist . . . we have to make the deal so attractive, so juicy, he won't be able to resist putting it through his own company. Naturally it must be extremely appealing, and so very big, so tempting, his greed will far outweigh his judgement. If the stakes for himself are high enough he'll act rashly, believe me he will.'

Sitting back, Philip crossed his long legs, glanced from Alexander to Paula and back to Alexander. 'Well, what do you say?'

Alexander now sat down heavily in the other chair, nodded slowly. 'I must admit, it's a smart ploy, and I'll go along with it, providing you can answer a couple of questions.'

'*Shoot.*'

'Philip, let's be practical, where the hell are *we* going to find this tempting deal to dangle like a carrot in front of Jonathan? That's for openers, and secondly, who are *we* going to get to offer it to him?' Alexander smiled narrowly. 'Let's not underestimate our wily cousin . . . he'll spot the holes immediately.'

'Ah, but there won't be any,' Philip replied evenly. 'I have someone who can offer the deal to Jonathan, a close friend who has his own real estate company here in London. So that answers your first question. As far as the deal itself is concerned, I believe my friend may have something up his sleeve that would be most appropriate, and tempting. All I need is your approval, and then I'll talk to him.'

'I suppose it's worth having a go,' Alexander said, fully aware of Philip's inbred shrewdness and discretion. He turned to Paula. 'What do you think?'

Paula said, 'I'm all for it, if you are, Sandy.' She eyed her brother. 'What's the name of your friend?'

'Malcolm Perring. Surely you remember old Malcolm – we were at Wellington together.'

'Vaguely. I think you introduced us once, when I came down to visit you at half-term.'

'I did. Anyway, he and I remained relatively close friends after we left school, and he was out in Australia for a year and – '

'Jonathan's bound to smell a rat,' Paula said sharply. 'You and Malcolm were at the same public school, then he was in Australia. Jonathan'll put two and two together.'

'I doubt it,' Philip said, sounding assured and confident. 'Malcolm's been back here for a couple of years. He inherited his brother's real estate company after that poor chap dropped dead of a heart attack at thirty-nine. Besides,

Jonathan's not going to ask a lot of personal questions, and Malcolm can be adroit and evasive, believe me, he can.'

'I trust you. I know you wouldn't embroil somebody in our affairs whom you couldn't rely on to be absolutely discreet. And you *will* have to take him into your confidence,' Paula remarked.

'Obviously. But Malcolm *is* reliable . . . true blue, Paula.' Philip chuckled. 'I'm sure he has a deal that is ready to go – Perring and Perring is a huge company, and wouldn't it be ironic if we were able to kill two birds with one stone? Catch Jonathan red-handed and do a bit of smart business for Harte Enterprises at the same time.'

Alexander began to laugh dryly, tickled at the idea. 'Oh how Grandy would love this!'

Paula half smiled. 'Perhaps we should go ahead then, Philip, since Alexander is all for it. And actually it must be his decision – as managing director of Harte Enterprises.'

Alexander exclaimed, 'We don't have anything to lose and, very frankly, I'm relieved we're taking aggressive action. This sitting around waiting for Jonathan Ainsley to tip his hand is most frustrating. I feel we must force him out in the open if we can.'

'I shall talk to Malcolm first thing tomorrow morning.' Philip glanced at his watch. 'If we're going to grab a bite of lunch before we go to John Crawford's office, I think we ought to leave. It's eleven-thirty. We have to be at John's at two-thirty, don't we, Paula?'

'Yes.' She stood up, brushed a piece of lint off her black dress. 'I'm not looking forward to this afternoon,' she began and stopped. Her upper lip quivered and her eyes filled with tears. She glanced away quickly. After a moment she managed to compose herself, and she smiled weakly at the two men.

'I'm so sorry,' she said. 'That happens when I least expect it – I think of Gran and just choke up. I can't get used to her not being here. It's just awful, such a gap in my life . . . all of our lives, I suppose.'

'Yes,' Philip agreed. 'Alexander and I feel the same way as you do. In fact, we were discussing it last night at dinner. It's hard to realize that she's not going to suddenly swoop down on us with a bit of unorthodox but frighteningly clever advice, or make one of those blunt or pithy comments of hers.'

Philip walked around the desk and took hold of Paula's shoulders gently, looked down into her white face. 'The reading of the will *is* going to be dreadfully upsetting, Paula, because it emphasizes the reality of her death. But you must be there . . . we all must.' He attempted a bit of levity as he finished, 'Grandy will be mad at us if we're not.'

Paula nodded, smiling faintly at his remark, knowing he wanted to cheer her up. Her sadness did ease slightly. 'I'll tell you one thing – it gets my goat when I think of the leeches who are going to be present later.' She sighed. 'Ah well, there we are, nothing we can do about it and my apologies to the two of you again. I think the less said about this afternoon the better. Now, come on, let's go to lunch. Emily's joining us – I've booked a table at the Ritz.'

'The Ritz!' Philip exclaimed in surprise. 'A bit fancy, isn't it, for a quick snack?'

She tucked her arm through her brother's, glanced up at him and then across at Alexander, a hint of genuine gaiety surfacing. 'Not really. It *was* one of Grandy's favourite places. And I chose it because it has such happy associations for the four of us . . . all those lovely treats she used to give us there when we were children.' Paula laughed, now addressed her brother, 'Besides, you and I might not be here if Emma and Paul hadn't indulged in a bit of romantic dallying at the Ritz over sixty years ago!'

'Correct,' Philip answered with a laugh. 'And in that

case I think lunch had better be on Paul McGill! Consider this my treat.'

'Jolly decent of you,' Alexander said as they left Paula's office and went out to the staff lift. Alexander engaged Philip in a few seconds of conversation about his friend Malcolm Perring as they rode down. Satisfied with Philip's answers, confident that his cousin had selected the right man to help them corner Jonathan, he asked, 'By the way, how long are we going to have the pleasure of your company?'

'I'll be here until the end of October, when I'm apparently going to Texas with Paula. So she told me before you arrived. Sitex business. From there, it's back to Sydney for a few weeks, and then I'm coming home again – for Christmas.'

'Oh!' Paula exclaimed. 'You didn't tell me.'

'I only just decided at breakfast this morning. I haven't had a chance to mention it. Mum's so done in at the moment, I think I ought to be here. It'll cheer her up. I've also agreed to go to Chamonix with them in January, and of course they're both delighted about that.'

'And so am I – this is great news.' Alexander beamed. 'Maggie and I have been invited to join Aunty Daisy and Uncle David.' He shot Paula a quick glance. 'Are you going to change your mind, now that Philip's coming along?'

'*No.* When *I* take a vacation I want to lie in the hot sun and bake myself to a crisp dark brown. The ski slopes have never appealed to me, as you both well know. Also, I have to be in New York in January. We're doing a big promotion of French and Italian couture fashions at the store, and I'm opening the Total Woman Shop at our Fifth Avenue branch then.' She gave them a wicked grin as they stepped out of the lift. 'Somebody has to work in this family.'

Laughing, they bustled her outside into Knightsbridge and into a taxicab and headed for the Ritz Hotel.

Emily was already waiting for them at a table in the restaurant. Elegant in a black suit, which was most flattering and showed off her blonde beauty to perfection, she nevertheless wore a mournful expression. Her green eyes were wistful as her cousins and brother sat down with her. 'I'll be glad when today's over,' she muttered to Alexander. 'The thought of hearing the will is so depressing.'

Alexander said, 'Come on, Emily lovey, cheer up. Philip and I have just been through the same recital with Paula.' He squeezed her arm. 'Grandy wouldn't approve. In fact, she'd be bloody furious if she could see us sitting around moping. Remember what she used to say?'

'Which particular thing?' Emily asked pensively.

'The remark she often made when we'd had some sort of failure or disappointment . . . she usually told us to forget yesterday, think of tomorrow and keep forging ahead without looking back. Don't you think that's what we should do, especially today?'

'Yes,' Emily admitted, giving her brother a more cheerful smile.

'Good girl,' Alexander said.

Philip said, 'I'm going to order a bottle of champagne and we're going to drink to the memory of that remarkable woman who gave us life, taught us everything we know and made us what we are.'

He motioned the wine waiter.

After Philip had ordered a bottle of Dom Perignon, and whilst they waited for it to be brought to the table, Paula leaned closer to Emily. She whispered, 'Philip has had a clever idea, thought of a way to possibly flush Jonathan out into the open. Once we've toasted Grandy, he'll tell you about it.'

'I can't wait,' Emily exclaimed. Her glistening green eyes narrowed with sudden shrewdness as she contemplated Jonathan's downfall. 'Now that would be a fitting tribute

to Gran – if we can uncover his treachery to her and deal
with him as she would have done.'

CHAPTER 45

John Crawford, Emma's solicitor, and a senior partner in
the firm of Crawford, Creighton, Phipps and Crawford,
hurried into the large conference room.

He glanced about and nodded with satisfaction. The
twenty-four chairs which were permanent fixtures around
the long mahogany table had been rounded out to twenty-
nine with the addition of five more. His secretary had
rustled these up from other offices within the law firm, and
the room could now accommodate himself and the twenty-
eight people who were due to arrive any moment.

John strode down the floor, placed the last will and
testament of Emma Harte on the table in front of his chair
at its head. His eyes rested on it briefly but thoughtfully. It
was a bulky document and he was facing a long session.
No matter, he thought, and half shrugging he stepped over
to the window, parted the curtains and looked down into
Upper Grosvenor Street.

A few seconds later he saw a taxi pulling up outside the
front door. David Amory alighted, followed by Daisy and
Edwina. Even from this distance he could see that Daisy
looked drawn, very sad, but she was still as beautiful as
ever. He sighed under his breath. No wonder his marriage
had failed. It was impossible to be married to one woman
whilst worshipping another. He had been in love with
Daisy for as long as he could remember. Most of his adult
life really. No hope there. She had married young, and she
had only ever had eyes for David. How special she was,
so sweet and unaffected, and not a bit spoiled by that
extraordinary wealth. They were good friends, and spent

two days a month working together, since it was Daisy who ran the Emma Harte Foundation, a rich organization devoted to charity. Daisy frequently needed his legal advice on other matters, and sometimes he was lucky, was able to spend a few extra hours with her. He was grateful for these small crumbs of her time, and looked forward with eagerness to their business luncheons.

He swung away from the window at the sound of his secretary's voice as she showed the Amorys and Edwina into the conference room. Smiling, he went to greet them, struck by Edwina's ghastly appearance. Like Daisy, she wore black and in consequence her face looked utterly colourless and drained of life. But this aside, she had become an old woman in the last few weeks. Emma's death had apparently affected her deeply.

He stood chatting to the three of them for a few minutes, and then they took their seats as the others began to arrive in rapid succession. By two-twenty everyone was present except for Jim and Winston. They came hurrying in five minutes later, apologizing, and explaining they had been held up in the traffic on the way from Fleet Street.

At precisely two-thirty John brought the room to order. He said: 'It is a very sad occasion that brings us all together today, but as Emma said to me the last time I saw her at the beginning of August, "No long faces after I'm dead. I've had an extraordinary life, known the best and the worst, and so there hasn't been one dull moment. Sing no sad songs for me." However, before I proceed with the business at hand, I would like to say that I personally mourn a very good and dear friend, who was the most remarkable woman – no, correction, person – I've ever been privileged to know. She will be sorely missed.'

There were a few scattered mutterings of approval at the expression of these sentiments before John said in a more solemn voice: 'This is the Last Will and Testament of Emma Harte Lowther Ainsley, who shall, hereafter, be known simply as Emma Harte throughout the reading of the will.' He cleared his throat, and his tone became more conversational as he said, 'Before her death Mrs Harte told me that members of her immediate family were aware of certain of the contents, since these were revealed to them by her in April of 1968. However, since the will covers the disposal of her entire estate, and because there are other beneficiaries I must read the will in its entirety. Also, that is the law. I must therefore ask you all to bear with me. It is a long document, I'm afraid, and one of some complexity.'

Paula, who sat between Jim and Philip, leaned back in her chair, folded her hands in her lap and directed her attention on the family solicitor. Her face was expressionless.

The first five or six pages dealt with Emma's bequests to the staff employed in her various homes, and all were generous, showed Emma's special consideration for each individual and their needs. Paula was genuinely gratified when she heard that Hilda was to receive a substantial pension when she retired, as well as the deed to one of the cottages Emma owned in the village of Pennistone Royal.

Hilda was not present, but Gaye Sloane was, and Emma's former secretary looked across at Paula and gave her a surprised smile of delight, after John had read out the details of Emma's gift to her. Gaye was to receive two hundred thousand pounds and a pair of diamond-and-gold earrings with a matching brooch.

The second portion of the will was concerned with Emma's considerable art collection. John explained, 'In the will drawn in 1968, Emma Harte left all of the art works to her grandson, Philip McGill Amory, with the exception of the paintings hanging at Pennistone Royal. This bequest has been modified.' He swung his eyes to Philip. 'Mrs Harte told me that she discussed this change with you and

707

gave you her reasons for making it, and that you were fully understanding of her motives.'

'Yes,' Philip said, 'Grandmother was seeking my approval and I told her this was not necessary, that she must dispose of her art as she so wished, since it was hers and hers alone. I am totally in accord with her.'

John nodded, glanced down at the document and read out Emma's words: '"In recognition of their many years of devotion, loyalty and friendship, I do give and bequeath to Henry Rossiter the Van Gogh landscape; to Ronald Kallinski the Picasso from the Blue Period; to Bryan O'Neill the Degas ballet dancer, each of which currently hangs in my Belgrave Square residence. To my beloved nephew, Randolph Harte, in appreciation of his love and friendship, I bequeath the four horse paintings by Stubbs and the two Barbara Hepworth sculptures, which are at present housed at Pennistone Royal. All of my other art works, *excluding* those hanging at Pennistone Royal, I give to my grandson, Philip. Also *excluded* from this bequest to Philip is the painting entitled *The Top of the World* by Sally Harte."'

Philip leaned into Paula and whispered, 'Uncle Randolph and the others are very touched. I'm glad she made those gifts to them, aren't you?'

Paula nodded, gave him a small smile.

John Crawford said, 'Regarding the matter of the Fabergé Imperial Easter Egg – ' The solicitor paused to take a sip of water, and went on to explain that Emma wished the Fabergé object of art to be auctioned, the money returned to her grandchildren who had purchased it for her as a gift for her eightieth birthday. Any balance of money left over, should the Imperial Easter Egg bring more than they had paid for it, was to be donated to charity in accordance with Emma's wishes.

Paula's eyes were surreptitiously wandering around the conference room. She had been aware of the mounting tension for the last fifteen minutes, had noticed the anxiety written on the faces of Robin, Kit and Elizabeth. Edwina, on the other hand, seemed oblivious to the proceedings, sat twisting her hands in her lap. She appeared more dolorous than ever.

As John began, 'I now come to the trust funds Emma Harte created for her children,' Paula could almost feel the anxiousness and nervousness emanating from her two uncles and her aunt. She quickly averted her eyes, trained them on John once again.

Leaning back in his chair, the solicitor said, 'The trusts, which became effective some years ago, have not been rescinded or changed in any way, shape or form by Mrs Harte. They remain intact, and the beneficiaries, Edwina, Kit, Robin and Elizabeth, will continue to receive the income from their trusts.'

John's voice droned on as he elucidated further details of the trusts, and just as she had sensed the apprehension in three of those four earlier, Paula was conscious of their profound relief. Robin and his twin, Elizabeth, were unable to conceal their jubilance. Kit's face was sober, but his eyes betrayed him as they flickered with triumph. Only Edwina was unaccountably distressed, weeping copiously into her handkerchief. Paula realized that her aunt was undoubtedly thinking of Emma, understanding yet again how eminently fair her mother had been.

'I will move on to the trusts which Emma Harte created for her grandchildren,' John announced, and Paula's grave face became very alert. She could not help wondering if Grandy had changed these. It soon became clear that Emma had not. Emily, Sarah, Alexander, Jonathan, Anthony, Francesca and Amanda would continue to benefit from the trust funds which Emma had provided for them in April of 1968. After spelling out the terms of the trust, the solicitor paused, shifted his position in his chair.

His glance rested on Paula, then moved on to regard Anthony. He remarked, 'At this point in the proceedings I must tell you that Emma Harte created three additional trust funds. These are for her great-grandchildren, Lorne and Tessa Fairley, son and daughter of Jim and Paula Fairley, and Jeremy, the Viscount Standish, son of Anthony and Sally Standish, the Earl and Countess of Dunvale. Each trust for these three great-grandchildren is in the amount of one million pounds.'

Picking up the will, John once more launched into a relatively long recitation of Emma's wishes which were couched in her own language. When this section was dispensed with, he moved on briskly, introduced the portion of the will that dealt with the dispersal of Emma's vast business enterprises and the enormous McGill fortune. She had again left the 1968 bequests intact. Alexander received fifty-two per cent of Harte Enterprises and was formally appointed head of this company for life. His sister Emily, as well as Sarah and Jonathan, each received sixteen per cent of the shares respectively. In the event of Alexander's death or disability, Emily would automatically assume control of the company, holding this position for her lifetime.

Paula eyed Jonathan and Sarah, and asked herself if they knew how lucky they had been. Jonathan could hardly conceal his glee, Sarah was smiling smugly, Paula noticed, and her face became closed and cold.

At the mention of her own name Paula gave John her full attention, even though she expected no surprises. She listened as he repeated Emma's words, written by her in 1968. Paula received all of Emma's shares in the Harte Stores which gave her total control of the company.

The entire McGill fortune went to Daisy McGill Amory, with the stipulation that her son, Philip, was to continue as Chief Executive Officer of the McGill Corporation of Australia, a conglomerate that owned the diverse McGill companies. Paula was to remain as her mother's representative in all matters pertaining to Sitex Oil. Upon Daisy's death, the McGill holdings were to be equally divided between Paula and Philip. Daisy inherited Pennistone Royal, all land and property attached to the house, all of its furniture, furnishings and works of art, as well as the McGill emeralds. The house, its contents, the land, and the jewels, were to pass to Paula on her mother's death. Paula received the remainder of her grandmother's considerable emerald collection.

'Mrs Harte's other jewellery is, for the most part, to be divided among her granddaughters. However there are other bequests – to Marguerite Barkstone, Alexander's wife, Sally Harte Standish and Vivienne Harte, her great-nieces, and Rosamund Harte Ellsworthy, her niece,' John told them. 'Emma made the selections for each individual, and these are as follows. "To my dearest granddaughter, Emily Barkstone Harte, I do give and bequeath my sapphire collection, comprising of . . ."' John intoned as he commenced to read from the long list.

It took the solicitor almost an hour to complete the reading of this part of the will, since Emma had owned a huge collection of jewellery, and those who were not beneficiaries became restless. There were rustlings and small muffled sounds as people moved around in their chairs. Cigarettes were lit. Someone poured a glass of water. Edwina blew her nose several times. Robin coughed behind his hand.

John Crawford was perfectly calm, as he always was, and oblivious to the scattered shufflings and odd noises. He read slowly, precisely, and it was obvious to everyone that he had no intention of being hurried. At last he finished, 'That completes the details of the disposal of Mrs Harte's collection of jewellery. I shall now proceed with the portion of the will that covers some of her real estate, mainly the house in Jamaica, British West Indies; the Avenue Foch apartment in Paris; the villa at Cap Martin in the South of France.'

The solicitor explained that the bequests Emma Harte had made in April of 1968 were unchanged. Emily Barkstone Harte was to inherit the Paris apartment, her brother Alexander Barkstone the villa on the Riviera, and Anthony was to get the house in the Caribbean.

At this juncture, John suddenly put the will down. His eyes roved from face to face and then his own face changed perceptibly as he brought himself up in his chair.

He enunciated in a most careful tone, 'It is now my duty to inform you that Emma Harte changed the remainder of her will.'

There were several audible gasps and the majority of those present stiffened in their seats. A number of worried glances were exchanged. Paula felt Philip's hand on her knee and she looked at him swiftly, her dark brows lifting before she brought her eyes back to Crawford. He was turning the page he had just read and perusing the one following.

Paula felt the tension flowing around her as it had earlier and there was a sense of great anticipation mingled with apprehension in the air. Her chest tightened as she clasped her hands together, wondering what bombshells were about to burst. I always knew it deep down, Paula thought. Unconsciously I knew that Gran would have a few surprises up her sleeve. She could hardly wait for John to continue.

The silence in the room was deathly.

Twenty-eight pairs of eyes were fixed unwaveringly on the solicitor.

Finally John looked up. He scanned their faces a second time, noting the expressions on each. Some were fearful or anxious, others avidly curious, a few merely interested. He smiled and read out in a strong voice:

'"I, Emma Harte Lowther Ainsley, hereafter known as Emma Harte, do hereby declare that the codicils attached to my Last Will and Testament on this Twenty-Fifth Day of April in the Year of Our Lord Nineteen Hundred and

Sixty-Nine are made whilst I am sound of body and mind. I do further declare and attest that no undue pressure or influence was brought to bear on me by any person or individual to make said changes in my Last Will and Testament and are solely of my own volition and doing."'

There was a brief pause on John's part as he turned the page, then gave his entire attention to the legal document in his hands.

'"Codicil One. I do give and bequeath to Shane Desmond Ingham O'Neill, grandson of my dearest lifelong friend, Blackie O'Neill, the diamond ring given to me by his late and aforementioned grandfather. I also bequeath to Shane O'Neill the painting known as *The Top of the World*, which I also received from his grandfather. Further, I do give to Shane O'Neill the sum of one million pounds in the form of a trust which I have had created for him. I make these gifts to Shane out of love for him, and in appreciation of his constant love and devotion to me.

'"Codicil Two. I give to Miranda O'Neill, granddaughter of my friend, Blackie O'Neill, the emerald bow brooch, presented to me by her grandfather. I do also make a gift to Miranda O'Neill of all other pieces of jewellery which were given to me by her grandfather during his lifetime. List of said pieces is attached to the end of these codicils. Further, I do give and bequeath to Miranda the sum of five hundred thousand pounds in the form of a trust. I do so in recognition of her affection and love for me and in memory of my dearest friend, Laura Spencer O'Neill, her grandmother.

'"Codicil Three. I do bequeath to my great-nephew, Winston John Harte, grandson of my beloved brother Winston, the property known as Heron's Nest in Scarborough, Yorkshire, and the sum of one million pounds, held in a trust similar to the aforementioned trusts. Also, I bequeath to Winston Harte fifteen per cent of my shares in my new company Consolidated Newspapers International, which he and I formed in March of 1969. I make these bequests to Winston Harte as a gesture of my love, and because of his love, devotion and uncommon loyalty to me over the years and because of his marriage to my granddaughter Emily, for the benefit of them both and any offspring of their marriage."'

At this point John stopped, took a quick sip of water and, aware of the taut atmosphere which now prevailed, he hurried on:

'"Codicil Four. I give to James Arthur Fairley, husband of my granddaughter Paula Fairley, ten per cent of my shares in Consolidated Newspapers International. This is a personal bequest to Jim Fairley and is in no way related to the trusts established for my great-grandchildren, Lorne and Tessa. This bequest is to show my appreciation of his dedication to me and my interests at the Yorkshire Consolidated Newspaper Company, and is also given as an expression of my affection for him.

'"Codicil Five. To my great-niece Vivienne Harte, granddaughter of my dear brother Winston, and to my niece Rosamund Harte Ellsworthy, daughter of my dear brother Frank, I do give and bequeath five hundred thousand pounds each in the form of trust funds which I have had drawn up for them. I do this out of my considerable affection for them both and in memory of my brothers.

'"Codicil Six. I do give and bequeath to my granddaughter Paula McGill Amory Fairley, and my grandson, Philip McGill Amory, my Fifth Avenue apartment in New York and my Belgrave Square house, both properties to be owned jointly by them. I make these gifts to Paula and Philip because the aforementioned residences were bought for me by their grandfather, Paul McGill. After long and careful consideration, I have decided that Paul McGill's grandchildren should rightfully inherit these homes. For this reason I have rescinded the original bequest made in my will drawn in April of 1968.

'"Codicil Seven. I give to my granddaughter Paula McGill Amory Fairley the remainder of my estate, including all motor cars, clothing, furs, and cash in my current cheque accounts. Further, I do give and bequeath to Paula Fairley all assets held in my private company, E.H. Incorporated. Said assets include my personally owned real estate, my personal stocks and shares, and cash balances. Total value of these assets is estimated at six million, eight hundred and ninety-five thousand pounds, six shillings and sixpence."'

The solicitor lifted his head, said to the gathering, 'That concludes the reading of the Last Will and Testament Of Emma Harte Lowther Ainsley, except for – '

'Just a minute!' Jonathan exploded. Seething, he jumped up. His eyes were wild, his face as white as bleached bone. 'I'm going to contest this will! I was left the Fifth Avenue apartment in her original will and it's mine by rights. I'm going to – '

'Please be so kind as to sit down, Jonathan,' the solicitor exclaimed coldly, glaring at him. 'I have not finished.'

Bristling, his rage apparent, Jonathan did as he was asked but not without crying, '*Dad!* Don't you have anything to say about this?'

Robin, also infuriated, nevertheless shook his head, motioned for his son to be silent.

Crawford continued: 'I was about to read the final statement made by Mrs Harte at the end of her will. I will now proceed to do so, and I must ask that there be no further unruly outbursts of this nature. This is Mrs Harte's last statement: '"I truly believe that I have been right, proper and fair in the disposal of all my worldly goods and possessions. I sincerely hope that my heirs understand why some of them are receiving greater inheritances than others.

'"However, should any of my heirs feel that they have been cheated or passed over for other members of my family, I must state again that this is not the case. Furthermore, should any member of my family contemplate contesting this will, I must caution them most strongly not to do so. Once again I attest that no undue influence, or influence of any kind, was brought to bear on me at any time. No one, other than my solicitor, John Crawford, knew of these changes and codicils which are entirely of my own creation. I must also state that I am not senile, nor is the balance of my mind disturbed. Attached to this document, which is my Last Will and Testament, are four affidavits signed by four doctors. These doctors were hitherto unknown to me before the date of this will, and are therefore uninterested parties. Two general practitioners and two psychiatrists examined me on the morning and afternoon of April Twenty-Fifth of Nineteen Sixty-Nine, prior to this will being drawn on the evening of that same date. The results of their examinations are contained in the affidavits and confirm that I am in excellent physical condition and perfect health, that I am mentally stable, and that none of my faculties are impaired.

'"Therefore, I must now point out that this will is irreversible, irrevocable and absolutely water tight. It cannot be contested in a court of law. I appoint my beloved and devoted daughter, Daisy McGill Amory, as executrix of my estate, and Henry Rossiter of the Rossiter Merchant Bank and John Crawford, of Crawford, Creighton, Phipps and Crawford as the co-executors of my estate."'

John sat back, waiting for the storm to erupt.

It did so instantly.

Everyone began to talk at once. Jonathan was on his feet and almost running down the long stretch of the conference room, looking as if he was about to physically accost John Crawford. Robin had also risen, and so had Kit Lowther and Sarah. These three also bore down on John, their expressions furious, their rage unconcealed as they began to rail at him shrilly.

716

Jonathan was apoplectic, shouted that the O'Neills had been favoured in his place and that Paula and Philip had stolen his inheritance. Sarah began to weep. Her mother, June, hurried to her, endeavouring to console her, and trying to hide her own considerable embarrassment without success.

Bryan O'Neill leaped to his feet. He went over to Daisy, and as the sole member of his family present, he protested that the O'Neills did not wish to accept Emma's legacies to them, in view of Jonathan's comments.

The brouhaha swirled around Paula. Jim, who had been sitting next to her, turned and said, 'Wasn't that lovely of Grandy to leave me the shares in the newspaper company?'

'Yes, it was,' Paula said, noting his shining eyes, his gratified smile.

Philip, who sat on her left, tapped her on the shoulder and leaned closer. Paula swung her eyes and stared at her brother. They gazed at each other knowingly for a protracted moment. Paula tried to keep her face straight but had difficulty doing so. She compressed her lips to prevent herself from laughing out loud. She murmured, 'Good old Grandy, as usual she thought of everything. What a brilliant stroke of genius that was, attaching those medical affidavits. The malcontents can do nothing – their hands have been firmly tied by Emma Harte.'

Philip nodded. 'Yes, but there will be trouble with them, you mark my words. On the other hand, knowing Jonathan's temperament, this sudden turn of events could easily make him behave in the most irrational way. He might act rashly. And we will probably uncover his treachery to Gran sooner than we think.'

'Let's hope so. Perhaps Grandy realized that too, Philip. I don't doubt her sincerity about leaving the McGill residence to us because we're McGills, but let's not forget how shrewd and wily she was.' Paula could not help smiling.

'You have to agree that Emma Harte has had the last laugh.'

'I would call it a loud guffaw,' Philip replied, chuckling.

Daisy pushed back her chair and came around the table rapidly. She bent over Paula and said, 'Poor John . . . he's being verbally castigated and most unfairly. Mummy's will was her own doing not his. He's only the family solicitor. Can't you put a stop to their disgusting behaviour. The Lowthers and the Ainsleys are getting out of hand.'

'Perhaps Daddy can say something,' Paula muttered.

'No,' Daisy answered firmly. 'Emma Harte made you the head of the family. It's your responsibility, darling. I'm sorry, but that's the way it is.'

Paula nodded and stood up. 'Please, everybody, do be quiet for a moment.'

Her natural reserve made it difficult for Paula to assert herself in a large group such as this, but when none of the rowdy troublemakers paid any attention to her, she leaned forward and banged her clenched fist on the table. She exclaimed fiercely, 'Shut up! All of you! And sit down!'

The Ainsleys and the Lowthers looked at her with antipathy, and although they did not budge from their positions around John Crawford's chair, they did stop quarrelling amongst themselves.

'Thank you,' Paula said, more evenly, but her voice reflected her icy eyes. She drew herself up to her full height and her inbred hauteur and imperiousness reached out to momentarily stun them all.

'How dare you behave in this unconscionable manner!' she reprimanded sternly. 'You're perfectly reprehensible, the lot of you. I think you might show a little respect for Emma Harte. My God, she's only been dead a few weeks and here you are, behaving like vultures, picking over her bones.' Paula's eyes were now riveted on Jonathan and Sarah, who stood together. 'My grandmother knew what

718

she was doing, and I think she has been overly generous to certain members of this family.'

Paula gripped the back of the chair tightly and continued in a tone that was almost threatening, 'Don't any one of you dare to even *think* about contesting Emma Harte's will. Because if you do, I shall fight you to the bitter end – and if it takes every hour of my time and every penny I have.'

The entire gathering stared at her. Most of those present were admiring of her, a few were condemning, but all were mesmerized by the aura of power she conveyed.

Winston edged closer to Emily and touched her arm. He whispered to his wife, 'Just look at her . . . she's Emma Harte personified. I think the legend lives.'

CHAPTER 46

Shane and Paula walked across the British Airways terminal at Kennedy Airport, took the escalator to the second level and went into the First Class lounge.

They found a quiet corner.

After helping her off with her wild mink cape, Shane shrugged out of his trenchcoat and threw it on a chair nearby.

'Let's have a drink,' he suggested. 'We have time before your flight.'

'That'll be nice. Thank you, darling.'

Shane smiled down at her, and ambled over to the bar at the other side of the lounge.

Paula watched him. How marvellous he looked. So darkly handsome and commanding, in absolute control. Her expression became soft; her eyes filled with love for him. In the year they had been having their love affair her feelings for him had only grown deeper. He was so much part of her now she felt lost when they separated and only half alive without him. He never ceased to surprise her. Although she had known him all of her life, she had never fully realized how truly dependable he was in every circumstance or emergency. He had a tremendous sense of commitment to her, and to every single thing that was important in his life. His strength of character was almost awesome. He has iron in his soul, she thought.

She gazed at him lovingly as he returned with their drinks. Shane smiled back, handed her the vodka and tonic and took the seat next to her.

He touched his glass to hers, said, 'Here's to next month, Paula, to the beginning of the new year.'

'To 1971,' Paula said.

'It *is* going to be our year, darling. Everything will be worked out with Jim. You'll be free, and just think, you'll be back here in January, not too long, really. We can start making our plans for the future. *Finally*.'

'Won't that be wonderful,' she said, but her luminous eyes darkened with incipient worry.

Shane noticed. He frowned. 'I don't like that look on your face, Paula. What's wrong?'

She shook her head, laughed gaily. 'Nothing. I'll just be glad when I've talked to Jim, settled matters with him. He's so frustrating, refusing to admit anything's wrong, burying his head in the sand. I know you probably think I've been ineffectual in dealing with the situation. However, it's hard to talk to someone who simply will not listen.' She reached out, squeezed his arm. 'Sorry. I'm going over old ground, repeating myself.'

'That's all right. I understand. But you'll tackle him when you get back.' A grin surfaced as Shane added, 'You should get him in a room, lock the door and pocket the key. That way he'll have to hear you out.'

'If necessary that's what I *will* do. I promise. I'm very determined to thrash this out once and for all. Of course, it's not a good time, with Christmas only two weeks away.

On the other hand, I suppose there is never a *right* time for discussing divorce ... emotional situations are always difficult.'

'Yes.' He leaned forward urgently. 'I know it won't be easy, Paula. I wish I could be in England with you, there in the background if you need me, but I have to go to the islands. I've no option. However – ' He stopped, stared at her intently. 'I'll fly to London immediately, if you can't cope alone.'

'I know you will, but I'll manage. Really I will, Shane.' There was a small silence and then she said, 'Thank you for this past month. It's been wonderful. And having an uninterrupted period of time with you has worked miracles for me. I feel so much better than I did when I arrived in November ... in every way.'

'So do I. And look here, Paula, it's been a triumphant month for you, if you think about it. Getting Dale Stevens's contract renewed and defeating Marriott Watson on so many of the issues at Sitex ought to make you feel good. And perhaps your success augurs well for the future. You've had a lot of sadness to deal with.'

'*You* pulled me through, Shane, you truly did. You've been so supportive and consoling. I'm stronger than I ever was because of you, your love and your understanding. And talking of Sitex ...' Her voice trailed off lamely. She eyed him carefully and wrinkled her nose. 'I know that *you* won't laugh when I tell you this, since you're such a superstitious Celt at heart ...' Again she stopped. Her eyes did not leave his face.

'I never laugh at you. So go on, tell me.'

Her fine mouth curved up into a light smile and she shook her head, suddenly laughing at herself. 'Well, when I first heard about the explosion in the *Emeremm III* I couldn't help thinking it was a bad omen, a sign of more hideous disasters looming ahead. And in a way I was right. Looking back, these past fourteen months have been fraught with problems . . . Min's death, the trouble in Ireland around the time of the explosion. Grandy's growing suspicions about Jonathan, Sarah's nastiness to me personally, her scheming to get her hands on the Harte boutiques. My marriage falling apart. Aunt Elizabeth's awful behaviour, the fear of scandal because of her divorce and Gianni's attitude. The continuing difficulties with Sitex, the internal fighting in that company, not to mention Jim's plane crash, then his nervous breakdown. The suddenness of Blackie's death, and Grandy going so soon after him, and all that horrendous quarrelling in the family about her will.' She pursed her lips. 'I feel as if someone put a curse on me, or rather, on Emma's family.'

Shane took her hand in his. 'In a sense, you *have* had more than your fair share. But let's be objective. First of all, Blackie was eighty-four and Emma was eighty-one, so it was to be expected that they would die soon. And they did have peaceful deaths, Paula, after long and productive lives. Secondly, you've put an end to the screaming and shouting about her will in certain quarters. You've settled many of the problems at Sitex, and Sarah's scheming against you was nipped in the bud by Emma. Jim has apparently recovered. Anthony and Sally are happily married and have a lovely son. Even your Aunt Elizabeth got off scot free and is seemingly happy with Marc Deboyne. As for your marriage, it was doomed long before the *Emeremm III* exploded.'

He put his arm around her, kissed her cheek, then drew away, looking into her face, so close to his. 'What about adding up the positives? Blackie and Emma were able to celebrate her eightieth birthday together, and they did have a wonderful eight months travelling the world. Emerald Bow won the Grand National which was a triumph for Grandpops. Edwina was reconciled with Emma, who lived long enough to see Emily married to Winston, Alexander

722

to Maggie. There have been many happy occasions, and a lot of good things have happened along with the bad.'

'Oh Shane, you're so right. How silly I must sound.'

'Not at all, and as you said, there's nobody more superstitious than I. Still, I do try to look for the rainbow. There usually is one, you know.' His face changed slightly and he peered at her through dark eyes grown quizzical. 'When you phoned me that night in October, after the reading of Aunt Emma's will, you said she'd made me one of her heirs because she loved me like one of her own, and because of her lifelong friendship with my grandfather. And I know you keep repeating that, but – ' He sat back, groped in his pocket for his cigarettes, took one, lit it. He smoked for a second or two, staring into the distance.

Observing him closely, her interest piqued, Paula probed, 'What are you getting at? Leading up to, Shane?'

'I can't help wondering if Emma had other reasons, or more precisely, *one* other reason.'

'Such as what?'

'Maybe Emma knew about us, Paula.'

'Oh Shane, I don't think so!' Paula exclaimed, giving him a curious stare. 'I'm sure she would have mentioned something to me. You know how close I was to Grandy. Anyway, she would have told Blackie, I know she would, and *he* would have certainly brought it up with you. He wouldn't have been able to resist doing so.'

Shane flicked ash into the ashtray. 'I'm not quite as positive as you are. Emma was the smartest person I've ever known. I doubt that she *would* have said anything, under the circumstances. For one thing, she wouldn't have wanted to intrude on my privacy, or yours, and she wouldn't have told Grandpops because she would have been afraid he'd worry. Let's face it, she did leave me the engagement ring. Hoping that *I* might end up giving it to *you* one day?'

Paula said, 'Perhaps she simply thought you were entitled

to own the ring, that it was rightfully yours, considering from whom it came. It is very valuable. Besides, she left you the painting which was another gift from your grandfather.'

'True. But Paula, a million pounds in trust for me . . . that's one hell of a hefty present by anybody's standards.'

'Agreed.' Paula smiled at him and her bright blue eyes, flickering with violet lights, filled with tenderness and warmth. 'My grandmother cared for you very much, Shane. She thought of you as another grandson. And look here, what about Merry? Grandy was awfully generous to her, too.'

'Yes.' Shane let out a small sigh. 'I'd love to know the real truth. But I don't suppose I ever shall.' Sudden laughter bubbled in his throat and his eyes danced mischievously. 'I must confess *I* like to think that Emma *did* know about us, and that she approved.'

'Well, that's one thing I can be sure of, Shane. I know she would have given us her blessing. Also – ' Paula stopped abruptly when an announcement was made over the loudspeaker. She glanced at him and pulled a face. 'That's it, darling, they're announcing the departure of my flight.' She made a motion to stand up.

Shane restrained her. He took her in his arms and whispered against her hair, 'I love you so much, Paula, remember that in the next couple of weeks.'

'How could I ever forget . . . it's part of my great strength. And I love you too, Shane, and I will for *all* of my life.'

Emily said, 'No, Jim, she hasn't arrived yet. I'm expecting her shortly, though.' Balancing the receiver between her ear and her raised shoulder, Emily zipped up her skirt as she continued to listen to Jim. He was phoning from Yorkshire and had caught her just as she was dressing.

After a few seconds, Emily exclaimed with impatience,

'I *know* the plane has landed. I checked with Heathrow and it *was* on time. It touched down at seven-thirty *exactly*. Paula has to clear customs and then get into town, you know.' Emily glanced at the clock on the bedside table. 'It's only *nine*, for heaven's sake, Jim. Look, I have to go. I'll tell her to ring you back the minute she walks in.'

'I'm about to leave the office, Emily,' Jim said. 'I'm driving up to London. Tell Paula not to bother coming to Yorkshire as she planned. I'll see her at Belgrave Square tonight. And you and Winston as well. Let's have dinner together, make it a *bon voyage* party.'

'Oh yes,' Emily muttered, 'I see what you mean, because Winston's going to Canada tomorrow.'

'Yes . . . and I'm going with him, Emily. I just hung up on him at our London office, and he's delighted that I've decided to tag along.'

'Oh,' Emily said, taken aback. 'Well, yes, it will be company for him, I suppose. I'll see you tonight, Jim. Bye.'

'Goodbye, Emily.'

She dropped the receiver in the cradle and stared at it for a moment. She grimaced, wondering if Winston was really as pleased as Jim thought. She doubted it. Neither of them had much time for Jim Fairley these days.

The phone rang again. Emily picked it up quickly, feeling quite certain it was her husband. 'Yes, Winston?' she said.

Winston laughed. 'How did you know it was me?'

'Because I was speaking to Jim a moment ago. He was looking for Paula. He told me he's going to Toronto with you. Aren't you thrilled to bits?' she asked sarcastically.

'Like hell I am,' Winston said. 'There's really no reason for him to come with me, but I couldn't very well tell him to get lost. He does own ten per cent of the new company, and he's curious about the latest acquisition, wants to look the new newspaper over. You know how odd he is these

725

days, a real fuss pot, and frankly he's getting to be a pain in the arse.'

'What a bore for you, Winston.' Emily sighed. 'Look, I hope he doesn't start messing around with the *Toronto Sentinel*. Editorially, I mean. That could delay you. You'd better be back here for Christmas, Winston.'

'I will, don't worry, lovey. As for Jim, well, I shall make short shrift of him if he starts interfering.'

'He suggested we all have dinner tonight. A *bon voyage* party, he called it. I'd prefer to be alone with you, but I suppose we'll have to join them,' Emily said, her tone grudging.

'We've no choice. Anyway, I only rang to tell you about Jim coming to Canada with me. Must dash. I'm about to start a meeting.'

After saying goodbye, Emily took her suit jacket out of the armoire and slipped it on. She hurried down the stairs in the Belgrave Square maisonette, where she and Winston had been staying for the weekend, heading in the direction of the study.

The lime-and-white room with its bright yellow and peach accents was filled with cold December light on this dreary Monday morning. Yet it had a cheerful feeling because of the bowls of fresh flowers, the blazing fire, the many lamps that glowed warmly. Emily noticed that Parker had brought in a tray of coffee and three cups and saucers. Her brother was due to arrive at ten o'clock, soon after Paula was expected.

Seating herself at the desk, Emily telephoned her secretary at Genret's London office and explained she would not be coming in that day. As she hung up she heard Parker greeting Paula in the foyer. She leaped to her feet and ran out to welcome her cousin.

'What a lovely surprise to see your smiling face,' Paula said warmly, rushing to embrace Emily. 'I didn't expect you to be in London, Dumpling. What are you doing here?'

'I'll fill you in shortly.'

Paula turned to the butler, 'Tilson's keeping the luggage in the car, Parker, since he's driving me to Yorkshire later today.'

Emily said, 'Oh, er, Paula, Jim rang a bit ago. He's on his way to London. He wanted you to know that, and suggested you stay here tonight.'

Paula bit back an exclamation of annoyance and murmured, 'I see.' She smiled weakly at the butler. 'Would you please ask Tilson to bring my luggage in after all, Parker.'

'Yes, madam.' Parker went to the front door.

Paula threw her mink cape on a hall chair and stepped after Emily, following her into the study. She closed the door, leaned against it and said heatedly, 'Damn it! Jim knew I was anxious to go *straight* to Yorkshire to see Lorne and Tessa! Did he say why he's suddenly coming up to town?'

'Yes. Winston's going to Toronto tomorrow, to review the situation at the new newspaper. Jim has decided to tag along.'

'Oh no!' Paula cried, her face tightening. She walked over to the fire and sat down heavily on the sofa. Her anger flared inside her. Jim was doing a disappearing act again, as he had in October when he had gone to Ireland to stay with Edwina. Did he have a sixth sense? Did he somehow *know* when she was about to broach the subject of divorce?

Emily stood near the fireplace, scrutinizing her cousin closely. Finally she said, 'You look awfully upset, Paula. Is something wrong?'

Paula hesitated, then confided, 'I don't suppose you'll be surprised, Emily, if I tell you that Jim and I have a lot of personal problems to discuss. And resolve. I'd hoped to get down to brass tacks in the next few days. Now he's leaving.

Again. Unless I can persuade him to cancel the trip with Winston, I'm going to have to wait until he gets back from Canada to talk to him.'

Emily lowered herself on to the sofa and patted her hand. 'I've known for a long time that things were difficult between the two of you, Paula. And you *should* talk to Jim – about a divorce, if you want my opinion. Winston happens to agree.'

Paula searched Emily's face and with alertness. 'So it's that apparent, is it?'

'Oh no, not to everyone, but certainly to those closest to you.'

'My parents?' Paula asked swiftly, sitting up straighter.

'Your father is aware there is great strain and he's concerned about the situation, but I'm not sure about Aunt Daisy. I mean, I don't think she realizes how bad it is, Paula. She's so nice, always making allowances for everyone.'

Paula sighed wearily. 'Do you think I can persuade him not to go to Canada?'

'No, I definitely don't. Because of those shares Grandy left him, Jim feels very much a part of the new company, and he wants to get his fingers into the pie. He's a bit of a meddler, these days.'

'I know.' Paula rubbed her face, feeling suddenly fatigued. She blinked. 'I hate these overnight transatlantic flights.'

Emily nodded. She took a deep breath, then said, 'You wouldn't be able to go to Yorkshire today anyway, Paula. Alexander needs you here in London. As a matter of fact, he'll be arriving in a few minutes to have a meeting with us.'

'What's happened?' Instantly, a look of comprehension flashed. 'Not Jonathan?'

'Yes, I'm afraid so.'

'Tell me all about it.' Paula stared at Emily anxiously,

thoughts of Jim and the divorce momentarily swept to one side.

'Alexander prefers to fill you in, Paula. He asked me to ask you to wait until he gets here. It's rather involved. And that's why I'm in London – because of Jonathan. Alexander wanted me to be here for the meeting with you. Actually, Alexander and I have thrashed the situation to bits for the past two weeks – '

'You mean you've known all this time and you didn't let me know!'

'We wanted to be sure, and get a plan together, also we had to talk to Henry Rossiter and John Crawford. We needed their advice. We're going to have to take drastic steps, Paula.'

'Is it that bad?'

'Pretty serious. However, Sandy and I have it well under control. Sarah is involved to a certain extent.'

'As we thought.' Paula sighed. Her dismay increased.

The door opened quietly and Alexander walked into the study. 'Morning Emily, welcome back, Paula.' He came over to the sofa, kissed them both and took a chair facing them. 'I wouldn't mind a cup of coffee, Emily,' he said to his sister. 'I walked over from Eaton Square and the weather's beastly this morning. I'm frozen.'

'Yes, of course.' Emily lifted the silver pot, poured. 'What about you, Paula?'

'Yes, thanks, I might as well.' Her eyes were penetrating as they rested on Alexander. 'You ought to have let me know.'

'To be honest, I thought about doing so, Paula. Emily and I discussed it at great length, and we finally decided there wasn't much point. You would have worried and you couldn't have contributed very much from New York. Besides, you had your hands full with Sitex. I didn't want to drag you back to London. Furthermore, I only just got to the root of it all at the end of last week. Well, more or less.'

Paula nodded. 'Tell me everything, Sandy.'

'Well, here goes. Philip's plan worked. Malcolm Perring helped me to flush Jonathan out, but I had another source of information. It was this source that enabled me to really nail him. But I'm jumping ahead of myself. I'd better begin at the beginning.'

'Please,' Paula said.

'Malcolm Perring *did* eventually come up with the perfect property deal for Harte Enterprises. He took it to Jonathan – who expressed considerable interest. Then nothing happened. Malcolm kept ringing him over a two-week period, and Jonathan stalled. However, in the middle of November, Jonathan invited Malcolm to come over to the office for a meeting. Apparently Jonathan waffled on for a while about it being an excellent deal, but finally he turned it down. He said Harte Enterprises could not handle it at that particular time. He suggested Malcolm take the deal to a man called Stanley Jervis at a new company, Stonewall Properties. He explained that Jervis was an old friend, very reliable, and in the market for big real estate deals.'

'Don't tell me,' Paula muttered, 'Stonewall Properties belongs to Jonathan Ainsley.'

'*Correct*. And get this – Sebastian Cross is his partner.'

'That odious man. Ugh!' Paula shuddered.

'Sarah also has money in the company,' Alexander told her. He shook his head. 'Foolish girl.'

'She's been duped by Jonathan again, just as she was when she was a child,' Paula remarked softly.

'Precisely,' Emily interjected. 'Only this time there are far-reaching consequences for her.'

'Yes.' Paula scowled in perplexity, now demanded, 'But how did Malcolm Perring manage to find all this out?'

Alexander answered, 'He didn't. I did. Malcolm Perring went along with Jonathan's idea, since that was the whole

730

purpose of our plan – catching him with his hand in the till, so to speak. Malcolm had two meetings with this Jervis chap, and then suddenly Sebastian Cross was on the scene. He's pretty much up front in the company now, even though Jonathan is obviously hiding behind straw men, his men, since his name doesn't appear anywhere.'

Alexander lit a cigarette, continued, 'Malcolm started negotiations with Cross and Jervis, playing them along, inducing them to believe he was prepared to close the deal with Stonewall. He didn't take to either of them, and suspected that the company was shaky financially. He did a bit of investigating, talked to people around the town, and his suspicions were soon confirmed. As planned, Malcolm began to back off, much to the astonishment of Jervis and Cross. They were scared of losing the deal, and started to boast about the big business transactions they had recently handled. Malcolm brought this information to me. I went through the files in our real estate division late one night, and discovered that *we* could have made all of those deals. Jonathan had passed them over to Stonewall. That clinched it for me, Paula. I knew positively that he was as guilty as hell. Malcolm finally cut off negotiations with Stonewall, explaining that another real estate company had come in with an enormous offer, one which his partners were insisting the firm accept.'

'And they bought it?' Paula asked.

'They had no choice. I was ready to swoop down on Jonathan and then quite unexpectedly some other information fell into my lap. And within forty-eight hours I had enough on Jonathan to hang him.'

'Where did the new information come from?' Paula leaned forward eagerly, riddled with curiosity.

'John Cross.'

'Alexander, you can't be serious!' Paula's astonishment was evident. '*John Cross*,' she repeated and her eyes widened as she drew back, looked at Alexander askance. 'I don't believe it.'

'It's the truth.'

'But why would he confide in you?'

'Actually, Paula, John Cross was looking to confide in *you*. He only got in touch with me because you weren't around. He asked me to come to Leeds to see him . . . he was in St James's Hospital.'

'Oh,' Paula said. 'What was wrong with him? Was he very sick?'

'Poor old man,' he murmured. 'He died, Paula. John Cross died just a few days after I saw him. It was cancer, I'm afraid. He was riddled with it, and obviously in great pain.'

'Oh Sandy, how awful.' Paula pursed her lips. 'Poor man. I wouldn't wish that on anyone. And he wasn't so bad. Weak, a little misguided maybe, and under the thumb of that rotten son of his.'

Alexander cleared his throat. 'I immediately drove to Leeds, and went to see John Cross at the hospital. I was with him for almost four hours. The doctor allowed me to stay that length of time, because – well, he *was* dying. John Cross talked about you for a while. He said he had a great deal of respect for you, Paula, admired your honesty and fairness. He then explained that you'd been very courteous to him in the autumn of 1969 when you saw him in London. I told him I knew about your meeting. He commented about your patience and your kindness to him that day, and said he understood why you hadn't been interested in re-opening negotiations for the acquisition of Aire Communications . . . because his company no longer had any real assets since the building had been sold. That's when he confided that Stonewall Properties had bought the Aire building for five hundred thousand pounds. Apparently his son persuaded him to sell. He insisted that he'd been cheated by them, because the building was worth a million at least. I had to agree with him. John Cross became very upset, and he said this to me, Paula: "Imagine my shock when I discovered six months ago that it was my son who robbed me, who ruined me, ruined any chance for Aire Communications to make a recovery. I was heartbroken that Sebastian could do such a terrible thing to me. My son . . . my only child." He began to weep, and I can't say I blamed him.'

'What a ghastly thing to happen to him . . . so Grandy was always right about Jonathan . . . she was very suspicious of him at the time of the Aire Communications negotiations,' Paula said.

'And with good reason.' Alexander crossed his legs, sat back. 'Mr Cross wanted *you* to know, *us* to know, that Jonathan was Sebastian's partner and that he had been working against Emma Harte for years. He mumbled something about despising family treachery, said he wanted to die with an easy conscience.'

Paula sighed, rubbed her weary face. 'What else did he reveal about Stonewall Properties?'

'Not a lot, at least, nothing I didn't already know through Malcolm. Mr Cross confirmed that Jonathan had been moving deals away from Harte Enterprises and into Stonewall, and he confessed that his son had bled him dry, taken every penny he had. The old man was very bitter when he explained that it was only because of his sister's generosity that he was able to have a private room at St James's, and private doctors. You see, Paula, old Mr Cross was destitute.'

Paula sank back against the cushions and for a reason she would never fully understand her eyes filled with tears. She coughed behind her hand and reached for one of Alexander's cigarettes. 'How sad that he had to end his days in such a frightful way . . . betrayed by his own son.'

Emily announced, 'Sebastian Cross is a bastard. And Jonathan Ainsley is no better, is he, Sandy?'

'No.' Alexander gave Paula a long look. 'John Cross told me something else, and this is the worst part of all.

However, because of it, I *am* going to get Jonathan. Really *get* him, Paula. In an effort to bail out Stonewall Properties, which is in grave financial difficulties, Jonathan borrowed a lot of money – against his shares in Harte Enterprises.'

Paula was momentarily dumbfounded and thrown off balance. She gaped at her cousins, then gasped, 'But he's not allowed to do that.'

'Exactly!' Emily cried. 'Don't you see, because he did that we can nail him . . . actually, he's nailed himself to the cross, hasn't he?'

Paula nodded, asked sharply, 'Are you sure there's no mistake?'

'None,' Alexander replied. 'John Cross knew about the loan, don't ask me how, but he did. He wouldn't reveal his source, nor did he realize the true importance of his information to us. He merely wanted to alert us to our cousin's activities. In a funny way, I think he blamed Jonathan for his son's transgressions, although I'm not so sure he's correct there. However, he *was* able to give me the name of the finance company who made the loan to Jonathan. Obviously Jonathan couldn't borrow from a bank – they'd want to know too much.'

'I can't believe he would be so foolhardy,' Paula said. 'He's fully aware he's not permitted to use his shares in Harte Enterprises as collateral, nor can he sell those shares unless it's to another shareholder – '

'That's right,' Alexander interrupted. 'He can only sell them to me, Emily or Sarah. Those are the company laws, which are very precisely spelled out in the articles of incorporation by Grandy. She wanted to ensure that Harte Enterprises remained a private company, a family concern, with no strangers or outsiders involved, and she made damned certain that that was the way it would be.'

'Which finance company did he get involved with?'

'Financial Investment and Loan.'

'Good God, Sandy, they're crooks,' Paula exclaimed,

horrified. 'Everyone knows that they're a shady outfit. How could he be so stupid?'

'I told you, he couldn't go to the bank. A bank would want to know everything as far as those shares are concerned, as would a reputable finance company.'

'How much did he borrow and against how many shares?' Paula demanded.

'He put up seven per cent of his shares, just under half of his sixteen per cent, and he raised four million pounds against them. However, the loan company gave him a poor deal. Those shares are worth twice that much, except, of course, that they cannot be sold to anyone – except to one of us. Still, the finance company weren't aware of that at the time they made the loan. They are now.'

Paula experienced a sudden sense of relief and her troubled expression lifted. 'You paid off his note and retrieved the shares, didn't you, Sandy?'

'I did. Last Thursday Emily and I met with the managing director of that dubious little company, along with Henry Rossiter and John Crawford. It was all very troublesome, and there were a lot of strong words, heated arguments and general unpleasantness. We returned again on Friday, all four of us, and I paid them back their four million pounds and they returned the shares. There was some interest due, but Henry and John were adamant, refused to let me pay that. They told the managing director to go after Jonathan. And there you have all the gory details.'

'Where did you and Emily get the four million from? Did you use your own money?'

'No. John Crawford figured out a way for Harte Enterprises to buy the shares back, rather than an individual. As you know, Paula, Grandy drew up a number of legal papers in regard to Harte Enterprises just before she died. I have extraordinary powers, a free hand in many instances, especially if the overall good of the company is involved. John and Henry agreed that this situation with Jonathan

735

was such an instance. However, I told them that Emily and I are perfectly willing to purchase those shares if they decide, at a future date, that this is the proper thing to do.'

'I see.' Paula stood up and walked to the fireplace. A thought struck her. 'Are Sarah's shares involved?'

'No. Stupid she might be, but she would never risk her shares,' Alexander replied.

'What are you going to do about Jonathan and Sarah?' Paula asked, her eyes sharpening.

'I intend to fire them both. At noon today. I've called a meeting. I'd like you to be present, Paula.'

CHAPTER 47

There was a sanguine air about Jonathan Ainsley as he walked into Alexander's office at Harte Enterprises.

Being an egotist who was convinced he was smarter and shrewder than anyone else, it never occurred to him that his double dealing might have been uncovered.

'Hello, Alexander,' he said, strolling nonchalantly across the room, shaking his cousin's hand. 'Sarah told me she's been asked to come to this meeting too. What's it all about then?'

Alexander sat down in the chair behind his desk and said, 'There are some important matters I have to discuss. It won't take long.' Alexander's clear blue eyes, so intelligent and honest, rested on Jonathan, but only briefly. He shuffled the papers on his desk, filled with contempt and loathing for the other man.

Walking over to the sofa, Jonathan sat down, lit a cigarette and lolled back against the leather cushions. He glanced at the door as Emily came in, and gave her a warm smile. This was entirely fraudulent, since he disliked Emily. But the feeling in no way matched his virulent hatred for

Paula, and that hatred flared when she hove into view, stood in the doorway a split second later.

Rising, he greeted Emily with a degree of cordiality, but his voice turned a shade colder as he said to Paula, 'You're not involved in the day-to-day running of Harte Enterprises, so what are you doing here?'

'Alexander invited me since I have a family matter to talk about.'

'Ah yes, family matters do seem to preoccupy you these days, don't they, Paula?' he said sardonically. He lowered himself into a chair, muttering, 'Not the will again, I hope.'

'No, not that,' Paula replied, her voice calm, betraying nothing. She followed Emily over to the sofa and sat down. Ever since his bitter outburst at the reading of the will, Jonathan had dropped all pretence with her. He did not bother to conceal his animosity and a minute ago she had seen the antipathy flickering. She had also noted that his anxiety had slipped through the bland façade he was trying so hard to hold in place. Paula looked down at her hands, half smiling to herself. Her presence had unnerved him, try though he had not to show it. After a second or two she lifted her head, studied him surreptitiously, her eyes objective. How attractive his appearance was. So fair of colouring and fine of feature. Yes, he *was* very clean cut, and there were times, such as now, that he had the look of an innocent choir boy. Yet she knew he was a schemer who would stop at nothing to gain his own ends.

Sarah swept in grandly, scanned the room. 'Hello, everyone,' she murmured coolly, and then spoke to Alexander directly: 'I'm in rather a hurry. I have a luncheon date at one o'clock with a very important buyer. I hope this isn't going to take long.'

'No, it won't,' Alexander said. 'I intend to make our meeting as short as possible.'

'Oh good.' Sarah swung away from the desk, looked at Emily and Paula on the sofa, and purposely chose a chair near Jonathan. Sitting back she offered Alexander a sweet smile.

He stared at her for the longest moment. Not an eyelash flickered and his face was suddenly cold and implacable. Sarah's smile slipped and she frowned at him, obviously puzzled by his manner.

'It seems odd to me,' Alexander began, 'that Stonewall Properties has such severe, such grave, financial problems.' He focused on Jonathan. 'Bad management, do you suppose?'

Jonathan felt a tightening of his stomach muscles and all of his senses were alerted for trouble. Secure in the knowledge that he could not be linked to Stonewall, he managed to keep a composed demeanour. He shrugged. 'How would I know. And don't tell me you've dragged us here to discuss another company?'

'Why yes, that is one of the reasons.' Alexander leaned forward, peering at Sarah. 'Were you aware that Stonewall Properties is likely to go belly up in the near future?'

Sarah opened her mouth and closed it swiftly. The disturbing information about the secret company, which she had invested so much money in, had stunned her. She did not doubt its truth, since it came from the reliable Alexander. She was anxious to speak to Jonathan alone, but she dreaded tackling him. He could be so difficult and now it was fear of his wrath that made her hold her tongue.

Alexander continued to regard her unwaveringly. She had paled under his fixed observation and her eyes were suddenly alarmed. He knew Sarah would crack if he increased the pressure.

But he addressed the room at large. 'What really baffles me, though, is how they managed to get into this state. Stonewall have closed an amazing number of genuinely good deals. I can't imagine why they are floundering so badly. Unless, of course, somebody has had a hand in the till.'

Rattled by this remark, Sarah cried, 'Do you think that's possible, and if – '

Jonathan interjected peremptorily, 'Now look here, Alexander, let's forget about the problems at Stonewall and get on with our own business.'

'Oh, but Stonewall *is* our business,' Alexander said in a murderously quiet voice. 'And you know it, since Stonewall Properties is your company, Jonathan.'

There was an involuntary gasp from Sarah and then she shrank back in the chair.

Jonathan laughed dismissively and threw Alexander a look that was both challenging and threatening. 'What bloody nonsense you do talk. I've never heard anything so preposterous.'

'Jonathan, I know everything there is to know about Stonewall. The company is jointly owned by you and Sebastian Cross, and Sarah has invested a great deal of money in it. It's run by Cross and Stanley Jervis, along with a number of straw men put in there by you. Cross and you formed the company in 1968. You've been channelling real estate deals intended for Harte Enterprises into your own company. You've lost us an enormous amount of business, important and highly profitable business, Jonathan, and you queered Grandy's pitch when she was in negotiations with Aire Communications. I'm appalled. You have been disloyal and a traitor to this company. You have betrayed Grandy's trust in you, and therefore I have no alternative but to – '

'Just try to prove it!' Jonathan shouted angrily, leaping to his feet. He slapped both his hands on the edge of Alexander's desk and bent over it, glaring into his cousin's face. 'You'll have the greatest difficulty doing so. There is not one shred of evidence to support or substantiate these ridiculous accusations.'

'You're absolutely wrong. I have all the evidence I need,' Alexander shot back evenly, but his tone was glacial, his look condemning. He patted the file of folders on his desk, which in fact had nothing to do with Stonewall, and said, with a thin smile, 'It's *all* here, Jonathan. Then of course there is your partner in – ' Alexander lifted his hands and shrugged ' – shall we *say* crime, for want of a better word. Yes, there she sits in stunned silence . . . Sarah Lowther.'

'Now you're trying to bring poor Sarah into this plot of yours,' Jonathan shouted. 'Yes, that's what it is – a plot to discredit us both. You've always been out to get me, Alexander Barkstone, ever since we were kids. And Sarah as well. But you're not going to get away with it. I'll see you in hell first. I shall fight for my rights, and for Sarah's. So just beware,' he threatened.

Alexander leaned back in the chair, and his blue eyes, so cold and hard a second before, instantly changed when he gave Sarah a look of pity. 'Yes, *poor* Sarah indeed,' he remarked softly. 'You've been duped, I'm afraid. Your money has gone down the drain, Sarah, sad for you really, but there's nothing you can do about it now.'

'A-A-Alexander,' Sarah stammered, 'I-I-I don't – '

'Be quiet, and let *me* do all the talking, Sarah dear. He's a crafty devil. He'll trap you into saying the wrong thing.' Jonathan brought his blazing eyes back to the other man. His lip curled. 'You're the biggest bastard alive!'

'All right, that's enough!' Alexander was on his feet behind the desk. 'Don't you dare call *me* a bastard.'

'Cut you to the quick, have I?' Jonathan laughed nastily. 'But that's what you undoubtedly are, and so is that sister of yours. You would do well to remember that it is *your* mother who sleeps around, not mine.'

'You're fired!' Alexander exclaimed, his anger spiralling into pure rage.

'You can't fire me.' Jonathan threw back his head and guffawed. 'I'm a shareholder in this company and – '

'Your holdings in this company have been considerably reduced,' Alexander interrupted in a steadier tone, taking full control of himself. 'By exactly seven per cent.' He lifted the top folder and took out the share certificates, waved them under Jonathan's nose. 'I just retrieved these . . . last Friday. It cost Harte Enterprises exactly four million pounds to pay off your loan to the finance company you borrowed from, but I was happy to do it in order to get these shares back.'

Jonathan had blanched. He stood gaping at Alexander in stupefaction. For once in his life he could think of nothing to say. For a moment he thought he was finished, and then he exclaimed, with a scornful smirk, 'I still own nine per cent of this company. Furthermore, there's no way you can fire me. Under the company laws, a shareholder cannot be fired.'

'Grandy made that ruling in 1968, when she drew her will and divided her one hundred per cent between the four of us. However, *she* still owned her one hundred per cent until the day she died, and therefore she owned the company outright. And as the sole owner of Harte Enterprises, Emma Harte could do anything she wanted, as you well know. And so, just before she went to Australia, Grandy changed all of the company laws. Actually what she did was to reconstruct the company and caused new articles of incorporation to be drawn. Under the new company laws, I, as managing director, chairman of the board and majority shareholder, can do practically anything I wish. I have extraordinary powers. I can buy out a shareholder, if that shareholder is agreeable. I can hire. I can fire.' Alexander leaned over his desk and impaled Jonathan with his eyes. 'And so I am firing *you*.' He looked past Jonathan, fixed his gaze on Sarah. 'You're also fired, Sarah. Your behaviour has been as shoddy as Jonathan's.'

Sarah could not speak. She seemed to have turned to stone in the chair.

'We'll see about all this bloody nonsense,' Jonathan railed. 'I'm going to pay a visit to John Crawford the

minute I leave here, and I'm taking Sarah with me. There's
– '

'Do go and see him by all means,' Alexander cut in, dropping the share certificates on the desk. He slipped his hands into his trouser pockets and rocked back and forth on his heels. 'He'll be perfectly happy to confirm what I've just told you. As a matter of fact, he does want a word with you anyway. He was with me at the two meetings I had with Financial Investment and Loan, and John was a little bit disturbed about the interest you owe to them. They're a shady bunch, Jonathan. You'd better pay up and smartly.'

Jonathan opened his mouth, and then snapped it shut, glaring at his cousin.

Sarah, having partially recovered, hurried to the desk. She appealed to Alexander tearfully, 'I haven't done anything with my shares . . . I haven't done *anything* wrong. Why are you firing me?'

'Because you *have* done something wrong, Sarah. You invested in a company which was in direct competition with the real estate division of Harte Enterprises. You've been disloyal, a traitor like Jonathan. I'm sorry, but as I just told you, I cannot condone your behaviour.'

'But I love Lady Hamilton Clothes,' she gasped, and began to sob.

'You should have thought of that when you threw your lot in with your reckless cousin here,' Alexander answered steadily, quite unmoved by her tears. 'And God in heaven only knows why you ever did.'

Jonathan cried irately: 'I intend to take this matter to another solicitor. I'm not convinced those papers Grandmother drew are quite as legal as you seem to believe.'

'I can assure you that they are . . . *very very legal*. John·Crawford and Henry Rossiter, as directors of Harte Enterprises, approved them, as did I. Don't try to challenge anything Emma Harte did, because believe you me you won't get anywhere. She outsmarted you.'

Suddenly Jonathan went berserk. He yelled, 'I'll get you for this, you bloody sod!' He swivelled on his heels and shook his fist at Paula, 'And you too, you bitch!'

'*Get out.*' Alexander made a move towards Jonathan. 'Before I personally take you by the scruff of your neck and throw you out.'

Paula jumped to her feet and ran to Alexander, put a restraining hand on his arm.

She stared at Jonathan and Sarah, pressing back her disgust and disdain. She said, very quietly, 'How *could* you? How could you do it to *her*? She who gave you so much, who was so fair and generous. She suspected you, Jonathan, for a long time before she died, and you, Sarah, latterly. And yet she gave you both the benefit of the doubt because she had no real proof. She did not rescind your trust funds, nor did she take back the shares in Harte Enterprises she so generously gave you.' Paula shook her head sorrowfully. 'You are both everything Grandy loathed and despised . . . treacherous, devious and dishonest, and liars and cheats besides.'

Neither of them spoke. Jonathan's face was ringed with bitter hatred, and Sarah looked as if she was going to pass out from shock.

Paula's voice took on a new note, one of calm resoluteness as she said, 'I'm afraid I'm not as forgiving as Emma Harte was. She tolerated your fathers long after their treacherous treatment of her. But I will not tolerate either of you. I only have this to add . . . neither of you are welcome at family gatherings in the future. Please remember that.'

Sarah, still white and trembling, became hysterical at Paula's words of banishment. She turned on Jonathan and cried accusingly, 'This is all your fault. I should never have listened to you. I've not only lost my money, but Lady Hamilton Clothes and the family as well.' She started to sob anew.

Jonathan ignored her. He leaned closer to Paula, his eyes

baleful, his face contorted in a mask of hatred. 'I'll get you for this, Paula Fairley. Sebastian and I will bloody well get you!'

Alexander finally lost his temper completely. He sprang past Paula, grabbed Jonathan's arm roughly, and dragged him to the door. 'I think you'd better leave before I give you the thrashing of your life.'

Struggling out of his cousin's tenacious grip, Jonathan yelled, 'Keep your filthy hands off me, you sneaky sod. And don't think you're immune. Don't forget what I said. We'll get you too, Barkstone. If it takes all my life I'm going to make certain you get yours.' Jonathan flung open the door and stormed out.

Sarah ran to Alexander, who still stood near the doorway. 'What am I going to do?' she wailed, brushing her hands over her wet face.

'I really don't know, Sarah,' Alexander answered in a cold and quiet voice. 'I really don't know.'

She looked at him helplessly, then brought her gaze to Paula and finally to Emily. She knew from their closed faces that her plight was hopeless. Cursing Jonathan under her breath, she found her handbag and left the office as quickly as she could, striving to quell her tears.

Alexander walked across the room, seated himself behind his desk and took a cigarette. He saw that his hands shook as he struck a match and lit it, and he was not surprised. 'That was all rather unpleasant,' he said. 'But no worse than I expected. I have to admit, I couldn't help feeling Sarah was in over her head and without knowing it.'

'Yes,' Paula agreed, and took the chair opposite his desk. She turned and glanced at Emily. 'There was a moment when I actually felt sorry for her, but it passed when I thought of Gran, and the wonderful things she did for them all their lives.'

'I didn't have one ounce of sympathy for Sarah!' Emily

cried indignantly. 'She deserved everything she got. As for Jonathan – he's despicable.'

'He'll try and make trouble but he won't succeed,' Alexander announced. 'He'll huff and he'll puff but he'll never blow our house down. All he did was make idle threats.' Alexander grinned. 'I couldn't believe it when he shook his fist at you, just like the villain in a Victorian drama.'

Paula laughed nervously. 'I know what you mean. On the other hand, Sandy, I don't think we should dismiss Jonathan quite so lightly. Not with Sebastian Cross – my enemy – in the background, egging him on to do heaven knows what. I've told you before, I have a very low opinion of Cross.'

Alexander sat back, observing her quietly, musing on her words.

Emily hurried over and stood next to Paula. She said, 'Honestly, Alexander, Paula's right. We've not heard the last of Jonathan Ainsley, Sarah Lowther and Sebastian Cross – not by a long shot.'

Leaning over his desk, Alexander smiled warmly and confidently. 'Forget the three of them, please. There's nothing they can do to us . . . not now or in the future. They're quite powerless.'

Paula was not so sure about this, but she said, 'Spoken like a true grandson of Emma Harte's.' Pushing aside her worry, adopting a positive attitude, she exclaimed, 'And as she would have said, let's get on with it. We've got a lot more to accomplish today. Now, Sandy, who do you have in mind to run Lady Hamilton Clothes?'

'As a matter of fact I was thinking of putting Maggie in there. She has a good business head, and with a bit of help from the two of you . . .' He stopped, looked at his sister and his cousin. 'Well?'

'It's a terrific idea!' Emily cried.

'I second that,' said Paula.

CHAPTER 48

The old nursery at Pennistone Royal, slightly shabby though it was, glowed with comfort and warmth. A huge fire crackled in the grate, lamps shone brightly and there was a feeling of gaiety and lightheartedness in the air.

It was early evening on a cold Saturday in January of 1971. Emily, sitting on the window seat observing Paula and her children, was filled with delight as she witnessed the happy scene being enacted in front of her. Paula was so very carefree tonight, and her eyes, which had been unusually troubled of late, sparkled with laughter. There was a new tranquillity in her face, and as always when she was with the children, her demeanour was gentle and loving.

The twins, who would be two years old next month, had already been bathed and were dressed in their night clothes. Paula was holding their hands, and the three of them formed a circle in the centre of the floor.

'All right, ready, set, go!' Paula cried and slowly began to move, taking small steps, leading the children around and around. Their freshly scrubbed faces shone with joy and their smiles were vividly bright, their eyes glowing.

Paula now began to sing: 'Half a pound of tuppenny rice, half a pound of treacle. Mix it up and make it nice. *Pop* goes the weasel!'

As they came to a standstill, Lorne broke free and flopped down on to the floor, giggling and laughing and rolling about. 'Pop!' he shouted loudly. 'Pop! Pop!' He continued to chortle and kick his legs in the air with the abandonment of a frisky puppy.

Tessa, clinging to Paula's hand, stared down at him and then up at her mother. 'Silly,' Tessa said. 'Rorn . . . silly.'

746

Paula crouched on her haunches and smiled into the solemn little face regarding her so intently. 'Not silly, darling. Lorne is happy. We're all happy after such a lovely day. Try and say Lorne, sweetheart.'

Tessa nodded. 'Rorn,' she repeated, unable as yet to properly pronounce her brother's name.

Paula's heart was bursting with love. She reached out and stroked the child's porcelain cheek with one finger. The green eyes surveying her reminded her of chartreuse liqueur that had only been slightly diluted, so startling was their depth of colour. She took Tessa in her arms and hugged her close, rumpling her burnished red-gold curls. 'Oh you're such a darling, Tess.'

Tessa clung to Paula for a moment longer and then wriggled free. She pushed her face at her mother, craning her neck, and pursing her lips. 'Mama . . . Mama,' she said and made small smacking sounds with her mouth. Paula smiled, leaned into her daughter and kissed her, ruffled her hair again. 'Run and give Aunty Emily a kiss, sweetheart. It's well past your bed time.'

Paula watched Tessa march purposefully across the floor. In her white flannel nightdress and blue robe she looked adorable, resembled a cherub. Turning to Lorne, Paula knelt on the floor and began to tickle him. He squirmed and kicked, enjoying every minute of the game, his peals of laughter slicing through the gentle silence. Finally Paula stopped and lifted him to her. She stroked his flushed cheek and swept back his hair, which was slightly darker red than his sister's, and endeavoured to calm him. 'Mummy's the silly one, Lorne, getting you so excited and just when it's time for bed.'

He cocked his head to one side and looked at her with great interest. 'Me,' he said. 'Mam . . . Mam.' Lorne now held up his face to be kissed, pursing his lips in the way his sister had done. This was a nightly ritual with both children, and Paula took his head between her hands and kissed his cheek, the tip of his nose, and his damp rosy lips. She drew back. 'You're such a good boy, Lorne,' she murmured, straightening the collar of his pyjama jacket, overwhelmed by tenderness for her little boy.

Lorne reached up, touched her face and then flopped against her, grabbing her arms tightly with his small hands, rocking to and fro. Paula held him close, also rocking and smoothing her hand over his copper head shining so brightly in the firelight. But after a few seconds she gently disentangled herself, rose and pulled him up off the floor with her. Taking his hand, she walked him over to Emily and Tessa who were cuddling on the window seat.

'The Sandman's about to arrive, Aunty Emily,' Paula announced, making this sound most important. 'Shall we go into the bedroom to welcome him?'

'What a lovely idea,' Emily said, taking Tessa's hand, helping her down off the seat. 'I haven't seen the Sandman for years.'

Together the four of them went into the adjoining bedroom where a small night light glowed on the table between the two beds.

'Off with your dressing gowns,' Paula instructed. 'And into bed with you both. Quick! We don't want the Sandman to go away because two little poppets dawdle.'

Tessa and Lorne struggled with their belts, and Paula and Emily went to their assistance. The twins scrambled into their beds and Paula pulled up the bedclothes, tucked them in and gave them a kiss in turn.

'Take a seat, Aunty Emily, and be very very quiet or you'll frighten the Sandman away,' Paula cautioned as she pulled up a stool and sat down between the two beds.

'I'll be as quiet as a mouse,' Emily whispered, going along with the game, seating herself on the bottom of Lorne's bed.

Paula gazed at her children. 'Sssh!' she said softly, bringing a finger to her lips.

'Pom,' Tessa said, 'pom . . . Mam.'

'All right, I'll say the Sandman's poem for you, but snuggle down, and close your eyes both of you.'

Each child did as she said. Lorne put his thumb in his mouth and Tessa clutched at the white lamb lying next to her in the bed, and began to suck on its ear.

Paula began to recite in the softest of voices:

'The Sandman has the swiftest wings
And shoes that are made of gold,
He calls on you when the first star sings
When the night is not very old.
He carries a tiny silver spoon
And a bucket made of night,
He fills your eyes with bits of moon
And stardust that's shiny and bright.
He takes you on a ship that sails
Through the land of dreams and joys,
And tells you many wondrous tales
Of dragons and magical toys.
So come now and rest your sleepyhead
And close your eyes very tight,
For should you stay awake instead
The Sandman won't pass by tonight.'

Paula stopped, stood up and went to peer at the twins. Both were already fast asleep. A tender smile flickered on her mouth. They had had an unusually hectic day and were worn out. Gently she kissed each of them and moved the stool out of the way. Emily went to Lorne and Tessa, also bent and kissed them, and the two young women crept out of the bedroom on their tiptoes.

By seven o'clock Paula was beginning to wonder what had happened to Jim. Emily had left over half an hour ago, after having a quick drink with her in the library. She had seated herself at the desk, intending to do some paperwork, but her worries had intruded.

It was 5 January. The day she had mentally set aside to have a serious talk with Jim. Her parents and Philip had returned to London three days ago, after spending Christmas at Pennistone Royal. They had already departed for their skiing holiday in Chamonix.

Christmas had been exceptionally quiet. Randolph and Vivienne had accepted an invitation to visit Anthony and Sally at Clonloughlin, and the O'Neills had made a last-minute decision to join Shane in Barbados. Emily and Winston, along with Alexander and Maggie, had come to stay for a few days, and the entire Kallinski clan had driven over on Christmas Eve. But the whole holiday period had been sad and depressing for everyone without Emma. She had always been the catalyst, the mover and the doer, and without her things were not the same.

Paula had somehow struggled through, making a supreme effort for the children and her parents, whilst counting the hours until today. And then Jim had suddenly rushed off to the newspaper this morning before she had had a chance to open her mouth.

Suddenly Paula swung around in the chair and jumped up as she heard the sound of a car on the gravel driveway outside. She stepped up to the window behind her chair, cupped her hands against the glass and peered out. The light over the back door shone brightly, clearly illuminating Jim's Aston Martin.

With a small intake of breath she held herself rigid as her eyes fell on the pair of skis sticking out of one of the back windows. So that was why he was so late. He had gone to Long Meadow first – to collect his skiing gear. He was going to Chamonix after all.

It's now or never, Paula muttered under her breath and flew across the library. Wrenching open the door she stepped out into the Stone Hall, waiting for him, suppressing her exasperation.

Jim came in a moment later and headed in the direction of the main staircase at the other end of the hall.

'I'm in here, Jim,' she exclaimed.

Startled, he pivoted swiftly, stood regarding her with uncertainty.

'Can you spare me a few minutes?' she asked, striving to bring her voice down to a lower pitch, not wanting to alert him or scare him off.

'Why not? I was just going up to change. Had a rather hectic day,' he announced, walking towards her. 'Surprisingly busy for Saturday.'

Not so surprising, she thought, stepping back, opening the door wider. You've been clearing your desk in readiness for your imminent departure. But she said none of this.

Jim strolled past her into the library, without kissing her or making any gesture of affection. There was a great deal of strain between them and this had lately turned into real coldness.

Paula closed the door firmly, thought of locking it, but changed her mind. She followed him over to the fireplace.

Sitting down in a wing chair, Paula glanced up at him hovering near the fire. 'Dinner's not until eight. You've plenty of time to freshen up. Make yourself comfortable, Jim, let's chat for a while.'

Throwing her an odd look, he nevertheless took the other chair, pulled out his cigarettes and put one in his mouth. After lighting it he smoked in silence for a second, staring ahead at the fire. Then he said, 'How was your day?'

'Fine. I spent it with the children. Emily came over for lunch and stayed all afternoon. Winston had gone to a football match.'

Jim said nothing.

Paula kept her voice very low as she said, 'So you *are* going to Chamonix.'

'Yes.' He did not look at her.

'When are you leaving?'

He cleared his throat. 'I thought I'd drive up to London late tonight, around ten or eleven. The roads will be virtually empty. I can make it in record time. That way I can catch the first flight to Geneva tomorrow.'

Anger rushed through her, but she clamped down on it, knowing that she had to keep a cool head and must not inflame him if she was to accomplish anything. She said, 'Please don't go, Jim. At least not for a few days.'

'*Why?*' Now he swung his head, levelled his silvery-grey eyes on her and a blond brow lifted in surprise. He said, 'You're going to New York.'

'Yes, but not until the 8th or 9th. I told you, when you came back from Canada, that I wanted to discuss our problems. You put me off because it was Christmas and we were expecting guests. You promised you wouldn't go to Chamonix until we had settled things, thrashed out our problems.'

'*Your* problems, not mine, Paula.'

'*Our problems.*'

'I beg to disagree. If there are any problems in our marriage you have created them. For over a year now you've been looking for trouble, insisting we had difficulties when we didn't have any. Also, you are the one who has . . . left the marital bed, not I. You, and you alone, Paula, are the one who has brought about the present untenable situation.' He smiled faintly, eyeing her more closely. 'Because of *you* we only have half a marriage, but I'm prepared to live with it.'

'We have no marriage at all.'

He laughed hollowly. 'We do have two children, though, and I'm prepared to share the same house with you for

752

their sakes. They need us both. And talking of houses, when I come back from Chamonix we are *all* going to move back to Long Meadow. That is *my* house, *my* home, and *my* children are going to be brought up there.'

Paula stared at him aghast. 'You know very well Grandy wanted – '

'This is not your house,' he cut in rapidly. 'It belongs to your mother.'

'You know very well Mummy and Daddy have to live in London so he can go to Harte's every day.'

'That's their problem, not ours.'

'Grandy didn't want Pennistone Royal to be left unoccupied half of the year. It was always a foregone conclusion that I would live here most of the time, that my parents would come for weekends when they could, spend the summer months and special holidays at the house.'

'I have every intention of moving back into Long Meadow. With the children,' he said in a rush. 'You are very welcome. Of course, I can't force you to move in with us – ' He broke off, shrugged. 'It's your decision.'

Paula looked at him, biting her inner lip. She said, 'Jim, I want a divorce.'

He said coldly, 'I don't. I will never agree to one. *Never*. Furthermore, I think you should know that if you decide to take such a step I will fight you for custody of Lorne and Tessa. *My* children are going to be with me.'

'Children need their mother,' she began, and shook her head. 'Surely you of all people know that. Naturally, you would have full visiting rights. I would never keep the children away from you, Jim. You would see them whenever you wanted, and they would come and stay with you.'

He smiled narrowly as he snapped, 'You're priceless, do you know that. Quite extraordinary, and the most selfish woman I've ever known. You want it *all*, don't you. Your freedom to do what you want, to live where you want, and

753

the children as well.' His eyes became icy. 'Do you also want to take my job away from me?'

Paula sucked in her breath. 'How can you think a thing like that! Of course I don't. Grandy renewed your contract before she died, and your job is safe for the rest of your life. And you also have the shares in the new company.'

'Ah yes,' he mused softly. 'The new company. I rather like Toronto . . . lovely city. I might move there for a few years. That idea had crossed my mind in December. I'd enjoy running the *Toronto Sentinel*. Naturally the children would go with me.'

'No!' she cried, her face paling.

'Oh yes,' he countered. 'But it *is* up to you, Paula. If you persist in this ridiculous idea of getting a divorce, if you break up *my* family, I will settle in Toronto and I have every intention of taking *my* children with me.'

'They're also mine.'

'Yes,' he said, 'they are. And you are *my* wife.' He softened his tone, gave her a warmer look. 'We're a family, Paula. The children need you, I need you.' He reached out, took her hand in his. 'Why can't you stop all this nonsense, put aside your silly and *unfounded* grudges against me, make an effort to patch up our marriage. I'm willing to try.' He flashed her his bland smile. 'Why not start right now – *tonight*.' He tightened his grip on her fingers and leaned closer to her, added in a suggestive tone, 'There's no time like the present, darling. Come on, let's go upstairs and make love. I'll prove to you that all of these differences you're forever talking about are imaginary, exist only in *your head*. Come back to my bed, come back into my arms, Paula.'

She did not dare say a word.

There was a long and painful silence.

Finally Jim murmured, 'All right, not tonight then. Pity. Listen, since I'm going off to Chamonix and you're about to head for New York, let us both take the rest of this month to come to terms with ourselves during our separation. And then, when we're both back home in a few weeks, we'll start afresh. We'll move into Long Meadow and begin again, build a better relationship than we ever had before.'

'There's nothing left between us, Jim, and therefore there is nothing to build on,' she whispered miserably.

He let go of her hand and gazed into the fire. After a short while he said, 'Psychologists call it compulsive repetition.'

Not understanding what he was suddenly talking about, Paula frowned and said, 'I'm not following you.'

Jim turned to face her, and repeated, 'Psychologists call it *compulsive repetition*.'

'What's that supposed to mean?' she asked sharply, wondering if he was attempting to sidetrack her as he so often did.

'It refers to the pattern of behaviour some people adopt – an offspring actually *reliving* the life of a parent or grandparent, repeating that life, mistakes and all, as if he or she is guided by some terrible inner compulsion.'

Paula gaped at him speechlessly. But she quickly found her voice. 'Are you trying to say that I am reliving my grandmother's life?'

'*Exactly.*'

'You're absolutely wrong!' Paula cried. 'I am my *own* person. I am living my *own* life.'

'Think that if you wish, but it's not true. You are compulsively doing everything Emma Harte ever did, and with great precision. You work your fingers to the bone, devote every moment of your time to that wretched business, selfishly flitting around the world, wheeling and dealing and neglecting your duties as a wife and mother. You make everybody toe the line, *your line*, and you lack emotional stability just as she did.'

Paula was furious. 'How dare you! How dare you criticize

Grandy! You're making her out to be something she was not, she who was so good to you! You've really got a bloody nerve. Furthermore, I don't neglect my children, and I never neglected you. Our estrangement came about because of the things which are lacking in you, Jim. I'm not emotionally unstable, but it strikes me that you are. I wasn't the one in a – ' Paula stopped herself, clenched her hands together in her lap.

'I knew you'd never let me live that down,' he said his face darkening. 'Has it ever occurred to you that you might be responsible for my nervous breakdown?' he challenged.

Paula gasped, 'If anybody's compulsive, you are. You continually want to blame *me* for everything that you yourself do.'

Jim sighed. He glanced away, ruminating for a few seconds, and then he brought his eyes to Paula. He gave her a penetrating stare. 'Why are you so keen to get a divorce?'

'Because our marriage is over. It's ridiculous to continue,' she murmured, adopting a calmer, more reasonable tone. 'It's not fair to the children, to you, or to me, Jim.'

'We were in love,' he mused almost to himself then asked, 'weren't we?'

'Yes, we were.' She took a deep breath. 'But being in love doesn't guarantee happiness, Jim. Two people have to be compatible and able to live with each other on a day-to-day basis. Being in love is never enough, I'm afraid. A marriage needs a solid foundation based on genuine friendship.'

'Is there another man?' he demanded. His eyes remained fixed on hers.

Unexpected though the question was, Paula managed to keep her neutral expression in place. Although her heart missed a beat, she said in her most convincing voice, 'No, there isn't, Jim.'

He did not say anything for a few seconds. And then he

got up, went and stood over her chair. He gripped her shoulder. 'There had better not be, Paula. Because if there is I will destroy you. I'll counter-sue you for divorce, and I'll have you declared an unfit mother. I'll get custody of my children, never you fear. No judge in England is going to give the children of a broken marriage to a woman who wilfully broke up that marriage and who is neglectful of those children, who travels the world in pursuit of her business interests to the detriment of those children.' He brought his face closer to hers, and tightened his hand on her shoulder. 'Or one who is screwing around with another man.'

Paula managed to throw off his vice-like grip. She leaped to her feet, her face blazing. 'Try it,' she said in a cold voice. 'Just try it. We'll see who wins.'

He stepped away from her and laughed in her face. 'And you don't think you're reliving Emma Harte's life. That's the joke of the century. Just look at you – why you sound exactly like her. And you think the way she did. You, too, believe that money and power make you invulnerable. Sadly, my dear, they don't.' He swung around and walked towards the door.

'Where are you going?' Paula called after him.

Jim stopped in his tracks and turned to face her. 'To London. There's not much point my staying here for dinner. We'll only continue to fight. Frankly, I'm weary of it all.'

Paula ran after him, took his arm, gave him a pleading look, 'But there is no real reason for us to quarrel in this way, Jim,' she said in a shaken voice. 'We can work this out like civilized people, like adults who are mature and intelligent. I know we can.'

'It's really up to you, Paula,' Jim said, also speaking in a more reasonable voice. 'Think about everything I've said and perhaps when I get back from Chamonix you'll have come to your senses.'

CHAPTER 49

John Crawford, the family solicitor, had been listening to Paula for over an hour.

He had not interrupted her once, deeming it wiser to let her unburden herself before asking any relevant questions. Also he had discerned, in his astute and insightful way, that she had not discussed her disastrous marriage with anyone else before tonight. Certainly not at great length, and he decided that in a sense talking to him was a catharsis for her. He believed that by talking, opening up, she would feel better.

Paula finally paused for breath. He instantly detected a relaxation in the way she held her body, a sudden slackening of her rigid facial muscles, and relief was mirrored in her startling blue eyes. 'That's about it,' she said, smiling a bit uncertainly. 'I don't think I've missed anything.'

John nodded, continuing to observe her. He recognized she was in total control, calm enough to accept what he was about to say. He cleared his throat. 'I don't want to alarm you, and this is only a suggestion, but perhaps we ought to make the children wards of court.'

Although she was startled, Paula said steadily enough, 'Oh John, surely that's far too drastic a step. It might even be begging for trouble. It's so inflammatory.'

John, who had long harboured a visceral dislike of Jim Fairley, clasped his hands together and brought them up to his face. He looked at her over them, his eyes reflective. 'It seems to me, from the things you've told me, that Jim virtually threatened to take those children out of the country, to Canada to be precise, if you don't do as he wants. Isn't that so, Paula?'

'Yes,' she admitted.

'By making children wards of court one prevents their physical removal from their country of domicile by a disgruntled and angry parent involved in this kind of distressing emotional situation.'

'Yes, John, I know what it means. But Jim believes I will change my mind about getting a divorce. He's not going to suddenly swoop down, grab the children and fly off to Toronto. He would certainly try to ascertain what I'm going to do first. Besides, he's in Chamonix.'

'And you, Paula, are going to the States in a couple of days. He knows that. He could easily try to pull something whilst you're absent. After all, Geneva is only a few hours away.'

'I'm sure he wouldn't – ' She stopped abruptly, alertly searching the solicitor's face. 'From your expression you obviously think he might.'

'There is that possibility.' John stood up and walked across the drawing room, poured himself another dry martini from the jug on the bar cart, swung around and apologized, 'I'm sorry, I didn't ask you if you wanted another drink. Do you?'

'No, thanks anyway.'

Returning to his seat, John sat down, continued, 'I'm going to ask you a very blunt question, Paula, a crucial question, and I would like you to think most carefully before you answer.'

She nodded.

He said: 'Do you believe that Jim is mentally stable?'

Without hesitation, Paula replied. 'Oh yes, John, I do. I realize he was in a nursing home an awfully long time after his nervous breakdown, but he's fully recovered now. He's behaving quite normally.' She smiled ruefully. 'If you can call his attitude to me normal, that is. He's stubborn, pigheaded really, but then he always has been. He blinds himself to the truth, to reality. He's convinced our problems are figments of my imagination, as I just told you. However,

I'll say it again, I do not believe he is unstable. Upset at the moment, yes, but that's all.'

'Very well, I trust your judgement, and I also understand your reluctance to take steps that would inflame him. However, I think it would be advisable for you to talk to Daisy, alert her to the situation. If Jim should leave Chamonix unexpectedly she must contact me at once.'

'No, not Mummy,' Paula exclaimed. 'I'd prefer not to worry her. Anyway, I've never confided in her, or anyone, to be truthful. Well, actually I have spoken to Emily and my father a few times lately, and they know how bad the marriage is, and, in fact, Emily and Winston have urged me to get a divorce. The point is this . . . Emily and Winston are going off to Chamonix the day after tomorrow. They'll be there for the next two weeks. I'll speak to her before she leaves, explain everything and ask her to ring you if anything untoward happens.'

John's face brightened. 'Good, good. Emily is level-headed and smart. I feel more confident knowing she's going to be staying at the chalet. As your grandmother always said, there're no flies on Emily. So in view of that and because you're against it, I'll drop the idea of having you make the twins wards of court.' He gave her a funny little smile. 'It's crossed my mind that you may think I'm paranoid, but I'm not. Still, I am prudent and fully aware that it's often wiser to take precautions to avert trouble.' He leaned forward intently. 'That's why I suggested the idea in the first place, also it struck me that you were worried about the children yourself, otherwise you wouldn't have brought them to London with you yesterday.'

'Yes, I was a bit concerned,' Paula agreed. 'I was badly shaken up on Saturday night after Jim left. On Sunday morning I decided I ought to have Lorne and Tessa with me. They looked so small and defenceless, so vulnerable, John. They're only babies, and I do love them so much. I even thought of taking them to New York with me, but that would be uprooting them unnecessarily. Nora is quite happy to spend a few weeks in London, and at least the weather's better here than it is in Yorkshire. They'll be fine, and Nora has Parker and Mrs Ramsey as back-up at the London flat.'

'Yes, they're both very reliable. Try not to worry, my dear. I'll keep an eye on things at Belgrave Square. Make sure Nora has my telephone numbers, though, and explain that she must ring me if Jim arrives on the scene.'

'I'll do that tonight.' Paula gazed past John, staring at the dark green damask curtains, her face suddenly thoughtful. She said a little haltingly, 'Jim can't take them away from me, can he, John?'

'Of course not. Don't even contemplate such a thing!' John patted her hand and, wishing to reassure her, said, 'Jim can threaten all kinds of things in an effort to make *you* do as *he* wishes, but threats are meaningless in the long run. Thankfully, we do have courts of law in this land and they are eminently fair, which is more than I can say about the judicial systems in a lot of other countries.'

'Yes,' she murmured, then let out a tiny sigh of weariness. 'He says I want it all, want everything my way.'

John laughed. 'That's like the kettle calling the pot black, Paula. Hasn't it occurred to you that Jim wants it *his* way?' Not waiting for an answer, the solicitor hurried on 'He's being selfish, expecting you to toe *his* line, regardless of your own feelings, and despite the fact that you have a disastrous marriage. It's already playing havoc with you emotionally, and it will inevitably start affecting the children. The only thing to do with a marriage that has failed so miserably is to end it immediately for everyone's sakes. Stop the flow of blood, in a manner of speaking. I ought to know.'

Paula looked across at him. 'Poor John, you went through hell too, didn't you?'

'To put it mildly, my dear,' he replied. 'However, those

troubles are behind me, and Millicent and I are good friends these days, most amicable really.'

'I do hope Jim and I can be friends eventually,' Paula said as if musing aloud. 'I don't hate him, far from it. To be honest, John, I feel rather sad for him . . . because he just cannot face reality.' She lifted her shoulders in a light shrug. 'But look, I came here to talk to you about a plan of action, and I want to say now that I wish to be scrupulously fair with him in every way. I want him to have total access to the twins, and of course there's no question about him staying on at the newspapers.' She scowled at the solicitor. 'I was stunned when he suggested I would take his job away.'

John stared into his glass for a moment, slowly lifted his eyes which were grave and intent. 'I don't want to delude you into thinking we're going to have an easy time with Jim, because we are not. I *know* we're going to have a fight on our hands. It's patently obvious, from what you've said, that he doesn't want to let you go, that he is prepared to put up with the worst kind of marital situation to remain your husband. Understandable perhaps. You are the mother of his children, you are a desirable and accomplished young woman, with immense wealth and power. What man wouldn't want to hang on to you. Also – '

'But Jim isn't interested in my money or my power,' Paula cut in rapidly. 'Why, John, he resents my business, does nothing but complain about my career.'

'Don't be naïve!'

Paula stared at him, her brows drawing together as she sat back, her expression changing to one of total disbelief. She opened her mouth, and then quickly closed it, wanting to hear what else John had to say.

'Of course he cares about your money and your power, Paula,' the solicitor remarked quietly. 'And he always has, in my opinion. Jim is not quite as altruistic as you seem to believe. As your solicitor I feel it is my duty to point this out to you, however unpalatable that might be to you. Jim has apparently been complaining very vociferously about your work, but he knew long before he married you that you were Emma's chief heir. He was also aware that you would not only inherit most of her wealth, but *all* of her tremendous responsibilities as well. He's merely using your career as an excuse to get at you, to hurt you, to punish you. At the same time it enables him to paint a picture of himself as the long-suffering, neglected and injured husband. In other words, he strikes a pose that will gain him sympathy. Please, my dear, do be aware of that for your own sake, and for your own peace of mind.'

'Perhaps you're right,' she conceded, knowing that John Crawford was a shrewd and brilliant lawyer and a man with great psychological insight into people. She leaned forward. 'If Jim *is* interested in money, as you imply,' she shook her head and laughed, 'no, *insist*, then let us give him money. I'm prepared to make a large financial settlement on him. Suggest an amount, John, and let's set a date when we can have a meeting with Jim. He'll be back at the end of the month, as will I, and I would like to put things in motion.'

'I can't come up with an amount tonight, off the top of my head,' John explained. 'That wouldn't be fair to anyone. It requires careful thought.' He took a sip of his martini, put the glass down and stood up. He walked over to the humidor on a side table, and took a cigar, not wanting her to see the cynical smile that had touched his mouth involuntarily. If my assessment of Jim is correct, and I'm sure it is, money will do the trick, John decided. Clipping off the end of the cigar, he strolled back to his chair, contemplating the settlement. It was a good card to have up his sleeve and would be a powerful negotiating weapon if Jim did prove to be intransigent.

Striking a match, John puffed hard on the cigar until it

ignited, then told her, 'As far as a meeting is concerned, we can get together any time you wish – ' He did not complete his sentence, but began to shake his head in a negative fashion instead.

'What's wrong?' Paula asked, clasping her hands together, experiencing a stab of apprehension.

'Nothing for you to look *so* concerned about, my dear. I think, however, that you're going to have your job cut out for you – getting Jim to meet with me, I mean. He's so dead set against the divorce and obstinate by nature. Maybe it would be better if I simply dropped by for a drink one night when he's in town. On his way back to Yorkshire after the Chamonix trip, perhaps?'

'Yes, that is a good idea,' Paula agreed. 'He did mutter something about seeing me in London in two weeks, before he left Pennistone Royal on Saturday.' Paula pushed herself to the edge of her chair and her face filled with sincerity as she reminded him, 'Don't forget that I want to be fair with Jim about the children, and I am willing to be very generous when it comes to money. It's important to me that Jim is financially secure for the rest of his life.'

'I'll remember everything,' John assured her. 'And whilst you're in New York I'll work on the terms of the divorce and make them most acceptable to Jim, I promise.' He gave her a fond smile. 'Not many women would be as kind as you. He's very lucky.'

'I'm sure *he* doesn't think that right now,' she ventured, rising to her feet. 'Thank you for being so understanding. I feel better after talking to you and much more positive about the future. And now I'm going to leave you in peace to have your dinner. I've taken up far too much of your evening as it is.'

He squeezed her arm affectionately as he escorted her across the drawing room and out into the small foyer. Loving her mother as he did, he considered Paula to be the daughter he had never had. He felt inordinately protective of her sometimes. Shrewd and clever in business though she was, she had had little or no experience with men, had been protected all of her life by Emma Harte and her parents. In many ways the harsher aspects of everyday living were unknown to her, and she might well be an easy target for an unscrupulous man.

As they reached the door, John turned her to face him. He bent forward, kissed her cheek, and with a chuckle, he said, '*You* can take up my time whenever you wish, my dear. It does a crusty old bachelor like me a lot of good to see your beautiful face. I'm only sorry we were meeting to discuss such a sad matter.'

Paula hugged him affectionately. 'You're not a crusty old bachelor,' she declared, smiling at him. 'You're the most wonderful friend – to all of us. Thank you for being that, and for everything, John. I'll speak to you before I leave for New York.'

'Please do, my dear.' He opened the door, then caught her arm as she went outside. 'It's going to be all right, Paula, really it is. Do try not to worry.'

'I will.' She ran down the short flight of steps in front of his house in Chester Street, turned and waved. John lifted his hand in response, went inside and closed the door, pressing back his concern for her.

Paula hurried down the street, making for Belgrave Square which was only a few minutes away. She had meant it when she had told John Crawford she felt relieved after talking to him. But this was not the only reason why her depression of the last forty-eight hours had lifted so unexpectedly. Making a decision, taking positive and constructive action, had worked wonders for her. Paula never vacillated. Like Emma before her, she was expedient by nature, always preferred action and commitment in preference to waiting. In consequence, marking time for the past year because of Jim's plane crash and subsequent sojourn in the mental home, had been unendurable. But she was nothing if not prudent, and she had schooled herself to be patient, had acknowledged months ago that if waiting was debilitating it was infinitely preferable to making rash moves she might live to regret.

But now, as she walked at a brisk pace, she experienced a great sense of release. The act of talking to John, of putting matters in his hands was liberating. She was confident he would work out an equable divorce agreement, and surely Jim would be convinced she was serious, in deadly earnest, when he knew she had taken this final step.

Paula glowed with a new optimism as she crossed Belgrave Square and went into the great mansion purchased so many years before by her grandfather, Paul McGill. She slammed the heavy exterior glass-and-wrought-iron door behind her, climbed the short circular staircase that led up to the front entrance of the maisonette and let herself in with her key.

Slipping off her tweed coat, she hung it in the hall closet and turned as Parker came hurrying out of the back quarters and into the large entrance foyer.

'Oh, Mrs Fairley, I was just wondering whether I ought to telephone you at Mr Crawford's house. Mr O'Neill is in the drawing room. He's been waiting for you for quite a while. I gave him a drink. Would you like anything, madam?'

'No, thank you, Parker.'

Wondering what Uncle Bryan wanted, why he had arrived so unexpectedly and without ringing first, she pushed open the drawing room door and stood stock still on the threshold. Fully expecting to see Bryan she was thrown at the sight of Shane. He stood up, grinning like a Cheshire cat from ear to ear.

'My God!' she cried, 'what are you doing here?' She pushed the door closed with her foot and ran into his arms, her face wreathed in delighted smiles.

Shane kissed her, took her by the shoulders and held her

766

away from him. 'I was so worried about you after those awful phone conversations on Saturday and Sunday I decided to come home. I arrived at London Airport about two hours ago.'

'Oh Shane, I'm sorry I worried you . . . but it is a wonderful surprise to see you, and several days sooner than I expected.' She drew him over to the sofa and they sat down, continuing to hold hands. Paula said, with a bright little laugh, 'But I'm leaving for New York the day after tomorrow, and you know that – '

'I thought we'd fly back together,' he interjected, his dark eyes roving over her lovingly. 'As a matter of fact, I concocted a rather good plan in the last half-hour. I thought I'd sidetrack for a few days, whisk you off to Barbados for the weekend on our way to the States. What do you think?'

'Oh Shane,' Paula began and hesitated, her face sobering. She said gravely, 'I told you Jim asked me if there is another man. And even though I denied it, I don't know that he's entirely convinced. What if someone should see us in Barbados? Or even travelling together? I don't want to do anything that would jeopardize my position and my custody of the children. He would be vindictive, I just know he would.'

Shane said, 'I understand your worry, darling, and I'd taken those points into consideration earlier. Now look, Paula, he's never going to be suspicious of me. It would be like him suspecting your brother Philip, for God's sake. Also, you do own a boutique in Barbados. You've every reason to go there, to check on it. And finally, no one will see us on the plane, and we can lay low once we get to Coral Cove.'

'Nobody will see us?' she repeated questioningly. 'What do you mean?'

'I have another surprise for you, Beanstalk. I finally took delivery of the private jet Dad and I decided to buy for the company. I just whizzed across the Atlantic in it, but let's forget that, and pretend our trip to the Caribbean is really its inaugural flight. Come on, say yes, sweetheart.'

'All right then,' Paula agreed, making a snap decision. Surely it was safe to travel with Shane. He was her childhood friend, after all. The grave expression fled and her violet eyes lit up. 'It's just what I need to give me a lift after the upsetting weekend.'

'Yes, it is.' He beamed at her. 'We have to think of an appropriate name for the jet, you know. Any ideas?'

'No, but I *will* bring a bottle of champagne and break it on the side, wet its bottom so to speak, even if we don't have a name,' she announced, enjoying the sudden and unexpected fun, the joyousness of being with him. Her heart soared with love for him, and she felt the old dizziness, the lightheadedness she experienced when she was with him again after a separation. Shane made all the difference in the world to her. And he made everything seem possible. The residue of her depression fell away so completely it might never have existed.

Shane now pulled her to her feet. 'I told Parker you were going out to dinner. I hope you don't mind me taking you over.' He gave her his boyish grin, and kissed her forehead. His face immediately turned serious. 'I want to know about your meeting with John. We can talk about it over a bottle of good wine and a pleasant meal at the White Elephant.'

CHAPTER 50

The chalet was deserted.

Emily realized this as she ran lightly down the stairs and stood poised in the circular entrance hall, her head cocked on one side as she listened for the usual morning sounds. Generally voices and laughter reverberated and the radio was always playing in the background. But all were absent on this Saturday morning late in January.

Swinging to her left, Emily went into the dining room. Her mother was standing near the window, holding a small hand mirror and peering at her face in great concentration.

'Good morning, Mummy,' Emily called in a cheery tone from the doorway and meandered across the floor.

Elizabeth turned with swiftness, smiled and said, 'Oh Emily, there you are, good morning, darling.'

After planting a kiss on her mother's cheek, Emily sat down at the long rustic table and lifted the coffee pot. She asked, 'Where is everybody?'

For a moment Elizabeth did not answer, continuing to examine her face in the bright sunlight pouring in through the window and then, sighing under her breath, she joined her daughter at the table. 'The devoted skiers left ages ago, as they always do. You've just missed Winston. He decided to go skiing at the last minute, and hurried off, hoping to catch up with the others. Apparently you were sleeping so soundly he didn't have the heart to wake you. He asked me to tell you he'll see you at lunch.'

'I just couldn't get up early this morning,' Emily murmured, stirring her coffee, eyeing the croissants longingly. They smelled delicious. Her mouth watered.

'I'm not surprised. It was awfully late when everyone left last night. I'm paying for it myself this morning –' Elizabeth cut herself short, glanced at Emily quickly. 'Do you think I need to have my eyes done?'

Laughing, Emily put the coffee cup down and leaned across the table, staring at her mother's eyes. She was accustomed to such questions and aware that she had to pay the strictest attention when they were asked. She shook her head several times. 'No, of course you don't, your eyes are marvellous.'

'Do you really think so, dear?' Elizabeth lifted the mirror and gazed at herself again.

'For heaven's sake, Mummy, you're a young woman, only fifty – '

'Not so *loud*, darling,' Elizabeth muttered. She placed the mirror on the table and went on, 'I must admit I have been toying with the idea lately. I think my lids look a bit wrinkled. Marc is so conscious of a woman's looks, and being older than he is – '

'I didn't know he was younger than you, Mummy! He certainly doesn't look it.'

This seemed to cheer Elizabeth and her face brightened. 'I'm glad to hear that, Emily, but he *is* younger, I'm afraid.'

'By how many years?' Emily reached for a croissant, no longer able to resist temptation and broke it in half.

'Five.'

'Good heavens, that's nothing. And forget about having facial surgery, Mum, you're a beautiful woman, and don't look a day older than forty.' Emily plunged her knife into the mound of creamy butter, lavishly spread it on a portion of the breakfast roll and added peach jam.

Elizabeth, distracted from her constant preoccupation with herself for a moment, stared at her in disapproval. 'You're not really going to eat that, are you, dear? It's loaded with calories.'

Emily grinned. 'Of course I am. I'm ravenous.'

'You know, you must watch your weight, Emily. You've always had a tendency to get plump very quickly ever since you were a child.'

'I'll starve myself when we get home.'

Elizabeth shook her head in exasperation, but knowing it was useless to argue, she remarked, 'Did you notice Marc flirting with that French countess at the party last night?'

'No, I can't say I did. But he flirts with everyone, Mother. He can't help it, and it doesn't mean anything,

I'm sure. I wish you'd relax about that man. He's lucky to have you.'

'And I'm most fortunate to have him. He's very good to me, the best husband I've had, if you want to know the truth.'

Emily doubted this and before she could stop herself, she exclaimed, 'What about *Daddy*? He was wonderful to you. It's a pity you ever left *him*.'

'Naturally you're prejudiced about Tony. He *is* your father. But you have no conception of how it was between us, dear. Latterly, I mean. You were only a small child. Anyway, I don't propose to start regurgitating all the details of my first marriage with you, Emily, picking it over and examining it under a microscope.'

'That's very *wise* of you,' Emily said with acerbity and munched on the roll, conscious they were touching on an explosive subject.

Elizabeth gave her daughter a sharp look but she, too, sagely held her tongue. She poured herself another cup of coffee and lit a cigarette, sat observing Emily, thinking how pretty she looked this morning in her emerald green sweater and trousers. They intensified the colour of her eyes. After almost two weeks in the French Alps, her hair was a lighter brighter blonde and her delicate face had the hint of a suntan. Elizabeth was suddenly glad that she and Marc had accepted Daisy's invitation to join them at the chalet they had rented. She had enjoyed being with her children and she had derived a great deal of satisfaction from Marc's attentiveness to them, especially to Amanda and Francesca.

Between bites, Emily said, 'I think I'll go into the town later. I need to buy a few things.'

'That's a good idea,' Elizabeth remarked. 'And perhaps you'll drop me off at the hairdressers, darling.'

Emily burst out laughing. 'You don't need your hair doing, Mummy, you were there yesterday.'

'Now, Emily, let's not get into a long discussion about my hair. *You* paddle your canoe and *I'll* paddle mine.'

'Okay.' Leaning forward, Emily propped her elbows on the table and continued, 'I have a vague remembrance of Amanda and Francesca barging into our room at some ungodly hour this morning and smothering Winston and me with kisses. I assume Alexander dragged them off to Geneva – screaming at the top of their lungs, no doubt.'

Elizabeth nodded. 'They *were* rather obstreperous. Neither of them seem to like the finishing school on Lake Geneva, and I can't imagine why. But they settled down when they knew Daisy was going to Geneva with them. She wanted to do some shopping and decided to go along with Alexander. They're planning to take the girls to lunch at the Hotel Richmond before returning them to the school. I do love that hotel, Emily, and in fact I promised the twins I'd fly up to Geneva from Paris at Easter to spend a few days with them.' Elizabeth had a sudden thought and it brought a warm smile to her face. 'Why don't you and Winston join Marc and me, as my guests at the Richmond? It would be fun, Emily.'

Pleasantly surprised at this unprecedented gesture, Emily said, 'That's a lovely thought, Mother, and very kind of you to invite us. I'll ask Winston and let you know later.' Emily reached out, her hand hovering over another croissant.

'Please don't eat that, darling!'

Looking slightly shamefaced, Emily pulled her hand back. 'Yes, you're right. They are awfully fattening.' Emily rose. 'I think I'd better go upstairs and get ready to go into the town. I know if I sit here chatting to you I'll demolish that entire plate.'

'I'll come up too,' Elizabeth said. 'I want to change.'

Emily groaned. 'You look perfectly gorgeous, Mummy, you don't have to bother . . . . you're only going to the hairdressers.'

'One never knows whom one might meet,' Elizabeth countered. Glancing at her watch, she added, 'It's not quite eleven. I'll only be half an hour. I promise.'

To Emily's relief her mother was true to her word for once, and a few minutes after eleven-thirty she was turning the key in the ignition and pulling away from the chalet. This was located in a small hamlet on the outskirts of Chamonix, the lovely ancient town that nestled at the foot of Mont Blanc. As Emily swung out on to the main road and cruised along at a steady speed, she could not help admiring the extraordinary scenery which never failed to make her catch her breath.

The Valley of Chamonix, bounded on one side by the Mont Blanc range and on the other by the Aiguilles Rouges chain, was like a natural platform from which to view the highest peak of Europe. And now, as Emily peered ahead at Mont Blanc and the surrounding mountains, she could not help feeling overawed by their grandeur and majesty. Their glittering snow-covered pinnacles thrust up into a high-flung sky that was clear cerulean blue, filled with white puff-ball clouds and brilliant sunshine.

As though reading her daughter's thoughts, Elizabeth exclaimed, 'Impressive, isn't it, Emily! And it's such a glorious day.'

'Yes,' Emily agreed. 'I bet our skiing enthusiasts are happy as larks, enjoying themselves on the slopes.' She glanced at her mother through the corner of her eye. 'By the way, did Marc go with Uncle David and the others?'

'Yes, and Maggie.'

'Oh,' Emily said, surprised. 'I thought she was driving to Geneva with Alexander.'

'She wanted to go skiing instead, make the most of it, I suppose, since they're leaving tomorrow for London.'

'Jan and Peter are travelling back with them, so Jan told

me last night,' Emily remarked, referring to the only non-family members who were house guests of her aunt and uncle.

'I tried to persuade them to stay on for a few days longer,' Elizabeth explained. 'I rather like them, and *he's* such a charmer.'

'Peter Coles! Honestly, Mummy, you do have funny tastes. I think he's a crashing bore. So pompous.' Emily giggled. 'But he is especially attentive to you, and I've seen Marc give him more than one filthy look during the ten days they've been here. I do believe the old Frog is as jealous as hell.'

'Please don't refer to Marc as an *old frog*, darling, it's a very unkind description and most inappropriate,' Elizabeth chastised. Then she laughed with sudden gaiety. 'So you think Peter makes Marc jealous. That's nice to know. *Mmmm.'*

'Very.' Emily smiled to herself, realizing how happy this bit of irrelevant information made her mother feel. But maybe it wasn't so irrelevant to her. The poor woman was dotty about Marc Deboyne. That snake in the grass, Emily thought. She detested him, and wouldn't trust him as far as she could throw him.

Elizabeth now launched into a glowing recital about her new husband's manifold qualities and Emily nodded and made small agreeable sounds, as if concurring. But she was only half listening. Her mother was quite irritating when she went on and on about him in this ridiculous way, and Emily was pleased when she saw the town of Chamonix looming immediately ahead.

After leaving the Citröen in the car park, Emily and her mother walked briskly down one of the main boulevards, heading in the direction of the small square where the hairdressing salon was situated. When they arrived at its door, Emily said, 'How long will you be?'

'Oh just about an hour, dear. I'm only having a comb

out. Why don't you meet me at that little bistro over there at the other side of the square. We'll have an apéritif before going back to the chalet for lunch.'

'All right. Bye, Mummy.'

Emily sauntered leisurely around the square, glancing in the shop windows. She only had a few things to buy and an hour to waste, so she took her time. After traversing the entire square she continued down the boulevard, making for a boutique that sold highly original *après ski* clothes, and went inside. The sales assistants knew her and she wasted twenty minutes chatting to them and trying on evening tops, none of which she liked enough to buy.

Back on the street, Emily wandered down to the pharmacy, purchased the small items she needed, tucked them in her shoulder bag, and left the shop. Slowly she retraced her steps, remembering she wanted to pick up some picture postcards to send to friends in England.

To her astonishment Emily saw Marc Deboyne coming towards her. He was hurrying, looked deeply preoccupied, and he had obviously not seen her.

As they drew level with each other, Emily said archly, 'Fancy meeting you, Marc. Mummy thinks you've gone skiing.'

Marc Deboyne, caught off guard, was both startled and embarrassed. Quickly recovering his equilibrium, he exclaimed, 'Ah, Emilee, Emilee, my dear,' and caught hold of her arm, squeezed it affectionately. He added, in his Gallic-accented but perfect English, 'I changed my mind. I decided to go for a walk. I have a headache.'

Leaning into him, Emily said pointedly, 'It's not the only thing you have, Marc. You've also got lipstick on the neck of your sweater.'

His smile was indulgent but his eyes reproved, and then he chuckled. 'Emilee, what *are* you implying? It's undoubtedly your mother's lipstick.'

Ignoring this remark, she said, 'Mummy's having her

hair done. I'm meeting her at the bistro opposite for a drink. At one o'clock. She'll be disappointed if you don't join us.' Emily's tone was all sweetness. Her eyes were chips of green ice.

'I would not disappoint Elizabeth. I shall meet you there. *Ciao*, Emilee.' He gave an odd little salute and moved on, walking at the same rapid pace.

Emily stared after him, watched him as he crossed the road and cut down a side street. She wondered where he was going. Bastard, she thought. I bet he was having a quickie with that ghastly countess from the party last night, who is no more of a Frenchwoman than I am. Filled with dislike for him, Emily grimaced in distaste and turned on her heels, marching up the street in search of a newspaper shop. She found one within minutes and browsed for a while, flipping through the latest magazines, still endeavouring to pass the time. Finally peeking at her watch she saw that it was almost one o'clock, almost time to meet her mother. Stepping up to the metal rack holding cards of Chamonix, she selected four and went to pay for them.

Putting the cards and the change in her shoulder bag, Emily smiled at the woman behind the counter. '*Merci, madame.*'

The woman started to respond and then stopped abruptly, cocking her head. At that precise moment there was a sudden extraordinary rumbling sound that rent the air around them and increased to thunderous and deafening proportions within the space of a split second.

Emily shouted, 'That sounds like a terrible explosion.'

The woman gaped at her through terrified eyes, screamed back, 'No! Avalanche!' She swung her plump body, grabbed the telephone.

Clutching her bag, Emily ran out into the street.

Shop doors were opening and people were emerging, all of them wearing the same frightened expressions, as were the passers-by.

'*Avalanche!*' a man cried to Emily and pointed in the direction of Mont Blanc as he sped on down the street.

Emily stood transfixed, mesmerized by the sight. Even from this distance she could see that great fractures boomed across the slopes of Mont Blanc and half the mountainside was rumbling down in a tremendous swathe that looked to be hundreds and hundreds of feet across. Gargantuan slabs of snow were hurtling forward at gathering speed, gaining momentum as they tumbled on their precipitous downward journey, sweeping aside all that lay in their path. And rising up into the brilliant blue air were enormous billowing clouds of powdered snow that had been pulverized by the turbulence of the slide into millions of tiny snow-smithereens.

Two police cars, their sirens screaming, raced along the street at breakneck speed. Their high-pitched wails broke the hypnotic spell that had momentarily held Emily in its grip. She blinked several times and then the blood seemed to drain out of her. *Winston was up there. Everyone was up there. David. Philip. Jim. Maggie. Jan and Peter Coles.*

She began to shake like a leaf and she could not move. Her legs turned to jelly as the fear rushed through her, swamped her, overwhelmed her. '*Oh my God! Winston!*' Emily cried out loud. '*Winston. Oh God! No!*'

It was as if the sound of her own voice galvanized her. She began to run, racing along the pavement, her head thrust forward, her feet flying over the stones as she ran faster and faster, making for the large cable-car terminal she knew was only a short distance away.

Her heart pounded in her chest, her breathing was laboured as she hurled herself on, blinking again, squeezing back the tears that stung her eyes. *Oh God, let Winston be safe. Please let Winston be safe. And the others. Make them all safe. Oh God, don't let any of them be dead.*

Emily became aware of other running feet, other people pressing around her. Some were outstripping her as they pounded past. They were also making for the terminal, which was now in her line of vision. A man jostled her as he leaped ahead, and she almost tripped and fell. But she recovered her balance and went on running, her fear propelling her.

She thought her heart was bursting when she finally reached the terminal. Only then did Emily slow down and come to a standstill, gasping for breath. She pressed her hand against her heaving chest. Rasping noises emanated from her throat. She leaned against one of the police cars parked near the cable-car depot, and fumbled in her shoulder bag. She found her handkerchief, wiped her sweating face and neck, endeavoured to marshal her swimming senses, willed herself to stay calm.

After a few seconds her breathing was more normal and she straightened up, looked around. Her eyes were frantic as they swept over the crowd that had already gathered in the space of fifteen minutes.

Emily hoped against hope that Winston had finished skiing before the avalanche had struck, prayed that he was somewhere amongst the tourists and townspeople milling around. She threw herself into their midst, her eyes darting from side to side, seeking him, her anxiety paramount. Instant dismay lodged in the pit of her stomach. He was nowhere in sight.

Turning away, Emily pressed her hands to her mouth, choking. Terror seized her, held her in a vice. She stumbled back to the police car, leaned against its hood, her heart clenching. *How could anyone have survived that avalanche? She had seen it hurtling down at such speed and force it would have crushed anything that stood in its way.* Emily closed her eyes. She ought to go and speak to someone, ask about rescue teams, but she had no strength. She closed her eyes. She felt her legs slipping and sliding under her as if she had lost all control of her body.

Suddenly two strong arms gripped her, pulled her upright.

'Emily! Emily! It's me.'

Her eyes flew open as she was spun around rapidly. It was Winston. She grabbed at his ski jacket, weak with relief, and then her face crumpled as she burst into tears.

Winston held her close, supporting her limp body and soothing her at the same time. 'It's all right, it's all right,' he kept repeating over and over again.

'Thank God! Thank God!' Emily gasped. 'I thought you were dead. Oh Winston, thank God you're alive.' She searched his worried face. 'The others?' she began and stopped when she saw his grim expression, the clenched jaw.

'I don't know whether they're safe or not. I hope to God they are. I pray they are,' Winston said, putting his arm around her.

'But you – '

Winston interrupted fiercely, 'I didn't go skiing this morning. When I got here I'd just missed a cable car. I waited around for a while, planning to take the next one, but I got fed up. I had a bit of a hangover and I was beginning to feel queasy. So I left, went in to the town. I bought the English papers, stopped at a café and had a *fernet branca*. By the time I felt better it was too late to go skiing, so I did a bit of shopping. I was actually in the car park, stowing the stuff in the car, when I heard a *whoomp* that sounded like a blast of dynamite. There was an American parked next to me, and he shouted something about an avalanche, that his daughter was on the slopes, and then he ran like hell. I followed him, knowing – ' Winston swallowed. 'Knowing that everybody from the chalet, well practically everybody, was up there too.'

An unexpected feeling of hope soared in Emily. She exclaimed, 'Perhaps they decided to ski on that other range.'

Winston shook his head. His face was bleak.

Emily grabbed hold of him. 'Oh Winston!'

He calmed her. 'Come on, Emily, you must be strong, very brave – ' He broke off and swung his head as he heard his name being called. He spotted Marc Deboyne and Elizabeth running in their direction and lifted his hand in a wave, looked down at his wife and said, 'Your mother and Marc are coming.'

Elizabeth almost flung herself at Winston and embraced him, crying. 'You're safe, you're safe. I was petrified for you, Winston.' She looked at him through anxious eyes. Her white face was stark, but she was exercising immense control. She hugged Emily, then said, 'What about the others, Winston? Have you seen any of the family, or Jan and Peter?'

'No. You see, I didn't go skiing this morning. I changed my mind.'

There was a sudden flurry of activity in the area. They all turned around. The rescue teams had arrived, professional skiers wearing backpacks and controlling a number of German shepherds. With them were additional police, a group of French soldiers and town officials.

'I will go and ask a few questions,' Marc muttered and strode off purposefully.

Winston exclaimed, 'It's stopped! Do you realize the avalanche has stopped.'

Elizabeth stared at him. 'It stopped when Marc and I were running down here. After that deafening noise the silence was awful, deathly.'

Before Winston could reply, Marc was back with them, explaining: 'The teams are going up now. They've got the best equipment in those backpacks. Listening devices, probing rods, and the dogs, of course. Let us be hopeful.'

'*Is* there any hope?' Winston asked in a low intense tone.

Marc hesitated, tempted to lie. But he elected to speak the truth. 'It's doubtful,' he murmured quietly. 'The avalanche must have been travelling at enormous speed, anywhere between one hundred and twenty to two hundred miles per hour . . . and then there is the force, the weight of the snow. And yet – ' He attempted an encouraging smile. 'People have been known to live through avalánches and snow slides as bad as this one. It depends where they are on the slopes when it strikes. Those near the bottom would have the best chance, providing they knew to throw away their skis and poles, make swimming motions with their arms. That creates air pockets in front of the face. Even if a person is felled by snow it is vital to keep the arms moving in that manner to provide air around the body. People have lived for days under the snow – because they had those air pockets.'

Emily said worriedly, 'David, Jim and Philip are experienced skiers, but *Maggie* – '

Elizabeth suppressed a cry of fear. She gasped. 'We must have courage and keep our hopes high. Please don't let's talk so mournfully. It makes me nervous. I must continue to believe that they are *all* alive.'

Marc put his arm around her protectively, 'You are right, *chérie*. We must be positive.'

Winston said to Emily, 'I think you ought to take your mother over to one of the nearby cafés. Wait there. There's nothing you can do here.'

'No!' Emily cried heatedly, glaring at him. 'I want to be here with you. Please, Winston.'

'Yes, we must stay here,' Elizabeth insisted. She blew her nose and got a grip on her diminishing composure. Silently she began to pray.

Exactly one hour after the avalanche had struck the rescue teams and the dogs went up in the cable cars.

In just under an hour they returned with the first eight people they had found. Five of them were dead. Three were miraculously alive. Two were young girls. One was a man.

'It's Philip!' Emily screamed and breaking away from Winston and her mother, she began to run towards her cousin.

Philip was being supported by a member of the rescue team. As he limped across to her, Emily saw that one side of his face was scraped and covered with congealed blood, and his bright blue eyes were dazed. But otherwise he looked as if he had escaped with no really serious injuries.

'Philip!' Emily exclaimed, drawing up beside him, 'Thank God you're safe. Are you hurt at all do you think?'

He shook his head. Despite the odd glazed look in his eyes, he recognized her, reached out to her.

A second later, Winston, Elizabeth and Marc were also by his side, asking questions. Philip simply went on shaking his head helplessly, remained mute.

The skier who had found him said in halting English, 'This man, your friend, has been lucky . . . he knew what to do. He did not panic. He discarded his poles . . . the skis . . . did the swimming. Yes, he was most fortunate . . . this man was at the bottom of the slope . . . had completed his run. He was covered with only ten feet of snow . . . the dogs . . . they found him. Now . . . if you please. We go. To the first aid station over there.'

Philip finally spoke. He asked, in hoarse voice, 'Dad? Maggie? The others?'

Winston said. 'No news yet.'

Philip closed his eyes, then opened them quickly, allowed himself to be helped away.

Turning to Emily, Winston said, 'You and your mother had better go along with Philip, lovey. Marc and I will wait here. Once you've ascertained that he has no internal injuries, I want the three of you to go back to the chalet.'

Emily started to protest. Winston cut her off sharply.

'Please, Emily, don't argue. Look after Philip. And some-body *should* be at the chalet . . . when Daisy and Alexander get back from Geneva.'

'Yes,' Emily acquiesced, realizing the sense he made. She kissed him and ran after her mother, who had walked ahead with Philip and the skier.

Winston and Marc stood around for another hour, smoking incessantly, occasionally talking to each other, and striking up conversations with other people who were keeping the same distressing vigil at the terminal.

The rescue teams continued to go up and down in the cable cars. Four more survivors were brought to safety, to be followed by nine who were dead.

At four o'clock one of the rescue teams which had been long and endlessly searching the higher part of the mountain returned. They brought with them five more vacationing skiers who had been trapped by the avalanche. The bad news spread quickly. All were dead.

'We must go over and check,' Winston said, throwing his cigarette on the ground, grinding his toe on the butt. Bracing himself, he swung to Marc. 'Will you come with me?'

'Yes, Winston. No use putting it off.'

The bodies were being laid on stretchers. When he was a few feet away from them, Winston came to a sudden halt. His strength ebbed out of him, but somehow he managed to take several more steps forward after this brief pause.

He felt Marc's strong hand under his armpit, heard the Frenchman say sorrowingly, 'I am so sorry, so very sorry. This is a tragedy for the family.'

Winston found he could not speak.

He gazed down at the five people who lay on the stretchers. Two of them he did not know, but the other three . . . For a moment his mind floundered. It did not seem possible that they were dead. Only a few hours ago they had all been laughing together at breakfast.

Sucking in his breath, and brushing his hand across his brimming eyes, Winston went to identify the bodies of David Amory, Jim Fairley and Maggie Barkstone, fatal victims of the avalanche. And he thought of Daisy and Alexander, driving back from Geneva, and of Paula, who was in New York, and he wondered how he was ever going to break the devastating news to them.

CHAPTER 51

Shane O'Neill stood in the kitchen of the barn in New Milford, waiting for the second pot of coffee to brew.

After lighting a cigarette, he reached for the wall phone and dialled the farm. When Elaine Vickers answered, he said cheerily, 'Top of the morning to you.'

'Hi, Shane,' Elaine replied. 'We thought you weren't coming up this weekend when we didn't hear from you last night. But Sonny saw your car earlier this morning, so we knew you'd made it.'

'It was late when we arrived,' Shane explained. 'The farm was in darkness and I thought twice about waking you. Paula didn't get back from Texas until early evening and it was after nine when we left the city. Sorry I didn't ring you before now, but we got off to a slow start this morning.'

Elaine laughed. 'I'll say you did. It's almost noon. But the way you two work you deserve to take it easy occasionally. I hope we're going to see you for dinner tonight,' she went on. 'We've been looking forward to it all week.'

'We'll be over around seven-thirty as planned,' Shane assured her.

Elaine exclaimed, 'Oh Shane, you'll have to excuse me.

That was the oven bell. My bread's going to spoil if I don't take it out immediately. See you tonight.'

'Bye, Elaine.' Shane dropped the phone in its cradle, stubbed out his cigarette and went to the sink. He rinsed the two mugs and dried them. He was just about to pour the coffee when the telephone began to ring. Putting down the pot, he picked up the receiver. 'Hello?'

There was no response at the other end of the phone, only the sound of static and a hollow echo. 'Hello? Hello?' Shane said again in a stronger tone.

Finally a muffled voice came down the wire. 'It's me. Winston. I'm phoning from Chamonix. Can you hear me, Shane?'

'I can now. Winston! How – '

Winston cut him off. 'Something terrible has happened here, Shane, and I don't know where Paula is, where to reach her, and I thought I'd better speak to you first anyway.'

Shane gripped the receiver tighter, frowned to himself. 'Actually she's staying here with me for the weekend. What's wrong, Winston?'

'There has been a disastrous avalanche on Mont Blanc, at about one o'clock today, the worst in years,' Winston began, his voice sounding more muffled and gruff than ever. 'Some of the family have been killed.' Winston's voice cracked and he was unable to continue.

'Oh Jesus!' Shane steadied himself against the counter, waiting to hear the worst. His heart had begun to thud in his chest and intuitively he knew that Winston was about to impart news that would devastate Paula. He knew it in his bones.

Thousands of miles away, in the dining room of the chalet on the outskirts of Chamonix, Winston Harte stood at the window gazing into the distance. Mont Blanc loomed up into the darkening sky, looked so peaceful now in the twilight after the havoc it had wrought only five hours ago.

He got a grip on himself, said in a controlled voice, 'Sorry for breaking down. It's been the worst day of my life. Look, Shane, I'm going to give it to you straight because it's the only way I know how.' Winston took a deep breath and began to speak, relaying the tragic news to his friend.

As he listened Shane felt the shock strike him like a body blow and ten minutes later when Winston finally hung up he was still reeling. He stood with his hand on the phone, staring blankly into the middle of the room. He began to blink as bright sunlight streamed in through the windows. How normal everything seemed here in this kitchen. It was so tranquil. Peaceful. And it was such a pretty day outside. The sky was a bright blue, clear and without a single cloud and the sun was radiant. But over in France the family he had been so close to for his entire life were living with unexpected death and sorrow. How abruptly, how suddenly lives had been changed, almost in the flicker of an eyelash. Oh dear God, Shane thought, how am I going to tell Paula? Where will I find the words?

He heard her step in the hall outside and swung around to face the door, then held himself very still, waiting.

She was laughing as she came in and said in a teasing voice, 'That's the last time I'll ever ask you to make the coffee. You've been on the phone for ages. Who were you talking to, darling?'

Shane took a step towards her. He tried to speak but nothing came out. There was a parched gravelly feeling in his throat and his mouth went dry.

'You've got the oddest look on your face, Shane. What's wrong?' Paula demanded, instantly tensing.

He put his arm around her shoulder and propelled her out of the kitchen and into the big living room, leading her to the fire. She demanded again, and with fierceness, 'Shane, what's happened? Please tell me.'

'I will, I will,' he said hoarsely, pressing her down on the sofa, seating himself next to her. He took her hands in his, held on to them tightly, and looked into that face he had loved all of his life. He saw the worry, the sudden apprehension invading it.

Shane's heart clenched as he said in the softest of voices, 'I just got some very bad news, some dreadful news, Paula darling. From Winston. There was the most hideous accident in Chamonix around one o'clock today. An avalanche on Mont Blanc. Some of the family have been killed.'

Paula gaped at him. Her eyes, opening widely, were pinned on his. He saw the horror mirrored in them and the draining away of all colour from her face. It turned chalky white. '*Who?*' she asked in a strangled whisper.

Shane's grip increased, his fingers biting into her flesh. 'You must be brave, my darling,' he said. 'Very brave. I'm here, I'll help you through this.' He paused, swallowed hard, sought the right phrases, the right words. But there were no such things, he knew that.

Paula, her mind racing, thought of the most dedicated skiers in the group. She cried harshly, 'Not Daddy? *Not my father?*'

Shane's throat constricted. He nodded. 'I'm so sorry. So very sorry, my darling,' he murmured in a dim and shaken voice.

For a moment Paula could not say a word. She continued to stare at Shane, stunned and stupefied, almost uncomprehending, unable to conceive what he was saying – or accept it.

Aware that it would be kinder to tell her everything at once, quickly, and without further delay, he said in the same saddened tone, 'Paula, I don't know how to tell you this, and I'm so sorry, but Jim was also killed. And Maggie. They were on top of the mountain with your father when it happened.'

'No!' she said. 'No!' She wrenched her hands out of his and clapped them over her mouth, looking around the room frenziedly, as if seeking escape, as if trying to run from this new and dreadful knowledge. Her eyes stretched and stretched in her ashen face. She jumped up jerkily and shouted in a frantic voice, 'It can't be so! *No!* It just can't be so! Oh my God! *Philip. My brother.* Was he – '

'He's all right,' Shane exclaimed, also leaping to his feet, wrapping his arms around her. 'Everyone is safe, except for Jan and Peter Coles. They haven't been found yet.'

Paula pulled away from him roughly, staring up into his face. Her violet eyes were black with the pain and horror of it all, and her face twisted in a grimace of grief and anguish and heartbreak. She began to tremble violently but as Shane reached for her once more, wanting to help her, to comfort her, Paula ran into the middle of the room, moving her head from side to side, denying, denying. Suddenly she wrapped her arms around her body and doubled over in agony.

She began to make small but high-pitched mewling noises like a terrified animal in immense pain. It was a keening really and it did not cease. Grief and shock continued to assault her, swept over her like giant tidal waves and engulfed her finally. She slipped to the floor unconscious.

The private jet owned by O'Neill Hotels International sliced through the dark night sky high above the English Channel. It was set on a steady course for London Airport where it would soon be landing after a seven-hour flight across the Atlantic.

Shane sat opposite Paula, who was stretched out on one of the banquettes and wrapped in several light woollen travelling rugs. He watched her closely, hardly daring to take his eyes off her. Occasionally he leaned over her, soothed her gently, as he had throughout the long and difficult trip. She tossed about restlessly despite the sedatives she had been given at different intervals since he had told her about the tragedy in Chamonix.

The local doctor in New Milford, instantly summoned by Shane after she had collapsed, had treated her for shock. He had injected her and given Shane a small box of additional sedatives in tablet form. Before leaving the barn he had instructed Shane to administer them during the flight whenever he considered it necessary, but to use his discretion.

Shane had rapidly come to realize that Paula was fighting the tranquillizing drugs, just as she had fought him at times during the night. Twice over the Atlantic she had tried to struggle up off the banquette, her eyes filled with panic and fear. She had vomited once, retching until there was nothing left inside. He had tended to her every need with infinite patience, tenderness and love, helping her in every way he could, murmuring consoling words to her, trying to ease her mental turmoil, ensure her physical comfort.

Now, as he sat observing her, Shane's worry accelerated. She had not broken down or cried once, and this was abnormal for her, she who was such an emotional woman by nature. Nor had she spoken to him and it was this extraordinary and protracted silence plus the wild and febrile look in her eyes that frightened him so much.

He glanced at his watch. They would be on the ground in no time at all. His father and Miranda would be there to meet them with a private ambulance and Paula's London doctor, Harvey Langen. Thank God for Harvey, Shane thought. He'll know what to do, the best way to treat her condition. And then he asked himself how a doctor could treat the overwhelming grief and anguish she was experiencing and he acknowledged miserably that he had no ready answers.

Shane sat in the small study of the Belgrave Square flat with his sister Merry. His expression was morose, his black eyes abstracted as he sipped his third cup of coffee, then drew on his cigarette.

Parker, the butler, had prepared breakfast a short while ago, but none of them had been able to eat a thing, and Shane had been chain-smoking since he had entered this room.

Bryan O'Neill, who had been showing the doctor out, came back in and hurried over to Shane. His hand rested on his son's shoulder, and he said in an optimistic tone, 'You were mistaken, Shane. Harvey says Paula's definitely not in catatonic shock. I tackled him about that, as you asked me to. She is in shock, of course, we're all aware of that, but Harvey believes she'll be pulling out of it later today, or tomorrow at the very latest.'

Shane looked at his father and nodded. 'Oh God, I hope so, Dad. I can't bear to see her like this, suffering so much. If only she would speak to me, say something.'

'She will, Shane, very soon,' Bryan said, squeezing Shane's shoulder affectionately. Sighing, he lowered himself into a chair and continued, 'This kind of catastrophe is devastating and sudden death, sudden loss, is always the hardest to bear because of its very unexpectedness, apart from anything else.'

'If only I knew how to help her,' Shane exclaimed. 'But I'm floundering right now. I haven't been able to get through to her, get a reaction from her, and yet I know she is in the most dreadful agony. I must find a way to ease the burden of her sorrow and pain.'

Miranda said, 'If anyone can help her it's you, Shane. You're the closest to her and perhaps when you come back tonight she'll be out of the shock as Harvey said she would. She'll talk to you then, I just know it. You will be able to console her, let her know that she's not alone, that she has you.'

Shane stared at his sister. 'What do you mean *come back tonight*? I'm not leaving her. I'm going to be right here

790

until she sleeps off the drugs . . . I wouldn't let her wake up alone.'

'I'll stay with you,' Merry announced. '*I* won't permit *you* to be alone.'

Bryan, who had been listening to this exchange between his children, instantly understood so many things that had baffled him in the last year. He said slowly, 'Shane, I didn't know – I didn't realize you were in love with Paula, that you loved her so profoundly.'

'*Love her*,' Shane repeated almost wonderingly, glancing across at his father in astonishment. 'Why, Dad, she's my whole life.'

'Yes,' Bryan said. 'Yes, Shane, I realize that now, seeing you like this. She'll recover, please believe me she will. People have enormous inner strength in times of trouble, and Paula is no exception. In fact she's stronger than most – one of the strongest women I know. There's a lot of Emma in her. Oh yes, she'll pull out of this eventually. In time everything will be all right.'

Shane threw him a dismal look and his eyes reflected his own pain. 'No, it won't,' he said in the bleakest of voices. 'You're wrong, Dad. Quite wrong.'

CHAPTER 52

The harsh winter had passed.

The spring came, bringing a new and wonderous greenness to her gardens at Pennistone Royal. And then, before she knew it, the summer was filling the air with its sweet fragrance as the flowers burst into bloom under warming sunlight and skies that were as blue as speedwells and filled with that glorious Northern light.

She was alone now. Entirely alone except for her children. Lorne and Tessa filled every waking moment of her time and she drew consolation and joy from their laughter, their carefree spirits and their childlike pleasures.

The grief that had shattered her at the end of January had been brought under control.

Paula had reached deep inside herself, had drawn on her inner resources for sustenance and strength in her time of loss and pain and trouble. She had had no option really. Too many people were dependent on her.

Her mother and Alexander had returned from Chamonix grief-stricken and crushed by sorrow. They had automatically turned to her, had needed her comfort and her support, her immense fortitude to help them through the difficult period of the funerals and the distressing weeks that followed. They were plunged deeper into mourning as their shock receded and reality took over. Her children had also needed the security of her love and devotion, every bit of attention she could give them now that they were without a father.

And finally her enormous empire required her to be at the helm, guiding its course at all times, and she devoted herself to the great legacy she had inherited from her grandmother, working around the clock to ensure that it remained safe and only increased in importance and wealth. And work had become her strong citadel in the way it had been Emma's in the past.

But as the grief lessened, grew a little easier to bear, her guilt only increased and intensified. And it was the guilt that continued to cripple her now, so many months after the tragedy that had decimated the family.

It was a many-faceted guilt . . . survivor guilt that she was alive when her father, Jim and Maggie were dead . . . guilt that she and Jim had parted with such animosity the day before he had left for Chamonix . . . and, worst of all, guilt that she had been with Shane when those three people she cared about had met their ultimately and hideous deaths.

As they had been suffocating under thousands of tons of snow she had been in Shane's arms, transported by passion and the ecstasy of fulfilment. Illogical as it was, she nevertheless felt responsible, blamed herself for their deaths. Intellectually she knew that she was not to blame, that it was wrong to feel this way, but emotionally she could not come to grips with true reality.

And she never wanted to make love again because in her mind the act of love was now associated with death and dying. In consequence, the mere thought of sex appalled her. She was desensitized, without feeling and emotionally and physically frigid, incapable of giving of herself as a woman.

Slowly Paula had come to realize she had nothing to offer Shane O'Neill. He was too virile, too passionate a man to settle for only a small part of her, and since she could not participate in lovemaking she believed the relationship to be doomed.

And so she sent him away. She knew his heart was broken and she loathed herself for inflicting pain and heartache on him, but she had convinced herself that she was doing the best thing for him, for them both ultimately.

Shane had remained by her side through February, always there when she needed him, giving her his continuing love, and friendship. Sensitive by nature, and knowing her as well as he did, he never made demands on her whatsoever. He shared her grief, her pain and her anguish, was consoling, became kindness itself. But after a month's sojourn in London and Yorkshire, he had had to resume his business activities. He had flown off to Australia to supervise the building of the new O'Neill hotel which Blackie had purchased on his trip with Emma.

Around this period, Paula had conceived the idea of sending her mother to Sydney with Philip, who was returning on the O'Neill private jet with Shane. At first Daisy had demurred, had protested that she must remain in

England to be with Paula and the twins, but Paula had persuaded her to go. At the last minute Daisy had hurriedly packed and travelled across the world with the two men. Her mother was still in Australia, trying to pick up the threads of her life without David, acting as Philip's hostess and taking an interest in the McGill holdings. And Paula was aware that her mother was starting to throw off her own pain and function again.

But Shane had returned to England in April and had come again to Yorkshire to see her. Once more, as was his way, he had been understanding of her dilemma. He had explained that he recognized that she needed time to adjust herself to the loss of her father, to whom she had been so close, to the loss of her husband, who though estranged from her was still the father of her children.

'I only wanted my freedom, a divorce from Jim. I never wished him harm, or wanted him to die. He was so young,' she had whispered on the day Shane was setting off for New York with Miranda.

'I know, I know, darling,' Shane had said with gentleness. 'I'm there whenever you need me. I'll wait for you, Paula.'

But she had not wanted him to wait, for she knew deep within herself that she would never be ready. She could never be Shane's wife. In a sense, that part of her life was over and she had adjusted herself to the knowledge that she would live alone with her children, would never share herself or her life with a man. It was not possible any more.

She had not told Shane about the dreadful nights when she awakened from the same terrifying nightmare, the nightmare that she was suffocating and one which constantly haunted her. It was so real she would sit up in bed with a start, her trembling body bathed in sweat as she cried out in terror and fear. And always in the centre of her mind there wobbled the horrifying image of her father and

Jim and Maggie being swept away by the avalanche, being buried under that icy snow that had smothered them, snuffed out their lives with such suddenness and so pointlessly.

But Shane O'Neill was no fool and it soon became apparent to him that Paula had changed towards him, and she *knew* that he knew. How could he not. She could not help her attitude or her demeanour, nor could she alter the circumstances that had wrought the shift in her emotional balance. Her remoteness, her detachment, her preoccupation with her children and her work combined to stun him initially, and then they eventually told him everything he needed to know.

Sometimes she was lonely, frequently she was sad and sorrowing, and occasionally she was afraid.

She stood alone. Her grandmother and her father, the two people from whom she had received so much support and love, were dead. She was the head of the Harte clan. Everyone looked to her, deferred to her, came to her with their problems both personal and in business. There were times when her responsibilities and burdens were crushing, overwhelming, too much for one woman to bear. But then she would think of Emma and draw strength from the memories of that beloved woman who was so much a part of her and whose blood ran in her veins. And every single day she thanked God for Winston, who was her rock, and for Emily, who was her greatest consolation, her dearest friend and her most loving, loyal and devoted cousin. Without them her life would be very bleak indeed.

The old familiar sadness enveloped Paula on this Saturday morning in August as she strolled slowly up the Rhododendron Walk which she herself had created. It seemed so long ago now – that spring when she had planted these bushes. So much had happened to her in the last few years . . . so many losses, so many defeats . . . and yet so many triumphs and gains as well. She smiled to herself as she suddenly thought of the children and the happiness and love they gave her. Her sadness lifted slightly and her smile widened. An hour ago Emily had arrived to take them, and Nora, off to Heron's Nest for the next three weeks. They would spend the remainder of August and the first two weeks of September in the old villa by the sea, whilst she herself was in Texas and New York on business. They loved their Aunty Emily, and their older counterparts, Amanda and Francesca, who would be joining them for the holiday in Scarborough. They had been so excited as they had toddled down the steps to the car, clutching their buckets and spades. And they had looked so adorable in their cotton sunsuits and matching sun hats. Little monkeys, she muttered affectionately, recalling the scene which had been enacted in the driveway a short while before. For once they had not been a bit concerned that they would be apart from her. After kissing her hastily they had clambered into the car and had been driven off without so much as giving her a backward glance.

No matter, she thought, as she turned and retraced her steps down the steep walk. They will enjoy the sun and the sea air and have a rare old time with Emily. And I know they are truly in safe hands in my absence.

Paula paused when she came to the lily pond at the bottom of the long sloping lawns. She stood reflecting as Shane edged into her mind.

The last time she had seen him the two of them had sat here on the stone bench near the pond. It had been a very hot sunny day towards the end of June. Almost two months ago. She had been exhausted, careworn on that Saturday, after a debilitating week rushing between the Harte stores in Leeds, Harrogate and Sheffield. He had arrived after lunch, unexpected and unannounced, and they had ended up having a violent quarrel. No, that was not actually true. They had not quarrelled. But he had lost his temper with her and she had simply sat there, letting his anger roll over her, aware that there was nothing else she could do. She had often been subjected to his outbursts as a child, and she had never won with him. It was always better to remain silent, let him rant and rave and get everything off his chest. That Saturday he had been justified. It would be wrong of her not to admit this.

Lowering herself on to the stone bench, Paula stared ahead and it was as if she was watching a piece of film as she sat back, saw herself and Shane as they had been on that stifling June Saturday only a few weeks ago.

'I can't go on like this, Paula,' Shane had exclaimed suddenly in the middle of their conversation. His voice had risen, and to an unnatural level for him these days, as he had burst out, 'I know it's only been five months, and I understand your pain, understand what you're going through. But you don't give me any hope for the future. If you did that, perhaps I *could* go on coping. But without hope a man has nothing. You turned away from me on that ghastly day at the barn, and you're drawing further away as you retreat deeper into yourself.'

'I can't help it,' she had murmured. 'I'm sorry, Shane.'

'But why? For God's sake tell me *why?*'

She had taken a while to reply. Then she had murmured in her quietest voice, 'If only I hadn't been with you . . . and I mean *with* you in the most intimate way, then perhaps things would be different now. But Shane, we were making love at seven o'clock on that Saturday morning. It was one o'clock in France, and the moment the avalanche struck. Don't you see, I can't face making love ever again. I just can't. When I envision doing so I fall apart emotionally. I link it to the tragedy, to the awful way Daddy and Jim and Maggie died.'

He had stared at her helplessly, his face tensing. 'I knew it. I knew that was it,' he had finally remarked in a curiously hoarse, choked voice.

797

There had been a short silence and then she had told him, had spelled out in actual words what she had long believed he knew within himself, understood in his heart of hearts. 'Shane, it's better that we don't see each other again,' she had whispered. 'Not even as friends. I have nothing to offer you, not even friendship right now. Look, it wouldn't be fair to you if we continued in this way. Perhaps one day I will be able to resume our friendship, be your friend, but . . .' Her voice had trailed off.

He had stared at her hard, his eyes piercing into hers, and she had seen the shock and hurt, the disbelief, and then the sudden anger reflected on his handsome face.

'I can't believe you're saying this to me!' he had cried heatedly, his face blazing. 'I love you, Paula, and even though you want to deny it at this moment, *you love me*. I know you do. We've had so much, and have so much together. That deep closeness that has grown from childhood affection to the mature abiding love of two adults, and compatibility in every way, and passion. Yes, I understand how you feel about sex because of the last time we made love, but that awful memory of the catastrophe will eventually fade. It has to. It would be abnormal if it didn't go away.'

She had shaken her head, remained mute, her hands clasped in her lap.

'You blame yourself!' he shouted, losing patience with her. 'Now I understand your attitude even more. You actually *blame* yourself and you're punishing yourself! Punishing me! You're so wrong, Paula. So wrong. It wasn't your fault. The avalanche was an Act of God. You didn't cause it to happen. And now you think that by flagellating yourself, leading a chaste life, you'll redeem yourself! *Is that it?*' Not waiting for her response he had rushed on, 'Whatever you do, Paula, you can't bring them back. Accept that. Accept that life is for the living. You have every *right* to be happy. And so do I. So do *we* – together.

798

You need a husband, you need *me*, and Lorne and Tessa need a father. I love the twins. I want to be a loving father to them, an adoring husband to you. You cannot be alone for the rest of your life. It would be a waste, the most terrible and wanton waste.'

He had paused for breath at this point and she had reached out, touched his arm gently. 'Please, Shane, don't upset yourself like this.'

'Upset myself! That's a joke, Paula! Here you are, telling me we must part . . . forever, seemingly, and you use a word like *upset*. Jesus Christ, I'm *shattered*, don't you realize that? You are my whole life. I have nothing if I don't have you.'

'Shane,' she had begun, reaching out again.

He had shaken her hand off his arm and leaped to his feet. 'I cannot continue this ridiculous discussion. I have to go. Get away from here. God knows how I'll ever find peace of mind again, but I don't suppose that's your problem, is it, Paula? It's mine.' He had stepped away from her, gazed down at her, his expression one she could not quite read. 'Goodbye, Paula,' he had said in a shaking voice and as he had turned away she had seen the tears glittering in his black eyes.

She had wanted to run after him as he had bounded up the steps to the terrace. But she had restrained herself, knowing that there was no point. She had been cruel to Shane but at least she had told him the truth and perhaps one day he would understand her motives. She hoped that he would come to realize that she had given him his freedom because she could no longer continue to hurt him by dangling the future in front of his nose. It was a future that did not exist.

Now, as she rose and went up the stone steps to the terrace in front of Pennistone Royal, Paula remembered how oddly detached she had felt that day. It had troubled her then and it troubled her now. Was she always going to be like this?

Sighing under her breath, she went in through the open French doors, crossed the Peach Drawing Room and hurried down the length of the Stone Hall. As she ran lightly up the grand staircase, heading for the upstairs parlour, she put all private and personal thoughts to one side. She was driving to London later in the day, taking a plane to Texas on Monday. She was about to do battle at Sitex and her plan of action needed every ounce of her attention, her total concentration.

CHAPTER 53

'Anyway, Shane, when John Crawford told me he was going to Australia to spend a month with Daisy and Philip, I was delighted,' Winston said across the luncheon table to his closest friend.

'So am I.' Shane lifted his glass, took a sip of red wine and continued, 'Daisy was looking much better, and she was certainly in brighter spirits when I saw her in Sydney in August. I think she's adjusting to life without David.'

'Daisy's a sensible woman.' Winston eyed Shane and then he laughed quietly. 'I must admit, I've always had a sneaking suspicion that John had a crush on Daisy.' Shrugging lightly, he added, 'Who knows, maybe he can give her a bit of love and companionship. After all, she's still a young woman.'

'Yes.' Shane's face changed. His expression turned morose and brooding as he gazed across the restaurant absently. He was lost in his thoughts, pondering his future, as he so often did of late.

Winston leaned forward and said slowly, carefully, 'Despite Paula's attitude at this moment, she could easily

800

reverse herself, you know. Women are unpredictable creatures at the best of times.'

'Not Paula,' Shane said after a few seconds of consideration. 'She's very strong, and once her mind is made up, it's made up.' He shook his head sadly. 'I'm going to have to do my damnedest to forget her, Winston, and make a fresh start. It won't be easy, but I'm certainly going to give it a try. I can't go around carrying a torch for her for the rest of my life. There's not much to be gained from that.'

'No, there isn't.'

Shane brought out his cigarettes, offered one to Winston. They sat smoking for a few minutes and then Shane said, 'I'm glad you stopped off in New York for a couple of days on your way back to London. It's been a – '

'So am I,' Winston interjected, and chuckled. 'I rather like the idea of flying home in style on that private jet of yours. Not to mention having you for company. And thanks again for delaying your plans, waiting for me. I appreciate it.'

'Yes, and what I started to tell you is that I've appreciated having your company.' Shane pursed his lips, gave Winston a pointed stare. 'As you're aware, I've never talked about women or my love affairs to you, but I needed to confide my feelings for Paula, unburden myself to someone I trust and respect. You've been very patient and helpful. Thanks, Winston.'

Winston sat back, finished his wine, and then puffed on his cigarette, looking thoughtful. Finally he murmured, 'I should have told you this the other night, but you seemed done in after your marathon session on the subject of Paula. Anyway, you weren't really telling me anything I didn't know. I mean about you being in love with Paula. I've known that for the longest time now. So has Emily.'

Shane said, very startled, 'And I thought no one knew. Just goes to show you, doesn't it.'

Winston said softly, 'Emma knew too, Shane.'

'She did!' Shane's astonishment was more pronounced and for a split second he was speechless, then he smiled faintly. 'Funnily enough, I've had the strangest feeling since she died that she was aware of our relationship. But Paula pooh-poohed the idea, dismissed it out of hand.'

'Aunt Emma didn't know you were involved, that's true,' Winston exclaimed rapidly. 'And to tell you the honest truth, neither Emily nor I were too sure about that either. Aunt Emma spotted a look in your eyes when you were observing Paula at the christening two-and-a-half years ago. That's when Emily and I also realized how deeply you felt about Paula.'

'I see.' Leaning across the table, Shane gave Winston a hard and questioning stare, asked, 'Obviously Aunt Emma discussed it with you. What did she say?'

'She was worried about you, Shane. She loved you a lot, you know, like one of us, one of her own. I think it was a disappointment to her that you hadn't spoken up earlier, before Paula married Jim. But she was philosophical about it really, knew she couldn't interfere. However, if she were alive she wouldn't be a bit surprised to know that Paula reciprocates your love for her, that I can guarantee you.'

'*Reciprocated* in the past tense, mate,' Shane muttered, and made a sour face. 'The lady has chosen to walk a solitary path.'

'She might change her mind,' Winston shot back, wanting to cheer him up. 'I keep telling you, women do that half a dozen times a day. Besides, it's only been nine months. Give her a chance, a bit longer to pull herself together. Look, Shane, I have an idea. Don't fly back to London with me this afternoon. Stay here in New York. Paula's been in Texas for a week, and I know she's due back in the city in a couple of days, either tomorrow or Wednesday. See her again, take her out, wine and dine her, talk to her. You can be very persuasive and – '

Shane held up his hand and shook his head with firmness.

802

'No, Winston, it won't do any good. She made it very clear to me in June that it was over. *Finished*. Besides, I can't delay my return any longer. Dad's due to go out to Sydney later this week. His turn, you know, and with Merry running this hotel, I have to be on the scene at home for a few months. I'll be racing between Leeds and London, but spending more time in Yorkshire, I hope.'

'Emily's looking forward to having you at Beck House at weekends, Shane, as soon as she's back from Scarborough. I hope you're not going to disappoint her, or me for that matter.'

'No. I'll be staying with you at weekends when I can, and thanks a lot. I want to spend some time at your father's stables, talk to him about Emerald Bow, and our racing programme for next year. Grandpops left me the racehorse to race, not to put out to pasture. And I haven't been on a horse for months. I'm itching to get into the saddle, give War Lord and Celtic Maiden a few good workouts.'

'That's great, Shane, it'll be –' Winston stopped, grinned from ear to ear and waved. To Shane, he said, 'Here's that gorgeous sister of yours.'

Shane swung around and his face lit up when he saw Miranda, who was hurrying across the restaurant looking as if she had something of vital importance to tell him. He smiled at her extraordinary costume, for that was all he could call it. She resembled a redheaded gypsy in her colourful patchwork cotton dress and masses of gold chains. Taking over as head of their New York operation had not induced her to change her spectacular style of dressing. Good for you, Merry, Shane thought. Stick to your guns. Be your highly original self, one of the genuine free spirits of this world.

'Hello, you two gorgeous men, and don't get up,' Merry exclaimed as they both made to rise. She flopped down into the empty chair and said, 'Come closer. I've something interesting to tell you.' Giving them both a conspiratorial

803

look, she went on, 'You'll *never* guess who I've just seen. Not in a million years!'

Winston looked amused. 'Then tell us, Merry darling. It'll save a lot of time.'

'Yes, do,' Shane remarked. 'Would you like a glass of this?' He lifted the bottle of wine, showed it to her.

'Thanks, that'll be lovely.' Merry settled back in her chair, waited until her brother had poured the last of the wine into their three glasses, then said, 'I was in the Terrace Café, talking to the *maître d'* when I spotted them . . . talk about the Terrible Trio!'

Both men looked at her blankly.

Grinning, Miranda wrinkled her freckled nose and hissed, 'Allison Ridley, Skye Smith and – *Sarah Lowther*. All lunching together and looking very, very chummy, to say the least. Can you believe it!'

'Sarah!' Winston chuckled sardonically. 'Well, well, well, that's very interesting. I wonder what she's doing in New York. Paula and Emily haven't heard anything about her for months, or Jonathan either, for that matter, since he went to the Far East.'

'Don't mention that bastard,' Shane said, scowling. 'He's always been a troublemaker, and as devious as the devil.'

Winston nodded in agreement.

Merry said, 'I suppose I ought to have gone over and spoken to them, but quite frankly I beat a hasty retreat. I wanted to warn you both that a couple of your old girl-friends were floating around our hotel. Thank God they didn't decide to lunch in here – then where would you have been?'

Winston said jokingly, 'Allison would have probably slipped a Mickey Finn in my drink.'

'Skye Smith was *never* a girlfriend of *mine*,' Shane announced, and winked at Merry. 'Not my type.'

'We all know *you* don't like blondes, that you prefer dark exotic beauties like my darling Pau – ' Miranda bit off the name and gave her brother an apologetic and concerned look. 'Sorry, Shane, I didn't mean to rub salt in the wound.'

'That's all right, Merry, and I'm a big boy. I might be still licking my wounds but at least I've managed to stem the flow of blood finally.'

'Yes, I know.' Merry took a small swallow of her wine and began to talk about their impending flight to London, making an effort to change the subject. Despite Shane's flippancy, the front he put up, she was aware that he was deeply hurt and still suffering inside. He yearned for Paula. He would all of his life, that was the depressing part. If only Jim had not been so tragically killed, Merry thought. Paula would have eventually been divorced and Shane and she would have married. Now Paula had put herself on a rack. And Shane too. Why is she doing this? Miranda asked herself. I don't understand her any more.

Shane said, 'Daydreaming suddenly, Merry? You started to say something about the car.'

'Oh yes, sorry,' Merry said, smiling at him. 'I arranged for the limousine to be outside at three o'clock. That gives you plenty of time to get to Kennedy before the rush hour.'

Skye Smith was the first to excuse herself after lunch. She could not wait to escape, and it was with a sigh of relief that she crossed the elegant lobby of the Plaza Towers Hotel, property of the O'Neills, and hurried out into the street.

She peered at her watch. It was just turning off two-thirty, and she had plenty of time to get back to the antique shop for her next appointment at three.

As she strolled towards Park Avenue she thought about Sarah Lowther. She did not particularly like her and she could not help wondering what Allison saw in her. Sarah was the bitchiest woman she had ever met, and not very bright in some ways.

On the other hand, Sarah had inadvertently dropped a gold mine of information on to the table over lunch, and had opened up in such a personal way about her private affairs, Skye was still slightly taken aback.

She smiled cynically as she waited on the corner for the traffic lights to change before crossing Park. *So Paula Fairley was the mystery woman, the love of Shane's life, the lady who had got her clutches into him. And so much so he was incapable of making it with any other woman.*

This news had staggered Skye. When Sarah had discovered that Skye had occasionally dated Shane, the Englishwoman had turned to stone at the luncheon table. Skye had thought for a minute that Sarah was going to scratch her eyes out, so venomous was the look on the redhead's face. It had become patently obvious to Skye that Sarah was madly in love with Shane, and she had quickly assured Allison's friend that they had only ever had a platonic relationship. This had seemed to appease Sarah, and she had relaxed again, confided more dirt about the family, and in particular about Paula. The hatred Sarah harboured for her cousin was frightening. Hell hath no fury like a woman scorned, Skye thought, hurrying along. I ought to know.

She hardly ever saw Shane O'Neill these days. He had become a world traveller as their holdings had increased, and apparently he spent a great deal of time in Australia. He was only in New York on rare fleeting visits since his sister had been made the president of their American hotel corporation. He had called her once, almost a year ago now, and they had had a drink together, but he had seemed preoccupied and restless, and she had decided against pressing him to take her to dinner.

Ross, on the other hand, was always taking Paula Fairley to lunch, especially in the last six months or so. He had let that slip accidentally. When she had teased him about Paula, Ross had said it was strictly business. And at heart she knew there was a great deal of truth in this. Ross had been close to Paula's grandmother, as had his uncle, Daniel P. Nelson. Still, Skye knew Ross as well as she knew herself. Business it might indeed be, but he no doubt hankered after the woman. Paula Fairley was everything Ross craved. Good looking. Young. Rich. Powerful. And available – now that she was a widow. Ross probably had some scheme up his sleeve, a plan to propel Paula Fairley into his bed, and possibly into matrimony. He had once told her that if he ever married again he would make sure his intended bride was wealthy. Yes, Ross would always continue to repeat his old patterns. He desired what he could not have. And after the things Sarah had told her there was no question in her mind that Paula Fairley had held herself apart, had not succumbed to Ross's charms. And why would she with Shane O'Neill in the background – her lover of long standing.

Skye now thought about her dinner date with Ross on Wednesday night and laughed under her breath. They dined once a week since they had become friends again. It had taken her a long time to forgive his shoddy treatment of her, but in the end she had forgiven him. She had done so because of their daughter Jennifer. When Ross had come begging to see their child she had consistently and categorically refused to permit this. The longer she had remained cold and unbending, refused to reverse her decision, the more his need to see his little girl had increased. How typical of him. What he could not have he did persist in chasing and forever tried to attain. She had taken great pleasure in making Ross implore and crawl on his hands and knees to her. And that he had eventually done – well almost.

With reluctance she had finally given in, but only because she had come to understand how much Jennifer loved her father, longed to see him on a continuing basis and to spend time with him. She could not deprive the child because of the man and his character.

The laughter bubbled up in Skye again as she continued walking at a steady pace, heading for her shop on Seventy-Third and Lexington. What fun she would have with Ross at dinner later in the week. She would adroitly drop a few spicy titbits about Paula Fairley and Shane O'Neill at the right moment, and then sit back and watch Ross choke on his food. It would drive him crazy when he knew that the sorrowing *widder* was, in reality, the Merry Widow, waltzing to Shane's tune and bestowing her very special favours on him. Although Ross and Shane had done business together in the past, Ross had always been disparaging about Shane behind his back, constantly referring to him as the stud.

Although she was not an unkind woman, Skye Smith was bitter about Ross Nelson. A cold gleam entered her eyes as she contemplated making her former lover squirm. I knew if I waited long enough I'd be able to twist the knife in Ross's back one day, she thought. And he deserves it, after all the pain and humiliation he's inflicted on me. I forgave him for our daughter's sake. But I've never forgotten and I never will.

She did not understand that she wanted Ross for herself.

Ross Nelson's sanguine expression vanished. His light hazel eyes clouded and narrowed slightly as he leaned back in his leather chair and stared harder at Dale Stevens.

Finally Ross cleared his throat and asked, 'Exactly what do you mean when you say Paula changed her mind?'

'She's decided not to sell her Sitex stock,' Dale told him and shrugged. 'We both misread her I guess. And badly.'

'She reneged? Reneged on our deal?' Ross exclaimed in a cold, tight voice. 'And where the hell were you, Dale, when all this was happening?' When Dale did not reply, he continued in a sharper accusatory tone, 'This is one hell of a disaster! I'm going to look like the biggest fool in the world. Milt Jackson is going to have apoplexy when he finds out.'

Dale sighed and crossed his legs, waiting for the banker to cool down.

The two men sat in Ross Nelson's private office in his bank on Wall Street. It was early on Thursday afternoon in the first week of September, the day after Dale had flown up from Texas with Paula.

'What am I going to say to him?' Ross pressed, leaning forward urgently across his huge partner's desk, endeavouring to control his considerable annoyance.

'Tell him the truth. That's all you can do.'

'Why didn't you call me after the board meeting yesterday? Give me a chance to collect my thoughts, come up with a reasonable story?' Ross demanded tersely.

'I felt it was better to tell you in person.'

'I just can't believe this,' Ross muttered angrily, shifting his weight in the chair. 'I was certain she was going to sell, convinced of it. I could wring her neck after the merry dance she's led us.'

Dale sighed wearily. 'Nobody was more surprised than I was when she pulled her stunt at the board meeting. But last night, when I could think dispassionately, I began to realize that she simply blinded us – with words, sweet talk, charm, and a lot of dissembling. And you know something, Ross, she *didn't* renege. I had time to analyse the situation last night, and as I ran everything through my head, replayed every meeting we've ever had with her and particularly in the last six months, I suddenly saw things very clearly. Yes, she talked incessantly about her problems, her worries, the burdens of running the Harte chain, and she did keep intimating she wanted to sell her mother's stock. But she never actually came out and said she would do so. In my anxiousness to render Marriott Watson helpless, have International Petroleum take over the company, and in your *own* anxiousness to please Milt Jackson, your valued client, we *assumed* she would unload. If anything, we're at fault, believing we could push her around, get her to do our bidding.'

'She listened to us both so attentively,' Ross exploded. 'She asked for our advice, seemed to be taking it. Not only that, she insisted on knowing who the prospective buyer was, and against my better judgement I told her!' Ross groaned. 'Oh Jesus, what a fool I've been! I should never have arranged those meetings between her, Milt Jackson and us.' The banker reached for a cigarette and lit it nervously. 'Milt thinks Sitex is in the bag. Jesus Christ, he's going to be convinced I misled him, or that I've suddenly developed flawed judgement, in the prime of my life. We've got to come up with a plausible story to tell him.'

'I repeat what I just said, we have to tell him the truth, explain that *she* misled *us*. He'll have to accept it, there's nothing else he *can* do,' Dale insisted.

Ross drew on his cigarette and then stubbed it out. He rose, walked around his desk and began to pace up and down, his hands behind his back as he contemplated the meeting with Milton Jackson, chairman of the board of International Petroleum, and an important client of the bank. Suddenly he stopped in his tracks and fixed his eyes on Dale. 'If this gets out we're going to look like the biggest idiots on Wall Street. Two grown men, seasoned businessmen, shrewd, tough and hard assed, taken by a slip of a girl.' He ran his hand through his blondish hair and grimaced with disgust at himself and Dale. 'Talk about Emma Harte. Paula Fairley puts her to shame. The double-dealing little wretch. I would never have believed it of her. I really thought she was taking our guidance.'

'I had my doubts about that on several occasions,' Dale remarked dryly. 'And then I admit I began to readjust my thinking about her, particularly in view of the events over the past year. There was Emma's death, that knocked her for a loop, and then she lost her Daddy and her husband. She was in shock. You witnessed her state with your own eyes. So there she was, all alone, and suddenly I believed it would be a cinch. I genuinely thought she would unload the stock. She indicated she'd be happy to do that, would be relieved to get out of the oil rat race. What a foul up.'

Ross said in a rush, 'I'm going to tell Milt that she *did* in fact renege. To hell with it. Guys renege on deals every day in the street and in the oil business. Why should a woman be any different. More likely to change her mind in my opinion. I can't afford to lose Milt Jackson as a client of this bank, or International Petroleum as a corporate account.'

'Okay,' Dale concurred. 'Basically he's your baby anyway. I don't owe him an explanation.' The oil man brought out a cigar, fiddled with the end, finally struck a match and brought the flame to the cigar. He said, 'You do realize my hands were tied at the board meeting, don't you, Ross? There was nothing I could do.'

'Sure, sure,' Ross mumbled and returned to his chair. 'Tell me exactly what happened on Tuesday.'

'Be happy to, Ross. Paula arrived looking like a demure little nun, wearing a black dress with a white collar and cuffs. She was unusually pale, even for her, and it gave her a waif-like look. She had a sort of innocence about her.'

'Save me the description, God damn it! I'm interested in what she said, not how she looked.'

'Her appearance is important,' Dale replied. Paula had played her role very well. He had realized, as he had sat in the Sitex board room in Odessa, that there was something of the actress in her. 'Don't you understand, Ross, she looked like a little girl, easy to handle, and some of those old buzzards on the board, who don't know her very well –

why they were rubbing their hands with glee. Metaphorically speaking, that is. Yes, Marriott Watson's cronies thought they were going to eat her alive.'

'As we did,' Ross muttered softly.

Dale smiled faintly. 'We weren't the only guys who were fooled, Ross, take comfort in that, cold as it is. Before we got down to general business, the North Sea oil situation and the renewal of my contract, Paula asked to make a statement to the board. Naturally, Marriott Watson had no choice but to agree. She said that it was her duty to inform her fellow board members that she was about to sell her mother's stock. The entire block – the entire forty per cent of it. Everyone was taken aback, and that was when Jason Emerson piped up.'

Ross nodded. 'He's still sharp, smart as hell, despite his great age.'

Dale agreed. 'Tough old wild catters like Jason don't change, not in my experience. I sat back, enjoying every minute, thinking it was going our way. It was only later that I began to realize Paula had made good use of the week she had spent in Texas, prior to the board meeting. She had done a lot of lobbying, entertained a number of the directors socially. Especially Jason. He was primed by her, no doubt in my mind about that. Still, he was close to Paul McGill in the thirties, and had remained loyal to Emma for forty years.'

'I know about that,' Ross snapped.

'Jason Emerson asked Paula who she was selling the stock to, and when she intended to sell. She told him, very sweetly, that she was selling all forty per cent to International Petroleum. *Immediately*. I thought that some of the board members were going to have a collective coronary. Holy hell broke loose. I said nothing, pleased at the way she had handled herself. There was a lot of heated talk about International Petroleum and Milt. It's no secret in the oil business that he has that company on a growth and expansion programme and that once he gets a foothold in a company he does his damnedest to swoop down and take it over. Also, certain board members seemed to be aware that Milt has been buying up Sitex's common stock, and that he now holds an enormous amount of it. Only a dunce could fail to miss the implications.'

'If I'm following the script correctly, as I think I am, presumably Jason spoke up again, asked her not to sell to International Petroleum.'

'You've got it, old buddy.' Dale shook his head regretfully. 'Sure as God made little green apples, once the shouting had died down, old Jason started to persuade her to reconsider her decision. It was a bit of real craftiness, I can tell you, Ross. Before I had a chance to jump in with a few comments of my own, the majority of the board were singing his tune. Except Marriott Watson. He looked as if he was about to spit blood. I'm not certain, but he may have deduced that the tough negotiating between Paula and Jason had been set up in advance.'

'And she capitulated of course.'

'Not at first. She said she would reconsider not selling her block of stock, providing she was guaranteed a stronger voice on the board and if certain conditions were met. *Her conditions*. To be precise, the continuation of the North Sea drilling and the renewal of my contract.'

'She blackmailed the board!' Ross shouted.

Dale shook his head very slowly and a gleam of admiration now entered his brown eyes. 'No, Ross, I wouldn't call it blackmail. It was the most brilliant bit of manipulation I've seen in a long time. In one way I've got to take my hat off to her because that's what business is all about — manipulation.'

'That's true,' Ross acknowledged. 'At least you got what *you* wanted, despite everything. Your contract has been renewed again and is secure for two years, Marriott Watson is temporarily muzzled and you have a free hand. But what's your position with Paula now, Dale?'

Dale grinned. 'My position remains the same. I'm president of Sitex Oil, she controls the stock of her mother, who is the largest single stockholder. Paula has more power on the board than she ever had. Naturally I'll continue confiding in her as I always have. I intend to remain friendly. You never know, she still might decide to sell her stock one day. International Petroleum isn't going anywhere.'

'Points well taken.' Ross laughed unexpectedly. 'Business is business. Not every deal works out the way one would wish. There's no point my being immature about this. The bank still handles some of her business in the States. Anyway, if I can't succeed with her in the board room maybe I'll get lucky – in the bedroom.'

CHAPTER 54

Paula Fairley was late.

Ross Nelson glanced at the carriage clock on the mantelpiece of his living room for the umpteenth time. He was growing impatient. When she had telephoned at six-thirty to say she was delayed he had told her to take her time. But he had expected her to arrive before now.

He strolled across the antique Chinese carpet and hovered in front of the bar contained in the ebony-and-gilt Chinese chest. He poured himself another dry martini, dropped in an olive and walked to the window, looking down on to Park Avenue. His thoughts continued to dwell on Paula.

She was one of the few women he had not been able to fathom. Or coax into his bed. He had desired her for the longest time now. Since the fall of 1969 when he had first become aware of her potent sexuality. She had always managed to keep their relationship on a cool businesslike basis. At first he had believed he would win her over. Women generally fell for him. Later he had become annoyed as she continued to be uninterested. But he had kept up his battery on the telephone, constantly invited her out to dinner and bombarded her with flowers. Since he was conceited, and had enjoyed much success with women from all walks of life, Ross convinced himself that Paula would one day be his alone.

After Jim Fairley had been killed in the avalanche, Ross had played the role of a concerned good friend whenever she had been in New York. In the past nine months he had seen more of her than usual, since she had wanted to divest herself of some of Emma Harte's holdings which she had inherited. He had been on hand to help the sorrowing widow handle her business. He had hoped to persuade her to sell the Sitex stock – and seduce her as well. Her grief and curiously distant manner had induced him to hold himself in check. He had bided his time. But he had no intention of doing so any longer. Not now, not after Skye Smith's revelations last night.

He focused on the gossip Skye had relayed about Paula and Shane O'Neill. He had been stunned and disbelieving, had demanded to know the source. Skye had been only too ready to further confide. At the end of the evening he had walked home bridling with anger and riddled with frustration. All these months, as he had held her hand and comforted her, Paula had been sleeping with Shane O'Neill. He knew Skye had not lied. After all, Sarah Lowther, Paula's cousin, had been the one who had spilled the beans.

He was delighted that Dale and his wife had been called back to Texas so unexpectedly. They had planned a foursome for dinner. He relished the idea of being alone with Paula tonight. His way was clear with her. *Finally*. At long last he was going to possess this most elusive of women.

Ross sat down on the sofa, put his martini on the Chinese coffee table and took a cigarette, suppressing the sudden grin that had begun to spread across his face. He had not told Paula that Dale and Jessica had returned to the ranch. Why alert her, give her the opportunity to cancel. But he had given his housekeeper the evening off, and telephoned the restaurant to change the reservation to ten o'clock. That would give him ample time to make his moves.

Thoughts of her slender boyish body, the voluptuous breasts, intruded, brought a sudden flush to his neck. He lifted the glass, downed the rest of the drink, and went to the bar to pour another one. It was his third. He hesitated. Oh what the hell, he muttered. I can handle my liquor. Ross prided himself on his ability to drink gallons and remain a potent lover. His glance fell on the bottle of champagne in the ice bucket and he smiled confidently. After a few glasses of that, and a little of his sweet talking, Paula Fairley would be much more susceptible to his masculine appeal.

Ross Nelson had almost demolished his third martini when the intercom rang. Leaping to his feet, he rushed out into the foyer to answer it, hardly able to contain himself. He told the doorman to send Mrs Fairley up and stood waiting for her.

A few minutes later he was kissing Paula's cool cheek, ushering her across the hall and into the living room.

She paused in the entrance and swung her head, looked up at him, her violet eyes quizzical. 'Haven't Jessica and Dale arrived yet?' she asked before she moved forward.

He gazed after her, watching the fluid movement of her body, the shapely outline of her long legs through the thin silk of the pale grey cocktail dress. He almost salivated with longing. He could hardly wait to remove the dress, to strip her naked and revel in her beauty.

Paula turned to face him, catching him off guard. He blinked rapidly, hurried into the room, explained, with a

816

nervous laugh. 'They had to fly back at the last minute. An illness in the family.' He stepped up to the bar, began to open the bottle of champagne. 'Dale sends his apologies and he told me to tell you he'll phone you tomorrow.'

'I see,' Paula said, seating herself on the sofa. 'I'm disappointed they're not having dinner with us. I did have a few more things to discuss with Dale.' She gave him a small smile. 'Never mind.'

'Yes,' Ross murmured and carried the drink over to her. Seating himself in the chair opposite, he lifted his own glass and grinned at her. 'Well, Paula, congratulations! You've certainly pulled off a coup at Sitex!'

'Cheers, Ross,' Paula said, took a sip of the champagne and then eyed him speculatively. 'You're probably annoyed with me, angry that I finally decided to hold on to the Sitex stock. But – '

'Of course not,' he lied blandly, wanting to keep the atmosphere cosy and totally free of conflict. 'It was your choice. Dale and I could only advise you. We only wanted to help you, Paula. As Dale said to me at the bank this afternoon, International Petroleum is not going anywhere. I think Milton Jackson would always be interested in buying you out.'

'I'm sure he would,' Paula responded quietly. 'And I do want to thank you for your concern, all of your help with the Sitex matter, and with my other American business. I'm most appreciative.'

'My pleasure.'

Paula leaned back on the sofa and crossed her legs, trying to hide her surprise at his attitude. She had expected Ross to be furious, knowing how much he valued Milton Jackson as a client of the bank. Dale, she knew, would always give her his support. But Ross Nelson was another kettle of fish. She was relieved that he was being so agreeable. He was always agreeable though, wasn't he? She sighed, realizing she would have to spend the next few hours alone with him. There was no way she could get out of dining with him. She decided to be gracious and get through the evening as best she could.

Ross began to talk about her brother Philip, whom he had met the previous autumn when they had both been in New York. And for the next half-hour the banker kept up a steady stream of conversation about the family in general, her grandmother, and Harte Enterprises. In between, he kept refilling her glass, downed another martini and lit endless cigarettes.

At ten to nine, Paula cut him short suddenly, and asked, 'Shouldn't we be leaving, Ross? For the restaurant I mean?'

'No, not just yet. I'm afraid I had problems with the reservation at Twenty-One. They couldn't give me a table before nine-thirty, ten o'clock. We might as well relax here.'

'Oh all right,' Paula said, but she was irritated. She disliked eating when the evening was almost over.

As he talked, believing he was being entertaining, Ross continued to drink. He also scrutinized Paula intently, admiring her elegance and beauty. The dress she wore was simple, with a draped cowl collar and short sleeves. She wore emerald earrings and, apart from a watch, these were her only pieces of jewellery. She looked stunning and the grey silk moulded her figure in all the right places. Suddenly he was unable to keep his distance.

He rose, strolled to the bar cabinet, topped his glass and joined her on the sofa. He rested his arm on the back, and sipped his drink. His eyes held hers and he smiled a slow warm smile. 'You're looking exceptionally lovely tonight, Paula.'

'Thank you, Ross.' She returned his gaze and her brow puckered. There was something in those hazel eyes of his that instantly alerted her and she drew back slightly, pressed herself closer to the arm of the small sofa.

She felt a sense of panic.

Ross placed his glass on the coffee table and in one swift move he pulled her into his arms, brought his mouth down hard on hers. She struggled with him, tried to push him away, but his grip was firm as he held her tightly. He forced his tongue against her mouth, forced her mouth open and began to suck on her tongue and her lips. Heat ran through him and he moved slightly so that he could grasp her left breast with his right hand. He squeezed it, pinched the nipple, increased the pressure of his fingers.

Paula continued to struggle, tried to disentangle herself from his arms, but he was a big man, and strong, and she had no chance against him. He somehow managed to pull her forward, sliding her body down the sofa into a supine position, and then he fell on top of her, working his tongue on her mouth again. She clamped her teeth shut and moved her head to one side rapidly. He ran his hand over her thigh, lifted her skirt, slid his hand underneath, stroked her upper leg and then worked his fingers against her crotch.

Paula, lying under the weight of Ross Nelson, was in a state of shock. She struggled hard to break free from his tenacious hold on her. He had leaped on her so unexpectedly, taken her totally by surprise, and only a split second after she had noticed the lust burning in his eyes. She was horrified, and revolted by him, and also terribly frightened. She knew she had to escape from him, from his apartment. Quickly. If only she could get her hands up to his face to scratch him. They were trapped under his bulk. She moved her head from side to side again, frantically avoiding his mouth without success. His hands were now ripping at her tights and dimly through the roaring in her head she heard the nylon tear as he tugged at the crotch of the tights. Oh my God. His fingers were against her skin, pushing into her as he slobbered against her face, his mouth slack and wet. Shudders rippled through her. She thought she was going to vomit. He was hurting her, trying to penetrate her with his fingers.

Tears sprang into her eyes, induced by the fear, the shock, the revulsion and the pain as he pushed his hand harder between her legs. He stopped kissing her at last, drew back for breath.

Paula opened her mouth and began to scream.

Ross was jarred from his exploration of her body and he sat up swiftly, looked down into her tearstained face, and clamped one hand over her mouth.

'Shut up,' he hissed. 'You know you like this, you bitch. Don't play the innocent with me. You've been getting it from Shane O'Neill for months. Now it's old Ross's turn.'

He laughed loudly and Paula realized that he was very drunk. She struggled, moving under him violently, easing herself to the edge of the sofa.

To pull her back he had to remove his hand from her mouth. The minute he did she began to scream again. Once more he covered her face with his large hand, wrapped one of his heavy legs around her body, and pinioned her under him. 'You've been playing the grieving widow with me far too long, Paula,' he gasped, his glazed eyes roving over her lasciviously. His lust was mounting by the minute, inflamed by the fight she was putting up. It brought a flushed and congested look to his face. 'Come on, let's go to the bedroom,' he mumbled, his words slurred. 'You know you want to screw me.'

Paula had been waiting for the right moment, and now she endeavoured to nod her head, as if acquiescing to this suggestion. She acknowledged him with her eyes, softening her gaze.

'No more screaming,' he muttered. 'Okay?'

She nodded again.

He took his hand away from her mouth and leaned into her as if to kiss her.

Paula whispered, 'I thought you wanted to go into the bedroom?'

He grinned at her drunkenly. 'That's the idea, baby.'

'What are we waiting for?'

Still grinning he got up off the sofa. Before Paula had a chance to do the same he bent down, took hold of her arms and pulled her to her feet.

She did not dare struggle, knowing his great strength. She would have to pick the right moment to flee. She swallowed as he dragged her to him and nestled his face against her hair. 'You're going to have to tell me everything liddle old Shane did to excite you, baby. Whatever old Shane can do, Ross can do better. And then some, baby.'

Swallowing her disgust and fear, summoning all of her strength, Paula pushed him away from her. Drunk, believing she was playing along with him, Ross was taken by surprise. He lost his balance, staggered back, and flopped down on the sofa.

Paula reached for her solid gold evening bag on the coffee table and swung around.

He was far too fast for her and grabbed her again. They struggled in the middle of the room. She kicked his shin and he yelled in pain, instantly loosened his grip on her. Finally she was able to pull away from him.

Ross snatched at her dress. The cowl collar ripped under his hand.

Paula kicked him again as he took a step towards her, his expression threatening, and then in a swift movement she raised her hand and smashed the heavy gold bag into his face with all her might.

He cried out in pain as the precious metal struck his cheek and backed off, stumbling against the Chinese coffee table immediately behind him. He went sprawling on the floor. 'You bitch!' he screamed, bringing his hands to his bleeding face.

Gasping for breath, shaking and terrified, Paula dashed

821

into the foyer. The Chinese rug skidded under her but she recovered her balance, hitting her face against the edge of the tall cabinet as she did. But ignoring the stab of pain she flew to the door, jerked it open and banged it after her as she ran out. She pressed the button for the lift, cowering against the wall, praying he would not follow her.

Tears rushed to her eyes as she fiddled with the collar of her torn dress. She pushed them back, attempted to compose herself. When the doors rolled open she almost fell into the car, avoided the curious glance of the uniformed operator. She moved further back, retreated into the shadow, opened her bag and took out her compact. She ran the powder puff over her face and then smoothed her hand over her hair, aware of her dishevelled appearance.

Within seconds she was stepping out into the marble lobby of the building, hurrying across it at her fastest pace, and then hailing a cab on Park Avenue.

CHAPTER 55

Paula somehow managed to keep a grip on herself until she reached the Fifth Avenue apartment.

After letting herself in quietly, she tiptoed upstairs, not wishing Ann, the housekeeper, to see her in this terrible state.

She slipped into her bedroom, locked the heavy carved-wood door and leaned against it, finally beginning to breathe a little easier. Her body was taut, rigid still with the fear that had swamped her when Ross Nelson had so unexpectedly launched his physical attack on her.

Eventually she found the strength to move forward on her trembling legs, and her hands shook as she unzipped her ruined dress and pulled it up over her head and discarded it. Once she had removed her underwear and her ripped stockings, she stumbled blindly into the bathroom.

Paula stood in the shower stall for ten minutes, soaping herself over and over again, letting the hot steaming water sluice down over her body. She felt battered and unclean, had the urgent need to erase the smell of him, the touch of him.

When at last she stepped out and looked at herself in the mirrored side wall, she saw that her body was bright pink, red in parts as if she had scalded herself, damaged the skin. But at least she felt cleaned of Ross Nelson. Pulling on a towelling robe without bothering to dry herself, she went over to the washbasin and peered at her face in the mirror. Her cheekbone was bruised where she had struck it against the cabinet. It would be black and blue tomorrow.

She continued to stare at herself.

Her blue eyes were dark, almost black, and they held the look of a wild hunted deer, were wide with fright and shock. She squeezed them tightly shut, wanting to forget what had happened to her only a short while ago. But she could not and she lifted her lids. His lustful face danced before her eyes, was reflected in the mirror, as if he was standing behind her in the bathroom. Paula shuddered and gripped the edge of the sink as she remembered how his hands had wandered so roughly over her body, how his horrible wet mouth had slobbered against hers, how his weight had trapped her under him. She had felt as though she was being suffocated.

Anger blazed through her. Ross Nelson had virtually tried to rape her. That he had been dreadfully drunk was no excuse. There was no excuse for that unconscionable behaviour. He was a disgusting specimen of a man. The worst. He was not a man. He was an animal. The shuddering intensified. How violated, how damaged she was feeling!

Nausea rose up in Paula. She began to vomit in the

washbasin, retching until she had nothing left inside. The dry heaving continued for a while and then eventually subsided. Lifting her head, she wiped her streaming eyes and her sweating face with the damp flannel, then leaned her head against the cool tiles of the wall. Her head throbbed, her eyes ached and her muscles were sore from struggling with him, fighting him off.

Blocking out the image of him, she closed her eyes, gulping air, calming herself as best she could, and when she was steadier on her legs she moved away from the washbasin and blundered back into the bedroom. She lay down on the bed.

It was only then that Paula Fairley fell apart.

Quite suddenly she was gripped by an internal shaking and then her whole body began to shake as if she had palsy. She pulled the eiderdown up over her. Her teeth began to chatter and she shivered as icy chills swept through her. Clutching at the pillow, she buried her face in it and she began to sob as if her heart was breaking.

Paula cried without restraint for the next hour.

And all of the pain and sorrow she had suppressed since the tragic deaths of her father, Jim, and Maggie broke free at last.

Her terrible grief overwhelmed her, but she let it wash over her, envelope her completely, gave herself up to it, recognizing finally that it had been wrong and foolish of her to bottle it up inside. But she had not known what else to do. She had had to be strong, so very strong for her mother and Alexander and her children. And so she had deliberately buried the grief. It had lain there dormant, yet it had gradually gnawed away at her, eating her alive, rendering her helpless in so many aspects of her life.

As Paula Fairley wept the bitter tears she should have wept nine months ago, and had not, she began to experience a measure of ease, a genuine relief from the searing heart-ache and anguish that had engulfed her since the avalanche.

When she had no more tears left inside her she lay quietly on the bed, her body limp and exhausted, her eyes red and swollen, wide open, staring up at the ceiling.

Slowly, but with her usual intelligence and analytical powers, she began to sort out her muddled thoughts, sift through the painful memories, examine her emotional and physical frigidity with a new and stunning objectivity.

It was as if the shock of Ross Nelson's violent assault on her had cleared her brain, startled her out of her state of frozen containment. She started to see herself with new objectivity, and she knew with sudden sureness that the burdensome weight of her enormous guilt had crushed all feeling in her, all emotional response to others except her children. *She had no reason to be guilty. She was not to blame for anything. Not one single thing.*

Shane was correct in everything he had said.

How cruel she had been to him, inflicting pain on him because her own pain had blinded her to the truth, to reality. *Shane.* She saw his face in her imagination, trans-ferred it in her imagination to the ceiling. If only he were really here now. She longed to have the comfort and security of his strong arms around her, keeping her safe.

Tears rushed into Paula's eyes. She had sent him away, had been so wilful in her determination to tread her solitary lonely road, believing it to be the only road for her. She wondered if he would ever be able to forgive her.

Ross Nelson's hideous, grinning, drunken face nudged Shane's to one side, obliterated him. Paula shuddered violently and sat up in bed. Fury ripped through her, momentarily, stunning her. *He had tried to rape her*. Never in her entire life had anything quite so disgusting happened to her. But then she had never been exposed to the harsher side of life. She had always been so protected. By Grandy. By her parents. By her large family. And by all that power and wealth. She did not know the streets, the hard world where other women had to live and fight and hold on to their sanity somehow, despite the burdens they had to carry, the punishment certain kinds of men made them endure.

Certainly she had never been exposed to men – not men like Ross Nelson, who were exploitative, pursued their own ends relentlessly. There had only ever been Jim. He had been her first lover and then she had married him. If he had been selfish and self-involved, and he undoubtedly had, if he had been swept along by his own needs, most certainly he had never been violent with her. He had never really forced himself on her, not once in all the time they had been married.

And then there had been Shane . . . theirs had been the grandest of passions, but physical desire had blended in with their deep abiding love, that love which he had said had grown out of their childhood affection and friendship. With Shane there had been a true bonding and on every level.

The brutalizing experience she had suffered at the hands of Ross Nelson had been terrifying. It was the worst kind of violation a man could inflict on a woman – an invasion not only of the body but of the mind and the heart and the soul as well. It had been cruel, painful and humiliating. She realized how lucky she had been to escape before he had committed that final act and a small series of shivers rippled over her and her anger surfaced yet again.

And yet his violence with her *had* shocked her into reality, brought her back to life, released the dam of her grief, destroyed the shell she had so carefully and deliberately built around her. But the carapace had cracked open and she was permitting herself to crawl out of it, to come back into the real world, to live again. Yes, she wanted to start afresh, to move forward, to put the past behind her, to look ahead to the future. Don't look back, forge ahead,

Emma had always said to her. And that was what she must now do.

It was dawn when Paula finally fell asleep.

She slept deeply, as if she had been drugged. Not once during the night did she awaken and sit up in sudden fear, crying out in terror as she felt herself being buried alive under tons of cold snow that brought with it icy death.

The nightmare that had haunted her nights for so long had been exorcized, along with so many ghosts, so many troubled memories.

When she arose the following morning, after only a few hours of rest, she discovered she felt lighter, freer. It seemed as if a great weight had been lifted and she recognized then that the guilt she had carried had started to dissolve. That too would disappear entirely . . . one day in the future.

A new strength came into Paula as she dressed to go to the store on Fifth Avenue. And with that strength came a steadiness, a calmness, and a sure and thrusting knowledge that reached deep into her heart. She knew where she must go, what she must do, and as she stood in front of the mirror she nodded to herself. Her way *was* clear. She was about to set out on a new road.

CHAPTER 56

He sat on one of the ancient ruined walls of Middleham Castle, daydreaming on this warm Sunday afternoon in September.

The high-flung canopy of the sky was a pewter colour, cloudy and overcast, presaging rain, despite the sun which was valiantly trying to push through. It finally emerged from behind the bank of cumulus and great rafts of brilliant silver light streamed across the heavens.

Shane lifted his head, looked up, was struck at once by the supernatural quality of that blinding light. It seemed to emanate from some hidden source behind those wild implacable hills and it held a shimmering clarity, a pure radiance that was unearthly, made him catch his breath.

His dark brooding eyes swept across the sky and then he glanced away, focused his attention on the ruined arch of Warwick's once-great stronghold, his mind turning inward. He was lonely and alone and yet he knew within his heart that he would find a measure of peace here in Yorkshire. He had made a decision when he had flown home from New York with Winston, at the beginning of this past week.

Shane O'Neill was going to end his long, self-imposed exile at last. There was too much pain in his life now to bring additional pain on himself and that he would surely continue to do if he persisted in exiling himself. When he was not travelling the world he would live here, surrounded by the beauty he had grown up with and which he so dearly loved. It was the one spot in this earth where he felt truly happy.

It would be hard for him at first but he would manage somehow. He was a man, mature, intelligent, and he had always been strong. Somewhere he would find the courage to create a new life for himself without her. And he fully intended to live out that life here.

War Lord was tethered nearby and he whinnied. Shane swung his head, looked about, expecting to see hikers or tourists. But he was still entirely alone. The ruined castle was deserted today and there was little sign of life, except for the occasional call of a kingfisher or a curlew, the *gawk-gawk* cry of a seagull which had flown in from the North Sea. His eyes lifted to the rolling moors, ranged up against the skyline, glorious today as the heather bloomed and rippling below were the lush green slopes of the Dales.

Shane sat there for a long time, feasting his eyes on the landscape, enjoying its stunning beauty. The grandeur and majesty of this place never failed to touch his Celtic soul which was so attuned to nature.

Suddenly he blinked, lifted his hand to shade his eyes. He saw a speck moving across the line of the hills coming steadily down the bridlepath, heading in the direction of the Castle.

When the lone horse and rider drew closer he stiffened on the wall and stared ahead, focusing his vision.

The rider was a young woman. She trotted at a brisk pace, handled the horse beautifully, showing great equestrian skill. Her long dark hair was blowing in the light breeze, streaming out behind a pale intense face.

In the passing of a moment he felt his heart leap and begin to clatter abnormally against his rib cage. The rider was spurring the horse forward. He recognized his own mare, Celtic Maiden, and he knew that girl, so clearly visible in that shimmering Northern light that washed the sky and the hills and the castle walls with its penetrating radiance.

It was his dreamlike child of his childhood dreams . . . riding through the dreamlike landscape of his childhood dreams . . . riding through the sunlight and the shadow . . . drawing nearer . . . nearer . . . nearer . . . raising her hand in greeting. His dreamlike child of his childhood dreams was coming to him . . . at last. But she had grown to womanhood now . . . as he was a man now . . . she was the dreamlike woman he loved, had always loved, would always love until the day he died.

The thud of the hooves on the rich dark earth drowned out the clattering of his heart. Slowly, disbelievingly, he rose from the wall, his eyes full of questions. But his face was still and without expression.

She swung down out of the saddle lightly, threw the reins over the tree stump where War Lord was tethered, took a step towards him and stopped.

'I thought you were in New York,' Shane heard his voice say. He was surprised he sounded so controlled, so normal.

'I took the overnight flight from Kennedy to Manchester on Friday. Tilson picked me up yesterday and drove me back home . . . to Pennistone Royal.'

'I see.' Shane stepped back involuntarily, sat down on the wall, feeling weak.

She joined him on the old greystone wall and studied him for a long moment.

Neither of them spoke.

Finally Shane said, 'What's happened to your face?'

'I fell. It's nothing.'

'What are you doing here?'

'I came looking for you. Randolph told me where you were. I came to ask you something, Shane.'

'Yes?'

'Would you please give me the ring . . . the ring Blackie gave to Emma?'

'You can have it if you want, Paula. She should have left it to you in the first place.'

'No. She meant you to have it. *She* never made mistakes like that. And I wasn't asking you to give me the ring as . . . you know, as a gift.' She hesitated only for the briefest second. 'I want you to give it to me as your future wife.'

He gaped at her.

She smiled at him.

Paula's uncanny violet eyes grew enormous in her pale face. 'I want to spend the rest of my life with you, Shane. If you still want me.'

He was incapable of answering. He put his arms around her and held her close to his shaking heart. And then he began to kiss her hair, her eyes and finally her soft and

830

tender lips. The kiss was deep and passionate yet there was tenderness in it and a depth of feeling that sprang from the recent pain they had both endured.

They sat for a long time on the ruined wall of Middleham Castle, their arms around each other. They did not speak, lost for a while in their own thoughts.

Paula felt safe at last now that she was with him. She would never leave him again. They would be together always until the end of their days. They belonged together, were part of each other.

Shane, his eyes scanning the gaunt bleak silhouette of the castle, was filled with a sense of timelessness that he always experienced here. And then slowly he was enveloped in a new and wondrous peacefulness and he knew it would never leave him now that she was to live with him for the rest of his life.

Paula murmured, 'If only Blackie and Emma knew . . . if only they could see us together.'

He looked into her face and smiled, and then he lifted his eyes to the dark hills, resplendent in that extraordinary supernatural light, his glance sweeping across the sky.

Then the Celt in him rose up and he reached out and touched her face with gentleness. 'Perhaps they can, Paula,' Shane said. 'Perhaps they can.'